LIGHT FIGHTERS

STAR CHILDREN SAGA:
BOOK TWO

By Palmer Pickering

C Palmer ♡

Published by Mythology Press

Stephanie,
Thanks for all your valuable
insights and help.
Starlight & Magic to you!
Barb

LIGHT FIGHTERS: BOOK TWO OF THE STAR CHILDREN SAGA

Copyright ©2022 Barbara Palmer Pickering

ISBN 978-1-7325688-6-0 (Trade Paperback)

FIC009000 **FICTION** / Fantasy / General
FIC009100 **FICTION** / Fantasy / Action & Adventure
FIC009010 **FICTION** / Fantasy / Contemporary
FIC028000 **FICTION** / Science Fiction / General
FIC028030 **FICTION** / Science Fiction / Space Opera
FIC028010 **FICTION** / Science Fiction / Action & Adventure
FIC028090 **FICTION** / Science Fiction / Alien Contact
FIC028070 **FICTION** / Science Fiction / Apocalyptic & Post-Apocalyptic
FIC061000 **FICTION** / Magical Realism

Cover art and design by J Caleb at jcalebdesign.com
Interior design and layout by Gretchen Dorris at www.inktobook.com
Peary Dome Maps by Melissa Stevens at www.theillustratedauthor.com
Pathways of Light Illustration by Nathan Hansen at www.nathanhansenillustration.com
Art on the Prologue and Part pages ©2017 Ashley Albright and reproduced here with permission of the artist. Find Ashley on Instagram @artby_albright
Compass icon art by musmellow
Moon maps, NASA

Published by Mythology Press

MYTHOLOGY
→PRESS←

www.mythologypress.com
Follow Palmer at www.palmerpickering.com
10 9 8 7 6 5 4 3 2 1

Dedicated to Lynda Emashowski at Nia Cú Herbs
for giving me a glimpse into the world of plant spirit medicine
and for the gift of the dancing bears.

"As you heal so does our world"

TABLE OF CONTENTS

MAPS

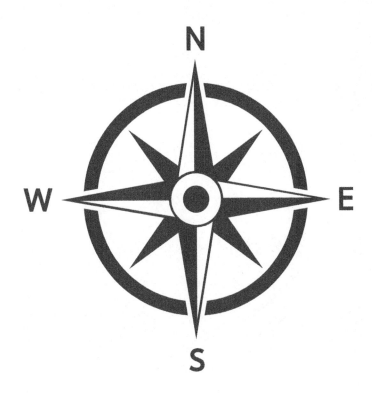

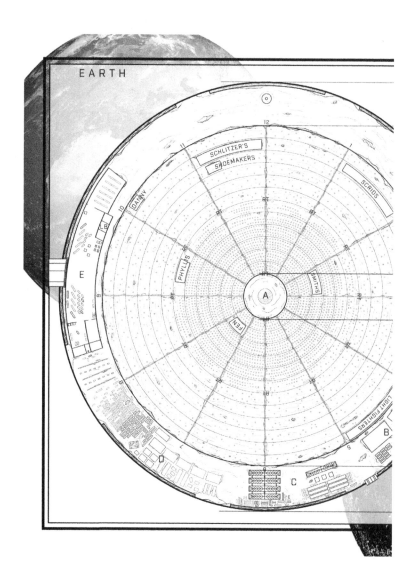

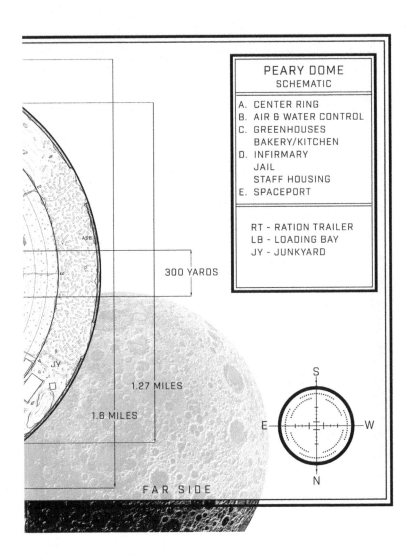

PEARY DOME
SCHEMATIC

A. CENTER RING
B. AIR & WATER CONTROL
C. GREENHOUSES
   BAKERY/KITCHEN
D. INFIRMARY
   JAIL
   STAFF HOUSING
E. SPACEPORT

RT - RATION TRAILER
LB - LOADING BAY
JY - JUNKYARD

300 YARDS

1.27 MILES

1.6 MILES

FAR SIDE

S
E ——⊕—— W
N

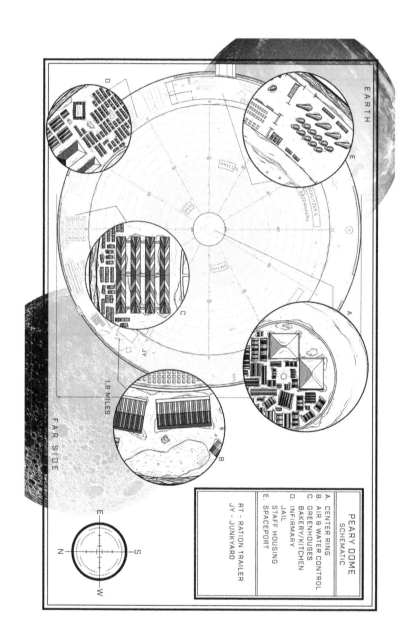

PEARY DOME
SCHEMATIC

A. CENTER RING
B. AIR & WATER CONTROL
C. GREENHOUSES
D. BAKERY/KITCHEN
D. INFIRMARY
JAIL
STAFF HOUSING
E. SPACEPORT

RT - RATION TRAILER
JY - JUNKYARD

Map of the Northwest Sector of the Near Side of the Moon

Credit: NASA/LRO_LROC_TEAM

Map of the North Pole of the Moon

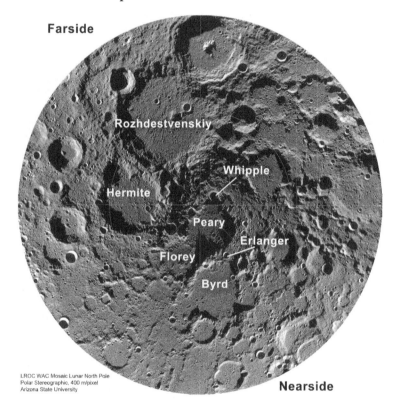

Credit: NASA/GSFC/Arizona State University

Map of Peary Crater (Peaks of Eternal Light)

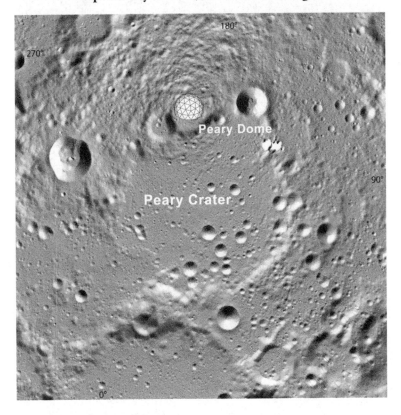

Credit: Lunar Reconnaissance Orbiter (LRO) laser altimeter data, NASA

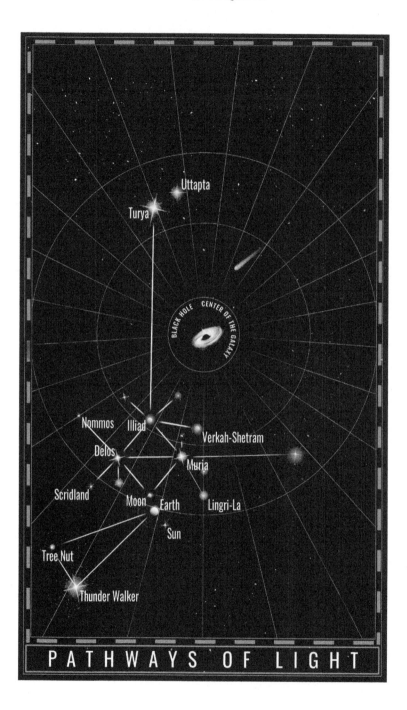

PROLOGUE

TURYA

Planet Turya

1

CONSTELLATİONS

L aris sat in the hollow of a fire pit below Father-Heart-of-Sky, contemplating the stars that shone in a clear sky free of volcanic ash. Out there among the jewels of the sky were the Descendants, living on planets settled by adventurers and colonists of long ago. The branches of the Totem had spread across the galaxy, a diaspora of the various Turyan humanoid races that had multiplied and become the dominant species on the far-off planets just as they had on Turya. The colonists had taken plants and animals with them, trying to make their new homes feel like Turya. Bears and gazelles, flying foxes and winged lions, tiny dragons and shoulder monkeys, giant ravens and hunting hawks, wild wolves and secretive shadow cats. Animals lived in the shadows between dimensions, slipping more easily between the worlds than the Turyans ever could, and they delighted in leaping across the chasm of time and space to discover new worlds.

Few of those animals still survived on the Home planet, but they came alive for Laris in the Illuminated Manuscripts of the Concha Scrolls, where they were drawn in great detail. And plants—plants that were largely only a memory. A few great-grandmother trees had still lived when Laris was a child, but the last of them were charred skeletons now. Long before he had been born, flowers of every imaginable color had bloomed, filling the air with a heady fragrance. Butterflies and dragonflies filled the skies with color. Fruits and flowers fell like

3

gifts into outstretched hands. At night the plants glowed and danced in cool, moist breezes. Or so Laris had read in the Scrolls.

He sighed, sat back on his heels, and picked out the constellations where the Descendants had settled. His eyes went immediately to the Flying Chariot, one of whose wings was outlined by the three stars of the three planets that formed the anchor trine of the traveling configuration—the three planets where the three smaller Hearts-of-Sky had been planted to form a stable matrix to traverse the galaxy: Iliad, Delos, and Muria.

Flying Chariot was so named after the legend of the winged lions who used to leap into Father-Heart-of-Sky ahead of the human adventurers, so excited were they to explore the new planets. The draft created by their swift exit from Turya would suck the human travelers in after them, making it feel as though they were flying on a winged chariot. *What should they call it now,* Laris wondered, since the first of the three anchor planets, Iliad, had lost its Heart-of-Sky, breaking the trine? *A grounded chariot,* he thought grimly, with no winged lions left on Turya to guide a new generation of travelers. The Turyans were stranded, awaiting help from the Star Children who might never come.

Laris supposed it was the circle of life. Still, he did not like it that parents eventually became dependent on their children. It didn't feel right or comfortable. He reflected on how, for the myriad Kalpas after the first travelers had left Turya, the Descendants had relied on reconnecting with their Turyan Ancestors to keep them healthy: to infuse them with the life force born of Uttapta and keep their fire meridians burning bright and their core helixes activated. How quickly the roles had reversed. Now the survival of the Ancestor Turyans depended on the Descendants. The Star Children must open the pathway between Turya and the colonized worlds so that the Ancestors could flee their burning planet before it was too late.

But Iliad's Heart-of-Sky was no more. That fact was the core worry that kept Laris awake at night. How could the Star Children ignite a pathway whose primary anchor point had been destroyed? Laris stared into the sky and located the next constellation and its central star, the star his teacher had called Lotus Flower. So named for the complex mandala the star and its planets formed as they spiraled together through space on their long journey circling Turya and the center of the galaxy.

Lotus Flower's third, small blue planet, Jaya, "gatekeeper," was home to a mixed race of Turyan Keeper Descendants tainted with the

blood of the Vardna. The planet with the crystal moon. The planet the
Descendants called Earth, whose name meant the soil upon which
one stood, the material plane between the ethereal world and the dark
eternity of the underworld. The planet where this age's Star Children
had been born. Turya's last hope.

Beyond Lotus Flower lay the dark shadow of the constellation
Black Dragon. The end of the line of Descendants. The farthest from
Turya and home to the Descendant race that was losing its light the
fastest. Resting on the dragon's head was a circlet of stars known as
Demon's Crown, and at the apex of Demon's Crown stood the binary
star system Bleeding Dagger, and around the larger of the two red
stars orbited two planets that formed the hub of the Cephean Empire,
home to the spawn of the Turyan Vardna tribe, the Descendant race
that surpassed even their ancestral tribe in violence and atrocities. The
Cephs had been responsible for destroying the Heart-of-Sky on Iliad,
and now they had invaded Earth, according to the Seers.

Laris settled into a cross-legged position, sheltered from the hot
wind by the fire pit hollow, and retreated to his Concha Scroll. He
faced the flames, which rose from a bronze brazier, and carefully
unfurled the stiff parchment and spread it across his lap. This one was a
simple copy in the precise script of his apprentice, Sannet, transcribed
in gold ink and devoid of illustrations. Perhaps the key to their survival
was buried in its symbols, right under his nose, waiting for him to find
it. He squinted in the firelight and read.

———————)———————

The sun blazed in the sky overhead, a massive fireball—Uttapta, Laris's
source and strength. It was calm today. When firestorms exploded
from its surface, everyone was forced to retreat inside thick-walled
stone buildings or underground. Chunks of flaming iron, drops of
molten gold, and gravel-sized diamonds, rubies, and sapphires hailed
down from the sky, the iron setting fire to whatever it hit—though
there was not much left to burn on Turya. Whenever Uttapta pelted
the land with fire and gemstones, Turya erupted in anger, belching
orange and blue lava from cones and crevasses and shooting geysers
high into the air, reeking of sulfur. The planet had become a barren
land of rock and ash whose mantle was cracking, lava and steam

leaking from its exposed veins. Stinking, bubbling mudpots scarred the Naraka Wastelands to the south and were spreading north to Purlan, pockmarking the foothills and valley with oozing sores.

Laris rubbed his cheeks. The sagging folds beneath his eyes constantly itched these days, and the ulcers had opened up on his scalp again, but he did not touch them nor tell his wife. She would only fuss, and there was nothing anybody could do about them. Uttapta had beaten down on his head for too long, and he refused to shield himself from its life-giving force, even though it was a harsh master. What gives life also takes it away.

And so he prayed on his bony knees in the shelter of one of the stone hollows that held the fires ringing Father-Heart-of-Sky, perched on the peaks of the Ageless Mountains. He prayed to Uttapta that he would be the last man standing on Turya after sending everyone else to safety and would die consumed in its flames.

He prayed until Uttapta set beyond the smoky horizon, painting the streaks of dark, sooty clouds blood red for a few glorious moments before they went dark again. In the distance, the peak of Mount Sagir rose majestically above the ash-cloud layer that ringed it, spouting orange lava streamers and bright blue methane flames into the black night, and sending rivers of crimson flowing down its slopes to disappear into the thick gray haze.

<hr />

Laris sat in a fire pit hollow to escape the biting wind and gazed across the stony escarpment at the three loves of his life standing on the Star Temple steps. His wife, Rocana, had seen a hundred Fires but looked nearly as youthful as their two daughters: Avala, who had seen forty Fires, and Irsili, who had seen thirty.

The three women saw things in Father-Heart-of-Sky. They had the Glimmering Sight. Father-Heart-of-Sky was not a normal crystal globe. It was not useful for communicating with other Turyan Seers across the land or Descendant Seers across the galaxy, as other viewing globes were. Father-Heart-of-Sky was a traveling portal, and as such had absorbed the memories of every being who had passed through its gate. Sitting high atop the Ageless Mountains and overlooking Purlan Valley to the north and the Naraka Wastelands to the south, it had seen and recorded the history of the Turyan civilization. And it had absorbed the life-giving yods of Uttapta for as long as it had sat there, for nearly three million Fires.

Laris, historian that he was, wished he could gaze into Father-Heart-of-Sky and access the information stored in its crystal matrix. But he was not a Seer—he could not read its memories. The Seers gathered around the massive globe in groups of twelve on special occasions to divine its secrets. It was an empty ritual, his wife had explained to him many times. Try as they might, no one was powerful enough to sort through the onslaught of information that flooded them when they gazed into Father-Heart-of-Sky. Rocana described it as a million streams of images burning through her mind that quickly converged into the red fires of Uttapta, forcing her to close her eyes lest her vision burn out forever. All the other Seers had similar experiences, and so they gathered infrequently, dutifully trying to make sense of the visions, and quickly surrendered to the flames.

At least he had the Scrolls. Laris was Eldest Keeper of the Concha Scrolls, charged with holding the wisdom of the Turyans and passing it onto future generations. He read the Concha Scrolls one after another. It took him ten Fires to read them all, and then he would start over. He had completed his twelfth reading not too long ago and had started from the beginning once again. Every day when he read, he hoped to find something new, something he had missed before. He sometimes wondered if the words changed between readings, or if his mind just could not absorb it all at once. Each reading felt different, as though the Scrolls slowly revealed their secrets to him over time. Perhaps it was simply that his understanding grew. Most of the Scrolls were written in the ancient script, a complex system of symbols with many subtleties, like any language. Although he had studied the ancient script from childhood, it was no longer a spoken dialect, so there was no real way to verify his understanding other than with the other Keepers. They would debate the interpretation of a symbol for days and finally agree on a common understanding, then mark it in the lexicon so that they would not need to repeat the same argument the next time someone came upon it.

No one argued over the significance of the time in which they were living. The Star Children were due. Overdue. The twin sister and brother had been born twenty Fires ago and should be well on their way to igniting the pathways and initiating the Joining. But it was a long journey fraught with danger. The bigger worry that incessantly nagged at everyone was that the primary node of the pathway had been destroyed. What if the bridge to the other worlds was irreparably broken? What if they would never see their Descendants again? The Seers and the Keepers had been trying for the past thousand Fires to ignite the pathways from Father-Heart-of-Sky, and they tried still. But the globe remained dark and dormant.

Laris shifted on the hard rock and looked up at their red, smoldering sun. He was anxious. Father-Heart-of-Sky awoke every thousand Fires—every Kalpa. The Concha Scrolls were very clear about that and had been verified numerous times. But in the previous Kalpa, Father-Heart-of-Sky had not awoken. The Star Children had not come. The Totem was not made whole. If they did not come this time, the Totem might well be forever shattered. The thought of the Star Children never coming Home made him heartsick and afraid.

Heartsick because the Star Children would never find the Ancestors and reunite the Totem. The Descendants would not be reminded of who they were and where they came from. Their energy bodies would slowly lose their fire, and the Descendant races would fall into darkness and despair, fighting each other in a desperate struggle to survive, only to die off in the end.

And he was afraid because the planet Turya was slowly burning as Uttapta grew darker and hotter. The oldest Illuminated Concha Scrolls depicted lush plants and flowers of vibrant colors on Turya—and clear water. Now, almost everyone subsisted on fungi, and the waters were dark with ash from submerged volcanoes spewing endless streams of primordial murk into the depths. The Keepers were certain that one day soon, during their children's lifetimes, Turya would no longer be able to support the population—the people would starve, or fire would consume them all. They needed to leave. But without the paths of light from Father-Heart-of-Sky, there was no route of passage off the planet.

Laris stood up on aching legs and joined Rocana as she approached. Together they walked to the gold platform that held Father-Heart-of-Sky and climbed the gold brick steps, which had been freshly laid several Fires ago in the ceremonial star pattern in fervent hope that the Children would arrive.

His wife shone with a golden hue, her nimbus shimmering pleasingly as she stood next to him. The orange flames from the Eternal Fires always seemed to heighten as she entered their circle, their light casting a golden glow as bright as her head dendrals, which cascaded in tight coils from her head to her waist. Her dendrals were thicker and brighter than they had ever been. Her coppery skin was smooth and taut over her cheekbones. It was said that communing with Father-Heart-of-Sky kept one young.

His head dendrals, by contrast, were losing their shine and straggled limply past his shoulders where they twined together with his long chin dendrals. His skin that once covered tight solid muscle now hung from his bony frame, and his arm dendrals cast hardly any light at all.

Rocana took his hands gently in hers. "Don't worry, they will come," she said, smiling reassuringly.

He nodded and tried to smile back, gazing into her fiery red eyes. He'd read in the Scrolls that some Descendants had blue eyes, and they had settled on planets with water and sky the color of the blue methane gas that burned across the Turyan landscape. Elaborate illustrations depicted such mythical worlds. His wife and daughters confirmed these wonders. The Sisters had Seen the planets. He could not imagine such impossible beauty. The skies and waters of Turya were the colors of the rocks that dominated the landscape: red, brown, or gray. During the occasional days when the clouds of ash cleared, the rocky mountains and valleys took on a fiery orange hue, reflecting Uttapta's light and resembling the rivers of glowing lava that crept down the slopes of Mount Sagir. *Turya, Fire Planet.* Hot and growing hotter.

Rocana's eyes were cool and calm. "They will come," she reassured him once again. "Tirili has Seen them."

He smiled, squeezing her delicate hands. Let her believe her words comforted him. It was sweet that she still trusted in her sister, even though by all accounts Tirili had lost her mind. Tirili had indeed Seen the Star Children twenty Fires ago, but then five Fires later had lost the connection, resulting in a mental breakdown that she had never fully recovered from.

Even if Tirili had Seen them since, as she claimed, he knew from the Scrolls that in the previous Kalpa the Star Children had also been Seen. They had been born. They had lived. But they had not made it Home. The Scrolls recounted the hardships that generations of past Star Children had overcome to fulfill their destinies. It was a wonder any ever made it at all.

"They will come," Rocana repeated.

2

AVALA

Avala and her blood-sister, Irsili, left their apartments in the Star Temple's residential wings, reserved for the upper echelons of the Sisters of the Glimmering Sight and the Keepers of the Concha Scrolls. The sisters stood between two pillars on the broad black stone terrace that served as the entryway to the Star Temple, waiting for their mother. The polished gold pillars soared far overhead, where they met a black stone ceiling streaked with gold and inlaid with diamonds to mimic stars in the night sky.

The temple was built upon a rocky crag of the Ageless Mountains adjacent to Father-Heart-of-Sky, with commanding views of the Naraka Wastelands and the Purlan Valley, both currently hidden beneath the haze that blanketed the broad flatlands. The fiery peak of Mount Sagir sat above the ash clouds far to the northwest like a massive pyre dripping red with blood.

Enclosing the Star Temple's mountaintop compound stood a massive black stone wall, which had been erected to keep out raiding Vardna and the justice of the Zura. The wall was a relic of the past, its single stone gate rolled to the side, the entrance standing wide open. Avala had never seen it closed. Her father said there was no point. Nothing could hold back the will of Uttapta. Still, Keeper guards patrolled the ramparts, walking the wall and looking out over the land from behind the parapets.

A hot wind blew across the jagged peaks, whistling over the wall and slapping the brown roughspun hood against Avala's cheek as she tightened it around her face and chest, covering her gold jewelry. Banners of Uttapta flew overhead, fully extended in the wind, golden rays displayed in all their glory on large squares of white silk, which were growing dingy from the ever-present soot in the air.

The clear soprano voice of Ribhana—her mother's childhood friend and second in the Sisterhood hierarchy—reached Avala's ears in snatches as the wind stole it away. Ribhana was leading the constant chorus of Sisters inside the Star Temple, in the central chamber, whose high domed ceiling was open to the sky in its center, amplifying and projecting the unending song across the heavens as a beacon to the Star Children.

Crowning the highest point of the Ageless Mountains' meandering ridgeline, Father-Heart-of-Sky reflected the fires of Uttapta. Twelve Eternal Flames stood sentinel around it, the flames flickering gently inside their protective bronze and crystal braziers, which were set into shallow pits hollowed into the rock. Her father sat cross-legged in one of the pits with his head bowed, intently studying a scroll in his lap.

Her mother emerged from the tall doorway and walked briskly to Avala and Irsili, her white robes rustling. Rocana always looked the part of the Mother, her face scrubbed and glowing, her golden head dendrals hanging in perfect luminescent coils that reached to her waist. An ornamental red and gold stole was draped over her chest and fell to her knees, and a gold satin cloak was clasped at her neck with a red fire opal and pushed back over her shoulders to hang down her back. Avala exchanged a quick glance with Irsili as they followed their mother to bid farewell to their father. She and her sister wore simple garments so as not to draw attention to themselves, but their mother refused to hide who she was.

Avala hugged Laris, his shoulders stooped and frail beneath her gentle embrace. Her father had already been elderly when she'd been born, having seen one hundred and ten Fires at her birth. She hated to admit that he was approaching the end of his life, but he was the oldest of the Keepers now. He swore he would live to see the Star Children come Home and then die in peace. That was small comfort to her, since her ardent wish to welcome the Children Home would mean saying goodbye to him.

"Take care, Father," she said into his ear so that he could hear her despite the wind. "Don't tire your eyes. The Scrolls say the same thing they said the last twelve times you read them." She gave him a kiss on the cheek. He chuckled. "You know I always find something new. Perhaps I will find the key to opening the dragon's mouth." He glanced at Father-Heart-of-Sky, which had slumbered in hibernation far too long.

"Perhaps," she said with a half-smile, and stepped away to join her mother and sister.

A troop of Keeper guards stood nearby waiting for them, swords at their sides in plain gold scabbards, fresh white tunics accentuating their broad shoulders, and polished red helmets gracing their heads. It was a new batch of young men, she noticed. Her father was always trying to find a husband for his youngest daughter, Irsili. Avala's sister ignored the guards as she strode past them, her loose brown robes pressed against her curves by the wind.

Laris insisted they travel with guards, whose main duty was to keep back the adoring throngs as they passed through the cities. They did not anticipate such attention on this trip, but the guards accompanied them by custom. Avala would prefer to travel without an entourage. So much fuss for no reason. There was little chance the crowds would rush to see them in these dark days, and even less danger the common people would attack them in anger over the failure of the Children to arrive—the Sikat were generally peaceful people. It was only the Zura and the Vardna who historically posed any real threat to the Sisters. The Zura were allies with the Seers and Keepers currently, and the Vardna stayed in the mountainous region far beyond the Naraka Wastelands. The few Vardna warriors the Zura allowed into their ranks were strictly disciplined and proud of their status. They would not risk their hard-won social standing by confronting a band of Sisters—particularly Rocana, the acting Mother, and Avala, wife to Azan.

Even if the Zura and Vardna should suddenly turn on the Sisters, as they had in previous Kalpas, the Keeper swords would be no match against the star-wrought swords of the Zura and the skill of the Vardna warriors. If it came down to it, it would be the Sisters who would protect the Keepers. All Sisters were trained in wielding energy—even novices could unleash bolts of lightning and fireballs from their palms.

The Zura practiced an ancient magic. In the olden days, they worked with plants and animals, before most went extinct. Now they were left only with minerals, and practiced divination using lava streams and drew their power from the pulsing core of the planet. Avala suspected the real reason the Zura allowed Vardna into their ranks was because the fierce mountain tribe trained in energy, as did the Seers, though their practice was darker and more sinister. The Vardna could not match the force of light the Sisters commanded, so they wielded their power from the shadows. Avala shivered and pulled her traveling bundle onto her back, turning her attention to the journey in front of her.

With twelve Keepers in the front and twelve taking up the rear, the traveling party passed single file through the arch of the black-and-gold-streaked stone gate. The banners of Uttapta flapped stiffly above the gate, bidding them farewell as they started on the long path down the Ageless Mountains. Even with her sturdy shoes and walking stick to help with the rugged dirt and stone path, Avala did not like this trek. The trip down the mountain would take a full day, then they would spend another day crossing the Purlan Valley, and a third to reach their Aunt Tirili deep inside the Sacred Chambers.

It had been almost an entire Fire since Avala had last visited Rocana's sister—she could not bear to see her once magnificent aunt so dejected and broken. Several Fires had passed since that terrible day when the strong and pulsating golden cord connecting Tirili to the girl Child of the Stars had suddenly and inexplicably been severed. Tirili claimed she could still See the Children and was almost able to connect with them. Avala did not know what "almost" meant. All the times they had sat around a viewing globe with their aunt since then, they had never Seen the Children. Tirili's assistants supported her assertions, but Avala did not know if they had actually Seen the Children for themselves or were just blindly devoted to Tirili. Perhaps they feared sending Tirili into a nervous fit if they disavowed her claims.

Irsili was younger than Avala and had been inducted into the ranks of Sisters too late; Tirili's connection had already been broken by the time Irsili was allowed to join the viewing circles, and it was a source of great disappointment for Avala's sister that she had never been able to connect with the twins. Irsili constantly begged to visit Tirili, desperately wanting to See the Children for herself. Avala preferred to avoid her aunt. Tirili was simply too crazy to take seriously. Even sitting around a viewing globe with her was exhausting.

Rocana had taken over the leadership of the Sisterhood after Tirili stepped aside, and although she said she believed Tirili, she made no official announcement that the Children had been found again. She and her daughters sat in the Star Temple's viewing circle daily, seeking a connection for themselves, but it was like fishing the dead oceans of Turya.

Avala vividly remembered the day Golden Star had been born. Avala had just been anointed into the ranks of full Sisterhood. No one knew which of the Sisters of Glimmering Sight the new girl Child of the Stars would attach herself to. They had gathered as custom decreed on the first day of the Twenty-Ninth Kalpa in the Sacred Chambers, seated around a viewing globe where they meditated and expanded their golden auras until the cavern glowed with a light so bright Avala had thought they were inside Uttapta itself. They had stood vigil for twelve sunrises when Tirili had suddenly collapsed, crying like a newborn infant. A golden cord of light sprang from her belly and flung itself through the rock ceiling towards the heavens. At the other end, far across the galaxy, the cord connected through the navel of the newborn Child of the Stars—the first of the twins to be born—the girl this time. The golden cord was thicker than Avala had imagined, a multitude of luminescent threads coiled into one fat living connection that pulsed with a power that had taken her breath away and sent hot tears streaming down her face.

Tirili had been anointed Sacred Mother that day, and they all paraded through the streets of ancient Purlan, the capital city of Turya. Tirili had been a sight to behold, robed in her ceremonial gold and white vestments, her golden nimbus extending out so far it illuminated everything around her. The people of Purlan had emerged from the underground city and thronged the streets, chanting and crying and falling prone, overcome with bliss.

Suddenly, Turya was a planet of joy. The Children were coming Home. The Sisters of the Glimmering Sight were officially returned to their Seat of Power atop the Ageless Mountains, with the Keepers of the Concha Scrolls at their sides to prepare for and record the momentous event of the coming of the Star Children. The common people, the Sikat, who were spread across Turya like grains of sand, made pilgrimages to get a glimpse of Father-Heart-of-Sky, climbing the last stretch of the stony mountain trail on their knees until they were bloody. The Sikat smeared the blood on their foreheads in a prayer that the fires of Uttapta would burn for all eternity and its flames spread to the darkest reaches of the cosmos, where they would ignite life in an endless stream of ecstasy.

Preparations had been made to receive the Star Children. Ancient gold bricks were brought up from the storerooms and laid around Father-Heart-of-Sky to receive their blessed footsteps. The common people wore white and gold to honor their coming. Rare plants were offered every dawn, and fires lit the city day and night.

Avala had learned how to follow Tirili's golden cord when they gazed into the viewing globe together and found Golden Star for herself. She was a fat and happy infant, bright with a golden nimbus of her own, and gazed back upon Avala as though they were in the same room, her big blue baby eyes calm and alert with the deep knowing of an ancient soul. Golden Star's twin brother, Flying Star, was often at her side, and Avala would gaze upon the infants for hours at a time, filled with such love she thought she would burst. She sang lullabies to them, songs her mother had sung to her.

She had continued singing to them as they grew. The girl Child was alert when she was awake, and so fecund in the golden filaments that grew from the seed stalk of Tirili that she connected to everyone around her until she became encased in a thick web of sensation that pulsed with the experiences of her people. Tirili became concerned that Golden Star could no longer distinguish her sacred cord from all the other cords that fought for her attention. So they sang to calm her, and tried to get her to sleep so that the constant barrage of sensations would subside and allow the Child to rest and the connection with Tirili to grow stronger.

It was during sleep that the boy Child became aware. Flying Star heard them singing when he slept and reached out with his little pudgy hands as he dreamt. He delighted in the songs so much that they sang all the traditional folk songs about the Star Children—songs celebrating their coming and wishing them a joyous life and a safe journey Home. He would sit with them in his dreams, laughing and clapping as they sang to him. He was happy and carefree, as the second of the Star Children was reputed to be. It was the primary Child who carried most of the responsibility for getting Home; the role of the secondary Child was to clear the way for the first and offer protection. That often included significant challenges, and often violence, so it was said that the second Child's carefree nature inevitably evolved into fierce determination, sometimes overshadowed with dark brooding.

And there was always a third, an assistant named Guiding Star who served as a forward scout. The Sisters believed they had Seen Guiding Star as well, a boy child leaning over the cribs of the twins, gazing at them in wonder and tickling them until they howled with laughter, and telling them stories that he made up about monsters and magicians and evil sorcerers.

The joyous connection with the Star Children had ended one day as abruptly as it had begun. Tirili had collapsed in a moaning heap, then screamed as though she were being murdered. Her golden nimbus faded to a pale brown sheath, and Avala had run to her side, afraid she was dying. When Tirili recovered enough to speak she told them a gray shadow had cut through the cord and all had gone black. That was all she remembered.

At first they feared Golden Star had died, but Tirili maintained some sort of connection to the boy Child and was able to sense through his dreams that his sister was alive and well. Or so she said. Tirili had retreated into the Lower Chambers where the monastic nuns resided, and Rocana had taken over the leadership of the Sisters of the Glimmering Sight, refusing to give up on the Star Children. She was given the title of acting Mother in a private ceremony attended only by the leadership of the Sisters and Keepers.

They tried to keep the broken connection a secret, but rumors spread. Pilgrims who climbed the Ageless Mountain to Father-Heart-of-Sky found a group of pale, haggard Sisters and nervous, tense Keepers. Soon the Sisters closed off the site to outsiders except for once a year during the high holy season, and most Sisters retreated to the Sacred Chambers at the western edge of Purlan Valley. Only the top members of the hierarchy remained at the Star Temple to watch over Father-Heart-of-Sky and await the coming of the Star Children—or suffer persecution and possibly execution if the Star Children never arrived.

Parades and celebrations ceased, and the population crept around in a state of confusion, unsure whether or not the Star Children still lived. Divisions emerged within the ranks of the Sisters of the Glimmering Sight, with branches of the Sisterhood going off in secret, seeking new connections. The Keepers of the Concha Scrolls scoured their libraries, trying to find historical records of past broken connections, but they could find none. The only record of a sacred connection being broken was during the previous Kalpa when one of the three Hearts-of-Sky on the colonized planets, the primary portal globe on Iliad, had exploded, and the Children had never arrived because of it.

Those records were sealed. Her parents had read them, of course, being the Eldest Keeper of the Concha Scrolls and the Sacred Mother, but they refused to speak of them, other than to say it was a completely different situation this time. When Avala asked about how the Star Children of this age would ignite the pathways of light without the Heart-of-Sky on Iliad, her parents said that there had to be another way to traverse the heavens. When she asked what that was, Laris and Rocana exchanged somber glances.

"There must be a way," her father would say. "The prophecies speak of the twenty-ninth Kalpa of the hundredth age, and how the Star Children unite the diaspora with the Ancestors. That's us," he would add, as though she did not know what every schoolchild learned when they were five.

"The Star Children will discover it," her mother would say with forced confidence.

It was an old problem, and Avala was tired of worrying about it. It was out of her hands.

Her mind wandered as they descended into the valley, the trail sometimes narrowing and the steep mountainside falling away beyond a hip-high wall that was too low to keep anyone safe if they should stumble. They used their walking sticks and stepped carefully, pulling their wraps tight as the wind whipped around them.

Avala passed the time daydreaming about the two nights Azan had spent at home recently, the first time they'd had two consecutive nights together this fire season. Azan had consulted the records, and it was true that the eruptions on Uttapta grew worse every year. But they had not spoken of the impending doom. Once when tensions were running high in the family, they had agreed that the two of them would trust with all their hearts that the Star Children would come and save them. To believe otherwise was too hard to endure.

Azan had made love to her like he had when they were newly married.

"What is it, my love?" she had asked after the first time.

He turned on his side and cupped her chin gently in his hand and kissed her. "I love you."

"I know you love me," she said, laughing. "But why are you treating me like a new bride?"

"Every day is new with you," he teased, nibbling playfully at her ear. She giggled and twisted away. He drew her close and began again.

But it still struck her as strange that before he left, he had insisted she wear her wedding jewelry on her journey. "It's heavy," she complained, "and ostentatious. I don't like to parade our status in front of the common people."

"They all know who you are," he said, helping her fasten the gold crescent around her neck. The gaudy piece was inlaid with alternating black and clear cut diamonds. It had been passed down to her through her maternal line, supposedly having belonged to the Sacred Mother of three Kalpas ago, and had been a gift from her mother on her wedding day. In turn, she was to pass it on to her female child, if she had one. If not, it would go to Irsili's daughter, or to a female cousin on her mother's side.

It was a treasure, and Avala preferred it stay in its box instead of weighing heavily on her collarbone. But Azan had insisted, and she could not deny her handsome husband this one small thing. He asked for so little from her. The only thing he wanted that she had not given him yet was a child. She was getting older, but there was still time. The energy a child took from its mother was something Avala could not spare right now while they sought Golden Star and Flying Star.

The wind pulled her from her reverie as she drew her robe tightly around her, her gold bracelets clacking against one another. She moved closer to the mountainside to try to shield herself from the wind, but it did no good. She made her way carefully down the smooth steps as they entered the series of switchbacks on the final descent.

She was almost happy when they descended into the gray haze, trading the wind for air that was thick with ash from the latest eruption of Mount Sagir. The air stank with sulfur from the constant venting of fumaroles and bubbling mudpots that ringed the valley. She and her sister and mother pulled white scarves from their traveling bags, drew them across their mouths and noses, and continued on.

They finally reached the base of the mountain in the stifling heat of the lowlands and spent the evening at a small temple with some Sisters

Avala knew from Novice training. They spent the evening catching up on the latest gossip, then slept until Uttapta rose.

They had to pass through the center of Purlan to reach the entrance to the cloisters beneath the Sacred Chambers where Tirili lived. The city above ground had been destroyed the previous Kalpa when tribal wars broke out after the Star Children had not arrived. No one had bothered rebuilding it, since Uttapta grew ever hotter and fire storms were more frequent. The population had retreated to the underground city, which was much cooler and safer, and just as glorious.

The central square of Purlan featured a large fountain whose waters had stopped flowing long ago. A circle of Sikat were sitting beside the dry fountain and singing mournfully. Avala recognized the song as one she used to sing to the Star Children, one of the boy Child's favorites.

When the dragon flames
Born of the king star
Reach through the skies
We fall upon the sacred ground
Where our Children return
Those who left us long ago
To travel to the stars
They ride the light to join us now
With tales of woe and glory

They passed the Sikat, who barely spared them a glance—not even faltering in their song, where once they would have flocked to them, showering them with blessings and kneeling with their foreheads to the ground as the Sisters passed. The singing faded into the distance as Rocana led her daughters from the square and into the labyrinth of ancient abandoned city streets, the voices haunting Avala. The people still had hope. They were reverting to the old ways, putting faith in the simple things since the formal institutions were failing them. Legends spoke of the common people of Turya singing in unison to guide the Star Children on their journey Home. It was an old grandmother's tale. A quaint notion that made the Sikat feel like they had some control over a life filled with despair, when everyone knew that only gifted and trained Seers had the skill to guide the Star Children across the heavens. If the Sisters of the Glimmering Sight could not guide the Children, then they would not come.

Avala's heart was heavy as they traversed the western edge of the city. The light from Uttapta was fading, and the gray clouds weighed down upon them. The guards lit torches to guide their way as abandoned stone buildings grew sparser and the fire-scarred terrain blended into the darkness before them. The light of the torches reflected off the white tunics of the guards, their decorative red helmets hiding the luminescence of their head dendrals, whose length trailed down their backs in masses of thick gold braids like fire snakes. Irsili's head dendrals were covered by the brown roughspun hood like Avala's, but Rocana's head was bare, and her coiled head dendrals glowed bright gold like the manes of the winged lions illustrated in the Illuminated Scrolls.

Avala wished for the ancient days the Scrolls depicted when winged lions roamed the plains and took to the sky, carrying Seers and Keepers on their backs. It was said that luminescent palm trees used to line the stone road to the Sacred Chambers, lighting the way with fronds of fluorescent green. But the path they traveled on was dark and devoid of life.

The stench of mudpots announced themselves before their gurgling reached Avala's ears. They passed the cluster of dark stinking sores. The road had been rerouted in spots where sinkholes had opened up and mudpots and sulfur pools had risen to the surface. One large pool was traversed via a new stone bridge. Avala drew the scarf tightly around her nose and mouth and tried to hold her breath for the duration.

Her feet were sore and her legs heavy when at long last the fires marking the entrance to the Sacred Chambers glinted in the distance. The white stone gates finally loomed before them, tall towers piercing the murky darkness like floating specters. Avala pressed her left hand to her belly in the ceremonial greeting to the Ancestors who lay below them as she passed through the stone arches. She prayed silently to Uttapta that its fires would continue to burn when she retreated into the catacombs the following day, the sun serving as a guiding light for the Star Children to find their way Home.

———————————)———————————

Golden Star was not a child anymore, but Avala recognized her. The shape of her cheekbones, the slant to her blue eyes, the curve of her pink lips. Even without the golden umbilical cord connecting her to Tirili, she was unmistakable. A few fine golden threads extended from Golden Star's belly and traveled through the air, but Avala did not want to break her concentration to see where they led.

Avala was skilled at maintaining her awareness even while dreaming. She resisted becoming totally subsumed in the dream and stored away her observations to recall later. She was connected to Golden Star, and through the most unusual of connections, the likes of which she had never seen.

One strand of Golden Star's core helix reached out and expressed itself back over the dimension of time, with nodes marking each past generation. Upon each node was imprinted the image of an Ancestor. The strand traced the journey of the matriarchal core helix that had been passed from mother to daughter generation after generation. A similar strand left Avala's abdomen and stretched back in time. Avala twisted to watch the strand as it unfurled and joined a distant node that was a Shared Mother to Avala and Golden Star, before their genetic lines had separated. The strand continued farther back beyond the Shared Mother and terminated at a large golden face—the face of Mother Sun, the First That Was. Avala remained transfixed on the First That Was, having only heard of her in legends. Mother Sun gazed back at her with waves of love that made Avala tremble.

Avala shifted her attention back to Golden Star, her distant cousin. She looked like a Turyan, yet different. Her head dendrals were not the luminescent gold of a Turyan, but a dull, dirt brown. At least they were full, though they extended only just past her shoulder blades, as though they had been severed at their ends, which made Avala shudder with pain. Golden Star's other dendrals looked dead and lay like brown fuzz along her arms. By comparison, the dendrals on Avala's head and arms and other parts of her body were translucent, living, glowing fibers and radiated the golden light that illumined all Turyans in a bright halo.

Golden Star's body structure and facial features were normal, but her skin was a pale, sickly white, having lost almost all of its gleam. The Star Child still emitted some faint light, but of a deep blue that extended only a hand's width from her body, except around her head where the nimbus was larger and still retained some golden tones. As a child, Golden Star had radiated a blinding gold light.

How Golden Star had lost her glow but still remained alive was confusing to Avala. Perhaps when the gray shadow had severed the connection to Tirili, it had nearly killed the girl Child, as it had nearly killed Tirili. Yet she appeared alive and well otherwise, her blue eyes bright, her posture strong, her breathing and heartbeat quick with excitement and wonder at their shared vision.

Avala awoke from the dream with a start and sat up. It was still dark out, and her sister and mother were asleep next to her in the large bed. She lay back and tried to sink back into the dream, but the vision of Golden Star and Mother Sun slowly faded. She pressed her hands to her chest, her heart pounding like a drum.

————————) ————————

Their guest bedchamber was in the Upper Chambers, which held the Sacred Library and school for apprentice Keepers. It was hot and musty, with only a faint gust of smoky air entering through a gap high up on the stone wall, which let in a shaft of dim red light that hit the opposite wall. Uttapta was rising.

They rose and breakfasted in the hall with the guards and apprentices, having been served the standard fare of tortula eggs and golden mushroom tea. While her mother was busy talking in hushed tones with an elder Keeper, and Irsili endured the flirtations of a guard, Avala walked casually towards the door, sternly gesturing at two guards who rose to follow her that they should stay put. They hesitated, and before they could determine what they should do, she slipped out the door into the courtyard where a stiff wind greeted her. She pulled her wrap close and lifted the hood over her head to protect her dendrals and crossed quickly to the towering gray stone library, pulling open the heavy metal doors. A gust of wind sealed the doors shut behind her. She slid the bar through the door brackets to keep her well-meaning guards from following.

It was peaceful and quiet in the entryway. She exhaled, grateful for a moment of solitude. She pushed the hood off her head, walked down the wide hallway, and tugged at the library's inner doors, but they were barred shut. She tried a second entrance, but it was also locked. She gritted her teeth in frustration. If her father were here, he would make sure the library was open at daybreak, like he had when she was a child. Better yet, if he were here, she would simply get a key from him so she could enter whenever she wanted.

Rather than face the wind that howled through the courtyard, Avala navigated the interior corridors, taking the long way around to return to the dining hall. Halfway to her destination, the door to a side room stood ajar, and she peeked inside. The room held several stone tables littered with half-finished scrolls. It was early yet, and only one apprentice was hunched over his transcription work. He looked up as she entered the room.

"Hi," she said, clearing her throat. "The library is closed."

The apprentice set his quill aside. "Yes, it is not open yet."

"Yes, well," she faltered.

"Sorry, I don't have a key," he said. He couldn't have seen more than fourteen Fires.

"I'll ask an elder Keeper," she said dejectedly, knowing her mother would want to rush them off into the subterranean chambers to complete the last leg of their journey, not spend all morning in a dusty library searching through scrolls. She couldn't tell her mother about her dream of Golden Star, or it would raise a huge fuss that would end with Avala locked in a viewing chamber with her aunt for countless sunrises and spawn jealousy among the Sisters. Or worse, they would think she was the next Sacred Mother, and then when they realized it was only a strange dream, hope would come crashing down. No, best she kept her vision to herself for now.

"I was wondering," she said, eyeing the stacks of scrolls that filled the floor-to-ceiling shelves spanning the entire width of the back wall. "Have you come across anything that describes the Star Children? You know, their skills. Their journeys."

The apprentice made a face and gestured to the shelves overflowing with scrolls. "All of them. Take your pick."

"Oh," she said, suddenly overwhelmed. She was accustomed to asking her father for what she wanted and having him pick the appropriate scroll for her. "May I look?"

He squinted at her. "Aren't you daughter of the Eldest Keeper?"

"Yes, I'm Avala."

"Well, then. You don't need to ask my permission." He waved his hand at the wall of shelves again, then turned back to his scroll.

Gold-leaf edges identified the Concha Scrolls, which took up the entire left side of the wall. She did not read the ancient tongue. The right side was filled with an assortment of rolled scrolls, and parchments bound into books. She pulled a few bound books randomly and cleared a spot on a table.

The first was a story her father had read to her as a child—battles between wolves and shadow cats, flying foxes and winged lions. She set it aside. The next was of the Ilian empire and the hierarchy of priests. The third was of a planet whose waters were rising and whose male Descendants were becoming infertile. The fourth was more interesting: "Characteristics of the Descendants—Modern Planetary Races," with a chapter on Earthlanders.

When they had first found Golden Star and Flying Star, it had come as a surprise to the Sisters that the new Star Children should come from a secondary planet. A team of Keepers and Sisters had conducted extensive research to confirm that the Star Children they were Seeing were indeed on the minor planet Earth instead of Iliad, Delos, or Muria, where all the prior Children had been born. Avala had been on heavy rotation in the viewing chambers to keep track of the Children, and had had no time to study scrolls. It had not mattered much to her where the Children came from, only that they had been born and had been found.

She flipped through the pages. There were chapters on the scattering of the Totem and the growth of populations on Iliad, Delos, Muria, and other planets she had never heard of. She scanned the chapter on Earthlanders. A section on physical characteristics described them as shorter in stature than their parent Turyan Keeper race while maintaining the primary features of the species. The Earthlanders' dendrals had lost most of their luminescence, and what light remained dispersed into various colors. The rare Earthlander maintained remnants of the gold nimbus. They retained the ability to connect through life threads, which were still gold or sometimes degraded to silver. If the Earthlanders were crossbred with some of the more malevolent races, the life threads could be gray, or in the worst cases, a sticky black. The life threads existed on a light spectrum that was not visible to anyone other than Seers and the occasional Zura or Vardna. Therefore, most Earthlanders, or most Descendants, for that matter, could not see them.

Earthlanders, though originally of Keeper stock, had suffered interbreeding with the violent Vardna tribe, which made the Earthlander race physically strong and sometimes brutal. The early Vardna explorers had journeyed across Earth on a warpath that had ended with the Vardna settling the Cephean planets and leaving Earth behind.

Avala flipped through the other chapters, scanning the history and evolution of each race over the nearly three thousand Kalpas since the Totem had first dispersed from Turya.

Ilians, modern-day Delosians, and Earthlanders originated from the same Turyan Keeper tribe. Ilian bloodlines were closest to Turyans' due to Iliad's position as the portal planet to Turya—host to the Heart-of-Sky that connected directly to Father-Heart-of-Sky. This propitious position had given Iliad's inhabitants a higher status than the rest of the diaspora, and more access to the invigorating life force and genetic material of the parent Turyan race at each thousandth-year Joining of the Totem. Ilians had actively sought out Turyan Seers to breed with, in order to better communicate with the Home planet during the millennium between each Joining. Over time some Ilian families had become very strong in the Sight and founded an exclusive caste of priests and priestesses.

Delos housed the second Heart-of-Sky, connecting to Turya through Iliad. Native Delosians were Descendants of a Turyan Zura mountain tribe, who were known for their magic. The same tribe had also settled a minor planet called Scridland. Those Zura who settled on Scridland interbred with a sect of Seers, who had also settled on that planet, having chosen it for its vast forests and powerful minerals.

On Delos, the native Delosians were slowly pushed into the mountains by the Ilian royalty who liked to vacation on the planet, enjoying the lush valleys and picturesque coastal areas. Ilian tribes established several towns to service the visiting royalty, and a Royal City built up around the Gate to Delos's Heart-of-Sky. Over time, the Ilian immigrants became known as Delosians, and the native Delosians were called the Mountain People. At the onset of the thousand-year war on Iliad, the Delosian population swelled with Ilian refugees and carried on the Ilian culture, which was all but destroyed on Iliad by the invading Cephs and the ravages of an endless war.

Delos also supported another population who were descended from a Turyan race that preferred to settle on islands and live off the fruits of the sea, back before the Turyan oceans had acidified, killing most of the food the Fish tribe had relied on. Many Kalpas ago, the entire Fish tribe had been on the brink of starvation and left Turya for their new planet,

Nommos, a wondrous land of oceans and idyllic islands where the tribe could carry on its traditions. But the sea level on Nommos rose over time, and after a thousand Kalpas little land remained. The population relocated to Delos, which had a single large ocean that took up half the planet. The Fish people had suffered a history of betrayals: starved by their native Turya, drowned by their colonized planet, and abandoned by their own internal oceans—the Fish tribe had isolated themselves for so many Kalpas that their genetic material had degraded to the point of mass infertility in the males, threatening them with extinction. They had found refuge on Delos, but they did not know how to reignite their internal fires, relying instead upon genetic engineering and genetic material from other races. The females of that race fled the infertile males, whose condition had driven some of the Fish men to insanity, and established their own colony on the planet Lingri-La.

Avala's favorite planet was Muria. A Turyan tribe of Seers had populated that strange jungle planet. Muria was the third leg of the primary triangle of the portal system, along with Iliad and Delos, and host to the third Heart-of-Sky.

The Murian race was reclusive and disliked the Ilians and Delosians. They were forced to interact with their cousins only at the Lighting of the Triangle, when the three Hearts-of-Sky were connected with golden pathways of light and connected to Turya via Iliad. Of all the Turyan diaspora, only the Murians' dendrals retained their full luminescence, and had even grown thicker and longer than Turyans'. Their dendrals vibrated with storehouses of Uttapta's fire, but strangely, the dendrals' color spectrum had shifted from gold to other more brilliant colors.

Suffering an opposite fate, the Vardna Descendants who settled the Cephean planets had maintained some of the taller stature of Turyans, but their dendrals had lost all luminescence. Their life threads had thickened to a sticky black and were used to aggressively control others.

Avala shuddered.

The Vardna were the most warlike of all Turyans, and were closely related to the Zura tribes, with interbreeding common enough that they were sometimes mistaken for one another. Her husband was Zura, but he spoke of the Vardna with respect. The Vardna whom he knew were fierce but fair, and their dendrals still glowed brightly. They would be ashamed to learn of the degradation of their distant Descendants. No doubt, that sort of consideration was why the Scrolls were kept secret, only available to Keepers and Sisters.

"May I borrow this?" Avala asked the apprentice.

He got up stiffly from his stool and examined the book, then found a duplicate on the shelf. "Yes, I'll tell an elder Keeper you have it," he said, giving her a shy smile.

Avala tucked the large book under her arm and went in search of her mother.

———————)———————

The tunnels that descended into the Sacred Chambers were dark and musty and stank of death. Winding passageways were lit by oil lanterns, which made the walls move with living shadows. Avala reluctantly followed her mother past the entrances to the Black Halls, where many of her friends lived. The Black Halls, also known as the Middle Chambers, had become a sprawling town built in the extensive cave system in the black lava beds that lay underneath the Purlan Valley. Over time, as fire and brimstone claimed more and more of Turya's surface, the Black Halls became home to hundreds of Sisters of the Glimmering Sight, most of whom aspired to reach the upper ranks of Sisters and stand vigil at the Star Temple and Father-Heart-of-Sky.

Avala and their entourage followed a maze of tunnels that formed a web beneath the lava beds, passing through several guarded checkpoints and continuing their descent into the deep and silent cave system of the Lower Chambers, which were lit by luminescent crystals set into wall brackets every hundred paces. Tunnels narrowed, forcing them to walk single file, and then opened up again into a series of small caves where stone statues of legendary Seers and Keepers kept vigil in their carved-out grottos, extending stone hands to assist the travelers in their journeys or following them with eyes of black volcanic glass.

Avala was almost happy to reach the subterranean village of Kala, where her aunt lived. White and gold banners of Uttapta draped the stone walls flanking the entrance, which was a low archway adorned with gold scrollwork inlaid with diamonds and rubies depicting extinct flowers. They passed under the ornate arch, and the ceilings disappeared into dark shadows overhead. The cavern held the ruins of a small amphitheater, or meeting hall, carved into the rock. Tiered seats faced a raised platform where the Sacred Mother had presided over the Sisters in days of old, when the governing body of the Sisterhood had made this their seat of power. Now it was a vacant, stale anteroom leading to a village most people had forgotten about.

The guards would be staying in the antechamber for the duration of the visit, guarding the entrance from threats that did not exist. Most likely they would pass the time playing cards or practicing their sword fighting—if for no reason other than to tone their young bodies. The women bid them farewell and went to the back of the large chamber where the inner gate to Kala stood gleaming in the shadows.

The gate was twice the height of Avala, and the closed door was fashioned of pure gold. It was simple in design, absent of gemstones or any decoration—appropriate for present-day Kala, a monastic community. Sisters and Keepers often retreated there in order to live in solitude and focus on cultivating their light essence, so that they could achieve the rainbow body upon death. Others simply chose to reside there in the twilight of their lives, leaving only when death took them.

Rocana rang the door chimes, and after a long wait the door swung open. They were greeted by an elderly Sister they all knew. They exchanged pleasantries, then continued on a long path that brought them to the main square of the village.

A small chapel was carved into the far end of the central cavern, where Sisters and Keepers would be laid to rest for a final viewing as their rainbow bodies flared in a final burst of glory before fading into eternal darkness. To the left were entrances to the administrative chambers. To the right lay the entrance to the residential neighborhood. The square had a fire fountain in the center that lit the vast room in a dancing yellow glow. Set against the walls of the cavern were a modest assortment of small stalls made of golden tenting, where various wares were sold. Avala, Irsili, and Rocana strolled slowly around the marketplace, exchanging greetings with the Sisters who were tending the stalls. They politely examined the bushels of dried mushrooms, small metal flasks of pure water from sacred springs deep underground, racks of silk scarves and ceremonial stoles, pillows for sitting in the viewing chambers, and assortments of crystal balls ranging from small ones that could be hidden in a palm or secret pocket, to the standard viewing chamber size, which stood at knee-height so that one could look into the globe but also see the Sisters sitting on the other side of the circle.

They shared the latest gossip from the Star Temple, purchased a flask of the precious water for each of them, and eventually made their way to the residential passageways. After several twists and turns they found themselves at the door to Tirili's chambers.

Aunt Tirili greeted them with tight hugs, her bony fingers digging into Avala's back, the scent of amber making Avala's nose wrinkle in distaste. The expensive perfume did not hide the stench of depression. It appeared as though Tirili had made some effort to ready herself for their visit—her dress was at least smooth and clean, though she still wore the gray silks of mourning, which gave her skin an unfortunate green tinge. It had been several Fires since she had donned the gray silks, and Avala figured she planned to die wearing them.

Her aunt looked worse than Avala remembered. Tirili's once vibrant head dendrals had a disturbing number of filaments that had lost all luminescence and lay in limp waves instead of the tight spirals all Sisters wore. Her skin, which used to be a radiant gold, was dull and hung in loose folds from her cheeks and jowls. Avala had not seen anyone with such a loss of light since her grandmother lay on her deathbed. Avala hoped her stubborn, independent aunt was allowing the healer Sisters to tend to her.

Tirili had taken up permanent residence in Kala, deep in the Lower Chambers commonly referred to as the catacombs. The Lower Chambers had been used for various purposes over the Kalpas. The most common use was as a burial ground for Keepers and Sisters. Other sections had been used as dungeons during the Dark Times, which often happened in the middle of the Kalpas between visits from Star Children when superstition and doubt reigned. The Dark Times had been longer and more brutal than normal this past cycle after the Children had not come, and when the Dark Times finally passed many of the dungeons had been walled off. West of the burial grounds lay Kala.

It was here that Tirili had lived since the connection to Golden Star had been severed. She was assisted by a small retinue of devotees who still viewed her as the Sacred Mother, despite her tragic failure. They had created a rather comfortable living environment, all things considered.

The two generations of sisters sat together in Tirili's outer room and shared a simple meal of yellow lichen and black beetles, with a sweet white mushroom wine. Tirili drank a lot of it, which softened her stiff demeanor. With her inhibitions weakened, Tirili managed an occasional laugh, but she also voiced her thoughts, which were not always pleasant. Avala shifted uncomfortably as her aunt filled her goblet again, watching warily as the conversation between Tirili and Rocana grew heated.

"You think I'm lying," Tirili said, silencing the room.

"I do not," Rocana said gently.

Tirili pushed back her cushion and stood up, her goblet of wine sloshing in her hand. "You don't think I know what my little sister is thinking?" she demanded, her eyes drilling into Rocana's. "I see him in his dreams."

"I hope you do," Rocana said. "I truly do."

"See?!" Tirili slammed down the metal goblet, splattering wine on the low stone table. "You *hope* I do? Don't patronize me. Come to the viewing chamber and I'll prove it." She gathered her gray skirts and swept away from the table, glaring over her shoulder for Rocana to follow. Rocana threw her daughters a frustrated glance, and the three of them got to their feet and trailed after Tirili.

The viewing chamber was a small stuffy room with low ceilings, chosen for the veins of gold that streaked the floors and ceiling. At its center sat a crystal viewing globe. Tirili was already seated on her pillow. Avala grabbed a pillow and sat on the floor to the right of her aunt and across from Irsili, with Rocana opposite Tirili. They all touched hands for a moment to create a connection, then settled with their hands folded in their laps and gazed into the globe.

The crystal ball was foggy, offering nothing. Avala relaxed and waited. Hours passed slowly, and she grew stiff and irritable. In the past, she had spent endless days locked in this room sitting around this globe. When the Star Children had been connected to Tirili, it had been a joy. Avala could not get enough and forwent sleep for the chance to see the twins. After the connection was broken, it became torture. Fires passed without even a glimpse of the Star Children. Finally, Laris convinced his wife to bring his daughters back to the Star Temple and take up vigil there. Avala was forever grateful to her father for that.

She had just let her eyes close when she heard her aunt gasp. Avala's eyes flew open and she searched the depths of the globe. It had cleared and rainbows streaked through it. A scene slowly took form.

A young man was walking slowly across a dry dusty plain littered with dead bodies. He stooped over the closest body and gently turned it onto its back and arranged the legs so that they were straight. He then closed the corpse's eyes and folded the arms over its chest. He went to the next body and did the same. The corpses seemed unharmed aside from being clearly dead.

Avala examined the young man. He had a glow about him, but it was violet, not gold. Still, there was something familiar about him. Seeing as Avala was in tandem with Tirili's Sight, she concluded it must be Flying Star. The face of the child Avala remembered had matured into the angular face of a man hardened by life. Her pulse quickened with excitement. Could it truly be him? She concentrated on her breathing to keep her mind and heart calm so as not to break the tenuous connection.

"Is he in a war?" Irsili whispered.

The four women kept their eyes fastened on the globe and spoke in low tones, as though a loud noise might awaken him.

"It's a dream," Rocana reminded them. "Could be present time, or it could be a memory. Or could be the future."

"He sees the future," Tirili stated flatly. She was the one holding the connection and was bordering on a trancelike state. "But he has been dreaming a lot about war lately. Earth has been invaded by the Cephs."

Her last statement hung heavily in the air. Everyone knew the Cephs had infested Earth, but seeing Flying Star embroiled in that mess made Avala's heart falter.

"I am going to try to contact him," Tirili said.

"No, you mustn't," Rocana said quickly.

"I must. With the three of you behind me, perhaps it will work."

Avala held her breath as her aunt attempted to enter the dream. It was a tricky maneuver, particularly over such a great distance and with a Descendant who had lost much of his golden essence. Avala relaxed her hands and concentrated, putting the weight of her own focus and energy behind her aunt's. She watched the dusty plain as her aunt stepped onto it.

Tirili's image flickered for a moment, then solidified. She gathered her skirts and crept up behind Flying Star, who was arranging another man's legs. Tirili stepped around the corpse to face him. When he rose, his eyes landed on her. Avala saw through her aunt's dreaming eyes as shock froze Flying Star's expression and he fell backwards, the dream image shredding as he awoke. The guttural call of his waking scream faded as Tirili was jerked out of the lucid dream and fully back into her body.

Avala's awareness returned to the viewing chamber with a jolt. When she looked at her aunt she saw what Flying Star must have seen as he left the dream. Her aunt's wrinkled face was twisted into a grimace, and her head dendrals were raised in a glowing mane that made her appear crazed and terrifying. The next moment, her aunt collapsed into a sobbing heap.

"He's frightened of me," she wept. Rocana hurried to her side and cradled her head in her lap. "I used to be an angel to him—now I'm a ghost haunting him."

Avala and Irsili locked eyes, and Irsili grinned. "We found him," Irsili said. The joy of finally seeing Flying Star shone in her eyes, and her bubbling laughter filled the room.

3

DRUMS

Laris stood at the black stone gate atop the Ageless Mountains, watching the mountain path where his daughter Avala's husband, Azan, was climbing its final ascent above the ash cloud layer. Laris's bones stiffened as Azan's helmet reflected a flash of gold and crimson from a glancing ray of Uttapta. Azan wore the Golden Helm as the reigning leader of the Zura Warriors of Mount Sagir, which meant he was here on official business.

The Zura protected the Totem from threats down below: the molten lava that erupted violently, bursting through the brittle rock to spew red fountains and clouds of ash into the skies. The Zura cleared the villages from the path of the blood of Turya. Azan ranged the countryside, carrying the Dowsing Rod and scouring the landscape, searching for the next eruption in time to evacuate the locals. He was correct eight times out of ten, so the villagers solemnly packed up when Azan detected stirring down below. Still, families from the villages where the ground did not erupt—where the stone hovels stood empty—those men and women bore down on him with stares of suspicion and contempt when he walked through the cave dwellings where the refugees gathered to live out their lives. Azan had driven them from their homes, and for no good reason. The dragon-ground had not attacked their homes, yet they were living in the honeycombed cave cities nonetheless. Being Zura Master and Dowser was not a light duty, and Azan's broad shoulders stooped from its burdensome weight.

The Ageless Mountains had been born of the flowing lava, but had long since died. There was no threat of eruption here. His son was not coming to evict him from the Star Temple. Laris knew why Azan was here. Laris had just recently reread the passage in the Concha Scrolls that told of this. The Zura were concerned that the Star Children had not yet arrived. Even the assurances of the Sisters of the Glimmering Sight, who vowed the Children were still alive, could not rest the hearts of the people.

Every Turyan knew what had happened the previous Kalpa, a thousand Fires ago, when the Star Children had not arrived and had been unable to unite the Totem. They knew what the Sisters had told them of that time—which the Keeper scribes had recorded in the Concha Scrolls. That a planet named Iliad, the primary portal planet for the Star Children to connect with the Turyans, had been invaded by Cephs, the Descendants of the warlike Vardna, and its Heart-of-Sky had been destroyed. Iliad, a planet with Seers advanced enough that they could connect with Turya's Sisters of the Glimmering Sight, was still ravaged by the war the Cephs' atrocity had unleashed, plunging the once-bright civilization into an extended dark age. The war was a struggle for power among the Totem's sons and daughters—the self tearing at its own body in a fit of insanity, unaware that the eyes it was gouging out were its own. The Ilian Seers who had fled from the marauding Cephs had begged the Turyan Sisters for aid, but Father-Heart-of-Sky did not awaken. There had been no way for the Turyans to send help.

Azan approached the gate, removing his helm and pressing his forehead against his father's in the tribal greeting. Laris was touched that even on Zura business Azan did not forget their familial ties. Laris had not objected when Avala had told him of her desire to wed Azan. It was customary for Sisters of the Glimmering Sight to wed Keepers of the Concha Scrolls. Zura normally wed weavers or goldsmiths. Or, rarely, the daughter of a Keeper and Sister before the daughter unveiled her Sight. But it was unheard of for Zura to marry full Sisters.

But Laris had read the Scrolls. He knew the past, which the Keepers did their best to let most Turyans forget. How during the last Kalpa, after the Star Children had not arrived, the Zura took up arms against the Keepers and the Sisters, wresting control of Father-Heart-of-Sky from them and casting doubt on their powers and the ancient ways. The Zura started questioning the Faith, and even the existence of Star Children at all, depicting those who gazed into Father-Heart-of-Sky as delusional witches, intent on bringing Turya to ruin. The Vardna had streamed up from the south and conducted extensive raids, where they ransacked the cave dwellings of the Sikat and broke into the smaller temples, raping Sisters and killing Keepers. It had been only through magic the Sisters wielded that the Sisters and Keepers had been able to regain control and protect Father-Heart-of-Sky from those who wanted to destroy it. Laris reflected sadly that the Turyans were not so different from their Descendants—that the traits displayed by the marauding Cephs on Iliad were hauntingly similar to those of their tribal Ancestors.

After generations of subjecting the people to the Sisters' strict obedience and hiding the truths of the Concha Scrolls from all but fellow Keepers, things had gradually loosened up. Openness and freedom reigned in Turya once again. Knowledge and truth, equality and self-determination had been allowed to return. Laris did not want to see the cycle of conflict and alienation repeat itself. The Turyan race might not survive it this time. He knew the Zura must not view the Keepers and Sisters as the enemy, or all hope was lost.

He looked into Azan's eyes. Waiting for the words he knew would come.

"We want to invoke the drums." The words dropped heavily from Azan's mouth. He knew it was a challenge to the Seers' authority.

Laris's heart fell, but he kept his expression open and gentle. "Of course," Laris said, patting his son-in-law kindly on the shoulder. "People want to take their lives into their own hands. Putting hand to drum makes men feel in control. It will strengthen their spirits. Let it be so."

Laris knew he was speaking sacrilege and defying the tenets of the Keepers. He was Eldest Keeper. What he was sanctioning would either save Turya or lead to its doom, and would either strengthen his claim as Eldest Keeper or send him into exile deep in the bowels of the catacombs. And he did not even want to think about what it would do to his relationship with his wife and daughters and the other Sisters of the Glimmering Sight, whom he had just formally discredited. Azan no doubt had the same worries regarding Avala, but he had sworn his life to the Zura before all else.

"Take me to the drum circle," Laris said. "I will bless the sounding."

He took a deep breath and held his son-in-law's gaze as Azan's large flame-red eyes shifted uneasily.

Laris shrugged and smiled gently. He let his formal tone drop and spoke to him as a man. "Don't look so surprised, Azan." Laris released a dry chuckle that more resembled a rasping cough. He grasped his son-in-law's forearm. "I haven't lost my mind. We will face the barren Father-Heart-of-Sky together, or we will die apart. Let us go."

Together, they descended the long trail from the peak of the Ageless Mountains, and by day's end made it to the vast rocky plain where the Zura warriors made camp. Uttapta sat upon the horizon behind the clouds, which glowed red like a blacksmith's fire. The sun finally sank, the embers of daylight slowly dying as orange reflections faded to ash.

At the camp's center was an ancient sounding pit, its rounded canyon walls carved with a whorling spiral pattern made to lift the sound of the drums to the skies, where it would travel across the atmosphere to the next drum circle and their response would travel back, in the ancient form of tribal communication. The legends of ancient drummers, as recorded in the Concha Scrolls, talked of how the drummers song could ride the spirals of the galaxy and travel to the dispersed Turyan tribes where they had settled on distant planets.

None of the Keepers really believed that the legends were true. They were ancient myths. Sound did not travel across galaxies. But Laris felt that, during this time of uncertainty, belief was stronger than truth. Belief made men strong and must be nurtured, no matter what its form, so long as it would not destroy them. And drums were not fire and they were not swords. Drums would not send the population burning and bleeding to their deaths.

One arm of the spiral wall was cut into stairs marked with lanterns that sent long shadows into the stone pit. Laris descended, followed by Azan. Down below, arranged in concentric circles, were rows of kneeling men with wood and hide drums grasped between bare legs. The Zura drummers wore the traditional woven garments that only covered their private parts, exposing their dark skin, which glowed with the golden nimbus of the Turyans. Steel helmets, armored tunics, and white crystalline swords lay neatly by their sides, the Zura ready to cast aside the drums in favor of weapons if need be.

Expectant faces clouded over with confusion as they spotted the Eldest Keeper of the Concha Scrolls entering their sacred space. Azan's firm look held the men in check as he followed Laris through the rows of drummers until they stood in the center, forcing the Master Drummer to step aside with a dark scowl.

Laris turned in a tight circle and met the eyes of the angry and suspicious men. Raising his hands, the billowing sleeves of his white robe falling around his elbows, Laris spoke loudly to the gathering. "I give you the blessing of the Keeper. May the drummers song reach the Star Children and bring them Home!"

The men fidgeted nervously, not sure what to make of this violation of tradition. Their eyes shifted to Azan, who was doing an honorable job of keeping his face stony and impenetrable. But Laris could feel his unease. Only because Laris was the father of Avala did Azan stand by his side. They both knew it was too late to turn back. Laris had lit the flame of destiny. Let it burn where it may. If the Star Children did not come, they would all burn to their deaths anyway.

Laris turned in a circle and intoned the ancient call of the drummers with a booming voice.

Eeeooooh Ratttaaaa Yyyrrllloooo

He lowered his arms, and the hands of the drummers fell in unison on the drumheads, the thundering sound shaking Laris in his bones. The Master Drummer reclaimed the center and led the waves of drummers in a pulsating rhythm that stirred Laris's blood, flooding him with an ecstatic rush that took him by surprise. Laris wondered suddenly if the ancient legends of the drummers song held some unknown mystery, some vein of truth. Laris looked up and prayed to the stars, their bright lights of hope hidden behind the ash-filled sky.

Let the Star Children hear them. Let Golden Star and Flying Star come Home.

PART ONE

BLOOD

Earth's Moon

1

THE ROOM

Rough hands tied Cassidy's wrists behind her back, twine cutting into her skin. Another set of hands bound her ankles together. Her body trembled violently as she tried to remain standing. Warm mucus ran from her nose onto the gag across her mouth. Shafts of light peeked in around the blindfold as fingers pulled off her necklaces and removed her belt and knife.

Gruff voices and the rustling of tent fabric surrounded her. She grunted and squirmed as iron hands lifted her legs out from under her. Her hip and shoulder hit the hard ground, and her back and head bounced against a dirt wall as more hands tugged at her shoulders and legs, stretching her out onto her back in what felt like a hole. Something landed on her belly with a melodic clinking of glass, and she recognized the weight of her green backpack. A board scraped over the ground overhead and sealed her in darkness. She followed the sounds of footsteps as they tramped above her, then everything grew quiet.

Her arms were pinned behind her, and the weight of her body pressed on her bound wrists. She maneuvered herself in the tight space and turned onto her side. Her backpack slid to the ground and the crystal ball slipped from her vest pocket and rolled slowly away, settling in a corner by her feet.

Cassidy focused on breathing. The gag in her mouth was tight, and mucus in her nose and throat threatened to choke her. She forced herself to relax her muscles, and drew in shallow lungfuls of stale, flinty air.

A scraping overhead, and then light.

Hard hands lifted Cassidy out of the hole and set her on her feet. She collapsed weakly onto her knees and mumbled through her gag, "What do you want?" But it came out as a garbled moan.

"What did you catch?" a male voice asked. Calloused fingers lifted her chin.

"Just like you said," another man responded. "Young and beautiful."

The first man grunted, and hands pushed under her vest and grabbed her breast through her t-shirt, squeezing painfully, and then squeezed the other. Cassidy held her breath and did not cry out.

"She'll do," he said. "But she doesn't look like a virgin. Are you a virgin?" the man asked, his hands on her face again, squeezing her jaw.

Cassidy frantically shook her head, not wanting them to check.

"Told you. Half a Solidi," the man said.

"You said a whole Solidi," the other argued.

"That was for a virgin. Half for a whore."

"A whole Solidi, or we keep her."

"I'll give you a Solidi for your two wives, and the baby girl."

The sound of scuffling broke out.

Finally, they settled on half a Solidi and ten sacks of rice.

"Put her in a fetal position and roll her up in a tarp. My transport's in the alley. I've got a crate," the man said, and his footsteps retreated.

Cassidy grunted and struggled in panicked protest as she was pushed down to the ground and her knees forcibly folded up to her chest, and then rolled tightly in dusty canvas. It was difficult to breathe again, and she blew snot out through her nose and tried to calm herself enough to pull in some air. Her thoughts flitted to her brother and Jasper and Berkeley. Had they escaped the attack? Were they searching for her?

Her thoughts were interrupted as she was lifted and carried, and then lifted again. The sound of an engine hummed around her. She was lowered into a dark box, her backpack thrown on top of her. The scrape of wood overhead closed her in completely. A hammer pounded, shaking her with each strike of metal on metal, as the lid to the crate was nailed shut. Doors slammed. The engine rumbled to life. The transport bounced over ruts and rolled along.

They stopped. More voices. Rolling forward. Doors opening. The crate tilted. Doors slammed. Wrapped tightly in her canvas cocoon, Cassidy shifted back and forth as the box was carried and moved from place to place. She tried to yell and kick, but the canvas muffled the sound.

Minutes dragged and then stretched. The fingers of panic tightened around her throat and loosened again in a sickening cycle. Adrenaline made her muscles shake, and the will to survive forced all thoughts from her mind as her body took over. Her cells screamed for oxygen, and she sucked in mouthfuls of air around the sodden gag.

She was on a ship. The buoyant floating sensation of a hovering craft was unmistakable.

Silence. Movement. Silence. Gliding. Accelerating. The nauseating press of high-speed flight. Settling out of rapid acceleration. More silence.

She tried to track where they were going, but she was floating in a dark void. She thought the acceleration would have lasted longer if they were leaving the moon, but she didn't know for sure. She tried to think, but she could not. All she could do was breathe and feel her heart rock her body in a primal pulse.

"If they are the Star Children ...," Brianna said, standing in their living room staring at Caden. Her green eyes burned with intensity and her dark hair floated around her head as she went on, *"... they need to stay alive. No matter what."* The fragment of memory flashed unbidden across Cassidy's mind's eye.

Her parents. Her brother. *She needed to stay alive. No matter what.*

Cassidy counted her heartbeats and tried to breathe.

———————)———————

Cassidy was lifted out of the crate, placed on the ground, and unwound from the tight grip of the tarp, turning over and over until cool air hit her face.

She greedily breathed in the fresh air, wheezing through her clogged nose and gagged mouth. She tried to see something through the gaps below the blindfold. She saw only slivers of light, but she knew where she was. The smell of bleach mixed with the gunpowdery scent of moon dust, and the distinctive echo and sounds of a cargo floor brought her back to her first moments on the moon. She was in Ridge Gandoop Spaceport.

She was pulled by the elbows to her feet and wavered on numb legs.

"What's this?" a stern voice asked.

"I brought her for the Nommos," her kidnapper said.

A cold sweat broke out over Cassidy's skin.

"The Nommos ship left this morning," the stern voice replied.

"Oh," the man said, followed by an awkward silence. "I thought they were leaving today."

"They did leave today, you numbskull."

"Well, can you buy her and send her off with the next ship?" her kidnapper asked.

"Do I look like a slave trafficker to you?" the stern man asked, his voice biting.

No response.

"I guess I'll take her to my place then, until they come again," the kidnapper said weakly. "But I need food."

"Not allowed to sell food to moon rats," the hard voice said.

The clicking of hard shoe soles against the floor approached.

"Who's she?" asked a deep resonant voice. "I thought the Nommos left already."

"They did, sir," the stern voice said in a subservient tone. "This here, um, far side trader wanted to sell her to them."

"Hmm," the deep voice said. "Where'd she come from?"

"Peary Dome, sir."

The clicking shoe soles walked around her. A hand ran over the braid hanging down her back, and she shivered.

"I'll take her," the deep voice said. "I'll give you a Solidi."

Her kidnapper replied, "I heard the Nommos pay two Solidi."

"I'm not a Nommos. And I dictate the prices around here. And I decide who stays and who leaves this port."

The threat hung in the air.

Her kidnapper replied, "One Solidi and two dozen sacks of rice."

"Fine," the deep voice said curtly.

The jangling of gold exchanging hands.

"Get him his rice," the deep voice said. "Fowler, help me take her to my speedster."

A gentle but firm hand gripped her elbow and tugged her forward. She hopped to keep up, her ankles still bound, until a second rougher set of hands took her other arm and helped drag her across the floor.

"Take this," her kidnapper's voice called.

Cassidy heard footsteps trotting over and the clink of her backpack being transferred to the one called Fowler.

Soon she was lying face down on the cold floor in the back of a craft. Doors clicked closed on either side. The sounds of the pilot working the controls filled the small cabin. The craft turned slowly, then floated forward. A decompression chamber door clanked closed behind them. She tried to stay quiet, struggling to breathe through a new onslaught of panic and mucus. The man cleared his throat and smacked his lips loudly, bringing bile to her mouth.

They flew out from the port, silent vibrations pulsating through Cassidy's bones.

Cassidy was dragged out of the craft and through an unfamiliar space by more men. Then a door shut, and she was left alone with the man who had bought her for a Solidi and two dozen sacks of rice. His hands groped around, searching her pockets. He found the crystal shaft in her vest pocket, and she heard him set it on a piece of furniture. Her pants pockets held loose change and a chunk of stale bread, and they joined the crystal.

He opened another door, pushed her forward, and said gruffly, "Clean her up. Be ready for me first thing tomorrow morning. Wear something nice."

The door slammed shut behind her, and she heard a lock slide into place. She stood, shivering. It smelled different here. Like perfumed soap and ... women.

A soft rustle of fabric, and more hands grabbed her arms. Tender hands—urgent hands.

"Come," two gentle voices said. "Sit here."

They guided her to sit on the edge of a bed, and fingers clawed at the knots behind her head. The blindfold loosened and slid up over her head. Cassidy blinked against the light.

She was in a bedroom that could have been on Earth. Two young women were behind her working on the knots of her gag and her wrist bindings. They finally got them off, then they set to work on the rope around her ankles.

As the rope fell away, the tension that had held Cassidy together since she had been abducted from the Peary road snapped, and she broke into shaking sobs. The women sat on the bed to either side of her, arms around her shoulders, hugging her.

"Where am I?" Cassidy asked, sniffling and examining the faces of her companions.

"We don't know," one said. She looked to be about fifteen. Petite, with blond hair in a jaw-length bob that was pushed behind her ears, which were a little too large and stuck out, making her look like an elf. She had round blue eyes and pale, flawless skin, and wore a short black silk negligee above thin bare legs. "I'm Anna," she said. "And this is Maria."

Maria looked to be about seventeen—tall, with long gangly limbs and small breasts under a white silk negligee. She had large green eyes, long red hair, and freckled skin. They both looked frightened and clung to Cassidy's arms, examining her in her dusty, oversized clothing.

"Where did you come from?" Maria asked Cassidy.

"Peary Dome."

"What's that?"

"It's the glass dome. The main lunar colony."

The women's eyes widened.

"We're on the moon?" Anna asked, tightening her grip.

"Yes," Cassidy said.

"They said we were going to another planet to be sold to a prince or something," Anna said.

"Where?" Cassidy asked.

Maria shrugged. "Nummo?"

Cassidy's brow furrowed. "The Nommos," she said, her throat constricting.

"Yes, that's it. Where is that?" Maria asked.

"It's not a place," Cassidy said. "It's an alien race. They're all males. And they're crazy."

"Oh. Uh-oh," Maria said.

"Yeah. It's bad," Cassidy said. She stood and turned in a circle, inspecting the room. It was dominated by a king-sized bed fitted only with white sheets and pillows. The walls were painted a plain beige, and wall sconces were illuminated with electric light bulbs. The floors were covered with a thick brown carpet, and the only other furnishings were matching bedside tables, an ornate straight-backed chair upholstered with a maroon brocade fabric, and a painting above the bed depicting ships in a harbor. Overhead, a skylight let in a vista of the star-filled sky. The ventilation system whirred loudly, and small vents high in the walls blew out gusts of warm air.

"How long have you been here?" Cassidy asked.

The two women huddled together, still seated on the edge of the bed. "Just a few hours," Anna said, pushing loose strands of blond hair behind her ear.

"What does he want with us?" Cassidy asked.

The two women looked at one another, then back at Cassidy. Cassidy returned their distressed gazes. There was really nothing in the room but a bed. She swallowed. "What's in here?" she asked, opening a second door.

It was a large walk-in closet, doubling as a dressing room, with a vanity with three mirrors and a small ivory silk-padded bench, and a laundrobot. The closet connected to a bathroom. Cassidy walked through the dressing room and into the spacious bathroom, which had a large bathtub, a separate shower, a toilet, and two sinks. She stared at herself in the mirror above the sinks. For a moment she didn't recognize herself—a disheveled young woman with the eyes of a trapped fox. She met her eyes in the mirror.

She needed to stay alive. No matter what.

———————)———————

Cassidy undressed in the walk-in closet and hid her rune belt behind a row of dusty high-heeled shoes that sat on a lower shelf. She went into the bathroom and slipped into the bath Maria had prepared for her. Alone in the fogged-up bathroom, Cassidy sank into the hot water and leaned her head back against the edge of the tub. She had longed for a bath ever since she'd arrived on the moon, but was now too terrified to enjoy it. She washed her hair with vanilla-scented shampoo, sinking her head under the water and losing herself in a brief moment of muted solitude and wondering what had happened to her brother, Jasper, and Berkeley, and if they had survived the attack.

She sat up, pushed the dripping hair away from her face, and picked up a bar of white, scented soap. The water was already gray from moon dust, which had coated her from head to toe. She washed her body, then took the hint from the row of new razors neatly arranged on the wide rim of the tub. With trembling hands she shaved her armpits and legs, nicking her shins in several places. Feathers of blood unfurled in the murky water, and Cassidy watched as the plumes dispersed, turning the water a hazy pink. Glimpses of her reflected face and the ceiling light fixture and spinning fan rippled in and out of focus.

Suddenly the water grew still and glassy, and she was looking down into a bright white room. Torr was lying on a cot with an intravenous tube taped to his arm. His forehead was wrapped with white bandages, his eyes were closed and framed by puffy red circles, and one side of his face was swollen and purple. A medic came into the room with a cup, lifted Torr's head gently, and put a straw to his lips. Torr sucked on it, his eyes cracking open, then he closed his eyes again.

The bathroom door pushed open, breaking Cassidy's vision. She looked up as Maria peered in.

"Are you okay?" Maria asked.

"Yes," Cassidy said, and returned her gaze to the water. Soap scum and clumps of dark hair floated on the surface.

Maria held out a white bath towel. Cassidy exhaled and stepped out of the bath.

"Thank you," she said, and pressed the soft towel to her face.

She had just water scried, she mused with a hint of wonder—but it brought her no joy. Just like when she was trapped in Gabira's cave, danger had drawn out her second sight. She preferred to be safe and shielded. But at least she knew Torr was alive.

She toweled herself dry and chose a pale pink negligee from the collection of satin garments hanging in the closet. She pulled it on over her damp skin, hating that she was preparing herself like this for a man who intended to rape her.

———————)———————

The three women huddled together under the bed sheet, watching the digits on the bedside clock count away the hours and waiting for the man to come into the room. They heard him enter the adjoining room at eleven in the evening, but it was not until six in the morning that the lock outside the bedroom door rattled and he entered the room.

The women sat up and fixed their attention on him.

He was a tall, imposing figure and exuded a brash confidence. He looked to be in his forties and stood bare-chested with broad muscular shoulders, curly black chest hair, and scars puckering his tight abdomen and slashed across one shoulder. A full head of sleek black hair and a tightly trimmed beard set off brilliant green eyes.

Cassidy's heart pounded in her throat, and she clutched the hands of Anna and Maria, their six hands gnarled together in a knot.

"You," the man said, striding across the floor and pointing at Cassidy and Maria.

Cassidy's heart faltered.

"In the closet," he said sternly. "Hurry up. If you come out, I'll kill her. Do you understand?" He reached out and grabbed Anna by the upper arm. The sour stench of stale alcohol overwhelmed Cassidy's sinuses, and his words reverberated in her ears. Anna's small hands slid from the frantic grip of Cassidy and Maria as the man dragged the fifteen-year-old across the bed until she was sprawled against the pillows.

Cassidy and Maria scrambled to the edge of the bed. Cassidy's bare feet landed on the carpet, and she staggered to the closet, pulling Maria by the hand. They shut themselves inside the dressing room and then retreated to the bathroom, closing that door behind them. They sat on the edge of the tub and gaped at each other in the mirror.

After a few minutes, the faint sounds of yelling and crying reached Cassidy's ears. Maria stood up and turned on the overhead fan. The fan whirred loudly, drowning out the sounds of the struggle. Maria returned to her side, and they clung to each other and wept.

───────────────)───────────────

Anna hobbled, naked, into the bathroom. Blood stained her thighs, and her face was bruised red, with one purplish eye nearly closed.

Cassidy and Maria rushed over and held her up.

"Don't wear panties," Anna slurred. "It makes him mad."

They led Anna into the bathroom, and Cassidy started running a bath. Anna was huddled in Maria's arms on the floor. Cassidy crept back through the closet and pressed her ear against the closed door. Hearing nothing, she cracked the door open and peeked out into the bedroom. The man was gone. The ventilation system hummed loudly, and the room stank of sweat and sex. The sheets were stained with blood, and Anna's black panties were on the floor, torn apart. Cassidy stripped the bed, her mind numb and her hands working from habit, pulling off the linens and stuffing them into the laundrobot.

When the bath was ready, Cassidy and Maria helped Anna step into the hot water.

There was nothing to say.

Anna lay back in the bath, stunned. Her one good eye was open and glazed, and the other was now completely swollen shut. A green tinge rimmed her lips.

Anna suddenly sat up and stepped, dripping, out of the tub, then rushed to the toilet. She bent over it and threw up. When she was done heaving, Cassidy and Maria helped her back into the bathwater.

Cassidy and Maria locked gazes, dreading their fate.

———————)———————

Cassidy filled a sink with water and stared down into it, waiting for a vision.

None came.

Her tears dripped into the water, making little splashes and forming expanding circles of ripples that merged into one another and disappeared.

———————)———————

Cassidy made the bed with the clean sheets, then crept around the bedroom. The bedside table drawers were empty. Stars stared down at her through the skylight. She tiptoed to the bedroom door and pressed her ear against the wood.

Silence.

She placed her hand on the door handle. It turned. She pulled at the door, but it was locked from the outside. A small peephole was at eye level, and she peered through it, but it was facing the wrong way. She cringed at the idea of him looking in on them whenever he wanted. She stepped away from the door and joined the other women.

———————)———————

The starry sky gleaming down through the skylight did not change to daylight, and so they tracked the passage of time by the digits on the clock. Cassidy's stomach growled from hunger. That evening, she ran herself a bath and slowly shaved her legs, afraid of what the man would do to her if her skin was rough and prickly. She stared into the water, begging silently for a vision to appear, but nothing came. Perhaps she was not scared enough.

Anna was curled up on the closet floor, refusing to sleep in the bed. Maria was in the bedroom, huddled under the sheet. Cassidy turned the light off and joined her, finally falling into a fitful sleep.

A faint noise awoke her, and Cassidy jerked upright. She remembered where she was, and her blood surged with a rush of adrenaline. She sat on the edge of the bed and stared at the clock.

5:30 am.

She tensed as the faint sound of a motor running vibrated the wall. It stopped. A minute later, the motor ran again, and then stopped for a short time, followed by another vibration. And then it was silent, except for the constant drone of the ventilation system.

5:45.

At precisely six o'clock, the lock rattled, and the man entered the room. He flashed her a grimace of a smile, and she held his eyes. They were greener than her mother's, with an odd, vacant look to them.

"Out," he told her, pointing to the closet.

Maria sat up and clutched the sheet to her chest.

Cassidy got to her feet and slowly backed away from the man.

"Don't hurt her," Cassidy said, glaring at him.

He turned his gaze onto her, a faint glimmer of surprise flickering in his eyes. Tan cargo pants were slung low on his hips, and long toes peeked out from beneath their hems. His bare abdomen tightened, his muscles sharply defined. He scowled at her, his eyes stony.

"I will save it all for you," he said, a leer spreading across his face. "Now, get out."

Cassidy reached for the closet door handle, her hands shaking. She opened the door and slipped into the dressing room, shutting the door behind her. She pulled Anna to her feet, and they hid in the bathroom, the fan spinning loudly overhead.

Anna sat on the closed toilet lid, hunched over with her arms folded across her belly and slowly rocking forward and back. Cassidy ran a hot bath for Maria, gazing at the clear, precious liquid as it slowly filled the tub.

2

BRUJ⊙

"Torr, can you hear me?"

It was Jasper's voice. Torr grunted in reply, his head pounding like a sledgehammer was hitting it. He opened his eyes and saw Jasper peering down at him. His vision split into two Jaspers, and Torr let his eyelids sink closed again.

"They haven't found her," Jasper said, his voice rasping.

"What?" Torr managed weakly.

"Cassidy. She's still missing."

Torr forced his eyes open again, trying to comprehend Jasper's words. Jasper wavered before him—his face was bruised and his nose was swollen and discolored. Nausea swept over Torr, and he closed his eyes to the soothing blackness. "What happened?" he muttered.

"We were attacked. Cassidy got taken."

"Where am I?" Torr asked.

"In the infirmary," Jasper said.

"Where are Mom and Dad? Are they looking for her?"

"We're on the moon, Torr. Your parents aren't here." Jasper sounded concerned.

It came vaguely back to Torr. The moon. His parents. Cassidy. "Where did she go?" he asked.

"We don't know—she got kidnapped."

"Oh, no," Torr said, his pounding headache chasing all thoughts away.

———————)———————

The next thing Torr knew, a medic was offering him water through a straw. Sucking on the straw made his head and eyes hurt, and he turned his lips away.

"Can you drink on your own?" the medic asked.

"It hurts."

The medic held each eyelid open in turn, shining a bright, painful light into his eyes. The medic let him close his eyes again.

He awoke to Jasper and Berkeley standing by his bed, telling him that Cassidy was still missing. He heard the words with a dull emptiness. They told him they'd searched the roads for her and were organizing a tent-by-tent search. Rodney and Kai had stopped all traffic out of the spaceport.

"We'll tear the camp apart until we find her," Jasper swore.

Torr opened his eyes and tried to sit up, but the hammering in his head drove him back into his pillows.

"Okay," he said, closing his eyes again and squeezing Jasper's hand. "Find her."

———————)———————

Torr opened his eyes. He was in a small hospital room that reminded him of the clinic at Miramar, but the air had the metallic tang of the moon. He vaguely recalled a medic and Jasper visiting him, but the passage of time felt like the oozing of hot tar. The room was empty and quiet, and the bright white walls and stainless steel counters made his eyes hurt. He slowly sat up, gritting his teeth against the pounding in his head.

He ripped the tape from his arm, pulled out the needle that was connected to a tube and an intravenous bag, and then pressed his thumb against the bruised prick mark. A raw pain in his dick brought his hands down there, and he carefully pulled out a catheter and tossed it aside. He swung his legs over the side of the cot and sat still until his brains stopped jiggling. He wrapped the sheet around his waist to cover his nudeness and tried to piece together what had happened. He remembered they had been walking down a road in Peary Dome. And then Jasper had woken him up to say Cassidy was missing.

Now he was alone in the infirmary. He didn't know what day it was. Jasper had not returned to say Cassidy had been found. Waves of panic rippled across his skin.

The pounding in his head had quieted to a dull throb. If he tried, he could resolve his vision into a single image, but as soon as he relaxed his eyes, the images split apart again. He breathed heavily and rose from the cot, wavering on unsteady legs, and stepped delicately across the small room, reaching out to grab a counter for support. His clothing was neatly folded on a chair, and his vest hung on a hook nearby. He sat in the chair and pulled on his boxer shorts, then one pant leg at a time, lifting his butt for a moment to pull his pants up all the way. He sat gratefully in the chair again and slowly pulled on his dirty socks and dust-caked boots. Every time he bent over, blood pounded in his head like ocean surf driving against a seawall.

He stood on weak legs and slowly pulled the jerkin over his head and arms, leaving the leather shirt open at the collar and the laces hanging loose. He put on his vest, and then his utility belt, which held an empty knife sheath. His heart stilled for a moment as he remembered the shrouded pouch at his waist, and he patted his skin frantically. The rune belt, along with his moon deed and gold, was gone.

He searched his vest pouches and cargo pants pockets, trying to avoid jerky movements that rattled his head. The crystals were there, but the rune belt was not. He patted along the counter, thinking perhaps it would be invisible until he touched it. Nothing appeared. No, he remembered, it became invisible only after the belt buckle was clasped against the skin. He would have found it if it were there.

He didn't like that the deed and his Solidi were gone, but Cassidy was more important. He needed to save his energy for her. Worry and fear warred within his muzzy head. He couldn't allow himself to get upset, he just needed to find her. Moaning, he staggered towards the door.

A medic in white appeared in his path. "Where are you going?" the man asked, rushing to his side and looping an arm around his back to steady him.

"I need to find my sister."

"You have a bad concussion," the medic said. "You need to rest."

"How long have I been here?" Torr shook off the man's insistent grip as the medic tried to steer him back to the cot.

"Two days," the medic said.

"Water," Torr croaked, and pressed his thumbs to his eyes to ward off a swirl of vertigo.

The medic hurried out of the room and returned with a tall cup with a straw.

Torr drank carefully, drawing gently on the straw, and then handed the cup to the medic. "Did you find a belt wallet under my shirt?" he asked.

"No," the medic said. "I undressed you myself and didn't see anything."

Torr tried to sense if the medic was lying. He looked sincere enough, though he couldn't focus on the man's eyes very well. The deed must have disappeared between the attack and the infirmary, but he had no recollection of how. He would puzzle it out later when his head didn't feel like a vise was squeezing it.

"Do you have my knife?" Torr asked.

The medic shook his head. "There was no knife on you when you arrived here."

Torr figured his assailants had disarmed him, and perhaps had taken the deed as well. He had no energy to think about it any further. Holding the wall for support, he hobbled down a short hallway and glanced into a wall mirror. He stopped in front of it, startled. Half his face was swollen and purple, and one eye was half closed.

"You have a skull fracture," the medic said. "You're lucky—it's just a hairline fracture. But your brain is bruised. You should rest for several more days. You must not reinjure it."

"Okay," Torr said. "I'll rest in my tent. Thanks for your help." He knew his speech was slurred, but the medic seemed to understand him.

"Stay here for another day," the man pleaded, taking his arm again. "You should be on an IV, and we need to monitor you."

Torr held the man's wrist, trying to right the tilting room. "I need to find my sister." He pulled away and found his way outside, closing his eyes painfully against the blazing sun. Leaning against the exterior wall, he tried to get his bearings. The medic appeared with a second medic, and the two watched him from the doorway.

Torr managed to lift his hand in a parting gesture of thanks, then gazed out over the colorless landscape of dusty roads and canvas tents. The gray dullness was soothing. But above the horizon Earth danced, a half-globe of blue bobbing upon a sea of star-speckled black, and the

sun pulsed at the periphery of his vision. He closed his eyes against an
onslaught of dizziness, fighting back nausea that welled up in his throat.

He kept his eyes lowered and stepped away, shuffling across the
outermost ring road towards the foot of the nearest spoke road, the
flat horizon tilting around him. Torr made his way slowly along the
endless spoke road, concentrating on keeping his balance and not tripping over the ridges of dust that reared up like waves rushing towards
shore. At each intersection he stopped to lean against the wooden sign-
post. He trudged forward, one foot in front of the other, and arrived
at Center Ring. He stumbled into a porta-potty, emptied his bowels
in a stream of liquid, and then turned around to puke mouthfuls of
yellowish water. The retching sent a lance of pain through his skull.
Maybe the medic was right—he should have stayed in the infirmary.

Torr left the hut and wove through the tents to find his camp.
Tatsuya and Faisal were sitting at one of the Fen's tables and hopped
up. They rushed to his side, asking if he was okay.

"Where's everybody?" Torr asked as Tatsuya gently felt his face and
skull and lifted his eyelids to look into his pupils.

"Searching for your sister. Somebody had to stay to guard the
place," Faisal said.

"You must lie down," Tatsuya said. His voice had none of the
pleading tone of the medic.

Torr felt like his head was an egg with the raw yolk jiggling frightfully close to the shell. He let himself be led by the elbow to the old
man's tent. Tatsuya made him drink water, and then guided him to
lie down on a thin futon and propped a small pillow under his head.

"I need to find my sister," Torr said.

"Jaz and the rest of our campmates are conducting a methodical
search," Tatsuya said. "You are in no condition to help."

Torr did not have the energy to argue. He closed his eyes, and the
sound of Tatsuya coming and going with a brushing of canvas and soft
footsteps was comforting. He felt the man kneel next to him, and with
deft fingers Tatsuya gently lifted Torr's head and held a cup to his lips.
Torr took a sip of the bitter brew, reminding him of his mother's concoc-
tions. He swallowed, then sank back onto the pillow. A cool compress,
fragrant with herbs, was laid on his bruised cheek, and another over his

forehead and eyes, and a third was wrapped against the side of his head where it hurt the most. Torr melted into the welcome darkness.

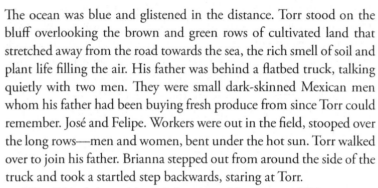

The ocean was blue and glistened in the distance. Torr stood on the bluff overlooking the brown and green rows of cultivated land that stretched away from the road towards the sea, the rich smell of soil and plant life filling the air. His father was behind a flatbed truck, talking quietly with two men. They were small dark-skinned Mexican men whom his father had been buying fresh produce from since Torr could remember. José and Felipe. Workers were out in the field, stooped over the long rows—men and women, bent under the hot sun. Torr walked over to join his father. Brianna stepped out from around the side of the truck and took a startled step backwards, staring at Torr.

"Torr," his father said, straightening with surprise. "What are you doing here?" Caden's face grew red, his expression flustered. "How did you get here?"

Torr's mouth pulled to one side. Why was his father acting so strangely? And what was his mother doing here? She never went on produce runs with them. "I rode here with you," Torr said. At least he thought he had. He couldn't really remember the ride down, but his mind often wandered when he and his father drove from farm to farm. He eyed the truck. It was not his father's—it was José's. "Where's your truck?" Torr asked.

His father's face turned from red to pale as his two companions also stared at Torr, as if he were a ghost.

"Brujo," the older man, Felipe, exclaimed under his breath. "It's his spirit, come to visit you."

"Honey, come here," his mother said. Brianna rushed to Torr and pressed her palms against the sides of his face. "You're hurt. Were you beaten up?" She stared into his eyes while Caden stood next to her, poking at his shoulder. "Did the Tegs get you?" she asked. "You weren't able to escape from Moffett Field? Where's Cassidy?"

"Are you ... dead?" Caden asked, his eyes wide from shock.

"No, I'm not dead. Are you?" Torr could not figure out why they were all acting so strangely. And why did his father have a TAFT assault rifle slung across his back, and why was his mother carrying his Browning 6 Creed across her chest?

Brianna's eyes narrowed. "What's wrong with your head?" She closed her eyes, and he could feel her hands growing hot as they pressed against his temples and his skull. "Your brain. It's injured," she murmured. "Your skull is fractured." Heat washed through his head, bringing a wave of comfort. He closed his eyes and let his head sink into her sure hands. A current of electricity tingled along his skull from branches of lightning that flowed from her fingertips. The currents forked in a zigzag pattern across the top and sides of his head, and then shot down the sides of his ribs and pierced the top of each foot in two painful jabs.

"Ouch," he said. He clutched her arms. "What was that?" He lifted his head, and his eyes popped open.

Her eyes opened slowly, and her hands lifted away from his head, hovering in the air by his ears for a long moment, before her eyes regained their normal clarity.

"Where's Cassidy?" she asked. Her hands dropped to his shoulders, gripping his vest.

"She's ..." Torr suddenly understood where he was. He was on Earth, but he did not belong here. He was on the moon, dreaming, but he was here as well. He met his father's eyes. "You got out of San Jose," Torr said, everything rushing back to him. José and Felipe's farm was on the coastal lands, south of Santa Cruz. "What are you doing here? You were supposed to head east, to the mountains."

"We tried," Caden said. "Too many Tegs—we had to turn back."

Torr froze. Topping the rise of the road from the south was a large gray transport. "Tegs," he whispered urgently.

Caden and the others stared at the Teg vehicles flowing over the rise, but no one moved.

"They already blocked Highway 1 from the north," Caden said in a monotone. "It was only a matter of time. We needed food. We had to take a risk. Bad luck, I guess."

Torr's throat constricted with panic, and he clutched his mother to his chest. "You need to hide." He looked around frantically. "The sheds. No, the hills." He looked to the forested lowlands that stood beyond the striped fields.

"There's no time," Caden said. "There's nowhere to run." Caden pulled the TAFT from his back and the pistol from his belt holster and slid the weapons under the truck. Torr wanted to fetch the guns, but his father pushed Torr and Brianna behind him and stood shoulder to shoulder with José and Felipe as they stared at the line of transports heading their way. The workers were running across the field, trapped between the road and the ocean. The women crowded into small equipment sheds, and the men gathered in a huddle under a shade structure, clutching hoes. Brianna broke away and crouched behind the truck.

Torr's legs trembled as the first transport rolled up next to them and an officer climbed out of the passenger side, toting an assault rifle. He stood tall and had a round baby face. His steel-gray uniform was neat and buttoned up to his throat. The Teg's blood-red shield insignia stood out on his chest pocket. He was followed by a dozen troops who streamed from the back of the carrier, followed by dozens more from the second and third carriers, with more vehicles coming. Soon, a hundred soldiers swarmed the road, surrounding Torr, Caden, José, and Felipe and fanning out over the field to herd the workers.

Though every cell of Torr's body constricted with fear, this was not dramatic like he'd imagined. There was no bloody battle. No yelling and killing. Simply a young officer looking at Caden, a small smile tightening the officer's lips. The Teg's eyes flicked to Felipe and José, and then back to Caden. The officer did not seem to see Torr, although he could not be sure.

Caden's palms opened. "Oh, thank goodness you're here," Caden said to the officer. Torr blinked in surprise but held still. Caden's blue eyes were wide and genuine, his face filled with relief, words rushing from his mouth. "I've been hoping to run into some of you. Our business has fallen off, and I know your troops will need food. We can help." He gestured to the truck and the fields. Caden's strategy became clear to Torr. If his father could become a supplier for the Tegs, then he would neither die nor go to the work camps. Maybe he could save Brianna from the same.

The officer stepped forward and struck Caden's face with the back of the hand. "Silence," he barked. "I do the talking here."

Torr flinched as his father cowered backward and lowered his eyes. Terror twisted in Torr's belly. He scanned the faces of the soldiers who lined the road, watching, assault rifles in hand. Most were young men.

Some were older. Some looked hardened by war. Others looked green—like Torr's squadmates—Gaia United soldiers turned Teg to save their own lives. Sour bile filled his mouth. Would it be so hard for Torr to turn to the Teg's side, given the options? Would it save his parents? Was he even really here? Should he take the rifle from under the truck and empty the magazine into a few of the Tegs before being cut down himself?

Torr stepped between the officer and his father. Caden stiffened, and Torr looked into the officer's brown eyes. They stared right through him. Torr waved his hand in front of the Teg's face. The man did not see him. He poked the officer's chest. The man flicked at his hand as though at a fly, batting it aside while not seeming to feel it.

Torr stepped away and he could see his father's legs weaken from relief. Felipe shifted nervously, his hands clasped in front of him, staring at his feet. Torr stepped backwards, nearly tripping over a rut in the ground. He suddenly felt drained and helpless. He was not really here. He could not do anything to help or to change the course of events.

The workers were being shepherded towards the road. Their faces were filled with fear and resignation. Their farming tools lay scattered on the ground behind them. A soldier walked behind Torr, heading around the side of the truck where Brianna was crouched. Torr jumped ahead of the soldier and lunged at his crouching mother, tackling her to the dirt and pinning her and the 6 Creed under his body, pressing the side of his head against hers. Her chest was heaving and he covered her mouth with his hand to quiet her frightened gasps. The soldier passed not two feet beside them but did not stop until he got to the other side. The soldier crouched and pulled the TAFT and pistol out from underneath the truck and started yelling at Caden and the Mexicans.

"We needed to protect the fields from looters," Caden explained, his voice pleading.

Torr heard the smack of a rifle butt hitting someone, followed by a groan. He struggled to stay silent and shielded his mother as his father's knees hit the ground. Torr tensed for another blow to his father, but none came.

"Good thing you had the sense not to use these," the soldier said harshly. He was joined by other soldiers, who surrounded the prisoners.

Torr peered underneath the truck as Caden was dragged to his feet. Torr watched the boots and legs of his father, José, and Felipe as they stumbled between gray-legged soldiers and disappeared from view. Torr held his mother's rigid, panting body and listened to the sounds of the farm workers being loaded into the carriers. Doors slammed. Orders and shouts passed up the line. The carriers rumbled to life and rolled by, gravel crunching, engines growling.

Soon the road was quiet. He released his mother and rose cautiously to his feet. His limbs were shaking violently. Brianna scrambled to her feet, staring desperately north at the empty road in the direction the convoy had left. Frantic whimpers escaped her lips, and he held her in his arms. "Shhh," he said. "Shhh." His mother's eyes met his, flooded with grief.

"Dad will be okay," Torr said. "He's strong. He's resourceful." She leaned her head against his chest, sobbing softly. Torr took a shaking breath and looked at the shimmering ribbon of road where his father had disappeared, a Teg prisoner.

They stood together, frozen in shock and disbelief. Fear for his father deepened as the reality of what had just happened sank in, and then concern for his mother rose to the forefront. His throat was dry, and he breathed in again, patting his mother's back. "I don't know if I'm really here, Mom. I don't know if I can help you anymore. I'm dreaming. When I wake up, I'll leave here. Unless I really am dead."

Brianna lifted her face towards the empty road, then turned her gaze to Torr. "You're not dead. And you're right, you won't stay here when you awaken." Her eyes held his as though she knew this for a fact. "You're a dreamwalker, Torr. Like Grandpa Leo." Tears flowed down her cheeks. "Did you and Cassidy make it to the moon?"

He nodded, and she smiled tremulously. "Cassidy's fine," he lied. "We found Jasper and Kai. They're fine, too."

"Oh, thank the stars," she said, leaning against him and clutching his vest. "I'm so glad I got to see you. I love you so much, Torr. Tell Cassidy I love her."

"I will. I love you, too," Torr said, his voice hoarse. "What about you?" Torr asked. "You must be a dreamwalker, too, if you can see me."

"No, not a dreamwalker," she said, wiping at her nose. "Just a lucid dreamer. I'm able to enter the dreamtime when a powerful dream-walker is present. Like I could with my father."

"But José and Felipe. They could see me too. And ... Dad?" The realization filled him with confusion. His father had always stood in the shadows while his mother had studied with the Shasta Shamans and pursued her plant spirit medicine. Yet he had been talking to Torr in his dream. "Felipe called me a brujo," Torr said, shifting uneasily. "What is a brujo?"

"The Mexican name for a shaman," she said. "Brujos are known for working with spirits, and shapeshifting, among other things." Brianna tossed her head towards an irrigation shack nearby. On its roof sat a lone crow. It was large—a raven. The shiny black bird peered at them sideways with its flinty eyes. "That raven has been watching us this whole time."

Torr's skin crawled. "So?"

"Crows and ravens are spirits from the abyss between the worlds," she said. "Just like coyotes and wolves. They come and go between the waking world and the dreamworld like shadows of clouds passing over the land."

Torr recalled stories of how Mexican immigrants used to creep across the borders, before the Free States had unified. How, when the borders had been closed and guarded, packs of coyotes would slip through the barbed wire fencing and disappear into the shadows. It was whispered that the coyotes were really men and women. Shapeshifters, fleeing through the night. He shivered. He had thought those stories legend.

Torr saw that his mother was looking around anxiously, and his heart tightened with worry. "You could take the truck," Torr suggested.

Brianna shook her head. "No, the roads are crawling with Tegs. I'll go back into the hills. We've been hiding out there, waiting for the Tegs to move on. We stashed our stuff in an abandoned barn. We came here to get food from Felipe and José and to warn them to leave. We were going to try to cross the central highways again tonight and head for the mountains."

Torr looked to where ridges of green rose to the east. Beyond the forested hills lay wide corridors of roads and decommissioned hover-craft lanes that connected the San Francisco Bay Area to Los Angeles. On the other side of the corridors stood a stretch of wilderness, then the San Joaquin valley. She had miles and miles to cross before finding the shelter of the Sierra Nevada Mountains. He took a deep breath. It was still summer. If she were lucky and could avoid Tegs, she could make it to Shasta in a few weeks, before the snows came.

"Even if I can make it to the mountains," she said, "I'll still have the Shaman's Shield to deal with."

Torr looked at the raven. "Maybe you can make it through," he said softly. "Across the abyss."

Brianna squinted, considering his words. Her emerald eyes turned to the raven. "Maybe I can."

Torr gathered his mother's hands. "You will make it. I will visit you in my dreams."

Brianna nodded, her eyes glowing with the instinct to survive. They scoured the fields for food, filling a small backpack with sandwiches and fruit that were to have been the farm workers' lunches, and as many bottles of water as she could carry. Torr helped her adjust the sling of the 6 Creed across her chest, wishing he had more ammo to give her. Wishing he had time to teach her how to kill.

His mother hugged him. "Go back to the moon," she told Torr. "Go back to Cassidy."

He hugged her tightly. Torr did not know how to get back, and he did not know Cassidy's fate, but he sealed his lips and walked with his mother across the field towards the hills. The raven lifted from its perch and flew in front of them, its wings beating in a determined rhythm.

3

THE BEAST

O n the third morning, Cassidy waited alone in the bedroom for the man.

Promptly at 6 o'clock, the lock rasped and the door opened. She stood and faced him.

"Ready for me?" he asked with a mocking smile.

She swallowed and did not answer, tensing her muscles in an effort to keep him from seeing her tremble.

"Did your redhead friend have a good time yesterday?" he asked. He dropped his pants, folded them neatly, and placed them on the chair. He was naked, and large, but not erect.

Maria had stumbled into the bathroom the morning before, nude, with fresh bruises covering her arms and legs. Her cheekbone had been split open, with blood dripping down her face. She needed stitches, but there were no needles or first-aid supplies to be found. Cassidy had held the torn skin together for hours, and finally wrapped Maria's face in a bandage made from strips she tore from a silk negligee.

Cassidy did not answer the man's sarcastic question, but stood, frozen, as he approached her.

He took her by the throat with one large hand and guided her onto the bed. She did not resist when he pushed her down and climbed on top of her. He felt up under her short silk gown. She was naked underneath, and he shoved his fingers inside her. She winced, and he smiled down at her.

"Have you ever been raped before?" he asked. She did not answer, and he laughed. "You'll like it," he said.

He was hard now and entered her with a sharp thrust. She let out a small cry as her tender skin tore. She closed her eyes, and a blow landed on her jaw, knocking her head to the side.

"Look at me," he commanded, and thrust again.

She opened her eyes against the burning pain. His teeth were bared as he thrust over and over, pounding against her. He stopped, looking slightly disgusted, and pulled out. He grabbed her arm and turned her over onto her stomach, and then started again. She bit her lip, trying not to cry out. Her mind went numb, and she tried to breathe.

He flipped her onto her back again and attempted to enter her, using his hand to help, but he was too limp. He struck her face with his open palm, a flash of white flooding her vision, then wrapped his hand around her throat and squeezed. The air was trapped in her lungs, and she opened her eyes.

His face lit up when he saw the terror in her eyes.

She might die here, she realized, and flashed on a memory of her and Torr as toddlers, squealing while the ocean surf crashed on the beach and sent foamy waves to bury their bare feet with sand. She saw her father scooping them up as another wave crashed, holding them one in each arm. She saw her grandmother and mother sitting around Grandma Leann's table with Great-Aunt Sophie, hinting that she and Torr were the Star Children. She saw herself sitting behind Jasper on his motorcycle, holding onto him as they took the hairpin turns of the mountain roads, redwood trees soaring up into the sky.

The rapist's eyes blazed, and he grew hard again, pumping her frantically and squeezing her neck. She struggled for air, but his grip was too tight. She counted the seconds, imagining she was under water holding her breath and would surface soon. She could see the daylight above her, murky blue and green and wavering. He loosened his grip, and she sucked in a lungful of air, gasping and praying silently that he would not kill her. His acrid musky scent filled her head. He propped himself up on his elbows, panting and grunting and slapping her when he grew limp, until he finally groaned and climaxed.

She was shaking uncontrollably and slimy with sweat when he climbed off. The metallic taste of blood filled her mouth and one ear was ringing from his heavy-handed slaps.

He ignored her as he wiped himself clean with a corner of the sheet and pulled on his pants. He took a small metal vial from his pocket and walked over to her.

She crab-crawled across the bed away from him as he unscrewed the top and came at her with a dropper. It was filled with green liquid, and she pulled her mouth to the side as he tried to insert it between her lips. He grabbed her by the back of the head and shoved it into her mouth. The bittersweet drug filled her mouth, numbing her tongue immediately.

He laughed and screwed the dropper back onto the vial, then left the room, locking the door loudly behind him.

——————————)——————————

The worst thing, Cassidy thought as she lowered herself painfully into the hot bath, was that she could die under the rapist's hand—or be shipped off to the Nommos—and her brother and Jasper would never know what happened to her. It would drive them crazy, and that made her want to stay alive and find her way back to them some day.

The next worse thing, she reflected, was if she got pregnant and had to bear the child of that monster. Her contraceptive herb, Waning Moon, was in her backpack somewhere inside this building. She had heard the rapist take her backpack from the speedster and hand it to another man with a gruff, "Do something with this." This was the moon, and Earth herbs were valuable, and so she doubted they would have recycled them. She had taken the last dose of Waning Moon three days before and its effects would be wearing off by now.

Blood from her lacerated flesh tinted the bathwater, and she washed herself repeatedly, trying to scrub off every last residue of him. She shivered, disgusted at what had happened to her. She had not even fought back. She could have at least yelled and punched him, instead of letting him have his way with her. But judging by the sick look in his eye when he had choked her, he probably would have enjoyed it if she had tried to fight him. It would have given him an excuse to beat her up even worse than he had. Prickles of fear stung her skin. He was too strong. And a psychopath. A *beast*.

She moved her jaw back and forth. It was sore, but no teeth were loose. The side of her head was tender, but she was not hurt as badly as Anna and Maria. They both had black eyes, and the sclera of Anna's left eye was red with burst blood vessels. Cassidy trailed her fingers through the water and noted oddly that she suddenly felt calm and happy.

Cassidy's thoughts were interrupted by an upwelling of nausea. She stood up and climbed out of the tub and rushed to the toilet, kneeling over it. Anna held Cassidy's hair back while she vomited. She was familiar with this routine by now—both Anna and Maria had done the same, and they had concluded it was the effect of the green drug he forced on them. Anna and Maria told her she would feel woozy, and then she would feel good. Cassidy had observed them both sink into a lethargic stupor that had lasted about twenty-four hours. She had originally attributed their condition to shock at having been raped, but more likely it was because of the drug. Cassidy wondered if it was a contraceptive drug and could only hope.

She stared into the toilet water between bouts of retching and tried to sense the nature of the plant essence, which turned her vomit green. Her plant spirit sensibilities were confronted with a confusing mélange of images and smells that reminded her of the jungle she and her family had visited in northern Puerto Rico when she was a child, hiking through thick foliage and exploring waterfalls while her mother gathered plants. But there was another essence she sensed, something pure and primordial. Her musings were interrupted by a cramp in her gut as she threw up again. She closed her eyes and breathed deeply until the nausea passed.

Trembling, she stood up and staggered back to the bathtub and lowered herself into the water. She splashed water on her face, gazing at her dazed reflection and a dimwitted half-smile that turned up one side of her mouth. The overhead light glinted off the water's surface, broken by the slowly spinning fan blades, and blurred images wavered and came into focus. She held her breath and squinted, trying to figure out what she was seeing.

She was looking down from above at a small brightly lit hangar with one gray speedster and an open area big enough for two or three more speedsters to park. A stool stood empty next to a door. Shelves lined the back wall. On a shelf sat her daypack. She let out her breath and leaned in. Yes, it was definitely her pack.

Her pulse quickened and she wondered if the speedster belonged to their captor. The view shifted and suddenly she was watching him step out of a steaming shower. She cringed and drew back but did not break the vision. She knew that body too well. Her blood ran cold as she watched him towel himself dry and dress in tan cargo pants, a tan field shirt, and a gray field jacket. A patch on a front jacket pocket read, "Balthazar." She swallowed and watched as he left the bathroom and dressing area, which looked identical to theirs, strode through a bedroom with two twin beds, and into a living area with a couch and two more twin beds. He pulled on socks and a pair of black boots, then stepped out into a corridor.

He entered a kitchen, where two men were cooking and two other men were seated at a table, drinking out of mugs. They engaged in conversation, but she could not hear anything. She watched hungrily as the cooks served plates of eggs and sausages. The previous day, about an hour after his raping session, the man—Balthazar—had brought them plates of scrambled eggs and sliced meats, leaving the plates on the floor inside the bedroom door, with no silverware. They had eaten with their hands. For water, they drank from the sink faucet with cupped hands.

Her mind started to grow muzzy, but she forced herself to focus on Balthazar lifting a forkful of food to his mouth. Wiping his mouth on a linen napkin. Stirring sugar into a cup of coffee. She could feel the drug warping her perception—the water seemed closer, and then far away, and the voices of Anna and Maria sounded as though the women were standing in a long tunnel. Cassidy thought they were talking to her but she couldn't be sure, and she did not want to break her remote viewing session. Her body felt warm and tingly from the drug, and she wondered vaguely why she had been so afraid of the man.

He finished eating and balanced three plates of food on his arm. She watched him press his free thumb to a lock pad and enter a room, which was filled with a large bed, a couch, a desk and desk chair, and two dressers. He approached a door locked with a sliding bolt. He slid the lock open, and she watched him place the plates on the floor of the rape room, look around the bedroom briefly, and then leave. Cassidy could faintly hear the door close through the closet door while she watched him bolt it shut. He grabbed a sensor from the top of a dresser by the bedroom door, and she stared at her crystal shaft, which also sat atop the dresser. She tried to track him as he left the room, but Anna was talking to her and shaking her by the shoulder. It was a weird sensation, to know she was being shaken but to not feel anything, while at the same time watching herself and Anna as she floated above her body and looked down.

"Come on, Cassidy," Anna said softly. "You've got to eat before you pass out." Anna pulled on her arm, and Cassidy rose, dripping.

She stepped out onto the cold tile floor, and Anna and Maria dried her off and wrapped her hair in a towel. "She's stoned already," Cassidy heard Anna say, her voice muffled and far away.

"Yeah, her pupils are pinpricks," Maria said.

Anna unwrapped Cassidy's hair and brushed it out, patting it dry as best she could, and Maria pulled a clean gown over Cassidy's head, letting the silky fabric drape around her hips. Cassidy stood on wobbly legs, staring at the marble wall.

"Come on, Cassidy."

They guided her into the dressing room and Anna put a plate of food in her hands. The food was tasteless, but Anna and Maria encouraged her to eat anyway, reminding her it was probably the only meal of the day. She finished half of the eggs and sausages, and then ran to the toilet and threw up. She staggered back to the closet and lay down on the carpeted floor with her head on a rolled towel. She looked up at her friends. They were talking, but she could not understand them. She loved them and took their hands and kissed their soft skin. They gently squeezed her hands and covered her with a large bath towel.

"Sleep, Cassidy," Anna said.

She did not want to sleep, she wanted to lose herself in the colors of the satin negligees hanging over her head. Sky blue and blood red and sunset pink. They were so beautiful. The carpet was soft and mushy, and she sank into it.

4

THE SEARCH

It took Torr a moment to realize he was in Tatsuya's tent, lying on a futon on the ground and covered with a clean white sheet. The air held a subtle herbal scent, and soft light filtered through the weave of the tent canvas. With the sun never rising or setting, he could not tell if he had slept an hour or a day. He tried to detect the angle of the sun, but the light was indirect and suffused across the canvas ceiling. He took in a deep breath and raised himself onto one elbow. His head was not throbbing any longer, nor did it feel like a bowl of quivering pudding. His face no longer stung nor ached.

He glanced around. The tent was artfully tidy. Clean rush mats covered the floor in a grid of perfect squares. A small glossy black table was centered against a canvas wall and displayed a framed photo of an old man. On the table in front of the photo sat a collection of small red lacquered bowls filled with rice grains and other offerings. In a back corner, a low table held a small, perfectly manicured, living bonsai tree. Torr could smell the earthy scent of juniper.

Outside the slightly parted doorway on a swept mat, his boots were lined up next to Tatsuya's tent sandals. Torr lowered his head back onto the pillow, wanting to steal a few more minutes of serenity before facing whatever it was his mind had dulled during the fog of sleep.

Overhead, three origami birds twirled slowly. They were crafted of multicolored paper: red, gold, blue, and green. They turned slowly on their strings, and Torr noted with satisfaction that he saw only one of each and was not made dizzy by their circling. Next to the birds hung a small circular web of sinew decorated with tiny white bones and gray and yellow feathers. A dreamcatcher.

Torr's heart skipped a beat as the memory of his dream came rushing in, as though the sight of the dreamcatcher had opened a door that let in streams of blinding sunlight. His mother fleeing to the hills, alone. His father captured by the Tegs. His mother holding his head in her hands—a surge of energy coursing through his body, making his skull vibrate and then grow quiet. Or was it Tatsuya's ministrations that had banished his throbbing headache? The dream had felt so real, unlike any he'd had before.

Growing up, his mother had made it a habit of asking him occasionally, casually, if he had dreamt of this or that. Often he'd have a murky recollection of something she mentioned. He told her about some of his strange dreams—of being lost in places he had never been, or running from people he had never met, or the flaming monster woman who had plagued his dreams as a child. Brianna told him about an elusive kind of dreaming, doggedly sought after by shamans—lucid dreams. Those in which the dreamer was awake and could influence the dream. *Could influence reality.* His mother had called him a dreamwalker—one who entered a higher form of dreaming than even lucid dreaming. He did not know what that meant, exactly, but apparently it ran in the family.

He'd never quite believed lucid dreaming was possible, yet this dream of his mother and father in the fields overlooking the ocean had felt as real as this tent. *More* real. He shivered. What was reality, anyway? If the dream had been real, then Torr had saved his mother from the Tegs. Shielded her with his ephemeral body. But he had been unable to save his father. Grief sank into his belly. His father was strong, he tried to convince himself. Caden would survive.

Torr rose to his feet and folded the sheet mechanically as his jaw muscles worked, holding back the panic that was building with a pressure that threatened to undo the work of ... his mother? Tatsuya? Both? It didn't matter—he believed his dream. His concussion was healed. His mother was alone, hundreds of miles from Shasta. His father was a prisoner. Torr's heart drummed against his chest and his cheek began to twitch. Cassidy must still be missing, or else she would be at his side.

Someone had clothed him in a clean pair of boxer shorts and his *Moon Star* t-shirt. Next to the bed, his other clothing was neatly folded. He pulled on his pants and donned his belt and vest, noting with displeasure the empty combat knife sheath, and then remembered the missing rune belt. He lifted his t-shirt and felt his skin. It was still not there. Patting his pants' right cargo pocket, he felt the long crystal shaft against his thigh, and the Bear crystal hung heavily from its vest pouch. He stopped only long enough to drink from his waterskin, then clipped it to his shoulder strap. He slipped on his boots and stepped out onto the dirt.

The blood he shared with his sister thrummed in his temples. If Cassidy had been killed, or if she had been trafficked away from the moon, he would leave Peary Spaceport by foot through the decompression chambers, plunge himself into space, and slowly explode.

But no, he could feel her heart beating with his heart. She was alive. He had to find her. And he had to stay alive to help his parents, even if only through his dreams.

Hiroshi peered up from where he sat cross-legged in front of his tent and hopped to his feet. Behind Hiroshi, Torr could see Tatsuya sleeping inside, having given up his tent for Torr. The Fen was cloaked in the silence of night curfew.

"Did you find my sister?" Torr asked.

Hiroshi rushed to him and clasped his shoulder. "No. We looked everywhere," the man said, his voice husky with sorrow. "We searched every tent. Every trailer. All the infrastructure buildings. The spaceport. Everywhere."

"Who's guarding the spaceport?" Torr asked, the sweat of panic blossoming under his armpits.

Hiroshi tightened his lips. "They've been searching every outbound flight. Nothing."

"What about underground, in that witch's cave?" Torr asked.

Hiroshi shook his head. "Jaz checked. I was with him. He asked Gabira. And he asked the Scrids. They both said no."

"And you believed them?"

Hiroshi nodded, his eyes keen like a bird's.

Tatsuya joined them. "You are better," the elderly man said, his gray eyebrows rising with surprise. He grabbed Torr's head and gently felt his skull, a look of wonder reflected in his small black eyes.

"Yes," Torr said.

"You are glowing," Tatsuya said, regarding him as though Torr were shining around the edges.

"Perhaps," Torr acknowledged, wondering what his mother had done to him. It had felt like a bolt of lightning had run from her hands through his body, though he did not know what lightning felt like. But it had felt like a current, and it had felt like light. Warm and throbbing. Jolting.

"I need my wolf knife," he said to Hiroshi.

The younger man disappeared into the tent and returned, handing him the sheathed blade with the bare metal tang.

Torr glanced at the wolf on the pommel, and its golden eyes stared back at him. He pulled the blade free and examined it briefly, noting it had been freshly polished, and then sheathed it and slipped it onto his belt. He thanked Hiroshi and strode out into the larger courtyard.

"Jasper!" he called, his voice loud in the silence. Fritz was sitting on a picnic table on night watch and frowned sadly at Torr. Jasper stumbled from his tent.

"Torr," Jasper said with surprise. His freckled face was bruised, and his nose was swollen and dark red, with blackened circles under blood-shot eyes.

"How can you sleep?" Torr demanded. He rushed towards Jasper angrily but stopped short when he realized Jasper's eyes were blood-shot, not from sleeping, but from crying. Torr could not recall Jasper crying since the days when Melanie had abandoned him and Kai had dropped him off at the Dagdas' house and left for the moon. Torr had sometimes heard Jasper's strangled weeping in the middle of the night when he thought Torr was asleep.

Torr clutched Jasper, and they embraced. "We couldn't find her," Jasper said, choking on his words. "We looked everywhere." Jasper's hands clung to the back of Torr's vest, and Torr pulled away to look into his near-brother's tortured eyes. "It's all my fault," Jasper said. "I should never have taken her out into the camp with only three men. I'm a fucking asshole."

"It's not your fault," Torr said firmly, hugging him and patting his back. "She's probably on a ship bound for the Nommos right now." Jasper's voice broke and his chest spasmed in a silent sob. Somehow Jasper's pain eased Torr's own, as though Jasper offered up enough sorrow for the both of them, leaving Torr filled only with stubborn resolve.

He closed his eyes and tried to sense Cassidy. Numbness greeted him. His insides clenched, and he wanted to flee from the rush of fear that assaulted him. He forced himself to stay present. He concentrated on his feelings, trying to determine where she was. He could not tell. All he knew was that she was still alive, and afraid. He opened his eyes and took in a shaky breath.

"Where did you look?" Torr asked. "You sealed all the exits?" He straightened and gripped Jasper's arms.

"Yes, yes," Jasper said. "We locked down the spaceports. No one can leave without a thorough inspection."

"What do you mean, *spaceports?* How many are there?" Snakes writhed in Torr's gut.

"There's a second spaceport, ASB," Jasper said. "Auxiliary Spaceport B. It's small."

Torr's spine grew rigid. "Ideal for whisking away a kidnap victim, don't you think?"

"Not from there," Jasper said. "It's safely guarded. The most reliable men run security at ASB."

"I want to see it for myself. Are there maps of Peary? I want to see them." Torr realized by Jasper's surprised reaction that he was barking out orders—Jasper was accustomed to Torr deferring to him.

"Montana has a bunch of maps," Jasper mumbled.

"In his office at the PCA?"

Jasper nodded. Torr turned and strode away while Jasper hurried to catch up. Torr made a beeline towards Center Ring, cutting between tents for the shortest route. "Torr, wait, I need to put on my boots." Torr stopped and looked down at Jasper's long hairy toes covered in dust.

"Meet me there," Torr said.

"But it's still curfew," Jasper said.

"You stopped searching for her during curfews?" Torr asked, staring him down.

"Yes, well, I mean," Jasper faltered. "We searched every day for eighteen hours straight, for three days in a row. We all needed to rest. We couldn't very well march into people's tents in the middle of the night."

Torr turned and left Jasper in the dust. A patter of footsteps came up behind him, and Hiroshi and Berkeley appeared at his heels, followed by Fritz and Frank. Torr nodded to them and kept walking. Berkeley strode with a slight limp, but his long legs kept pace with Torr's.

"You okay?" Berkeley asked, looking at Torr oddly.

"Yeah. You?" Torr asked, returning the appraisal. Berkeley appeared to be in pain.

"Twisted my knee," Berkeley said lightly. "Got a couple of cracked ribs. Some nice bruises." He gestured down his body. White tape bound his left ring finger and pinky finger together. "Couple of busted fingers. Got some boots to the head, but I got my hands up in time so they didn't ruin my pretty face. Not like you and Jaz."

Torr nodded. He hadn't even inquired about Jasper's health. "Did Jasper break his nose?" Torr asked.

Berkeley shook his head and said, "Medic doesn't think it's broken. But you had a concussion. How did you get better?" Berkeley asked, a puzzled look wrinkling his brow.

"I'll tell you later," Torr promised. They continued walking in silence for a few paces. "Thanks," Torr said. He didn't know exactly what for. For getting beat up for his sister, he supposed. For standing by him right now, even though he was bruised and battered.

Berkeley glanced at him and smiled. "Don't mention it," he said, and they walked on.

Heads poked out from tents as they passed by, curious to see who was disturbing the stillness of the nighttime hours. Two young men Torr's age stepped out of a tent in front of him. Torr stopped as the pair blocked his path.

"Did you find your sister?" one of the young men asked. Torr didn't know how the man recognized him, but if Jasper had led a tent-by-tent search, everyone in the camp would be aware of Cassidy's disappearance by now.

"No."

"We want to help. I'm Li-Jie. This is my cousin Zhang-Yong." The man was earnest, his serious expression mirroring Torr's own. Torr shook the men's hands. They ran back into their tent and soon caught up with him and walked at his side. Raleigh and Roanoke trotted up behind them, still bleary from sleep. Not far behind were Sky and Thunder. Torr kept walking, and his followers fell in behind him.

Jasper caught up to them, with Ming-Long and Khaled. Center Ring was abandoned, except for a lone guard on duty in front of the PCA tent, the second of the two large Peary Central Administration tents. It was not Bratislav, but a broader, huskier man with a bushy blond beard and shaved upper lip and scalp, and watery blue eyes. Jasper introduced them. The guard, Sid, allowed the party into the large tent. Jasper led them past the tables and around back to Montana's office, where they gathered around a table strewn with maps.

The topmost map showed a Peary Dome camp that must have been from some earlier, more orderly time. Tents were indicated in neat, curved rows, filling the ever-expanding blocks that radiated out from Center Ring. Each tent was numbered. It hardly resembled the current chaotic collection of tents and jury-rigged structures. But the PCA tents, gravity bar, and storage containers of Center Ring, as well as the ration trailers, porta-potties, and sauna shacks seemed to be in the same locations, as were the infrastructure buildings that filled the exterior ring. Air and Water Control. Greenhouses and bakery. Infirmary. Staff container shantytown. Spaceport. Jail—he hadn't noticed that before—on a triangular plot between the staff housing and the infirmary, and not visible from the road.

Torr traced his finger to where Jasper pointed. On the opposite end of the dome from Peary Spaceport, at the end of Spoke Road Three, was a collection of containers, with a small notation inside one of the rectangles: "ASB." Torr raised one eyebrow.

"It's underground," Jasper explained, reading Torr's expression.

"I see," Torr said. "Let's go."

"I told you," Jasper said. "I checked there already. The security there is rock solid."

Torr rolled up the map, clutched it in his fist, and left the PCA. He set out across the broad circular yard and headed towards Spoke Road Three.

"You won't be able to get in," Jasper called and hurried to catch up, his face growing red.

"You'll get me in," Torr said gruffly.

Jasper sucked his teeth loudly and walked reluctantly at his side. Berkeley sidled up on the other side, and the three men walked in silence as they entered the spoke road, their companions trailing behind. Tent doorways parted, with confused, bleary faces peeking out at them. A man emerged from his tent, fastening his pants with a wide leather belt hung with various knives and tools. He ran after Torr, his belt clanking. "I recognize you," he said, pointing to Jasper and Berkeley. "You were looking for that girl. You get her back?"

Jasper shook his head sullenly. The man peered at Torr. "You her brother?"

Torr nodded and met the man's eyes. He was middle-aged, but his brown eyes were young and lively. "I'm William. I'll help you find her," he said, falling into step beside them. "I hate them dumb bastards. Rapists should have their cocks chopped off."

Torr swallowed and marched forward. The man walked jauntily at Jasper's side. Four more men volunteered as the group made their way up the long straight road. They reached the end of the spoke road, and Torr told his swelling ranks to wait while he went ahead with Jasper and Berkeley.

Under the curving wall of the dome, in the no-man's land beyond the perimeter road, stood an extensive collection of metal shipping containers. Jasper led them through the maze to a dark-green container at the far edge.

Jasper rapped loudly on the metal door using a metal rod that hung by the door. Jasper folded his arms and leaned against the metal wall. "It'll be a few minutes," he said, his eyebrows knitting together as he examined Torr. "Where'd your bruises go?"

Torr shrugged. "Tatsuya's a good healer." He folded the rolled map and tucked it into his left leg pocket.

Jasper lowered his brows at Berkeley, who was inspecting Torr closely. Berkeley's brown eyes squinted, half closed. He tugged at one of his beard points and spoke softly. "Are you aware that you're glowing?"

Torr pursed his lips and adjusted his vest. Jasper scrutinized him as well, searching for the glow he had missed. "Tatsuya said the same thing," Torr said hesitantly. "Glowing ... like how?"

"Well, it's purple. Like a nimbus of flames around your whole body. I have to squint to see it, but in the shadow here it's blazing like a fire." "I can't see it," Jasper whined.

Berkeley glanced at him. "You need to practice more, instead of obsessing about your trading business."

"I do not obsess," Jasper said, and Berkeley rolled his eyes. "I work," Jasper insisted.

"Ramesh told you to meditate two hours a day, minimum. When's the last time you meditated?" Berkeley asked, and Jasper shrugged guiltily. Berkeley continued, "I used to meditate six hours a day when I was with Eridanus. You don't need to sleep much if you meditate that often. And everything seems easier to do. Time is slower, and action is smoother. You notice things you never noticed before."

Torr wondered what he meant exactly by meditating.

A noise from the container brought them all to attention. A metal latch scraped from the inside, and the door swung slowly outward. A stocky bearded man clad in green military fatigues and cradling an assault rifle looked out at them crossly. "No flights in or out," he said sharply. His eyes narrowed, adjusting to the bright light of the outdoors. "Oh, it's you, Jaz. What do you want? Isn't it curfew?"

"Yeah." Jasper brushed by the man into the container, which was lit by a strand of solar filaments. Torr and Berkeley followed. Jasper introduced the man, Jericho. The ASB guard had a surly swagger to him, his moustached lip curling down as Jasper told him that Torr was worried Cassidy would be taken out through the port.

Jericho looked at Torr. "Sorry about your sister," he said grimly. "My sister got taken by the Tegs."

"Oh," Torr said. "I'm sorry."

Jericho held his gaze. "It was a long time ago. I can't think about it much. Except when something like this happens—brings it all back."

"Sorry," Torr repeated.

"Ain't no way your sister will get taken out this way. But if you want to check the place, be my guest."

Torr nodded, and Jericho led them down a long ladder that descended into a dark hole in the ground and terminated in a stone tunnel with rounded walls and ceiling. They walked down the dim tunnel and came upon a large cave. Four more men with assault rifles were sitting on stools by a wide metal compression bay door. Two dusty gray speedsters were parked in the back of the small underground hangar. A radar panel and a control board sat on a table against the far wall. A large air vent mounted on the ceiling let out faint puffs of air with a soft whirring sound.

"This is it," Jericho said, waving his hand through the air. "Our humble spaceport. Was the original one. Built inside a natural lava tube. Like I said, we ain't had no traffic, in or out, since last week. Days before your sister went missing. I swear it."

Torr nodded. He believed him.

Jericho's eyes shifted and settled onto the wall beyond Torr's shoulder. Torr glanced behind him. In the shadows stood two cloaked figures. The nape of Torr's neck tingled. He gasped as one of the figures pushed its hood back to reveal an alien face. The man's skin was a translucent white, glowing like candle wax from the reflected light, and stretched tautly over wide cheekbones and a prominent jaw that showed not even the hint of a beard. But it was his eyes that made Torr go rigid. They were large and wide and fluorescent green, lit from within. They reminded Torr of a leaf covered with dew and sparkling in early morning sunshine, with glowing fronds for eyelashes. Torr held his breath as a long strand of hair fell loose from the shelter of the man's cowl. His hair was the same color green as his eyes and glowed like a light tube. Torr stepped backwards, and Jasper put a hand to his back.

"It's okay," Jasper said softly. "They're Murians. Their eyes and hair glow. Otherwise, they're mostly like us. You don't need to fear them." Torr's startled surprise retreated and was replaced by curiosity. "They stay in the caves because they can't tolerate the sun," Jasper said. "And they wear robes to help keep the dust off their sensitive skin, and their, uh, tendrils. There's a small community of Murians who have lived underground here for years."

Torr held the Murian's eyes, which were locked onto his. Large horizontal pupils within the glittery green irises were dark, and Torr stared as the man blinked his eyes, revealing the full length of the glowing green eyelashes.

"Hello, Murugan. Guruhan," Jasper said, and bowed his head, pressing his left hand to his belly. The Murians bowed in the same manner. Jasper looked at Torr sideways, and Torr imitated the bow, as did Berkeley. Jasper stepped forward into the shadows to greet the men, and Torr and Berkeley followed.

"Jasss, Buckla," Murugan greeted them in a fair approximation of their names. He looked at Torr and rattled something off in a series of clicks and hisses. Jasper gave a few awkward clicks in response and glanced at Torr. The men were taller than even Berkeley, wide of shoulder, and stood on strong legs. Their moss-green cloaks were parted in the front, and underneath they wore pants and tunics of the same shimmering green fabric.

Murugan spoke in his strange clicking language to Jasper and Berkeley, all the while looking at Torr.

"He sees the glow, too," Jasper said. "He says you have the light of the old priests who guarded the Star Globe. He wants to know if you have passed the three trials." Jasper shrugged at Torr with round eyes. "I'm just translating. I don't know what it means."

"Tell them I don't think so."

The two Murian men spoke rapidly to one another, and then to Jasper.

Jasper clicked back and turned to Torr with his brow furrowed. "They asked if you have a twin sister. They want to know if she glows too," Jasper said.

"Only when she's angry," he said, trying to make a joke. Cassidy's face flashed before his eyes, reminding him with a rush of panic why he was there. "Do they know where she is?" he asked in vain hope.

The Murians and Jasper exchanged a few sounds.

"No," Jasper said. "But they said you must find her and take her to Muria."

"Right. We've got to go," Torr said. "Tell them I'd like to talk with them more another time." He bowed, and the Murians bowed in return. Torr called his thanks to Jericho and the other guards, and then led Jasper and Berkeley at a trot through the long tunnel and up the ladder. Jericho came up behind them as they exited into the sunshine, wishing them luck before swinging the container door shut and clanking the latch into place.

———————)———————

The group had added two more followers while Torr had been down below. They cut across Spoke Road Three on a straight path towards

Peary Spaceport—their next destination. They collected two more men between the auxiliary spaceport and Center Ring. At Center Ring, three men were scraping open the doors of the ration trailer, indicating that morning gong was about to sound. Bratislav and Sid were standing at the corner of the PCA tent, and the blond-bearded Sid ran to join them.

"I'm coming with you," he said, as he fell into step beside Berkeley.

Morning gong sounded. The deep rolling tones of several gongs converged and resonated through the still air.

The globe of Earth shone in an even half, the unlit side dark against a darker sky. Torr squinted briefly, looking to see if he could detect the Free States. The western hemisphere was shrouded in shadow. He resisted the urge to take his binoculars from his belt, and instead strode resolutely forward. There was nothing he could do for his parents right now. Cassidy was the dagger impaling his heart and requiring immediate attention.

The men attracted stares as they marched up Spoke Road Nine. Small groups of sleepy-eyed men headed towards the porta-potties or nearest ration trailer. Several men inquired as to Cassidy's fate. Before the group had reached the spaceport, a dozen more men were marching with them.

Torr paused at the perimeter road before entering the spaceport. He told the group to wait outside, and several of the men ran off to gather their friends to help. Torr wasn't sure what they were going to help with, but he let them go, not wishing to have a conversation nor quell their enthusiasm.

Torr stepped inside the spaceport with Jasper and Berkeley. The guards inside the door directed them to an Earth freighter at the far wall. Rodney and Kai were watching with arms folded as a forklift loaded drums of titanium powder into a shipping container that sat in the ship's hold.

"Torr," Kai called out and rushed over to greet him, taking his arm protectively. His face was lined with weariness. "You feeling better? You look ... good." Kai tilted his head with a confused frown.

Torr gave him a curt nod. "What's going on here?"

"We can't hold ships here any longer," Kai said. "We've cleared her for departure."

Worry knotted in Torr's gut, and his cheek throbbed. "What if Cassidy's hidden in there?"

"She's not," Kai assured him.

"Are you sure?"

Kai squeezed his shoulder. "Positive."

"What about smuggling compartments?" Torr asked.

Rodney must have sensed his misery and motioned for Torr to follow him up the ramp. Rodney took a crowbar and tapped it along the floor until the tone changed. Torr stooped and felt around in the dust and found a small gap in the metal floor. Rodney handed him the crowbar, and Torr pried at the floor until a metal plate lifted. His heart pounded. Together, they pushed the heavy plate aside. Lying in a wide shallow recess were coils of rope, large hooks, and a collection of winches.

The captain of the ship stood by with his hand on his hips. "They checked already," he told Torr sourly.

Rodney glanced up at the captain as he and Torr slid the plate back in place. "Let him do this," Rodney told the captain softly.

Torr met Rodney's eyes, then tapped along the floor with the crowbar until he found another floor compartment. Inside was a pile of netting that Torr pulled out, and then stuffed back into the hole. They went to the side walls where Rodney and the ship's captain removed one panel after another, revealing bundles of wiring and nothing more. Torr peered into the two shipping containers, which were filled with metal drums.

"We're not unloading those again," the captain said in a strained voice.

"No need," Rodney said, looking firmly at Torr.

Torr lowered his eyes.

The captain led them into the front cabin, where they inspected small closets and lifted a hatch on the floor that revealed tanks of oxygen in a square compartment. Torr sighed with resignation as Rodney laid his heavy hand on Torr's shoulder. "She's not here," he said.

Torr nodded, tears hovering at the edges of his eyelids. He straightened, struggling to maintain his composure, then climbed down out of the cabin and onto the hangar floor.

"Torr," Kai said, holding both his shoulders. "We're doing everything we can."

Torr swallowed. "Really?" His voice came out thin and cracked. "Then why isn't there a security force maintaining order in Peary Dome? Why are people left to do whatever the hell they want?" He glared at Kai, who looked taken aback. Rodney had overheard and glanced at Torr sharply, then looked away.

"Tell me more about the camp search you conducted," Torr said, turning to Jasper. He refused to abandon himself to despair. He could only go on the assumption that Cassidy was still inside Peary Dome. If she was hidden in Gabira's cave, then she was safe for now. Jasper and Berkeley promised they'd take him down there to look, although they insisted they had checked there already. The Scrids were more urgent, with their supposed portal. If the Scrids had not taken her—Jasper had assured him they had not—then Cassidy was prisoner in a camp somewhere inside the dome.

Jasper and Kai described the search they had conducted of the tent city. They had found one young woman, who said she was being held against her will, and had taken her to a female Traders Guild member for care. A young boy, as well, appeared to have been held prisoner and was being cared for by the same woman. Torr nodded, pleased that the effort had saved a couple of people but agitated that Cassidy had not been among them.

They told him about a large gang run by a man named Schlitzer, who ran a whorehouse and the bar Jasper had told him about. Schlitzer had spies all over the camp and had deployed them to see what they could uncover. Torr scowled at this. Spies could be bought both ways. But his ears pricked up with more interest at the mention of a few people who said they had witnessed the attack that had resulted in Torr's concussion and Cassidy's disappearance. Two people had separately thought they'd recognized the attackers as the men who ran a shoe shop out of their camp on Ring Road K.

"What did you find there? Who searched the shoemakers' camp?" Torr asked.

"I led the search," Jasper said. "We all went. They have a big compound and several men, plus two women and children." The hairs on Torr's neck tingled with electricity. "They didn't like us coming inside, so I thought maybe we'd found her," Jasper said quickly. "They threatened us with knives and scissors, but finally relented when we threatened to come back with a bigger gang. We scoured that camp down to the last speck of dust, I swear to the stars." Kai and Berkeley nodded in agreement. Torr wished his squad from Miramar were there. He wished he had his guns. "We searched their shop and all their sleeping tents," Jasper continued. "She wasn't there." The men nodded again, and Torr's heart thudded.

"We will look again, after we visit the Scrids," Torr announced. "I want to make sure all exits from the camp are sealed. The Scrids could take her out through their portal, right?" Torr's frantic gaze darted between the exhausted men.

"They haven't played their drums," Berkeley said. "They always play their drums when they use the portal. That's what I understand, anyway," he said, his voice trailing off.

A tempestuous anger stirred in Torr's blood. He rarely lost his temper, but he felt his self-control weakening. He did not want to lash out at his friends—it wouldn't help find Cassidy.

"We should check in with Schlitzer, to see if he's learned anything," Jasper said. "It's on the way to the Scrid camp." Anguish and guilt still haunted Jasper's eyes.

Torr clamped his jaws shut, wishing his cheek would stop twitching. "Okay," he said, sighing. "Let's go."

"I'll stay here," Kai said. "If someone tries to take her out this way, we'll have their heads." The sad resignation behind Kai's bravado clutched at Torr's heart. "If anyone can find her," Kai said to Torr, "you will."

Torr's confidence wavered. A thorough search had already been conducted of the camp. Who was Torr to think he could find Cassidy when Jasper and Kai had not? Torr stiffened his resolve. He had to try. He refused to believe her captors had somehow slipped the security net of the spaceports. Kai gave him a gentle cuff on his back, then returned to Rodney's side at the freighter.

Torr led the way out of the hangar. Outside, the band waiting for him had doubled in size again. Torr quickly met the newcomers, then looked out across the sea of tents.

He and his band headed around the perimeter road towards Earth, attracting more followers. Their next stop was Schlitzer's camp. The bulk of Torr's group split off to wait for them at the end of Spoke Road Twelve. Torr trotted down the long block to Ring Road L with Jasper, Berkeley, Khaled, and Ming-Long.

Schlitzer's compound was a well-established camp, encompassing an entire block and surrounded by storm fencing. Two large round pavilion-style tents stood inside the main entrance, which was guarded by two men who nodded at Jasper and Berkeley and let them pass without question. The pavilions had been connected together to form one continuous space, with the sides rolled up halfway. A collection of smaller tents, shipping containers, and other outbuildings stood beyond the pavilions.

Torr ducked under a wall of the pavilion, and his eye was immediately drawn to a long Earth-style bar made of polished wood stretching along one side of the tent. The bar was lined with stools and was backed by a wooden wall with a large mirror in its center, flanked by tall shelves filled with glinting bottles.

It was early in the day, and the place was empty except for a woman stocking the bar. Jasper spoke to her, and she left the tent, returning a couple of minutes later with a puffy-eyed man. The man was tall and strapping, with wild brown-and-gray-streaked hair that billowed about his head. A short-cropped goatee framed his smiling mouth.

"Jaz," he said, clasping Jasper's arm. "How'd the search go? You get your woman back?"

"No. This is her brother, Torr, who I was telling you about."

Schlitzer shook Torr's hand and grasped his arm with kind concern. Torr felt himself relaxing under the beaming gaze of the man's deep-set blue eyes, but caught himself. The man ran a whorehouse and a spy network. No doubt he was successful due to his ability to make people trust him despite everything. Torr gripped his hand, veiling his distrust behind a polite smile. Torr's eyes flicked to the patch on the man's vest pocket—*Peary Dome Traders Guild*.

Schlitzer spoke in a deep resonant voice. "Tell me about your sister. What does she look like? How does she behave? What do you think her next move will be?"

Torr didn't like the man asking him questions. Surely Jasper had already given him a detailed description. Schlitzer was supposed to provide information, not interrogate. Torr did not have time to waste.

Torr asked in return, "Did you find out anything? Have you heard rumors? Anything feel unusual in the camp?"

Schlitzer's gaze hardened. He ran a thumb and forefinger thoughtfully over his moustaches, smoothing them in an apparently futile effort to tame the straying whiskers. "Well, now. Nothing I can tell you right off."

Torr's back bristled. Jasper stepped closer to Torr, casting him a stern glance, and took over the conversation, describing Cassidy to Schlitzer. Torr wondered if the man had found Cassidy himself and was planning on demanding a ransom for her return. Had they searched this camp? He stepped back and muttered his question to Berkeley.

Berkeley put his lips near Torr's ear and whispered, "Yes. As best we could. I don't think she's here. At least she wasn't."

Jasper and Schlitzer were engaged in conversation, and Schlitzer assured Jasper he'd let him know if he learned anything.

"What do you know about the shoemakers?" Torr interrupted.

Schlitzer's bushy eyebrows rose. "They sell shoes. I know that much." Torr wanted to punch him. "And they have two women and two kids. But I haven't heard about a third woman there." His eyelashes fluttered innocently. "I'm sure I'd know." He smiled, showing straight white teeth, daring Torr to sink his knuckles into them.

Torr bowed his head. "Thanks for your help," he said, and turned to leave the pavilion. Two young women were entering as he ducked under the canvas wall. They were dressed in short sheer negligees that showed their nipples and didn't quite cover their shapely behinds as they bent to duck under the canvas. They couldn't have been older than sixteen. Torr looked away, disgusted at himself for the reflex that stiffened his dick. The girls seemed happy and bubbly, and Torr wondered what would drive a young woman to sell her body. Schlitzer was not as charming as all that. Jasper and the others followed in his wake, all of them glancing sideways at the scantily clad females. Torr sighed and went to rejoin the others.

They were at the end of Spoke Road Twelve, standing around the sundial. He turned his attention to Jasper. They had not spoken since they'd left Schlitzer's camp. Torr and Jasper stepped away from their party. "Thank you for introducing me to your royal pimpness. What the fuck?" Torr demanded.

Jasper's eyes grew wide with consternation. "What do you mean? Schlitzer's the best source of intel around. He knows everything. Even more than me." Jasper sounded envious.

"He's a lying cocksucker, that's what he is," Torr retorted.

"What do you mean?" Jasper asked again, waving his hands helplessly.

Torr pressed his lips together. Apparently charm was indeed Schlitzer's trick—one which Torr had somehow deflected, much to Schlitzer's displeasure. "Never mind."

If Schlitzer did have Cassidy, Torr thought he would have felt it. Maybe he should have been friendlier. It was probably unwise to make enemies with a spymaster, but he didn't have time to worry about that now.

"Okay," he said, turning to Jasper. "Next stop, Scrids."

This time he took the whole group, whose numbers had grown again, anticipating that he might need a large force to overwhelm the Scrids if it came to that. Many of his ragtag band had clubs and knives, and some appeared by their postures to know how to use them. Others seemed to wear them just for show. He figured the band would naturally organize themselves with the capable fighters in the front and the less experienced ones hanging back. He took a deep breath and headed to the Scrids' block.

At the entryway to the Scrid compound, Torr, Jasper, and Berkeley approached the guard who stood in the open yard that surrounded the large donut-shaped tent structure.

"Ho, Stump," Jasper called out to the guard, who stomped his feet, making the little bells on his boots jingle and a stone club sway at his side. A chuckle escaped Torr's mouth. The man did look like a stump. Wide and squat, with straggly hair trailing from his head and face like Spanish moss.

Jorimar and Helug appeared at the doorway and strode out into the yard on short, thick legs. They stopped in momentary surprise, then rushed forward. Jasper tried to hold Jorimar back, but he pushed past him and lunged at Torr, butting his barrel chest against Torr's, almost knocking the breath out of him. Torr felt his troop straining behind him, held back by Berkeley's waving hands. Helug chest-butted him next, and Torr accepted this as a respectful greeting. The two men beat their fists against their bear hide vests and yelled up to the star-studded heavens. Their thick guttural voices filled the air. Jasper translated as they spoke.

"Moon Wolf has arrived. Prepare the fires. The stars are descending."

The drumming of metal against wood emerged from inside the tent in a loud complex rhythm that reverberated off the glass panels of the dome. Chanting rose from within the tent, and the boom of a bass drum filled the yard. Jasper translated, his head cocked with concentration.

"Prepare the fires. The eyes of the wolf have opened. The golden flames of the stars descend."

Torr stepped forward and grabbed Jorimar's thick forearm, shaking it. "Stop it! What is going on? Are you activating the portal? Do you have my sister?"

The Scrid leader's amber eyes, already glowing with a sort of fanatical ecstasy, grew even brighter at Torr's touch. Jasper translated the man's guttural tongue.

"The violet flames of the stars have erupted around you. The wolf shadow stands by your side. It truly is you, Moon Wolf. The stars have answered our call."

The man fell to one knee and clutched Torr's hand, pressing it to his cheek where Torr felt the wetness of tears. Torr sucked in his breath, speechless. They had named him *Moon Wolf.* Torr gently raised the weeping man and pressed the man's thick hand between his own and held Jorimar's eyes.

"Listen. My sister is missing. Do you know where she is? Stop that drumming! Are you opening the portal?" he repeated.

Helug and Stump disappeared inside, and the drumming and chanting quieted while Jasper translated Jorimar's response. *"Portal? No. Where's Golden Cloud? You have not found her?"* Distress tarnished the copper glow of Jorimar's eyes. *"We must find her. Where is she? Can you feel her?"*

Torr said, "Yes. No. I don't know." He closed his eyes and tried to sense her location. His eyes opened and he looked around in dismay. "I don't know where she is. Can you feel her crystals?"

Jorimar's bushy eyebrows lowered, and Jasper rushed to translate the Scrid's quick speech. *"You have the Bear crystal in your vest. And another against your leg. And another in your chest pocket. Yes."*

"No," Torr said impatiently. "Not mine. Can you feel hers? She carries two."

Jasper responded with dismay, "She's carrying crystals? Of course she is. I should have taken the Scrids with us from the beginning."

Jorimar closed his eyes, then opened them and said through Jasper, *"There are several crystals around the camp. I do not know which are hers. I am sorry."* He looked ashamed.

"Okay, good enough. Come with us." Torr was praying that Cassidy was at the shoemakers. Torr could not think about what he would do if she were not there. He wrenched his mind from his dark thoughts. One thing at a time. He gathered his courage and looked around.

Jorimar gathered a dozen Scrids and joined him. Torr's followers exchanged glances with surprised acceptance, leaving a wide berth around the squat warriors as everyone headed out onto the road together. Torr stopped and faced the jostling band. "We'll go back to the sundial to regroup, and I'll tell you our plan," Torr announced loudly. The crowd yelled with approval.

Torr had no idea how he'd find Cassidy when the others had failed. He hoped the Scrids would be his secret weapon. Still, their team would need to plan a coordinated attack. Their best bet was to catch the shoemakers by surprise. Should they march in through the front? Sneak in from the back? Take hostages? He needed to pull this off without anyone dying. Particularly Cassidy.

At the sundial, Torr huddled with the men from the Fen. They would split into squads, guard the alleyway behind the shoemakers' camp, and storm the front. If the shoemakers did not admit they had her, he would tie the bastards up and tear the place apart, taking down every tent if he had to. Then, if she still had not been found, he would tear into the men one by one until they told him where she was.

If the shoemakers did have her but held her at knifepoint or some other horrid situation, he didn't know what he'd do, but he had to start somewhere. He held the pommel of the wolf knife, turned to the waiting crowd, and began assigning squad leaders.

———————)———————

"Radios off," Torr snapped as he led his force towards the shoemakers' camp. The tinny chatter silenced as people with radios turned them off.

They approached the shoemakers' block, and several people split off to guard the rear alleyway while Torr and the rest continued along the spoke road.

They turned the corner onto Ring Road K and stopped in front of a tent whose canvas doors were tied back, opened to the road. Inside the tent, a table displayed an assortment of shoes made from tire rubber and tent canvas. Two men stood behind the table and tensed up nervously as Torr's men streamed into view.

Three heavyset men pushed out through flaps of a neighboring tent. "What's this?" one of them demanded, a wooden club in his hand.

Torr met his angry eyes. He recognized that face. The square jaw and unkempt beard. The pudgy bags around the eyes. The same leer Torr remembered as clubs swung at his head, until next thing Torr knew he had woken up in the infirmary.

"We're here for my sister," Torr said, squaring his shoulders.

"We don't have her," the man said.

"Like hell you don't," Torr said. His hand went to the wolf knife pommel. The man gripped his club and hesitated.

"Take him down," Torr said to Ming-Long and Khaled, who jumped on the man and wrestled him to the ground, while Hiroshi took down the second heavyset man with quick precision, and Fritz and Frank took care of the third man.

Torr turned to a commotion in the other tent. The shopkeepers had turned over the display table, and one of them leapt over it and lunged at Jasper. Jasper threw his hand forward and, without touching the man, cast him to the ground. The man scrambled backwards over rows of sandals and cowered at the back of the tent. The second shopkeeper fell to the dust, writhing at Berkeley's feet, while Berkeley glared down at him and clutched empty air.

Raleigh and Roanoke rushed forward and helped lash the shoemakers' wrists behind their backs.

"Knock down the tents," Torr said to the Scrids.

The thick squat men pulled up stakes and poles, and canvas billowed to the ground, exposing a large open yard hemmed in by several tents arranged in a square.

A group of men stared out at them from a central courtyard, and a tall man strode forward angrily, a deep scowl scoring his bearded face.

"What's the meaning of this?" the man demanded.

Torr stepped over the tent canvas, followed by his forces, and confronted the man. "We're here for my sister."

"We don't have your sister," the man said, a sneer lifting his upper lip. "Get out of my camp."

Torr quickly assessed the situation. More than a dozen shoemakers were gathered in the center of the yard, and four more stood in the back of a large workshop tent, knives and scissors in hand. Torr had three times as many men, but a fight could get ugly. A baby started crying from behind a row of tents, and one of the men glanced over his shoulder towards the sound.

"Jorimar, Helug," Torr said, directing the Scrids towards the shoemakers in the courtyard and workshop. "Guard them while we search the camp."

The shoemakers shifted on their feet and the leader objected loudly as several Scrids encircled them and the other Scrids walled off the open workshop tent, trapping the other four. The Scrids glowered at the shoemakers, slapping stone clubs against thick palms. The shoemakers eyed them warily.

"Search the camp," Torr shouted to his followers, waving them forward. "Take down every tent."

Tents fell all around, and belongings were thrown into piles. Five men, two women, a toddler, and the wailing baby were herded into the courtyard to join their clan.

"Torr!" Raleigh called out as Roanoke pulled up the canvas floor of the kitchen tent. The brothers lifted a large piece of plywood off the ground, revealing a dirt pit.

Torr and Jasper ran over, and Torr dropped to his knees. In a dark corner of the empty pit a small crystal ball glimmered. His heart dropped and he grabbed Cassidy's crystal. Panic and rage surged through him, and he jumped to his feet.

"Torr!" Sky called from a tent nearby. Hawk held up Cassidy's black web belt with her combat knife still attached.

Torr's heart jumped into his throat and he turned to the shoemakers huddled together in the yard, their eyes darting between Cassidy's belt and the crystal ball in Torr's palm.

"Cassidy!" Torr called out and ran into the tent where Sky and Hawk stood. Jasper ran in behind him, followed by Berkeley. They looked around frantically in the dim interior, which was strewn with sleeping blankets and clothing. They rifled through the bedding and clothing, and in the pocket of a pair of men's pants Torr found her golden amulets—the coin of the water goddess, and the triangular Heaven's Window pendant, dangling from their gold chains. Adrenaline coursed through him as he searched more pockets.

"Is her rune belt here?" Torr asked, flinging aside dirty clothing. "Mine is gone," he grumbled.

"No it's not," Berkeley said. "I took it off you at the infirmary."

Torr glanced gratefully at the tall man, his heart lifting momentarily. "Thank the stars," Torr said, and continued searching, but they found nothing else.

They ran outside, yanked up the tent's stakes, and pulled away the canvas flooring. Others felled the remainder of the tents, looking underneath for more hidden holes in the ground. The crew who had been guarding the back alleyway came in and helped. They found Torr's combat knife, and Jasper's and Berkeley's knives and radios. But Cassidy was not there.

Torr's pulse was thready, and for a moment he was afraid tears of panic and frustration would overwhelm him. He turned his gaze onto the shoemakers and stalked across the yard. The Scrids parted to let him pass.

"You!" Torr said, pointing at the leader with a trembling finger. "What is your name?"

The tall man lifted his bearded chin and did not answer.

"Bring him here," Torr said to Jorimar.

Jorimar and Helug marched into the center of the circle and hauled the leader across the dust by the upper arms. Torr grabbed the man by the throat, wrapping both hands around his corded neck. The shoemaker struggled, but the Scrids held him firmly.

"Where is my sister?" Torr demanded, squeezing harder.

The man's eyes bulged, and Torr loosened his grip. The shoemaker gasped and spit in Torr's face, the warm phlegm hitting Torr's cheekbone and sliding down. Torr wiped away the spit with the back of his hand, then punched the man in the face. The man's head jerked back, but he recovered and stared levelly into Torr's eyes. Torr punched him in the gut. The man lost his breath for a moment but remained stubbornly silent. Torr tackled him to the ground and straddled him, punching his head and face. The man tried to fight back, but Scrids held his arms and legs.

"If you won't talk, maybe your women will," Torr said.

Torr got to his feet and went to a huddle of shoemaker men who were encircling the women and children protectively, but several friends of Jasper wrestled the men away and two grabbed the woman with the toddler screaming in her arms. They prodded the woman forward until she was standing over the man at Torr's feet, who was yelling and trying to get free from the Scrids.

Torr regarded the frightened woman and child. Tears were streaming down both of their faces.

"I'm not going to hurt you," Torr said hoarsely, warm tears wending down his own face. "I just want to find my sister. Where is she?"

"I don't know," the woman said, wiping her cheeks and looking beseechingly at the man on the ground.

Torr turned to him. "Please. It's my sister. Where did she go?" Torr fell to his knees and grasped the man's hand. "Please."

The man did not pull his hand away but met Torr's eyes. He hesitated, glancing up at the woman, and then exhaled and said, "My name is Shiraz. I don't know where she is. A man took her."

"What man?"

"A far side lord," Shiraz said. "He said his name was Joe. He had been bothering us for weeks, wanting us to sell him one of our women. Then he hired us to help him kidnap a stranger, since we have so many men in our clan." The man gazed up at Torr fearfully.

"Go on," Torr said.

Shiraz swallowed and words tumbled from his lips. "We kept saying no, but he kept bothering us and threatening our women and children, and then you appeared. It was only the three of you and your sister. It was spur of the moment. He gave us five gold Tetras. We needed food. No one is buying shoes, and my wife is pregnant again."

"Five Tetras? You sold my sister for *five Tetras?!* Where did he take her? Tell me." He shook Shiraz's shoulder.

"I don't know. He took her away in a box truck." Shiraz hesitated, then grimaced and said, "He always talked about how much gold the Nommos paid for young women."

Torr hopped to his feet and met the blazing eyes of Jasper and Berkeley.

"What did this far side scum Joe look like?" Torr asked Shiraz, his gut twisting into knots.

Shiraz sat up as the Scrids stepped back. "Medium height and build. White with brown hair and eyes. He had a Free States accent. He was scruffy. Dusty. Like everyone."

Torr gritted his teeth, trying to stay rational. "You hid her in the hole. For how long? How long after you attacked us did he take her away in the truck?"

"I'm not sure. No more than an hour. We found him at Schlitzer's bar, where he always hung out. It's not far from here. But he drove your sister away towards the spaceport."

"Come on," Torr said, motioning to his friends. "To the spaceport."

"What do we do with them?" Ming-Long asked, gesturing at the shoemakers.

"Leave them. But you're coming with us," he said to Shiraz. Torr offered him a hand up, and the shoemaker grabbed it and got to his feet. The leader brushed off his clothing, exchanged glances with his wife, and nodded.

———————————)———————————

Torr, Jasper, Berkeley, and Shiraz went inside the spaceport and found Rodney.

"Did a Nommos ship leave here after we were attacked?" Jasper asked Rodney.

"Nope," Rodney said. "Just the one you traded with, but that one left the day before."

"What trade?" Torr asked Jasper.

Jasper shrugged. "I trade with everybody. They usually want Earth spices and other stuff I sell."

Berkeley raised an eyebrow at Jasper. Jasper's mouth drew into a thin line and he returned his attention to Rodney. "What about any other ships bound for Gandoop?" Jasper asked. "The Nommos usually go to Gandoop after they stop here. They could have intercepted them at Gandoop."

"Who?" Rodney asked.

"Just check the passage logs," Jasper pleaded.

"Alright. Hang on," Rodney said, and strode away. He came back with a handscreen and frowned at it. "Looks like an Earth freighter left here the day you were attacked. Before we went on lockdown."

"When, exactly?" Torr asked.

"As soon as we heard," Rodney said.

"When did you hear?" Torr asked.

"I called my dad from the infirmary," Jasper said. "They stole our radios." Jasper glared at Shiraz, who was staring down at his feet. Jasper turned back to Torr. "I thought you were dying. We searched for Cassidy for a while, then we took you to the infirmary."

"How long did that take?" Torr asked. "You should have let me die."

"Shut up, Torr. Maybe an hour," Jasper said.

"Then we had to decide what to do," Rodney said. "We don't just lock down the port on a whim."

"A whim," Torr said bitterly. "When did the ship leave?"

They pieced together their memories and compared them to the passage logs.

"That Earth freighter left in the gap between when we were attacked and you went on lockdown," Torr said. "Cassidy could have been on it. Call Gandoop."

Rodney sighed and unclipped his radio from his belt. "Ramzy," he said into it, and walked away, talking privately. He came back and held the radio out so they all could hear Ramzy's gruff voice coming through the small speaker.

"I talked to Ishmar Gandoop two days ago. He said the Nommos ship left Sunday."

Torr and Jasper stared at one another. They had been attacked on Sunday.

"What time?" Berkeley asked into the radio.

"He didn't know," Ramzy said, the signal crackling with static. "He said they have a new crew and they only recorded the date. That's all I could get out of him. He didn't want to talk much. I'm happy he took my call at all. Things have been tense lately, with the food shortage and all."

"I'm sorry," Rodney said, clicking the radio off and placing his hand on Torr's shoulder.

Torr looked frantically at the men surrounding him. Jasper had grown pale. Berkeley gazed sadly at Torr. Shiraz stared at the floor. Rodney patted his shoulder, then walked away to inspect some cargo.

"I can find her on Nommos," Torr said, grabbing Berkeley's sleeve. "Right?"

"The planet Nommos is uninhabited," Berkeley said. "The Nommos live on the ocean in Delos, in their floating sea-cities. None but Nommos are allowed there."

"Except Earth women," Torr said bitterly. "I'll find a way. When is the next ship to Delos?"

"No one knows," Berkeley said. "Delosian ships arrive here randomly. It could be a while."

Torr fought back a wave of frantic helplessness, then turned a hard gaze on Shiraz and said, "I want to find that far side scum." Then he turned to Jasper. "Wouldn't he have to be a Guild member to do business with an Earth freighter? He must have bought passage for Cassidy."

"You don't have to be a Guild member to buy passage for a person," Jasper said. "But," he turned to Shiraz. "He must have hid her to get her through security, right? They wouldn't let an unconscious or bound woman be shipped out of here. And she wouldn't have gone without a fight, if I know Cassidy."

Shiraz looked up, anguish shimmering in his eyes. "They gagged her, and we rolled her in a tarp and hid her in a wooden crate."

Torr's hands curled into fists, and his seething glare sent Shiraz back a pace.

Jasper sighed. "Sometimes they take bribes to skip security inspection."

"Who takes bribes?" Torr demanded.

"Rodney's men."

Torr stormed across the hangar floor to Rodney, and the big man turned to face him.

"What now?" Rodney asked, not unkindly.

"One of your men took a bribe to ship my sister out. She was in a wooden crate."

Rodney's mouth dropped open, and Jasper rushed to his side. "I didn't say for sure that's what happened," Jasper said. "The guy could have been a Guild trader, I don't know. Rodney, can we figure out who loaded the ship?"

"Human smuggling is strictly prohibited," Rodney said stiffly. "Any box that could hold a human is always inspected. Unless ..."

"... Somebody took a bribe," Torr said, glaring at Rodney.

"For Algol's hell," the big man muttered. Rodney waved his hand at them and said, "I'll find out what happened. But give me a few hours. This could be delicate." Rodney's eyes were bloodshot, and he fixed them on Torr.

Torr huffed out an agitated breath. "Okay," he said. "In the meantime, how did the guy get a transport?" Torr turned to Shiraz.

Shiraz shuffled over. "I don't know."

"Does it matter?" Jasper asked.

Torr glowered at him, and Jasper glared back. "Listen, Torr, I'm as upset as you are. But she's gone."

"Shiraz said they found the scumbag trader at Schlitzer's," Torr said. "I knew that dirty pimp was trouble." He turned on his heel and left the spaceport, his companions scurrying after him.

Outside, Torr cast unfriendly gazes at his waiting forces. He needed some space. Some time alone.

He headed south along the perimeter road and stopped beyond the far corner of the traders pen in the vacant stretch of land that formed a wide arc between the spaceport and the sundial, affording an unobstructed view of the lunar landscape. Earth floated in the star-speckled sky like a ship lost at sea.

Torr searched the stars. The planet Delos with its Nommos sea-cities was near the Orion constellation in Canis Major. The warrior's belt glinted at him from above the horizon to his left and pointed to a brighter star. Cassidy was headed there.

He felt for her, closing his eyes. A vague hint of torpor overcame him, his muscles relaxing and weakening and his mind growing muzzy. He opened his eyes and blinked hard. She felt asleep. Or drugged. They must have sedated her for the passage to Delos. He swallowed, remembering their passage to the moon, floating in the darkness in the cargo hold of the *Calico Jack*. He had been annoyed with her then. Or, rather, he had been grieving over their parents and the friends he had abandoned, and the men he had killed. The familiar stab of guilt pierced the fogginess he sensed from his sister. At least she was still alive. A hollow loneliness settled into his bones as she drew farther and farther away.

Torr cupped her crystal ball in his pocket. It was cold and felt heavier than normal. He pulled it out and gazed into it. Webs of rainbows shimmered within. He imagined he saw his sister's eyes, drowsy and vacant. "Cassidy! Cassidy!" he hissed, squeezing the sphere. Her eyes stared listlessly, and the image slowly faded. "Cassidy ...," he pleaded, wiping dust and tears from his eyes. He gazed into the crystal ball, but it was foggy now, and he saw only his own desperate eyes reflected back at him.

He raised his eyes to Earth. "Mom. Dad," he said, and stumbled towards the moat tanks lining the edge of the dome.

Torr found a gap between tanks and pressed his palms against the dome glass. He gazed helplessly out at Orion the Hunter and picked out the two hunting dogs and their quarry, Moon Rabbit.

5

THE TRAP

"I hate him," Anna said softly.

The three women were lying on the closet floor—no one wanted to sleep in the bed anymore. The closet was dark except for a bit of light cast from a nightlight in the adjacent bathroom. Anna was staring up at the ceiling, and Maria was in a drug-induced sleep, breathing slowly and evenly. Anna and Maria had both been abused three times, and the next morning it would be Cassidy's turn again.

Cassidy did not respond to Anna. She was too busy being petrified to think about hating Balthazar. Anna was the shortest in stature but the strongest among them. The small blond elf-like woman said she fought back sometimes, but he liked it, and so she was the most bruised and bloody of them all.

Cassidy had not fought him, but he beat her anyway. The second time, everything she had or had not done was wrong, and the only thing that excited him was seeing the fear in her eyes when he strangled her. She had passed out and woken up with him huffing and grunting over her. Afterwards, he had grabbed her by the hair and shoved the dropper into her mouth, the green liquid burning and tingling down her throat as she swallowed. Later, she had stared down into the bathwater, but only her bruised and swollen face gazed dully back at her. She had thrown up, barely making it to the toilet, and then slid into a groggy haze on the bathroom floor.

After the drug wore off, she had obsessively stared into a sink full of water, trying desperately to scry, but nothing worked. Her prior glimpses must have been temporary cracks in her shield, but it had repaired itself, leaving her stranded here in this madman's lair.

Morning came, and she heard him open the bedroom door. She stood on unsteady legs and entered the rape room. He glanced up as he folded his pants and set them on the chair, and then twisted a length of rope around his hand and smiled at her.

———————)———————

Cassidy soaked in the tub, her wrists and ankles chafed and bruised where he had tied her to the corners of the bed. He had left her there, and it had taken Anna and Maria half an hour to free her from her bonds. By that time, she had vomited onto the bed sheets. She was gaining some sort of tolerance for whatever the drug was and fended off the encroaching oblivion, taking advantage of the sensation of total surrender that muted her fears and allowed her to think rationally, if only for a few minutes, before the drug pulled her under completely.

Her lip was split and she spat a mouthful of blood into the bathwater. The blood unfurled in a stringy web, forming shifting patterns that slowly dissolved.

She could see her red swollen face in the reflection. She could barely open her jaws. She wondered if the man intended to beat her to death, or more likely strangle her. Her mind was already growing hazy from the drug, the familiar sense of well-being taking over, as though her ordeal were a bad dream disconnected from the reality of the blood flowing through her veins. She grasped at the fleeting moments of lucidity and considered his motivation for force-feeding them the drug. It was possible it was a contraceptive, but if so, it seemed like overkill. More likely it was a narcotic that he was using to control them. If so, it was working.

She stared down at the water. Her face glowed with a brassy sheen. Her hair was a river of gold, and her eyes were red rubies lit from within.

"Cassandra." Her name was whispered from coppery lips.

Cassidy gazed into the scarlet eyes. "I am here," she whispered back.

"You can hear me?" the golden voice asked, surprised. "Can you see me?"

"Yes," Cassidy replied softly. "You are me."

"No. I am Avala. You are Cassandra. I have been trying to communicate with you for such a long time."

Cassidy stared into the eyes in the reflection. They were not her own eyes. They were larger and more beautiful and contained a thousand shining suns.

"Who are you?" Cassidy asked, transfixed by the angelic vision before her.

The voice flowed like sweet nectar. "I am a priestess of Turya, and you are the Golden Star Child. Blessed Water Carrier. *Jalavahini.* Are you in the blessed water now? I can feel it."

Cassidy shook her head, drowsiness pulling at her eyelids. "No. What blessed water?" Cassidy asked, hoping the dream would carry her off to another world for all of eternity.

"Stay with me," the melodic voice begged, the words merging together like a violin string vibrating on one long note, yet still clear in their meaning.

"I am in a bath," Cassidy said. "I am trapped by an evil man."

Avala's eyes narrowed. "Yes, you are trapped. But you are trapped by fear."

"No, I am trapped by a man," Cassidy said.

"But I sense that you are more trapped by fear. Fear has saved you so far, but soon it will kill you. It is time to let it go."

"I can't," Cassidy said, closing her eyes and sliding further into the warm bathwater.

"You must," Avala said.

"Cassidy, did you say something?" Anna was at her side and held a cool towel to her bruised face.

"I can't be afraid anymore," Cassidy mumbled.

"Me neither," Anna said. "No more fear. I'd rather die than be afraid."

"Me too," Cassidy whispered.

6

MİRRORS

If he hadn't needed to go to the bathroom, Torr wouldn't have gotten out of bed at all. As it was, his body forced him from his fitful slumber long after morning gong had struck. Cassidy's sleeping bag lay where she had left it, still rumpled as though she just slept in it that night. Her cast-off clothing sat next to her pack in a tangled clump. Torr did not have the fortitude to roll up the sleeping bag and arrange her things.

He shuffled out of the Fen. The Boyer brothers and Sky and Thunder saw him leaving the camp by himself and hurried to follow him. He nodded at them wordlessly, proceeded to Center Ring, and found an empty porta-potty. When he came out, he eyed the long line at the ration trailer.

"Let's come back later," Torr said. "I'm not hungry, anyway."

Back at the Fen, Torr headed straight towards his tent but was intercepted by Tatsuya. The small Japanese man stood in front of him with a set of quick little bows and motioned towards the picnic tables. "I made you breakfast, Torr-san," Tatsuya said.

"I'm not hungry," Torr mumbled.

"Of course you're not hungry," Tatsuya said, grabbing his wrist with a clawlike grip and leading him to the table. Torr sat down, and Tatsuya scurried to the kitchen countertop and removed a frying pan from the hot plate. He returned to the table with a plate of eggs and rice.

"Jaz bought eggs, special deal," Tatsuya said. "And hot sauce." He handed Torr a small red bottle.

"Hmm," Torr grunted, and unscrewed the cap. He dribbled some hot sauce on the fried eggs and rice, sprinkled on some salt and pepper, and ate silently.

Tatsuya set a mug of steaming green tea in front of him, and Torr sipped at it.

When he was done eating, Torr thanked Tatsuya and retreated to his tent. He burrowed into his bedding, turned away from Cassidy's side of the tent, and closed his eyes.

———————————)———————————

Torr was lost in random dreams of desert scrubland and hot red-rock terrain, searching for his sister. The sudden specter of a woman with glowing snakes for hair, calling his name, jerked him awake.

Peary Dome was humming with midday activity. Torr got out of bed and stretched. Cassidy's belongings still lay untouched across the tent. His heart sank, and he averted his eyes. He had to go on, no matter how much it hurt.

He pulled on his vest and boots. Berkeley had returned his rune belt to him, and he secured it around his waist, with his moon deed and gold hidden safely within it. He removed Cassidy's crystal ball from his pocket and forced himself to gaze into its glassy surface and look for her. The crystal ball was dark, and he felt nauseous. He was almost glad it revealed nothing, and dropped it into a vest pouch.

Outside his tent, he gazed at Earth and numbly reviewed what he had learned over the past few days. Rodney had found the Ranger who had taken the bribe to let the wooden crate pass through cargo security without inspection. He was now in jail with the shoemaker clan leader, Shiraz.

They traced the truck she had been transported in to Schlitzer, but he claimed no knowledge of the abduction. He said he had rented out the vehicle, as he often did, with no questions asked. Another trader had sold the far side mining lord the wooden crate but didn't know anything else. They had determined that the mining lord was not in the Guild, and no one knew where his claim was in the lawless expanse of the far side, which was riddled with thousands of craters to hide in.

There was nothing else to do. No one else to blame. Cassidy was on her way to the Nommos islands on Delos, and Torr was stuck here, pathetic and impotent. He took in a breath and gathered his remaining shreds of courage. He would go to Delos and make his way to the Nommos floating cities and rescue her. Rodney had promised to alert him the moment a Delosian ship landed at Peary. In the meantime, he would hone his fighting skills. And he would learn magic.

He turned to Faisal, who was sitting in his lawn chair in front of his tent.

"Faisal," Torr said.

"Torr," Faisal replied.

"Let's throw some knives," Torr said sullenly, unsheathing his combat knife.

Faisal rose from his chair and went into his tent, reappearing with a collection of small throwing knives nested in black sheaths.

They went into the back area and leaned the top of the Delosian crate up against the metal container wall. Torr went into the workshop tent for something to mark it with, and greeted Tatsuya, who was at the work table bent over Torr's new wolf knife handle, with Hiroshi looking on.

"How's it coming along?" Torr said, leaning over and admiring the polished olivewood handle Hiroshi had made, newly attached to the hilt. The amber eyes of the wolf gazed dully up at him from the pommel, which was sitting to the side, detached from the knife.

Torr's heart leapt into his throat. "What did you do? You took the pommel off?" Torr grabbed the pommel and shook it, then stared down at the wolf who was seated on his haunches facing forward, his golden eyes dull and lifeless. "You killed him?"

Hiroshi glanced up. "I had to remove the pommel to attach the handle. That's how it is done. The wolf will be fine."

Torr turned the pommel over, and the pattern of petals on the back was motionless as ever. He turned it over again, and the wolf was showing Torr his profile and howling at the moon.

A rush of air left his lungs. "Oh, thank the stars," Torr said. "He's alive."

Hiroshi smiled and said, "I told you so."

"What are you doing now?" Torr asked Tatsuya.

The elderly man held something like a soldering gun, which Torr determined by the faint scent of fire to be a wood-burning pen. He was etching a pattern into the wood and did not look up.

"He's putting snakes on it," Hiroshi said.

"Ah," Torr said, and grabbed a red crayon from a shelf.

He went outside and marked the wooden target with the outline of a life-sized man, adding eyes, nose, mouth, an X for the heart, and a V for his groin.

Torr and Faisal took turns throwing, and Hiroshi came out to join them. After an hour, Torr went back into the workshop tent. "Are you done yet? I want to try throwing it."

"No," Tatsuya murmured, still concentrating on the snakes. "I am coloring it in, and then it needs to dry. And then Hiroshi will wrap it with shagreen."

"You're going to cover that up?" Torr asked. "It's too pretty." The snake was a detailed copy of the carving on the metal tang, now hidden beneath the wood. Tatsuya was laying down green ink in the snakeskin's scales.

Tatsuya glanced up at him with his black bird's eyes. "I will make you a snake tattoo, so that you will not forget," he said, smiling.

Torr returned the smile and rolled his right shoulder, sore from knife throwing.

"Practice throwing with your weak arm," Tatsuya suggested, then turned back to his artwork.

Torr practiced throwing lefty, missing wildly, but improved after several tries. Faisal appeared to be ambidextrous and could hit his mark with either hand. Raleigh, Roanoke, and Hawk joined them with their slingshots. Roanoke was a dead aim. When they grew tired of target practice, they found some plastic tent stakes in the container to use as training knives. Faisal showed them techniques for slashes and thrusts, and Hiroshi demonstrated footwork. Berkeley joined them, followed by Fritz and Frank, and soon they were embroiled in a melee. One by one, they feigned dying, until they were groaning melodramatically, writhing on the ground and clutching imaginary knife wounds.

Berkeley stood victorious, broken fingers and all, and the dying moans dissolved into laughter.

———————)———————

Two days later, the wolf knife was done and Torr wrapped his fingers around the new handle. The pebbly sharkskin grip was the perfect texture—like coarse sandpaper, but not scratchy. The pommel was firmly attached and provided a counterweight to the substantial blade. Torr stared at the wolf, and the wolf stared back.

"You okay in there?" Torr asked. He thought the wolf blinked but could not be sure. He assumed everything was fine and threw the knife at the target.

"Oh, man," Berkeley said, approaching the board. The blade had hit the target's eye, piercing the board and sinking in all the way up to the winged crossguard.

"Not bad," Faisal said, pulling the knife free and handing it back to Torr.

"Your spirit wolf is eyeing the target. Try it again," Tatsuya said, walking over and pointing to the ground at Torr's side.

"Don't tease me," Torr said, his spine tingling at the memory of the Scrids' talk of a wolf shadow.

"I am not teasing. You don't see him? He's right here, looking up at you."

Torr looked down at the dusty ground at his feet, and then at the knife. The metal-inlay wolf sat on its haunches, staring up at him from the pommel.

"Is he sitting down?" Torr asked.

"Yes, he is," Tatsuya said.

"How come I can't see him?" Torr asked.

"Your mind is not calm enough," Tatsuya said, his eyes sparkling. "Can you see it, Berkeley?" Tatsuya asked.

"Yes," Berkeley said, squinting. "I think so. I see a gray outline. Like a ghost."

"Stop making things up," Torr said, throwing the blade again.

Later, in his tent, Torr sat on his bedding and stared at Cassidy's sleeping bag and scattered clothing. Warm tears trickled down his face. He was able to keep up a strong front when he was with the others, but alone inside their tent he shook with silent sobs.

The wolf knife was poking his side. He removed the sheathed knife from his belt and set it beside him on the blanket. The metal wolf figure stared up at him from the pommel.

"Brother Wolf," Torr said to the creature, wiping away his tears. "I am Moon Wolf, and you are my brother."

The wolf stared back at him. Torr let his gaze stray across the tent, peering into the shadows for a hint of a canine form. He saw nothing, and clutched the knife's new handle, the wire-wrapped shagreen rough beneath his hand. He felt power at his fingertips, hovering just beyond his grasp.

A mirror. He needed a mirror. His mother and grandmother had always said mirrors were useful for many things, one of which was to see that which hid in the shadows. Two mirrors were better, looking one into the other. The last time he had tried it was several years ago, sitting between two facing mirrors with a candle flame behind his head. His own face had turned into another's—that of a young dark-skinned man with bright black eyes heavy with responsibility. It had scared him so much he'd not tried it since.

His fear now seemed childish, and he went outside. He slipped into Jasper's tent and grabbed his friend's square shaving mirror, tucking it under his arm. Back in his own tent, he fished inside Cassidy's backpack until he felt Grandma Leann's hand mirror. He pulled it out by the handle, and a pink t-shirt fell out of the pack. It was Cassidy's favorite shirt—studded with multi-colored gems arranged in the form of a butterfly. A fresh onslaught of sobbing shook him.

When he recovered, he carefully folded the pink t-shirt and tucked it into the pack, and then quickly folded and stuffed her other clothing in with it. He rolled up her sleeping bag and set it against the tent wall. He exhaled and sat back on his heels and pulled out Cassidy's crystal ball, wondering if he could summon a vision of her again. The rainbows cleared, and he saw ripples of water. He furrowed his brow, trying to understand what he was seeing. He was about to discount it, when he recalled that Cassidy had seen water while Torr and Bobby were escaping up the coast with *Moon Star,* and she had dismissed that because it did not make any sense to her at the time. Perhaps she had reached the Nommos floating city already. He had thought the trip to Delos took longer than a few days, but he didn't know for sure. He froze as threads of blood extended through the water. His mother had said visions were sometimes symbolic and the viewer needed to inter- pret them. There was no interpreting blood as anything other than bad, so he stuffed the crystal ball back into his pouch.

Shaken, he tried to distract himself with the wolf mystery again, and gazed into Grandma Leann's mirror, wiping dusty tear tracks from his cheeks. He regarded his face from different angles. He looked older than he thought himself to be. His gray eyes were deep and serious, and his jaws were strong and defined, showing the scruffy start of a beard. He was tempted to abandon his weekly shaving ritual and let his beard grow out like most everyone else did in Peary Dome. He took Jasper's mirror and propped it up on top of a plastic storage crate he'd bought from Berkeley, resting the mirror against the tent's back wall. He grabbed the wolf knife and sat with his back to the square mirror, then angled the hand mirror until he could see the square mirror in its reflection over his shoulder. The second mirror was what he focused on, scanning the dim interior of the tent through the double reflection.

He breathed deeply and curled his fingers around the pommel of the wolf knife, studying the reflection of the interior of the tent and looking into the shadowed corners. He flinched, nearly dropping the mirror. In the far corner, from the deepest shadow, two golden eyes stared at him. Torr's hands shook, but he held the mirror up with one fist, clutched the knife pommel with the other, and met the glowing eyes.

Slowly, the form of a wolf came into focus. It was a large animal, its jowls and neck bushy with thick silver fur. It had a black nose and white muzzle, and its ears stood tall and alert. The eyes were intense and intelligent. Torr slowly shifted his gaze from the mirrors to look directly at the shadow, goosebumps rising over his whole body. The corner was dark and empty.

He sucked in his breath, scared that he had lost the vision, and gazed into the mirrors again. The wolf was still there.

"Brother Wolf," he said softly. The wolf pricked up his ears. Torr made clicking sounds with his tongue. The wolf's ears twitched, and the proud animal cocked his head to one side. Torr whistled softly. The wolf stared at him, its golden eyes boring into him. Torr hummed the funny little tune his father used to hum to their German shepherd, Silver.

Brother Wolf's ears stood up tall, and then he slowly lowered himself onto his haunches and placed his nose between his front paws. Torr found himself laughing—a deep laugh that started down in his belly and shook his chest. The wolf's eyes rolled up to look up at him questioningly, and then he slowly wagged his tail.

"You are a good wolf," Torr said, catching his breath. "Good wolf." He breathed slowly, and his heart raced with excitement. "Will you stay by my side?" The wolf wagged his tail again. Torr blinked, and the wolf was gone. He realized he'd let his hand leave the knife and cursed himself. He placed his hand back on the pommel and peered hopefully into the mirrors. The tent held nothing but a dim shadow. Angry with himself, he moved his hand to the shagreen handle, but still nothing. He tried again and again to summon the wolf spirit, but the shadows revealed nothing but canvas and moon dust. He was trying too hard. He had lost his calm, open mind.

Torr exhaled with disappointment and crept slowly into the corner, sniffing and peering around the dusty canvas for any sign of the wolf. Paw prints, tufts of fur, anything. But there was nothing. Even so, he was convinced that he had seen the wolf. It was real. Well, as real as a spirit animal could be. He took the knife from its sheath and looked at the wolf on the pommel. It was down on its haunches, looking up at him curiously. A shiver ran up Torr's back. He clicked his tongue at it, and suddenly it was in its frozen, seated pose. Torr swallowed and slipped the blade slowly back into its sheath.

Torr was determined to learn more. His adrenaline was flowing, and he began exploring his crystals. He had only three now, after trading the garnet to Jasper. He took turns examining the long dagger-like shaft, the heavy Bear crystal, and the green fluorite octahedron. He had some notion of the Bear crystal—not of what it did, but at least it had a name. The other two he had no clue about. He sat on the ground with his back to the square mirror and his legs straight out in front of him. He set Grandma Leann's mirror on his front ankles, propped up against his toes so that he could see his head and shoulders while leaving his hands free. In his left hand he held the fluorite, in his right the long shaft, and lifted them to either side of his face so that he might see them both in the reflections of the mirrors. Narrowing his eyes in the dimness, he gazed at himself holding up the two crystals. Their facets caught the light from the small tent windows and glinted at him. He let his vision soften and blur, fixed on his silhouette. Little tongues of purple light flickered around his head, like a fire dancing across embers. He widened his eyes in astonishment, and the flames disappeared.

Torr relaxed and softened his gaze again, and shortly the purple halo became visible. He held still this time, not daring to breathe. He softened his gaze further, and the violet flames expanded outward. A thin sheath of green shrouded his body, feeding fuel into the flickering violet aura. The light extended across his shoulders and down his arms, then engulfed the crystals, casting up taller purple flames as though from two torches. Torr held his breath, and his hands tingled sharply.

He stared at himself in the mirror. He was himself, but not himself. He blinked his eyes and moved his mouth, and his reflection did the same. But his skin was a dark velvety brown. His eyes were large and black, staring back at him in wide-eyed shock. The hands clutching the crystals were large, with long strong fingers and pink nail beds.

"What in Algol's hell," Torr said. His voice was deep and resonated with a strange accent. Torr dropped the crystals and jumped to his feet, the hand mirror tumbling onto the canvas floor. He fled the tent, running headlong into Jasper.

"Whoa," Jasper said, grabbing Torr's shoulders and laughing. "What's up? Did you find your wolf? Is he that scary?"

Torr stared at Jasper, his mouth working silently. He processed the question, then croaked, "Yes. No. He's good. I mean, he's nice. I just scared the shit out of myself."

"You are scary, I agree," Jasper said, chuckling. "You serious about the wolf?"

Torr patted at his own arms, checking to make sure he was himself again. His skin was white. His hands were the proper size. He lifted his gaze to meet Jasper's. "Do I look normal?" he asked Jasper hesitantly. "Am I myself?"

Jasper gave him a lopsided grin. "Uh, normal? I don't know about that. Yourself?" Jasper patted Torr's cheek, teasing. "I think so. Who else would you be?"

"I don't know," Torr said, and Jasper's smile faded.

"Come on, Sundance. Let me get you some tea." Jasper put his arm around Torr's shoulders and led him to the kitchen area.

7

THE DRUG

The next time, Cassidy didn't even care what he did to her. She just wanted more of the drug, and he laughed when she turned her mouth to the dropper and sucked on it, trying to get every last drop.

The next day when she awoke from her stupor she obsessed about the drug, picking at her skin and pulling at her hair, and counted the days until she would see the sadistic creep again and get some more of the green elixir. It made everything okay. At least for a little while.

She shuffled stiffly into the bathroom. Everything hurt. She glanced at the mirror above the double sinks. She did not recognize herself. Her face was swollen and discolored, and her lip was puffed up on one side. She opened her mouth. Her teeth were all still there, although they were stained green. She found a new toothbrush in a drawer and real toothpaste, and brushed her teeth, trying to avoid the cuts on her lip and inside her cheek. She rinsed out her mouth and drank water straight from the faucet, then splashed cold water on her face, trying to get rid of a splitting headache and trying to remember how her mother had cured addictions. Usually she treated addiction with herbs. But sometimes she taught people mind tricks, such as telling yourself you can have the drug whenever you want, just not right this second, but later ... always just a little bit later. It sounded too easy. Besides, Cassidy didn't have any of the drug to save for later. She just wanted more of it and knew she would do anything to get it.

She went into the bedroom and rattled the door handle. The knob turned, but the door was locked from the outside with a bolt. She pounded on the door with her fists and yelled, but no one came. She finally gave up and paced back and forth across the carpeted floor. Finally, she sat cross-legged in a dark corner of the closet, facing the walls and staring down at her wrists, and picked at her scabs until they bled.

8

SİGNS

"Let's go see the Murians," Torr said to Jasper over breakfast the next day. "Maybe they can teach me some magic."

Jasper chewed on a piece of bread and nodded.

Torr, Jasper, and Berkeley made their way to Auxiliary Spaceport B. Jasper's new band of protectors trailed them and waited outside the container—seven friends Jasper called the Alphabet Boys—Arden, Buck, Copper, Dang, Elvis, Febo, and Guy.

Jericho let them in and followed them down the ladder and into the stone hangar.

"I heard about your sister," Jericho said. "I'm sorry. Nommos are bad news."

"Yeah," Torr said, meeting the man's sympathetic eyes. "I don't want to talk about it."

"I understand," Jericho said. They embraced and Jericho patted his back. Jericho's body was warm and solid, and his steady presence comforted Torr.

They parted, and Torr thanked him.

Berkeley led Torr and Jasper to a shadowy cleft in the back wall. They headed down a dark tunnel towards a hint of purple light up ahead. Soon they emerged into a large cave. The air was still and silent. The rock wall to their left was studded with crystal points, which glowed purple and cast a diffused violet light throughout the chamber. On one side of the large space, several bedrolls were pushed against the wall alongside small stacks of clothing and other supplies. On the other side of the chamber a green blanket was spread out on the ground next to an assortment of baskets, jugs, and stacks of plates and cups.

Torr admired the glowing walls.

"Veins of pure crystal," Berkeley explained. "They extend through the rock to the exterior of the cliff, tunneling in sunlight. That's why the Murians chose this cave—the crystal walls remind them of home."

"They must be in the back," Jasper said, and led them down another dim tunnel.

They entered a smaller chamber. This one was lit, not with veins of crystal embedded in the rock, but with crystal shafts mounted onto the walls in metal brackets and glowing a soft white. On a large green blanket in the center of the floor, four hooded men were seated around a game of some sort—polished black stones and white stones arranged in a pattern—and two other hooded men watched. The men rose and turned to them. They were all Murians, their eyes and hair glowing a fluorescent green. They lowered their heads in respectful bows, and two of them approached. The others bowed again, clicking and hissing softly, and then sat down to resume their game.

Torr returned the bows and greeted the two men he had met before—Guruhan and Murugan. Their hoods were pushed back to reveal wide foreheads, and Torr examined their facial features. Flattish noses with round nostrils. Wide reptilian eye sockets with the horizontal pupils of goats cutting across green, glowing irises. Their jaws and chins were strong and square. Stray strands of luminescent hair fell from their bell sleeves and reached nearly to the ground from their forearms. Torr swallowed and tried not to stare. He lifted his gaze to their faces. Their skin was pale white and slick, reminding Torr of the underbelly of a snake. He did not want to touch the men and was glad they did not extend their hands for a handshake.

"Come, come," Guruhan said, in his strange, breathy accent.

Guruhan and Murugan led them back to the first chamber, invited them to sit on the blanket, and set a round copper tray in the center. Torr, Jasper, and Berkeley sat on the ground around the tray. Guruhan opened one of the jugs and brought them small cups filled with a dark purple liquid.

"Whafkan juice," Berkeley said, gesturing for Torr to drink.

Torr sipped at it. It tasted like strong, sweet wine, and he took another sip.

"Torr wants to learn magic," Jasper said to Murugan and Guruhan, who sat down with them, tucking their arm fringes inside their sleeves.

Torr was mesmerized by their glowing filaments, and swished the whafkan juice around in his mouth, savoring the tart, fruity taste.

"Magic ...," Murugan repeated slowly, as though liking the sound of the word. He then broke into his clicking, hissing language. Jasper translated for the rest of them. "What do you mean?" he asked.

Torr replied, "I don't know. I want to be able to see, like my sister can. I thought I saw her eyes in the crystal ball, and then I saw water. Does that mean she's on the Delosian ocean already?" He held Murugan's gaze, afraid of the answer.

Jasper attempted to translate Torr's question for the Murians.

"She is the blessed water carrier," Murugan said through Jasper. "She knows water."

Torr turned up one side of his mouth and exchanged glances with Berkeley and Jasper.

Jasper shrugged. "I'm translating the best I can."

Guruhan started speaking again. Jasper listened intently, then turned to them.

"He says that by modern ship it takes two weeks to get to Delos from here, but there are other ways to get there, the way the priests and priestesses used to travel, back in the olden days when they were still powerful."

Guruhan gazed at Torr ruefully, as though mourning days gone by.

"Does he mean through the Star Globes?" Berkeley asked, tracing a big circle in the air with his hands.

Guruhan replied through Jasper. "No. There are other ways. Golden Star and Flying Star will learn." He smiled at Torr, showing small stained teeth, and Torr felt slightly ill. "But it is not likely your sister's thieves are skilled enough to travel as the ancients did," Guruhan said.

Murugan nodded in agreement and spoke with Jasper.

"They want to see your crystal ball," Jasper said.

Torr reached into his vest pouch and passed it to Murugan.

The Murian examined the small shining globe. "Aaaahhhh," he hissed. "This is from Muria," he said in Globalish, then continued in his own language.

Jasper said, "He wants to know where you got it."

"My aunt got it on Delos, I think," Torr said.

Murugan hissed and clicked, and Jasper said, "Those thieves."

"Since when do you know how to speak Murian so well?" Berkeley asked.

"I can't speak it well," Jasper said. "I can only understand it. Same as you."

"Let me see that," Berkeley said, holding out his hand.

"What? This?" Jasper asked, handing the garnet crystal to Berkeley.

"Why were you holding it?" Berkeley asked.

"I like to hold it," Jasper said.

Berkeley turned to the Murians. "Say something," he said.

They gazed at him, perplexed.

"Tell me ... do you think he is the male Star Child?" Berkeley asked, pointing his chin towards Torr.

They replied in their language. Berkeley's eyes grew wide, and he translated, "We think he could be. He glows like the old priests." Berkeley held up the dark-red garnet, inspecting it closely. "Well, Hermes' wings," Berkeley said. "This must be an interpreter's stone."

"Let me see that," Torr said, taking the garnet from Berkeley.

"What is that?" Guruhan asked, and Torr stared at him, understanding the Murian's breathy hisses as though he had spoken in Globalish.

"I can understand him," Torr said, gaping with wonder and turning to Jasper. "This stone is magic. You ripped me off, you shyster. You knew what it did."

"I did not," Jasper said, spreading his arms innocently. "I swear."

Torr glared at his old friend. "I should have known not to trust you. You always tried to rip me off, like that cracked surfboard you convinced me take for my bow and arrows. You are such a snake."

Jasper laughed. "We were kids, Torr. Geez. Your parents made me give you that bow back, anyway."

"I should have known not to trade away anything from Great-Aunt Sophie," Torr grumbled.

"It was a fair trade," Jasper said. "You got a spirit wolf in exchange."

"I suppose." Torr rested his free hand on the knife pommel, gazing into the shadows for Brother Wolf, but saw nothing. "Do you see a wolf?" he asked, directing his question to the Murians. "My spirit guide."

They looked confused, and Guruhan asked in Globalish, "What is 'wolf'? What is 'spirit guide'?"

Torr pursed his lips and with a shiver of apprehension held out his hand to Guruhan. Guruhan stretched out his hand, with its waxy white skin and the glowing arm tendrils falling from his sleeve. Torr clasped the man's hand with his own. Torr had expected it to be cold and fish-like, but it was warm, and the Murian's grip was strong. The garnet was pressed between their palms, and Torr repeated his question.

Guruhan's fluorescent eyes widened in surprise. "Ah. You have a whisperer's stone. How extraordinarily useful." Murugan clicked in agreement. Torr smiled and nodded. He described the wolf and how he sometimes appeared at Torr's side, but that most people could not see him.

"Ah," Guruhan said. "No, I do not see any spirit drifters. But I am not a priest."

"Spirit drifter?" Torr asked.

"Yes. You call it wolf?"

Torr described the animal, and Guruhan nodded with comprehension. "Ah, yes. Wolf is one of certain magical beings who can travel across time and space. Dimensions you could say. This particular being with the sharp fangs and bodies thick with filaments, we call Verkah. They come from a wild place, Verkah-Shetram, a planet of tangled forests where men go to die."

Torr tried to understand his meaning, and the Murian continued speaking.

"It is said that the male Star Child often has a Verkah companion." His eyes glowed more brightly. "But we are concerned about your sister, Golden Star. You must get her back."

"I know," Torr said. "I plan to go to Delos and look for her."

"You must be cautious," Guruhan said. "The Nommos are very jealous of men who retain their virility. They do not allow males of other races on their floating land. If you go there they will try to kill you. But if you are indeed Flying Star, you will be successful—most likely." Guruhan's horizontal pupils narrowed to a thin slit for a moment, then widened again. "You must bring your sister back here," the Murian said urgently. "You cannot abandon the moon at this time."

"Why not?" Torr asked.

"And then she needs to go to Muria and awaken the Star Globe," Murugan added.

"Yes, yes," Guruhan agreed. "After you bring her back to the moon, she must go to Muria and awaken the Star Globe there, and then she must go and awaken the Star Globe on Delos."

Torr felt overwhelmed suddenly. "But why must we return to the moon?" he asked.

The Murians looked relieved, as though that were the easier question.

"You cannot allow those poisonous snake Cephs to gain control of it," Guruhan said, patting the ground at his side. "You must defeat them. And then you both can go to Muria."

"Me? Us?" Torr asked, shifting uncomfortably. "Defeat the Cephs? Why us?"

Murugan answered, having understood his simple questions. "Assuming you are the Star Children—as it appears that you are— then it is your job to remove all obstacles to the Joining with the Star People. The Cephs are here on the moon. I can feel them. Or at least their half-kin—those unholy mongrels."

Torr grimaced and glanced at Jasper and Berkeley, who were frowning at them. Torr translated the conversation. Berkeley looked thoughtful, and Jasper grew more grim.

Guruhan released Torr's hand, and Torr clutched the garnet, hiding it from Jasper's glare. Guruhan moved to the edge of the blanket, smoothed a thin layer of dust on the stone floor, and then traced shapes in it with his finger. He drew a square with a small circle at each of its four corners, a fifth circle an arm's length away, and a pair of small circles beyond the opposite side of the square.

"This is planet Turya," Guruhan said, pointing at the lone, distant circle. "Home of our ancestors, the Star People. No maps reveal its precise location. But it is somewhere beyond the hungry black star," he said, drawing a spiral between the square and Turya.

He then pointed in turn to each of the circles at the corners of the square and named them, "Muria, Iliad, Delos, and Earth." He drew a line connecting Muria and Delos, bisecting the square and creating two triangles, and then drew a small circle next to Earth. "Earth's moon," he said.

Guruhan then pointed at the pair of circles outside the square. "These are the ruling planets of the Cephean Federation: Thunder Walker and Tree Nut. And here's Scridland," he said, drawing another circle next to the square, and then drew more circles around the square. "This is Lingri-La. Verkah-Shetram. Nommos, the abandoned water planet. And a few other minor planets that are not very hospitable to life."

Guruhan looked up to make sure Torr understood. Torr nodded and translated for Jasper and Berkeley.

Guruhan continued, "Back before the Cephs destroyed the Star Globe on Iliad, every Kalpa, or great age, a trine was formed by Iliad, Muria, and Delos." Guruhan traced the triangle connecting the three planets. "When the trine came into the proper configuration, the twin Star Children ignited a pathway of light between the three planets, which opened the star bridge between Iliad and Turya for a period of about one Earth year." He drew a long line connecting Iliad and Turya, passing near the spiral. "The Turyans and their descendants who have settled the planets—that's us—traveled the star bridges to visit each other. The Joining commenced, and a new age of enlightenment was born.

"Over the period of the Joining, the light paths branched out, extending from one or another of the primary trined planets to the peripheral planets for shorter durations of time—months or weeks, depending on the planet." Guruhan drew lines connecting the surrounding planets to one of the primary planets. "This enabled travel between all the colonized planets."

Guruhan then pointed to the Earth and moon. "Earth is unusual in many ways. First of all, the planet was always accessed via its moon." Guruhan patted the ground. "Star Travelers had to hop quickly from the moon to Earth—often perishing in the process." Murugan erased the triangle connecting Muria and Delos to Earth and redrew the lines to connect the two planets to Earth's moon. "Supposedly, there are many landing spots on the moon and on Earth," he said, adding several lines between the moon and Earth.

"Also," he continued, "Earth is the connecting pathway to the Cephean Federation. The pathway of light only illuminated for a brief time to Thunder Walker, and a shorter period of time to Tree

Nut—and for an even shorter time they were both illuminated at once. During this small window of time, a path of light ignited between Tree Nut and Thunder Walker, creating a triangle and allowing direct passage between the two Cephean planets. Thunder Walker and Tree Nut could not access the primary planets directly. Therefore, Earth is considered a bridge planet—the only one of its kind. In addition, and most importantly, Earth's moon is the only body that connected to two of the trine planets at the same time." Guruhan pointed to Muria and Delos, his glowing green fingernail tracing the connecting lines of the triangle.

"Therefore, we think the moon might be able to form a new primary trine, replacing Iliad, and ignite the star bridge to Turya." Guruhan met Torr's eyes. "Earth's moon could be the key to establishing a new pathway to the Star People. That is why we are here." Hope flickered in Guruhan's and Murugan's eyes.

Shivers swept across Torr's skin, and he translated for Jasper and Berkeley.

"But it will be up to the Star Children to make that happen," Guruhan said, smiling at Torr with luminescent green lips, and taking Torr's hand again with the garnet pressed between them.

"I don't have any idea how to do that," Torr said.

"You will learn," Guruhan said confidently. "Follow the signs."

"I don't see any signs," Torr said.

"Well," Guruhan said. "You have made it to the moon. That is a good first step. Now you just need to get your sister back, and then move on to the next step."

The mention of his sister set his back bristling. "I need to go," he said, releasing Guruhan's hand. He felt jittery all of a sudden and sitting still was not helping any.

"See if he knows how to work your crystals," Jasper said.

"Oh, yeah," Torr said. He took out the long crystal shaft, the green fluorite octahedron, and the large squarish Bear crystal that the Scrids wanted. He knelt down and set them side by side on the green blanket.

Guruhan and Murugan gathered around and inspected the crystals, and Murugan placed the crystal ball next to the others. "Crystal balls are tools of Seers," Murugan said. "They focus the mind's eye."

Guruhan picked up the long shaft and said, "I think this is a weapon."

"Like a knife?" Torr asked.

"No," the Murian said. "It should emit a stream of light, but it is not responding to me. You need to ask a priest." Guruhan picked up the fluorite. "This one feels very heavy for something so small." He tossed it up and down on his palm. "Intriguing."

"And this one," Murugan said, holding the large chunky crystal. "This looks like an inter-dimensional crystal, but I can't be sure. If so, it is very rare and exceedingly valuable."

"The Scrids called it a Bear crystal," Torr said. The Murians looked blankly at him, and Torr passed the interpreter's stone to Murugan and described a bear.

"Ah, yes," Murugan said, and handed the garnet back to Torr. The Murian examined the Bear crystal with interest and said, "Yes, well, the Scrids are very strange. They worship the furry bear creatures, Ballukah."

Torr interpreted for his friends, then collected his crystals and rose to leave.

Jasper held out his hand for the garnet. Torr hesitated, and Jasper smirked and said, "Give me the garnet or the wolf knife. Your choice."

Torr glanced at Berkeley, who shrugged and said, "Interpreter's stone or spirit animal. Tough choice."

Torr frowned and scanned the empty shadows, resting his hand on the wolf knife's pommel. He sighed and reluctantly returned the garnet to Jasper, and said under his breath, "Looks like you're stuck with me, Brother Wolf."

They thanked the Murians, promised to return soon, and climbed back up to the surface. They bid farewell to Jericho, who clanged the container door shut behind them, then gathered their security detail and left for the Fen.

———————)———————

Torr spent his nights haunted by dreams, and his days battling despair. Tatsuya had given him the dreamcatcher, saying he had found it in Torr's tent on a stack of clothing when he had gone in search of clean clothes for Torr when he was sick. Torr assumed it was Cassidy's but had not recalled seeing it in their tent before. He hung it over his bed. The twirling sinew web was decorated with dangling bones and feathers around an empty center that reminded him of an eye, which seemed to stare at him. Instead of granting him a dreamless sleep, the dreamcatcher seemed to make his dreams more vivid. He left it hanging there because dreamcatchers were supposed to offer some sort of protection.

The only thing that kept him sane was working out. Pushups, situps, running laps around the perimeter ring road. Throwing knives. Grappling with his campmates in the Fen's yard.

Tatsuya and Hiroshi taught them Judo moves: locks and throws. Febo and Elvis taught them kickboxing mixed with regular boxing. Ming-Long, Khaled, and Faisal taught them knife fighting.

The sessions became aggressive and competitive and attracted small crowds of onlookers. The friends-of-friends and Peary Dome citizens who had helped Torr hunt for Cassidy found him in Center Ring over time, and the Fen's courtyard became full to overflowing during the day as people took turns grappling and boxing.

Jasper suggested that they claim a block at the end of Spoke Road 5, which was largely vacant. They convinced, or bribed, the few inhabitants of the remote block to relocate, and then moved their training sessions out there. They started formal classes and invited their new friends to participate. Berkeley added a meditation class, which Tatsuya made a requirement to take his Judo class, which everyone wanted to do.

Jasper took them scavenging in the junkyard behind Air and Water Control, where they found several sets of metal scaffolding and dragged them to the yard. They were useful as monkey bars, for pull-ups, and to hang rolled-up tents for punching bags. Torr purchased two big tractor tires to drag around the yard for strength training, and the junkyard workers offered them torn and patched ground tarps for their classes, and more tarps to provide shade over two beat-up picnic tables. Jasper purchased a wagon, and Torr paid for a five-hundred-gallon tank of water, which they wheeled back and forth to the practice yard every day—and had to replenish after several days, which Torr gave Jasper gold for again. Their numbers had expanded to nearly two hundred.

Jasper sat with Torr at a training yard picnic table late one afternoon when most everyone else had left.

"Do you have an endless supply of gold, or what?" Jasper asked, propping his sunglasses on top of his mop of red hair.

"Not endless," Torr said. "Enough to buy some water for my friends."

"Enough to buy passage to Delos?" Jasper asked, holding his gaze.

"How much does it cost?" Torr asked.

"I can maybe negotiate your passage for two Solidi. One way only." Torr swallowed and nodded, and Jasper raised one eyebrow.

"Why, is a ship expected soon?" Torr asked.

"I don't know. One will come eventually," Jasper said. "Are you serious about going after Cassidy?"

"Yeah," Torr said, screwing and unscrewing the cap of his ration jug. "What am I gonna do, abandon her?"

"You could die at the hands of the Nommos," Jasper said.

"Without Cassidy I'm half-dead anyway," Torr said. "Are you coming with me?"

Jasper's jaws tightened and his normally mischievous eyes were grave. "Yes."

9

THE VİGİL

That morning Cassidy and Anna had found Maria sprawled across the bed, vomit and blood dribbling from her lips, and rainbows of light shining down on her naked body from the skylight. The brute Balthazar had knocked a tooth out, and an hour later Maria's gum was still bleeding.

The tall, leggy woman was passed out on the closet floor, dosed up on the green drug and lying on her side with her head resting on a rolled towel. Purple and yellowish-green bruises, and some fresh red ones, covered her face, neck, and arms. Cassidy knelt at her side and wedged a rolled strip of silk into the gap where her tooth had been, and wiped drool and blood from her swollen lips with a damp washcloth.

Cassidy went into the bathroom and submerged the washcloth in a sink basin filled with cold water, scrubbing it to get the blood out. She froze. On the surface of the water she saw the image of the raping bastard. He was entering the room outside their bedroom. He opened their bedroom door and deposited plates of food on the floor. He left again, locked the door with a sliding bolt, and then grabbed a sensor from the dresser by the door and left the room.

She followed him in the scrying water, viewing the scene as though floating above him. He walked down a corridor past an open living room. He stopped at a door on the left and pushed it open. Cassidy followed him into the room—it was the hangar. One of the other men

124

was sitting on a stool inside the door—he stood up and saluted, then pressed a large yellow button on the wall.

Balthazar pointed the sensor at the lone gray speedster, and the pilot-side door slowly lifted. He climbed into the craft, and she watched as he pressed a sequence of buttons and switches, illuminating the instrument panel. The craft's door lowered and sealed shut. She could not hear anything—she could only see. He moved his thumb on a control stick by his left leg and pumped his feet on floor pedals. The craft rose off the ground and pivoted slowly to face the rear wall, which was opening to expose a decompression chamber. He pushed on a throttle in the center console—it looked the same as the layout of the craft Kai had piloted to explore their land, and not so very different from her mother's hovercraft, although with many more controls on the panel.

Cassidy watched as he glided into the decompression chamber. She waited, holding the vision in focus, until the front wall opened and he entered a second chamber. When the outer wall opened, she watched him push on the throttle and pull on the side stick, flying out over the bright lunar landscape. Earth hung in the sky, largely shrouded in shadow, and the sun blazed in the black sky.

He flew above the silvery terrain and before long came upon a gaping pit, vast and deep. He flew down inside it, and Cassidy recognized the ghostly white spaceport and monstrous black cubes of Gandoop Spaceport and Mine. He was inside Anaximenes crater. *Her* crater. Anger welled up inside her, and she shoved her fist into the glassy water, shattering the image. She grabbed the washcloth and wrung it out, then stormed through the closet and into the bedroom. Anna was sitting on the floor, eating from a plate with her fingers. Cassidy stepped over the plates and rattled the bedroom door handle. The door was locked, as usual. She turned to Anna, fuming.

"That bastard. No-good dirty thief. I'll kill him," Cassidy said.

Anna stared up at her, her mouth full of eggs, and nodded.

———————)———————

Cassidy gazed into the sink filled with water, trying for the millionth time to scry. Her magical skills were not within her control, and it was maddening. The clear liquid winked up at her, teasing her. She gritted her teeth and glared at the glistening surface, rehashing all her successful viewing sessions. Her baths. The sink when she was washing Maria's face towel. Maybe it was the green drug that induced her visions. Or fear. *Or blood.*

Cassidy bit down hard on the inside of her cheek and spat a mouthful of bloody saliva into the basin.

The view of the room next door came into focus, and she stared, transfixed. Balthazar's dark hair made a sharp contrast against his white pillow.

It was morning already, and she watched him roll out of bed and walk across the large dwelling to another suite to use the bathroom.

When he came back and entered the women's prison, she was waiting for him, standing with her arms crossed.

He lifted an eyebrow at her as he removed his pants and picked up his coils of rope.

"What do you want with us?" Cassidy demanded.

"I want you to keep quiet and spread your legs, that's what I want," he said, striding across the floor and backhanding her across the temple.

Her head whipped to the side with a flash of white light. She stumbled backwards but kept her footing. "You are a rapist and a thief, *Balthazar,*" she sneered.

He froze and stared at her. "How do you know my name?" he asked, anger darkening his olive-toned skin.

He came at her and punched her face. She fell to her knees, pain lancing through her head.

"How do you know my name?" he repeated, kicking her in the stomach.

She gasped and clutched her belly, the breath knocked out of her. He lifted her head by the hair and kneed her in the face, her nose crunching.

"Tell me," he demanded.

Her reckless courage fled, and she trembled at his feet. "I ... I ... heard them call you that in the hangar ... when I ... a ... a ... arrived," she stammered.

"Liar," he said, slapping her.

"Before you g ... g ... got there," she said, blood trickling from her nose down to her lips.

"You lying bitch," he said, pulling her around onto her hands and knees. He grabbed her silk negligee at the back, breaking the thin shoulder straps and tearing the fabric, ripping the gown off her body.

He whipped her shoulders with the rope while he raped her from behind, and she fell onto her elbows, crying out as he tore her flesh. He dragged her back up onto her hands by the hair and wrapped the rope around her neck and tightened it.

She choked as he twisted the rope and thrust into her from behind. She couldn't breathe, and all went black.

————————— ☽ —————————

When she came to, she was crumpled on the floor, her face buried in the brown carpet. She heard the rustling of his pants as he approached, and he kicked her in the back, and then dragged her over by the shoulder and crouched above her, squeezing her cheeks between his thumb and fingers.

"Are you going to tell me how you know my name?" he demanded, his breath reeking of sour alcohol.

"I told you," she muttered.

"You are lying. No one calls me Balthazar."

One of her eyes was swollen shut, but she trained the other on his livid face as he loomed over her. "They do when you're not there," she said, not caring anymore. *"That asshole Balthazar,"* she said, spittle flying from her lips.

He slapped her hard, and then squeezed her face again and held the dropper filled with the green drug over her head. "You want this? You want food? Then tell me how you knew my name."

"I told you," she said, staring greedily at the dropper.

He wrapped his hand around her throat and squeezed, a grimace transforming his face into a grotesque gargoyle. She pulled at his thick wrist with both hands, trying to break his suffocating hold, but he only squeezed harder. The familiar panic and pressure in her head overwhelmed her, and she kicked, writhing helplessly. Right before she lost consciousness, he let go of her throat and slammed her head to the ground. He stood up and kicked her in the ribs, then turned to leave.

"Wait," she called after him, coughing and struggling to stand up.

He turned and sneered at her as she swayed unsteadily on her feet. She bit her lip and said nothing.

His face was red, and his eyes drilled into hers. "I don't even need to send you to the Nommos," he said, a cruel smile creeping across his face. "No one knows about you. I can keep you forever."

Cassidy's courage turned to pale, cold dread.

He smirked at her, then lowered the still-full dropper into the vial, screwed the cap shut, and slid the vial into his pants pocket and left the room, locking the door loudly behind him.

"Wait," she called, running to the door and pounding on it. "Just give me a little bit and I'll tell you everything, I promise."

She heard the outer door slam shut, and all was quiet.

———————❧———————

Cassidy was lacerated and bruised more than usual, and her muscles were jittery, but her mind was sharp and agitated from skipping the drug dose it was expecting. The craving ate away at her belly, and her skin felt like a million bugs were crawling all over it.

She soaked in the bathtub, trying to make the itching stop, and watched through blood-tinged water as Balthazar showered and ate breakfast. She watched him return to his bedchamber without the usual plates of food for the women. She gaped at him, but he couldn't see her. He didn't care if they starved. He didn't care that she needed the drug, which he had made her dependent on. It was all her fault. Next time she would be quiet and let him do whatever he wanted. But she couldn't tell him how she knew his name. She moaned, her belly aching with hunger and her nerves twitching. She watched him leave the room, walk down the corridor, and enter the hangar. The guard pressed the large yellow button on the wall, and the decompression chamber door parted as Balthazar climbed into the speedster. She watched him press a round ON button on the instrument panel, then the same short sequence of buttons and switches. The craft rose into the air, and he turned it and passed slowly through the decompression chambers, and then flew out over the flatlands towards the main Anaximenes crater. The sun was higher in the sky, and the ground was shining like sand-blasted aluminum, gritty and blinding.

She got out of the bathtub and apologized to Anna and Maria over and over for making him so angry that he did not feed them. They were not mad at her, but instead lay down on the closet floor and tried to sleep. Cassidy slipped on a new silk gown, then went back to the bathroom, feeling nauseous, her skin clammy. Her muscles were weak, and she wondered if she had the flu. She knelt by the toilet and threw up. She flushed the toilet and spit a mouthful of bloody saliva into the toilet bowl, hanging onto the toilet seat as she hung her head over the water and found him again in her vision.

He was inside the Gandoop Spaceport hangar. He walked by himself into an office, where he met with one officer after another, barking out silent orders. The men would salute and walk stiffly away, and then once out of view of the one-way glass of the office, their shoulders would slouch as they went about their business. She followed one man across a walkway and into a massive building that looked like a metal foundry, with an enormous cauldron of molten metal, mounds of moon dust, and sacks marked "Titanium Dust." Another cavernous room held huge steel tanks and lines of shelves filled with small tanks. She followed more men into bunk rooms and a cramped dining hall, then found a warren of storage rooms further down a cement hallway.

She grew dizzy and stood up, leaving her explorations for another day. She retreated to the closet floor but could not sleep, and the next morning she was still nauseous and shaky. She resumed her vigil at a bathroom sink and saw Balthazar drag Anna onto the bed. Cassidy could not watch, but instead explored the rest of the house they were captives in.

A guard left his post in the hangar, spent ten minutes on the toilet, and then joined the other three men in the kitchen where they were cooking eggs and steak and frying diced onions and potatoes. Her mouth watered, and she licked her lips hungrily.

When Balthazar was done with Anna, he showered and ate. He brought them eggs and steak, but only on two plates instead of three. Cassidy got the point, but Maria shared her food with her. Anna pushed her plate away, but they set aside her portion for later, when she would wake up from her delirium, famished.

Cassidy resumed her vigil at the sink, spying on Balthazar while the other women slept. That evening, Balthazar arrived at the house, ate dinner with his four men, and then sat alone in the living room, drinking one glass of whiskey on the rocks after another. He finally went to bed, and the other member of the household arrived home, gliding into the hangar and greeting the sleepy guard who was posted on the stool by the hangar door.

The loner was tall and lean and wore a plain black flight suit. He walked with a purposeful gait and went directly into his private suite. She wondered who he was and why he was hardly ever there, and why he did not have sex slaves like Balthazar did.

She spent all night waiting for morning to arrive, sitting on the marble bathroom floor and staring into the toilet. Her eye was purple and puffy, and she could not breathe through her swollen nose. But it was easy to cough up blood and spit it into the water, making her visions come alive. She told Anna and Maria that she felt nauseous, so they left her slouched over the toilet and retreated into their own miseries.

As morning approached, Cassidy switched her viewing to one of the sinks and watched the loner rise before the others. The illuminated clock on his bedside table read 5:30. He showered quickly, got dressed under a skylight, and left the house without even eating. Then the guard in the hangar followed his morning routine—first the bathroom, and then he joined the other guards in the kitchen where they were drinking coffee and one was cracking eggs into a bowl.

Five minutes before six, Balthazar rose, went to the bathroom in the other suite, and then came into their bedroom for his turn with Maria. While he conducted his vile business, Cassidy explored the exterior room where he slept. Her crystal shaft was still sitting on the dresser where he had left it that first day, next to his speedster sensor. The crystal glinted at her, the facets catching shafts of colored light that streamed in through the small skylight in the ceiling, glittering violet, green, red, and gold.

Cassidy swallowed. Her heart was pounding, and a desperate rashness took hold of her. Balthazar always left the bedroom door unlocked during his raping sessions, apparently unafraid that any of them would be bold or stupid enough to try and escape.

Avala's words rang in her head. *But I sense that you are more trapped by fear. Fear has saved you so far, but soon it will kill you. It is time to let it go.*

She could take his sensor and fly right out of there. The idea was suicidal. He would catch her and kill her. He would punish Anna and Maria. The hairs on her arms rose, tingling.

Cassidy crept into the closet. Anna was still lying on the floor, in the late stages of the drug fog when the headache and muscle cramps came on. Cassidy fought back a craving for the drug and changed quickly into a black gown that reached to her knees. Her entire body was trembling, and a cold sweat dampened her skin. She hesitated and considered the alternatives. He had threatened to keep her as his slave forever. Or, if she were lucky, he would sell her to the Nommos. She grabbed her rune belt from behind the unused shoes and clasped it around her waist under the gown.

"I love you, Anna," she whispered.

Drool hung in a transparent thread from Anna's lip to the carpet, and she stared listlessly at the wall.

Cassidy pressed her ear to the closet door. She heard the smack of a slap and Maria whimpering. He always followed the same routine. Beat them, strangle them, and then huff and puff while he tried to prove that he was still a man. Cassidy waited until he was grunting during his long effort towards orgasm, and silently turned the doorknob.

He was facing away from Cassidy, hunched over Maria, who was on her belly under him, her wrists outstretched and tied to the corners of the bed. Cassidy held her breath, silently closed the closet door behind her, and tiptoed on bare feet across the bedroom carpet, hoping the sound of the ventilation system would mask her movements. He was grunting loudly. Cassidy reached the bedroom door, carefully turned the knob, and pulled the door open. She slid out while he was still grunting and closed the door softly behind her.

She gulped in a mouthful of air, grabbed her crystal and the sensor, and then ran to the hallway door. She opened it and slid out into the corridor. She could hear the guards talking faintly from the kitchen around the corner. She turned the other way and ran on tiptoes to the hangar door. It was unlocked, and she slipped inside. She was panting, and her heart was thundering in her ears. Sitting on top of the guard's stool was the man's handscreen, showing a video feed of her inside the hangar.

She swallowed and ran to the shelf, grabbed her daypack, stuffed the crystal inside it, and then stared at Balthazar's speedster. Was she really going to do this? *She could do it. She had to.*

She pressed the yellow button on the wall to open the decompression chamber, and then pointed the sensor at the speedster, pressing a button with a picture of one door on it. The pilot's door rose, and she climbed into the seat, and then pressed the sensor button again to close the door, nearly dropping the sensor from her violently shaking hand.

"Calm down," she whispered to herself as the door sealed shut. "I am only trapped by fear. I must let it go." She looked over her shoulder through the side window. The decompression chamber door was opening behind her. She stared frantically at the speedster's control panel. There were so many gauges and buttons.

She forced herself to slow down. She had watched Balthazar navigate the craft several times. There was the green ON button. She pressed it, along with the other buttons and switches she had watched Balthazar use, and the craft vibrated to life. She found the knob to move the seat forward, and then pulled the harness over her shoulders and clipped it between her legs. The hover control was just like in her mother's hovercraft. She flipped the switch up, and the craft rose off the ground, and the landing gear buzzed beneath her and then was silent.

Cassidy fumbled with the control stick on her left and pushed gently on the throttle in the center console. The craft jerked forward, and she pulled the throttle back. She worked the foot pedals, the metal cold and rough on her bare soles, and found the toe brakes, just like on a hovercraft. Gently, she tried to pivot the craft in order to face the decompression chamber, but the craft jerked to the right and a red flashing button beeped at her. Her heart was in her throat. *She did not have time for this.* She gripped the side stick and tried to remember Balthazar's hands on the controls. Under her left thumb was a small round knob. She pushed it gently, and the craft inched forward. She breathed in and moved the knob in a circle. The craft slowly pivoted until it was facing the open airlock chamber. She pushed the knob forward, and the craft glided slowly into the chamber. She was breathing heavily and sweat dripped down into her eyes, stinging. She looked around frantically for a button to close the decompression chamber door, but it started closing on its own.

She exhaled and sat back in the seat. Balthazar's seat. *Balthazar's speedster.* He would kill her if he caught her. But first he would torture her. The wall-sized door slid shut behind her. She waited, her blood pounding. Images of her childhood and Earth flitted across her mind—Torr and her parents. Grandma Leann and Great-Aunt Sophie. Jasper as a gangly teenager. Peary Dome. She wanted to pee. The door in front of her opened and she glided into the second chamber. The door sealed shut behind her, and she inspected the cryptic collection of gauges until the outer door opened.

The surface of the moon spread out before her, blinding her with its brightness. She pushed on the thumb knob and glided out of the hangar. She tried to coordinate the stick in her left hand with the throttle in her right. After a few jerks and almost driving the nose into the ground, she managed to lift the nose upwards and pressed on the throttle, rising above the landscape.

She knew where Anaximenes was on the map, and she knew where north was in relation to Earth, and so she turned the craft and headed towards Peary.

She did not know how long it would be before Balthazar discovered she was gone, but he had no speedster to chase her with—unless he radioed Gandoop Spaceport and sent out patrol speedsters, or those swimming Mantas.

She bit down on her lip, clutched the throttle, and pushed it all the way forward, trying to set a trajectory that would keep her from crashing into the mountainous crater rims that rose and fell below her but not propel her out into space. The black firmament beckoned with the glowing bridge of the Milky Way forging a path across the starry sky, but that way would lead to her death.

She inspected the various controls, trying to figure out how to go into high gear, but there were too many gauges and screens she did not understand. And so she gripped the side stick and throttle, and sped towards the north pole, glancing over her shoulder every few seconds, trying to see behind her through the small side window. Nothing was there but vacant land and empty sky. She thought about turning on the radar screen, but didn't know how and was afraid to touch any unfamiliar buttons.

She tried to relax but could not. What if she missed her mark and wandered aimlessly across the moon, lost among fields of impact craters, until he caught her? She exhaled and thought of the golden woman. A Turyan priestess. Avala was her name. She felt like a sister to her.

And she thought of Anna and Maria and winced at how he would take out his wrath on them. They would understand. Wouldn't they?

Her brother. He was waiting for her. Or had he lost all hope? She closed her eyes for a moment and tried to feel Torr. He was jittery and impatient. Or was that her? And Jasper—did he really even love her?

She stared straight ahead, trying to recognize land features, but everything looked the same. The moonscape passed beneath her, and she thought of her mother and father crossing the wilderness to Shasta. Afraid, like her. Craters loomed and retreated, and bare land scraped across her consciousness. The specter of Balthazar hung over her shoulder, but she shut him out.

There was nothing here. No air. No life. Time lost all meaning, and she prayed to the stars.

She used the position of Earth in the sky and the direction of the shadows as her reference points and kept heading northeast, adjusting course until a glint flashed in the distance. She held her breath and headed towards it. Yes, it was Peary Dome. A cry of relief escaped her lips, and she pulled back on the throttle, steering in an arc to approach the long white landing tunnel.

"Identify yourself."

The sharp voice made Cassidy jump. She looked around for a way to talk into the radio, but there were so many buttons, and she had to focus on aiming towards the mouth of the tunnel.

"This is Peary Control. Identify yourself."

Cassidy headed for the mouth, slowing down, but the ground reared up at her and she jerked the nose up, missing the tunnel. She pulled up hard on the stick and barely avoided crashing into the curved wall of Peary Dome. Its facets blinded her with flashes of reflected sunlight and then fell behind her.

"Are you from Gandoop?" the voice asked. *"What's your call sign? Did you bring food?"*

Her heart was racing and she was drenched in sweat. She made a tight arc around Peary Rim, the battered landscape of the moon's far side coming into view. She circled towards the tunnel mouth again.

Behind her a speedster appeared and got on her tail. Her hands were slippery on the controls. She hoped it was only Kai. But he would not know it was her. Or maybe it was a patrol ship from Gandoop, here to snatch her up just when she was on the doorstep to freedom.

She tried to steady her breathing and slowed the craft, nudging at the thumb knob and biting her lip as she steered the craft towards the opening and made a vertical descent, just as she would if she were dropping her mother's hovercraft into a traffic pattern.

She made it this time and blew out her breath. Her whole body was shaking as she glided slowly through the landing tunnel and brought the craft to a hovering idle in front of one of several compression chamber doors. A set of doors slowly parted, and she glided Balthazar's speedster inside and brought it to a stop. The airlock door closed behind her, and tears sprang from her eyes. She leaned back against the headrest and waited, the hot salty tears streaming down her face and stinging her cuts.

The door in front of her opened, and she glided into the second chamber, then waited anxiously for the pressure to equalize. Her pulse was throbbing, and suddenly she was desperately thirsty. She licked her parched and swollen lips and drummed her fingers on the throttle.

The inner door finally opened, and she navigated the speedster into the massive hangar, following the hand signals of one of Rodney's Rangers and parking in the spot he indicated. She stopped the craft and flicked the hover switch down. The landing gear whirred and clanked, and the craft slowly settled onto the floor. She killed the engine, grabbed her pack, opened the door, and climbed out. Her legs were weak and trembling, and she turned to the group of Rodney's Rangers and traders who were gathering around, staring at her.

"Cassidy?" Jasper broke from the group and ran to her. "Cassidy!"

She collapsed into his arms, and he held her up, screaming for someone to get a transport.

———————)———————

Cassidy squeezed her eyes shut and let the medic at the infirmary examine her. She hated having a stranger touch her, but she wanted to make sure Balthazar had not irreparably damaged her body or impregnated her. The medic covered her with a sheet, and she pulled her rune belt above his reach as he gave her a pelvic exam. She wished she had more of the green drug, and tried not to think of Balthazar as the medic gently felt around inside her.

When the medic was done, she sat up on the table, clutching the sheet around her. He told her she would heal and that she was not pregnant, but he gave her a pee stick to check again for pregnancy after two weeks. She had not had her period since she'd arrived on the moon several weeks

before, and he told her that was normal. Her cycles would resume eventually, he assured her, after her body adjusted to the strange lunar environment. He gave her a few washable pads for whenever that happened.

He gave her a shot of antibiotics and a bottle of antibiotic pills that
she was to take for two weeks. Nothing serious, he assured her, and
asked her to come back in six weeks to check for other types of infec-
tions. The other bruises on her face, neck, and the rest of her body were
superficial wounds, he said. No bones were broken, and no organs were
damaged. The lacerations in her private parts were not deep and were
already healing well. He was concerned about the psychological trauma,
however, and suggested she seek out a woman named Phyllis to talk to.

She told him that she felt sick to her stomach a lot, and weak and
shaky, but she did not tell him about the drug, which she suspected
was the cause. He thought she might have some kind of a flu bug
and that it would pass. He gave her a gallon of water to take with her
and electrolyte powder to mix with her water for a few days. Then he
gave her a long white paper gown to cover her body better, and paper
slippers for her bare feet until she could get real clothes.

Cassidy thanked him and left the examination room. Torr was in
the waiting room and rushed over to her. They embraced, and her
thready heartbeat synchronized with his strong and steady pulse.

"Oh my god, Cassidy. I'm so sorry," he said, hugging her. "I was so
worried. Are you okay?"

She hung onto him, wishing it had all been a bad dream. "Yes. No,"
she mumbled into his shoulder. "I will be, I hope."

He rocked her gently for a long moment. When they separated,
she glanced down at a flicker of shadows. At Torr's side stood a large
wolf, gazing up at her with amber eyes. She squeezed her eyes shut, and
when she opened them again the hallucination had vanished.

They stepped outside as Jasper rolled up in his borrowed box truck
and pulled to a stop. He climbed out of the cab and placed his hand
gently on her shoulder. "Are you okay?" he asked.

She nodded and leaned against him as he put his arm around her
protectively. He was warm and smelled like Earth. "Did you talk to
Ramzy?" she asked.

"Yeah," he said. "He wants to talk to you."

"Now?" she asked, feeling slightly nauseous.

"Yes," Jasper said. "Sorry."

"Ugh," she said. "I hate him."

"I know," Jasper said. "But he doesn't know where the house is that you said is near Anaximenes, and he doesn't know about any human trafficking rings operating out of Gandoop."

She stepped back and met his concerned gaze. "Alright. If it'll help my friends. We need to get them out of there." A wave of panic overtook her. "Let's go," she said, taking in a shaky breath. She could hang on for just a little bit longer—force herself to behave rationally, even though all she wanted was to go back to the Fen and curl up in a ball inside her tent and block out the world.

They drove to the spaceport and went inside. Ramzy was waiting for them in his stuffy office, seated at his table.

She stood inside the doorway, her arms wrapped around herself, and stared at the floor.

"Where is this structure you were held at?" he asked gruffly.

She glanced up to find his eyes wandering over her bruised face and neck and white hospital gown. She could not tell if his sour expression was one of sympathetic horror or disgust. She swallowed, suddenly feeling small and dirty. Torr placed his hand on her back, and she leaned against him.

"North of Gandoop Spaceport," she said quietly, and dropped her eyes again.

"Where?" Ramzy asked. "In a crater?"

"No," she said. "On the flatlands."

"There is no structure out there," he said.

Just then, Kai came through the door and stopped short when he caught sight of Cassidy. His face fell, and she gave him a brave smile.

Relief welled up inside her at the comforting presence of the man from her childhood—her parents' close friend and Jasper's father. She blurted out a short version of what had happened to her.

He listened quietly, his eyes smoldering with hurt and anger.

"It's dangerous on the moon," Ramzy said. "I suspect you understand that now."

Cassidy broke away from Kai's worried gaze and turned her attention to the leader of Peary Dome. Ramzy glared sternly at her over his reading glasses, and his tone sounded as though he was blaming her for what had happened.

Fury rose in her blood, and she sneered at him. "I was kidnapped, and two other young women are still trapped there. Are you going to help, or what?" she asked.

"I don't know where they are," Ramzy said.

She repeated her observations of the house's location for Kai's benefit, and he rubbed his chin.

"Must be an underground bunker," Kai said. "I heard the Gandoops have a compound out there somewhere," he said, glancing at Ramzy. "But I've never seen it myself. It's hidden, apparently."

Cassidy nodded.

"Who held you?" Kai asked, pulling out a chair for her.

She sat down gratefully, and Ramzy rose from his chair to make tea.

"His name is Balthazar," she said. Saying his name brought his leering face to mind, and she held her stomach. Her pulse fluttered nervously as she thought about what he would do to her if he caught her. He must have discovered that she was gone by now—he always left for the spaceport right after breakfast and would find his speedster was missing. He would erupt in a violent rage and take it out on Anna and Maria. Cassidy squeezed her eyes shut and tried to breathe. "We need to save my friends," she said, wringing her hands and trying not to weep.

"I don't know anyone named Balthazar," Ramzy said. "What does he look like?"

She swallowed and inhaled, struggling to get hold of herself. She opened her eyes and described Balthazar's tall stature and his dark hair and green eyes.

"How old?" Ramzy asked.

Cassidy shrugged. "Forty, maybe? Forty-five? I don't know."

"Not Ishmar," Ramzy said.

"Maybe one of his sons?" Jasper asked. "Ridge, maybe? Ali?"

She shook her head. "Not Ali."

"Was he tall and skinny with a crew cut?" Kai asked.

She shook her head. "No. He was big and had a full head of hair. But another guy in the house was tall and thin with a shaved head, and he always wore a black flight suit. Balthazar worked at the spaceport. He was in charge of something."

"I don't know the guy," Kai said. "But it sounds like he's working with the Gandoops. Ridge always wore a black flight suit, though I haven't seen him in years. Can you call Ishmar?" Kai asked Ramzy.

Ramzy harrumphed and handed Cassidy a small glass of tea. She blew on the hot tea and took a sip. If that loner was Ridge Gandoop, owner of the spaceport and mine, then he was behind the whole sordid business. They were running human trafficking rings on *her* land. Outrage, fear, and self-loathing swirled in her head, drowning out any coherent thoughts. She stirred sugar into her tea and sipped at it as the men talked.

"And just what am I supposed to say to Ishmar?" Ramzy asked. "Accuse his son of harboring a kidnapper?"

"Yes," Torr said stiffly.

Ramzy snorted. "I can barely get Ishmar to return my calls as it is, trying to clear up this food shortage nonsense. Now I'm going to insult his son?"

Cassidy closed her eyes and swallowed a mouthful of the hot, sweet tea, turning her mind to Anna and Maria and blocking out the horrible man sitting across from her.

"And what if it is true?" Ramzy continued. "You think whoever it is will hand them over just because I ask? Do you think I'm going to raid their compound and start a war with the Gandoops over a couple of girls?"

Despair crushed Cassidy's heart as she realized Ramzy was not going to help save Anna and Maria. She wondered if the blustering man really had a daughter, and if he knew what love was.

Cassidy finished her tea while Ramzy and Kai debated about whether or not the Gandoops were letting human traffickers use their port. Jasper sat silently at her side, and she could feel Torr fuming, but he said nothing.

She set down her glass and stood up. "I feel sick. Let's go," she said, and left the room.

————————)————————

Cassidy rode with Torr and Jasper over the bumpy roads towards the Fen.

Everything felt odd, as though she weren't really there. People walked the roads as though everything were normal—as though she hadn't been kidnapped and held captive on this very moon—abused and drugged and damaged. She looked up to the heavens. She had always thought the stars were looking down upon her, protecting her. But now she realized they were just balls of fire, and planets were just chunks of stone, hurtling through empty space in a mindless dance. Living creatures were nothing but brief bursts of light, sparks that ignited in a painful flash and then quickly turned to ash.

"Are you okay?" Torr asked, nudging her with his elbow.

She was sitting between him and Jasper on the single bench seat of the box truck's cab, with her hands pressed between her knees. "Yeah," she said numbly. Jasper glanced at her with concern, and she avoided his gaze, staring down at her bruised wrists and wondering again if Balthazar had discovered her absence yet. Of course he had, and he was furious. He would have sent out patrols, trying to track her down. She shivered with dread and bit down on the inside of her cheek, drawing the metallic taste of blood.

The truck bounced and turned onto Spoke Road Seven, and then turned into the alleyway behind the Fen's kitchen tents. Jasper stopped the vehicle, and Cassidy followed Torr down onto the dust.

The men of the Fen were sitting at the picnic tables and looked up, staring at her. Hawk's eyes were round, and she tried to smile at him. Berkeley stood up, but she walked past the tables and into her tent and tied the door flaps shut behind her.

It was dim inside, but she liked it that way. She rummaged through her pack and found clean underwear and her pink butterfly t-shirt and changed into them, and then unrolled her sleeping bag and curled up inside it, zipping it all the way up and hiding her face in its welcome darkness.

PART TWO

LIGHT FIGHTERS

10

THE ASSİGNMENT

Ridge was in his spacesuit repairing the crane at the rare-earths mine in a large crater on the floor of Anaximenes H. Moon dust inevitably clogged everything, requiring regular equipment maintenance, no matter how hard he tried to enclose movable parts. The crane's gears had jammed so badly the operator was afraid he would break something if he tried to fix it, and so Ridge had to do it himself. He had just finished when his radio vibrated at his hip. He glanced down at the digital readout. Balty was calling him. He ignored it and waved to the crane operator, closed his toolbox, and began the climb out of the pit to the rim where he had parked his speedster. His radio vibrated again. He glanced down at the text readout.

Where the fuck are you? Get to the house immediately.

Ridge inhaled the oxygen mixture through his face mask and kept climbing, bounding up the terraces in great, floating leaps, the heavy toolbox nearly weightless in his hand. He got to his speedster, stashed his toolbox in a storage compartment behind the seats, and sealed himself inside the craft. He removed his helmet and gloves, set them on the co-pilot's seat, and headed to the house.

He stepped out of the speedster into the home's hangar and gazed around. Things felt odd. The stool where Balty's thug usually sat was empty, and in place of Balty's speedster was one of the regular Gandoop patrol speedsters. It wasn't possible that Balty's speedster had broken down—it was brand new. Balty's men had recently intercepted a ship bound for Peary Dome and stolen the four speedsters it was carrying, and Balty had claimed one, painting it gray in a weak attempt to conceal his crime. Balty loved that speedster, and if he was here without it, something was very wrong.

Ridge peeled off his spacesuit, hung it in the de-dusting chamber, and brushed off his black flight suit, running an anti-static wand over himself. He then vacuumed the moon dust out of his speedster and brushed off his flight suit again. Finally, unable to think of another delay tactic, he steeled himself and stepped out into the corridor.

Balty's harsh voice and the angry clinking of the ice-maker depositing ice in a glass came from the kitchen, and Ridge followed the familiar noise. Balty was pouring a whiskey on the rocks for himself at the counter and pointedly ignored Ridge.

Balty's four thugs were seated around the table, along with Fowler and the new half-breed officer who had arrived with the most recent shipment of Tegs—Harbin. Harbin seemed a friendly enough sort and had the distinctive half-breed triple widow's peak like Balty and Ridge, and was nearly as handsome as Balty.

Ridge sat in one of the two remaining chairs and glanced around the table. Everyone's eyes were downcast or shifting nervously. The guard who usually manned the hangar during the day was holding an icepack over what looked like a recently punched nose.

Balty pulled back the chair at the head of the table and sat down heavily, scowling at Ridge.

"What happened?" Ridge asked.

"That bitch escaped," Balty said in a growl, tilting the glass to his lips and loudly slurping down half of its contents.

"What bitch?" Ridge asked.

"The one from Peary."

"What one from Peary?" Ridge asked, frowning. He normally tried not to pay attention to Balty's sex slaves. It was too depressing, and made Ridge feel like he should do something about it. "I don't know what you're talking about," Ridge said, folding his hands together on the table.

"One was being trafficked from Peary, and I borrowed her," Balty said, the whites of his eyes showing dangerously above drooping lower eyelids.

Ridge had thought human trafficking was prohibited in Peary. The moon rats must be getting desperate for gold. Ridge tightened his grip and tried to maintain a calm voice. The other men glanced at him hopefully, as though he had the magic cure for Balty's insanity. Ridge cleared his throat and asked, "How did she escape?"

"She stole my fucking speedster. That bitch." Balty's jaw squared and his eyes turned on the man with the icepack. "This imbecile left his handscreen in the hangar while we were having breakfast." The guard sank lower in his seat, melting under Balty's glare.

Ridge nodded. He had set up everyone's handscreens with the video feed from inside the hangar, as well as the security cameras outside the house, but he wasn't surprised at the guard's breach of protocol. They never had unexpected visitors. No one knew it was there except a select few, and Ridge had camouflaged the home, coating it with a radar-absorbing graphene mixture to conceal it from view. Ridge himself had muted the hangar's interior door's security beeps, since they annoyed everyone. No one had considered a threat from the inside or that one of the sex slaves might be brazen enough to defy Balty and escape.

"She stole my fucking sensor and walked right out. We watched the hangar footage. She got in the speedster and flew away. Just like that."

Ridge tried to keep a straight face. He thought Balty kept the girls locked in his bedroom—Ridge had installed the slide bolt himself—but he didn't want to ask. Balty had originally wanted a camera installed inside the bedroom to monitor them, but Ridge had teased that he would watch Balty perform. Balty had changed his mind and asked Ridge to install a simple peephole instead.

"Whore," Balty said, and drained his drink. "By the time this jackass noticed the speedster was gone, it was too late."

The guard stared down at the table.

"We got confirmation from one of my contacts that she landed at Peary Spaceport," Balty said. "That sly cunt."

"She must have taken an indirect route," Harbin said apologetically.

Ridge raised his eyebrows and nodded again. They had disabled the transponders on all the stolen speedsters.

Balty directed his gaze at Ridge. "I want you to get her back."

Ridge tried not to flinch. "Me? Get her back?"

Ridge had been slightly surprised that Balty had admitted any weakness or failure, but now he understood why. Balty wanted him to do his dirty work, as usual.

"Yeah," Balty said, leaning back in his chair. "You know Peary Dome, and I need to keep a low profile. Best none of my men show up there right now." Balty's eyes narrowed and a sneer lifted his upper lip. "No one disrespects me and gets away with it."

Ridge sighed and drummed his fingers on the table. He didn't think escaping from a sadistic rapist qualified as disrespect, but Balty's view of the world centered on himself. And once Balty set his mind to something, there was no swaying him. "I'll see what I can do," Ridge said reluctantly.

Balty flashed his gregarious smile, stretched his arms up, and laced his fingers together behind his head—the very picture of ease. The hairs on the back of Ridge's neck stood on end. He hated the way the schizophrenic creep flipped between vicious rat and charming fox in the blink of an eye.

"Sure thing, Balty," Ridge said. He scraped back his chair and fled to his private chambers.

———————)———————

A pounding at his suite's door wrenched Ridge out of a deep sleep.

Ridge threw back his bed covers and staggered to the door, opening it to find Balty leaning against the door frame, stinking of whiskey.

"Come look at this," Balty said, grabbing Ridge by the arm.

"Wait a second," Ridge grumbled, shaking off Balty's hand and shuffling back into his bedroom. He pulled on his flight suit and slippers and followed Balty out to the living room.

"I ran the bitch's hair through a DNA analyzer," Balty said, slurring. "Look what the database spit out."

Ridge walked over to the wall screen where a document written in calligraphy was displayed. "Lunar Deed," Ridge read aloud. "Is this her?" he asked, pointing at the name at the bottom, "Cassandra Cethlejan Dagda."

"Yes. Cassidy. But look at this," Balty said, pointing to a metallic seal. "The Salmon Seal of Metolius. And his signature and fingerprints." Balty turned and confronted Ridge, his face puffy and red from alcohol, and his eyes bulging. "She's a fucking spy," he said hoarsely, waving his hands through the air. "Sent by that scumbag, Metolius."

"Spy? Metolius?" Ridge asked, stepping back a pace to get away from Balty's foul breath.

"Why else would she appear out of the blue? So conveniently. And so cheap. And so pretty. Such a good fuck. How else would she escape so easily? She knew how to pilot a speedster. And she *knew my name.* That sneaky whore. I'll kill her."

"What? I don't get it," Ridge said. "Metolius? I thought you worked for ..." Ridge's voice trailed off. It seemed unlikely that President Metolius would have dropped a female ninja warrior into Balty's lair, but it was curious that she had managed to escape—and that she knew how to fly a speedster. Regardless, he wasn't going to challenge Balty while the maniac was in the midst of a paranoid rage.

Balty bared his teeth, his bloodshot eyes livid. "Metolius has been plotting against Tegea for years. And now he has the gall to send his agents to foil our plan. She has a twin brother." He turned to the wall and changed the image to another deed, signed by a Torrance Brenon Dagda. "Don't you see, you idiot? Look." Balty flipped back to the girl's deed and pointed to the land coordinates.

The blood drained from Ridge's face. "Those are ... that's for ...," Ridge faltered.

"Yeah," Balty slurred. "Anaximenes. The spaceport. The facilities. Everything. And ...," Balty said darkly, flicking back to the boy's deed, "Anaximenes G and H."

Ridge's heart dropped into his stomach. "I'll be damned," Ridge said softly. Legal deeds to the land he was standing on. His regolith fields. His rare-earths mine. Rightful ownership of the empire he and his father and brother had built over the past twenty years. Had poured their sweat and blood into. Their souls. "Well, they're not going to take Gandoop, I can assure you of that," Ridge said, meeting Balty's fiery gaze.

Balty's mouth curled into a smile. "I thought you might feel that way. Get the deeds. And bring me that bitch of a girl. And kill the boy."

Ridge suppressed an eye roll at Balty's orders. Ridge was not a killer, and Balty knew it. But he *did* want the deeds. The trick was how to get them. Faint snoring came from the guards' quarters. They were all

Tegs. Trained warriors. Scouts. Why was it always up to Ridge to deal with the difficult tasks?

Balty changed the screen to passport photos of the young sister and brother. The contrast between the young woman's sweet innocent face in the photo and the battered creature Ridge had seen in the security footage was sickening. He inhaled and examined the photos. The twins bore some resemblance, but it was the intensity in their eyes that caught Ridge's attention. Eyes that seemed to be watching him—to see inside him.

Ridge shivered and went to the wet bar to pour himself a drink.

"And my speedster," Balty said, waving his fist at him. "Get back my fucking speedster."

Ridge sighed and scooped half-melted ice from the ice bucket into a glass and poured whiskey over it, the ice shifting and settling into the golden liquor.

11

VİALS

Life on Earth seemed like a dream to Cassidy. A distant fantasy. A make-believe time when things were beautiful. When she had parents who loved her. When she took air and water for granted. When she could bury her face in soft fragrant flowers whenever she wanted and be transported by their sweet scent into a state of bliss. Plants and animals—they were just part of life, right? They would always be there. Just like the ocean. Wind and rain. A snowflake. A waterfall.

She sat cross-legged on her sleeping bag, clothed in her old gray sweatshirt and jeans. She looked around at the dusty tent she shared with Torr and clasped her hands together in her lap so that he wouldn't notice them shaking. She had been taking various herbs to try and quell her nausea and emotional turmoil, but nothing seemed to help. Even her mother's red notebook had shown her nothing but squiggly snakes filling the pages with indecipherable gibberish.

Torr was sitting on his blankets across from her and glanced up from the knife he was polishing. Worry creased his brow. His bruises were completely gone, and he looked stronger and healthier than she remembered. A faint purple aura outlined his body. She tried to give him a reassuring smile, and he returned the smile hesitantly.

He returned to polishing his wolf knife. She recalled the illusion of the wolf by his side at the infirmary. The majestic animal had emerged from the shadows, and then it had vanished. It reminded her of a plant

149

spirit, but more ferocious somehow. As though it were real. An animal spirit. Rather, a spirit animal. Torr's spirit animal. Maybe she had been delirious from the stress of her captivity and escape. Or perhaps, she dared hope, her second sight was coming back. She was able to water scry now, after all.

She breathed deeply and closed her eyes, pressing down a sense of dark foreboding. Her vision came at a price, she knew. She had seen all sorts of things as a child, before Grandma Leann had shielded her from her powers, insisting it was too much for a child to bear—that Cassidy shouldn't have to feel the grief of the world. Especially a world at war. But now Cassidy was a victim of the cruelty of the world in real life. Her blindfold had been torn off by Balthazar. There was no escape now.

Cassidy opened her eyes and yawned, overcome with a heavy fatigue. The dome was growing quiet as night curfew approached.

"Hey, Cass," Torr said gently. She looked up. His face was drawn and somber. "How'd you get all those bruises?" he asked.

She considered lying, but what would she say? She swallowed and said, "The guy who held me captive was very violent."

"Oh," he said. "I'm sorry. That must have been awful."

"Yes, it was," she said, wishing she had some of the green drug to make it all fade away. "But, what about you?" she asked. "You got beat up when we were attacked. When I saw you in the infirmary, your face was a mess."

"You saw me in the infirmary?" he asked, his eyebrows lifting.

"Yes," she said with a hint of pride. "I learned how to water scry."

"You did? It really works?" he asked.

"Yes, it works," she said, sinking back into despondency. "Do you know who attacked us?"

"Yeah," he said. "A bunch of guys who make shoes. The leader is in jail, locked up in a shipping container over by the infirmary. They did it for money. But we never found the guy who smuggled you out of Peary."

"He was a far side lord, I think," she said.

"Yeah, we figured that out," Torr said. "Maybe he'll resurface again."

"I hope not," she said nervously.

"I meant so we can catch him."

She nodded. Her skin was clammy, and she didn't want to talk about it any longer, but he looked like he had more to say.

"What?" she asked, sitting rigidly in anticipation of personal, prying questions.

"I had a lucid dream. I found Mom, and she healed me."

Her mouth dropped open, and her shoulders relaxed. "In your dream?" Cassidy asked. She had never heard of such a thing. "How did she do that?"

"I don't know. She just held my head, and my skull got all hot and tingly. That's all I know."

"I wish I could ask her what she did," Cassidy said, inspecting his unblemished face. His eyes were bright and steady.

"Cassidy," he said, holding her gaze. "Dad got taken by the Tegs."

Pain sliced through her as though she'd been struck.

"And Mom, she's on her own," Torr said gravely, and related a story of Tegs and brujos and a raven.

Cassidy could not breathe, and her arms and legs started shaking. Torr's eyes melted into hers in shared despair.

"What will happen to Dad?" she asked, her voice quavering. She had told herself her parents would be okay. That they would make it to Shasta and find safety there.

Random details captured her attention as her careening consciousness tried to avoid processing what he had told her. Light-brown stubble covered her brother's chin and jaws and above his lip. The pores on his nose stood out as tiny black dots. His irises were pools of gray ringed by darker gray.

Images of her father kept trying to work their way into her mind, clawing like cats at a door. She ignored their insistent scratching. *Scratch, scratch, scratch.* Glimpses of a scene forced their way into her consciousness before she could slam the door against them. *Soldiers in gray Teg uniforms. Guarding. Watching. Taunting. Rows of disheveled men standing in a paved yard, facing forward. Hands tied behind their backs. Out under the blazing sun. Standing ... standing ... No water. No shoes. Sweating. Burning. Falling.* The air tremored around her. She struggled to hang onto the vision and find her father among the prisoners, but at the same time wanted to turn away from the agony of it.

Torr was speaking, his voice wooden. He was sitting cross-legged, facing her, his elbows resting on his knees. She tried to understand his words, but she felt as though she were being held under water, unable to hold her breath much longer. The pressure of it pushed against her eyes. Her eyes—they were like her father's. Blue as the sun-kissed ocean. *Her father's eyes. She could see them. Azure blue and scared.* Her mind scrabbled for something to hang onto. Something solid and grounding to keep her from slipping into the current of her father's reality and losing hold of her own. Her eyes traced the metal pommel and winged cross guard of the wolf knife, now resting at Torr's side, and followed the spiral of wire that curled around the new black handle.

Cassidy got hold of herself and thought hesitantly of her mother. Brianna was strong. She would hide in the forest. She would find allies in the plants. Cassidy closed her eyes. *Darkness. Warm stale air that smelled of decaying soil. A rectangle of light framed a door. Rakes and shovels leaned against a wall.* Brianna was hiding inside a shed. She was thirsty.

Cassidy opened her eyes. Her head ached and her heart was racing. She realized she was accessing her vision all on her own, and it hurt like hell. She longed for the comforting, darkening blanket of Grandma Leann's shield, and it settled around her.

Taking a deep breath, she tuned in to Torr's words. He was telling her how a group of followers had formed around him. Friends-of-friends and strangers had rallied around him as he'd gone in search of her. He told her he'd met Murians in a hidden underground space-port. Their hair and eyes glowed, and they had told him that he also glowed.

"They said I needed to find you, and that we need to save the moon. And then we need to go to Muria, and you need to wake up a big crystal globe. And something about you and water."

"You met the Murians?" she asked. "You need to introduce me to them."

"I will," he assured her. He described their hooded cloaks and rasping, clicking language. "You know what else?" he asked. "You know that garnet I traded to Jasper for the wolf knife?" She nodded. "It's a translation stone."

"A what?" she asked, sitting upright.

He explained how he had communicated with the Murians as though they were speaking Globalish, even though they weren't.

"We should have never traded that away," she said. "We should never give away anything of Great-Aunt Sophie's."

"I know," he said glumly.

"I'm going to borrow it from Jasper," she said.

"Good luck," Torr said, chuckling. "I think the trade was worth it, though," he said, and told her that the Scrids had seen purple flames around him and a wolf at his side. "And then I found the wolf in a mirror."

She stared at him.

"What are you looking at?" he asked.

"Well," she said slowly, and squinted. Faint wisps of purple danced around his head. "I see a purple aura around you. And I saw a wolf next to you at the infirmary."

Torr slipped his knife into its belt sheath, hopped to his feet, and took Grandma Leann's mirror from the top of a plastic crate. He peered into it, and then angled it towards a square mirror propped up on the crate. He gazed into the hand mirror hopefully, but soon disappointment clouded his face. "I can't see anything. You say you saw the wolf with your bare eyes? That's not fair," he said, glaring into the mirror. He set it down and paced in the small space. "How come you can see stuff so easily, and I can't?"

Cassidy shrugged. It had always been like that. Even with her sight shielded by her grandmother, she was still able to see obvious things like auras and emotions rippling off people. She shivered. She had really seen the wolf. A small sense of triumph raised her energy a notch. "You dream," she said, trying to cheer him up.

He frowned and sat heavily on his blankets, pulling his knees to his chest and resting his chin on a knee. "It's my wolf," he muttered. "I should be able to see him whenever I want."

They both peered into the shadows, but the tent was empty.

"You say you saw him in a mirror, though?" she asked. "That's something. Mirrors are powerful," she said, and he nodded.

The conversation turned back to her. She told Torr a little bit about her ordeal, leaving out the most personal, violent details.

"I abandoned my friends," she said, guilt stabbing at her heart.

"I know how that feels," he said, his expression reflecting hers.

"Balthazar will probably kill them," she said.

"He probably won't," Torr said.

"He will," she said, panic rising and wrapping around her throat. "We have to rescue them. We have to go back there."

"Cassidy," he said, crawling over and kneeling in front of her. "I wish we could help, but we can't do it alone."

"I have a speedster now," she said, grabbing his shoulders. "We have to save them. *We have to save them!*" She realized she was screaming from the surprised look on his face. Her fingernails were digging into his shoulders, and his hands were gripping her forearms.

"Cassidy," he said. "It's okay."

"It's *not* okay," she said, and suddenly she was crying. "Ramzy won't help," she said through her tears, "but maybe Rodney will. He has all the guns, anyway. Will you ask him?" She peered up at her brother.

He wore a pained expression but nodded. "Okay. I'll ask him," he said, releasing her arms.

She returned her hands to her lap, wringing them together and taking in shuddering breaths until the panic attack subsided.

Torr sat on his heels, worry creasing his brow. "I'm just glad you got out," he said softly. "I could hardly stand it. Jasper and I were going to go search for you on Delos."

"You were?" she asked.

"Yes. Of course," Torr said. "We weren't going to give up on you."

She forced a smile, and his worried expression relaxed.

"Hey," he said. "Look. We found your crystal ball and your necklaces. And we found your knife." He took the crystal ball and necklaces from his vest pocket and unclipped her knife sheath from his belt and handed them to her. "But we didn't find your rune belt."

"I still have it," she said, pulling her necklaces down over her head. He produced her utility belt from his pack, and she clipped the knife onto it and strapped the belt over her blue jeans. "I hid it." She patted her belly where the rune belt rested under her sweatshirt. He sighed with relief, and she gazed into the crystal ball. She examined the rainbows glimmering inside the small sphere and wondered if blood had somehow been captured inside the quartz—cellular remains of dead animals from millions of years ago.

The rainbows resolved into shadowy images. She peered at them, then froze. Balthazar was sitting in a recliner in the living room, across from the sour-faced loner in the black flight suit, who was sitting on a couch. *Ridge Gandoop.* The two men were drinking alcohol and talking. She shifted her attention to the bedchamber and found Anna and Maria huddled together, asleep on the closet floor. She detected their rib cages rising and falling with silent breaths, and her own chest felt as though the air were being squeezed out of it.

"Do you see something?" Torr asked.

His voice pulled her out of her vision. "Yes," she said, inhaling. "My friends are still alive. They're trapped. We need to get them out."

Torr swallowed but did not look away.

Movement outside the tent door caught her attention. Jasper's long legs were visible through the gap between the door flaps. He was pacing back and forth.

She slipped the crystal ball into her sweatshirt pocket and went to the door. She poked her head through the canvas flaps and squinted up at Jasper.

"Did I wake you?" he asked.

"No." She slid her bare feet into the paper slippers and stepped out into the light. Several friends of Jasper's who had been hanging around all day were making themselves at home. Some were playing cards, and others were lying on a canvas ground covering spread out at the side of the yard next to the half-container. A shade tarp had been erected above the ground covering, creating a small sheltered pavilion. The men lounged against colorful floral-patterned pillows and dusty bedrolls and looked to be settling in for the night.

"They're the Alphabet Boys," Jasper said, following her gaze. "They're helping us with security. They volunteered."

"Volunteered for what?"

"To help guard you."

Cassidy frowned.

Jasper said, "They may look kind of rough around the edges, but they're the nicest people you'd ever want to meet."

Cassidy knit her eyebrows together.

"We need more of us," Jasper hurried to explain. "They're trustworthy. They do security gigs for some of the Guild traders and offworlders, and sometimes they help me with my business. I've known them for years. My father introduced us." He went on, "We call them the Alphabet Boys because their names are all in a row—A through G. Arden, Buck, Copper, Dang, Elvis, Febo, and Guy."

He rushed to continue, as though afraid he would lose her attention if he stopped talking.

"Arden is the small one with the ponytail. He's like an alley cat, and fights like one. Buck is the tall white guy with the big yellow teeth. He said his teeth used to stick out real far until they got knocked out in a fight. With a baseball bat," he added, peering at her to see if she was still listening. "His teeth are fake, but there are no dentists here to replace them when they get old. He tries not to smile, but he forgets a lot."

Cassidy glanced over at the men as Jasper described them. Arden was arranging his bedding, and Buck was big and hulking, with obvious discolored false teeth.

Jasper went on, "Copper's the beefy one with the red hair and freckles. He goes by Copper because he was a cop, plus his hair is more orange than mine. Dang is the wiry Chinese guy. And Elvis is the skinny, bowlegged Black guy with the messed up nose. He was a boxer and got his ass kicked a lot, I guess. He thought Elvis would make a good boxing name for when he got famous. He won't tell us his real name."

Cassidy recalled Jasper and the Alphabet Boys following her and Torr and their friends earlier that day when she'd gone to the porta-potties. Dang had walked with an even, measured pace. Elvis, on the other hand, sort of hopped as he walked, like he was ready to pick a fight with anyone who looked at him sideways.

"And Febo's the guy with the pretty black hair and enormous mouth. He teaches kickboxing. He thinks about everything backwards. I can never figure out how his mind works, but he's good at the strangest things." Jasper smiled, and Cassidy acknowledged to herself that Febo's hair was indeed pretty. Thick black curls tumbled to his shoulders, and his mouth could easily accommodate an entire sandwich in one bite. Cassidy had also noticed he laughed at inappropriate times, making people stop and look at him oddly.

"And Guy is French. You're supposed to pronounce his name 'Ghee,' but nobody does, so he gave up."

"And you think I want them hanging around me all the time?" she asked.

"I know, Cass," Jasper said. "You've been through hell, and the guys look like scurvy moon rats. But they're real sweet. They'd do anything for you. I swear. I would never bring in anyone I didn't trust."

She sighed. "Yeah, okay, but keep them away from me."

"Sure, Cassidy. They won't bother you."

He touched her shoulder, and she flinched. "Cass, look at me." She focused on him. He was searching her eyes. "You're going to be fine. We'll protect you."

She nodded, and Jasper let out a pent-up sigh, pulling her into an embrace. Cassidy clutched his shoulders, and then gently pushed him away, goosebumps nettling her skin.

She tried to calm her pounding heart. She had escaped. She was safe now. She breathed in and out, trying to remain in the present. The nightmare was over. Everything was going to be alright. *Except for Anna and Maria ...*

Jasper lifted his fingers to touch her cheek. "You're hurt," he said.

"I'm fine," she said, not wanting to talk about it. She turned her face away from his touch and glanced again at the seven men in the pavilion, and more prickles of apprehension stung her skin.

"Come inside so we can talk," Jasper said, stepping aside and holding open the door flap to his tent.

She reluctantly followed him inside, and they stood facing one another in the shadowed space. He took her hands, and they trembled in his large upturned palms like two frightened birds. He gently kissed the bruised, scabbed skin of each wrist. He raised his head and carefully kissed her tender cheek, and then kissed her forehead. Cupping the back of her head in one of his large hands, he drew her close.

She clamped her jaws together and set her chin on his shoulder as he wrapped his arms around her.

"Stars, Cassidy, I was worried like hell." His words came to her as a vibration through his chest. "I didn't know what happened to you. I thought ..." His words broke off. "I was afraid they had taken you ... *off-world.*"

She shivered, and he tightened his hug. She squirmed out of his arms and finally spoke, trying to sound calm. "Well, they were going to. Probably."

He furrowed his brow at her. "Will you stay with me tonight?" he asked. His gaze was steady, his question lingering in the air.

She folded her arms across her chest. She had promised to come to his tent weeks ago—a lifetime ago. She whispered a reply, "I'm in no condition to ..."

"I know that," he said. "We'll just sleep. Pretend like we're camping in the mountains back home. I'll hold you."

She managed a tremulous smile. "I'm sorry. I can't."

His face fell, and she diverted her gaze, her eyes wandering across the cluttered tent. The glint of a small metal vial on a shelf caught her attention. She stepped over to it and unscrewed the top. The dropper was filled with green liquid. She sniffed it, and the familiar pungent aroma made her shiver.

"Cassidy, what are you doing?" Jasper asked as he came up behind her.

She tilted her head back and emptied the dropper into her mouth. The bittersweet liquid landed on her tongue with its welcome bite.

"Cassie, what the hell?" Jasper demanded, grabbing the vial from her hand and staring at the empty dropper. "Did you just take that whole thing?"

She nodded and met his eyes. "Yeah," she said, the liquid burning down her throat and into her stomach.

"You're only supposed to take two drops," he said, screwing the cap on and frowning at her worriedly. "Why did you ...?"

"What are you doing with this stuff?" she interrupted, placing her hands on her hips. "It's a drug."

"I know it's a drug," he said. "I sell it."

"You *sell* it?"

"Yeah, it's my main product."

"Your main product?" she asked with disgust.

"Yeah. My main money-maker. Well, one of them."

"You know what this does, don't you?" she asked, pointing her finger at him and holding it an inch away from his nose. "It makes everything feel good, and it makes you sick. And addicted. And it makes you let anyone do whatever they want to you, just to get more of it."

She glowered at him, fire burning in her eyes, and his mouth dropped open.

"He fed it to you?" he asked.

"Yes. Me and the other girls. I hope you didn't sell it to him," she said, narrowing her eyes as his gaze shifted away from hers.

"I don't know who ... how ... it was ... where," Jasper said.

"Is this the stuff Berkeley said you cornered the market with?" she asked, sorrow and anger mixing in her belly. She was in the short window of clarity between when the drug sharpened her senses and when she would get ill, and then everything around her would soften into a tranquil numbness.

"No. Yes. I'm the main supplier. But others resell it, I'm sure. I don't know who this man was who kidnapped you. I swear."

"But you still sell this ... narcotic, or whatever it is. It's evil, Jasper. Balthazar used it to control us." Her voice was rising. "Give me that," she said, snatching the vial from his hand. "How much more of this do you have?"

"Some," he said, lifting his shoulders in a guilty shrug.

"Get rid of it," she said, sneering at him.

"I can't get rid of it," he said, wresting it out of her hand and closing his fist around the vial. "It's worth too much. We need to eat."

"I'll buy it off you," she said, frantic desperation taking hold of her. Her mind ping-ponged between opposing thoughts. She would dump it all out. She would keep it all for herself. She hated it. She needed it.

"It's too expensive, Cassidy, be reasonable."

"I'm rich," she said. "Where's the rest?" She turned and started pushing aside the junk on his shelves, looking for more vials.

"Stop it, Cassidy," Jasper said, grabbing her arm.

"What's going on?" Torr's voice cut through their argument.

Torr pushed through the canvas door flaps and stepped into the tent. "What's wrong? Stop it," Torr barked, pulling Jasper away from Cassidy.

"Jasper's a drug dealer," she said, sweeping things off the shelves and onto the floor.

"Torr, make her stop," Jasper said as Cassidy began emptying a crate.

She dumped its contents onto the floor, and then went to the next crate, pulling out random items and tossing them onto the floor as Torr and Jasper argued. At the bottom of the crate she found a row of silver vials.

"Aha," she said, standing up. "Is this all of them?"

Jasper's face was red, and Torr's arms were wrapped around his shoulders, restraining him. Jasper frowned and sighed. "Yes. I'm almost out. I need to get more."

"Over my dead body," she said, pulling out the vials and lining them up on the shelf. "I need to get my pack," she said to her brother. "Hold him back for another minute."

"No, Cassidy," Torr said, joining Jasper's objections.

Not trusting Jasper, she shoved the vials into her sweatshirt pocket and ran barefooted to her tent. Jasper and Torr were right behind her.

"What is that stuff?" Torr asked, looking between Cassidy and Jasper as she stuffed the vials into her green daypack.

She felt amazing. Warmth permeated every cell of her body, and now she had an unlimited stash of the good stuff. She smiled at her brother and best friend. "I love you guys," she said.

Jasper rolled his eyes and turned to Torr. "She's high. Next, she will get sick. Very sick. She took a lot. Then she will pass out."

Jasper left the tent and returned with a large cooking pot, set it next to Cassidy, then sat on Torr's blanket next to him. They both watched as she sat on her sleeping bag and rocked back and forth, humming that elusive tune from the stars.

"I miss Anna and Maria," she said. "I hope they don't hate me. But I love them. I wish we had a bathtub here. Jasper, do you think we could get a bathtub?"

Jasper and Torr sat silently as the minutes floated by and she thought of home and her parents, and the angel, Avala, wondering if the Turyan goddess was watching her right now. And then she wondered if Balthazar missed her, or if he hated her and wanted to kill her. She really did not care either way. He could go fuck himself. And then she grabbed the pot and threw up a stream of dark green liquid from way down deep in her gut.

12

TRAİNİNG

Torr stared up at the dreamcatcher turning slowly overhead. Night gong had rung hours ago, but he was wide awake. Cassidy was breathing evenly across the tent. He tossed and turned until he finally slipped into a fitful sleep. Dreams came and went—flashes of Earth, and endless rambles around the labyrinth of Peary Dome.

The snap and hiss of a can being opened lifted Torr's gaze. Edgemont sat across the table in the bunker at Miramar, slurping beer from a can. The can was shiny blue and red, with the image of a curling ocean wave against a sunset sky. In golden script it read, *California Special Brew.*

"What do you want?" Torr asked. "I thought I'd seen the last of you."

Edgemont threw back his head and laughed. "Very funny, Torrance. You can't get rid of me that easily."

Torr glared at him.

"I'm not any less dead," Edgemont said. "So why should you see any less of me? Did you think the passage of time would bring me back, or settle my soul gently into a peaceful grave? You murdered me."

"It was war," Torr said, pulling back the metal tab and cracking open his beer. He took a swig of the cold, frothy ale.

"Doesn't matter. You still killed me."

"It was self-defense. You were going to kill me."

"True," Edgemont said, grinning at him. The Teg leaned back in his chair and clomped his feet up onto the tabletop, crossing one ankle over the other. Small gray pebbles were wedged between the boot's big black treads. Edgemont's snide voice drilled into Torr's head. "But I'm still dead, and you're a dreamer. A necromancer, so it seems. And so you're stuck with me."

Edgemont's mocking laughter grated on Torr's nerves. Torr took another swig of beer. It was sharp and bitter in the back of his throat. He looked up and asked, "So then what're you gonna do for me? Seeing as you insist on tormenting me."

"What do you *want* me to do for you?" the Teg asked, amused.

"How can I fix my sister?" Torr asked.

A grim shadow darkened the Teg's eyes. "You can't fix her, bro. Any more than you can bring me back to life. She will move forward in a new configuration. She will heal, in her own way, but you will never get your old sister back."

The beer was sour in Torr's belly and he took another gulp, letting the cold brew bite back his warm tears.

"But watch out," the Teg said, his eyes glinting again. "She's angry, and she could take it out on any man."

"Oh, I know," Torr said. "Believe me, I know."

Torr rolled over and opened his eyes. Light filtered in through the yellowed canvas walls, illuminating a myriad of dust motes floating in the air. He lifted his wrist and glanced at his watch. It was four in the morning. His internal clock was all messed up now, after playing nursemaid to Cassidy for three nights in a row and napping in the afternoons. That Greenwash drug had nasty side effects, and Jasper was a shithead for dealing it.

Torr sat up and caught sight of himself in Jasper's mirror propped up against the wall, and grabbed Grandma Leann's hand mirror from the floor by his bed. He thought of his mother and how she had healed his skull. The medics had called him back to the infirmary and imaged his skull twice, not understanding how he had healed so quickly and so completely.

"His mother's from Shasta," Jasper had told the medics.

The medics had stared at Torr and let him go without any further questions.

Torr gazed into the mirror, searching for Brianna. Cassidy had said she had learned to water scry during her captivity, and that using the crystal ball was even easier—but the small sphere was clutched in her hand as she slept. His mother said mirrors could be used for scrying, so he stared into the hand mirror, looking for her.

Nothing.

He crawled across the tent and tried the double-mirror trick, but saw nothing, not even Brother Wolf, who appeared in his mirrors intermittently and did not seem to like to be summoned for no reason.

Torr got back into bed and closed his eyes. Dreams had always been his bridge to the other side, so he let himself drift off.

It was dark and smelled of fertilizer. A wide fallow field was faintly lit by a half moon. Torr floated over the dry stubbly grass, looking for his mother. He peered at dark mounds, but they were only piles of rotting straw. A line of twisted junipers bordered the field and he floated over to them, trying to discern the shapes of knobby clumps on branches. Ravens. There were two of them. Large black birds, their feathers glistening in the moonlight, their beaks tucked under their wings, sleeping. One stirred and lifted its head, two shining coals staring at Torr. The other lifted its head, holding a luminescent, frost-green octahedron crystal in its black beak. The first raven leaned forward and lifted its wings with a loud squawk.

Torr's eyes popped open. His hands were shaking. He rolled up onto his knees, pressing his palms on the tent floor to ground himself. He took in a deep breath. *Two ravens.*

He reached for his vest and removed the pale-green fluorite crystal from the inside pocket. The raven had held this crystal in its mouth. Torr hefted it in his palm. The crystal was cool to the touch. He examined the eight triangular sides that made up the octahedron, the facets uniform in size and shape. He pushed at one side with his thumb, turning the crystal over and over in his palm. He sat in a cross-legged position and relaxed his eyes and let his mind rest, slipping into the half-sleep state he had become expert at during the long days on the shooting platform at Miramar staring at the shimmering Shaman's Shield.

His mind wandered in and out of murky memories and waking dreams. He was in a cool forest that smelled of pine sap. He scanned the forest floor and ranks of tall tree trunks, searching for the wolf whose howl wailed mournfully from the hillside.

He felt dizzy, and the scene shifted to a rocky plain. The rock was the color of blood-soaked clay. Long crevasses in the crimson ground spewed fountains of glowing lava, orange and blue and stinking of rotten eggs.

Suddenly he was at Miramar, gazing out over the hills, insects buzzing in the dry brush. He turned around, looking for the Shaman's Shield, but it was gone.

Then he was standing at an open window, looking out over a churning gray ocean. A brisk wind lashed at the water, sending white foam splashing along ridges of the choppy sea.

His hands leaning on the stone window frame were large, with long fingers. The skin was dark brown, and the nails were well polished over pink nail beds. Torr knew in his half-awake state that they were not his hands, but he held himself under, staying with the vision. He recognized those hands. Though they were not his, he knew them as if they were his own. He felt comfortable in these hands. Capable. Deeply troubled.

"We cannot find the path in one lifetime, Darius," a young dark-skinned woman said to him, her black eyes blazing. She was so familiar—like Cassidy, but not Cassidy. "The path of ages has been broken. We cannot just change the trajectory at will. It does not work like that." She was frowning fiercely at him, and he was filled with helpless remorse. As if it were all his fault, though he knew it was not. Or was it? His stubbornness. His arrogance. No, it was the priests' greed and power-hungry insanity that had blown the Star Globe to bits.

"Then what do we do?" he asked, his deep voice soft and scared.

"Stop feeling sorry for yourself," his sister snapped at him. "We must plan for the next time. Prepare the way for those who will come after us. They will need help."

Torr looked down at his hands. White skin. Dirty fingernails. The pale green crystal sat in his palm. Light filtered in through the yellowed canvas. Cassidy's breathing was soft and steady. He took a deep breath and lay down, afraid of what more his dreams had in store for him.

———————————)———————————

It was mid-afternoon. The Fen was quiet, aside from the gentle strumming of a guitar, which drifted pleasantly through the tent wall. Torr sat on his sleeping bag while Cassidy took a nap. He searched through his mother's red herb notebook for something to help his sister, but all the writing was incomprehensible, as it had been the last time he had checked. The aftereffects of the narcotic were harsh and lingering—abdominal cramps, nausea and diarrhea, headaches, debilitating depression, fits of rage. He went outside and caught Jasper coming out of his tent.

"What's that herb you got from Cassidy to treat addictions?" Torr asked.

"What herb?" Jasper asked. "Oh. Douleia? I sold it."

"You sold it? Why?"

"Sold it to a far side lord who used to buy Greenwash from me. He wanted to kick the habit, so I sold him the bottle of Douleia instead, for twice the price of a vial of Greenwash." A smile bent across Jasper's face.

"Don't you think you needed that for yourself?" Torr asked.

Jasper shrugged. "Nah. I'm not addicted."

Torr shook his head and went back into his tent. He carefully dumped the contents of Cassidy's herb bag onto his blankets and sorted through the collection of small bottles, searching for Douleia. There was none. He frowned and searched the dried herbs. No Douleia. He exhaled with exasperation and returned the herbs to her bag, then gazed at his sister, who was twitching in her sleep.

Torr let his mind wander to a place he rarely allowed his thoughts to go. *Reina and Jenna.* Had they managed to escape into the desert wilderness east of LA? More likely they were in a work camp. Or a breeding center. Torr swallowed. What was a breeding center, anyway? A euphemism for a rape camp, to service Teg soldiers? He brushed at his eyes and took in a deep, shuddering breath.

———————)———————

Torr left Cassidy in the care of Jasper and the Fensters while he went to the spaceport with the Boyer brothers and Sky and Thunder. He asked his friends to wait outside.

"Is Rodney here?" he asked the customs guards, peering through the dim space.

"I'll get him," one of the guards said, and spoke into his radio.

A few minutes later, Rodney strode across the hangar and stood in front of Torr, towering above him by a head.

"How's your sister?" he asked.

Torr shrugged. "She's okay. Recovering."

Rodney nodded. "She's lucky."

"Yeah, I guess," Torr said, and stepped with Rodney into the

shadows. "Listen. Your guys are the only armed men in the camp. Do
you think you could help us raid the compound of the guy who held
Cassidy? Or at least lend us some weapons?"

Rodney crossed his arms and gazed down at Torr, his nostrils
flaring. "We're not guns for hire."

"I know that."

Rodney sighed out a breath. "Ramzy told me about it. The guy
who held her is associated with the Gandoops, apparently?"

Torr nodded. "We think so."

Rodney shook his head. "Even if I could break the rules, which I
can't, we can't go up against the Gandoops."

"Why not?" Torr asked.

Rodney pursed his lips, giving him a sardonic look.

"Well, okay," Torr said. "They're kinda powerful. I get that."

"Kinda?" Rodney laughed. "They've got our ass over a barrel." He
raised an eyebrow at Torr. "Look," Rodney said, placing a hand on Torr's
shoulder. "Think of the Gandoops as a powerful street gang. You don't
just go raiding their leader's house unless you're ready for an all-out war."

Torr frowned. "You do if they raped your sister," he said.

Rodney swallowed and dropped his hand. "Sorry," he said. "I wish
we could help." He gave Torr a curt nod, then walked across the floor,
leaving Torr by himself.

———————)———————

Torr and his friends crossed the camp to the auxiliary spaceport, and
Torr met Jericho in the green shipping container. Torr didn't even bother
going down the ladder, but asked Jericho if he could help Torr rescue the
other women held by Cassidy's captor, or at least lend Torr their guns.

Jericho gazed sadly at Torr. "Rodney warned me you might come
by," he said. "No can do. Boss's orders."

Torr considered begging or bribing, but he could tell by Jericho's
solid stance and grieving face that he had his final answer. Torr shook
the man's hand and left the container.

———————)———————

Torr had canceled training for the fourth day in a row, and he could
hear Ming-Long and Khaled grappling outside the tent. The Alphabet

Boys were cheering them on, with Febo's loud voice rising above the others in a raucous laugh.

Cassidy was sitting cross-legged on her sleeping bag, staring into the crystal ball cupped in her upturned palms on her lap. She was wearing the knee-length black gown she had arrived in, and her feet were bare. Her hair was tangled, and wisps of dark hair floated with static electricity.

She had gone into a lethargic stupor for twenty-four hours, as Jasper had predicted, waking now and then for a bite to eat, which just made her throw up or stagger to the porta-potties. The next day, she'd had a searing headache and snapped at him and Jasper whenever they'd tried to talk to her, and intermittently moaned and cried over Anna and Maria. The third day, she had alternated between weeping and yelling obscenities at no one in particular.

She refused to leave the tent, except to get her rations, plus an occasional visit to the porta-potties where she kept getting sick. Whenever they went out, she wore her tight blue jeans and gray sweatshirt, and an old pair of Hawk's work boots, which were coming apart at the soles and were secured by duct tape. She would gaze around at the curious men with a threatening leer, and then hunch her shoulders and stare forward.

Torr, whichever Fensters were available, plus the ubiquitous Alphabet Boys accompanied her wherever she went, but she would not talk to the seven newcomers.

Cassidy was angry at Torr for getting rid of Jasper's supply of Greenwash. At the same time, she shot scathing remarks at Jasper for dealing it.

Torr had taken the vials from Cassidy's pack the first day when she was passed out. Jasper had grudgingly accepted a Solidi as payment for all ten vials. It was market rate, but Jasper complained that his customers would be upset with him for running out—it wasn't like he could just hop over to Muria to get more. And even if he could afford passage there, the Greenwash was hard to find—small puddles of the stuff hidden in inaccessible caves.

Torr didn't care about Jasper's problems and had secretly dumped the green liquid into a porta-potty, draining the small vials onto the mound of shit and then pissing all over it. He had rinsed the vials and droppers with the Fen's wastewater and dumped the water onto the dusty alleyway behind the kitchen tents, where it had soaked into the dry dust immediately, leaving nothing but a dark stain. He'd then returned the clean vials to a grumpy Jasper.

It was done, and four days later, she seemed to have mostly shed the effects of the drug—aside from an infrequent tremor or sprint to the por-ta-potties. Tatsuya had prepared her an herbal tea and checked several times a day to make sure she was drinking it. A half-filled cup sat at her side.

"Balthazar and Ridge Gandoop and one of Balthazar's guards are gone all day, every day," she said, looking up at him. "That leaves only three guards in the house. We could break in and rescue Anna and Maria."

Torr suppressed a sigh and considered her implicit request. "What's their security like?" he asked. "Do they have cameras? Weapons?"

Her face tightened and she nodded. "There's a camera in the hangar. I know that much. And they carry handguns."

"Are the handguns black?" he asked. "Kind of large, and shiny?"

"Yes," she said.

"Lectros," Torr said, his skin prickling. "Tegs carry them."

"They're not Tegs, I don't think ...," she said, her voice trailing off and her complexion blanching.

"They could have bought Lectros on the black market, I suppose," Torr said. "But if Tegs are at Gandoop, and Ridge Gandoop lives at that same compound, then maybe that guy who kept you was a Teg."

Torr was sorry he'd stated that possibility out loud as his sister's breathing grew shallow and erratic.

"I'm sorry," he said.

Her eyes were big and watery. "It's just ...," she said weakly. "If he was a Teg, I can't even ..."

Tears welled up in her eyes, spilling onto her cheeks. Torr moved to her side and put his arm around her shoulders. "I'm sorry, Cassidy. He's probably not a Teg."

"He probably is," she said through her tears. "He's that horrible, and cruel, and strong. We'll never get Anna and Maria out."

She lowered her face into her hands and sobbed. He patted her back. "We can find a way," he said.

She sniffed and wiped her eyes. "I don't know how," she said. "We can't get inside the place. And we don't have enough weapons. Do you think Jasper could get some guns? You guys are all soldiers," she said, gesturing towards the Fen yard.

"He said he can't," Torr said. "And like I told you, I already asked Rodney and Jericho. But, maybe, somehow ..."

They sat in silence for a time. Cassidy resumed gazing into the crystal ball, and Torr returned to his side of the tent.

"Cassidy," Torr said. She ignored him and continued staring into the crystal. "Cass, we're going to resume training tomorrow, in the yard at the other side of the dome. You'll need to come with us."

Her lips pinched. "I'll stay here with the Fen guards," she said. "But not those weird seven alphabet-whatevers."

"No," Torr said. "We only leave two people here. You'll have to come with us. There are picnic tables and a shade tarp over there, and water. You can watch us practice."

Silence.

"Do you want to go to the road markets today and look for new boots?" he asked. She shook her head, and he sighed. "I'm going out, then," he said. "I'm going stir-crazy here. Berkeley, Tatsuya, and Hiroshi are in the back. Maybe you should go hang out with them."

She lifted one shoulder and dropped it again.

He didn't know what that meant. But she needed new shoes and another pair of pants besides tight blue jeans. She had arrived from her captivity in bare feet and nothing but the black silk negligee. Berkeley had offered her a pair of brand new cargo pants, but she had refused them, claiming that they were men's pants and she didn't want to wear them.

"Why do you keep wearing that gown?" Torr asked. "Doesn't it remind you of bad things?"

She looked up at him and sighed. "Torr. My sisters are still trapped in a closet waiting to be raped."

Torr swallowed. "I'm sorry," he said, returning her frown.

"Go out," she said, waving her hand at him and returning her attention to the crystal ball. "I'll be fine."

Torr got up and left the tent, grateful to be out in the open air. He gathered the Boyer brothers, Sky and Thunder, and Prince Faisal, and asked Durham Boyer to keep an eye on Cassidy. Durham was seated at a low table in front of his tent working on a radio and said that he would. Torr asked the same of Ming-Long and Khaled, who were circling each other on the ground tarp. They lifted their hands to their foreheads in a salute, and the seven Alphabet Boys nodded at him from their shaded pavilion.

Jasper had said he trusted the seven men with his life, and so Torr had decided he would too. What choice did he have? Jasper had hired them to guard Cassidy, and they were always around. Torr couldn't babysit her every second, and Jasper felt confident enough to leave her at the Fen with them while he left for hours at a time to conduct his trading business. Torr shook off feelings of claustrophobia and guilt, and he and his band set off to wander the roadside markets.

They scoured every collection of junk they came across, but there were no decent boots that would fit Cassidy. He bought himself a brand new pair of knee-high Teg combat boots. They were made of black leather and steel-gray Kevlar, with straps across the front, and were so comfortable he couldn't resist them. He kept his beat-up Gaia United boots for backup, hanging them by the laces from a back strap of his vest, and kept looking for something for Cassidy.

They wandered the circular grid aimlessly and turned onto Ring Road K. After two long curved blocks, the shoemakers' storefront tent came into view on their left, and Torr slowed his pace. Their camp had been reassembled, with the compound sealed off from the road by two tents and tarping. The two men in the sales tent recognized them, and their postures stiffened. The same three heavyset men stood up from plastic-crate seats in front of the neighboring tent and puffed up their chests.

Torr considered passing them by, but brand new shoes and boots were lined up neatly on the display table, and sandals filled the floor space underneath the table. Torr nodded warily at the three guards. The heavyset men stepped back, and Torr and his friends approached the sales tent.

"I need boots for my sister," Torr said, eyeing the selection and glancing up at the shoemakers standing behind the table.

The two men shifted nervously, and one of them said, "I heard she came back."

"Yeah," Torr said.

"Take whatever you want," the shoemaker said. "For free. Here," he said, picking up a pair of boots made of tent-canvas uppers and tire-rubber soles. "These should fit her."

Torr frowned. They were the same drab lunar desert gear all the men wore, and he was afraid Cassidy would reject them. He picked up a pair of red-and-yellow-beaded sandals.

"Sandals aren't practical," Raleigh said. "Except for maybe around the camp. Those paper things she's wearing are falling apart."

Torr nodded and set them aside.

The man offered him another pair of tent-canvas boots.

"She doesn't like men's stuff," Torr said, and the man set them back on the table, frowning.

The shoemaker turned to his companion and said, "Get those new boots from the back. The red ones."

The other man raised an eyebrow but left and returned with a pair of odd-looking boots. The foot uppers were soft black leather with long pointed turned-up toes, set atop truck-tire soles two-inches thick with large treads. The uppers around the calf area were a plush maroon velvet, with black lacing up the front. Torr examined them. They were lightweight, aside from the soles.

"Those are Delosian," one of the men said. "Except we re-soled them for the moon. The original soles were just one thin layer of leather. Look," he said, loosening the laces and showing Torr the inside of the boot. "They're lined in leather, and the insoles are shaved shearling or something similar," he said, handing the boot to Torr. The interiors of the velvet uppers were supple white leather, and the insoles were soft and fuzzy. "The calves are silk velvet, as far as we can tell," the shoemaker said. "They repel the dust. See how clean they are?"

Torr ran his hand over the soft velvet. Cassidy would love these, he reckoned, and she wouldn't even need socks. The boots were unusual, but practical. And definitely feminine, but with beefy soles to navigate the Peary Dome roads.

"Okay," Torr said, tucking the boots under his arm. "How much?"

"Free. I told you," the shoemaker said, while the other man nodded.

Torr figured anything Delosian was very expensive, and the shoemakers had probably intended to find a private buyer who would pay a large sum for the off-world boots. But the men seemed to want to try and make amends.

"Here, take the sandals too, no problem," the first man said, pushing the beaded sandals towards him. "She can wear them around your camp."

"Thank you," Torr said, accepting the sandals and handing them and the boots to Hawk to carry.

"Sure, sure, no problem," the shoemaker said with a small bow.

Torr looked through the men's sandals and picked out a pair for himself and a second pair for Tatsuya, then tossed the shoemaker a tenth-gold bit.

The man tilted his head but accepted the coin, then cleared his throat and asked, "Do you know when they will release our cousin, Shiraz?"

"From jail?" Torr asked. "I have no idea."

"No one will talk to us," the man said. "People say you know Ramzy and Rodney. Shiraz's wife and child want to visit him, at least. And see if he's being fed."

Torr recognized the fear and helplessness in the man's eyes. The worry of not knowing the fate of a loved one.

"I'll see what I can find out," Torr said.

"Thank you," the man said, trying to smile. "I hope your sister is okay."

Torr met his eyes. "She's alive," he said darkly, and turned away, heading out over the dusty road. "No thanks to you," he muttered under his breath.

He stuffed the sandals into his cargo pants pockets and strode along the ring road with his friends, lost in thought. Cassidy's condition worried him. Her body was healing, but she was retreating further and further into her shell, and her emotions were erratic. Torr wished their mother were there. She would know what to do. And he wished Caden were there to help him figure out how to save the moon from the Tegs, like the Murians wanted him to do.

"How can you talk to those guys?" Sky asked, interrupting his thoughts. "After what they did to you and your sister."

Torr shrugged. "The leader's in jail. They seem remorseful."

"They're thugs," Sky said, walking at his side.

Torr did not respond, and Sky did not press the issue.

Torr was upset at the shoemakers for their part in his sister's trauma, but as for them beating him up, he barely remembered that. Maybe the hole in his memory was from his head injury. Or maybe it was like his mother always said, that when a person was completely healed by a good healer, they would have no recollection of ever being sick. Torr wished his mother were there to heal Cassidy.

They walked in silence to Spoke Road Nine, where several vendors always had tarps out along the main thoroughfare between the spaceport and Center Ring. They sorted through mounds of clothing and other goods, looking for something Cassidy might like. The pickings were slim. They ended up with a red t-shirt, a short, yellow puffy vest

with a wide blue waistband, a few yards of black denim with an iridescent sheen that glistened a silvery purple in the right light, and a box
of random fabric and leather scraps.

Roanoke found a box of surgical tubing, which the Boyer brothers purchased to make slingshots with. They combed the junk bins for anything
with a Y shape that they could use for a slingshot handle and collected an
assortment of kitchen implements and other tools that might work.

They ended up at the foot of Spoke Road Nine across from the
spaceport and wandered over to the chain-link fence enclosure of the
traders pen and looked for Jasper. He was standing in the row where
he had his own half-container and spotted them.

"Hey, what'cha got?" Jasper asked, walking over and pushing back
his overgrown auburn hair.

They held up their purchases, and Jasper frowned.

"Is she still wearing that black nightgown thing?" Jasper asked Torr,
hanging onto the fencing that stood between them.

"Yes. It makes me ill every time I look at it," Torr said.

"Me too," Jasper said. "You know, I've been thinking ... I haven't
been able to sell that Delosian dress. The long purple one with the gold
beads. I might as well give it to her."

Torr cocked his eyebrow. "That thing looks like it's for a princess."

"A priestess more like. From the Teller clan. You see Teller Seers
wearing dresses like that on the streets of Delos City sometimes.
Cassidy liked it, remember?"

"Yes, I remember," Torr said.

"She can have it," Jasper said. "It might cheer her up. I'll meet you
back at the Fen later."

When they got back to the Fen, to Torr's relief, Cassidy liked
their choices, especially the boots. She was wearing her jeans and her
Delosian leather jerkin and went with Torr to Berkeley's sewing station,
where they showed him the black iridescent fabric.

"What do you want me to make with this?" Berkeley asked, unfolding it. "This is high-quality stuff. Where'd you find it?"

Torr told him, and Berkeley looked at Cassidy. "I'm good at making
cargo pants," Berkeley said. "But you said you didn't want to wear
them anymore."

Cassidy shrugged. "Maybe if they were tighter. Like girls' pants. And I still need lots of pockets."

"I can do that," Berkeley said. "It's got a nice stretch to it," he said, tugging at the fabric.

Torr fetched the box of scraps, and Cassidy and Berkeley looked through them.

"Can we make something with these?" Cassidy asked, fishing out silver and gold metallic fabric, glossy black patent leather, a roll of white neoprene, wide strips of carbon fiber fabric, and lengths of midnight blue and dark purple satin. "Like armor? You know, with overlapping scales."

Torr made a face, but Berkeley smiled and nodded as though it were a good idea. "We can figure something out," he said, and Torr silently blessed the man. Berkeley and Cassidy went into the workshop tent and began laying out fabric scraps on the table.

Torr took leather scraps from the box for slingshot pockets, and then brought the sandals and red t-shirt to Tatsuya. The elderly man thanked him profusely for the sandals and agreed to paint a dragon on the t-shirt to replace the one she had lost—the one item she had mentioned missing. Then Torr went into the main Fen courtyard where his friends and the Alphabet Boys were seated in the pavilion, making slingshots. He joined them, and Roanoke showed him how to assemble his. They were easy to make, and soon they were testing them with moon rocks against the side of the half-container.

Jasper arrived later that day and handed Cassidy a bundle wrapped in tent canvas.

Her face scrunched up with curiosity, then brightened as she held up the purple gown. She immediately changed into it and came out of the tent to model it. It hugged her body and flared out below her hips, draping all the way to the ground and just clearing the dust with her new platform boots on. The gown sparkled with tiny gold beads, casting shards of light as she turned. The floor-length dress with her pointy Delosian boots peeking out from under the hem made Torr imagine she really was a Delosian priestess and they were in Delos City mingling with the Teller clan, searching for the pathway to the Star People. She wore a genuine smile for the first time since she'd returned, and although her face was still a patchwork of mottled bruises, she looked almost like herself again.

13

THE PLAN

Ridge stretched out on his bed and held up his handscreen, reviewing the video of Balty's captive escaping from the house's hangar. Her face was swollen and bruised, and Ridge felt a familiar, gnawing guilt. He watched as she crept furtively to the hangar's back wall and snatched a small backpack from the shelf. Then she fumbled with the sensor to open Balty's speedster's wing door, hesitated for a moment, and then climbed into the pilot's seat. The wing door slowly lowered and sealed her inside.

The craft rose into hover mode while the landing gear folded up into the wheel wells. He cringed as she nearly crashed the speedster into the wall, but she stopped just in time, and with a few fits and starts pivoted and glided into the decompression chamber. He had to admire her courage—defying the sadistic madman and stealing his craft. He chuckled as the decompression chamber doors closed.

Ridge turned off the handscreen and stared up at the rainbow skylight to think. There was no way in Algol's hell he was returning her to Balty. But he did want the deeds to his land. The boy he wasn't so worried about, but he needed a plan to secure both deeds while at the same time keeping the girl out of the hands of Balty and the Nommos.

He considered various options. She was not safe wandering the roads of Peary Dome. Sooner or later, Balty would go after her if Ridge did not bring her to him. Balty was a vengeful man, and in his twisted logic she had wronged him. Balty would never rest until he got payback.

There was only one place Ridge could think of on the moon where she would be safe. He had avoided the women's cave his entire time on the moon, based on the reputation of its leader, Gabira ben Najam, and the cult-like fascination and muddled thoughts he had observed in men exiting her hidden den. But despite Gabira's wily ways—or perhaps because of them—she had managed to create a safe haven for females in Peary Dome. The only problem was that she had stopped accepting new girls ever since Ramzy had stuffed his own daughter down there. The cave was full, or so the story went.

Ridge held the Truthsayer above his chest and asked the dimly glowing pendant, "If Balty gets the girl, will he end up killing her?"

The blue crystal orb glowed brighter, and the pendulum slowly circled in a counterclockwise direction. *Yes.*

His heart quickened, and he asked, "Do the twins want to take back their land?"

Yes.

Ridge's concern for the girl shifted to possessiveness over his family's lunar empire.

Ridge sighed and asked, "Is Gabira's cave safe?"

The pendulum grew still, and the blue crystal suddenly brightened in a blinding flash.

Ridge squeezed his eyes shut, then tentatively opened them again— the crystal had dimmed, and blue dots danced before his eyes. With a trembling hand, he returned the amulet to its box and quickly closed the lid.

———————)———————

Ridge stopped by the Gandoop warehouse to get a load of food and other goods to bribe his way into the women's underground community. He directed workers to load an assortment of perishables and sacks of grains. He knew the matriarch had a thing for gold, so while the men were loading the ship with food, he rummaged through the warehouse's hard goods for something suitable.

He found the section filled with jewelry and trinkets and came upon a small gold statue of a peacock, with tiny, multi-colored gems decorating the tail feathers. It was delicate and beautiful, and fit easily in the palm of his hand. Next, he decided on a small pineapple paperweight. It was solid gold and heavy in his hand, with spiky leaves made with layers of gold leaf. He kept looking, and found a box filled with smaller boxes, each holding a piece of twenty-four-carat gold jewelry. He didn't know what a woman might like, so he took six random boxes and stuffed them into a burlap sack with the statuettes. He knew Gabira had two daughters, so he searched for a third statuette and finally found a small solid gold prowling panther, with dark green emeralds for eyes and covered head to tail with small black diamonds. On his way out of the jewelry aisle, he detected a wooden crate on the floor with Delosian runes. He stopped and stared. The buck sigil of Antler Kralj stared back at him. He wondered if it was part of the same haul the Guild trader, Jaz, had procured.

Ridge pried the lid off with a crowbar and sorted through a mound of Delosian ruffled shirts and leather goods and found a stash of smaller boxes on the bottom. He looked through them all, wondering if he might find another treasure like the Truthsayer. Though every piece was beautiful, he found nothing unusual. He chose a necklace and a gem-laden ring he thought Gabira might like and stuffed them in his sack.

Out on the hangar floor, he picked through the food being loaded into the old cow and filled a burlap sack with an assortment of fresh produce that had just arrived from Moffett Field: plums, pears, peaches, apricots, cucumbers, peppers. Back in the warehouse, he found small sacks of shelled walnuts and roasted pistachio nutmeats and added those to his bag, along with some pink candy-coated wedding almonds, dried dates, and dried apricots. Plastic bags of sugar candies caught his eye, and he dropped several of those in as well. The aroma of roasted coffee beans pulled him over to a pile of bulging burlap sacks. He hoisted a fifty-pound bag onto his shoulder, returned to the hangar, and deposited the coffee and his bag of gifts on the co-pilot's chair. The workers filled the rest of the cockpit with a random assortment of items Ridge chose from the overflowing warehouse shelves: pickled herring, caviar, goose liver pate, canned hams, vodka, truffles, lemon curd, shortbread, vanilla extract, anise seed, sparkling mineral water. The cockpit was filled to the ceiling by the time he was ready to take off.

Ridge sped out into the glaring sunlight, rose up out of the massive crater, and headed south to Last Chance. When he landed at the new facility, Murphy smiled at him obsequiously, grateful to Ridge for transferring him there after Balty's Tegs had pushed him out of his logistics role at Gandoop Spaceport.

Murphy insisted on taking him on a tour of the recently completed work. Things were looking good. Construction had progressed quickly under Murphy's watchful eye. The residential wing's exterior walls and air systems were in place. That was the toughest part: using heavy equipment and sharp tools in a space suit. Ridge was proud no one had died at this job site.

One large room would soon house the kitchen and open living space. He had designed a picture window with automatic shutters in the southern wall facing the Black Mare. The shutters were open, the blaring sun shielded by the roof's overhang, which he had designed to block direct sunlight for much of the sunny period. The view was breathtakingly beautiful, in a minimalistic sort of way. The vast black lava sea stretched to the horizon, where it met the star-speckled sky. Floating in the heavens was Mother Earth, which was a thin crescent today. He had also installed one helical rainbow skylight in the ceiling, with his retracting roof design, bathing the room in a violet glow.

Three men stopped their work preparing for the kitchen fixtures and eyed Ridge warily, then shuffled silently along the side wall and disappeared into the hangar to stay out of their way. The second large space would be divided into four private quarters, each with its own bedroom, sitting room, and bathroom. The interior walls were framed and the plumbing and electrical had already been installed. He was satisfied with the progress, happy that Murphy had taken to his new role so well. The man was adaptable, a crucial trait on the moon.

Ridge accomplished the freight transfer and his identity change from Ridge, the rich clean-cut inventor, to Jidna, the scummy outer rim mining lord, then flew the Korova from his lab's hangar and carved a wide arc northward.

A tall antenna tower appeared on a crater rim below him and fell away as he sped along, one of several relay stations various mining lords had erected to enable radio communication between the mines and Peary Dome. Ridge had installed several between Peary and Gandoop himself, taking advantage of the high peaks of the large craters, and another series between Gandoop and Last Chance, and more between Last Chance and Peary. With no atmosphere to refract the radio signals, line of sight was required. A lunar grid of communication satellites had supposedly been part of the multi-national consortium's plan after Peary Dome was completed, but fell by the wayside when Metolius and Tegea disrupted the world order. Not only that, the Global Alliance jammed most signals that had connected Earth to the moon. One day, Ridge would venture into the business of lunar satellite communications himself.

After going in and out of high gear, Jidna approached Peary Dome, where it perched atop the Peaks of Eternal Light. Peary Crater was nearly as large as Anaximenes, but was situated on the north pole, granting it the unique qualities of perpetual light on the mountainous rim and perpetual darkness in its depths. A large area below the southeastern peaks was always out of reach of the sun and held ice lakes that Peary Dome mined for water. The rest of the crater floor, as well as the entire area surrounding the north pole, were dotted with several large impact craters filled with impenetrable darkness, holding additional reservoirs of ice that Peary Dome had claimed. The Gandoop family had purchased ice mining rights in one of the craters at the edge of the polar region, Hermite, which they sub-leased to a couple of smaller mines.

A security vehicle intercepted his, surfacing from the shadows. Jidna flew slowly towards the mouth of the landing tunnel with the security cruiser on his tail.

He radioed Peary Control. *"Last Chance 2224, outer rim, requesting entry for trading business. Traders Guild member 1859. Out."*

A voice blared into his cockpit. *"Bay Two, Last Chance."*

Jidna angled for the tunnel, and the cruiser left him and shot off over the dome. Jidna sat inside the tunnel until the middle-sized airlock opened for him. After passing through the dual compression chambers, he glided into the reception area and showed his Traders Guild patch to two of Rodney's guards, who were shouldering assault rifles. They directed him to a parking spot at the side of the cavernous structure.

The scale of this facility still made Ridge jealous. It dwarfed Gandoop by comparison. He sighed. It was okay, Gandoop Spaceport served its purpose and provided the Gandoops a lucrative income. Besides, he noted with a twinge of guilt-laced satisfaction, there were relatively few freighters here today; there were more at Gandoop. Jidna climbed out of the cockpit and jumped down onto the hard floor. The mood of the guards was severe, and they roughed him up a bit during an unusually thorough weapons search that made him want to knee the guards in the groin. A tall steely man in a navy blue flight suit strode with an uneven gait across the floor. The tall man looked familiar, but Jidna couldn't place him. He approached, jerking his head to glance over his shoulder repeatedly. His name patch read, "KUJO."

"Who are you?" Kujo demanded.

"Jidna," he said shortly. Kujo's eyes were a bit too close together, making him look mean and a bit crazy. "I've got a cargo hold filled with food," Jidna said. "Are you a trader?"

The man wore a Peary Pilots patch, not a Traders Guild patch. Kujo frowned and took his radio from his belt, stepping away to speak into it. Guild traders started straggling in and converged on Jidna's vessel. Ramzy showed up a short time later and stood with Kujo as the freight was sold and loaded onto transports.

Ramzy spoke abruptly to Jidna. "They got any potatoes at Gandoop?"

Jidna met Ramzy's eyes, which peered at him through black-rimmed glasses. Ramzy's skin was oily, and his rounded shoulders were tight with stress.

"I don't know," Jidna said. "I'll have to ask."

"And cucumbers, and tomatoes, chickpeas, and onions. Eggs. Olives. Olive oil. Tuna." Ramzy spoke as if he were placing an order. "Oh, and peanuts, and salt. And parsley, or better yet, cilantro."

Jidna glared at Ramzy. "What do I look like, the commissary?"

Ramzy glared back.

Jidna glanced at the traders, who were standing to the side, listening. "You guys want any of that stuff?" Jidna asked, to keep up his pretense of not selling directly to Peary.

The traders vied for his attention. They all wanted all of it.

Jidna turned to Ramzy and said, "I'll see what I can do."

"How soon?" Ramzy asked.

"As soon as I can get back in there," he said. "They're not always friendly. I can't risk annoying them."

Ramzy's lips puckered, then he blew out his breath and marched off, with Kujo at his heels.

The traders were all still standing around, like dogs waiting for table scraps. They wanted to see what was in the cockpit. Jidna led them around to the side, followed by the armed guards.

Jidna opened the door and handed down the cargo. Fierce bidding ensued, and a fistfight broke out over the canned hams. The guards pulled the men apart. Evidently meat was hard to come by at Peary. Ridge had never thought about that. He wasn't overly fond of meat and didn't eat pork but had enjoyed a fine beef tenderloin steak the other night that one of Balty's bodyguards had prepared, and he ate chicken almost every day with his father and brother, which they ordered from the mess hall kitchen. He supposed he was spoiled. He'd have to bring more meat over for these poor bastards.

The coffee was the last to go and seemed almost as precious as the meat. Jidna cut open the sack, divvying up the dark aromatic beans into several smaller bags one of the traders produced. He sold all of them except four, which he held back for bribes.

When the cargo hold was empty and the traders had turned their attention to transporting their goods, Jidna took his burlap sack of bribes and gifts with him and locked the craft.

Jidna left the spaceport through a back door. Once outside in the open air, he breathed deeply, smelling the swampy odor of the moat. He'd always wondered how much oxygen the phytoplankton really produced. It was not a bad idea. He should have thought of it himself.

He put on his sunglasses and walked along the rear metal wall of the spaceport, stopping to sit on the ground for a moment, alone in the vacant zone between the spaceport wall and the glass dome. Leaning back against the building, he enjoyed the sunshine that always shone in Peary, and gazed out at the open sky through the glass triangles, reveling in the spaciousness. His mind wandered to the caves directly below him. He recalled one time when he was younger and his father had come here to meet Gabira—a woman from their part of the world, filled with spice and fire, as his father put it. His father had proposed marriage to the woman and offered his two sons for her two daughters.

Ali, as the eldest son, had accompanied Ishmar into the cave, while Ridge had stayed behind to guard their vehicle. Ridge had bristled at being left behind. He would have expected the family dynamics to have changed after he'd invented everything that made their lunar enterprise the success that it was. But when it came to some things, the old ingrained traditions still ruled. He was the youngest son, and he was not to forget it. And when it came to a wife, Ishmar expected to choose her for him, though he was taking his sweet time about it. Not that Ridge was waiting for him. Not that he really expected a wife to live with him on the harsh moon. What could he offer her for a life? Any reasonable woman would want to live on Delos. He had considered moving to the planet himself many times, but even with the vast wealth he would bring with him, he would forever be a second-class citizen there. His only route to integrating with the Delosians would be to serve his lifetime as an apprentice to a trader in the Monger House. If he did well, his children might be accepted into the House as junior members. Only those of Ilian descent could become senior Mongers. No, he preferred to be a big fish in a small pond.

He knew his father and brother shared similar sentiments, but Gabira had apparently made Ishmar lose his head, and he had proposed to her on the spot. According to Ali, Gabira had laughed in Ishmar's face. "Do you think I fled Earth and fought for my freedom in this hell-hole, in order to turn over my body and that of my daughters to men? Are you nuts?! I would rather kill myself, my daughters, and all the women with me." That had been her indelicate response to Ishmar's sincere offer and had turned Ridge off from wanting to meet her. He didn't need a man-hater in his life. He'd had more than his fill of that being raised by his grandmother.

Ridge pulled his lips tightly against his teeth, wishing his life had been different. That he could have been normal and had found that elusive thing called love. He wasn't sure exactly what that meant, but he knew he didn't have it. He hadn't had much luck with women, other than with Danny. The bad luck had started when he'd killed his mother while she was birthing him. He had been too much for her, he guessed. His head was too big or something. In any case, she had died, and he had never known her. He didn't know if Ishmar blamed Ridge for it. If so, he never acted like it, but Ridge knew that somewhere buried deep in his heart, Ishmar hated him.

Ridge's brief romantic and sexual forays during his infrequent trips to Delos and in the early, reckless days at the Peary brothels had not been particularly satisfying. The sex he liked, but as for any sort of relationship, he was too shy and socially awkward. Oh, he could be charming on the outside, but once he got past initial flirtation and down to true relating, he didn't know how to act. Even his interactions with Danny never lasted more than a couple of hours, nor ventured beyond superficial conversation. So, he supposed having his father choose a bride for him wouldn't be any worse than what he could manage for himself.

If they'd stayed on Earth, where women were plentiful and eager to marry, he might have found a wife, or two, like his father had. He dug into the dust with his heels, feeling sad all of a sudden. He didn't like feeling sad and hopped to his feet. Anger displaced the sadness. What right did the Tegs have to ruin Earth for everybody? And now Balty was bringing that curse to the moon.

While he was in Peary Dome, his feelings didn't matter. He was Jidna here, and no woman would fall in love with him. Jidna headed into camp to find Danny, taking the long way around so that he could pass by the greenhouses.

Jidna was happy simply to stretch his legs and walk under the glass dome. It felt like such freedom. He took his time, walking with long easy strides around the perimeter road in a counterclockwise direction. The Gandoops had considered building a glass dome on their property but had chosen instead to prioritize practical buildings for mining operations, and then the spaceport. A dome was an unnecessary luxury.

Balty had never set foot in here, so he didn't know what he was missing. Ridge should convince him to visit—then Balty would get his men to erect a small dome at Anaximenes. It should be a simple matter of buying the materials of the original dome from Ramzy. The current dome had been built around the much smaller one, which had then been disassembled. The glass triangles and titanium girders were stacked outside the dome near the landing tunnel, covered in canvas, waiting for Ramzy to do something with them. Or for Ridge to buy them.

He slowed as he approached the greenhouses, the glass buildings bursting with life. He walked along the sides and pressed his nose against the glass of the second house from the road. The tall twining soybean vines were thick and lush, dotted with clumps of purple flowers, and the faint sound of birdsong reached his ears. He felt heartsick and longed to step inside and breathe the moist air.

A greenhouse was another thing Ridge wanted to construct to bring a bit of Earth to Gandoop. He could turn the small glass dome into a giant terrarium—but Anaximenes had two weeks of constant light and two weeks of darkness. Maybe he should just build a grow room in one of the cubes. He had more than enough power. Plus, it would be easier to regulate light and darkness in an enclosed facility, unlike here where the black tarps that sat rolled up at the peaks of the houses were lowered nightly to plunge the plants into darkness. He sighed. So much to do, so little time. Especially with Balty ordering him around like a serf.

After a long moment, he pulled himself away, briefly stopping to peer into the standalone greenhouse where they grew edible greens and other vegetables. The stacked growing beds were unusually sparse, some filled with new seedlings, and others with bare brown soil. He could smell bread baking in the kitchens behind the vegetable greenhouse.

Jidna moved on along the perimeter road past Air and Water Control and the scrapyard. On the block across from Air and Water Control, someone had dragged scaffolding and ground tarps out into the vacant area and set up what looked like a makeshift gym, with punching bags, plywood figures with red bullseyes painted on them, large tires and coils of thick ropes, and a shaded table area. A pair of men were sparring on a ground tarp, and a few others were doing exercises and lifting tent poles, which had bags of sand tied to each end for weights. He watched for a minute, curious about this new development, then strode on.

Beyond Spoke Road Four, populating the outer ring of land, a large collection of shipping containers formed a random grid. These were long-term storage containers, or emergency supplies, or who-knows-what. This sector of the dome was built close to the edge of the crater's rim, which dropped off precipitously in a sheer cliff to the terrain far below. The entrance to the original spaceport, which was set into the side of the cliff in a lava tube, was hidden amongst the warren of containers somewhere, but its exact location was closely held, and Jidna had never bothered to bribe anyone to find out exactly where it was.

Jidna continued on. At Spoke Road Twelve, he stopped at his favorite installation: a large sundial, whose diameter was longer than a man was tall. The thick, flat bronze disk was set on a raised platform at hip-level, with a gyroscope set into its base that adjusted for the wobble of the moon. A long central spike cast a sharp shadow across the face. The disk was divided into twenty-nine days, which were further divided into twenty-four-hour increments, with even finer tick marks denoting ten-minute intervals. He counted and compared it to his watch. The hour was fourteen-thirty. The designers had conveniently calibrated the dial to Earth time, even though it was an artificial construct here. Jidna stood near the metal disk and watched time move. When twenty minutes had passed, he felt calm and refreshed, and moved on.

The two brothels were situated within a block of each other. He bypassed Schlitzer's and stopped first at Danny's place. Her real name was Danielita, but she preferred Danny. She was a sweet woman. Large and plump. Fat, really, but solid, with dreamy blue eyes and peach-colored skin. She hadn't always been fat. When he'd first met her, she had been merely voluptuous. Ridge had liked the way her breasts overflowed his hands and how her hips were soft beneath him. Now he liked her because he felt comfortable with her.

She made a good madam. Her girls adored her. Danny could size up a man in two seconds. If she didn't like him, she sent him on his way. Even if she allowed him in, if none of the available girls liked him, he had to leave. They could be pretty choosy, and he had seen many a man leave the tent sad and dejected. Ever since his Jidna persona had come into being, he'd only dared go with Danny, and she seemed fine with that. She took few customers these days, and he felt special that he was one of them. Today, however, he was not here for sex. She could tell with one look that he was not and did not seem particularly disappointed.

She kissed his cheek, smelling flowery with a hint of citrus. "Jidna, you're looking handsome," she said, gently patting his scruffy beard. She lied, of course, and they both knew it. They both preferred Ridge.

He gave her a grin. "Thank you, Danny."

They ducked under hanging canvas walls and entered the reception tent. Several smaller tents had been disassembled and sewn together to form a large, shaded pavilion. The walls hung halfway down, letting in air and daylight but providing some privacy. She led him to a seating area in the center of the canvas floor, which was scattered with small woven rugs and pillows that reminded him of the bazaars back home. He sat on a rug and leaned his elbow on a large pillow, folding his sunglasses and slipping them into a breast pocket. No girls were to be seen, but the tent was pleasant just to be in. Colorful fabric was draped from the tent ceiling, and misters had been installed at the corners, which sent a fine spray of scented moisture into the air every few minutes.

Two girls ducked under a canvas wall and came to sit by him. Small scrawny brown-haired things. He didn't recognize either of them. He smiled politely and returned his attention to Danny.

She read the expression on his face and shooed the girls away to sit across the tent beyond easy listening range.

"Do you have some cold tea? It's hot and dry in here," he said.

"Of course, dear. How rude of me not to offer."

They smiled at one another. He was happy she felt comfortable enough with him to dispense with formalities, and he was happy he could ask for what he wanted without worrying about being impolite.

He watched her swaying behind as she left the tent. He sat back on his pillows and recalled the days when Peary Dome had first been completed, not long after he'd arrived on the moon. Unlike the small dome, which had been stuffed to the gills with smelly construction workers, the new dome had offered up a whole new life. All of the settlers with small mining claims scattered across the moon had suddenly found a place to congregate. The dome had immediately turned into a thriving trading hub. Soon it became a destination for Earth adventurers who sought the new frontier or an escape from the marauding armies of Tegea and Metolius. It had been exciting as a young man to come to this wild boisterous place, where willing girls could be found and exotic treasures from other planets discovered and traded for enormous sums.

Ishmar had disapproved of the debauchery and rarely took his sons to the dome, but as Ridge and Ali got older they often snuck away on their own. It was during one of those visits that Ridge had lost his virginity to Danny. Ishmar had been worried when Ridge had disappeared for three days, and, despite his disapproving frown, had said nothing when the flush on Ridge's face told him all he needed to know. Back then, gangs and kidnappings, thievery, rape, even murder, were common. Gangs started fighting for control of the water supply, then the spaceport. Ridge had been here at this very brothel when a gang had taken over Air Control, holding everyone's lives hostage in a bid to control the spaceport. Ridge had bribed his way out of the dome before a series of battles ended the siege. But the struggle for power had continued. Things had gotten so bad, a militia of men banded together under a leader named Ramesh, calling themselves the "Free Men," and started the Peary uprising.

After several bloody confrontations, Ramesh and the Free Men kicked out the worst of the mining gangs and their leaders—the "mining barons," or "mining lords," as they preferred to call themselves. Ridge had always found that title to be a joke. Lords of piles of dust. How proud and noble.

The Free Men had succeeded in making this a peaceful little enclave. Ramesh had left for Muria, and Ramzy had taken the helm. A few years later, Rodney arrived with his gang, and somehow endeared himself to Ramzy, who made him second in command.

Danny returned with two glasses and handed him one. "How is the outer rim?" she asked as she settled down onto the pillows.

"Dull and dreary. It's much more pleasant here."

"I'm sure," she said.

"Heard there was some excitement at the camp a few days ago," he probed casually. "Some girl who went missing?"

Danny nodded. "A newcomer was kidnapped a few weeks back. She stole her captor's speedster and made her way back here. How about that?" she asked, batting her eyelashes.

Jidna laughed. "Wow. Good for her." He stroked his unkempt beard. "This kind of thing been happening often?" he asked. "Kidnappings and such? Reminds me of the old days."

She chuckled. "Yeah. Well, not as bad as that. But there's been more and more petty theft and assaults. Mostly over food. Rations are pretty meager these days. Some sort of food shipment shortage from Earth, or something. The gangs have been getting restless, roaming the roads and making trouble. Ramzy should do something."

"Ramzy won't do anything," Jidna predicted. "He's not like Ramesh—he doesn't like to fight."

"So I hear," Danny drawled. "A grumpy introvert is what I understand. An intellectual. Or a fool, I don't know which. But I've never met the man. He's never shown his face here."

Jidna nodded. Ramzy was not dumb, he was just fat and comfortable. "What about Rodney?" Jidna wondered.

"What, show his face, or do anything?" Danny laughed. "He's shown more than his face here plenty of times," she chuckled. "But will he do anything? I don't know. He could, but he defers to Ramzy for some reason I can't figure out."

"Respect?" Jidna ventured.

Danny's blue eyes gazed across the tent as the spritzers sprayed arcs of lavender mist into the air. She looked thoughtful. "Respect. Perhaps," she said.

"Do you know the girl?" he asked, keeping his voice bored, as though he were making idle chitchat.

"The kidnap victim? No," she said. Danny turned her eyes to him. They were clear like an Earthan sky. She smiled, knowing that men loved to look into her eyes. "I don't know who she is. But I hear she was beat up pretty badly. Nasty stuff, that."

She tipped her forehead to the two mousy girls who were sitting quietly on the other side of the tent. "Interested?" she asked softly.

"Not today," he replied. "Lovely, though." A twinge of hurt brushed against his heart. Did she really think he would choose one of those pubescent girls over her? Would she so casually hand him off to another? He sternly reminded himself that she was a madam and he was a client. He forced a smile and got up to leave. "Thanks for the tea, and the company."

She kissed his cheeks goodbye. "Always a pleasure," she murmured in his ear. "Don't be so serious next time," she scolded him. "I prefer you in my arms."

His heart warmed, and he gave her a brief hug, then dug out a gold Eagle. She pocketed it with a gracious nod.

"Oh, you might want some of this," he said, opening his burlap sack. "Take some fruit and sweets."

She selected a few plums, peaches, apricots, a white mesh sack of candy-coated wedding almonds, and a bag of coffee beans, and set them onto a brass tray that sat among the pillows. She gestured the girls over and handed them each a plum, and the young prostitutes hurried away across the tent to eat them, as though fruit were the most precious thing in the world. He needed to remember to bring Danny food every time, acknowledging to himself that he was a self-centered jerk.

"Do you need any jewelry?" he asked.

"No," she said, dropping her eyes.

She always wore the same gold necklace with a simple gold cross pendant, and small diamond stud earrings. He knew she was frugal and did not waste her hard-earned gold on baubles when she had a stable of girls to care for.

"Here," he said, sitting back down among the pillows with her. "Let's see what I have." He hadn't even looked inside all the boxes he had grabbed in the warehouse. He opened three of the smaller ones. They were all gold necklaces with glistening pendants. One was a gold crescent moon studded with diamonds. Another was a diamond and sapphire dragonfly. The third was a large diamond solitaire encircled with smaller diamonds.

He looked up. She was inspecting them all, trying to look like she didn't care. "Choose one," he said.

"Oh, no, Ridge, I couldn't," she said, her face flushing. "They are too expensive."

"Don't call me that, babe," he said, leaning over and kissing her gently on the lips.

"Oh. Sorry. Jidna," she said, meeting his eyes and blushing a darker red.

He was afraid he had just made a misstep. She was reading more into this gift than he had intended. To him, they were random trinkets he had grabbed as bribes for Gabira and her daughters. To Danny, his gesture was a sign of affection.

He stifled a sigh. It was too late now. "It's nothing," he said. "Whichever one you want." He gave her a strained smile.

She chose the crescent moon, and he helped her clasp it behind her neck. It glittered next to the cross, and her eyes regarded him fondly.

"Uh, well, I should get going," he said.

She smiled. "You work too hard."

"Yeah, I guess," he said, and stood to go. He gave her an awkward hug and left the tent, taking a deep breath of relief when he set foot onto the ring road.

———————)———————

Jidna put on his sunglasses against the glaring sun as he approached Schlitzer's viper's nest. He headed down the long dusty block, nodded to the guards, and poked his head under the half-rolled-up canvas wall of Schlitzer's double pavilion. This was not nearly so genteel an operation as Danny's brothel. Here, there were as many males as females for the buying, and other members of Schlitzer's gang who just hung out. The hookers who were working congregated at the bar or lounged on pillows in the large covered area. He could hear a baby wailing in the background.

Jidna stooped under the canvas wall and stepped into the tent. The pavilion was loud with laughter and the clinking of bottles. Schlitzer had constructed a proper bar, and Jidna sat on a stool, leaning his elbow on the polished wood. A woman brought him a cold beer in a twelve-ounce glass, and he took it, even though they charged a tenth-gold bit. Schlitzer probably made more gold on beer than on sex. Several other men and women were sitting at the bar, but they ignored him. The beer was cold and sharp with carbonation. He drank half the glass in one draught and belched happily.

A woman from across the tent wandered over to him. Wanda, her name was. Long blond hair, overlarge breasts. Small hips. A pug nose. Thirty years old, he would guess. He had been with her a few times, years ago, when he had been Ridge. She had been pleasant for a short visit. Good with her mouth and didn't expect him to carry on a conversation. He smiled, and she smiled back. She didn't recognize him as Ridge but knew Jidna carried gold. All the girls did, and they vied for his business, perplexed that he never went with any of them. He'd let them know he preferred Danny's place and only came here for the beer. But they still pursued him, as though they had a bet going for who could seduce him.

"Jidna," Wanda purred.

He bent and kissed the back of her hand. It smelled like she'd had sex not too long ago, and he met her eyes, concealing his revulsion. "Wanda. Good to see you. Will you sit with me? What's new with you?" he asked as she settled onto the stool next to him. He pretended to listen as she talked about herself and brothel gossip, his mind wandering. Eventually she got around to the kidnapping. She didn't know much more than Danny. He soon tired of her and handed her a tenth-gold bit for her troubles. "Where's Schlitzer?" he asked.

She directed him to a bartender who led him across an inner yard of the sprawling compound and gestured to a nondescript tent. Inside, Jidna found Schlitzer holding court with some of his gang. Eight men were squeezed around a plastic picnic table, listening to Schlitzer, who was sitting at the far end on an aluminum beer keg, telling an animated story.

"Yo," Schlitzer greeted Jidna, interrupting himself mid-sentence. Schlitzer had frizzy brown and gray hair that he kept in a short ponytail, a neatly trimmed goatee, and an amiable grin that made Jidna feel good. "Whatcha doin', Jidna? Got anything good for me?" Schlitzer asked, edging sideways behind the bench and giving him a bear hug.

Jidna smiled, grasping the man's shoulders in an awkward effort to return the embrace. He always felt grateful when Schlitzer paid attention to him. He thought everyone must feel that way about the man.

They stepped outside. "Let me see," Jidna said, searching in his burlap sack. He always brought something special for Schlitzer. The pimp had access to most anything he wanted, so it was a little game they played to see if Jidna could find something Schlitzer couldn't get a hold of, or better yet, had never heard of.

Schlitzer opened the small bundle. "Aha," Schlitzer said, his eyes flashing. "Dried mushrooms?" He looked at Jidna curiously.

"From Muria," Jidna said. "Ever had any?"

"No," Schlitzer said, pleased. "Are they for eating, or, you know, for feeling good?"

Jidna grinned happily. "First they'll make you vomit, then you'll feel good."

"Excellent," Schlitzer said, pocketing the mushrooms. "What do I owe you?"

Jidna motioned for him to walk with him through the maze of tents to another tent where Schlitzer conducted his private business. Once inside, Jidna sat in one of the lawn chairs arranged in a small circle and asked, "You hear about the girl who was kidnapped?"

"Yeah," Schlitzer said, casting him a sidelong glance. "I heard they took her to Gandoop to sell her to the Nommos, but they missed the ship and sold her to some local guy instead. She said she was taken to a place not far from Gandoop."

Jidna scowled inside but kept his expression neutral. Of course Schlitzer would know what had happened—he had ears everywhere. "I heard that too," Jidna said. He shook his head with regret.

Schlitzer's eyes narrowed. Schlitzer knew very well who he was, and Jidna knew the pimp was hinting that he had had something to do with it. Ridge suddenly felt ridiculous in his hairy disguise. He removed his sunglasses and dropped all pretense of Jidna. Notwithstanding his greasy hair and shabby clothes, the jocular, irreverent demeanor of his alter ego fell away, and Ridge's formal courtesy displayed itself in the level set of his eyes and the straightening of his spine.

"Do you know where she's staying?" Ridge asked bluntly.

"Yeah, why?" Schlitzer asked, leaning back in his lawn chair and pressing his long fingers together in a steeple as he inspected Ridge.

Ridge considered the pimp and spymaster in return. They had tacitly agreed years ago to trust one another. As two of the most powerful men on the moon, they each had access to knowledge and resources that the other often needed. Ridge had to give Schlitzer credit for building a little shadow empire within Peary Dome. The man was clever and resourceful, controlling the majority of the alcohol, drugs, and prostitution in the dome, and much of the secondary food market. He even had his own speedster parked at the spaceport.

"She has something I need," Ridge said. "And her brother, too."

Schlitzer pressed his palms together and rested his forefingers against his lips for a moment, then asked, "What do they have?"

Ridge weighed how much to tell him. He admitted to himself that he could not do this without Schlitzer's help.

"You know who I am," Ridge stated.

"Of course," the pimp said.

"How much can I trust you?" Ridge asked.

"The more you trust me, the more valuable I am to you. Think of me like a wife," Schlitzer said, grinning crookedly. "You trust me, I won't cheat on you. You assume the worst, and I'll find the first opportunity to prove you correct."

Ridge gave a wry chuckle. "Small comfort, that."

Schlitzer smiled widely. "I'm just sayin'."

"What are you saying?" Ridge asked flatly.

"I'm saying, trust is a mutual agreement, to benefit both parties. It can't be halfway."

Ridge thought on this and nodded slowly. "Okay," Ridge said. "They're carrying deeds to Anaximenes."

Schlitzer's eyes grew round as Ridge's words sank in. "Legitimate deeds? To all of Anaximenes?"

Ridge nodded, and Schlitzer's mouth turned into a half-smile, half-grimace, reflecting Ridge's mood exactly. He almost wanted to laugh. In fact he did laugh, but it came out more like a dry cough that turned into a hacking bark and ended with his head in his hands as Schlitzer laughed nervously with him. Ridge lifted his head and met Schlitzer's bloodshot eyes.

"I understand," Schlitzer said. "How can I help?"

Ridge relaxed back into his chair, confident again, and turned back into Jidna. He burped loudly and said, "See if you can find out where they keep the deeds. And show me where their tent is."

"How much is it worth to you?" Schlitzer asked, grinning.

"What, you want more than a bag of Murian mushrooms? Those are impossible to get. Plus, it's an easy assignment."

They haggled a bit and settled on an Eagle, and Jidna tossed him a gold coin.

"Consider it a down payment," Schlitzer said slyly. "Whatever you decide to do about your little problem, it could get tricky. You might need more help. In the meantime, I'll get one of my guys to show you their tent. They're staying at Jaz's camp. Do you know where that is?"

"Jaz's camp?" Jidna asked. "Hmmm. That's interesting. No, I don't."

"It's in the middle of the block between 7B and 8C. About a dozen tents with two picnic tables and a gray half-container. Can't miss it. Nine men in the camp, plus your twins make eleven. Plus six new guys who seem to be friends of the twins. And the Alphabet Boys have been hanging out there lately. Jaz, the twin brother Torr, and Jaz's sidekick with the dreads were beat up as well during the kidnapping. So now they're all kind of jumpy."

Jidna nodded. He was familiar with the band of seven men dubbed the Alphabet Boys. They made themselves available as a private security detail to off-world traders or paranoid mining lords who wanted to wander the dome. They had a reputation for being tough and honest. Schlitzer left and returned a few minutes later with a man he introduced as Maui. He had a medium build, light brown skin, dark hair, and wore dingy fatigues, same as half the inhabitants of the dome. They shook hands.

"Maui will take you around," Schlitzer said, and turned to the man. "Take Jidna by the duck blind and show him the ducks in the pond. Especially the new pair. He can hang out at the blind whenever he wants."

Maui's eyebrows knit together involuntarily, but the rest of his countenance said he wasn't particularly interested in Jidna, though that was a lie. Anyone joining Schlitzer's ranks was a potential threat in all sorts of ways—competition for Schlitzer's attention and the best jobs, or possible betrayal. Anyone could mess it up for everyone else. Jidna wondered if Maui knew he was a client and not one of Schlitzer's lackeys. It didn't matter—Maui would follow Schlitzer's orders without question.

Jidna walked out of the camp with Maui, making idle chitchat about the weather. Dry, hot, and dusty. The conversation soon ended, and they zigzagged across the tent city. They passed a ration trailer at a G ring road intersection, and Jidna slowed, watching the scene inside the open container. Jidna could hear a man complaining, "But we always get peanuts on Saturdays."

The ration guard replied, "We *used to*. Just like I used to suck my mama's tit. Now move along."

The man snapped his metal camp dish shut and stalked to the water container to fill his jug. Others who left the canteen were grumbling and looking into their dishes, as though counting the grains of rice and realizing they'd been shorted. They had been. Half their rations were sitting at Gandoop warehouse, overflowing the aisles—again. Jidna couldn't keep up with all the incoming shipments. Half the perishables were rotting and would end up in Gandoop's recycler. The other food was making its way slowly to the Cephean Federation of Planets, none of which needed more food, as far as he knew.

They made their way to Spoke Road Eight, and after crossing Ring Road C, cut into a densely populated block and navigated through clusters of tents. Maui stopped at a tent and held the door flap open for Jidna.

Inside were two lawn chairs, a small plastic crate being used as a table, and a bedroll on the floor against a side wall. Maui took a pair of binoculars from his cargo pants pocket, lay on his belly with his elbows propped up on the bedroll, and peered through the binoculars out a small mesh window.

After a minute, Maui moved aside and handed the binoculars to Jidna. Jidna took a turn looking through the window. Two lines of several tents stood back-to-back, creating a narrow field of view into another camp.

"You see that laundry line?" Maui asked.

"Yeah," Jidna said, adjusting the lenses.

"See the lawn chair facing this way?"

"Yes."

"The chair is in front of the third tent in a row. See it? That tent belongs to Prince Faisal the Clean. The first tent belongs to Jaz the Trader Man. And the second tent belongs to the chick who was kidnapped and her brother—Cassidy and Torr."

Jidna lowered the binoculars and looked over his shoulder at Maui, who had moved to a lawn chair. "Why are you watching them?" Jidna asked.

Maui shrugged. "Best you ask Schlitzer that."

Jidna nodded and lifted the binoculars again.

"She rarely comes out of her tent these days," Maui said. "Except to go to Center Ring for rations and to use the porta-potties."

Jidna wondered if the girl were in the tent right now—and wondered how well she was recovering from the damage Balty had inflicted on her. Probably not very well, he surmised, if she spent all day hiding in her tent.

A young man stepped across Jidna's line of sight and went into the second tent. A few moments later he re-emerged. Jidna recognized him as the twin brother, Torr, but he stepped out of view before Jidna could get a good look at him.

Jidna spent a couple of hours spying on the twins' tent. The girl never came out, but various men passed in and out of view along the well-traveled corridor that fronted the row of tents.

He would let the spymaster figure out where they stored the deeds, then they would figure out their next steps. Jidna returned to Schlitzer's camp and found the pimp at the bar, and they walked together out to the sundial.

"I need something else," Jidna said, gazing at Earth and then back at the tall man. "Can you get me into Gabira's cave?"

Schlitzer chuckled. "You can't get in yourself?"

"Never tried. I heard she won't let just anybody in there."

"True enough," Schlitzer said. "Especially outer rim mining lords. She hates them."

"So I hear."

"She might let a Gandoop in," Schlitzer said with a wink. "She likes rich men."

"Jidna's rich."

"Jidna's not very attractive."

They both burst out laughing.

"What are you trying to say?" Jidna asked. "Are you saying I smell?"

"A bit," Schlitzer teased. "It wouldn't kill you to wash your clothes once in a while. Or your hair. Even mining lords take showers. Or at least a sauna."

"I took a shower this morning."

Schlitzer guffawed. "You'd never know it. I'm just giving you shit. But yes, I can get you in to see Gabira. I need to check in at the Guild pen anyway."

They walked back to Schlitzer's camp and climbed into a small open jeep, which Schlitzer navigated through his compound. Their conversation died off as the jeep bounced over ruts and potholes, leaving a wake of dust behind them. Schlitzer turned onto an oiled ring road and headed towards the spaceport. Jidna hung onto the roll bar and gazed blankly at the tents lining the road.

Schlitzer parked his jeep at the far end of the spaceport. They walked down the narrow lane that ran along the north wall of the spaceport and stopped at the steel door that led down to Gabira's cloistered caves.

"Let me know if you find out more info," Jidna said, trying to pat down his beard. "If you get the chance, just nab the deeds. I'll make it worth your while. When you have something to report, radio me at the mine and say my order of raisins came in."

"Sure thing," Schlitzer said, and rapped on the door.

Schlitzer introduced Jidna to the guards, then bid him goodbye, with a warning not to fall into Gabira's trap. Schlitzer laughed good-naturedly as he said it, but Jidna was left with the uncomfortable feeling that he wasn't kidding.

———————)———————

Jidna dispensed bribes of gold and coffee beans and made it through the first layer of Gabira's guards. A third guard inside the airlock disappeared and returned a few minutes later, saying Gabira had agreed to see him, but then made him wait a full hour. The guard finally led him down a long set of stone stairs and along a straight lava tube tunnel with a series of wooden doors. They stopped at a large olivewood door with matching brass doorknocker and door handle in the form of a lunging dog. Jidna thanked the guard, who knocked on the door and trotted away as the door swung open.

The first thing Jidna thought of when he saw Gabira was Janjabar's wig shop. The portly woman had so much hair piled on top of her head that she could have been one of the mannequins in Janjabar's window. Jidna wanted to laugh but did not want to be rude. She also wore an entire jewelry store around her neck and forearms. He bowed stiffly and let her usher him into a gaudily decorated chamber, complete with wall and ceiling murals of an olive orchard painted on gold walls under a blue sky. Small rugs were stacked everywhere, serving as divans, backed by pillows against the walls, and the cloying smell of patchouli filled the room.

He sat down, and Gabira sat across from him on a pile of rugs and pillows. Her large almond-shaped eyes regarded his tangled hair and beard with open distaste. She reminded him of his grandmother, both in the way she sat upright with her chin wrinkled as if she were about to tell him to comb his hair but held her tongue because he was a man now, and in the way her slightly crossed eyes seared into his, making him feel faintly dizzy.

Ridge's grandmother had been good at bewitching people to make them do what she wanted, and this woman seemed to have the same power. It was hard to resist, but having grown up under his grandmother's manipulating influence, he had learned the warning signs and had some tricks of his own.

Softening his gaze, he used the center spot on his forehead to reach out to the same spot on Gabira's forehead, which his grandmother called the "true eye." He probed, reaching inside her forehead to see what he could discover about her intentions. She recoiled, her eyes widening, and then she scowled at him, her plum-colored lips tightening into a dried prune. He ignored her and kept probing. She had been trying to access his true eye with her energy tentacles, which had caused his dizziness, but he'd thus far deflected her attempts. She was still trying—and she was strong.

He held her off with part of his attention, while the rest of his energy focused on bypassing her defenses. She was clearly intent on controlling him, but he did not know why. Perhaps it was her way of defending against marauding men. Yes, that felt right—that was what she believed. She was paranoid, as well as power-hungry. He pressed into her true eye. Something was preventing him from going very deep, and the shield seemed to be coming from her heart area. He shifted his gaze and spotted a glimmering crystal shaft hanging from a gold necklace. An amulet of some sort.

Ridge's grandmother also had worn a power object, but it had been an obsidian ring. It had been impossible to get beyond his grandmother's stubbornness, and he'd sometimes suspected it was the ring's fault. But her knuckles had swollen with age and the ring could not come off, and so he was never able to test his theory. She had been buried with it still on her finger.

He relaxed and withdrew his probe. He'd learned with his grandmother that a simple friendly conversation could accomplish more than an endless power struggle. He smiled his charming grandson smile, and Gabira lowered her eyebrows. She knew he had yielded voluntarily. She withdrew her tentacles as well, having been unable to pierce the titanium-like shield he had instinctively envisioned in front of his own true eye. It was a new shield—he would never have thought of titanium as a child—but from all the titanium he produced these days, it was the first material that had come to mind.

He remembered the first time he had discovered how to use such a shield, when his grandmother had been trying to control him through his true eye at the dinner table. He had lifted his soup spoon and placed the rounded metal on his forehead, the concave side facing his grandmother's piercing eyes. Her controlling energy filaments had hit the spoon and deflected back at her. He knew it worked not only because he saw the energy curve back on itself, but because his grandmother had pushed up from her chair, waddled around the table, and wrenched the spoon from his hand. "Do not talk back to me, you little snot," she'd sputtered, which did not make any sense, but Rjidna knew what she meant as he'd covered his head to avoid the spoon as she beat him about the head with it.

Jidna met Gabira's eyes, so like his grandmother's in the way they tried to grab him and twist him to her will. "I have a niece coming to Peary," he said. "She'll need a place to stay." He held the woman's steely gaze. She knew he was lying.

"Bring her here and I'll see," she said shortly.

He smiled a thin smile. "She's not here yet. But as soon as she arrives, I'll bring her straight to you."

"Wonderful," she said flatly. "Is that all?"

"That's a relief," he said, brushing his hand through his bushy wig. "I'd heard you weren't taking any more women."

"That all depends," she said, her voice sharp with irritation.

"Depends on what?" he asked.

"On how easy they are to work with. Hopefully she's not like her *uncle.*"

He smiled graciously. "Not to worry. She's very … malleable."

Gabira glared at him coldly, and his eyes were drawn to her crystal shaft. It was spinning slowly on its chain as she leaned forward, elbows on her knees and her ample bosom spilling from her robe. Another large disc-shaped pendant hung next to it, set with glistening sapphires of various colors and tiny black diamonds.

He shifted his eyes back to the crystal shaft, pretending to be transfixed by it, amused that she was still trying to enchant him. The crystal, in addition to acting as a shield, exuded some sort of somnolent effect, a narcotic-like, dreamy bewitchment that tugged at the edges of his mind, trying to take hold and pull him under. Interesting, but easy to spot, like a green ooze that moved slowly enough to avoid as long as he held it in his awareness. He let his face look sleepy, then snapped his eyes to hers.

"Nice crystal," he said brightly, grinning at her.

Her face reddened, and he suppressed a chuckle.

"I believe you've met my father," he said.

"Really?" she asked icily. "I'm sure I don't remember."

"He's tall, with a balding head. Long nose. Handsome brown eyes. He offered you marriage." He did not know why he was telling her this. Ishmar was Ridge's father, not Jidna's. How awkward. Perhaps some of her charm had gotten past his defenses, after all.

She snorted and rolled her eyes. "I've had as many offers of marriage as I have necklaces."

Jidna glanced at the collection of gold chains hanging from her neck. There were at least two dozen. At least she realized she was overburdened with gold. He suddenly felt stupid for bringing jewelry to try and woo her. He could see it was not a very original idea. He opened the burlap sack, determined not to be intimidated by this peevish woman.

"Let me see," he said casually. "I'm not sure if there are any necklaces in here or not. To add to your collection."

She followed his hands as he pulled three jewelry boxes of various sizes from his bag. He opened them one by one, flipping the velvet tops open and setting them on the round brass table, facing her. She hadn't even offered him tea, he noted. How rude.

She examined the contents of the boxes: the Antler Kralj gem-studded gold ring, which Jidna suddenly realized with embarrassment was a man's ring; a gaudy gold necklace thick as a collar with dangling diamonds; and a gold lizard brooch set with diamonds, emeralds, and rubies. Jidna watched from behind lowered lashes as Gabira hungrily eyed each piece, lingering longest on the ring, which glittered with tiny sapphires of various colors and a single black diamond in the center.

"I'm sorry there's no simple gold chain for your elegant taste," Jidna said apologetically. "But I'll be sure to tell my father to bring you one." Jidna showed his teeth in a wide smile as he started snapping the boxes shut.

Gabira licked her lips as he put them into his sack.

"Oh, did you like something?" he asked innocently.

Her eyes hardened.

"I brought other gifts, but I was hoping to offer them to your daughters in person, over tea," he said.

The statuettes clanked against the brass table as he set down the pineapple, the peacock, and the panther.

Avarice gleamed from behind her tightly controlled eyes as she studiously avoided looking at the chunks of solid gold sitting on her table. Each of these pieces was worth more than the whole lot of jewelry combined—aside from perhaps the Antler Kralj ring. She looked instead at his nose and bellowed out in a piercing voice, "Tea!!" She jerked at a thick gold rope that snaked down the wall behind her.

After a minute, two women scurried into the room, carrying trays with steaming tea in small metal cups that reminded him of home. The women were obviously entranced, looking down at their trays in a subservient posture. One woman wearing a bright pink silk robe knelt in front of him. He took the hot teacup from the tray, trying to catch her eyes, but they were glazed over. These women were not Gabira's daughters.

Gabira waved the women away, yelling after them with a stern command, "Fetch Giselle and Daleelah." The door shut behind them, and he was left alone with the angry woman in her colorful den. They examined one another, searching for weakness.

"You remind me of my grandmother," he said.

She frowned. "And you remind me of my son, Hasan."

"Oh? Where is your son now?"

"Dead." Silence echoed. "Where is your grandmother?"

"The same," he answered. "Died when I was thirteen. Right before we fled Earth and came here. That's twenty years ago. A long time to live on the moon."

"A long time," she agreed, her face softening a touch.

"My grandmother raised me," he continued. "My mother died when I was born."

"I see," she said. "Your grandmother taught you well."

"What I know I learned on my own. For self-defense. For survival. *For my sanity.*"

Gabira glared at him, knowing what he was insinuating, and judging by her deepening scowl she did not like being called on her shit. He didn't care. He didn't like being controlled by presumptuous women. Or by anyone, for that matter.

He recalled one day when he was little, sitting next to his grandmother on the couch, when she'd tapped at the true eye spot on his forehead. He must have been about six. His grandmother had crooked her finger and curled it at his forehead. It had felt as if she were reaching inside his head and pulling out his brains. Only they were masses of golden threads. She'd pulled them out and twirled them with her fingers. He'd leaned over and reached inside her head, imitating her, and pulled silver threads from her true eye and lifted them as though he were stretching a spider's web.

"Here," his grandmother said. She took her strands from his fingers and tied them together with the strands she had pulled from his head. "Now we will always be connected."

He remembered the sickening feeling of her silver tendrils creeping into his true eye and traveling down his throat, past his heart, and into his belly. It felt like he was being invaded by parasites.

He had reached in front of his forehead and made a clipping gesture with his fingers, like they were scissors, and cut the twining threads, hers and his together. "There," he announced. "Now we are apart."

His grandmother had cuffed him hard on the side of the head, making his ear ring. But at least the squirming worms inside his belly were dead.

The heavy wooden door of the colorful room opened, and a younger, slimmer version of Gabira glided inside, clothed in emerald-green robes and bedecked with gold jewelry. Her gleaming black hair was coiled on top of her head, and wide exotic eyes flashed up and down Jidna's body, checking him out. His dick stiffened, and he met her deep brown eyes as her full lips puckered into a smug smile.

"Giselle," she murmured in introduction, dipping in a brief curtsy.

"Jidna," he said, rising and stepping forward to take the hand she offered him, and bent to touch his lips to her smooth skin, breathing in her lemony scent as he kissed the back of her warm hand. He suddenly wished he was not disguised as this repulsive creature, but had presented his true self, the fastidiously groomed Rjidna. His own odor assaulted his nose, and he cringed away from himself but could not escape.

She retreated to sit next to her mother, across from Jidna, and raised her eyebrows curiously. Giselle looked back and forth between him and her fuming mother, as though realizing he was not captivated by her mother's spell. Her attention fell on the gold statuettes.

Jidna turned his attention to Gabira. "There are three statues, to be given as a set," he told her pointedly. If his appearance marked him as an uncouth slob, he was intent on letting his behavior speak differently. He was a man to be taken seriously.

Gabira's lips thinned. "Where is your sister?" she growled.

Just then the door creaked open and a young woman slipped into the room and sat next to Giselle, knocking a pillow to the floor and quickly picking it up and setting it on her lap. She looked at her mother with large brown eyes framed by long black lashes.

"This is Jidna," Gabira said curtly, nodding towards him. "Be polite and say hello."

The young woman's eyebrows knit together as she, too, was surprised that he was not spellbound. She lifted her eyes to him shyly.

"Nice to meet you. I am Daleelah."

His reaction to her was not as strong as for Giselle. Daleelah was like a startled deer, whereas Giselle was a prancing show horse who basked in the attention of the crowds. He preferred the show horse.

"I brought you gifts," he said. "To brighten the endless dark days below the surface." He glanced at the coils of solar filaments hanging neatly from the ceiling. "Although I see you have the next best thing to the sun." He wished he could claim to have invented solar filaments. They were a brilliant and simple invention, funneling pure sunlight from the surface through the coiling tubes.

He lifted the peacock. "The gifts are well suited to each of you," he said, handing the delicate bird to Giselle. "The peacock, both elegant and flamboyant."

Giselle took the peacock and cradled it in her palm, a smile turning up her succulent lips.

To Daleelah he gave the panther. "The panther, sleek and strong, who prefers the shadows."

It was almost more satisfying to see a tender smile light the face of the timorous Daleelah than it was to please her sister, who Jidna suspected was quick to smile at everyone.

The pineapple was for Gabira. He offered it to her and she snatched it from his hand. "The heaviest, purest gold," he said, leaving out the round and prickly part.

"Thank you," Gabira managed to choke out, her thanks echoed sincerely by her daughters.

"My pleasure," Jidna replied, having earned a few more minutes with them. He dug into his sack and set food on the table. A sharp clap from Gabira was quickly followed by the serving girls bringing tea to Giselle and Daleelah and refilling Jidna's and Gabira's cups.

The servants left without so much as glancing at the food, which Gabira and her daughters could not take their eyes off of. It made a colorful display, with the purple plums, green pears, orange peaches, and golden apricots. Next to the fruit, he laid out three cucumbers and two yellow bell peppers, then opened the paper bags of walnuts and pistachio meats. Lastly, he pulled out the bags of sugar candies, candied almonds, dried fruit, and the single remaining sack of coffee beans. The aroma of the dark roasted beans filled the air.

"Ooooh," Giselle sighed. "Smell that, Ami, real coffee!"

Gabira harrumphed and tried to hide her excitement by tightening her jaw and flaring her nostrils disdainfully. Daleelah's fingers stroked the small black diamonds on the panther's back, which she had set atop the pillow on her lap.

"Shall we?" He slipped a small knife from his belt and sliced a pear into quarters, handing them each a section. He passed the sacks of nuts across the table to Daleelah, and she made two small piles on the pillow next to the panther, one of walnuts, and one of pistachios, and then passed the bags to her sister.

Giselle's nipples were poking at her silky robe, drawing his eyes as she took a small handful of each variety of nut. She saw him looking at her breasts, and he lowered his head and sliced up a firm peach, sharing that as well.

He sat back, taking a bite of pear, while taking pleasure in the fact that Gabira was suffering his company even though he knew she itched to throw him out. He let his gaze wander over to Giselle again, noting her nipples had subsided. Her legs were crossed at the knee under her peacock-green robe, but her bare ankles peeked out from below the hem. She wore sandals on her graceful feet, and her toenails were painted red. He forced his eyes back to her fuming mother, whose nostrils were still flaring.

"I'd be honored to take a tour of your facility," he told Gabira, realizing awkwardly that facility was not the right word. He'd been spending too much time at the mine. "To inspect the women's quarters in anticipation of my niece's arrival."

Gabira choked on a nut, covering her mouth and coughing loudly. Giselle pounded on her back. When Gabira recovered she glowered at Jidna, her eyes cold and watery. "Visitors are not allowed inside."

He had suspected as much but had accomplished his goal, which was to learn where the women's quarters were located. Her mind had flashed to the quarters when he'd asked his question, which she'd tried to cover with her coughing fit. But he'd been able to track her mental marker, which appeared to Jidna as a small light beacon flung out like a fishing lure on the end of a long glowing line. The women were located a few hundred yards to the rear, and down. He considered going straight there when he was done visiting, out of curiosity more than anything, but he figured that path would end with several daggers in his back.

He smiled amiably. "Of course, I understand. No matter. I trust you." He squinted his eyes with sincerity. Gabira sneered at him.

He rose and bowed formally, then took his leave, exiting into the corridor and striding towards the stairway, with Gabira's eyes burning into his back as she stood at the doorway and watched him go.

14

IGOTRA

Gunfire went off around Torr, echoing in the bunker, deafening him. Reina had traded her spotting scope for her TAFT, and Torr fired his Dashiel at ants spilling out of disabled Teg vehicles on the hills. Millions of black ants flooded from doors and broken windshields and descended the hills towards the Scripps Ranch Company. His squadmates sprayed the ants with automatic fire, and Jessimar frantically loaded a new chain of bullets into his machine gun. But they kept coming. The army of ants swarmed the bunker, flowing up over the rampart and crawling up Torr's arms and face, biting him with a thousand pinpricks.

He woke himself screaming, and Cassidy was sitting up in her sleeping bag, wiping dust crust from the corners of her eyes.

"Stars, Torr," she said. "Your nightmares are getting worse."

The dreamcatcher turned slowly overhead.

"Tell me about it," Torr said, grabbing his dusty t-shirt from the floor and wiping sweat from his face. "I can't beat it, hard as I try," he mumbled. "And my cheek is getting worse all of a sudden. I thought it had stopped." A sharp electrical current jabbed at his cheek every few seconds, making his eye squint. He slapped at his cheek, trying to get it to stop.

She gazed at him, her bruises having turned a sickly green, and suddenly he felt stupid for complaining. "It'll be okay," he said.

"No it won't," she said, frowning. "It's just going to get worse. For both of us."

He met her gaze and wondered at what point exactly their waking life had become the real nightmare.

———————) ———————

Torr carried two cups of tea into their tent for breakfast and sat across from his sister. Lately, she refused to leave the tent for anything other than rations and a single visit to the porta-potties—she had started pissing into a pot so that she only had to leave the Fen once a day. She didn't even want to eat meals at the table with everyone else. He had set up a little pantry for her in the back of the tent—shelves made from stacked plastic crates, which held a few dishes, a water pitcher, a jar of honey, a tin box to hold her stale bread, some sweet sticky-rice balls Hiroshi had made, a small sack of dried figs Jasper had bought for her, and two strips of Murian gish from Jasper's stash.

"Do you want to come to training today?" he asked, as he had every day for the past week.

She shook her head and stared down into her tea, slowly stirring in a dollop of honey.

"I can only scry in water when there's blood in it," she said vacantly. A shiver ran up Torr's spine. "But with the crystal ball," she continued, "I can see whenever I want."

She glanced up at him, and Torr nodded. Her black eye had faded to a yellow circle.

"Just like Grandma Leann said," Cassidy said, and took a sip of her tea.

"What do you see?" he asked hesitantly, almost afraid to ask.

"I check on my friends Anna and Maria on the Nommos ship. The ship captain drugged them, which is a blessing, I guess. They are crammed together with ten other women, lying in a cramped compartment with no room to even sit up. And I'm checking in on the two new women Balthazar is torturing."

Her voice was absent of emotion, and her eyes were like blue ice. He swallowed and changed the topic.

"Do you want to come outside and sit at the picnic table later? Or maybe play cards in Sky and Thunder's tent?" he asked.

She pursed her lips and focused on him, scaring him with the intensity of her gaze. "I told you," she said. "Someone is watching me. I don't want to leave the tent."

He swallowed again, and his cheek twitched. He did not want to indulge her paranoia, and pressed, "Sky and Thunder have a tent. What's the difference?" he asked.

She shrugged her shoulders, set the tea cup on the tent floor, and stared down into her crystal ball.

"I was going to get you another knife," Torr said. "Hiroshi has a collection from Earth. He said he'd sell us each one."

"That's great," she muttered, gazing into the crystal.

"Cassidy," he said, his patience wearing thin. "I wish you would leave the tent. It might help you if you interacted with your friends. Training is really fun—you'd like it. You can't be a hermit here forever."

Torr had started going to the training yard in the mornings and entrusting Cassidy's care to Jasper and whoever else in the Fen was not an instructor. When Torr got back, the others took turns going to the training yard, and Jasper rushed off to do whatever it was he did. The instructors were running several shifts, and the group's numbers were growing every day as word spread.

"It's too far across camp," she said.

"Well, then, you can train here in the evenings with us. Don't you want to learn how to fight?"

Her gaze lifted to meet his, and she tilted her head. "What about that four-wheeler in the container? Can Jasper fix it?" she asked.

Torr's hopes lifted. "Would you feel more comfortable with a vehicle to drive around in?"

She nodded, and the shadow of a smile parted her lips.

He focused on the faint glimmer of light in her eyes and said, "Maybe Kai can help us find an engine and wheels. It's just a frame right now."

"Okay," she said, and sipped her tea, staring off into space.

Torr fidgeted, trying to think of something that would make her happy. "How about we invite Hawk to come hang out with you while I go to practice this morning? He wants to keep translating Mom's blue and gold book with you."

"Oh," Cassidy said, as though he had awoken her. "I'd forgotten all about that. Yes, that's a good idea. Can you ask him to come by later?"

Torr nodded, pleased that she liked his idea, but disturbed that she would not simply poke her head outside and ask Hawk herself. "Sure," he said. "I'll tell him."

They ate their stale bread in silence. He returned their cups to the kitchen, rinsing them out in the two inches of gray dish water.

"How's Cassidy?" Jasper asked, elbowing Torr aside and cleaning his own cup.

"Weird," Torr said. "She stares into that crystal ball all day long."

"Still?" Jasper asked, flashing a concerned look at Torr.

"Yeah. I don't know what to do. But she agreed to hang out with Hawk. And she wants to fix up that four-wheeler in the container."

Jasper raised an eyebrow. "Really? That's Berkeley's. It was a moon rover before it got stripped for parts. Now it's just a steel frame."

"I know. That's what I told her. But if it will get her to leave the Fen ... Plus, maybe we can use it to tow the water wagon to the training yard every day. I'm tired of dragging it like a mule."

Jasper sighed and set his cup on the drying rack. "I don't know. I'll ask Berkeley if he wants to rebuild it. But engines are hard to come by. I'll ask my father to check with the maintenance crew. Does she like the figs?"

"Yes, Jasper, she loves the figs."

"She does?"

Torr shook his head at Jasper's pathetic expression. "Just go ask her yourself. She doesn't bite."

"She hates me," Jasper muttered.

"She doesn't hate you. She's just a little mad at you." The last words she had spoken to Jasper had been a snide remark about the Greenwash drug and how he was the equivalent of a slimy eel lurking in dark shadows stalking unsuspecting prey. Torr gestured across the yard. "She needs company. Go talk to her."

Jasper sighed again, and Torr folded his arms and watched the tall redhead cross the yard and duck inside their tent. He didn't immediately step back outside, so apparently she wasn't going to throw him out. Torr waited, and after a few minutes Jasper returned to the picnic table, where Torr was sitting by himself.

"What'd she say?" Torr asked.

Jasper's face was paler than normal. He plopped down next to Torr, looking beaten. "She said her friends are on their way to Delos in a Nommos ship. Then she started crying, saying she abandoned them. I tried to hug her, but she pushed me away and told me it was all my fault."

Jasper wiped a tear from his freckled cheek. They sat quietly until

Jasper got hold of himself. "I'll talk to Berkeley and my dad about the moon rover," Jasper said and set his elbows on the table, resting his chin dejectedly on his fists.

Torr got up and went to the Boyers' tent and asked Hawk if he wanted to help Cassidy continue translating the blue and gold book. Hawk jumped up and disappeared into Torr and Cassidy's tent. Torr stepped inside to make sure Cassidy wasn't going to ask the boy to leave, but they were both sitting on her sleeping bag, spreading out scraps of paper next to the off-world book.

Torr smiled at Cassidy. The pink flush had returned to her cheeks, and her eyes were clear. Torr grabbed his things and went outside, exhaling a sigh of relief. He volunteered to pull first and strapped on the chest harness Hiroshi had made and leaned into it, tugging against the weight of the water wagon until it started rolling, then headed for the training yard with Tatsuya, Hiroshi, Berkeley, and the other instructors.

Ming-Long and Khaled took turns pulling the wagon. When they arrived at the training yard, several dozen men were already there, waiting for classes to start. Jorimar and Helug stood a hundred yards away in their customary spot at the intersection of Ring Road L and Spoke Road Four, thick arms folded across burly chests. They smiled at Torr and struck their fists to their chests in their daily salute to him. Torr returned the gesture and turned away, shaking his head. The Scrids were there every day, watching the training from a distance.

Torr introduced himself to a few newcomers and organized them into a squad. Other squads were gathered around the kickboxing teachers, Elvis and Febo. Elvis was a traditional boxer, whereas Febo used everything: fists, elbows, knees, and shins. They liked to spar with each other to warm up.

"Come on, badass," Elvis taunted, jabbing at Febo.

The two men circled one another. At first, Torr thought Febo would get the better of Elvis, with his long legs and fancy moves, but Elvis was quicker and landed most of his punches. Soon blood was trickling from Febo's nose.

"Okay, okay," Torr said, pushing them apart. "Febo's ugly enough as it is. Knock it off."

The two men wiped at their faces, their eyes flashing. The crowd urged them on. They went at it again. The more brutal the sparring became, the happier the two men looked. When they were covered with sweat and blood, the opponents shook hands, laughing, and exchanged sweaty hugs.

"Okay," Torr called out. "Let's get going."

Torr's regular squad was back at the Fen guarding Cassidy, so he randomly joined another group and stood on the tarp waiting for Hiroshi and Tatsuya's Judo class to begin.

They started the class by lining up on their knees and bowing. Then they warmed up with pushups and stretches, and then practiced hip throws and shoulder throws and sweeping their opponent's legs out from under them. Then they learned some new standing armlocks and practiced on one another. They ended class with kneeling again, closing their eyes, and breathing in to the count of seven, holding their breath for the count of seven, and breathing out to the count of seven. They repeated the breathing meditation, then ended the class by bowing to Tatsuya and Hiroshi and thanking them in Japanese.

Next, Torr took the kickboxing class, where they took turns at the punching bags and then practiced footwork, kicks, jabs, feints, and blocks, followed by sparring. After the class ended, some people were too tired to continue and wandered off or stood on the sidelines to watch. Torr was sore, but he liked it. It meant he was getting stronger. Besides, he didn't worry about Cassidy while he was fighting.

After a break, Torr joined the knife-fighting class taught by Ming-Long, Khaled, and Faisal. They used short lengths of rolled-up canvas instead of real blades. They started with a review of anatomy and the locations of vulnerable arteries, tendons, and organs. Then they learned three new forms—Lady's Fan, Figure Eight, and Dead Man's X—and then practiced single-handed stabbing and slicing techniques with their weak hands. Finally, they practiced defending against a two-on-one attack.

Afterwards, Torr brushed off a spot on a mat to sit for a meditation session with Berkeley. Berkeley instructed the class to sit on the ground cross-legged, gaze softly at the ground three feet in front of them, and focus on their breath. That was it. Torr chose a small moon rock to focus on, and felt his abdomen rise and fall. His hips were stiff, and with his ankles crossed together his knees stuck up in the air, unlike Berkeley, whose legs were folded flat against the ground.

Instead of bringing him peace, meditating for forty-five minutes straight made Torr jittery. He was surprised at how undisciplined he was. Sitting in front of a gun and focusing on a target was one thing. He could pass the time on the shooting platform at Miramar observing his surroundings with all his senses and looking for any movement— detecting lizards scurrying across the parched landscape or calculating wind speed based on the motion of plants or heat ripples rising from the ground. Or he would settle into a half-sleep state to see where his waking dreams took him. But sitting still for so long with no goal and without letting his mind wander was harder than he'd imagined.

Berkeley listened and nodded when Torr complained about it after the session had ended, standing together at the water tank.

"How can I ignore all my thoughts?" Torr asked skeptically. "That's what the brain does. It thinks."

Berkeley's eyes were wide and round. "Your mind is an untamed beast. Just focus on the breath, and don't give those thoughts any more attention than to acknowledge them and let them go on their merry way." Berkeley read the look on his face and said, "Thinking is overrated."

"One needs to think to live," Torr said. "Man does not live by breath alone."

"A wise man thinks each thought only once," Berkeley replied.

Torr laughed. "Yeah, right."

Berkeley did not break his gaze, nor did he smile.

Torr swallowed. "What about planning? Or reasoning through an issue? Or doing math problems? How can you do any of that if you don't think?" Torr lifted his chin at Berkeley. "Huh?"

"You're thinking too much," Berkeley said, cracking a grin.

"Ha ha," Torr said and smirked at his friend.

"Sometimes you do need to think," Berkeley admitted. "But many thoughts are repetitive and bound together with an emotion, making them powerfully addictive and a waste of energy. Believe me, you will be much more productive and effective if you control your mind, instead of your mind controlling you."

Torr frowned. He understood what it meant when it came to shooting. He had to dismiss his vagrant thoughts in order to hit a target, but he had never practiced the same kind of mental discipline during his daily life, other than for brief periods to calm his nerves and control his cheek twitch. "Maybe it'll work," Torr said.

"Oh, it works," Berkeley assured him. "But it takes years of training. Do you have that much patience?"

Torr scowled, and Berkeley's eyes darted past Torr's shoulder. Torr turned to follow his gaze. Crossing the dusty yard was a large group of women, coming straight towards them.

"Smith gang," Berkeley said to Torr under his breath as the group stopped a few paces away.

A tall woman stepped forward. "Hi," she said. "Are you in charge here?"

Despite her strong bearing and typical Peary cargo pants, t-shirt, and field vest, Torr was immediately struck by her overwhelming ... female-ness. Aside from his sister, Torr's life was sorely devoid of the half of the human population that made the world go round. Having so many women suddenly standing in front of him assaulted his senses. There was something so ... *liquid* about women. They exuded an indefinable something that seeped through Torr's skin and into his blood, making his cells hum.

He tried not to stare, realizing suddenly that he was not replying.

Berkeley cleared his throat and elbowed Torr.

"Uh, yes," Torr said. "I am ... I guess. All of us ... are. He is ..."

Berkeley interrupted. "He's in charge. His name is Torr. I'm Berkeley," he said, and stepped forward with his hand outstretched.

"I'm Blaire," she said, shaking Berkeley's hand, and then turned to Torr.

Torr shook her hand. Her grip was firm, and her light brown eyes shimmered with streaks of gold.

Torr released her hand, and Blaire wiped her palms on her hips. "So, you're Torr," she said, holding Torr's gaze. "This is your gang."

Torr shrugged. "It's not really mine, and we're not really a gang. We're just learning how to fight to protect ourselves."

"Everyone calls it *Torr's gang,*" Blaire said, the corners of her mouth quirking up.

Torr could feel his face getting red and shrugged again. "Whatever. But Jasper started it, and Berkeley and the others lead the training."

"They say you're the leader," she said, seemingly amused by his embarrassment. "That you were sent by the stars. Some sort of god or something." He felt his blush deepen and started to object, but she continued, "If you don't like the word *gang,* you could call yourselves *Torr's Fighters.*" She pointed to his upper arm.

He glanced down at his tattoo, where the word *Fighters* peeked out below his t-shirt sleeve. "Is that Earth?" she asked. He lifted his sleeve to reveal the rest of the tattoo. "Ah," she said. "That's it. You could call yourselves the *Light Fighters.*"

Torr considered the idea and nodded. "Lightfighter is actually just the name of a road near my house," he said sheepishly. "I always liked it."

"It's a much better name than the *Smith gang,*" she said with a wry chuckle.

"Light Fighters is a noble name," Berkeley agreed. "And a noble task. Light must win over darkness. There is no other option. We will save the moon, and Earth too. You'll see."

Torr laughed good-naturedly, but Berkeley stared at him with his serious round eyes and did not join in his laughter. Blaire nodded, and Torr began to warm up to the idea.

"It's settled, then," Torr said, chuckling. "We are the Light Fighters, and we shall defend the universe from darkness."

"I'll make us all patches," Berkeley offered.

"That's a great idea," Blaire said, as though it were her gang as well.

"You know how to make patches?" Torr asked.

"Of course," Berkeley said, rolling his eyes. "I make all the Peary Dome patches," he said, gesturing to the assortment of embroidered patches covering his vest. "What, do you think I belong to all of these?" he asked, pointing to Air Control and Peary Pilots patches.

"Oh," Torr said. "So you're not a Peary trader?"

"I am," Berkeley said. "Even I wouldn't be allowed to wear that patch if I weren't officially in the Guild. But the others are just for show. Well, I did work for Air Control for a while, back when everyone took turns shoveling dirt into the oxygenators."

"You're full of surprises, Berkeley. Light Fighters patches would be awesome," Torr said. He glanced past Blaire, where the other women were waiting.

Blaire followed his gaze, then turned back to him. "We're wondering if we could train with you guys. I heard you're accepting new students?"

"Uh, yeah," Torr said, his blush returning. "We have enough ... um ... room, don't you think, Berkeley?" His heart suddenly began pounding at the thought of so many women in such close proximity every day. Torr turned to his friend.

"You mean for the morning sessions?" Berkeley asked. "I suppose we could take ..." Berkeley quickly scanned the group of women. "Twenty more?"

"Yeah, around that many," Blaire said. "But we have eighty total. That's probably too many, though. We can teach the others what we learn, back at our camp."

"Okay," Berkeley said, and Torr nodded dumbly.

"You're the one whose sister got kidnapped, right?" she asked, returning her gaze to Torr. "I heard she escaped. How is she doing?"

Torr's momentary elation subsided, and he met her concerned gaze with a grim look. "She's recovering, I guess. I've been trying to get her to come here, but she won't leave our camp."

"Maybe she would if there were other women to train with," Blaire said, and several women behind her nodded.

Torr's heart lightened again. "That's a great idea. Will you come to our camp and talk to her?"

"Sure," she said. "We'd be happy to."

"Now?" he asked hopefully.

She shrugged and exchanged glances with her companions. "Sure," she said. "There's not much going on in Peary Dome, in case you hadn't noticed."

He gathered his things, winked at his gawking friends, and left with the Smith gang. The instructors trailed not far behind, deciding it was a good time to take their lunch break.

Torr felt like a giddy teenager as he walked across the dome with the women. Blaire introduced him to her three younger sisters: Becka was the second oldest, then came Britta, and Bailey was the youngest. Blaire appeared to be in her mid-to-late twenties, Becka and Britta in their early-to-mid twenties, and Bailey looked to be a couple of years younger than Torr. The sisters shared similar features and stature. Their skin was light brown and smooth, their noses were small and flat, and their hair was long, thick, and black, tumbling down their backs in frizzy waves or plaited into ponytails. Their large brown eyes were intelligent and kind. They stood tall, with strong shoulders, narrow hips, and long legs. Another much shorter dark-skinned woman named Darla, who had a closely shaved scalp and wore a multitude of ear and nose rings, walked at Blaire's side.

The Smith sisters were from Denver and had left their parents behind. Torr told them he and Cassidy had left their parents back on Earth as well. No one asked if their parents were still alive. Earth hovered above the horizon, blue and white and ghostlike.

They arrived at the Fen, and Torr found Cassidy still inside the tent with Hawk. Torr introduced them to Blaire.

Hawk rose awkwardly to his feet. "Nice to meet you, ma'am," he said, turning red and shaking her hand.

Cassidy stood up, and the two women shook hands. Cassidy's face relaxed with relief and a flash of joy.

Torr chided himself for not thinking of finding female companions for her sooner. "Cass, Blaire and her sisters and their friends are going to train with us at the training yard. She thinks we should name ourselves the Light Fighters. What do you think?"

Cassidy nodded and gave him something close to a smile. "Just like your tattoo."

Torr nodded. "Yep. I'll let you guys chat," he said, and motioned for Hawk to follow him outside.

Hawk left the tent and stood with Torr.

"She's pretty," Hawk said, his eyes gleaming.

"Blaire?" Torr asked. "Yeah."

Hawk's gaze landed on the other women who were gathered around the picnic tables.

"Whoa," Hawk said. "A whole bunch of them."

Torr laughed. "How was your morning?" he asked.

"Good. We translated a lot of words," Hawk said, still staring at the women.

"That's great," Torr said, patting the boy's shoulder. "Have you been working on it this entire time?"

"Yep, mostly, except when my dad made us some rice."

"Thank you, Hawk." Torr was grateful for the gentle boy who had somehow worked his way into his sister's heart.

After a few minutes, Blaire came out of the tent and nodded. "We'll come by tomorrow morning to get her. Is that okay?"

"It's more than okay. It's fantastic. Thank you," Torr said, bowing his head. "Morning sessions start at eight o'clock."

"Okay. We'll come by around seven thirty," Blaire said, and shook his hand.

Torr bit his lip and watched as she walked away to join her friends. The women filed out of the camp, and the men of the Fen stared after them, then moaned and groaned when they were out of earshot and began talking about their favorites in graphic terms.

"Shut up, you idiots," Torr said, directing his glare at the men and gesturing towards his tent where Cassidy was still silently lurking.

———————————)———————————

The next morning, the Smiths returned as promised, and Torr and his campmates happily followed the women across the dome, leaving Fritz and Frank to guard the Fen.

Jasper showed up at the training yard, and Torr watched as Jasper approached Cassidy, where she had assembled with the women to form squads.

"Cassidy," Jasper said. Cassidy turned to him with one hand on her hip. "Don't you think you should train with some men?" Jasper asked. "You should take the Alphabet Boys as your squad."

Torr curled his hands into fists, wishing Jasper would leave well enough alone.

She folded her arms and gave him a dark look. "So, I suppose you think you're going to tell me what to do now?"

"Cassidy," Jasper said. "If you train with the Alphabet Boys, you'll learn faster."

"I am not a child, Jasper Manann," she said. "And I don't need your advice. So why don't you just take your smart ass and walk straight back to Algol's hell?"

Torr bit his tongue. She never used to talk that way to anyone, but at least she was angry instead of curling up in her shell. Torr feared Jasper would go stomping off at her harsh words, but instead he took a deep breath and said, "If you disappear or get hurt again, I will be in Algol's hell, I can assure you of that."

She stared wordlessly at Jasper, hints of emotion breaking through her stiff countenance.

Two new male recruits stepped forward. "We can train with them," the tall one offered. He had slick dark hair and a friendly way about him. His companion was small and tight-lipped. "Name's Stanley," the man said. "And this here's Gerbil."

Gerbil was short and skinny with a patchy brown beard and a small forehead. It was an unfortunately fitting name for the rodent-like man whose front teeth stuck out too far and whose cheeks looked like they were stuffed with nuts. Stanley, by contrast, was tall and muscular, with neatly trimmed hair, icy green eyes, a strong chin, and a smooth-shaven face.

Cassidy turned up her nose, glancing at the dark-haired man, who smiled genially and showed off his biceps by folding his arms casually over his chest. The smaller one nodded, and the handsome one gave Jasper a friendly, reassuring smile. Jasper's expression hardened.

Cassidy turned away, pulling Blaire and her sisters over to the side to speak with them. At length, Cassidy turned back to the men and said, "If Sky and Thunder want to join our squad, that would be okay with us." She avoided looking at Stanley and Gerbil.

Sky exchanged glances with Thunder.

"Sure," Thunder said, and Sky nodded.

"And in exchange, Blaire and Darla will join Torr's squad," she said, directing her attention at Torr.

His eyes widened involuntarily, and Blaire and Darla looked at him expectantly.

"Uh, sure. That'd be ... fine. Yeah," he said.

"Good. It's settled then," Cassidy said.

Sky and Thunder joined the women while Stanley and Gerbil wandered off to find another squad, and Jasper stalked out of the yard, his radio pressed to his ear.

Blaire and Darla approached, and together with the Boyer brothers and the Alphabet Boys Arden, Buck, Copper, Dang, and Guy, Torr went to a tarp and waited for the Judo class to begin.

"Are we your official squad now?" Hawk asked, his eyes big and serious.

"Yes, I suppose so," Torr said, laughing and patting Hawk's shoulder.

"Fritz and Frank don't need a squad?" Hawk asked. "Don't they need to train? They always get stuck staying behind at the Fen."

Guy was listening and said, "Those twins were special ops in Germany. They can fight better than any of us. But they prefer to make music. Can't find better guards for the Fen, if you ask me," he said, and the other Alphabet Boys nodded in agreement.

"Our squad's an odd number," Arden said to Torr. "We need another person. What about Durham?"

Torr glanced over to where Durham sat at a picnic table, watching.

"He's only got one leg," Hawk said.

"I know," Arden said. "So what?" Arden was small and wiry, and his dark brown eyes were keen.

"Sure," Torr said, and waved Durham over.

Durham got up on his crutches and came to the mat.

"We need you on our squad, to make twelve," Torr said.

Durham's face fell with surprise. "I couldn't," he said.

"Why not?" Arden asked. "My dad lost his leg in the Early Wars too. He still beat the crap out of me. Come on." Arden tilted his head at Durham.

"I don't want to hold you guys back," he said, glancing at his sons, Blaire and Darla, and the other Alphabet Boys.

"We already know how to fight," Dang said, gesturing to his fellow Alphabet Boys. "We're just staying in shape. We could use the challenge. You know, figure out the best moves for you." Dang's friends nodded.

"Yeah, Dad," Raleigh said. "You're stronger than most people."

Hiroshi and Tatsuya were listening and came over.

"Yes, you can practice Judo, Durham-san," Hiroshi said with a series of short little bows. "We will help adapt the moves for your strengths. No crutches during drills, though."

"I can hop for a little bit at a time," Durham said.

"Good. You'll be hanging onto your opponent a lot of the time, anyway, or down on the mat," Hiroshi said.

Hiroshi and Tatsuya bowed at Durham, and Durham bowed back.

They lined up, facing the instructors. Durham set his crutches down behind him and lowered himself to the mat as they did a kneeling bow and began class.

———————)———————

Torr was walking in a forest, looking for his mother. A raven circled overhead, and then lazily flapped northward over the treetops. Torr followed, striking out through the woods, trying to keep sight of the raven through gaps in the branches. The forest thickened, obscuring the sky, and he cursed as he lost the raven.

A tickle at the back of Torr's neck made him freeze in his tracks. Someone was watching him. He turned slowly, peeking over his shoulder. "Torrance."

The silhouette of wild floating hair emerged from behind a tree trunk. "Mom?"

"Torrance, don't run away from me." The head grew larger, and the black hair turned into a flaming halo of yellow and orange snakes reaching out to him. The creature loomed over him, arms outstretched.

Torr jerked awake and sat upright. His heart was pounding and his skin was bathed in sweat. He was in his tent, blankets twisted around his legs, and Cassidy was sound asleep, curled up in the fetal position with her back facing him. He grabbed his ration jug and drank gulps of warm water. The dreamcatcher twirled slowly overhead.

The flaming monster woman was a recurring figure who had appeared randomly in his dreams since childhood, but it had been years since she had shown her face. Now, suddenly, she kept reappearing, scaring him awake. He set the jug down and pulled his knees to his chest, wrapping shaking arms around his shins and resting his chin on one knee. The pale gray face loomed in his vision, her expression twisted in agony.

Focus on the breath.

He shifted his awareness to his rapid breathing and the air brushing against his upper lip. The image of the monster woman faded, and his pulse returned to normal. He sat upright and crossed his legs in the meditation pose. His knees did not touch the floor, so he rested the weight of his legs on his crossed ankles instead, placed his palms on his thighs, and set his gaze on a random clod of dirt at the tent doorway, and breathed.

Who was she, and what did she want?

Return to the breath. Why did she always chase him? And why did she frighten him so much?

Thoughts come and go. Berkeley's instructions echoed in his head. *Emotions are just thoughts. Let them go and focus on the breath.*

Torr's eyelids grew heavy. He forced his eyes open. The image of the monster woman haunted him as he stared at the clod of dirt. He returned his attention to his breath, over and over again. She punished him every time his attention wandered, taking the opening and inserting herself into his consciousness, calling his name and reaching her flaming tendrils towards him.

"Tell me who you are without frightening the crap out of me," he muttered. "Where do you come from?"

His breath was an anchor, keeping him moored to his body. He blinked stubbornly, and his cheek twitched. "Oh, for Algol's hell," he said. *Return to the breath.*

Minutes passed, and he jerked his head up. He had dozed off. He sat up straighter and focused his eyes on the dirt clod. But Berkeley had said to soften his gaze. His eyelids drooped, and the torpor of sleep tugged at him.

He was standing on a broad rocky plain ringed with mountains. The stink of sulfur filled the air. Ribbons of fire flanked the hills, and lava snaked down the slopes or spurted from gashes in the reddish ground in fluorescent plumes that shot up from the rocks in tall arcs. The rivers of molten lava that flowed down the mountain range to his right were orange. The rivers of fire on the distant hills to his left were blue.

Another mountain loomed behind him, dark and dead. A glimmer of light reflected off a point at its peak, reflecting the red of the massive sun that hung like a giant glowing coal in the sky and cast off waves of heat.

Torr tightened the pack straps on his shoulders and headed across the plain towards the dark mountain. He kicked at glittering gravel that covered the ground and stopped with surprise. He scooped a handful into his palm. The small stones were not stones at all but appeared to be uncut gems. Small chunks of what could have been ice—if it weren't so hot out—but could well be diamonds, he thought, as he remembered the gem shows he and his family used to attend. Dark blue and purple stones looked to be sapphires and rubies. He stared in wonder across the land strewn with raw jewels. He stuffed a handful into his pocket and kept walking.

A light but steady wind carried sulfur fumes across the flat valley, filling the air with the stench of rotten eggs. As he walked, the red sun climbed higher in the sky, the wind shifted, and faint strains of singing reached Torr's ears. He adjusted his course and headed towards the voices. As he drew nearer, he came upon stone ruins of what must have once been a magnificent city. He walked through the abandoned streets, trying to carve a straight path towards the faint singing.

Skeletons of red stone buildings stood empty on either side of wide boulevards paved with smooth, gray stones. No trees were to be seen, nor plant life of any kind. The buildings were made of man-high cubes of stone fitted perfectly together. Some of the stones were scattered or piled in mounds, having tumbled over like giant children's blocks. Windows and doorways were bare eye sockets and gaping mouths. Facing a large square, black pillars of what once must have been a great temple stood atop broad steps of black marble, the upper lintel still intact but the roof behind it caved in—huge slabs of black stone leaning precariously against one another. Headless statues of men and women lined the vast empty square, worn breasts and flaccid penises hanging impotently.

Torr continued hiking through what could have been a residential neighborhood at one time. The city looked as though it had been bombed, or perhaps there had been a catastrophic earthquake. Block after block of skeletal structures and mounds of stone rubble stood silent where once a civilization had thrived.

Finally, the singing became clearer. He turned a corner, and another great square opened up before him.

At the center of the square stood a massive round dry fountain of black marble crowned by four one-horned antelopes rearing below a pair of winged lions, who were in flight and engaged in battle. The lions' wings were outstretched, and their mouths gaped open in snarls, but no water flowed from them. At the far end of the dry stone pool, two dozen people were gathered in a ring, some sitting on the edge of the pool, others standing. They sang in a chorus, high and low voices in harmony, weaving a melody that pulled at Torr's heart.

He cocked his head and listened. Yes, it was that same tune. The elusive song from his childhood dream. He hummed along, trying to commit it to memory.

A youth from the group saw him, and the young man's face lit up. He stopped singing and waved at Torr, gesturing at him to join them.

Torr approached, and the teenager broke away from the group to meet him.

"You are here! *Ranapriya!*" the young man cried, his face dominated by the wide smile of the intellectually disabled and small eyes that were nearly crossed.

"Where is here?" Torr asked as he grasped the hands of the teenager who clung to him with radiant joy.

"You are home! You have come to save us!"

"Save you from what?" Torr asked.

"The fires," the youth said, freeing one hand from Torr's grip and waving at the burning mountains, and then up at the blazing sun. "Uttapta is angry. He burns in the sky, and rains down fire on our lands."

"Ah," Torr said, echoes of familiarity niggling at him.

"I am Igotra," the young man said. "Come, come."

Igotra tugged at Torr's hand, and Torr followed him to the group, who were still singing plaintively.

> *Children, come home*
> *Uttapta burns*
> *Drink of the golden yods*
> *Remember who you are*
> *Show us the pathway to the stars*

"Igotra," a woman said, gesturing to the teenager. "Come back and sing."

"I found him," Igotra said. "He has come."

"What are you saying?" the woman asked. "Come and sing."

Igotra dragged Torr to the edge of the circle. Some in the group glanced at Igotra but did not break from their song.

"They don't see me?" Torr asked.

Igotra frowned and turned to Torr. "They are stupid," Igotra said, disappointment furrowing his brow.

"Igotra," said the woman. "Stop talking to yourself and join the chorus. We must keep singing for the Children of the Stars to find their way back home."

"But he is here," Igotra said with tears of frustration pooling in his eyes. He tapped repeatedly on Torr's shoulder. "I found him. I found the Son of Uttapta."

"Igotra," the woman said in a gently scolding tone.

"I am here," Torr said.

No one else heard him.

"How do I get here in real life?" he asked Igotra.

The group kept singing, oblivious to Torr and Igotra. The two locked gazes.

"I need help finding this place," Torr told the boy.

"Come whenever you want," Igotra said, his sadness suddenly gone and his eyes brimming with happiness. The boy threw his arms around Torr.

Torr returned his warm hug and opened his eyes.

The clod of dirt sat at the threshold of the dusty tent while the dreamcatcher spun slowly overhead.

Torr rolled onto his knees. Paper. He needed paper. He had none. Why hadn't he brought his journals from Earth? Cassidy's notebooks were in her pack next to her peacefully sleeping form.

Rather than disturb her, he rubbed his hand over the dust on the canvas floor on the other side of his bed, smoothing it out, and wrote with his finger:

Children, come home
Uttapta burns
Drink of the golden yods
Remember who you are
Show us the pathway to the stars

15

SEER

Cassidy waited for Jasper to come looking for her, which he did after night gong struck. She met him at her tent door.

"You still mad about the Greenwash?" he asked.

"Yes," she said, lowering her eyes.

"So you're gonna just ignore me?"

"Yes," she said and ducked back inside her tent. She heard him exhale in exasperation and walk away. She sighed and got ready for bed.

The next morning, Jasper confronted her outside her tent. His hazel eyes flashed. "It's tough out here, you know? It took me five years to build this camp. When I got here, all I ate was rations. My dad barely got anything extra. I give him food now, did you know that? I bet you didn't know that, did you?" Cassidy met his eyes. "How did you think I could afford all this food, huh?" he asked, grabbing her arm. "You gonna stop eating it now that you know how I paid for it? Are you?"

"Don't be a jerk," she said, shaking off his hand. "I can buy my own food."

"Yeah? From your stash of gold coins? How did you get all that gold, anyway? For that matter, how'd you and Torr get off Earth? Your brother said he paid two Solidi. How do you think he got that gold? Huh?" She pressed her lips together. "Yeah," he said with a wry grin. "He stole it, that's how."

"He did not."

Jasper looked at her with a flat gaze. "Are you kidding me? How else would he get a bunch of Solidi, Cassidy?" Jasper threw up his hands. "It's wrong to steal, but it's not wrong to buy passage to the moon with the stolen money, is that what you're telling me?"

She couldn't think of what to say to that. He was right. She had never thought about it that way. She had never pressed Torr on how he had gotten all that gold. She looked up at Jasper, unable to say anything in return.

"And this," he said, tapping the Heaven's Window pendant at her neck. "How do you think I could afford a crate of Antler Kralj goods? You going to give this back to me?"

All she could do was stare at him.

"I didn't think so," he said. He turned his back to her and strode out of the Fen without looking back. She watched him leave, her mouth open. She stepped inside her tent and glared at the faded walls. Sounds from the camp drifted in through the canvas. How much of Jasper's livelihood was based on his drug trade? She guessed a large portion of it. Her hand curled around the Heaven's Window pendant. Anguish rose in her throat.

She removed the gold chain from her neck and looked at the triangular pendant, the three blue gems winking at her. She should give this back to Jasper. Throw it at him and tell him she wanted nothing to do with his ill-gotten spoils. She knelt down on her sleeping bag and gazed into the blue gems of the Star People. The ones she was supposedly seeking. She and Torr. And Jasper.

She laughed darkly at herself, the gems staring back at her. She knew she would not give it back. And she knew she would continue to eat the Fen's food and drink the water. She was a hypocrite. Suddenly she hated herself. She was party to Jasper's dealings, whether she liked it or not. She was a detestable human being. Before she realized what was happening, she was pulled in a downward spiral into the Heaven's Window's gem eyes—a three-pronged vortex bathed in a fire of blue, red, and orange. The air left her lungs. Her eyes were glued to the gems, her forehead pulsing with heat. A rush of golden light flooded into her. She felt herself growing faint and slumped over onto the bedding.

She awoke to Blaire nudging her shoulder. "You okay?" Blaire asked. "Are you still up for going to training today?"

"Uh, yeah," Cassidy said blearily, raising herself onto an elbow. "I'll be out in a second."

"Okay," Blaire said, and left the tent.

Cassidy stood up, clasped the Heaven's Window necklace around her neck, and gathered her things.

———————)———————

Later that morning, Cassidy pulled Torr aside at the training yard.

"How did you get all those Tetras and Solidi?" she asked, holding onto his arm. "Tell me the truth."

He met her gaze and took a breath, his shoulders stooping. "I stole a yacht and sold it." His eyes were steely gray and did not flinch.

"You stole a yacht?"

"Yes. I escaped from the Tegs and stole a yacht, to get my sorry ass back home. Any more questions?"

Cassidy blinked. "Whose yacht was it?"

"I don't know, Cassidy. Some guy named Earl T. Morrow. Some poor sucker who probably needed his yacht to save his family, and when he got to the marina to make his escape his boat was gone, and he and his family ended up in a work camp."

He tore his arm from her grasp and walked away, calling for his squad to assemble on the mat.

———————)———————

Cassidy was awake but could not open her eyes. It was her turn. Balthazar would be here soon, and if she was not in the bedroom waiting for him he would storm into the closet and drag her out by the hair and punish her. But her muscles were leaden and would not move. Maybe she was dead and she hadn't realized it yet. Maybe it was better that way. But then Anna and Maria would suffer alone.

She forced her eyes open. They were filled with sand. She crawled onto her knees, then slowly stood up and staggered across the closet.

She jerked back. He was there. She was too late. His chest muscles were hard under her hands, and she scraped her fingernails against his bare skin as she fell to her knees and begged, "Please, I'm sorry. I was on my way."

"Cassidy."

She snapped her head up. Torr was lifting her by her arms, steadying her as she rose to her feet.

"Cassidy. It's okay. It's me."

The tent was cast in shadow, and she turned in a circle, disoriented, her heart racing.

"You were dreaming," Torr said.

"What day is it?" she asked, struggling to catch her breath.

"Tuesday, I think."

It meant nothing to her. "When did I get back?"

"A couple of weeks ago."

"Oh," she said, and slumped down onto her sleeping bag. "Are Mom and Dad okay?"

"I don't know," he said.

"I want to go home," she said, and started crying.

"I know, Cassidy," he said, sitting down next to her. "I do too."

"I don't know what's happening to me," she said through her tears.

"It's probably post-traumatic stress," he said gently. "It's normal to be confused and to have nightmares. Believe me, I have all sorts of crazy dreams about the war, reliving stuff over and over as if I were still there, only weirder. Then when I wake up I don't know where I am."

He rubbed her back, and she looked up at him, sniffing and wiping her nose.

"I don't like it," she said.

"I know," he said and smiled sadly. "But I'm here for you. We can look out for each other."

"Okay," she said, sniffing again, and returned his smile.

---------------)---------------

"Sorry about the other morning," Jasper said. He had cornered her at the water wagon after dinner, and she took a step back. They had not spoken since their argument.

"It's okay," she said, shrugging. "You were right. Torr stole the money. Or stole a boat, actually, and sold it." She met his gaze.

Jasper lifted his eyebrows. "Smart," he said.

"Yeah," she said sarcastically. "We're all lowlifes. You happy now?"

Jasper frowned and held out a cap. It was made from a fine tan weave like parachute material, with a long stiff brim. It looked brand new. "I finally got you a hat," he said. "Tarmac crews used to wear these at Beersheba." A blue rocket ship was embroidered on the front, with the characters עבש ראב. "Don't worry, I traded it for some food ... from a Guild trade ...," he said, his voice trailing off.

She accepted the gift and tried on the cap, adjusting the headband. It was lightweight and comfortable, and shielded her face from the rays that constantly beat down through the filtered glass of the dome.

"Thanks," she said awkwardly, and dropped her eyes to the red and gold beard that he seemed to be neglecting.

"Looks cute," he said, with a tentative smile.

"Thanks," she said, and chewed on her lip, lowering her eyes further to examine the Traders Guild patch on his vest's chest pocket. The shooting star pin glinted from his other pocket, but she studiously avoided looking at it, afraid it would spark a conversation of the past and what they meant to each other. He might reach over and take her hand, and then she might fall into his arms—or lash out in an uncontrollable fury.

She felt slightly nauseous and wanted to get away from him and clear her head. She appreciated his concern, but he was so worried about her that it made her even more nervous. She made a weak parting gesture with her hand and edged around the far corner of the wagon. She hurried across the yard, past the shaded pavilion area where the Alphabet Boys were hanging out, and headed towards the sounds of laughter and shuffling cards coming from Sky and Thunder's tent.

"Can I join you?" she asked, a wave of relief washing over her as she stepped inside the familiar tent and dropped the canvas door closed behind her. Raleigh and Roanoke shifted over to make room for her. Sky shuffled cards on a scrap of plywood that served as a low table.

"Hey, Cass," Thunder greeted her.

"Hiya, Cassafrass," Hawk said, with a big grin plastered across his face. She frowned at the nickname he had picked up from Jasper.

"Nice hat," Thunder said as she settled into her spot.

"Thanks," she said, tugging at the brim.

"Looks new. Where'd you get it?" he asked.

"Jaz."

"Aha," Thunder said with a half-smile. "He has access to the good stuff."

"I thought you guys were fighting," Hawk said.

"Hawk," Raleigh scolded, glancing at Cassidy apologetically. Everyone else looked at her expectantly, waiting for her response. She lifted one shoulder and watched as the cards interleaved together with a pleasing whirr as Sky expertly shuffled the deck.

"Did you guys make up?" Thunder asked.

She took in a breath and met his curious eyes. "We're friends."

He lifted an eyebrow but did not push any further.

"Star Man's Double," Sky said, announcing the hand's game. "Red Knights are wild."

Everyone threw in a copper bit for ante. Sky dealt the cards, and Cassidy examined her hand. The Knight of Hearts and the Queen of Globes stared up at her, next to the Prince of Stars and the Princess of Stars. Her breath caught in her throat, but she forced out a casual sigh of disappointment. She discarded the Jack of Spears and drew the Knight of Daggers. She relaxed her face into a bored look laced with a tinge of annoyance, as though she hadn't gotten the card she needed, and casually bet as high as people would go without folding.

Everyone else revealed their hand and then turned to her.

"Star Man's Double," she announced, and lay down her cards to a chorus of groans.

"No way," Raleigh said with astonishment. In all the weeks they'd played together, no one had drawn the rare combination.

"How'd you get both red Knights *and* the Star Twins?" Roanoke complained.

"And the Queen of Globes," Sky added suspiciously. It was the highest value card in the deck, and notoriously elusive.

Cassidy replied with a triumphant grin. "Must be my lucky hat," she said, and scooped up the pile of coppers.

———————)———————

Cassidy lay on her back in her sleeping bag, her eyes closed, waiting for sleep to come. Torr mumbled incoherently across the tent, already deep in his dreamworld.

She missed Jasper. He was only a tent away, but she may as well still be back on Earth, as distant as she felt from him. She had always thought they'd get married. But that was back when the world was normal. Now their old life was dead and gone. A scene from home popped into her head of when she was a young teenager.

She was in the workshop off the kitchen, hanging herbs for her mother. Jasper came into the room, looking for a jar of honey. She grabbed one off the shelf and held it behind her back.

"Come and get it," she said, teasing. He rolled his eyes and grabbed for it. She held on, and they struggled, laughing, until all four of their hands were clutched around the jar between them. His large hands were strong from playing high school lacrosse, but she had a better grip. She pulled the jar to her chest, stood on her tiptoes, and kissed his mouth.

He pulled away. "What are you doing? Stop that." His voice was taut.

"Why? You don't love me?"

He stared at her, his pupils large and black. "I love you," he stated, like it was an obvious fact everyone knew.

"You don't want to kiss me?"

"You're not even fourteen, Cassidy."

"So? Answer the question. Do you want to kiss me or not?"

He pursed his lips in frustration. "Yes I do. That's the problem."

That was all she needed to hear. She grabbed the back of his head and pulled his mouth to hers. He resisted for a moment, and then gave in, returning her kisses fervently and wrapping his arms around her. Sounds of her mother came from the kitchen just outside the workshop door, making them freeze.

They straightened their clothing, and he left the workshop with the honey. She came out a minute later. Jasper was at the counter making a peanut butter and honey sandwich, and her mother looked up from the sink. Brianna turned and leaned back against the counter, wiping her hands on a towel and regarding both of them, her expression partly amused, partly concerned.

"Listen, you two," she said, grabbing both of their sleeves and pulling them to her. She looked each of them in the eye. "Jaz. Cassandra. I know you love each other, but you're too young. Cassidy is too young." She focused on Jasper. "Do you understand me?"

He nodded, his pale, freckled cheeks a deep crimson.

"And you, young lady," she said, turning to Cassidy. "Don't you tease him. It's nothing to play around with, and it's not fair to him. You understand?" Cassidy lowered her eyes sheepishly. Her mother was not stupid. She knew Cassidy had been the instigator.

"When Cassidy is twenty-one, if you two still love each other, then you can get married. Or something. Okay?" She raised her dark eyebrows, her icy green eyes drilling into Cassidy's and then Jasper's.

"Yes, ma'am," Jasper said. "May I go now?" He cast an accusing glare at Cassidy for getting him into trouble. Brianna released him, and he grabbed his sandwich and fled from the room.

"Twenty-one?" Cassidy asked with a grimace.

Brianna held Cassidy's arm with a talon grip. "Do not tempt him. Do you understand?" She shook Cassidy's arm. "Knock it off." She released Cassidy and turned back to the sink.

Torr mumbled, "No, no," and then snorted in his sleep and turned over.

Cassidy opened her eyes and stared up at the faded canvas ceiling, where the dreamcatcher slowly turned.

---------)---------

Cassidy felt free with the Smith gang. Almost like herself again. Almost as though she were back on Earth. She lined up with them at the ration trailer, happy to be surrounded by women instead of all men.

The server behind the table gave her a scoop of rice, three wilted spinach leaves, and a small chunk of tofu. At the bread station, the server apologized as he handed her half a loaf of bread.

"Bread rations got cut today," he said.

"I see that," she said despondently, and shuffled to the water tank to fill her jug. She had already heard that rations had been cut—people had been talking about it at training that morning. Everyone relied on the bread for breakfast and to hold them over between the small daily rations. She was lucky that the Fen served dinners of rice and beans. Many people weren't fortunate enough to have their own food supply and would suffer even more than she would. Still, her stomach growled. She exchanged glances with Britta and stood at the side of the road with the Alphabet Boys while they waited for the rest of their group.

After lunch they wandered the dome, looking for junk to repurpose into art or something useful. The Alphabet Boys, except for Elvis and Febo who taught kickboxing all day, shadowed them, and Cassidy let them. Back at the Smith camp, Cassidy sat at a picnic table with Blaire and her three sisters.

Blaire's sisters and several other women were busy making small figurines from pieces of metal, glass, and anything else they could scavenge. Bailey was fashioning an elephant from pieces of aluminum cans that Britta was cutting up for her, and Becka was making a soap dish from the base of a green bottle. Cassidy sorted through a crate of junk, and at the bottom discovered a large chunk of black glassy rock as big as a dinner plate, but thicker. It was misshapen, with curved facets reflecting the light.

"Obsidian," Blaire said from her seat on the bench next to her, where she was repairing a solar panel.

"Oh, yeah," Cassidy said. "My dad showed us how to make arrowheads from this stuff."

The thought of her father made her tense up for a moment. She closed her eyes and felt for him. He was alive. That's all she could bear to find out right now. She opened her eyes and took the heavy black obsidian stone and set it on the table in front of her, remembering that her father had used a stick whose tip was wrapped in copper to chip off slivers of the mineral. She sorted through the items in the crate and found a short length of narrow copper pipe that she thought might work.

First, she put the obsidian chunk in a canvas sack and set it on the ground, then struck it with a sledgehammer until she had small pieces to work with. She sat on the bench and gripped a piece in her lap, then pressed the copper pipe against the edge until a small flake came off the glassy stone. She moved along the edge, pressing off one flake at a time.

The black stone glinted back at her, and the repetitive motion of the knapping was soothing. She focused on her work, and time flowed by.

The finished arrowhead was not exactly symmetrical, but not bad for her first attempt. She had carved a little fishtail shape at the base, around which she wrapped a length of black cord, then tied it around her neck with the Golden Falcon medallion and the Heaven's Window pendant. A sense of calm settled over her.

"Want to take a walk?" she asked Blaire, who was soldering a connection on the solar panel. "I'm supposed to meet a woman named Phyllis. Britta said you guys know her."

"Yeah, sure," Blaire said. "I need to get more rice from her anyway."

When Blaire finished her panel, a group of them gathered. The five Alphabet Boys had been invited into the Smith camp and were sitting on upturned crates, learning how to knit. They got to their feet and set their needles and yarn carefully on a table.

"That shit is hard," Copper said. "Save mine for later."

"Gonna make me some socks?" Darla asked. "I like purple."

"Yes, dear," Copper said, and grinned as she playfully scowled at him.

The band crossed Peary Dome and arrived at the trader woman's camp.

Blaire introduced Cassidy to Phyllis, and they shook hands. Cassidy remembered the gray-haired woman from her first day in Peary Dome. Phyllis had been sitting inside the Guild traders pen next to potted plants and a bird cage holding two finches. Cassidy told her she had seen her.

"Oh, yes," Phyllis said. "I sold the plants to a mining lord who lives on the south pole at Aitken basin, and the birds went to Dragan at the greenhouse. He buys all my birds. He says they make the soy plants happy, and they grow better that way."

Cassidy returned the woman's glowing smile, feeling at home. Phyllis gestured for Blaire and Cassidy to follow her into a tent. The tent was lined with shelves, which held a sparse collection of industrial-sized cans of food, a few sacks of rice and beans, and some root vegetables. Blaire began counting out silver bits as Phyllis measured cups of rice from a large burlap sack into a smaller sack.

"You want your usual forty cups?"

Blaire nodded.

"Price of food is going way up," Phyllis said gravely. "This is the last batch I'll be able to sell you at the old price."

Lines furrowed in Blaire's forehead as she stacked silver bits on top of a crate.

"How's business?" Phyllis asked.

Blaire shook her head. "Only so many knickknacks people want to buy these days. The solar panel repair business is what's keeping us going." She pushed four stacks of coins across the crate.

Cassidy could see the anxiety straining Blaire's face as her golden eyes scanned the other items in the tent, resting on cans of vegetables and a sack of beans. Cassidy knew forty cups of rice was barely enough to make one meal for the eighty Smiths.

"I'll take fifty cups of beans," Cassidy said. "And one of those big number-ten cans of stewed tomatoes, and that can of carrots. And a dozen of those onions," she said, nodding at a sack of sprouting onions.

"That'll cost you ninety-six global credits altogether," Phyllis said, her brown eyes sliding to the gold medallion at Cassidy's neck.

"Okay," Cassidy said, pulling out a gold bit coin.

Phyllis raised an eyebrow at the gold bit and counted out four silver bits in change, then gathered the food for Cassidy.

"What do you do for water to cook rice and beans?" she asked Blaire, eyeing five-gallon jugs of water in the corner of the tent.

"Everybody chips in a cup," she told Cassidy. "You guys have your own water supply, apparently," Blaire said. "So you should be good for those beans."

"Everybody chips in something for the water at the Fen, too," Cassidy said. "I'll take one of those," she told Phyllis, nodding at a jug. That cost her two tenth-gold bits. She wouldn't tell Blaire the extra food and water were for the Smiths until they got back to their camp, knowing Blaire would refuse them.

Cassidy's gaze roved over a small bookshelf by the door that held a collection of tattered paperback novels.

"Take some," Phyllis said. "They're free. When you're done, just pass them around. And bring me some different books if you find any."

Cassidy took a small assortment for the Boyer brothers and the Alphabet Boys and stuffed them into her daypack. On the bottom shelf, coated with dust, sat a stack of leather-bound journals. Cassidy squatted down, brushed the top one off, and thumbed through it. Her skin tingled. It was a blank journal, with a thick tooled leather cover and unlined paper, white and silky.

"What did you find?" Blaire asked, squatting next to her and lifting the next journal off the stack. It was also brand new, with clean, ivory paper.

"Torr forgot to bring his journals from Earth," Cassidy said. "He needs paper."

"How about this one?" Blaire asked. "People say he has a spirit wolf."

Blaire handed her the third journal in the stack. Tooled into the russet-brown leather cover, a wolf head stared up at Cassidy with a steady gaze, its ruff up.

"This is perfect," Cassidy said.

Phyllis was looking on and said, "Those are for sale. And they're not cheap, sorry to say. Paper is getting hard to find."

"How much?" Cassidy asked. "And do you have pens or pencils?"

"I believe I do, somewhere," she said. Phyllis opened a crate and began sorting through its contents. She held up a small cardboard box. "Here," she said, handing the box to Cassidy.

Inside the box was a random assortment of pens and pencils—some used, some new. There was one pack of twelve new black wooden pencils wrapped in plastic. Most of the pens were used and dried up, but there was one new fountain pen in a fancy velvet-lined box. The pen was marbled blue with gold details.

"That's a luxury European pen," Phyllis said. "This goes with it." She handed Cassidy an inkwell.

Cassidy pulled the cap off the fountain pen and examined the metal nib, and then snapped the cover back on.

"How much for six journals, this pack of pencils, and the fountain pen and ink?" Cassidy asked.

Phyllis tightened her lips. "Six journals? That only leaves me with two."

Cassidy knew she was being greedy, but she wanted the books and held Phyllis's gaze. Cassidy's father had taught her to buy up goods in short supply when you had the opportunity. You might not get another chance.

"Well, let me see," Phyllis said, scratching on a small pad of paper with a stub of a yellow pencil. "One gold bit per journal, another gold bit for the pencils, and an Eagle for the pen and ink."

"An Eagle?!" Blaire exclaimed.

Cassidy's shoulders tightened. One hundred global credits for a blank journal was outrageous, even on the moon, but a thousand global credits for a pen was robbery. And pencils back on Earth were pennies. But then again, there were no trees or hemp here to make paper with, and no animals to get hides to make leather. No wood for pencils. And no factories to make fancy pens, and nothing to make ink from.

Phyllis shrugged. "Can't get good pens anymore, and it's my last one. I'll throw these in for free," she said, digging through the box and handing Cassidy a small pencil sharpener and a pink rubber eraser.

"An Eagle for everything," Cassidy said.

Phyllis sighed. "One Eagle and six gold bits. I'll give you the pencils for free. A good deal, just for you."

They finally agreed on an Eagle and two gold bits. Phyllis showed her how to fill the fountain pen, and then wrapped everything in a length of clean tent canvas, secured it with twine, and handed the bundle to Cassidy in exchange for the gold coins.

"Thank you," Cassidy said. She hesitated and threw Blaire a pointed glance. Blaire caught her meaning and left the tent, leaving Cassidy alone with the older woman.

"Uh ...," Cassidy faltered. "The medics suggested I speak with you."

"Ah, yes," Phyllis said, unfolding two lawn chairs and inviting Cassidy to sit down. "You are the one who escaped those kidnappers, are you not?"

"Yes, that's right," Cassidy said, taking a seat and resting the bundle on her lap.

"How are you feeling?" Phyllis asked.

"Fine. Good. Not good. I don't know." Cassidy looked down and fiddled with the twine.

Phyllis let the words hang in the air.

"I just don't know ...," Cassidy said, tears pooling in her eyes. "I don't know how people can be so cruel."

"It's hard to understand," Phyllis said.

"It doesn't make sense. I mean it does make sense, I guess. If people have power, they abuse it. Isn't that so?" She lifted her eyes and met Phyllis's. The woman mirrored Cassidy's pained expression, and Cassidy went on, "They treat other people as playthings, then toss them aside, the way a cat mauls a bird and then forgets about it, as though a life of joy and wonder had not just been cut off for no good reason."

Cassidy sniffed loudly, and Phyllis nodded. Cassidy wiped at her nose and said, "And just like a bird, I feel like my wing feathers have been yanked out, and I'm stumbling around, lost and confused and unable to fly. What is a bird if it can't fly?" Tears spilled over, and she wiped them away.

Phyllis said, "If it gives you any comfort, my dear, my wing feathers were pulled out too. It took time, but they did grow back. I can fly again, but I am not the same bird as I was before. I was a dove, I think. Now I am an eagle." She gazed at Cassidy with a pinched grin. "And eagles hunt."

Cassidy swallowed and sat up straighter. "Yes. I suppose that's so," Cassidy said and returned Phyllis's sad smile.

"It's not easy, my dear," Phyllis said as they stood up. "It's not easy." Phyllis gave her a warm embrace. When they parted, Phyllis leaned in and peered at Cassidy's necklaces.

"What are all those power objects you're wearing? May I?" Phyllis asked.

Cassidy nodded, and Phyllis took the obsidian arrowhead in her hand and closed her eyes.

"This one will save your life one day," Phyllis said in a soft murmur that made Cassidy's skin prickle.

Cassidy held her tongue, sensing ripples of knowing coming off the woman, reminding her of her mother. Phyllis kept her eyes closed and felt with her fingers for the next pendant, clasping the Golden Falcon medallion next. The corners of her eyes wrinkled in thought. "This one resonates with a part of yourself and will help you open a door in the future. And this one," she said, clutching the Heaven's Window triangle. Cassidy could feel the woman's hand tremble. "This one will lead you nearly to your death but will help you save the world."

Phyllis's eyes popped open and held Cassidy's surprised gaze. The woman's mouth broadened into a wide smile.

"Very interesting," Phyllis said, patting Cassidy's shoulder and winking. "I will need to keep my eye on you."

They walked together out of the camp. "Stop by anytime you need a little rest along your journey," Phyllis said, and squeezed Cassidy's hand.

"Thank you," Cassidy said. "I will."

She joined the Alphabet Boys and her friends, who had been waiting for her on the side of the road. They walked north around the perimeter road, taking the long way back to the Smith camp and stopping at the greenhouses to gaze upon the glorious greenery. One soy house was thick with foliage, blooming with thousands of small purple flowers. Birdsong was faintly audible through the glass. The sight of all that greenery and the sound of birds singing made her heart hurt. They moved along. The smell of baking bread made everyone stand outside the bakery building, as though the smell could fill their bellies. Further on, they stopped at the junkyard, where Cassidy bought a big blue plastic tarp. Guy offered to carry it for her, and they headed back to the Smith camp.

In the late afternoon, Torr, Jasper, and a bunch of Fensters showed up at the Smith camp to walk her home. Cassidy and the Alphabet Boys got to their feet and said goodbye to the women.

"Don't forget your food," Blaire said, motioning to the items Cassidy had purchased from Phyllis.

"You can cook it up here and save me a plateful," Cassidy said.

"No, Cassidy," Blaire said, lowering her brow sternly. "It's too expensive."

"It's no problem," Cassidy said. "Please."

"Really? Are you sure?"

Cassidy nodded. "I'm sure."

"Thank you," Blaire said, looking embarrassed.

"Thank you for making me feel normal again," Cassidy said.

They smiled and exchanged a brief hug, and Cassidy walked out to the road.

Hawk approached, and Cassidy patted him on the shoulder.

"Hey there, Kitty Hawk," she said. "Want to carry this for me?" she asked, handing him the bundle of journals.

"What is it?" Hawk asked.

"I'll show you later."

Cassidy headed down the ring road surrounded by her friends and the Alphabet Boys. She found herself looking over her shoulder, reminding herself of Kai and his nervous tic. She told herself not to worry—there were too many of them to get attacked.

"Did you make that?" Hawk asked, pointing at the sculptures in her hand.

Jasper appeared at her other side. "Whatcha got there, Cassidy?" he asked.

She held up the two metal flowers she'd fashioned by cutting petals and leaves from the sides of aluminum beer cans and attaching them to wires.

Jasper looked at her with a hesitant smile and bright eyes, hoping she was no longer angry with him. She saw his gaze rest on the Beersheba hat she was still wearing. He looked pleased.

"Do you want ...," she started to ask, holding out one of the flowers. He abruptly turned away as his radio chirped at him. He crossed the road and talked into it, then clipped it to his belt. "See you guys later," he said, and trotted off, leaving her staring after him. She lowered the flower and kept walking.

"They're pretty," Hawk said.

"Thanks," she said sullenly, and offered him one. Hawk took it and gazed down at the metal blossom as though it were a real flower.

"What's Jasper up to?" Torr asked, dropping back to walk with her.

"I don't know," she said, kicking at a ridge in the road.

"He's on that radio all the time," Torr said.

"I know," she said, meeting his eyes.

Back at the Fen, Cassidy and Guy hung the blue tarp on the clothesline that stretched between Fritz and Frank's and Jasper's tent, creating a barrier along the southwest corner of the camp.

"What are you doing?" Torr asked.

"Hanging a tarp," she said. "What does it look like we're doing?"

"*Why* are you hanging a tarp?" Torr asked, frowning at her and the tarp, which reflected off his sunglasses like a bright blue sky.

"Because someone is watching us, and I don't like it," she said. She met his skeptical frown with a glare. "I know you don't believe me, Torr. You probably think I'm crazy, but I don't have the energy to care what you think. But someone *is* watching us."

Torr pressed his lips together, and she turned away and ducked inside their tent. She changed out of her jeans and butterfly t-shirt and into her purple, gold-studded gown, which she wished she could wear everywhere, but which Torr had insisted looked ridiculous and was not practical to train in. She had determined it would get too dirty if she wore it everywhere, and so she only wore it when she was at the Fen. She tightened the laces of the boots Torr had bought her and ran her hands over the soft wine-colored velvet. She had worn the boots all day, including at practice, and they still looked brand new.

She left the tent, swept by Torr and the Alphabet Boys, then went into the back, where she sat on a crate next to Berkeley at his sewing machine. He was making her a new pair of pants from the black iridescent fabric.

"Make them tight, like girls' pants," she reminded him as she arranged her long gown so it would not touch the dusty ground.

"I know, Your Highness."

"But with lots of pockets."

"Yes, Your Grace," he teased as he guided a seam under the whirring needle.

"And tight around the calves. To fit under my boots."

"Your wish is my command."

She lifted the dress hem above her shins to show off her boots and waved a foot in the air until he glanced up.

"Yes, oh Jewel of the Stars, those are lovely boots. They're Delosian, you know."

"They are?" She examined them more closely.

"Yes, all except the soles. Those are standard moon soles, made from tires."

"I like them," she said, putting her foot on the ground and letting the dress drape down over the boots. "Look what I made," she said, holding up her remaining metal flower.

Berkeley finished the seam and looked up. "That's pretty cool," he said. "Reminds me of home." He got a wistful look in his eyes, and she felt tears welling up in hers. The tears overflowed and trickled down her cheeks.

"What's the matter, Cassidy?" Berkeley asked, setting aside the black fabric and pulling his seat next to hers. He put his arm around her shoulders.

"I just ...," she said, wiping at her cheeks. "I just never thought I'd never see another flower ever again." Silent weeping took hold of her, and she buried her face in his dusty dreadlocks as he squeezed her shoulder.

"The soy plants in the greenhouses have flowers," he said gently. "And the tomato and pepper plants flower. Even the lettuce has flowers if they don't harvest it soon enough."

"I know, but those flowers are tiny. And I can't go in there."

"Muria has flowers," he said.

"It does?" She sniffled.

"Yeah. Big, crazy flowers," Berkeley said. "They grow really fast, and they glow at night."

"Really?" she asked. "They glow?" He rocked her gently, and she felt like a child being told a bedtime story. "What do they look like?" she asked.

He described orange flowers that hung upside down with whorled petals, and big cone-shaped purple flowers that held pools of nectar, with little flying blue lizards nesting in them.

"I would like to go to Muria someday," she said. Her tears had stopped, but she stayed snuggled against him. "What about Delos? Do they have flowers?"

"Oh, yes," Berkeley said. "They cultivate them, and the noble ladies make big headdresses out of them and walk around like they're in a parade or something, except they're very serious about them. The bigger their headdress, the more important they feel."

Cassidy giggled, and Berkeley described the huge wigs the women wore, with their fake hair piled high like wasp nests to hold the floral arrangements, making her laugh even harder.

Her spirits lifted. Maybe it was not so bad after all, out here in space where there were friends to be made and worlds to discover. She placed the metal flower in an empty bottle on a shelf next to the sewing machine, then she got an idea. Berkeley volunteered to donate a length of tent canvas for her project. They went into the craft tent, spread the fabric out on the table, mixed up several colors of paints, and set to work.

--------------------)--------------------

After dinner, Cassidy distributed her spoils from Phyllis.

She brought the novels to the Alphabet Boys' tarp and set them on a crate and called the other Fensters over. "These are for you guys to share," she said. Within minutes, the books were all taken, and the men dispersed to read.

Then she went into the back and stacked the blank journals on the craft table. There were five left, of various tooled leather designs— she had left one in Blaire's tent with two pencils. She kept one for herself, stashing it in her daypack, and then passed out the others, along with two pencils each, to Berkeley, Hiroshi, and Tatsuya. Tatsuya was extremely touched and bowed repeatedly. "I've been wanting fine paper to sketch my bonsai," he said. "I like to capture the shape as it grows and transforms."

"Bonsai?" she asked, her breath catching in her throat. "You have a bonsai tree?"

The man's small eyes widened. "Yes, I do. You didn't know? Would you like to see it? It's in my tent. Go on inside and take a look. You can visit it whenever you want." He waved towards his tent. "Go ahead," he said, bowing again.

Cassidy crossed the small yard to Tatsuya's tent, her heart quickening. She was about to step inside when she saw that the tent's floor was covered with clean rush mats. She removed her boots and set them on a mat outside the door, and then went inside in her bare feet. An immediate sense of peace enveloped her. The tent felt spacious, with a futon rolled up neatly against the back and a meditation cushion sitting in the center of the floor facing a small shrine. On the other side of the tent, a set of black lacquered shelves held Tatsuya's neatly folded clothing and an assortment of baskets. Three colorful origami birds twirled slowly overhead.

In a corner on a low table stood the bonsai tree, the subtle scent of juniper reminding her of the coastal woodlands back home. The small tree looked almost like an animal—a forest sprite—living and breathing, with two arms raised up and bearing clumps of manicured greenery. They stared at one another, and Cassidy bowed to it.

"You must be very strong and brave to survive in such a hostile place as the moon," she said.

The bluish-green needles shivered and shimmered.

"Tatsuya is about the best guardian you could imagine. You lucked out," she said, half expecting the tree to answer.

Cassidy sat cross-legged on the floor and meditated with the bonsai for a long while. When her legs grew numb, she got to her feet and stretched, yawning. She slowly backed out of the tent, bowing to the tree as she left through the canvas door flaps, then pulled on her boots and went in search of Torr.

She found him in their tent and sat next to him on his blankets. She handed him the canvas bundle.

"What's this?" he asked.

"A present."

He unwrapped the bundle and regarded the wolf journal, his face lighting up as he examined the detailed wolf design and flipped through the blank pages. "Wow, Cass," he said. "Thanks."

"Blaire picked it out for you."

"She did?" he asked, glancing up. "Do you think she knows about my wolf? Can she see it?"

"I don't know if she can see it, but yeah, she mentioned it. People talk. Everyone's a little bit intimidated by you."

He gave a wry laugh. "Really? That's too bad."

Cassidy shrugged. "Respect is not such a bad thing."

"I would rather be loved than feared," he said.

"Oh, they love you too, don't worry about that," she said.

"And Blaire?" he asked, raising an eyebrow.

"What, love you?" Cassidy laughed. "I know she *likes* you."

"That's a start," he said, chuckling. He inspected the pencils, then the fountain pen and inkwell. She showed him how to draw ink up into the pen by twisting its base.

"This is great," he said. "You're the best. Let me copy this down before it's gone forever," he said, crawling to the other side of his bed to a strip of dust that bordered the tent wall. "I learned the words to a star song in a dream. I visited the planet Turya, and they were singing it."

"You did?" she asked, her pulse quickening. "They were?"

He squinted at barely discernible markings in the dust and wrote in his journal. "I meant to tell you. But I can't remember the melody for the life of me."

Cassidy looked over his shoulder, and he read out loud as he wrote:

Children, come home
Uttapta burns
Drink of the golden yods
Remember who you are
Show us the pathway to the stars

"I thought *they* were supposed to show *us* the pathway to the stars," she said. "And what are golden yods?"

"I have no idea," Torr said.

"Did you ask them how to get there?" Cassidy asked. "You know, in real life?"

"Yes," he said. "Kind of."

"Well?" she asked.

His mouth turned down. "The only guy who could see me doesn't seem to know."

"Oh," she said, her voice heavy.

"I'll try to go there again," he said.

She struggled to keep her hopes up. If they could miraculously find their way to the mythical planet Turya, maybe this entire nightmare would end.

———————)———————

Later that evening, Cassidy stole some time alone in her tent and gazed into her crystal ball.

"I'm hunting," she said softly to the crystal. It glimmered and glowed in response and settled on an image.

It was Balthazar again. Exactly the person she did not want to see.

During her first week back, she had barely left the tent and had spent most of her time spying on Balthazar in the crystal ball. Even just watching the man made her body hurt, but she had grown accustomed to the heavy feeling of dread after all the water scrying sessions during her captivity. Only now she was free. But her friends were not. They were on their way to an unknown fate, and a new pair of women were trapped in Balthazar's lair. The guilt ate away at her, but still she watched.

Tonight she found him in his new speedster—identical to the one she had stolen—flying slowly out of Anaximenes crater and over the highlands. Her latest distraction had been to learn how to properly pilot the craft by observing his every move, and she had slowly begun to decipher the control panel. She watched as he approached the dwelling, which blended perfectly into the colorless landscape, and pointed his key fob at the camouflaged landing bay. He pressed a number sequence on the tiny keypad—5733—and the compression bay door slowly opened. He glided inside, and she turned her attention away from the house. She did not have the stomach to watch him strut around the house while two women were locked away in his rape room. Instead, she searched for the loner—Ridge Gandoop—who shared the dwelling with Balthazar and the other four men. Cassidy had determined the four men were Balthazar's personal guards, or more like house servants, except for the lucky one who got to leave the dwelling with Balthazar and follow him around the spaceport complex. Ridge seemed to be an introverted loner and separate from Balthazar and his guards. He interacted with them very little and came and went as he pleased. He had his own bedroom suite and his own speedster. He walked with his head held high, and roamed around the spaceport and attached buildings as though he owned the place, which apparently he did. She tightened her jaw. He was a land thief. A trespasser. An immoral man who allowed human trafficking to operate from his spaceport and a lunatic rapist to share his dwelling. A tall, lean man, Ridge always wore an immaculately clean black flight suit, kept his scalp and face shaved, and never smiled. She found him in one of the black cube buildings, watching a stream of orange molten metal flow from an enormous crucible into a large trough. He was standing next to two other men. She left him there and began exploring.

Remote viewing with the crystal ball offered her more control than scrying with water. With the crystal, she could direct the vision with her thoughts, although sometimes it seemed to have a mind of its own, leading her in a new direction or showing her something unexpected. Like when it had plopped her right in the middle of the shipping container that held a dozen young women, from which Balthazar had plucked two at random and then shoved Anna and Maria into the arms of the remaining ten. The vision had left her suffocating with fear and guilt. At least Anna and Maria had made it out of Balthazar's den alive.

Cassidy gripped the crystal ball, hoping fervently that the Nommos were not as bad as everyone said, and prayed that the two new women would survive Balthazar's sadism with their bodies and souls intact. *Golden stars, may your light shine down upon them and bring them peace.*

She took a breath and shrank away from the suffering of the women and recalled what Great-Aunt Sophie had said about crystals: *We don't use them, they use us, if they deign to. Crystals are sentient beings, and we ignore that fact at our peril.*

Shivers tingled across Cassidy's shoulders and head. "Show me only good things," she murmured to the crystal.

She wanted to wander through the Gandoop buildings and see what she else could discover. She exited the smelter, floated down a hallway, and emerged into another passageway. At its end, she passed like a wraith through the closed door and found herself in the bustling hangar of Gandoop Spaceport.

She followed a small transport across the floor and through a large doorway. Her mouth dropped open. She was in an enormous warehouse, stacked floor to ceiling with row after row of shelves crammed with food. Crates of canned goods. Sacks of grain. Bags and crates of sprouting onions and garlic, and all other varieties of fresh produce. Crates of eggs. Tanks of spring water. Dried meats. Wheels of cheeses.

Hunger reared up and clawed at her belly, and her muscles burned with hunger that she had suppressed, convincing herself that she was lucky to be at the Fen with enough to eat. Then a fiery rage welled up and spilled from her eyes in hot tears. The heartless hoarding made her nauseous and sad. They were intentionally restricting the flow of food to Peary Dome. There was no other explanation. And whose office overlooked everything? *Balthazar's.*

A new level of hatred merged with terrified fury. It collected in her throat, choking her.

"Cassandra, my dear. There you are."

A warm golden glow permeated her consciousness, chasing away her tears. Her cells buzzed, and a radiance surrounded the crystal ball, lifting it from her palms. The glowing orb floated, suspended between her hands, and Cassidy stared into it.

Avala peered back at her with concern. The Turyan priestess's eyes shone vermilion-red, alive like flames of a hot fire.

"Where have you been?" Cassidy asked, distraught and relieved. "I've been looking all over for you."

"I'm sorry, *Jalavahini*. I have been trying to reach you as well."

"How come I can hear you, but I can't hear anything when I view others?" Cassidy asked.

"That is simple," Avala said. "We have a two-way connection. That is why."

"Oh," Cassidy said. "That makes sense. So if I find my mother, and she is scrying at the same time, then we will be able to speak with one another?"

"That is correct," Avala said. "She searches for you sometimes in pools of water."

"She does?" Cassidy asked, her heart aching. "I am afraid to look for her."

"Why?" Avala asked.

"I feel her sometimes. And my father. They are both frightened. I'm afraid if I see them, the grief will overwhelm me. I already feel so fragile. Sometimes I think I am going to literally fall apart and crumble into a million pieces."

"I understand," Avala said. "You have been attacked. The darkness is creeping forward. It is scary, I know. But that makes it all the more important that you succeed in re-establishing the pathways of light so that we can be together. Otherwise, the dark forces might win, and we will all perish before our time. You must be strong. But beware, the attacks will continue. You are a beacon of light, and dark is attracted to light, even though light extinguishes darkness. They seek to put out your flame."

Cassidy stared at the floating crystal ball, and Avala's eyes seared into hers.

"But how can I re-establish the pathways of light?" Cassidy asked. "I don't know anything about that, and I'm stuck here on the moon where there's nothing except starving people. And a few greedy, selfish, cruel people. I hate it here. But Torr said the moon is important, and we're not to abandon it. The Murians told him so."

"Ah, yes. The Murians. There are many teachers available to you, as is the way with the Star Children. Forces conspire to help you—as well as to stop you," Avala said. "I wish I knew the solution, but no one knows how to establish the light pathways since the primary portal was destroyed. It is up to you to find the answer, I'm embarrassed to say. The Star Children and Guiding Star are the navigators of the stars. The Blessed Trinity. Perhaps the Murians will be able to assist you. They know crystals, and many other secrets they have protected through the ages. But those particular Murians who reside on the moon are not priests. You must go to the planet Muria to learn all it has to teach you. That is where one of the remaining Star Globes sits. It waits for you."

Shivers ran up Cassidy's spine. Avala continued, "But the Murians are right about your moon. It is made of crystal sand and is a node along the pathways of light. Some say it is a key to the puzzle, but the Concha Scrolls are vague about this. Or so my father says."

Cassidy shivered again. "Moon of crystal sand. It says that in a book I have."

"A book?" Avala asked. "That is a sign for you. Perhaps that book contains ancient wisdom. You must consult it for more clues."

"Yes, I need to," Cassidy agreed. "I am trying, but it is in a different language. There are so many things I need to do," she said. "I don't know what to do first."

"Just do what is in front of you. You will know. But regarding your parents," Avala said. "They will benefit from your strength if you visit them, even if they cannot see you."

"Will they know I'm there?" Cassidy asked. "Can others detect me when I spy on them?" She was suddenly frightened at the prospect, and Balthazar's face loomed in front of her.

"Your parents will probably feel you. Others—if you mean the man who attacked you—he may sense you. Or he may not. I'm not sure. He may think of you and not know why. In any case, there's nothing he can do to you from such a distance while you both remain on the physical plane. I do not believe he is a sorcerer, from what I have observed."

"You have observed him?"

"I have," Avala said. "He is cruel, but there are much worse than him."

Another wave of shivers shook Cassidy.

The crystal ball shimmered. "I awaken," Avala said abruptly, glancing over her shoulder. "My sister awakens."

The view expanded, and Cassidy could see that Avala was lying in a large bed, her golden head cradled on a pillow of shimmering white silk.

"I will find you again," Avala whispered, and she was gone.

The crystal ball settled into Cassidy's palms, and she stared down at it. She clamped her teeth together while she still had courage and searched for her mother in the crystal ball. She found Brianna immediately. It was a bright night, lit by the light of the moon. Brianna was stalking silently across a fallow field. A large raven was perched on her shoulder, its beak nuzzled in its wing feathers, sleeping. Brianna stopped and looked around her, sensing the air.

"Mom," Cassidy said. "Can you feel me?"

Brianna tilted her head for a long moment, then turned and began slinking forward again.

Cassidy shifted her thoughts to her father and found him in a bunkhouse. He was lying on a bottom bunk, which was only a bare piece of plywood, with a thin blanket covering him. He was asleep, his body exhausted and hungry. Cassidy bit her lip and stayed with him for a short while. He was breathing steadily. He was not sick. He felt at ease with the men surrounding him in the tightly packed bunkhouse.

Cassidy backed away and floated across the sky, and then alighted on the surface of the moon and searched for Jasper. He was in the traders pen, sitting on a stool and fidgeting with his pocket knife, snapping it open with a flick of his wrist, and then pushing it closed with his thumb. Over and over. He looked as though he were waiting for something. Cassidy didn't know why he couldn't wait here in the Fen with the rest of them. She wondered if he felt her presence—if he was thinking about her right now—but she could not tell.

She exhaled with hurt annoyance and closed her fingers around the crystal ball. "Thank you," she said idly to the small glass globe. It was warm in her hands. She slid it under her pillow, then rubbed the Golden Falcon pendant at her throat between her thumb and fingertips, the warm gold soothing her jagged nerves.

———)———

"Torr," she said as they were getting ready for bed. "There's a code to get into Balthazar's bunker. I can punch it into the key fob and open the hangar door."

Torr peered at her. "Really? A code?"

She nodded.

"I thought your friends are on their way to the Nommos," he said.

"They are," she said. "But there are two new women trapped there. We could get them out."

Torr sighed. "Even with the code," he said, "we still have the issue of getting past their security. Is the hangar airlock a dual chamber?"

She nodded again.

"Well, then, by the time we got through the second chamber, they'd be there waiting for us. We'd be sitting ducks, with no weapons against their Lectros."

She pursed her lips, trying not to blame him for her feelings of helplessness. "Well, we're going to have to do something," she said. "And not just about the women. They're hoarding food at Gandoop Spaceport."

"How do you know that?" he asked, pulling his blanket up under his chin.

"I saw it in the crystal ball. An enormous warehouse packed with food. It makes me sick with anger."

He raised himself on an elbow and looked at her.

"Are you sure?"

"Yes," she said. "My vision has returned. At least with the help of the crystal ball. Just like Grandma Leann said."

"What else can you see?" he asked.

"Everything. It's a little overwhelming. I can't look at it for too long."

"Seems like that's all you like to do lately," he said.

"Yeah, well ... I found someone on Turya. A priestess." She related their conversations. "But what about the food?" she asked. "We need it."

"Of course we do," he said, resting his head on a rolled-up towel and closing his eyes. "They are obviously putting us under siege. We need to make a plan. And we'll try to figure out how to rescue those women. Tomorrow. Or the next day. I'm exhausted."

"Take me to see the Murians," she said. "Maybe they have some ideas."

"Okay," he muttered.

"We can't wait," she said. "The hungrier we get, the weaker we'll be."

The deep breathing of sleep was his only reply.

———————)———————

The next day at practice, Berkeley and Cassidy proudly unrolled the banner they had painted. It read *Light Fighters* in big colorful letters, next to a large version of the image from Torr's tattoo. They had filled in the Earth outline with blue, green, brown, and swirling white clouds. A bright yellow moon was dotted with round craters, and silver swords crossed above the planet's horizon. Torr was surprised and gave Cassidy and Berkeley a group hug. They hung the banner from the shade structure above the picnic tables, then formed into squads for practice.

During the knife-fighting class, Cassidy practiced grabbing Thunder from behind by the chin and cutting his throat with her rolled canvas knife. He was nearly as tall as Balthazar, and the act of killing him, even if it were pretend, gave her shivers of terror and glee.

"You're pretty good at that," Khaled said to her, coming up to the pair as she reached up to grab Thunder's chin again. "But he's letting you do it. Try it on me."

Khaled turned away from her, standing with his arms folded. She approached from behind, but before she could get a grip on his goatee-covered chin, he turned and tackled her to the ground with his hand around her throat. She froze in terror, images of Balthazar flooding her vision.

The next thing she knew, Torr body-slammed Khaled to the ground and started grappling with him. Cassidy staggered to the picnic tables and crawled underneath, folding her knees to her chest and struggling to breathe.

"You're a fucking asshole," Torr's said, his angry voice making its way through the frantic drumming in her ears.

Her whole body was shaking, and she desperately wished she had some Greenwash. Why had Torr hidden all of it? He wouldn't tell anyone what he had done with it—he just said it was gone and there was no getting it back. Maybe if she begged him he would retrieve it for her. Maybe Jasper had more and wasn't telling her. She squeezed her eyes shut and began counting her breaths. *One two three.* Balthazar smelled of French milled soap and whiskey. *Four five six.* Counting like she did in Berkeley's meditation class, even though he said counting was thinking and that she should just focus on the breath.

"Cassidy."

It was Torr. His leg appeared over a bench, and he wormed his way under the table and sat with her.

"I'm sorry, Cassie. Khaled's an asshole."

She looked up. "He was just trying to teach me."

"He shouldn't have done that," Torr said.

"I don't want anyone putting their hands around my throat."

"I know, I'm sorry," he said. "He won't do it again."

Even though she had not shared all the details of her captivity, her throat had been bruised red and purple when she had arrived at Peary. Torr must have figured out what had happened. Khaled should have known too. Maybe he *was* an asshole.

Later, when she emerged from under the table to sit on a bench, Khaled came over and apologized.

"You can teach me another time," she said, keeping her voice steady. "I want to learn how to never let anyone put their hands around my neck ever again."

"Okay," he said, bowing his head. "I can do that."

She skipped the rest of knife-fighting class but returned to her squad for Judo. She liked the anatomical precision of the lock holds. Even the tiny, elderly Tatsuya could disable the giant Buck with a deft twist of a joint.

The day moved on, and after spending the afternoon at the Smiths' she returned to the Fen and changed into her purple gown. Everyone had become accustomed to her odd ways and no longer exchanged concerned glances whenever she appeared dressed in the Delosian Seer's garb. After they ate a dinner of rice and beans with stewed onions and tomatoes, and cleaned the dishes, Tatsuya and Hiroshi invited her and Torr into the back. Tatsuya presented her with a red t-shirt with a black dragon he had painted on it. She admired Tatsuya's artwork. This dragon was even nicer than the dragon on the t-shirt she had left behind in Balthazar's closet. This one had its wings outstretched, flying, and its eyes followed her. Torr explained that Hawk had found the shirt for her. Berkeley joined them and handed her the new black pants.

"These are done, too," he said. "Try them on when you get a chance."

She went to her tent and changed out of the purple gown and into the new pants and shirt, pulling on the yellow and blue vest Torr had bought for her and lacing the Delosian boots up over the pants. The clothes were comfortable, and she examined herself in the square mirror Torr had taken from Jasper's tent. She liked the look. Feminine, but not too much. She transferred items into her pockets and strapped on her belt, which now held her combat knife, a wooden club, a slingshot Hawk had made for her, and a couple of belt pouches.

She returned to the back courtyard, where she modeled the clothing. Berkeley and Tatsuya looked pleased with their handiwork.

"Do you want to look at those knives now?" Hiroshi asked.

He brought out a large wooden case. Inside, several knives were neatly displayed. Cassidy's breath caught in her throat. The steel blades shimmered and rippled like water reflecting sunlight. The handles were either made of wood of various colors and grains, or polished gemstone. Homesickness washed over her as she inspected each of them. Black walnut, ironwood, ebony, rosewood, sandalwood. Flame agate, lapis lazuli, red river jasper, tiger iron, green jade, fossilized coral, amethyst, snowflake obsidian, tiger eye, malachite. Each one was more beautiful than the next.

"Why do you still have all of these?" Jasper asked, coming up behind them. "You could sell these for a fortune."

Hiroshi shrugged sheepishly. "I have a hard time parting with them. They are my last pieces of Earth."

Everyone was struck silent and reverently passed around the box of knives.

"But I will let each of you have one, since you are also part of Earth," he said, turning his gaze to Cassidy, Torr, and Jasper. "They tell me you three are the chosen ones. The Star Children. You must save us all, so we can one day return to our homes."

Cassidy traded glances with Torr and Jasper. The prophecy haunted her. She felt horrible letting Hiroshi believe it was true, when she had been such an abject failure.

"I couldn't," Cassidy said. But then she thought of Avala. The Turyan priestess existed. Somewhere. The beautiful golden goddess believed in her. Cassidy inhaled and stood taller.

"You must," Hiroshi said. "I insist." He held up the lapis lazuli knife—midnight blue awash with flecks of gold. But her eyes kept returning to the plainest of the knives—the snowflake obsidian. She lifted it from the case. The handle was black with splotches of white, the blade was long and single-edged—and very sharp—and the metal of the bolster and butt was polished and unadorned.

"Obsidian," Hiroshi said. "Good choice. The healer's stone. Protector against evil influences." It was cool in her hand, and her fingers wrapped around the polished handle. "It is yours," he said with a bow.

"And which do you choose?" Hiroshi asked, turning to Torr.

Torr's face wrinkled with indecision. Hiroshi disappeared into his tent and returned with a suede bundle, which he unrolled to reveal six more knives with bone and horn handles.

"This is it," Torr said immediately, pointing at one, and Hiroshi passed him the knife.

Cassidy found it to be relatively ugly. It was a plain, brown handle with raised ridges spiraling around it, a brass butt and bolster, and a long blade.

"Horn from an antelope," Hiroshi said. "Sacred creatures."

Torr nodded and turned the knife over in his hand, and Cassidy considered that maybe it was not so ugly after all.

"And what about you?" Hiroshi asked, turning to Jasper. "Which do you choose?"

Jasper pointed at himself. "Me?"

"Yes. You are the third, or so I understand. The *Friend*. Are you not?"

Jasper shrugged and looked helplessly at Torr and Cassidy.

"You were in the book at the Pegasus dealer," Cassidy said.

"And in the blue and gold book," Torr said.

"There are always three," Berkeley said. "The twins, plus the one who must clear the way. It is said to be the most dangerous role. So perhaps you need a good knife."

Jasper's face flushed, and he turned his attention to the gemstone knives. He was fascinated with the Australian tiger iron. It was a beautiful grain of metallic gray, deep red, bright orange, and warm gold, flowing like molten lava. The steel blade was long and double-edged with a serrated section by the top of the bolster.

"I thought you would go for the red river jasper," Cassidy teased.

"This has red jasper in it," Hiroshi said. "Plus hematite, quartz, and tiger eye. It's the most powerful knife here, in my opinion."

"Good for star travel, then," Berkeley said, his eyes flashing to Jasper, whose face grew a deeper red.

"Indeed," Hiroshi said. "Air, fire, water, and earth. Ethereal yet grounding. Perfect."

They accepted the knives and gave Hiroshi some gold coin, despite his objections. Lastly, Hiroshi brought out the matching sheaths. Jasper's was ostrich, Torr's was antelope hide, and Cassidy's was buffalo hide. She felt guilty and grateful at the same time. She examined the snowflake obsidian handle and jewel steel blade again, then slid it into its sheath and onto her belt.

"Thank you so much, Hiroshi-san," she said, returning his jerky little bows. "I am honored to receive such a beautiful knife from a master such as you."

"It is I who am honored that a Star Child would carry the work of my humble and unworthy hands," Hiroshi said, bowing again.

Torr and Jasper bowed, and Hiroshi bowed to them. They exchanged more thanks and self-deprecating words in the seemingly endless ritual of politeness that Hiroshi and Tatsuya were teaching them in Judo class.

"Hey, Dad," Jasper said.

Cassidy looked up to find Kai standing there, grinning at them. After Kai admired the knives, he revealed the purpose of his unexpected visit.

"Ramzy thinks the speedster you brought back is one of the missing ones," Kai said to Cassidy. "He wants the key so he can check it out. Do you mind grabbing it for me?"

Cassidy chewed on her lip and considered his request. "I will take it to him myself," she said.

Kai's eyebrows rose and he shrugged. "Okay. Whatever you like."

The key was in her rune belt hidden under her shirt. She went inside her tent and transferred it to her inside vest pocket, then waited in the yard while the Alphabet Boys assembled to accompany them to the spaceport.

When they got there, Cassidy went inside with Kai, Jasper, and Torr, and found Balthazar's speedster in the row of small craft where she had parked it. She suddenly felt lightheaded and broke out in a cold sweat. She leaned against Jasper and he put his arm around her.

"Are you okay?" he asked softly.

"Yeah," she said, taking in a deep breath and standing on her own again.

Kai radioed Ramzy. While they were waiting for him, they walked around the speedster, and Kai pointed out the unique lines of this particular model.

The portly leader of Peary Dome waddled across the floor, huffing and puffing. Ramzy barely acknowledged her but held out his hand for the key fob.

"What do you need?" she asked.

Ramzy glared at her, finally making eye contact. "The key."

"Why?" she asked, glaring back at him.

Ramzy's complexion darkened, and he glanced at Kai as though needing help with a recalcitrant child.

"He wants to look for the serial number inside the door," Kai answered.

Rather than asking which door, she took out the key fob and pressed the button for both doors, and the wings slowly elevated, smoothly and silently.

Ramzy turned his back to her and inspected the inside of the left-hand door seal with Kai.

"They ground it off," Kai said.

Ramzy grumbled with annoyance, then climbed into the pilot's seat and began fiddling with the controls.

"Tell that girl to give me the key," he said to Kai.

Kai looked over his shoulder at Cassidy with a pleading look. She pointed the key fob at the instrument panel and pressed the remote start button like she had seen the loner do. The speedster hummed to life and the instrument panel lit up.

Ramzy snorted but did not ask again. "This is definitely my speed-ster," Ramzy said. "What are the chances they would get this exact model at exactly the same time as my order? She says he was from Gandoop?"

She hated the way he spoke about her in third person as though she weren't there. Kai turned to her again. She gave him an icy look and refused to answer.

"Close by Gandoop, apparently," Kai replied. "As we discussed before, it could be that the man is staying at the Gandoop's private compound, but there's no way to know for sure."

"Look," Torr said. He pointed to the inside of the raised door. Cassidy went over and looked at where he was pointing. A thin seam of red was exposed where the gray paint transitioned to polished metal. "This used to be red," Torr said.

Ramzy climbed out and examined the door. "Those lying thieves," he said, his eyes bulging. "I'll have their heads."

Cassidy stepped back and folded her arms. *Big words for a cowardly man,* she thought to herself.

Kai went around to the other door and began searching the interior and opening hatches she hadn't known were there. There were small compartments in the front panel and large compartments in the rear floor. Behind wall panels in the rear hung four space suits and eight oxygen tanks. She exchanged looks with Torr, and he arched his eyebrows happily.

From a center console hatch, Kai pulled out a long length of bright blue silk, and Cassidy's blood ran cold.

Jasper and Torr turned to her.

She leaned into Jasper's embrace again, shaking.

"That's Cassidy's," Torr said stiffly.

Kai silently handed the Delosian silk to her, and she wadded it up and stuffed it into her vest's side pocket.

Ramzy seemed oblivious to what was going on. He turned to her and said, "I'll take the key now."

She pulled away from Jasper and said, "No you won't. This speedster is mine now." She gritted her teeth and slipped the key fob into her inside pocket, zipped up the front of the yellow puffy vest, and snapped the waistband closed, daring him with her eyes to take the key from her.

His face flushed again, and he glanced up as Rodney approached.

"What did you find out?" Rodney asked. "Is this one of your missing craft?"

"Yes, it is," Ramzy said, looking pointedly between Cassidy and Kai, as though Kai were her father. "This is mine," Ramzy said firmly, regarding her with a cold glare.

"Not any longer, it's not," she shot back. "We told you Gandoop had them weeks ago. You could have gotten them yourself, but you were too scared. I got this one back all by myself. I paid for it with my *blood.* Do you understand me?"

Her eyes drilled into his. Next to Balthazar, this man was a pathetic puppy dog. "Don't think you frighten me, Mr. Ramzy." She spat on the floor, and he took a step back, horrified.

"Well you can't park it here," Ramzy sputtered, glancing at the men for help. No one stepped forward to intervene. "It costs five Eagles a month for a long-term parking spot," he said, raising his chin at her.

"That's no problem," she said, digging in her pocket and counting out five gold Eagles.

His lower lids sagged, exposing the whites of his eyes. "We don't have any spare spots," he said stubbornly.

"I thought you were expecting four new craft," she countered, closing her fingers around the gold coins. "Where did you think you were going to park them?" She glanced around. There was plenty of open floor space.

"They would be out on patrol," he said in a patronizing tone. "Like aircraft are meant to be. In the air."

"There's no air on the moon," she said, narrowing her eyes at him.

"This is ridiculous," he said haughtily, waving his hands around. "Kai, take care of this. And don't you think it's time you sent her downstairs with Gabira?" He flashed his eyes at Jasper and Torr. "Haven't you learned your lesson yet?"

Anger was coursing through her veins, and it felt much better than fear. She brushed past Ramzy and hopped into the pilot's seat, then pressed the control buttons on the panel to lower the doors. The men stepped back in surprise. The doors clicked closed, sealing her in welcome silence. She got her bearings and flipped up the hover switch. The craft slowly rose off the floor. She turned on the center console display, as she had learned from spying on Balthazar, so that she could see behind the craft. She ran her thumb over the knob on the side stick and slowly backed out of the parking spot and pivoted into the lane. The men were standing to the side, staring. Ramzy was irate, yelling at Kai and waving his hands. They couldn't see her through the reflective glass, and she couldn't hear anything in the airtight cabin, which was fine with her.

Jasper and Rodney were conferring with each other, and Torr wore an amused grin, watching her taxi slowly away from them.

Torr, Jasper, and Rodney followed as she navigated the speedster across the hangar floor away from the decompression chambers. Ramzy and Kai disappeared from view behind another parked craft.

She headed to the front of the hangar towards the loading bays where large garage doors stood open to the perimeter road. Workers stepped out of the way, and a crane lifting a water tank swiveled aside as she passed by. There was a clear path through an open bay, and she taxied slowly through it and out onto the road, chuckling to herself.

Passersby stopped and stared at the strange spectacle of a speedster floating above the roads of Peary Dome. She kept it at ground hover height, unsure of her skills and not wanting to launch into the glass panels by mistake. She slowly headed north along the outermost ring road, passing the staff quarters, the infirmary, the greenhouses and bakery. A maintenance vehicle pulled over to the side of the road to let her pass, and the driver gawked at the winged craft. The Light Fighters training yard came up on the left, and she turned into the large open area beyond the picnic tables away from everything, and gently settled the craft onto its landing gear. She smiled with smug satisfaction.

"Thank you, Balthazar," she said into the empty cabin, and laughed out loud.

16

ILLUSİONS

Balty demanded immediate results, and despite Ridge having urged the Teg general to be patient, Ridge found himself loading up the Korova to head to Peary again. He found all the food Ramzy had asked for, and then some—sacks of potatoes and onions, cases of cucumbers and celery, carrots with the leafy tops still on, hard pale tomatoes, and fresh spinach. Ridge tore open a box, and deep-green spinach leaves drew Ridge's nose downward. Dirt still clung to the bundled roots. He held a brown clump to his nostrils and stood there, eyes closed, inhaling the scent of Earth.

He found no fresh parsley or cilantro, but found a case of dried cilantro, which would have to do. The other stuff was easy. Barrels of olive oil were taking up more than their fair share of space, and he was glad to get rid of some. Peanuts, tuna, salt, olives, chickpeas, all were available in abundance. Fresh eggs—apparently something Peary had always ordered—appeared at Gandoop like clockwork. He supposed hens kept laying, and since Gandoop kept buying, they kept on arriving. In a walk-in freezer he found sides of beef and crates of chickens and had the workers load several of each.

He was granted access to Peary and sold off his cargo quickly. The traders were ecstatic over the meat. Ramzy appeared and looked on silently, the hungry look in his eyes saying more than words could have. Rodney and Kujo were there as well. Ramzy actually thanked him, which filled Jidna with shame.

Jidna locked up his Korova and made his way directly to Schlitzer's. He hoped the pimp had made progress locating the deeds, to pacify Balty. Jidna reflected on how he was more concerned about Balty's reaction than his own feelings anymore. Sometimes he felt nothing these days except cold calculation, mostly about whether or not it would be suicide to try and kill Balty. He always ended up admitting that it would be and put the thought out of his mind.

Jidna found Schlitzer at the bar, and they went to his private consultation tent and sat across from each other.

"They're carrying the deeds on their persons," Schlitzer said without ceremony. "Under their clothing in waist belts."

Jidna raised one bushy eyebrow. "Is that so? That's unfortunate."

Schlitzer nodded. "It does complicate things a bit."

Jidna sat back to think, wondering how the girl had managed to keep hers from Balty, unless the original kidnapper had stolen it, in which case it was out in the wild somewhere. Jidna rubbed his temples.

"What's wrong?" Schlitzer asked.

"Are you sure the girl's deed didn't get taken when she was kidnapped?" Jidna asked.

"Good question," Schlitzer said. "I'll see if I can find out. We might have to ask the kids outright. You know, offer to buy the deeds."

Jidna nodded. "That might be the easiest way. Can you broker it for me? I don't want them to know who I am."

"Of course," Schlitzer said.

"And I don't want to pay an outrageous sum."

"Of course not. Only what it's worth. Which is ..." Schlitzer's half-finished sentence hung in the air.

"A lot," Jidna said glumly and furrowed his brow. "Would it be enough to simply possess the deeds, I wonder? Or should I get them signed over to me?"

Schlitzer shrugged. "If you want to settle this once and for all, then you probably need them signed over to you. In which case, you really do need to buy them."

"Unless I forge their signatures," Jidna said, contemplating how he would do that. "But I would also need their fingerprints. Although they're already on the deeds once. So, I could forge those too."

Schlitzer chuckled. "This is getting complicated."

"I know," Jidna said. "You know what's really odd, though? The documents also have Metolius's signature and fingerprints on them. And his Salmon Seal."

Schlitzer's normally composed countenance broke for a moment. "President Metolius? That's bizarre."

"I know, right?"

Schlitzer stroked his graying goatee. "There's something else strange," Schlitzer said.

Jidna frowned. "What?"

"We had to move the duck blind. The girl put up a tarp that blocked our view. Word has it she said she was being watched."

Shivers ran up Jidna's back. "How did she know that?"

"I'm not sure. But I'm confident my guys didn't leak. And I don't think you did."

Jidna shook his head. "Wasn't me."

"They say," Schlitzer continued, "that she's been acting really oddly since she got back. She stares into a crystal ball all the time." Schlitzer cocked an eyebrow.

"Really?" Jidna said.

"Yeah. Maybe she's psychic," Schlitzer said. "We'll see if she senses our new location." Schlitzer laughed, as though enjoying the game of cat and mouse.

Jidna was not amused. Goosebumps rose on his arms, nettling his skin. His grandmother used to spy on him in the reflection of her tea, which she drank from a large saucer-like porcelain cup painted with purple roses. When he was a child, he had tried staring into the yellowish tea when his grandmother was not looking, but all he ever saw were reflections of the room and his own face. He would dump the tea out when she wasn't looking, but she would just tut-tut at the configuration of tea leaves clinging to the porcelain, and then refill it. One day he broke the tea cup on purpose. She beat him over the head with a spatula and locked him in his bedroom until his father came home from work.

"He's just a boy," Ishmar had told his mother.

"He's an evil spawn," she said in her language.

"He's not. He's a kind boy. I know you wish I had had a daughter, but it's not to be."

Their conversation turned to the topic of finding Ishmar a new wife, and Rjidna had escaped outside to play.

Jidna glanced up to find Schlitzer eyeing him thoughtfully. "They also say the twins are the Star Children," Schlitzer said, forcing another laugh. "And Jaz is supposedly part of the holy trinity. That's a lot of Star Seeker crap, don't you think?" the pimp asked, smirking at Jidna.

"Yeah, I don't believe in all that star stuff," Jidna said. "I think people look for spiritual solutions whenever the world falls apart, like it's doing right now."

Schlitzer nodded in agreement. "That's for sure," he said. The pimp fished two cans of beer out of a cooler and handed one to Jidna.

Jidna gratefully wrapped his hand around the ice-cold can and cracked it open.

———————)———————

Jidna avoided Danny's and headed across the dome towards Gabira's caves. He had been unable to get Giselle off his mind. The luscious curves of her breasts and hips. The gleam of her eyes, the plumpness of her lips. He wondered if she ensnared every man she met. Surely his reaction was laced with some sort of enchantment. He normally wasn't so overcome with lust. Did she enjoy luring men to her lair for the sheer joy of rejecting them? Like some cruel flower that swallowed the ants and bees who dared venture into its nectar-filled blossom?

He was able to get into the caves this time without Schlitzer. He still needed to bribe the guards, but Gabira knew who he was now. And although she might find him vexing, she also knew he brought gold. Perhaps that was the scam. Giselle drew men with fantasies of sex. Men bought their way in through Gabira. She was a madam, selling her daughter for gold. He wondered how far Giselle's services went. He didn't think they went as far as sex. It was pure seduction. The most intoxicating form, based on illusion and fantasy. Gabira and her daughters were masters at it, Jidna suspected, and it made him all the more excited. Maybe he would be the one to break through the fantasy and get Giselle's flesh in his hands for real. He chuckled to himself at his lecherous thoughts. Giselle's skill at enthrallment was good ... very good.

The numb serving women, on the other hand, were strange. He didn't sense any sexual exploitation there. No, Giselle kept that game all for herself. The serving women were held below for some other sinister purpose, he was sure. He did not know what—and was not particularly interested. There were worse fates for women on the moon than being bewitched by Gabira and her daughters.

Gabira opened the blond olivewood door after he rapped politely using the leaping dog knocker. He entered the room, which reeked of Gabira's patchouli scent. He smiled and kissed her hand. Giselle was not there. That was okay, he knew the drill. Bribe the mother. Entice the daughter. Take it from there.

He had not been very successful with Giselle the first time, but he would get further today. The women did not have the advantage of controlling him with magic. That must surely intrigue them, if not scare them a little bit.

He sat on a stack of colorful rugs and looked around the small cave room and the mural of an olive orchard. It was quite a good likeness of the gnarled trees. "Who painted the mural?" he asked, folding his sunglasses and tucking them into a chest pocket.

Gabira's lips puckered in a sour sneer, finding it impossible to smile at him. "I did."

"Wow. Very nice," he said cordially. "Reminds me of home."

"Me too," she said, eyeing him. They were not from the same region—he could tell by her accent and the tone of her skin. She was from the south, and he was from the north. But they no doubt had more in common than the many moon inhabitants from the Free States.

He smiled at her. She was delicately feeling around his body with her energy filaments, looking for a gap. He peeled a sticky tendril off his throat with his mind's fingers and flung it back at her where it recoiled into her belly like a frog's tongue. Her eyes bulged. He smiled widely at her. Where was her daughter?

He sat awkwardly and slowly uncurled his fists, which had invol- untarily tightened on his knees. Ridge forced himself back into Jidna's persona. Jidna was much happier and laid-back than Ridge was. Jidna settled into the pillows and gazed at the devious woman.

"That ring you admired last time looks to be a match with your necklace," he observed. He did not wait for her response but felt around in his sack and retrieved the small black velvet box. He opened it and flashed the ring at her. It was gold and studded with gems. A man's ring that would no doubt fit her index finger. The gems in the ring were similar in color and arrangement to those in her pendant. He asked if he could examine the pendant, but she merely scowled at him, and the crystal shaft glinted from where it lay next to the multi-colored pendant in the deep crevasse between her pendulous breasts.

Two glassy-eyed serving women entered the room. This time they bore polished brass chalices of ice-cold water. The water was delicious and cooled his dry throat. Hot tea followed in small metal cups, with sweet brown biscuits served on small hammered brass plates.

Gabira did not ask to see the ring that he set on the brass table, though her eyes flicked to it occasionally, against her will, he was sure. She was weak without the use of bewitchment, and terribly grumpy. He wondered why she had agreed to see him at all. They sat in uncomfortable silence, nibbling at cookies.

Finally, Gabira asked, "Where's your niece?" She was asking just to needle him. She knew there was no niece.

"Couldn't get out. Moffett Field has been taken by the Tegs. She's stuck there. Very sad." He made a big frowny face, his eyes overly grieved. "That's what I came to tell you. I knew you'd be waiting and worried. It's hard for me to talk about it." He dabbed at his eyes with his sleeve and peered over his arm at her. "I'm still trying to find a way to get her out."

She was glaring at him, and he held back a mischievous grin. No need to provoke her. She could have tricks up her sleeve still. Giselle being one of them. That was a trap he was anxious to get ensnared in.

"Where are your lovely daughters?" he asked, digging into his carrying sack for the blue velvet bag of gold he'd brought. He dumped the coins gently onto the table and began sorting them into small stacks.

From Earth there were Kroners, Apollos, Eagles, Pandas, and Springboks. From Delos there were Stags, Urns, Falcons, and Angels. From Lingri-La there were Goddesses, Glass Orbs, Eyes, and Spears.

From the Nommos colony there were Fish, Serpents, Turtles, and Mermaids. From the Cephean Federation were profiles of stern men, and large square buildings on the reverse.

He had two or three of everything, having searched through his multiple stashes for a fair representation that was sure to awaken her avarice.

"I'm sure you have all of these," he said, straightening the stacks. He lifted his eyes slyly. Her gaze was fastened on the gold, trying to determine which coins he had. Her pink tongue lashed out and retracted.

"What do you want?" she asked.

"To be friends." He lifted the ring from its velvet nest. "You really must have this. To complete your set." He reached his hand across the table. She wiped her palm on her purple silk gown and reluctantly opened it to him. He dropped the ring onto her pink flesh, then went back to his coins, arranging the stacks in a neat line. He watched from under veiled eyelids as she tried the ring on various fingers, finally settling on her left forefinger.

"Come," he said, gesturing to the coins. "Take a look. See if you need any of these for your collection." He stood and stepped aside, indicating his seat, which was nearest the glittering stacks.

She huffed and pushed herself to her feet and shuffled around the table. She sat heavily on his pile of rugs, and he politely backed away, folding his hands in front of him. She fingered all the stacks, resting longer on the ones she did not recognize, which to his satisfaction were several. He prided himself on his collection, and it did not disappoint. The ones from Lingri-La were the most rare.

"Giselle would enjoy seeing these," Gabira said, her voice suddenly honey-sweet. His guard went up, but he nodded agreeably.

"Certainly."

"You must come with me to find her. She is in the caves, overseeing the women where we mine our ice."

"Okay," he said, curious to see her caves.

"It's down deep. Are you sure you are up for it?" she asked, her long eyelashes batting.

If she could make the walk, he would have no trouble. "I'd be pleased to visit your ice mine," he said. "Sounds most unusual."

She smiled, her teeth tinged with green. His eyebrows rose at the sight. Murian Greenwash was the only thing that stained teeth like that. A strong narcotic that interstellar travelers favored. Few could resist its addictive properties if consumed too often. It was extremely hard to come by and frightfully expensive. He understood Jaz had cornered that lucrative market. If she liked Greenwash, it was a weakness he could exploit. He could get a hold of some to tempt her with, and in the meantime, he better understood her need for gold.

Jidna held the door for her as she lumbered heavily through the doorway. He took his carrying sack but left the stacks of gold on the table. He did not fear thievery here—at least, not outright thievery.

He followed her rotund form down the tunnel past several doors, her purple robe shimmering in the soft glow of the solar filaments. They passed through a doorway at the end of the tunnel, traversed a short curving tunnel, then entered a long chamber with a ceiling of interlocking tree branches and solar filaments. The chamber narrowed into another tunnel, which twisted and turned, and soon the light faded. Gabira fished a tallow candle from her pocket and stopped to light it with a match, accepting his help as she fumbled with the striker. The flame flared when the wick caught, then settled into a steady flame. Fire was not allowed up above in the dome, or anywhere, really, on the moon. But there was not much that was flammable down here, and the oxygenators he had sold to Peary Dome pumped out plenty of oxygen. Still, it was wasteful, and he made a mental note to bring her some battery-powered flashlights.

They resumed walking single file, with Gabira in the lead. The tunnel descended and curved again, coming to a fork. She took the left fork and led him deeper into the dark cave system. Twinges of unease crept up his spine, but memories of Giselle's scent strengthened his resolve. They would fetch the ravishing beauty and bring her back to the sitting room. He would sit next to her on the rugs and fondle her hands. She would interlace her fingers with his, and he would stroke the velvety skin on the inside of her wrist. Gabira would leave to squirrel away her gold coins, and Ridge would lower Giselle onto the pillows and kiss her neck. He would part her robe and trace the roundness of her breasts with his tongue. Rising blood warmed his skin, and he unfastened the top button of his shirt, letting the cool cave air caress him as they ventured ever deeper.

He kept track of the twists and turns as he followed the flickering candle. "How far is it?" he asked.

"I told you it was deep," Gabira said.

He straightened his back and marched forward. Of course the ice was deep. The tunnels were cold as a crypt. Gabira trundled along at an even pace. After several more minutes of treading through the darkness, Jidna felt a breath of warm air. He stopped, confused. A scent filled his nostrils. Subtle but spicy. Like leaves baking in the sun. It could not be the scent of Giselle—hers was of fresh lemons.

Gabira felt him stopping, and turned to look at him, the candlelight casting grotesque shadows across her face from where it glowed under her chin, making dark hollows of her eyes and sharp daggers of her chin and nose. "We are almost there," she said, the light reflecting from the dark-brown breccia walls and turning her pupils red.

He lost his balance for an instant, catching himself with his hand against the hard stone. The sudden lightheadedness took him by surprise, and he closed his eyes, breathing steadily to regain his composure. He took a deep breath and opened his eyes. Gabira's narrow eyes were examining him, her dark lashes fanned out, their shadows appearing as wings. He felt a strange pressure in his skull but attributed it to the depth of the cave. He wondered idly how air was pumped down here and how vast the tunnel network was.

Jidna followed Gabira as the path leveled out. A faint light softened the blackness into a penumbral gray. It grew brighter as they climbed a gentle incline. Gabira labored forward and blew out the candle. They turned a corner, and a bowl of light appeared before them. It was the mouth of the cave, with daylight visible beyond and sand beneath his feet. He wondered when Giselle would appear, but his thoughts were lifted away by a light breeze that ruffled his hair.

He ran past Gabira and out into the balmy air. The open sky was cobalt blue with wisps of clouds. The air was dry and redolent. He spun on his feet, elation filling his lungs. The rocky outcropping topped a tiered hillside lined with ancient, gnarled olive trees. They were heavy with fruit, which was smooth and purple with hints of green where olives met stems. He ran down the terraces, scrambling down short rock walls that kept the earth from sliding down the hill.

He glanced over his shoulder. Gabira stood majestically on the

uppermost terrace, gazing out over her domain. She turned and walked
slowly through the trees, stroking the small fruit as she passed under
the shadowed branches. She was beautiful in her amethyst robe in
the dappled sunlight, patterns of gold shimmering through the leaves
and burnishing her glowing skin. She was ripe and smooth like the
fruit, and smiled down at him with a secret, knowing smile. His heart
reached out to her, adoring her. He turned to face the small valley.
Before him rose another tiered hillside of olive trees, gray-green leaves
fluttering in the breeze.

He made his way down the last terrace to the foot of the hill, crossed
a short expanse of ancient orchard, and began climbing the facing set
of terraces. Dry grass crunched under his boots, and he bent down,
scooping a fistful of dry crumbling dirt into his hand and lifting it to
his nose. He breathed in the glorious scent. *Earth. Gaia. Mother.* The
source of his bones and teeth, his blood. Excitement invigorated him,
and his muscles trembled with joy. He leapt from terrace to terrace,
climbing like a buck in spring, testing the air with his straining nostrils, tasting for a female. Yearning for life and love, to dip his soul in
the well of creation.

Atop the crest he looked out over the vastness of the blue sky, its
limitless expanse filling him with wonder. He dropped his eyes to
the next valley below, and his heart stopped for an instant, and then
thudded against his chest. Before him lay a field of gray stumps on dry
cracked earth. Bare olivewood limbs lay scattered like bleached bones
on a forgotten battlefield. The skeletons were stark in their realness,
and the blood that pounded in his neck awoke him. *Where was he?*

He turned his head to the green valley he had ascended from. It was
shimmering like a dream, the colors jewel-like, the air fresher and sky
bluer than the dull grays on the other side. Turning back to the field
of bones, he was sure that was real. Looking back at the green valley,
he was sure that was an illusion. At the head of the illusion was a large
purple-robed woman, walking purposefully towards a rocky outcropping, stealing a look over her shoulder to where Jidna stood. He stared
at her. *She had trapped him in her magic. Fucking hell.*

Gabira's lip curled in an insolent grin. She tossed her head and
turned away, heading for a shadowy cleft in the hillside. Anger boiled
inside him, spilling from his eyes. He shot an energy tendril from his

belly, sending it across the vale like a grappling hook, sinking it into Gabira's fleshy back as her voluminous hips jiggled from side to side and she disappeared into the gash in the rock.

Jidna ran down the glistening green hillside, leaping down terraces then up the other side, following the line of his energy filament still buried in her back. He hoped she did not become aware of it. He knew from experience that tendrils planted in the back were difficult to sense, attaching into the subconscious. Those without experience could easily disregard the telltale twinges. If she'd never been attacked in such a fashion, he might stay attached and find his way out of her enchanted grove, trailing after her life force. If she did detect the line and was able to pull out his hook, he could be left there forever—lost in the nether region between her glittering illusion and the dry valley of lifeless trees of he knew not where.

His blood pounded in his arms and legs. He did not stop to wonder where the gray boneyard was in truth but sprinted towards the cave opening. He wished with the tiny part of his mind that watched himself run that the fragrant leaves were real, that the shining fruit would ripen to perfection. He would soak them in brine and eat them with cheese and fresh bread, and watch the sun set a rosy peach over the emerald hills.

His boots crunched over dry soil and sank in the sand of the cave mouth as he ducked into the dim hollow. He followed the golden thread that extended from his belly and curved through the dark passageways. Daylight faded behind him, and he was shrouded in darkness. Only the faint shimmer of his life thread cut through the black void. He slowed, his breath coming in faint gasps. Feeling the stone floor with his feet and the rough walls with one hand, he waved the other hand blindly in front of him, pushing through the blackness, fervently hoping the tenuous connection with Gabira would not break.

After countless minutes of stumbling through pitch-dark tunnels, a faint hint of light lifted the ghoulish gloom. He broke into a run, able to discern the twilight-gray of the walls and floor. He turned a corner, and up ahead limped Gabira, her weight too heavy for her swollen feet. She turned, startled at the sound.

He surged forward, causing her to back away in fright. He slid to a stop, his rage pressing her against the cave wall, her eyes round with shock and her hands clasped pleadingly in front of her, the candle flickering in her fists. Jidna tore his hook and line from her back, her body responding with a small shudder. He turned and trotted down the passageway, wooden doors on either side. A thick coil of solar filaments snaked across the ceiling, illuminating Giselle's startled face as she peeked out through the sliver of a doorway. She closed the door firmly as he trotted past. He did not spare her even a glance.

At the door with the brass dogs, Jidna pushed his way in. His gold coins were gone. He growled in annoyance and left the room. Gabira was hobbling down the long tunnel towards him. He walked stiffly away from her and up the stairs. He passed through the airlock without a word to the guard, then pushed past the other two guards and out into the light of Peary Dome.

He shook with rage and horror at how close he'd come to being trapped in her spell, or whatever that was. Wherever. Earth? He could not fathom how that could be. His legs trembled weakly as he made his way around to the main entrance of the spaceport, passed through security, and climbed thankfully into the familiar cocoon of his cockpit.

His pulse had almost normalized by the time he passed through the decompression chambers and flew out over the blessed, barren moon.

17

DREAMWALKİNG

Torr found himself in the dry red heat of Turya, crouched on a flat rocky plain strewn with raw diamonds, rubies, and sapphires. He scooped up a handful of the hot, unpolished gems, and let them fall through his fingers. He did not know how to transport material objects from one world to another but seized up in a moment of realization that he was aware he was dreaming. Asleep in his tent at the Fen and awake on Turya. *Dreamwalking.*

He tried to calm his pounding heart by breathing the sulfur-tainted air. *Inhale. Exhale.* He really was dreamwalking. He was afraid of awakening himself on the other side, so he stood up slowly, silently, and gazed around the flatlands. Heat waves rose from the ground, and the fiery Uttapta beat down on his shoulders.

The sound of singing reached his ears in faint, wispy threads. The voices came from the direction of the stone city, which stood on the horizon in jagged clusters of red and brown teeth. Torr hiked across the plain towards the singing and followed the mournful strains through the maze of abandoned city streets until he arrived at the broad square at the city's center. He approached the dry fountain, topped by its towering sculpture of one-horned antelopes and winged lions.

The same group of people he had found the last time formed a rough circle at the far side of the fountain, singing an intricate melody. Torr slowed his pace and tried to distinguish the various vocal parts.

There were bass and baritone, tenor and alto, soprano and high soprano. Six parts. He crept around the large round wall of the empty pool and examined the sculpture. The antelopes were ramming each other to get at the pair of lions who were fighting above them, wings outstretched and fangs bared. Or, maybe the lions were in a mating dance, or climbing together into the sky, fleeing the antelopes—he could not tell which. For a moment the animals seemed alive as the red light of Uttapta glinted off their wings and horns.

His friend Igotra spotted him with an outburst of delight and separated himself from the group.

"Igotra," a woman called. Igotra ignored her and ran around the fountain, throwing himself into Torr's arms.

"Beloved Son of Uttapta, Flying Star, *Ranapriya,* Lover of Battles. You have returned!"

The youngster's language flowed like water across river rocks, smooth and clearly comprehensible, though it was a stream of sounds Torr had never heard before. He was not at all offended by the warrior name the Turyan had given him but was filled only with joy at having been recognized.

"Igotra, my friend," Torr said. He squeezed the solid body of the young man, and then held him at arm's length, gripping his shoulders to contain the excitement of the trembling Turyan. Igotra had the slightly stunted, stout body of someone with Down syndrome or another such genetic condition, with slightly misshapen eyes, and a wide gaping mouth, showing rotted teeth. But he glowed. His hair glimmered like spun gold in the crimson sunlight. Each strand of hair not only reflected the light, but shone from within, as though Uttapta's light entered the shaft and continued vibrating inside. His skin also radiated a reddish-gold aura. And his eyes. They were a brilliant, reddish-copper, and held Torr's gaze with open adoration.

"Flying Star, where is your sister, Golden Star, *Jalavahini,* Blessed Water Carrier? Is she coming? Has she brought the divine water?"

"No, she's not here," Torr said. "I'm not really here, either," he said, releasing Igotra and pulling at his own jerkin. It felt real.

"You *are* here," Igotra stated matter-of-factly, placing his stubby hands on his shapeless hips.

"I'm dreamwalking," Torr explained.

"Oh." The boy tilted his head and looked at him from crossed eyes. "That is good. I dream too. I dream when I'm awake."

Torr laughed, and the boy joined in with a funny, hiccupping laugh. "My mother tells me not to," Igotra said. "She says I might get lost."

Torr nodded and said, "My mother used to tell me the same thing about my dreams."

"Good," Igotra said, grinning with delight. "We will get lost together."

"Igotra!" The voice of Igotra's mother pierced through the singing.

Igotra ignored her and turned to a range of dark mountains that dominated the skyline. He gestured to the highest peak. "Did you come through Father-Heart-of-Sky?"

"What is Father-Heart-of-Sky?" Torr asked.

"It's the big shiny globe where the starlight comes through. Where the Children of the Stars come and go." Igotra narrowed his eyes in puzzlement. "Don't you know?"

"No," Torr said, squinting at the summit and detecting a pinpoint of reflected red light.

"You should go there," Igotra said, pointing at the glinting beacon. "Go look for your sister. Maybe she has come."

Torr bobbed his head in a noncommittal nod. "Perhaps. But even so, I would like to see this Father-Heart-of-Sky. Can you tell me how to get there?"

"Yes, of course. Everyone climbs the Ageless Mountains on the pilgrimage. Every winter when Uttapta stops raining down fire. Just follow the southeast road, and it will take you right up there." Igotra nodded to a stone gate at the far corner of the city square, which Torr had not noticed before. "It's easy," Igotra said. "Well, it's a little steep. But you can do it."

"*Igotra!* Come join us. We need your voice."

"I have to go," Igotra said, puckering his lips in a pout. "You go find your sister and bring her back here. We need the divine water very badly."

"Yes, Igotra. I will try." He gave Igotra a parting hug, and then headed towards the stone gate.

Torr's steps in his dream were like a giant's, covering several paces in one step. It seemed normal, as though one should be able to skim across the ground when one wanted to move quickly. In four strides he was under the huge red stone lintel that spanned two pillars. The tall, thick pillars were carved into masses of twining snakes, which climbed up in spirals of slithering knots. Carved into the lintel overhead, a line of large stone bats hung upside-down and stared down at him. Torr shivered and passed through the gate.

Igotra had not been exaggerating when he said the way up the mountain was steep. Torr climbed a seemingly endless number of switchbacks that hugged the side of the mountain. Many of the spans were so steep that long flights of stairs had been carved into the red rock, each step worn smooth by what must have been centuries of footsteps. His magical, giant steps slowed to the opposite sensation— every step was an effort, and his legs were as heavy as wet sandbags.

Eventually, the incline grew more gradual, and the path straightened out, hugging the mountainside to his right. A waist-high stone wall to his left was the only thing that stood between him and a drop of thousands of feet down a sheer cliff face. A hot gust brought the foul stench of volcanic brimstone with it. Torr pulled his bandana up over his nose and mouth, bent his head into the wind, and continued his ascent.

By the time he made it to the top, Uttapta was low in the sky, painting a sunset of coppery orange that reflected off streaks of soot-gray clouds. Torr passed beneath a towering gate of polished black stone veined with gold, topped by white and gold banners flapping in the wind. He climbed one last set of wide stately stairs. Each step was newly polished and leveled, and was flanked by a pair of large winged lion statues made of gold. They sat alert with their wings tucked tightly against their sides and watched Torr. He nodded to each one as he mounted the steps. He could not tell if they were scowling or surprised to see him.

He stepped into a stiff wind as he crested the summit, and surveyed a high plateau dominated by an imposing temple of polished black stone streaked with sparkling golden flecks, and soaring pillars of gold. Across from the temple, the plateau narrowed to a serpentine ridge, and upon its crest sat a massive crystal globe, twice as tall as Torr. It was mounted on a gold pedestal in the center of a large stone circle ringed by flickering fire pits.

A ray of Uttapta's light reflected off the globe in a blinding flash that drove Torr to his knees. He shielded his eyes against the piercing shaft, and when he looked up again, he was kneeling on his blankets in the tent. Cassidy rolled over and turned her sleepy gaze to him.

"What's the matter, Torr?" she asked. "You dreaming again?"

"Yes," he muttered, rubbing his eyes.

"Nightmares?"

"No. I visited Turya again." He lifted his gaze, and the dreamcatcher spun slowly overhead, casting its eye on him.

"Oh, good. Tell me later," Cassidy mumbled, then turned over and fell back asleep.

Torr got out his journal and fountain pen, turned to the second page, and recorded his dream. Then he drew a map of the Turyan valley within the ring of volcanic mountains. He marked the ancient city, the central square and fountain, the mountain path, and the temple and giant crystal globe sitting atop the peak. He drew a small arrow pointing to the sphere and wrote, FATHER-HEART-OF-SKY.

———————)———————

Torr lined his crystals up next to his pillow and stretched out for an afternoon nap, luxuriating in peaceful solitude. His muscles were heavy with fatigue from so much training. He yawned and mused about how he would ever find his way across the stars to Turya. He could only surmise that the feat required magical powers that he did not possess. The familiar anxiety to achieve some sort of miracle tightened his jaws.

He forced himself to relax and clear his mind. The dreamcatcher twirled slowly above him. The sinew web and bones shone a pearly white, translucent in the filtered light, and the feathers cast shadows like fingers running over the tent walls.

He felt his eyelids growing heavy and forced them back open. Some of his most powerful dreams happened when he napped during daylight hours. His mother had said lucid dreamers could dream day or night, and dreamwalkers could dream at will. She used to tell stories of finding Grandpa Leo rocking in his porch chair or leaning on a shovel, staring out into space. She would pull on his hand, and after a few moments he would turn to her and tell her he had been visiting another world. Grandma Leann had said that he could put himself into a trance-like state and dream awake whenever he wanted to. She said dreams provided information, and sometimes when Grandpa Leo could not find an answer to something, he would go into a dream and wake up with the solution. As he got older, he spent more and more time living in his dreamworlds, until one day he never came back. She found him lying on the couch with his hands folded over his chest, staring up at the ceiling, dead.

"The more you practice, the stronger you will get," Grandma Leann had told Torr. "But it's important to ask for what you want to learn before you enter your dream," she said. "You must ask."

Torr gazed up at the dreamcatcher and thought about what he wanted to know. Something that would not be too disturbing. If his parents were dead or suffering, he was not sure he was ready to learn that right now. Not today. But this dark-skinned man who kept turning up and taking over Torr's body. That was disturbing, but also very curious. And his crystals. What did they do?

He grabbed the fluorite crystal and the dagger-like shaft. Lying back on his bedding, he examined the two crystals.

"What are you for?" his whispered. "Where did you come from?"

He flung his limbs wide in a spread-eagle position, with his hands open and the crystals resting on his palms, and stared at the ceiling. The dreamcatcher circled slowly one way and then the other. Soon his eyelids closed, and he let himself be pulled into the current of the dreamtime.

———————)———————

Torr found himself in a large chamber. His bedroom. But not his bedroom. He turned in a circle, confused. And then the confusion left him the way a lingering dream fades away and is replaced by the imposing solidity of the world.

He stood in the large stone bedchamber, which held a massive canopy bed with dark green velvet curtains and a large desk covered with scrolls. The gray stone walls were decorated with embroidered tapestries of stags and hounds and curling vines, and the floors were of dark mahogany-red wood, with a large woven rug of beige and brown diamond shapes in the center of the floor.

It was a nice enough room, he admitted. Or it would be, if it weren't in essence a prison. He could more easily throw himself from the high window to his death than escape the greedy clutches of his current keepers. Priests, they called themselves. Wisemen. *Captors.* They claimed to be tasked with training the Star Children—to prepare them for welcoming the Star People. As though welcoming them was their only role. He knew better. It wasn't as simple as that.

He, Darius, was the male Star Child, not Zinz, nor any of the other arrogant Star Priests. His twin sister, Danute, was the other Star Child. They were the "Blessed Ones." The fabled Prince of the Morning and Princess of Light. The only ones who could forge the connection with the Star People and bring salvation to the galaxy. They were the ones who should be in charge. If they hadn't been found when they were still children, they would be. But they had been lured here too young and were now prisoners of the stupid priests. It was time he and his sister did something about it. They were twenty now, and the time of Joining with the Star People was rapidly approaching.

Darius pulled on his heavy ruby-red velvet longcoat with the ridiculous gold piping and voluminous sleeves that reached almost to the floor. He dropped the Memory Keeper into his inside left pocket, where the fluorite octahedron fit nicely. His first teacher on Delos—the best one, Rigel—had told him he was to carry the crystal everywhere. That it recorded his memories for the next Prince of the Morning, adding his to the vast collection of memories from past Princes that were stored in the cloudy green double pyramid. The memories were supposedly helping Darius, though he was rarely conscious of any. Though he supposed he could attribute his eerily accurate intuition to the crystal. Regardless, the fact that he knew what it did, and his keepers did not, delighted Darius to no end. He would not let any of them touch it, which irked them terribly.

Darius chuckled to himself as he left his chamber and strode down the wide stone stairs for his lessons. His four guards rushed after him. He turned into the Star Hall, its white marble floors awash with multi-colored light cascading from the large stained glass windows that lined the upper walls of the cavernous chamber. Darius walked across the polished floor and came to a stop, facing his least favorite keeper.

Zinz glared at him from under wiry gray eyebrows, wisps of musky incense swirling around the man's tall wiry body from the ornate censer that swung from his hands. Distaste filled Darius's mouth at the sight of the old priest. He recalled all too well that it had been Zinz who eight years ago had taken him and Danute from the happiness of their mountain home, with promises of adventure and riches at the royal court on Iliad. Zinz—who had confined them to the cold stone castle. Zinz—who had ordered Darius beaten the first few times he had tried to leave the walled grounds. But it was when Zinz had ordered Danute to be beaten that his hatred for the sneering, smiling man had truly blossomed.

"And how is the Prince this morning, Prince of the Morning?"

"Ha ha," Darius said. It was the same joke every morning. "What are you teaching me today?" Light fell in multi-colored shafts from the windows, illuminating the aging priest.

Zinz stiffened and smoothed his purple silk robes. The wrinkled man hated that question. "Our lessons are subtle, young Prince. As I tell you every morning. It is not what I teach you, but what you learn, that is important."

Darius sighed and glanced up as his sister swept into the hall, her long golden gown swirling behind her as she yanked the train from her attendant's hands. She hated this as much as he did. Being plucked from their humble home in the thick Delosian forest and whisked off to a seaside castle on the planet Iliad had at first seemed like a fairy tale. Magical and enchanting. Quickly, they had learned it was one of the bad fairy tales, filled with cruel idiots intent on making their lives miserable and hoarding power for themselves. He nodded to Danute, relieved to have her company. She was his one source of sanity. Zinz allowed them to be together only at certain times, and never alone. And they were rarely allowed to speak with one another. No doubt because they'd plot their escape if they could. As it was, neither wanted to abandon the other to this horde of crazy Star Priests.

Darius met Danute's eyes. Large and black like his, as dark as their velvety skin. The Scrids on Delos called their kind hairless bears. Darius did not mind the comparison so much. Legend said the bears on Scridland were powerful, holy creatures.

Zinz handed the censer to an attendant and held aloft his wooden scepter, the one topped with the glowing purple crystal ball. He always held this when they trained with the crystals.

Darius pulled a six-sided crystal shaft from the sheath at his hip and held it in the air as Zinz invoked his magical incantation. Darius rolled his eyes. The Destroyer crystal worked for Darius whether or not Zinz was there, and it didn't work at all if Darius didn't want it to. Intention, Rigel had taught him, was the key to everything.

Zinz glared at Darius with rheumy brown eyes as he chanted, foul-tempered as usual when his chanting did not immediately cause Darius's Destroyer crystal to light up. Darius snickered to himself. When he'd realized this vexed Zinz, he'd started delaying the illumination just to watch Zinz's face turn sour.

Darius held the elderly priest's eyes. The chanting broke off, and Zinz took in a deep breath and spoke with a voice like shards of glass. "Focus, my dear Prince. Keep your eyes on my staff, as I have instructed you countless times. The amethyst globe will help you reach a heightened state of awareness." The man closed his eyes and resumed his sonorous chanting.

How about if I focus on planting this crystal in the center of your forehead? Darius asked silently, envisioning the shaft protruding from the man's furrowed brow and turning crimson with blood. Perhaps then he and Danute could escape. Run from the great hall in the hubbub of shrieking acolytes. His mouth turned down. No, more likely it would serve only to get Darius locked in an underground cell. Still, the idea was tempting.

Rigel's admonitions echoed in his head. *Be mindful of your thoughts, young master. The seed of your intention will bear fruit, whether you desire it or not.* A shiver ran up Darius's spine, and a twinge of guilt made him turn his eyes away from the wrinkled brow of the old priest. Darius had not quite figured out all the intricacies of intention, having been pulled from Rigel's tutelage too soon.

He recalled when the Ilian scholars had discovered Darius and Danute. A cadre of Ilian priests led by Zinz had appeared at the doorstep of their home on Delos. A week of tests had ensued, and before autumn waned to winter he and Danute had been shuttled off to the Star Globe in the Old City, where they had stepped into a beam of golden light and found themselves in a stone palace on the planet Iliad. Darius remembered that glorious, horrible day when they'd stepped from Iliad's Star Globe, navigated a labyrinth of secret passageways, and finally emerged into a vast hall surrounded by rays of light that splashed across white marble floors—the very room they stood in now. Darius looked up at the huge window that depicted the coming of the Star People. White-robed men and women bearing flaming red torches descended on thick shafts of golden light that cut through the midnight blue sky, as though calmly stepping down a spring waterfall lit by the dawning sun.

Little had Darius and his sister suspected that they were pieces in a complex game of court and priestly politics, to be traded back and forth like land holdings. More valuable than children from the royal bloodlines. Danute had already been promised in marriage to some Ilian prince she'd never met. White-skinned, blond teenage girls had been paraded in front of Darius weekly, accompanied by promises of large dowries in the hope that he would choose a bride. Or two. Darius knew it nettled Zinz and the nobility that he and his sister were of the dark-skinned Delosian mountain tribes. That didn't stop the simpering noble families from offering their daughters, if it meant a chance of bearing an heir to the Prince of the Morning. Parasites, all of them.

Regardless, Rigel would not approve of his hateful thoughts. Darius shamefully bowed to the memory of his teacher and tried to wipe away the vision of the shaft jutting out of Zinz's forehead. He did not know exactly how to do that. Could he erase it somehow? Reel in time? Retract the intention like a fishing line? Darius shrugged. If Zinz was half the teacher Rigel had been, Zinz would have taught Darius the reversal technique already. The perfumed priest probably didn't even know what a line of intention was.

Zinz's nasally voice grated on Darius's nerves. The old priest had been a hindrance more than a help in his education. Zinz seemed to think all the power was contained in the crystals, and Darius's task was merely to submit to the will of the ancient minerals. Zinz was a fool. All the same, Darius took back his unkind thoughts. He blew out his breath and let his crystal light up with its purple flames, just to get Zinz to shut up. The sound of the flames fluttered like bird's wings. The old man opened his eyes and stopped chanting, giving Darius a smug smile.

"Very good, very good. Today, my young Prince," Zinz said, not bothering to mask his patronizing tone, "you will evaporate diamonds into their essence. Think of diamonds as little stars. No more than light trapped in a solid matrix. Release the light from the binding of its internal forces, and let it dissipate the darkness."

Darius's eyes wandered across the stained glass windows, examining the depictions of Iliad's two suns and three moons that surrounded the golden waterfalls of light and the legendary ancestors. Darius was part of a timeless cosmology that had nothing to do with Zinz's drivel. The priest was a speck of space dust. Darius and Danute were the stars in the sky. By rights, Darius should be able to burn the man out of existence merely by looking at him.

"Draw your focus, young Prince, as you would draw a bow. Hold it steady and loose the arrow."

Darius ignored the man's ramblings—he'd already envisioned how it must be done. He trained his eyes on the row of glinting diamonds, which sat atop tall narrow pillars at the far end of the chamber, bathed in light streaming down from the high windows.

Darius had always had uncanny aim, though he knew the real trick of the Destroyer had nothing to do with hand-eye coordination. Like everything, it had to do with his line of intention. He breathed slowly to prepare himself. His gaze locked onto the center diamond. He allowed the surge of energy to enter through his head and feet and course through his body and then shoot out through his palm and fingers, where it was amplified and focused by the crystal. A beam of purple light flowed from the crystal shaft and struck the first diamond with a sharp ringing that pierced the air in a painful screech. The diamond exploded into rainbows of light with a deafening crack, streams of sparkling mist radiating out from the center point and filling the room.

The next moment, an ominous scraping came from above, like the sound of an ice sheet shearing off a mountainside. Darius stared as the blue, red, and gold stained glass panels folded in slowly away from the walls and fell through the air. Darius jumped backwards, twisting and taking Danute with him to the floor, flinging his wide sleeve over their heads. The glass hit the marble floor with a crash, which exploded through the chamber, rebounding off the stone walls and ceiling in a musical cacophony. A brief sliver of silence was followed by the tinkling of glass shards falling to the ground the way raindrops drip from trees in the forest long after the storm has passed. Darius felt a shower of small fragments land harmlessly on his thick velvet cloak.

Darius lifted his head and checked to make sure Danute was not hurt. She gazed up at him, wide-eyed.

"That was amazing!" she gushed, and Darius grinned proudly. He looked up to see the shocked face of Zinz, who had a dark rivulet of blood trickling down the bridge of his nose from a spear of red glass that was lodged in the center of his forehead. Darius realized with a flash of horror that Zinz's glazed eyes were those of a dead man as the old priest collapsed onto the floor in a puff of silken robes.

His next thought was of Rigel and his look of grave rebuke, and Darius was filled with shame.

———————————)———————————

Darius jerked awake. His body was trembling and his hands were slimy with sweat. He sat up with a start, and the fluorite octahedron and crystal shaft rolled from his hands onto the blanket. Remorse and shame filled every cavity of his body, quickly replaced by fear for himself and his sister. He had to fight and run. Darius sucked in mouthfuls of air as his heart hammered in his chest. He and Danute needed to escape the castle while the court churned in chaos at Zinz's death. They had no time for a plan. No time to retrieve their belongings. They just needed to flee.

He surged to his feet and looked around at the dusty tent, disoriented. The ground seemed to tilt, forcing him to his knees. He squeezed his eyes shut and sat back on his heels, rubbing his face as he slowly made his way out of the murkiness of the dream and into the present.

"Holy stars," Torr said, and jumped to his feet. *"Hermes' wings!"* he bellowed. He slipped the fluorite Memory Keeper into the inner pocket of his vest and slid the Destroyer into his right leg pocket and hopped outside the tent, where the eyes of his friends trained on him with wary curiosity.

Torr was vibrating with energy. The revelations about his crystals made his head spin. He yelled with happiness, sliding his feet across the dust in Rashon's little dance, to the twisted smiles of his companions.

"What girl did you just dream about?" Ming-Long asked.

"Angels from heaven," Torr replied. He laughed merrily and went into the back courtyard to find Berkeley.

"Berk," he said, greeting the man who was hunched over his sewing machine, attaching a pocket to a length of tent canvas that looked destined to be a trouser leg.

"Hey, Torr."

Torr sat on a plastic crate next to Berkeley and watched him work. Berkeley's long fingers fed the fabric under the sturdy sewing needle. "Have you ever heard of Prince Darius?" Torr asked.

Berkeley pulled the canvas away from the needle, clipped the line of thread with little scissors, and looked up at Torr. "Prince Darius of Delos?" Berkeley asked.

Torr nodded. His heartbeat, which had been strong and steady with excitement, thinned to a rapid patter.

"You mean the last of the Star Children?" Berkeley asked, setting down his scissors.

Torr's heart faltered, and Berkeley looked at him strangely. "You look like you've just seen a ghost," Berkeley said. "What's wrong?"

"What was Darius's sister's name?" Torr asked, his voice unsteady.

Berkeley thought for a minute, his round eyes narrowing. "I think it was Danu."

Torr swallowed and took a breath. "Danute," he finally said, and Berkeley raised one eyebrow. "Did you know they were dark-skinned, like you?" Torr asked.

"Really?" Berkeley looked surprised, and then pleased.

"Yeah, they came from the mountain forests on Delos," Torr said.

"Ah, that makes sense. They must have come from the northern mountains," Berkeley said, then his lips fell and his eyes rounded. "How do you know?"

Torr shrugged innocently and stood up, taking the Destroyer from his pocket.

"They were killed when the Star Globe on Iliad blew up," Berkeley said.

Torr turned slowly to Berkeley. "Oh," Torr said, feeling as though he'd been punched in the stomach. A deep sadness washed over him. "Oh." He clutched his belly and sat back down.

"Torr," Berkeley said. "What's wrong?"

"Oh," was all Torr could say, leaning his elbows on his knees and struggling to breathe. He pulled himself together and tried to clear his head. Lifting his eyes, he saw Berkeley, Tatsuya, and Hiroshi peering at him worriedly. He sat upright and rubbed his eyes. "It's nothing," he said hoarsely and got to his feet.

Torr stooped and picked up a fist-sized moon rock, one of many that accumulated at the tent borders. He placed it on top of the wooden Delosian crate and stepped back into the middle of the yard, trying to shake off the heavy grief that had taken hold of him. His campmates eyed him with concern.

"I'm fine," he assured them, forcing a grin. He inhaled sharply and pointed the Destroyer crystal at the moon rock and tried to send violet flames out its tip, like Darius had done so easily. Nothing happened, and Torr lowered his arm with disappointment. Maybe it had been just a regular dream, after all. Maybe he'd learned the names of the last Star Children during one of the many Star Seeker meetings his mother had hosted at their house in Shasta when he was a small child. The fact had lodged itself somewhere in his subconscious and resurfaced in his dream.

"What are you trying to do?" Berkeley asked.

"Hit the moon rock. With my energy. I think."

"Using the crystal?" Berkeley asked.

"Yeah. Something like that." Torr focused again and pointed the Destroyer at the rock. He closed his eyes, trying to remember how it had felt to be Darius. His eyes popped open. He had not *watched* Darius. He had *been* Darius. The realization unnerved him, and his pulse raced again. He breathed deeply. If he could only remember how it *felt* to use the crystal shaft. He had drawn light down through the top of his head and up through his feet and torso. He tried to imagine it, but the crystal remained inert in his hand.

"Are you trying to harness the light?" Tatsuya asked, squinting at him.

"Yeah," Torr grunted. "I don't know ... I forgot how. Something about taking in energy through my head and my feet."

"The light entering the head is white, almost purple," Tatsuya said. "From the ground it is red. They mix together in the heart. Like a flame fueled with lava from the earth and starlight from the heavens."

Torr closed his eyes and practiced pulling in the energy as Tatsuya had described. That felt better. He envisioned the two streams of light mixing in his heart, igniting into flames that coursed through his arm and into the shaft.

"Open the pathways," Tatsuya coached. "Do not pull in the light. Let it pour in like a waterfall. You must simply open yourself to it. Be like a riverbed that collects and channels the relentless flow of water."

Torr thought of the American River during spring thaw, cascading ferociously over rocks and surging against its banks. He opened himself, surrendering himself to the torrent, his face tilted upward and his feet planted solidly on the ground. A heat rose within him, and his hand burned with a strange sensation. The trick to the Destroyer was his "line of intent."

Torr opened his eyes and lifted his arm so that he could gaze down its length and that of the crystal shaft as though it were his pistol. He drew a bead on the moon rock and let loose the flow of light.

A flash of purple struck the rock with a crunch and a puff of dust. Torr gaped at the crystal. His arm trembled with a buzz of electricity. He ran to the crate and inspected the small mound of dust that moments ago had been solid rock. He fell to his knees and leaned his head against the crate, awed that he had succeeded, and heavy with grief that Darius and Danute had been blown to bits with the Star Globe.

Torr sat back on his haunches, a thought occurring to him. If the Memory Keeper and Destroyer had belonged to Darius, the crystals had somehow survived. So, then, perhaps Darius and Danute had also survived. Torr held onto that small sliver of hope and stood, gesturing to his concerned and astonished companions that he was okay.

He collected more moon rocks and set them on the wooden crate. Had the shard of glass that killed Zinz been part of Darius's line of intention? Torr shivered. He would need to be careful with this crystal, he realized, rubbing his thumb over the striated ridges of the faceted shaft. More importantly, he would need to be careful with his thoughts. He steeled himself as he stepped back and took aim at another moon rock.

18

CRACKS

Cassidy sat in her tent and languidly brushed the tangles out of her hair, looking at her reflection in Jasper's mirror. She braided her hair slowly into one long plait and let it hang limply over her shoulder. No matter how much she brushed it, she could not get the moon dust out.

She frowned and regarded her face in the mirror. She barely recognized herself anymore. If anything, she was reminded of Grandma Leann's haggard, wrinkled face in her waning days as life slowly departed, replacing her once vibrant ruddy complexion with an ashen shadow of herself.

Cassidy's own face was gaunt, and her skin was dry. She examined her face, leaning in for a better look. She squinted as several dark cracks appeared and then deepened. She watched with detached curiosity as the cracks spread, as though her face were an eggshell, crushed in an angry fist. She felt numb inside, but another part of herself, which was still aware and concerned, watched from above in fascination and horror as her face crumbled into fragments and fell piece by piece into the dust.

19

TWO SOLIDI AND A FAVOR

Torr woke up, ate a quick breakfast, and dragged himself to the training yard. The Smiths and other squads were already assembling on the various classroom tarps. Torr caught sight of the Scrids at the far intersection, and they exchanged their fist-to-chest salutes. Cassidy's speedster stood like a grounded bird, a glorious piece of machinery abandoned on a vacant stretch of dust.

"I will," Cassidy had said the other day when he'd asked if she was ever going to take it out.

"I want to learn how to fly it," he said.

"Me too," she had said distractedly. "I'll ask Kai."

But she hadn't, as far as Torr knew. Thankfully, she had not brought up rescuing the captive women again—a mission he should be down for, but only found himself recoiling from the idea. Perhaps he was no better than the Gaia United generals, giving up when the odds were stacked against them. Magic seemed to be the only thing that offered any hope of defeating the Tegs, but he didn't have any magic to speak of, aside from brief flashes of intuition and vivid but useless dreams. And his intriguing new skill with the Destroyer crystal. He cocked his head, still unsure what to make of that.

He wondered how he would react if it were Reina and Jenna trapped in that house instead of two strangers. Probably he would move heaven and Earth to get them out. But here he was, hiding out in the relative safety of Peary Dome—a weak and pathetic man. He had abandoned his friends on Earth and was kidding himself if he thought he could ever free them. He was a hypocrite, letting people think he might be the Star Child. He was no better than a false prophet. A fake messiah. A fraud.

Torr sighed and scanned the training yard for newcomers. There were a few. He greeted them and helped them find squads.

His squad started their day with Ming-Long, Khaled, and Faisal's knife-fighting class. The smiling, serious Ming-Long had them do pushups and run in place, and a host of other exercises. Then he taught them some martial arts forms that he said would help their knife-fighting technique. They waved their hands from side to side and from the ground to the sky. Then they made figure eights that ended with their arms spread like wings. Torr's favorite form was the motion of drawing a bow. Then they jumped forward and back and from side to side. They ended their warm-up leaping like frogs around the tarp. Durham had been able to do many of the exercises and showed off on the leaping drill by going into a handstand and hopping around on his hands.

Ming-Long made them hop until they could hop no longer. Then they reviewed their footwork, making patterns with their steps— crosses, squares, circles. Durham did this drill with one crutch substituting for his missing leg and flowed through the patterns with ease. Next they practiced knife strikes—defensive parries and offensive slashes and thrusts. They spent the remainder of the class slowly combining the knife strikes with the footwork. Ming-Long and Faisal made it look so easy.

They took a break, then lined up on the Judo mats. They did their ritual bows and warm-ups, and then Hiroshi and Tatsuya told them to break into pairs. Blaire appeared in front of him again. She had a glint in her eyes that made him smile.

They started off by practicing falling and rolling. They learned a new throw where Blaire attacked him from behind and Torr wrapped an arm around the back of her neck and pulled her over his hip onto the ground. She took a turn throwing him. She was strong. And she smelled good. They practiced that a few times, and then Tatsuya reviewed anatomy—how the shoulder and arm bones were arranged, and how the joints worked. Then Tatsuya and Hiroshi introduced a standing arm lock flow—a series of a dozen efficient moves that pinned the arm in various holds and incapacitated the opponent. They explained certain moves that could injure the opponent and were prohibited during training.

Hiroshi came over and demonstrated the flow on Torr, then Blaire tried the first hold, twisting Torr's wrist and fingers gently to the point of pain. He tapped his chest for her to ease up. Fingers and wrists were followed by arm bars and shoulder locks. They each practiced the flow a couple of times on each other while Hiroshi demonstrated on Tatsuya at the front of the class.

"Try harder," Blaire told him when they were instructed to make it more like a real fight. He realized he had been letting her twist his limbs with little resistance.

"Okay," he said. They started again. Joint locks were by their nature painful, and she seemed to enjoy getting the better of him. When it was his turn, she resisted him, forcing him to handle her more roughly than he wanted to, but he understood that it was the only way to really practice.

Tatsuya told everyone to trade partners. Torr paired up with Durham, and they ran through the lock flow again.

"Damn, Durham," Torr said as Durham grabbed hold of his arm. "Your hands are like vice grips."

Durham smiled and shrugged. "Comes from hauling my body weight around with my arms for so many years."

"I guess. Wow," Torr said, wincing and laughing as Durham twisted Torr's arm and immobilized him with an elbow lock.

They each completed the flow one more time.

"That's enough for today, we will pick this up this again tomorrow," Tatsuya announced loudly, clapping for them to line up on the mats to stretch. They ended with their parting bows.

After a break, they paired up for kickboxing. Durham partnered with Dang, and Torr paired up with Blaire again. They warmed up, and then wrapped their hands in canvas and set to sparring. Torr soon got over his reluctance to strike her. He caught her once in the eye, which made him feel bad, but she came back at him harder than ever, punching him until they were both laughing. When the session was over, he examined her eye. It was watery and starting to get puffy. "Great," he muttered. "First thing I do is give you a black eye."

"You were just trying to get back at me for hurting your little pinky finger," she said.

"No, I wasn't," he said, laughing and turning his shoulder away as she jabbed at him playfully.

Next, they sat for Berkeley's meditation session. Blaire sat behind him, beyond his peripheral vision. That was just as well. Otherwise he'd spend all his time stealing glances at her instead of focusing on his breathing.

He survived meditation class, then walked next to Blaire as a group of them hurried to Center Ring for their daily rations. The canteens were serving slices of beef today, which was unheard of, and Torr's stomach growled just thinking about it.

Torr strode silently and examined the woman at his side. He realized that he knew almost nothing about her. He knew that she was from Denver and had arrived at Peary several months before the city was bombed. She was the oldest of the four sisters and had formed the Smith gang. But that was all he knew, other than that she was smart and funny, stubborn and kind, strong and beautiful.

"What did you do? On Earth?" he asked.

Blaire's eyes darted to his. "I was getting my Ph.D., doing research at the Front Range Aerospace Center."

His eyebrows rose. Front Range had been second only to Moffett Field in aerospace research and development. Some would say it had been ahead of Moffett in some areas. "What kind of research?" Torr asked.

"Well, it was top secret." Her lips pursed for a moment. "I guess that doesn't matter anymore. We were reverse-engineering a Cephean aircraft that had been recovered in New Mexico."

Torr's mouth fell open with surprise. "So you're a rocket scientist," he said.

She shrugged. "Yeah, I guess. Or almost one, anyway. I had to leave before I finished the program."

"And I'm a twenty-year-old high school grad whose biggest talent is shooting a rifle."

"Oh, Torr," she said. "You fought in the war. That's important."

"What was your Ph.D. in?" At least he knew enough to phrase the question properly. He hoped.

"Advanced interstellar off-world propulsion technologies."

Torr barked out a short laugh. "Holy stars, Blaire."

She regarded him with amusement. "It's not such a big deal. My parents were aerospace engineers, so it was a natural course of study for me."

"What about your sisters?"

"I'm the only one. Becka was in marketing, and Britta was studying math. Bailey's the baby and wanted to be a softball coach."

"Softball coach," Torr said weakly.

"Yeah. We're all athletic. We all swam competitively in high school, and I played soccer and lacrosse. Britta and Becka played basketball, and Bailey was a softball pitcher."

That explained the broad shoulders, strong limbs, and confident swagger of the sisters. "What about your parents?" Torr asked. "Where are they?"

Blaire's merry eyes darkened as though a cloud had passed in front of the sun, and Torr instantly regretted his question. She tightened her lips and looked forward.

"I'm sorry," he said quickly. "If you don't want to talk about it ..."

Her nostrils flared as she breathed. Her eyes were wide and stared as if not seeing. She spoke slowly, her voice monotone. "They stayed behind at Front Range. They were on a team that was building a defensive weapon they thought would protect us from the Tegs. They were almost done and wanted to see it through." She swallowed and kept walking.

He reached for her hand. She flinched, and then took his fingers. He held her hand gently, and she went on, her voice raspy. "They convinced me to leave with my sisters and come here. They were going to follow when they were done." Her eyes were watery, and Torr's heart tightened as her face stretched into a grimace of grief.

Torr pulled her to a stop and embraced her. Her chin dug into his shoulder as she held onto him, her breath blowing in short puffs against his neck.

"I'm sorry, Blaire," he said. He rocked her gently until she raised her head and gave him a brave smile, her eyes a bottomless chasm. They turned and continued walking, hand in hand.

They did not speak as they walked, their legs swinging in unison. He wondered if her parents had died when Tegea destroyed Denver. It sounded as though her parents had worked at the Front Range aerospace complex and spaceport, the epicenter of the attack. If they were at work at the time, they would have been incinerated along with everything else. If they were home, well, he did not know how far from the blast radius their home was and did not want to ask. If she wanted to talk about it more, she knew he would listen.

He thought of his own parents. He thought of LAX and Moffett Field. The spaceports and surrounding cities were in Teg hands now, but they still stood, as far as he knew. The thought crossed his mind for the first time, like shafts of sunlight cutting through the Shaman's Shield, that perhaps the Gaia United generals were not so stupid and cowardly as Torr had thought. After the Shaman's Shield had fallen, all that remained to Gaia United was conventional warfare. If Gaia United had resisted in California the way they had in Colorado, how long before Tegea would have gotten fed up and destroyed another spaceport and city? Torr had always figured Tegea would never destroy Moffett Field because of its advanced aerospace program. But the general had bombed the Front Range into oblivion. Perhaps the Gaia United generals had decided to save everyone's lives, rather than sacrifice them out of stubbornness.

Torr did not know if death was better than slavery—or turning Teg. But he was glad his father was still alive, so he guessed he had his answer. He was even glad Johnson was alive, and Smiley, Rashon, Bates, and Jessimar. If Torr were one of the Gaia United generals, what choice would he have made? He did not know, but somehow the musings put his heart at ease.

They lined up for rations, and Torr stared hungrily as the server placed two thin slices of medium-rare beef, a small baked potato with a pat of butter, and steamed spinach into his camp dish. It was a real meal. They grabbed a full-sized loaf of bread, filled their water jugs, then everyone rushed off to their respective camps to eat.

The Fensters took seats around the picnic tables and ate silently. Torr chewed slowly, savoring the food, not knowing when they would be served such riches again.

Later that evening, Blaire, Darla, and her sisters stopped by to visit with Cassidy, and huddled in the tent. Blaire wandered outside and sat down across from Torr at the picnic table, and he offered her some tea. She stirred in some honey, and Torr brought the conversation back to her story.

"I saw Cephean craft in California, after the Shaman's Shield moved north," Torr said, studying her face carefully to make sure he wasn't getting too close to a tender spot. She lifted her eyebrows with interest, with no sign of her brooding pain. "Whole groups of them," he continued. "Flying in formation. They were like manta rays."

"Mantas," she said, her eyes lighting up. "That's the ship we were studying. But it was too damaged to fly. I never saw one fly in real life, I only saw footage." She listened intently as Torr tried to describe how they flew.

"And we saw two here," Torr said, his voice low.

"Here! Where?" The excitement lighting her face quickly turned to concern.

"In the northwest quadrant," he said, gesturing over his shoulder.

They discussed the disturbing implications of Cephean craft on the moon and the long-term Teg presence it pointed to. He told her about the men Torr suspected had been Tegs at Gandoop Spaceport, and how they had been chased off when they'd done a flyover. Since there was no need to tell her about the deeds and their land, he left that part out, but described the Manta craft as best he could.

She gazed across the table at him. "I want to see them. Can you take me?" she asked.

"I don't think that's a good idea, Blaire. I think they might attack us if we went near the spaceport again."

Disappointment was sharp in her eyes, but she didn't press him. "The wings were made of some sort of strange membrane," she said. "We think it might have been living tissue, attached to a mechanical body. But whatever it was, it was dead by the time we got hold of it. Anyway, I left before the biologists figured that part out."

She started to explain an interstellar propulsion mechanism that she and her research partners had been studying. It quickly became another language to Torr, and he smiled and nodded, trying to follow what she was saying. Her voice faltered, the spark in her eyes fading as she realized she had lost him.

Faisal was standing behind Blaire, heating water for tea. Torr had barely noticed him standing there, until he turned and spoke to Blaire. Faisal posed some technical question Torr could not decipher, and the fire in Blaire's eyes rekindled as she turned to converse with him. Torr remembered Faisal had a Ph.D. in Astrophysics. Torr gnawed on a hunk of bread, listening to the two of them go back and forth about whatever it was they were talking about. Faisal poured tea for himself and sat next to Blaire, the two of them engrossed in a discussion about tight pulsar white dwarf binary gravitational waves, or some such incomprehensible topic.

Faisal was animated like Torr had never seen him before. The handsome man perched his ever-present sunglasses on top of his head among glossy waves of black hair, revealing large intense eyes. White teeth flashed with enthusiasm as Faisal spoke more words in one sentence than Torr had heard out of him in all the days they'd camped together. Torr excused himself and left the table, with barely a flicker of Blaire's eyes registering his departure.

Torr went to the back courtyard and took a seat on a crate next to Berkeley at his sewing machine. He watched despondently as Berkeley finished a Light Fighters patch and added it to his stack, and then took another blank round of canvas and placed it under the needle. The sewing machine whirred as the needle moved robotically in its programmed embroidery pattern.

"Is Blaire okay?" Berkeley asked as they watched the machine work. Torr assumed he was asking about her sadness on the way to Center Ring earlier that day.

"Yeah. Her parents were at Denver Front Range when it was destroyed."

Berkeley took a deep breath and nodded, his eyes on the embroidery. Torr found himself hoping Blaire's parents had been captured, or that her father had joined the Tegs. Odds were, though, that they had been killed. If they were rushing to finish their project, no doubt they spent all their time at the facility. Torr wondered again which of the possible fates was worse. Torr's thoughts strayed to his own parents, pondering if he could learn to dream of them at will.

The sewing machine whirred in the background as Torr's thoughts returned to Blaire. She was maybe too much for him. Or he was too little for her. Or too young. He guessed she was at least five years older than he was, if not ten. How could he compete with the likes of Faisal—a strikingly handsome man who was a few years older than Blaire. Faisal was obviously highly intelligent, well educated, filthy rich, and to top it all off, he was a prince. Torr rose to his feet, disliking his train of thought. *Focus on the breath.*

He scoured the small yard, gathering moon rocks. After stacking them in a pyramid on the Delosian crate, he stood back to practice using the Destroyer. It took all his concentration to gather his energy and shoot it through the crystal, taking several seconds or even minutes each time to get it to work. Dissatisfied with his progress, he went in search of Raleigh and Roanoke, cutting in between tents to avoid the picnic tables. He found them in Sky and Thunder's tent with Hawk and Durham. They were playing Galaxy and looked up from their cards as Torr poked his head into the tent.

Torr convinced them to come into the back courtyard with him, confiding with them about the Destroyer and his challenge with using it. They stared at him with a mixture of awe and fear and agreed to try and help him. All except Sky, who shifted nervously.

"What's the matter?" Torr asked.

"I don't think you should be messing with magic." Sky's voice was grave.

"Why not?" Torr responded, examining Sky's worried blue eyes.

"Because you don't know what could happen. You could do something you regret."

Torr hesitated. He hadn't thought about that. What if something unexpected happened, like it had with Darius and Zinz? He frowned as they regarded each other sullenly.

"The Shaman's Shield kept the Tegs out of the Western Free States for three years. That didn't hurt anybody," Torr ventured, attempting to convince himself as much as Sky.

"That you know of," Sky said. "I heard if people went inside the Shaman's Shield, they disappeared forever."

Torr scoffed. "No." Although he had heard the same thing. His mother had even said as much. The same was said of the mist over the Great Isles. "No one can enter the Shaman's Shield," he told Sky. "Solid objects can't get through. I used to shoot bullets at it, and they would bounce right off and fall to the ground."

That seemed to appease Sky somewhat, but not completely. Torr left out the part about the Gaia United scouts who had entered the dissipating shield and never returned. Everyone assumed they had been killed or captured by the Tegs. Then he thought of his mother's goal of finding a way through the Shaman's Shield to reach Mount Shasta and was struck with worry.

"The Shaman's Shield was raised by shamans," Sky said. "Those people from Shasta have some sort of, I don't know, uncanny connection with nature and spirits. It's black magic, if you ask me."

"If it keeps out the Tegs, I don't care what you call it," Torr argued. He waited for Sky's comeback, and when it didn't come he realized Sky was staring open-mouthed at his chest. Torr had taken off his vest, and his red t-shirt displayed the snow capped peak of Mount Shasta, with SHASTA MOUNTAINEERING printed clearly around it. His impulse was to cover it up, but he stood straighter and held his ground. He shouldn't be ashamed of who he was.

"I'm a shaman," Torr claimed, holding his chin high. That part felt like a lie, but he did not flinch. "I'm from Shasta."

Sky's mouth worked silently, his face blanching. The Boyers and Thunder stared at him.

"Well, I moved away from Shasta when I was a kid, but I visited my grandmother there all the time, growing up. She was something strange, I'll tell you. And my mother and father, too. They both studied with the shamans when they were younger, especially my mother." The men were silent and regarded Torr as though he were from another planet. "Jaz, too," Torr added, in an effort to diffuse the shocked stares.

"And Cassidy?" Hawk piped up.

Sky's eyes narrowed suspiciously. "So you didn't really train with them."

"Well ... no. Not exactly." *Not at all, really, but he had picked up things along the way.*

"I don't think God wants us messing with magic," Sky said stubbornly.

Thunder snorted. "You think God wants the Tegs to make us all slaves?"

Sky scowled at Thunder, who glared back at him and said, "This God of yours seems to play by some mysterious set of rules that makes no sense whatsoever."

"Look, are you going to help me, or not?" Torr asked.

Sky's blond eyebrows lowered petulantly over stormy eyes, but he followed Torr and the others across the main yard towards the back area.

Blaire and Faisal were still at the picnic table, sitting close to one another and leaning over a piece of paper that Faisal was sketching on. They didn't even look up as the band of men trooped by. Torr acted as though nothing were wrong and led his friends into the back court-yard, where Berkeley showed off his new inventory of Light Fighters patches. The tall man rose and stretched, shaking out his legs and dusty locs, then joined the others as they gathered to evaluate Torr's problem.

"See how long it takes me to prepare?" Torr asked as he focused on a rock, which exploded in a small puff several seconds later. "That is unacceptable." The onlookers stared at the mound of dust, their mouths agape.

Only Berkeley seemed to have his wits about him and stepped forward. "Let me try," he said.

Torr watched as Berkeley attempted unsuccessfully to get the Destroyer to work for him. Berkeley grew more and more disgusted with himself, and finally passed the crystal to Durham. Everyone took a turn, including Sky, whose face screwed up with such a look of horror as he pointed the crystal that Torr was afraid of what would happen to Sky if he actually made it work.

"I know," Raleigh said. "We'll throw rocks in the air, and you try to hit them."

"Good idea," Torr said.

Raleigh, Roanoke, and Hawk took turns tossing rocks in a slow arc, but the violet flame spurted impotently from the crystal a couple of heartbeats later.

"You're thinking instead of feeling." Tatsuya's voice came from across the yard, and the small man walked over. "You are trying to direct your power from up here," the man said, tapping his forehead. "That is the upper star. Thought." Tatsuya moved his fist down to his lower belly. "You must drive your will from down here. The lower star. Hara. Life force."

Torr listened, reminded of things his father had taught him during archery practice.

"Don't think so much. *Feel.* It's all about intention," Tatsuya said, sending tingles across Torr's skin. "Try it again."

"Okay," Torr said, casting Tatsuya a curious glance. "Throw a rock," Torr said to Roanoke.

Torr did not think. He did not prepare. He just planted his feet firmly on the ground and waited for Roanoke to heave a small rock into the air. Torr shot a thin line of shimmering purple that hit the rock and sent a burst of dust motes spinning through the air, catching the sunlight and refracting into a thousand tiny rainbows that flashed and faded.

The courtyard was still. No one breathed. Then the yard erupted in low murmurs as everyone turned to one another, all speaking at once. "Did you see that? Did you see the rainbows?"

Torr's hands trembled with excitement, and Raleigh threw another rock. Torr shot the stream of light from the Destroyer, catching the rock in its downward arc and exploding it in midair. The onlookers broke out in a cheer, and Torr's adrenaline surged.

He tried again but could not get the crystal to light up. Again and again, nothing happened. He tried not to think. He tried to imagine the purple light. He tried remembering Darius, but nothing worked. Torr found himself completely exhausted after several such attempts. He tried one last time, and purple flames shot out from the Destroyer, hitting a rock and sending Torr to his knees. His mind was numb and his entire body was shaking when Tatsuya helped him up and led him away, supporting him on his strong wiry arm.

At the edge of the small courtyard, Torr found himself face to face with Blaire and Faisal, who were staring at him with open-mouthed wonder.

"May I?" Faisal asked, holding his hand out hesitantly.

Torr put the Destroyer in Faisal's hand and watched, too tired to be jealous, as the man turned it over in his palm and then handed it to Blaire. They began discussing possible scientific explanations for what they had just witnessed. Torr plucked the crystal from Blaire's hand and turned away, letting Tatsuya lead him to his tent, where the man forced him to drain an entire waterskin and fed him a handful of almonds before allowing him to collapse onto his blankets in a dazed heap.

———————)———————

Late the next afternoon, Torr went to refill his waterskin at the water tank and Tatsuya appeared. "Come with me," the man said to Torr, bowing at him. "Please. I want to show you something."

Torr followed the small gray-haired man into the back. Tatsuya went to his bench and held out a piece of paper.

It was a detailed black ink drawing of the snakes that were etched onto the wolf knife's tang, now hidden by the handle. The twining snakes coiled around each other, and wings spread above the snakes' heads, like those that formed the knife's guard. Tiny scales and feathers were drawn with intricate detail.

"It's a beautiful likeness," Torr said. "A work of art." The snakes on the paper seemed almost alive.

"Your tattoo," the small man said, beaming happily at him.

"Really?" Torr asked. He lifted his left forearm and turned it up to expose the smooth skin. Tatsuya lay the paper over his arm. The size was perfect.

Tatsuya sat on the bench next to his tray and arranged his ink vials. He looked up at Torr expectantly, patting the paper with the snakes that sat on a stack of towels in the middle of the bench.

"You want to do this now?" Torr asked.

"Yes, if you do." Tatsuya smiled.

Torr straddled the bench, facing Tatsuya, and laid his arm on the stack of towels between them.

Tatsuya shaved and cleaned Torr's arm. He transferred the stencil to Torr's skin, making a dark blue outline, and then set to work. The strum of Fritz's and Frank's guitars drifted in from the main yard and blended with the buzz of the ink gun. The needles were not very painful, and before too long, the ink outline was done. Torr chose the colors: green and gold, like the garden snakes back home.

Tatsuya first laid down the gold ink, coloring the eyes and the stripes along the backs, and small accents on every scale and wing feather. They skipped dinner, and Tatsuya continued working, applying greens of various shades. Hints of red and indigo, like shadows, added depth to the edges. He used the same red and dark blue to make two long forked tongues. Then he moved to the golden wings and started adding purple shading.

Tatsuya worked silently, intent on his art, and Torr let himself relax into a languid half-sleep. Images of twining snakes writhed across his vision. Dozens of them … hundreds … thousands … rising in paired mating dances across an endless field. Towering cliffs rose in the distance.

After a time, Tatsuya finished and Torr inspected the tattoo. The snakes were lifelike and wriggled when Torr clenched and unclenched his fist. Prickles ran up his spine as gold snake eyes gleamed up at him, the serpents' bodies slithering.

"What did you do, Tatsuya?" Torr asked with a nervous chuckle. "Add in the snakes' spirits?"

Tatsuya's mouth turned up in a sly smile. "I always ask the assistance of spirits when I work. That is why my tattoos are so sought after." His eyes narrowed to slits. "I never tell anyone my secret, but you guessed it on your own. You still have violet flames flickering around your head. They must have attracted the snake spirits, for they came to watch, competing for the best view." Tatsuya's black eyes sparkled with amusement at Torr's expression. "Your snake spirit came and bit into your arm, releasing its magic venom with its needle-teeth."

Torr tried to laugh with him. "Tatsuya, don't joke."

"Who's joking, young wolf?" Tatsuya asked. "Your snake spirit is very powerful. It spoke to me."

"What did it say?" Torr asked, shivers running across his skin.

The old man peered at him. "He said your spirit has wings. When you dance the dream, you are more powerful than ten thousand snakes crawling on the ground." Tatsuya raised one gray eyebrow, and Torr didn't know what to think.

Tatsuya took Torr's arm again, resting it on the stack of towels, and applied ointment to the tattoo and wrapped it in a bandage. When he was done, he turned to clean his ink gun. Torr rose from the bench and insisted Tatsuya accept two gold bits for the tattoo.

"Come back soon and I will color that in for you," Tatsuya said, pointing to Torr's Light Fighters tattoo.

They exchanged bows, and Torr went to the kitchen to cook some eggs for himself and Tatsuya.

Torr glanced at his watch. It was already twenty-two hundred hours, and Cassidy wasn't back from the Smiths' yet. Raleigh radioed the women's camp and handed the handie-talkie to Torr.

"Hello?" a woman's voice said.

Torr recognized Blaire's voice. "Hey, Blaire," Torr said, clearing his throat. "Can I talk to Cassidy?"

"Hang on."

Torr could hear an electric grinder in the background, and the high-pitched pinging of a hammer cut through the loud buzzing.

"She's busy learning how to solder," Blaire said. "She said to come on by."

"Over there?" Torr asked. "To your camp?" He winced. What a stupid question.

"Yes, Torr," Blaire said, chuckling. "Over here. We don't bite."

"Yes, ma'am," he said, smiling, and turned off the radio.

"Come on," he said to the Boyer brothers. They gathered Sky and Thunder and Fritz and Frank, then left for the Smiths.

"When're you going to take us to the gravity bar?" Roanoke asked Torr as they entered Center Ring. "You promised."

"Whenever you want," Torr said.

"Now?" Roanoke asked, lifting his brow hopefully.

"Uh ... okay," Torr said, glancing at his watch again. They still had almost two hours until night gong. "Sure, come on," he said, gesturing for his friends to follow.

"Awesome," Fritz said.

"You've never been back there?" Torr asked.

"No. You can't just go back there," Fritz said.

Torr shrugged. "I'll see if I can get us in."

The ration trailers were closing up, and the yard was relatively quiet, with only a few small groups wandering across the empty space. Sid was on guard duty at the PCA tent and waved them through without even a word. Fritz cocked his eyebrow at Torr, and the blond twins followed Torr inside.

Hawk gawked at the ping-pong table and star shooters table. Pablo and Diego were playing ping-pong and stopped when they saw them.

"Where are you going?" Pablo asked.

"Out back to the gravity bar," Torr said.

"We're coming," Diego said, setting down his paddle.

Torr peeked into the back office. Montana was talking to another ration guard, and Torr gestured for permission to go into the back. Montana waved his hand and turned back to his conversation.

Torr smiled, and his friends filed out into the back courtyard and encircled the shimmering white pillar.

"I love this thing," Diego said, spreading his arms and leaning against the pillar with a big hug.

"Me, too," Torr said, placing his palms against the warm stone.

The others imitated him, placing their palms against the gravity bar and staring up at its enormous height. Torr leaned in, closing his eyes and resting his cheek and chest against the stone. It almost felt like the gravity bar was pulsating, and he let his heartbeat and breathing synchronize with its rhythm. The throbbing lulled Torr into a partial slumber, and soon he was rolling across the Milky Way star bridge like a tumbleweed made of branching light fibers.

His eyes popped open, and he tore himself away from the pillar and led the others up the ladder to the roof of the red shipping container.

Torr gazed overhead while he awaited his turn at the telescope. The Milky Way stretched across the sky in a cloudy web of darkness, its edges flooded with light. Jupiter, Mars, and Saturn floated overhead— beacons staring down at him.

Beyond the planets, the number of stars was unfathomable. Where was Uttapta, he wondered, closing his eyes and listening for star music. All he heard was the constant din of ten thousand souls echoing off the glass geodesic dome.

Torr took his turn at the scope and focused on Earth. The planet was a thin sliver of blue and white, almost at new Earth, and the rest of the globe revealed dark shapes of Eurasia against darker oceans, faintly illumined by moonshine. The continents were speckled with orange light where cities were lit by electricity. The bright clusters were dimmer and fewer than in photos he remembered from the past. Many cities had been razed by the Cephs. Perhaps work camps were dark at night. His stomach grew heavy, and he thought of his father. He sighed. *Focus on the breath.* Warm air left his nostrils. *Inhale. Exhale. Emotions are only thoughts. Let them go.*

He stepped away from the telescope to let Thunder take a turn.

"Look, Torr," Pablo said, gesturing down at the yard.

Jorimar and Helug were sauntering slowly across Center Ring, looking up at them and grinning widely.

Roanoke came up beside Torr and dropped down into a prone position, slingshot in hand.

"What are you doing?" Torr asked.

"Just having some fun," Roanoke muttered.

Pablo laughed and lay down next to Roanoke, peering over the edge.

"Don't hit them in the head," Torr warned, crouching down.

"I won't," Roanoke said. "Besides, it's just chalky regolith. It won't hurt 'em none." Roanoke aimed and let the rock fly.

Torr peered over the edge in time to see Jorimar's hand flick out, quick as a frog's tongue, and catch the rock, and then hurl it back at Roanoke. Torr drew back, and the rock flew over the lip of the container where Roanoke's head had been. It thudded onto a container behind them. Torr raised his head and stared at the Scrid.

"He caught it!" Hawk said. "From a slingshot throw! Did you see that?"

Torr burst out laughing. Jorimar and Helug were laughing, too. Torr had never seen such quick reflexes.

"Scrids have eyes like hawks," Frank said.

Jorimar was tossing another moon rock in his palm, smiling mischievously.

"Now you've done it," Fritz said.

"We'd better go," Torr said. "Before Montana bars us from the courtyard." He was still chuckling as he climbed down the ladder.

They kept their distance from the Scrids, who followed them with their eyes as Torr's group left the PCA and cut across the yard and onto Spoke Road Three on their way to the Smiths.

Cassidy was just getting up from the table with Blaire's youngest sister, Bailey. Cassidy held out a small square solar panel. "I fixed this," she said proudly.

Torr nodded with approval. She was happy, yet somehow she looked different than the sister he knew. Her bruises were gone, as were all signs of the drug addiction, yet she had changed. Her face was longer, and her eyes were larger. And her hair floated like their mother's.

Cassidy and Bailey went to put away the soldering guns, and Torr scanned the bustling yard until his gaze settled on Blaire's strong back. She was wearing a black racerback tank top, and her sculpted shoulder blades moved under smooth brown skin as she gestured while talking to her sisters, Becka and Britta. Blaire felt him looking at her and glanced over her shoulder. She met his gaze for a moment and lifted her hand in greeting, then turned back to her conversation.

Torr stood around chatting with the Alphabet Boys while Cassidy got her things together, then they headed home to the Fen, each lost in their own thoughts.

———————)———————

Torr retreated to his tent before night gong struck and collapsed onto his blankets. The dreamcatcher turned slowly above his head, and he gazed at the tiny, fluffy feathers. After a few deep breaths, he drifted off to sleep.

He awoke briefly when night gong rang and Cassidy entered the tent and crawled into her sleeping bag, and then again to the sound of laughter nearby. He propped himself up on one elbow, trying to identify the voices.

He frowned and lay back down, listening. It was Jasper in the tent next door. A very drunk Jasper. And a woman who most assuredly was not Cassidy. He glanced across the tent, and his sister stirred.

"Who's that?" Cassidy asked.

"I don't know." Torr closed his eyes with dismay. Certainly no one from the Smith gang would be so heartless or stupid as to hurt Cassidy by climbing into bed with Jasper. Torr exhaled loudly. "I'm going to find out," he said.

"No, don't," Cassidy said.

Ignoring her objections, Torr pulled on his clothes and boots, then untied the door flaps and stepped out onto the dust.

He stood outside Jasper's tent and scowled as giggling erupted from inside.

"Oh, Jaz," the female voice slurred. "You are so mean. I'm sure it's not worth that much." Torr could not decipher the low murmur of Jasper's response. "I'll stay here," she said loudly, then giggled again. "Here," she said. "Have some more."

Torr glanced across the yard at Fritz and Frank, who had pulled curfew guard duty and gave Torr a helpless shrug from their seats at the picnic table. Torr walked over to them.

"Who's in there?" Torr asked.

"One of Schlitzer's girls," Fritz said.

Torr looked up at the stars with disgust and crossed the yard again. "Jasper," he called quietly at the doorway, not about to let the drunken fool break his sister's heart by sleeping with a prostitute within earshot of Cassidy.

"Huh?" was the drunken response. "Torr?"

"Let me in," Torr demanded.

"Ho. Wait a second. Yeah, come in."

Torr pushed through the door flaps. Anger burned in Torr's chest. The only good thing was that Jasper and the girl were not having sex. They were fully clothed and sitting on Jasper's blankets, peering into a crystal shaft that lay on a square of purple satin. The crystal glinted in the dim light. Next to them on the canvas floor stood a half empty bottle of tequila.

"Look, Torr," Jasper said, waving him over. "Delly got my crystal for me. From Gabira."

"Debbie," the girl corrected him, and hiccupped.

"Tha's what I said. Delly. She got my crystal from Gabira, 'cause that witch won't give it to me." Jasper gave Torr a crooked smile, his eyes staring off in different directions. "Damn witch don't like men. But Delly here, she can get Gabira to do it 'cause she's Schlitzer's girl and the bitch won't mess with Schlitz. Right, Delly?" Jasper's eyes closed halfway, and he jerked his head up, then bent over to peer into the crystal with one eye. "Wha's it do?" Jasper leaned on one palm, holding himself upright with effort.

"Alright, alright," Torr said, leaning over and pulling Debbie by the arm. He hoisted her to her feet. She wavered and leaned against him. Her breath was thick with tequila fumes.

"What's your name?" she asked, gazing up at Torr, her blue eyes glazed and slightly cross-eyed. Her breasts pressed against his chest, and he took in a breath.

"I'm Torr, and I'm taking you home. You live at Schlitzer's camp?"

"Yah. It's nice there. We got showers and a cook." Her head lolled against his chest, and her knees started to buckle. Torr got his arms under her armpits before she fell. He held her upright while he pushed through the door flaps.

"Say goodbye, Jasper," he said to Debbie.

"Bye, Jazzy." She smiled crookedly at Jasper. "Thanks," she hiccupped. "You're welcome," she said.

Torr dragged her from the tent and motioned for Fritz to come help him. "Here," he said to Fritz, rolling Debbie into his arms. "Hang onto her for a minute."

Torr slipped back into Jasper's tent. Jasper was sprawled on his blankets. His eyes were half-open, and he was snoring.

"What a fuck-up," Torr muttered. He took a quick glance at the mystery crystal and placed it on a shelf, then grabbed the bottle of tequila and left the tent.

Fritz was standing tall, with a half-sleeping Debbie leaning on his chest, her head resting on his shoulder. He wore a lopsided grin.

"Most action you've seen in a while, eh, buddy?" Torr joked.

Fritz nodded. "Sad but true."

"Enjoy," Torr said, and left her in his arms while he gathered the Alphabet Boys, who were already awake in the pavilion and watching curiously, and the Boyer brothers, who dragged themselves out of bed, and Ming-Long and Khaled, who emerged from their tents, bleary-eyed and grumpy. Torr left the tequila on a picnic table, knowing it wouldn't last long. Fritz and Frank eyed the bottle with interest. Torr asked Faisal, Sky and Thunder, and Durham to help Fritz and Frank guard Cassidy, then looped his arm around Debbie's back and left for Schlitzer's camp.

They took turns propping Debbie up between them and escorting her to the side of the road where she retched loudly into the dust. Torr finally scooped her up like a bride he was carrying over the threshold. She was lighter than he'd expected and stank of tequila.

Peary Dome was quiet. It was past one in the morning, and curfew was in full effect. At Schlitzer's bar, a half-dozen patrons sat quietly with an assortment of drinks and girls. Schlitzer rose from his stool at the bar and came to meet them.

"What's this?" Schlitzer asked, not looking pleased as he regarded Torr with Debbie passed out in his arms. Schlitzer's wiry brown and gray hair was pulled back in a short ponytail, wisps of vagrant curls floating in the air. His blue eyes were wide and alert, with no hint of alcohol or fatigue.

"She was with Jaz," Torr said as Schlitzer took the limp, sleeping body from his arms and held her in his own. Torr continued, rushing to explain. "She apparently helped Jaz retrieve a crystal that he had purchased from Gabira but failed to remove from her cave. They were both very drunk and made it as far as Jaz's tent. I figured it was best to get her home." Torr bowed his head slightly. "My apologies."

Schlitzer sat on a stool with Debbie slumped in his lap and lifted her lip with one finger. Torr saw that her teeth had a greenish tint to them. Schlitzer glanced up at Torr with annoyance. "You fed her Greenwash?" the pimp asked.

Torr's hackles rose. "I didn't feed her anything. I told you. She was with Jaz, and he passed out."

Schlitzer flicked his eyes at two men, who hurried over and took Debbie from him. Schlitzer folded his arms and regarded Torr. His eyes were steady, but not angry. "Not your fault. Thanks for bringing her over." He smiled cordially. "However, Jaz failed to pay for her, and now I've lost her services for an entire night. Since you're taking care of things, I assume you'll fix that little oversight?"

Torr didn't really know why he should be the one to fix it. Jasper was the idiot who'd taken her out and gotten her drunk. And Torr thought he had destroyed Jasper's stash of Greenwash. They would be having a conversation. And why did Torr always feel like he needed to step up and take responsibility? That's how it had been at Miramar, too. That's how he had become squad leader. He sighed. "How much?" he asked.

"Two Eagles," Schlitzer said.

Torr did not blink. That was robbery. "One." Torr forced a smile. "I'm sure Jaz didn't pour the tequila down her throat, or the Greenwash, or anything else, for that matter."

Schlitzer laughed. "I like you. Okay. One. And you owe me a favor."

Torr raised his eyebrows, resisting the warm flow of charm that exuded from Schlitzer. "Owe you a favor for what?" Torr asked.

"For me not getting angry," the pimp said.

Schlitzer had said it in such a friendly tone, Torr found himself wanting to feel grateful. His cheek twitched.

"Oh," Torr said. So that's how it was. A threat. Making Torr take the blame for something that was not his doing, and trading money for loyalty while making it seem like Schlitzer was being magnanimous. Some backwards sort of manipulation. He hated that shit. He wanted to tell the cocky man to fuck off but took a deep breath instead.

"Tell you what," Torr said, releasing his own stream of charm while trying to still his cheek. He dug into his pocket and came out with a gold Eagle and a handful of smaller coins. "Here's the Eagle for her time, and a gold bit for the bottle of tequila, which I assume came from your bar." It was twice what the tequila was worth, but Torr did not want to count out smaller coins and look cheap. Torr smiled into the smoldering eyes of Schlitzer, who looked not at all happy that Torr was immune to his powers.

"As for the favor," Torr said softly, "I just did you a favor by bringing her back, after curfew, unfucked. And if I ever find another of your girls passed out drunk somewhere, I will do the same."

Torr had tried to keep his tone courteous, so that if any of the other patrons overheard them, they would not sense anything amiss. Only Schlitzer had heard his actual words. Torr met the man's steely gaze and held out the gold coins.

Schlitzer hesitated, then opened his palm. Torr dropped the coins into it, and a smile spread across Schlitzer's face.

"I know I can count on you," the pimp said, and nodded graciously.

Torr let out a silent breath and turned to leave. He had narrowly avoided challenging Schlitzer's honor in front of his customers, a mistake that would have put a target on his back. Torr ducked under the half-lowered canvas wall and walked casually out onto the road with his men.

The stars stared down at Torr and his friends as they crossed the silent roads. Jupiter, Mars, and Saturn were all bright in the sky, looking on like curious companions.

When they arrived at the Fen, all was quiet. Fritz and Frank were at their posts at the picnic table. The tequila bottle sat on the table, empty. Soft snoring sounds came from inside Sky and Thunder's tent.

"Ming," Torr said. "Can you stay up tonight and walk the Fen boundary?"

"Sure thing, Torr." Ming-Long smiled. "Who needs sleep, anyway?"

"Oh, never mind," Torr said. "You need to teach tomorrow."

"It's okay, I fell asleep right after dinner, anyway. I'll be fine. Or maybe I'll get Faisal and Khaled to cover the afternoon classes tomorrow, and I'll cut out early."

Torr nodded. He wished they had more men like Ming-Long. Torr glanced up at Earth, then went into Jasper's tent and knelt at his side, gently lifting the upper lip of his friend. Jasper's teeth were the telltale green. Torr got slowly to his feet, trying not to feel betrayed. He rummaged through Jasper's pockets and belongings but did not find a silver vial of the green drug.

He went into his tent, stripped down to his boxer shorts, and lay on his blankets. Cassidy was sound asleep. His breathing slowed and his heart rocked his body gently as blood coursed through his veins. The encounter at Schlitzer's bar haunted him, the pimp's friendly grin dancing across his vision as he fell into his dreams.

The image steadied, and Torr held Schlitzer's gaze, the pimp's blue eyes dark and glittering. Torr's friends were hovering in the shadows near the bar. Schlitzer's girls were staring at him from the multi-colored pillows, their pretty faces drawn into spiteful, ugly leers. Debbie stood at Schlitzer's side, hanging onto his arm with her pink lips pursed in a seductive pout. The edges of the tent seemed to waver in the darkness.

"You owe me two Solidi and a favor," Schlitzer said, his large eyes boring into Torr's. Torr's hand went to his wolf knife, the metal pommel cold and hard in his hand. Filaments of light snaked from Schlitzer's abdomen and reached around, worming their way into Torr's back.

Torr's rage overflowed like lava seeping from deep fissures. He unsheathed the knife and swiped it smoothly behind his back, severing the creeping tendrils. Schlitzer flinched, as though he'd felt the sting of the blade.

"Tell you what," Torr said. "I'm returning your girlfriend for free. Next time, I'll charge you a Solidi for bringing her back safe." Torr smirked at the snarling man, then waved his blade at his friends to leave the tent.

Torr purposefully turned his back to the pimp. As much as Schlitzer might like to put a knife in Torr's back, they both knew such a thing would kill his business. However, Torr was sure Schlitzer was a patient man and would consider this exchange a debt to be paid, for much more than two Solidi and a favor. Torr ducked under the half-lowered canvas wall, walked casually out onto the road, and pointed his men towards home. Stars danced overhead. Orion's shield was directed at Torr, his two dogs bounding at his heels.

Torr approached a raised platform at the juncture of two roads.

Edgemont and Matthew were standing up on top, wearing Light Fighters patches on their chest pockets. They met Torr's eyes and saluted. "Stay alert," Torr said, stopping below them. "Schlitzer's dogs will be on the prowl." The two men nodded and put their hands to the black Lectros at their belts. "We're on it," Edgemont said, tightening his jaw. Matthew raised binoculars to his eyes and scanned the sleeping camp.

Torr sat upright in his blankets, rubbing the dream from his eyes. At least, he thought it had been a dream. He reached his hand around his back to feel for any light tendrils hanging off, but his skin was smooth and unbroken. Lifting his gaze, he found the dreamcatcher hanging motionless from the tent ceiling. The hole in the center of the small sinew web stared down at him.

Torr shivered and crept out of the tent, clothed only in his shorts and sandals, and nodded at Fritz and Frank. Torr peered inside Jasper's tent. He was still sprawled on his back, snoring lightly. Torr crept around the outside of Jasper's tent and trod silently behind the row of tents, looking and listening. At the end of the row, he turned the corner and hopped backwards into a defensive stance. Ming-Long crouched in return, brandishing a shiny blade.

A grin stretched across Ming-Long's face, the scar on his lip making his smile crooked. "Worried about something?" Ming-Long whispered.

They relaxed their stances, and Torr nodded and stepped away from the tents. "Bad dreams. That guy Schlitzer spooked me for some reason."

Torr was still groggy from sleep and wondered for a panicked moment if this was real or if he was still in the dream. It was all starting to blur together. *Focus on the breath.* He breathed in deeply and slowly exhaled, feeling the air leave his nostrils. Yes. He was pretty sure this was real.

"I'm awake, right?" he asked Ming-Long.

Ming-Long laid his hand on Torr's shoulder. "Get some sleep," Ming-Long said. "Frick and Frack and I have everything under control."

"We need to post guards on the roads," Torr whispered. "On raised platforms. Lookout posts."

Ming-Long inspected him from hooded eyes. "Let's talk about it tomorrow."

Torr nodded and retreated to his tent. He knotted the tent doors closed and curled up in bed with the wolf knife clutched in his fist.

———————)———————

The next morning, Torr caught up to Jasper shuffling towards the kitchen and dragged him into the back alley.

"How you feeling, Jaz?" Torr asked snidely.

Jasper moaned and rubbed his eyes.

"What in Juno's name were you doing bringing a hooker to your tent last night?" Torr asked.

"Who, Debbie?" Jasper picked grit from the corner of his eye. "She got my crystal from Gabira for me. Now I just need to figure out what it does."

"You were going to let her sleep in your tent," Torr scolded.

"Really? I don't remember. She wasn't there this morning."

"That's because I took her home, you dust brain."

"You did?" Jasper glanced at him. "That's cool. Thanks."

Torr gritted his teeth. "Don't you think it's kind of cruel to bring a hooker to your tent, not two yards from Cassidy? I mean, are you trying to fuck with her head, or what?"

"No," Jasper said defensively. "Of course not. Debbie's harmless."

"You're a fucking idiot. She's a prostitute."

"Well, I didn't sleep with her. She's not my type. Besides, she doesn't sell her body anymore. She and Schlitzer are dating. I'm not that stupid."

"Well, I paid Schlitzer an Eagle for her. For you."

"What'd you do that for?" Jasper's bloodshot eyes focused on him.

"Schlitzer tried to get two Eagles out of me," Torr said.

"It was her night off," Jasper said bitingly, and then huffed with irritation. "All she does anyway is hang out with Schlitzer and take care of his baby for him. She hired a babysitter. Schlitzer must have been fucking with you. Now I suppose you'll want me to get your stupid Eagle back."

"Baby?" Torr asked, trying to maintain his composure. He didn't know whom he was more upset with, Jasper for being such an insensitive prick, Schlitzer for conning him out of an Eagle, or himself for being such a Boy Scout and trying to fix everything for everybody.

"I'll get it myself," Torr snapped. "And you'd better tell Cassidy what Debbie was doing in your tent. You hurt her feelings. And what's with the Greenwash? Your teeth were bright green last night. You swore to me you gave me all your stash. Are you lying to me now?" Torr grabbed Jasper's shoulder.

"No," Jasper said, shaking off his hand. "Gabira sold us a little— made me pay for my own damn shit. She and Debbie are mad at me for running out. Everyone's going to be pissed at me. Did you hide it somewhere?" Jasper asked hopefully.

"No," Torr said. "I got rid of it. I told you. I dumped it into a porta-potty. It's long gone."

Jasper groaned. "Oh, man. You're killin' me."

"So are you a Greenwash addict?" Torr asked. "How come you're not getting sick and passing out?"

"Because I took the normal dose," Jasper said. "It just makes you high for a few hours. And no, I'm not addicted anymore. I used to be, when I first discovered the stuff. But I kicked it years ago. It takes several doses to get you hooked, and I'm not stupid enough to do that again. Cassidy took way too much. But don't tattle on me. She'll hate me even worse."

Torr rolled his eyes. "Just apologize to her about Debbie."

They went back to the kitchen, made some tea, and sat across from one another as more Fensters straggled over to the tables for breakfast.

Cassidy came out of their tent, robed in her purple dress. She strode past the table, ignoring everyone, made herself some tea, and then swept by and disappeared inside their tent again.

Jasper turned his eyes to Torr. "Did you feel that arctic blast blow by?" Jasper asked wryly.

"Yeah, I felt it," Torr said. "You'd better go talk to her."

"You talk to her for me," Jasper said.

Torr set his cup down. "You guys are supposedly in love. You go work it out."

"Do you really think she loves me?" Jasper asked, glancing sideways at their campmates, who were pretending not to listen.

"Do I think the moon orbits Earth? Now, go," Torr said.

Jasper sighed and rose from the bench. He went inside Torr and Cassidy's tent and returned to the table a few minutes later. His face was drawn.

"What'd she say?" Torr asked. "Did you apologize?"

Jasper dunked the last of his stale bread crust into his tea. "Yeah. She acted like she didn't care. Then she made me lend her the garnet."

"Made you?" Torr asked.

"You know how she gets," Jasper said.

Torr nodded.

"And she wants me to get another tarp," Jasper said.

"For what?" Torr asked.

"She thinks whoever she said is watching her moved. Now she says they're spying on her through the alleyway entrance."

Torr met Jasper's gaze.

"She's scaring me, Torr. She had that crystal ball in her lap, and her eyes are like ... like she's not all there. And her hair is floating like your mother's."

"I know," Torr said. And his cheek started twitching.

20

FİGHTİNG GHOSTS

The garnet was still warm from Jasper's pocket, and Cassidy pressed it against her cheek, trying to absorb his body heat. She had wanted to run into his arms, but instead she had sat stiff as a rod and her face had frozen in a pinched sneer. Words had jumbled up in her throat and she could not get them out.

He had seemed as uncomfortable as she, mumbling, "Sorry about last night and Debbie ... We're just friends ... I didn't mean to hurt your feelings," which sounded like Torr's words, not Jasper's. Still, she appreciated the apology. What hurt the most was how he and Debbie had laughed and giggled together, whereas she and Jasper barely looked at one another anymore, and when they did they exchanged awkward silences. Maybe he considered her to be damaged goods now. Or maybe that's just how she viewed herself. She would never be whole again—she was certain of that. She could still feel Balthazar's hard hands on her body, and even though she had scraped her skin raw with the sauna sticks, she could not rid herself of the numb sensation. It was as though parts of her had turned dark and dead.

Finally she had blurted out her request for the garnet, and he had handed it over without his usual haggling. And when she told him about being spied on, she knew he didn't believe her, and she didn't blame him. She sounded crazy, even to herself.

Cassidy gazed down at the garnet's reddish-purple facets. She could see nothing in them, not even light or shadows. But it was supposed to be a translation stone, not a Seer's stone, she reminded herself.

She pulled the blue and gold book from her backpack and regarded the gilded Heaven's Window cover design and the runes, which meant *Songs of Sirius.* It was so clear, she was perplexed that she had not understood the markings before.

She set the garnet on the floor in front of her. The runes became illegible. She picked up the garnet and could read them again. She exhaled, not having realized she had been holding her breath. With the garnet clutched in her left hand, she opened *Songs of Sirius* to the first page. It was handwritten in ornate calligraphy, as though carefully transcribed from the original.

Introduction

In this journal, I am collecting songs about the Star Children and the path home to the Turyan Ancestors. The songs are from many sources across the galaxy. The Ilian priests are teaching us songs that have been passed down to them, although sometimes I do not trust the priests because I know they keep editing the translations. The songs I like the best are the ones my mother used to sing to me and Darius when we were little. I sang one for Zinz once, but he scoffed and said that it was just a folk song sung by the common people of Turya and was meaningless. But I think those common people are probably wiser than the priests and priestesses, who think they know everything. If they knew everything, why wouldn't they just open up the portal to Turya themselves? And the songs from the Cephs are even more suspect, since those songs are always about themselves and how great they are, even though everyone knows their planets are the farthest from Turya, and therefore their energetic material is the most corrupted. Anyway, I am copying down the lyrics here. I wish I knew what they all meant. And I wish I knew how to transcribe the musical notes, because I think the melodies themselves have some power in them. All the songs have so many parts, creating complex harmonies. That is one thing I like here on Iliad—listening to the choirs sing the divine star music.

—Danute Stormbringer

Torr came into the tent and glanced down at Cassidy. "Ready for practice?" he asked.

Cassidy handed him the garnet and the book. His face lit up, and then grew somber as he read.

"Danute. Darius," he said, and turned the page.

"Hey, wait for me," she said, jumping to her feet and tugging at the book. "Don't skip ahead."

He reluctantly released the book and passed her the garnet. "We have to go to practice anyway," he said. "We'll read it later."

She put the book away, hid the garnet in her rune belt, and got ready for training.

———————————)———————————

That afternoon, Cassidy invited Blaire and Darla into her tent to show them the blue and gold book. They were passing around the garnet and translating a passage when the door flaps parted and Torr appeared.

"Knock, knock," he said.

Cassidy squinted against the light and invited him in with a sweep of her arm. Torr ducked inside and stood at the entryway.

She, Blaire, and Darla were sitting on her sleeping bag with *Songs of Sirius* open before them. "I transcribed another stanza," she told him, holding up the garnet. "It's a lot faster with this."

"I'll bet," he said, smiling.

Darla handed Torr the book, which was opened to the page with the section they had just translated.

He read it aloud.

> *Crystal castles glisten in the glow of the dogs*
> *Big dog fights little dog, battling for starlight*
> *Black tide pulls at the pack, they strain against the current*
> *Do not drown yet, big dog, little dog*
> *The golden people need you*

He handed the book back to Darla. "Does that mean Cassidy and Jaz are speaking again?" Torr asked, nodding at the garnet. "Seems to me he took back his crystal at the training yard this morning, and now she has it again already."

Cassidy shrugged and closed her fingers around the garnet. "I needed it," she said.

Darla gave her a pointed look and arched her eyebrows. "She goes, *'Jasper Manann,'*" Darla said, mimicking Cassidy's sarcastic tone. *"'Would you be ever so kind as to lend me your garnet?'"* Darla hopped to her feet and thrust her hip out to the side, with one hand propped on her hip and the other palm outstretched. Darla made like she was tossing long hair over her shoulder.

Torr and Blaire burst out laughing, and Cassidy sucked her teeth loudly. "I did not do that."

"What did Jaz say?" Torr asked.

"Nothin'," Darla drawled. "Not one little word. He just goes like this." Darla gave an oversized swoop of her arm as though dropping the garnet into a hand, then turned up her nose and spun on her heel, jutting her hips out side to side in an exaggerated saunter. Darla's voice sang out, "Then he just *swaggers* away, like he don't have a *care* in the world, and certainly not about *Miss Cassandra*. No, he don't care *one little bit.*"

"Darla," Torr said, laughing harder. "He does his pirate walk, right?"

Darla nodded, smirking. "That's it. A *pirate.*"

"And when Cassidy's not looking," Torr said, "he smiles like this, right?" Torr twisted his mouth into a crookedly lecherous grin.

Cassidy couldn't help but giggle at his silly face.

"That's right," Darla said. "He think he some big, *baaaad* pirate," she said, shimmying her shoulders. "Like he don't care *one little* bit. Then, at night, when he alone in his tent, he be like," she made crude motions with her fist at her groin.

Cassidy shrieked and threw a sandal at Darla, who caught it as she howled with laughter. Cassidy's smile faded, and she said, "I was going to have a civil conversation with him, but then he brings some *girl* into his tent. Ming-Long said she's a hooker, Torr." She glared at him. He had no response to that, and she repeated, "A *hooker!* What am I supposed to do with that? Huh?" Her lower lip was trembling now.

"Look, Cass," Torr said. "They're just friends. He didn't do anything. She helped him get that crystal from Gabira, that's all. Remember? Jasper gave Gabira that Pleiades necklace and he left without the crystal. You know that. You dragged him away, actually, so technically it's your fault."

"My fault?" Her trembling lip stiffened with anger. "Jasper was so drunk from that witch's spell, he never would have remembered it anyway," she said.

"Well, he asked for your help, but you made it clear you would not go near Gabira again," Torr said.

"Damn straight," she said. "She's an evil sorceress. And why are you defending him?"

"I'm sorry. I'm just teasing," Torr said. "Debbie helped him get it, that's all. They didn't *do* anything."

Cassidy exhaled with a loud huff. "*Debbie,*" she said, the name tasting badly on her tongue. "Still. How am I supposed to act?"

"Try acting normal," Torr said. "Instead of like a twelve-year-old."

She sniffed and returned to her book. "Mind your own business, all of you," she said, wiggling her fingers in the air at them.

Blaire left the tent with Torr to make some tea, and Darla cocked an eyebrow at Cassidy and peered over her shoulder at the book.

———————)———————

The following day at the training yard, there were more new people who wanted to join the Light Fighters. Cassidy watched as Torr walked around and talked to every single person, shaking their hands and asking their names. Joking with those who'd been there from the beginning. He was a born leader, and people gazed at him with open admiration. She smiled to herself. He was a handsome man. Sure of himself. Gracious. His newly colored Light Fighters tattoo was raw and shiny from ointment. It looked nice. Tatsuya had done a good job.

Cassidy partnered with Thunder for kickboxing. Elvis and Febo had them do a drill where one person was to use only their arms and hands, and the other person was to use only their legs and feet. It was Cassidy's turn to use her feet, and she clamped her jaws together as Thunder tied her hands behind her back. He knotted the tent strap loosely around her wrists, and then faced her, his hands up in a defensive guard, waiting for Febo's whistle.

Her heart was already pounding, but she could do this. It was only Thunder. Shy, gentle Thunder. And besides, her legs were strong and she was flexible, unlike Thunder who could barely touch his toes.

Febo's whistle blew, and Cassidy and Thunder danced around each other, waiting for the other to make the first move. Cassidy faked with her left knee, then lashed out with her right foot. Thunder parried her foot aside easily, and they circled, grinning at each other.

"Come on, Thor, god of Thunder," Cassidy taunted him. "Show me what'cha got."

"You'll be sorry when my rain and hail falls down upon you, Child of the Stars," he retorted, throwing fake jabs.

"Come on," Elvis said as he and Febo wandered from pair to pair. "You have to hit each other if you want to learn. Kick him, Cassidy. Try the spinning kick we taught you yesterday."

"Shush, Elvis, now he'll know what's coming," she said as she hopped and delivered a flying kick, catching Thunder in the shoulder.

"Good," Elvis said.

Thunder bounced from foot to foot, peering over his canvas-wrapped fists.

Elvis moved on to the next pair, and Cassidy and Thunder traded gentle strikes. Cassidy kicked him hard in the thigh, then Thunder hit her with a hook, catching her on her cheekbone and snapping her head to the side. She struggled against her bonds, and Balthazar's face leered at her. A dark shroud tightened around her, suffocating her. A scream tore from her throat, and she attacked him in a frenzied onslaught of feet and shins. His hands reached out and grabbed her shoulders, and she jabbed her knee hard, catching him in the groin. He fell away from her and stumbled to the ground. She stood over him, hot and panting, and the scene crystallized before her. It was Thunder on the mat, curled up in pain.

"Oh, I'm sorry, Thunder," she said, crouching beside him. "I'm so sorry, I didn't mean to do that."

He groaned, and Elvis came over. "Ouch," Elvis said. "Geez, Cassidy, you got him good. But that move is forbidden, remember? You get docked five points."

In Judo class, Cassidy was paired with Sky. He glanced at her warily. "Don't worry," she said. "I won't freak out again."

"No worries, Cassidy," Sky said. "Just don't damage my family jewels."

She smiled apologetically. "I won't."

They watched as Hiroshi and Tatsuya demonstrated head-lock escapes.

When it was Cassidy's turn to try the escape, they lay down on the mat. Sky was on top, putting the weight of his torso across her chest and wrapping his arm around her head in the Kesa-gatame mat hold.

"Stay on your side, Cassidy," Hiroshi instructed, standing over them. "Link your hands together around him."

She grabbed her own hands and squeezed Sky's chest. Sky pressed his weight down on her.

"Now scoot your hips over," Hiroshi told her.

She shifted her hips close to Sky's.

"Bridge up," Hiroshi said. "Press his head down and roll him."

Cassidy pulled Sky over her, and she rolled on top.

They changed positions, and Sky tried it. He rolled her over and ended up on top.

"Now make it harder for your partner," Tatsuya said from the front of the class. "Switch positions." Cassidy shifted to the bottom again. Sky wrapped his arm around her neck, and she moved her hips over, trying to get him into position to roll him over, but he kept scooting away. "Increase the pressure on their chests," Tatsuya said to the attackers. "Lean into them, don't let them roll you."

Cassidy squeezed Sky's chest and tried to get her hip under his. He pressed down, pushing her flat onto her back. Her face was in his armpit, and the sharp stench of male sweat made her recoil. He leaned harder, and she couldn't breathe. Her heart pounded. She knew she couldn't win. She surrendered to him, lying limp and waiting for it to end. He could do whatever he wanted, as long as he didn't kill her. He would give her the green drug afterwards, and everything would be alright.

"What's wrong, Cassidy?" he asked, loosening his grip and rising to his knees. "Are you okay?"

She looked up. A man's face with broad cheekbones and spiky blond hair loomed over her. Tears stung her eyes. She could not respond. Her vision was foggy and mucus blocked her nose. She rolled onto her knees and rested her forehead and elbows on the ground, coughing and shaking.

"Cassidy," a woman's voice said, and a gentle hand rested on her back. She looked up. A woman with silky brown skin and bright golden eyes gazed down at her. "It's me. Blaire. Are you okay?"

Cassidy sat up, and Torr was kneeling in front of her. She leaned into his arms, and he helped her to the side of the mat and over to the picnic tables, where they sat on a bench. She was still shaking. "I don't know what's wrong with me today," she said, wiping at her nose and resting her head on his shoulder.

"It's okay, Cassidy," Torr said, rocking her and patting her back. "You're safe now."

———————————)————————————

"I can't be afraid to fight," Cassidy said to Torr. They were sitting next to each other at the table after dinner at the Fen. She had on her new black pants, and she slipped her hands into the front pockets. She curled her hands into fists against the stretchy fabric, as though by squeezing her hands tight she could hold herself together.

"Just give yourself some time," Torr said. "You'll probably have some good days and some bad days."

"I hate the bad days," she said.

"I know," Torr said, putting his arm around her shoulder.

They got up and stood in the shade of the Alphabet Boys' pavilion, watching Buck and Arden grapple in the middle of the yard on the tarp that Jasper had bought for her. Before dinner, she had unfolded it to hang over a laundry line in the back of the yard to shield herself from the prying eyes, when the Alphabet Boys had asked her if they could borrow it for their evening grappling sessions. The one they had been using was plastic, but this one was canvas and better to fight on. She had agreed and hung the tattered blue plastic tarp on a line strung between Khaled's tent and a pole that secured a corner of the kitchen tarp, obscuring the alleyway entrance. She was pretty sure it would block the laser-like sensation she felt of someone watching her, as though they had gun sights trained on her. She glanced over at the tarp. So far, she did feel a little better.

She and Torr watched the scrappy, wiry Arden wrap his legs around Buck's thick waist in a scissor hold, until Buck tapped out. They got up, and Guy stepped onto the mat to challenge Arden.

Ming-Long joined Cassidy and Torr, folding his arms across his chest with a smirk on his face as he watched Guy and Arden wrestle.

"You think you can beat Arden?" Torr asked Ming-Long.

"I'm sure of it," Ming-Long replied.

"Awfully humble of you," Torr said, laughing.

"What happened at training today?" Ming-Long asked, and Cassidy realized his question was directed at her.

She lifted one shoulder in a half-shrug. "I don't know. Flashbacks, I guess."

"Yeah," Ming-Long said. "Those happen. You can't let them stop you, though, or you'll be paralyzed. And then those motherfuckers will have won after all. You know?"

Cassidy lifted her gaze and met Ming-Long's black, hooded eyes. "I guess," she said.

"You have to conquer your fear. It's the only way," Ming-Long said, squaring his shoulders.

"But what about when the fear sneaks up on you?" Cassidy said.

"Yeah, it's like an ambush," Torr said. "Dreams are even worse."

"True," Ming-Long said. "I just look those ghosts in the eye and tell them I'm alive and they're dead, and to suck it up."

Torr laughed again, with an edge of bitterness.

"What if your ghosts aren't dead?" Cassidy asked, and the men grew quiet.

She turned her gaze to the two men grappling on the tarp. Guy had Arden in the Kesa-gatame headlock. Arden rolled over on top, but Guy still had his arm wrapped around Arden's neck. Arden got his leg over Guy's hip and started pressing his forearm against Guy's jaw, and then levered himself loose and got Guy in an armbar.

The crowd clapped and cheered.

"Wanna try?" Ming-Long asked.

Cassidy turned her head. He was looking at her. "Me?" she asked. She shook her head with a rueful chuckle.

"I'll take Arden," Ming-Long said, "and then you fight me, Cassidy."

Cassidy laughed again, and Torr said, "No, Ming. That's a horrible idea."

"I'll either knee you in the balls, or whimper away," Cassidy said. "And embarrass myself in front of everybody, once again."

"No, you won't," Ming-Long said. "It'll be fine. Thunder and Sky don't know what they're doing. I do."

She lifted an eyebrow at him, and he grinned his lopsided grin, the scar on his upper lip making it look almost like a sneer.

"Alright," she said. "We're among friends, right?" She broke out in a nervous sweat and her pulse quickened, but she focused on her breathing like Berkeley had taught them, and soon her heartbeat normalized. But her skin was still clammy.

"Time me," Ming-Long said to Torr, and stepped out onto the mat to face off with Arden.

The crowd hooted and hollered. Arden and Ming-Long circled one another for a few moments, sizing each other up, then Ming-Long took Arden to the mat with a flying scissor takedown, and before Cassidy could figure out what he was doing, Ming-Long had immobilized Arden with a legbar, and Arden was tapping out.

The crowd cheered wildly, and Ming-Long and Arden got to their feet and bowed to one another.

"How long?" Ming-Long asked Torr.

Torr glanced at his wristwatch. "Twelve seconds."

The crowd whistled and clapped, and Arden left the mat. Cassidy noticed Hiroshi and Tatsuya watching from the entrance to their yard, and she stood up straighter.

Cassidy took a big breath and walked onto the mat.

The crowd grew quiet.

Cassidy and Ming-Long bowed to one another, then she stepped back, not sure what to do. In class, they had always practiced prescribed moves, and their freestyle sessions were always a combination of whatever they had just learned.

"How about you take me down with a regular leg sweep. Osoto gari," Ming-Long said, crouching and circling with her. "I'm going to grab your collar. You ready?"

Cassidy breathed and nodded. He came at her in slow motion. She stepped forward, swung her leg around his and dropped him to the ground with a loud thud. The force of her throw pulled her over, and she rolled out of it and landed on her feet, facing him. She beamed proudly as the crowd cheered, and Ming-Long got to his feet.

"Good," he said. "But you let go of my arm. You always need to stay in control. Try again. This time, keep my arm and get me into an armbar before I can get up."

Hiroshi was on the sidelines now and said to her, "You remember the one. One foot in his armpit and one foot on the other side of his head. Then lie back and pull his arm between your legs."

"Oh, yeah," she said. "I'll try."

It took her four attempts to get it right, but finally she had Ming-Long on the ground with his arm pinned to her chest and his elbow hyperextended. He tapped the mat, and the crowd hooted and whistled. She and Ming-Long stood up, brushing themselves off.

"Want to try it at full speed now?" Ming-Long asked.

"Oh," she said, laughing. "That wasn't full speed?"

They went at it again, and after several tries she got it right. She was dripping with sweat and her muscles were trembling, but she was not afraid. She knew he was going easy on her, but he applied just the right amount of pressure to challenge her without breaking her spirit.

"Thanks," she said, "I'm done. Unless you want to box." She playfully threw jabs at his chest, and he caught her up in a big bear hug and lifted her off her feet, growling and swinging her in a circle. She shrieked and giggled, and his growls turned to laughter. He set her on her feet and his eyes held hers, his pupils melding with the solid black of his irises.

Ming-Long shifted his attention to look past her shoulder, and she followed his gaze. Jasper was watching from a bench at the table, and his eyes were not laughing.

"What's his problem?" Cassidy muttered.

"He doesn't like anyone else touching his property," Ming-Long said as they walked off the mat together.

"I'm not anybody's property," she said, and turned her back to Jasper.

21

---)---

BLOOD FİGHTİNG

Night curfew was approaching. Torr sat on his blankets and peered up at the dreamcatcher, which hung motionless, staring at him. He thought the magical sinew circle was supposed to protect against dreams, but if anything, his dreams had been more vivid and disturbing since he had hung it over his bed. His body was exhausted, but he was afraid to go to sleep and lose himself in the dreamworld. He glanced over at Cassidy, who was sitting with the blue and gold book in her lap.

She looked up and met his gaze. "I need to borrow the garnet again," she said. "But Jasper's not talking to me." Her eyes were somber.

"I notice you're not talking to him, either," he said. "What's going on with you two?"

She shrugged. "He probably thinks I'm crazy."

"No, he doesn't. You went through a terrible time. Don't worry about it."

"How can I not worry about it? He's been avoiding me."

"Maybe he thinks you're scared of him. Scared of men," he said, broaching the topic hesitantly.

Her mouth closed. "Oh. Yeah, well. I am, a bit. But not of Jasper."

"Uh-huh," Torr murmured, staying quiet and waiting for her to continue. Her shifting eyes told him there was more.

"I just ... I don't want to belong to anybody. You know what I mean?" Her blue eyes searched his.

"Yes, I do. But I don't think Jasper wants to own you."

"I know," she murmured.

He took a breath and continued, trying to think of words that would help. "There's belonging *to,* and there's belonging *with.* They're not the same thing." She tilted her head, looking unconvinced. "Cass, Jasper blames himself for your capture."

Her brow furrowed. "It wasn't his fault," she said.

"Jasper thinks he should never have walked through camp with only the four of us. And he's beating himself up for not locking down the spaceport sooner," Torr explained.

"Oh," she said, the lines deepening across her forehead.

"You should talk to him, Cassidy. He loves you."

"He does?"

"Yes. Of course. Do you love him?" Torr asked.

"Of course I do," she said.

"He doesn't think you do. He said you've never told him."

"Well ... I don't know. Maybe I haven't ..." She bit her lower lip. "I'll talk to him. If I can ever get him alone. Where is he now, by the way? Durham said he left a while ago with Ming-Long, Khaled, and Faisal, and they haven't come back."

"Hmm," Torr said. "I don't know where they went. I'm sure he's fine." Cassidy forced a smile.

"Let me go find out where he is," Torr said.

Cassidy nodded and turned back to her book.

Torr put on his boots and went outside and looked inside Jasper's tent. It was empty. Normally everyone was back at their camps by night gong. Torr hadn't noticed any enforcement of curfew, but it seemed to be generally respected. He looked at his watch. It was twenty-three forty-five. He needed a radio badly.

"Call Jaz," Torr said to Raleigh, finding his friend at the picnic tables.

"Can't," Raleigh said.

"Why not?"

"I can't access the Guild channel, and no one ever gave us the code to the Fen channel."

"Why not?" Torr asked, irritated.

Raleigh frowned, and Torr walked around the camp. Fritz and Frank were in their tent.

Torr shook their tent door. "Can you radio Jaz?" Torr asked through the canvas.

"Come in," Fritz said. Torr pushed through the doorway. Fritz and Frank were sitting on their beds, and Fritz turned on his radio, hailing Jasper. There was no response.

"Try the Guild channel," Torr suggested. "He's glued to that thing."

"We're not in the Guild," Fritz said apologetically.

Torr went into the back and asked Berkeley to reach him on the Guild channel. Berkeley tried, but Jasper did not respond.

Torr drew his lips together. He had a sneaking suspicion where Jasper was and gathered a small group to accompany him: Fritz and Frank, Raleigh and Roanoke, Sky and Thunder. Hawk whined at being left behind, but Durham shot his youngest son a stern look. Hawk clamped his jaws closed with a petulant scowl. Berkeley was busy at his sewing machine, and the Alphabet Boys were settling down in the pavilion for the night, fighting over the flowered pillows, when night gong rang.

"Watch Cassidy," Torr said to them.

"Yes, boss," Arden answered.

"Why do you think we're here?" Elvis added. "Not for your pretty face, that's for damn sure."

Torr grinned.

"You're not allowed to walk the roads after night gong," Febo said.

"Have you ever done it?" Torr asked.

Febo shrugged. "Well, yeah. A few times."

"What happened to you?"

"Nothin'."

Torr cocked his head at Febo, then led his friends from the encampment. They strode silently along Ring Road B, which was eerily vacant. The entrance to Schlitzer's camp was near 12L. When they got to Spoke Road Twelve, they turned left and headed towards the perimeter.

In the sky beyond a crescent Earth shone a bright cloud of stars that reminded Torr of the halo around Darius's exploding diamond. He searched the skies for constellations and found Orion's belt and

shield and the dogs at his heels. The star Sirius shone brightly at the
big dog's throat.

Iliad orbited Sirius. Supposedly the planet was completely torn apart
from the thousand-year war. Most of the population had been killed
during the centuries of endless conflict, and the rest hid underground.
That's what Great-Aunt Sophie had said. Torr hoped Darius and Danute
had escaped the planet and lived to a ripe old age somewhere safe, their
bones or ashes buried in the embrace of a peaceful planet. He peered up
at the heavens as he walked silently along with his mates.

Just as Torr had suspected, he found Jasper sitting at Schlitzer's bar.
The spacious pavilion-style tent was bright and cheerful, even at this
hour. Large colorful pillows were strewn across patterned rugs, and
groups of men and women lounged against them, holding drinks or
each other. The sound of twittering laughter and deep voices melded in
a pleasing hum. At one cluster of pillows sat Ming-Long and Khaled,
both with crooked grins on their faces and a female on each arm. They
waved a greeting to the group, who lingered at the edge of the tent.
Torr's companions chose a vacant group of pillows and sat down while
Torr went to say hello to the grinning pair.

"Where's Faisal?" Torr asked.

"Conducting some business," Khaled drawled, raising a meaningful eyebrow.

"Oh? What about you guys?" Torr smiled politely at the four young
women who were looking him up and down.

"We don't have that kind of gold," Khaled said. "We just get to sit
here while Faisal has all the fun. I think these gals are hanging around
with us, hoping Prince Faisal has energy for another round. Right,
Jenny?" Khaled slid his arm around the waist of one of the girls, who
smiled innocently at him.

"Alright, well ..." Torr's voice trailed off. As much as he would love
to have sex, he couldn't see doing so as a business transaction. He would
much rather be with Blaire—a woman with depth and spirit—over
these beautiful young things who sold their bodies like the shoemakers
sold shoes.

He left them at the pillows and went to talk to Jasper, who was
sitting alone at the bar, a half-finished glass of beer and an empty shot
glass in front of him.

"Yo, Torr," he said, his voice slurred. Torr tried to catch his eyes, but they were glassy and kept sliding away from Torr's gaze.

"Bambi, another," Jasper called to the barmaid, who strolled over and filled his shot glass from a bottle of tequila, then wandered to the other end of the bar, where Torr saw Schlitzer sitting with a group of a half-dozen men and women.

"What's up, Jaz?" Torr asked.

"No' much." Jasper tilted back the glass of amber liquor and smacked his lips. "Wan' one?"

"Sure." Torr signaled to Bambi, who came over. "Whatever he's having." Torr motioned towards the shot glass.

She poured him a glass. Torr inspected the gold label on the square tequila bottle and drank. It tasted good. Bambi raised her blond eyebrows. "Another?"

"Sure." The hard alcohol reminded him of a night on the yacht with Bobby when they'd raided the liquor cabinet. A twinge of sadness tightened his heart at the memory of his friend, and he tried not to imagine his fate. He thought of the elegant vessel, *Moon Star*. The sea. Open sky and endless waves.

Images of his Gaia United squadmates flashed through his mind. *Reina*. If he had the choice of Reina or Blaire, whom would he choose? Reina had been his best friend at Miramar, after Bobby. Blaire, on the other hand, though he'd known her for only a short time ... there was something about her that made his blood throb.

Torr drank the second shot and placed some coins on the bar. "Beer for those guys, please," Torr said, pointing to his companions who sat awkwardly on the pillows. He doubted any of them had gold to spend. "And those two Casanovas over there," he said, gesturing towards Khaled and Ming-Long. Bambi nodded and took a tray filled with cold glasses of beer over to the grateful men.

"Where'd you get all this?" Jasper asked, his eyebrow rising crookedly as he turned over some of Torr's coins. His breath reeked of alcohol.

"It's a long story," Torr said.

Jasper grunted and didn't press it.

"I talked to Cassidy," Torr said.

"She hates me," Jasper mumbled.

"She doesn't hate you. You need to talk to her."

"What good am I if I can't protect her? Kidnapped and sold by some fucking assholes to a psychopath. Heh?" Jasper raised bloodshot eyes to Torr. "I'm worthless."

"You're wallowing in self-pity, that's what you're doing. Snap out of it."

"I'll never be good enough for her."

"Maybe you never want to be good enough for anybody. Maybe you'd rather spend your life drunk at a pimp's bar."

"Shut the fuck up, Torr," Jasper snapped. "You goodie-two-shoes perfect fucking Boy Scout."

Torr stood up and shoved Jasper off his stool, sending him sprawling onto the dusty canvas floor. Torr was suddenly filled with rage and loomed over Jasper as he crawled to his feet.

"What the fuck'd you do that for?" Jasper's eyes were offset, one eye glaring at Torr while the other wandered aimlessly to the side. He rubbed his elbow painfully.

"'Cause you're a drunken fool, that's why. You don't know anything about me. You haven't seen me in five years." *Goodie-two-shoes.* He wished he were a goodie-two-shoes, not some murdering bastard who shot a man in the back and then shot his eye out for good measure. "Let's go. I'm taking you home." He grabbed Jasper's arm, gripping it tighter as Jasper tried to squirm away.

"How much do we owe you?" Torr asked Bambi, who was watching them with a twisted grin. Schlitzer ignored them, though Torr had no doubt he had witnessed Jasper's tumble. Torr paid the barmaid, left her a tip, and pocketed the rest of the coins. He gestured for his companions, who downed their beers and scrambled up from the pillows. They followed as Torr pulled Jasper along. Ming-Long lifted his glass of beer to Torr, and Khaled was too busy sticking his tongue down Jenny's throat to notice them leaving.

Torr decided to take the long way home, around the perimeter road past one o'clock, hoping Jasper would walk off some of his drunkenness. Jasper swayed and stumbled along. Torr offered him some water, shooting a stream of liquid into Jasper's mouth from his own waterskin. "Those nasty lips are not touching my nozzle," Torr muttered.

"You're such a priss, nobody's lips will ever touch your nozzle." Jasper laughed at his own joke. "Are you a virgin, Torr?"

Torr was tempted to punch him, but it wasn't worth it. He wasn't about to confide in Jasper while he was so drunk. He would just make fun of Torr no matter what his answer was. He'd just better shape up, or Torr would stop encouraging Cassidy to make things right between them.

Jasper continued to heckle Torr as they walked past the lower-numbered spoke roads where the camps thinned out. The roads were empty, and the dome had settled down for the night. It was kind of nice being out here when everything was so quiet and the stars were so bright.

They passed Spoke Road Three when a group of men appeared around the curve up ahead. His companions saw them at the same time. They stopped and exchanged glances. Raleigh took his club from his belt, and Roanoke took out his slingshot.

"Maybe we should turn around," Torr said warily.

Jasper squinted. "Nah, I know those moon rats. *RENO!*" he called out, his voice booming across the silent dome. Torr cringed. Torr clamped his hand over Jasper's mouth as he was about to bellow something else. Jasper twisted in his arms and finally shook him off. "You my fucking mother? Lay off, Torr."

The two groups approached each other, and Torr hung back as Jasper sauntered up to the man leading the strangers. They clasped forearms in a hearty handshake.

"That crystal you sold me is worthless, Reno," Jasper slurred. "Piece of crap."

"I told you," the thin man replied, "you need to be a wizard to use it."

"I am a wizard."

"And I'm President Metolius."

The men bantered while the others stood by. They finally parted ways with curses and promises of a deal that was bigger than any deal the other had ever seen. Jasper sauntered cockily at Torr's side as they and their campmates cut across Center Ring. Torr waited for Jasper to collapse inside his tent before retreating to his own.

He sighed and stared up at the dreamcatcher as he lay on his blankets and listened to Cassidy's steady breathing, thankful for a few precious hours of peace and quiet. He rolled onto his side, clutching the Memory Keeper in one hand and the Destroyer in the other, and fell asleep.

———————⟩———————

Edgewood wriggled out of the overturned vehicle on the hillside and got to his feet, brushing his clothes off, and then looked up and caught Torr watching him from the bunker. Torr had the Teg's face in his sights, the crosshairs pegged to the spot between his eyes. Edgewood slowly raised the black Lectro in his hands. The two men held their guns pointed at one another.

"You gonna shoot?" Edgemont called to him, his voice faint from the distance.

"You first," Torr called back. Torr could see the man was smirking.

"You chicken?" Edgemont taunted him.

Torr lowered his sights to Edgemont's shoulder and squeezed the trigger. The Teg jerked from the impact but did not fall. Torr felt a searing pain as the snake jaw of the Lectro dug into his left arm. He expected to die on the spot, but it merely stung. He swatted at the snake jaw and it fell onto the plywood shooting platform.

Edgemont lowered the Lectro and propped an assault rifle against his shoulder, took aim, and fired. Torr jerked back as the bullet tore through the same arm. Blood gushed down his skin, but otherwise the wound did not seem to impede his movements. He aimed his gun at Edgemont's exposed abdomen and took a shot. Edgemont stumbled backwards, then regained his footing and shot again.

Torr breathed slowly as the two men exchanged fire, blasting holes in one another and yelling curses. *"Die, you motherfucker!"* Torr shouted. *"You die first, you stubborn rat's tick!"*

Torr could see tears streaming down Edgemont's face, mixed with blood. The Teg's body was riddled with gaping black holes, but still he fired on Torr. Torr raised the sights to Edgemont's right eye. If he blasted out both his eyes, the man wouldn't be able to aim anymore. Torr stumbled backwards in fright. Edgemont's eyes were a steely gray and focused with clear intention. His face was smooth, his skin tanned, and sandy-brown whiskers covered his jaws and chin. It was Torr's own face, bleeding and crying, twisted with anger and shame, staring back at him. He was shooting at himself, but he would not die.

Of course he would not die. It was only his reflection in a mirror. He took his TAFT and let loose round after round, blasting the mirror into a thousand pieces, which flew at him like darts, piercing his arms and chest, striking his face. A large shard pierced his forehead, and warm blood trickled down the channel next to his nose.

Torr jerked awake and sat upright on his blankets, panting loudly and soaked in sweat. He rolled onto his hands and knees, bowing down and resting his head on the dusty floor, trying to catch his breath and slow his galloping heart.

"*Fucking Algol's hell!*" he cursed. He unsheathed his combat knife and drove it through the canvas floor and into the hard ground underneath, pulling it free then driving it in again and again. "*I fucking hate you!*" he yelled, not knowing whom it was that he hated, and not caring. He just wanted it to stop.

Spent and trembling, Torr lifted his head and looked across the tent. Cassidy's sleeping bag lay flat and empty. He sat back on his heels and rubbed his eyes. That's right, it was the afternoon. He had pulled curfew guard duty, which would start at midnight, and had taken a nap after lunch. He got dressed, pushed aside the canvas door flaps, and went over to the kitchen to make himself some tea.

He stood there, listening to the water heat up in the teakettle, when Blaire appeared at his side and rinsed out a cup in the dirty dish water.

"Hi, Torr," she said, glancing at him. "You okay?" she asked, furrowing her brow.

"Yeah. What are you doing here?" he asked. "Where's Cassidy?"

"In the back. Berkeley's helping us cut patterns for some clothes."

"Oh, nice," Torr said, turning the burner off and pouring steaming water into a cup and adding a big pinch of loose black tea leaves. "Want some tea?"

"Sure," she said. "I'll never refuse hot tea."

"Me, neither," he said. "At least not since I arrived at Peary Dome. I used to dislike the stuff."

She held out her cup, and he poured water into it and offered her the tin of tea leaf.

They stood next to each other, waiting for their tea to brew.

"What's the matter, Torr?" she asked, turning to him.

"What do you mean?" He inspected the black eye he had given her the other day, sparring. It was shiny and purplish, but at least the white part of her eye was not bruised. "Why?" he asked.

"You were yelling," she said.

"Oh, that," he said, dropping his gaze. "I was taking a nap and had a nightmare. That's all."

"Sounded like more than a nightmare," she said. "It sounded like you were killing someone—or wanted to."

He gave a dry chuckle. That was closer to the truth than she knew.

"Who is it that you hate?" she asked gently.

He lifted his gaze to meet hers. Her irises were such a golden brown they reminded him of polished brass. He shrugged, overcome with a wave of exhaustion. "I don't know ... myself?"

"Why do you hate yourself?" Her voice was searching. Like she really wanted to know.

The breath escaped Torr's lungs. He hadn't spoken of the killings to anyone. He hadn't had to tell his squadmates in the bunker. They had been there. They had seen it. There had been nothing to discuss other than his phenomenal aim. He had wanted to tell his father about it, but there hadn't been time. And Cassidy. She knew, although they had not spoken of it.

He had hoped the gnawing ache would go away on its own. But if anything, it seemed to be growing deeper. Like a hunk of shrapnel working its way ever closer to a vital organ. He held Blaire's gaze, trying to keep the pain from his eyes, but they squinted on their own. "I killed two men. Back on Earth."

Her eyes widened and her lips parted. "Oh." She hesitated, keeping her eyes trained on his. "In the war?"

"Yes." He let out a little half-sob, half-laugh. "It feels like another lifetime ago—yet it feels like yesterday."

His jaws tightened, but he forced himself to speak. "One of them was going to shoot at us. At my squad. I killed him first. I'm a sharpshooter. I hit him right between the eyes. But the second one. He was running away."

Torr choked on his words but kept on with a ragged voice. "He was a scout. I thought he would reveal our positions, so I shot him in the back."

He was not looking at Blaire anymore. He saw the hills of Scripps Ranch. The foggy remnants of the Shaman's Shield. The ash-covered ground. The man fleeing. "The thing is ..." Torr swallowed, tears stinging his eyes. "I could have let him go. Gaia United surrendered two days later. It made no difference to the war that I killed him, and ... he would still be alive now, and I killed him for ..." He breathed in loudly through his nose. "For nothing. *He died for nothing.*"

Torr bowed his head and realized he was crying. Blaire took hold of his shirt and pulled him to her, pressing her forehead against his. Tears dripped down his cheeks, and he could feel her breath on his skin. It felt good to let it all come out. He closed his eyes, and she kissed one tear-soaked cheek then the other, and then softly pressed her lips to his. He returned the kiss and forgot about everything for a long tender moment.

She gently broke their kiss and pressed her forehead against his again. She nestled her hands against his chest, creating a private little cave between them. He wrapped his arms around her and drew her closer, pressing his cheek to hers and breathing deeply to control his tears. He'd cried enough. It would not bring the men back, nor remove the spear that impaled his gut. He buried his face in her hair, breathing in the scent he had come to know so well during hours of training together. He kissed her neck, and she leaned into him and stroked his head.

She didn't tell him that it would be okay or that she understood. Or that it was good what he had done or that it was bad. She just held him, and he loved her for it.

———————)———————

The next day, Torr's squad found room on a canvas tarp where Ming-Long, Khaled, and Faisal were waiting to begin their knife-fighting class. Faisal and Khaled stood to the side while Ming-Long stood at the front, smiling, thick arms folded across his bare chest. His spiky black hair was coated in a film of dust, and his black eyes flashed.

"The most important thing to learn about knife fighting is how to not fight at all," Ming-Long announced, his voice cheerful. "Knife fighting usually ends with one or both people bleeding or dead. The best strategy is to avoid contact altogether." His smile widened, showing bright white teeth with chips on the inside corners of his two front teeth, making a little half-moon gap.

"If you do get close enough for contact, your first goal is to immobilize your opponent. After he's been immobilized, you disarm him. And remember, anyone who comes at you with a knife is trying to kill you. You'll need to quickly disable your opponent, and if you have no other choice, kill him. And that's not as easy as it sounds. The human body is amazingly resilient and holds an enormous amount of blood." Torr's toes curled in his boots. *Blood fighting* was what Ming-Long called his style. He went on about what it was like to get cut, pointing at scars on the side of his ribs and across his palm, and the ones on his face. Torr watched Roanoke's complexion fade to a pale, ashen white. "These," Ming-Long said, pointing to the scars on his forearm, "are laser scars. They do not bleed, but they hurt like hell. Knife wounds both bleed and hurt." He went on to list the best places to stab someone. When he described stabbing an eyeball, Torr fought down an upwelling of nausea.

Ming-Long clapped his hands together. "Okay, enough of that. Let's get down to business, shall we?"

Torr nodded weakly with the rest of his squad.

"Okay," Ming-Long said. "What is the first thing you should do if someone threatens you with a knife?"

Torr thought for a second. "Immobilize him?"

"No," Ming-Long said sharply.

Torr frowned. *That's what he had said.*

"Raleigh?" Ming-Long asked.

"Disarm him?"

"No." Ming-Long pressed his lips together and looked disappointed. "First thing you should do is run." He looked at them, his eyes hooded with heavy eyelids. He was no longer smiling. "Got that?" he glared at everyone.

"Yes," they said in unison. "Run." That sounded good to Torr.

"What if you can't run? What if you're cornered?" Ming-Long asked.

Raleigh and Torr looked at one another, afraid to answer.

"What you do is scream. Not a frightened scream. A loud, war scream. A battle cry to scare the piss out of him. Let him know you're crazy." Ming-Long got a wild-eyed, demented look on his face. "I want you to look crazy. Let me see your crazy faces."

Torr twisted his mouth and tried to look crazy, glaring at Raleigh and Roanoke, who started cracking up. Hawk bared his teeth and crossed his eyes, rolling them up into his head. Torr's war face dissolved into laughter, and Ming-Long jumped at them with raised fingers bent like claws and a loud yell, startling them.

"Try again. Look mean this time. This is serious. Show me your warrior faces." Ming-Long's scar tugged at his mouth as he struggled to suppress a smile while the squad pulled themselves together. Faisal stood by, having no problem looking fierce. Khaled looked bored.

Torr made an angry face at Ming-Long.

"Good, now make fire in your eyes," Ming-Long encouraged him.

Torr imagined violet flames shooting out of his eyes, burning whatever was in his path.

"Now think of someone you hate and pretend I'm that person."

An image of Schlitzer smirking at him filled Torr's vision and melted into the blue flame at the hottest part of the fire.

Ming-Long gazed back at him. "Good," he said, meeting Torr's eyes with understanding.

Torr glanced at Blaire, who was making a snarling, animal face, and he wondered what vision of hatred was haunting her.

"Good. Now scream."

They practiced their war cries until Ming-Long was satisfied, attracting curious looks from the other classes. "Do you feel energized now?" he asked.

Torr nodded. He did, actually. Good thing too, because Ming-Long believed in physical fitness. "You need to build up the stamina to keep fighting even after you've been stabbed several times," he told them in all seriousness.

Torr had never liked the idea of knife fighting and was liking it less the more Ming-Long talked about it. Fortunately, they were soon distracted by exercises. Ming-Long started off by handing them all ropes. Ming-Long held one himself, wrapping an end around each hand.

After several sets of skipping rope, Ming-Long pressed on with more exercises, finally relenting when Torr's legs and arms were heavy and his breath came in quick even gasps. Everyone bent over and leaned their hands on their knees, their heads hanging with relief.

Faisal pulled out a knife, one of several that hung from the back of his belt. Ming-Long told the squads to fetch their real knives. Everyone ran to the edge of the tarp where their belongings were strewn, excited to finally work with real weapons. Torr chose to practice with his combat knife.

Ming-Long demonstrated different positions for the thumb and
how to change to a reverse grip. They practiced the different grips with
each hand, then practiced the various stances they had been learning.
"Turn your shoulder like this so you make a smaller target." Ming-
Long demonstrated, and Torr imitated him.

Torr held his knife hand forward and his free hand up near the
chin to protect the neck, with the forearm angled across his chest to
protect the heart and lungs. Half-step forward, quick retreat. Then
they changed hands and repeated the drill.

"Good," Ming-Long said, and began running through the forms
they had been practicing.

They started with the figure eight, cutting slowly on the diagonal
to form an X in the air. "Pay attention to where the cutting edge of the
knife is," Ming-Long instructed.

Torr began to get comfortable with the feel of the knife and sped it up.

"Keep it flowing," Ming-Long said. "Same move in the opposite direction."

Torr stopped and reversed the path of the knife, taking a couple of
figure eights to get up to speed.

"Keep your guard hand up and switch it to the other cheek when
you cross the knife hand over," he reminded them.

Faisal demonstrated and Torr mirrored him, moving his guard
hand from one jaw to the other as he flowed through the figure eight.

"Now try it with the other hand."

Torr switched the knife to his left hand and adjusted his stance. He
concentrated, willing his left arm to flow as smoothly as his right. This
side required more focus, and his forehead tightened from the effort.

"Don't think so much," Faisal said, coming to his side. "Relax and
let your arm learn on its own. Do not think of it as the reverse of the
other side. Let it find its own way."

Torr did as Faisal instructed, and soon his left arm was moving
gracefully through the X shape.

"Keep the knife's edge toward the opponent," Ming-Long
reminded them.

Torr slowed down, paying attention to the position of the blade.

"Okay, good," Ming-Long said, and then led them through the

next move—a cross instead of an X, the cuts moving along the horizontal and vertical axes.

Torr started slowly, then sped up as he grew more comfortable, then switched hands and repeated it.

"Keep the movements tight," Ming-Long said. "You only need to cut the length of the body. Don't waste any motion."

They then combined the X and the cross to make a star, then added the remaining moves of the flow: an arc at various angles, Lady's Fan, nine angles of thrusts. Then Ming-Long had them do the whole sequence from the beginning. They took a short break, then repeated the entire drill using the reverse grip Ming-Long called the hammer. Torr's muscles were burning.

Ming-Long slid his knife into his sheath. "Good work. Tomorrow, we'll combine it with the footwork we learned earlier."

Torr tried to imagine combining the complex knife patterns with the different footwork drills, while remembering to keep the blade edge toward the opponent and the free hand in the right position. His head hurt just thinking about it.

—————————)—————————

They took a break, everyone sitting and drinking from their water containers. Then they moved on to Judo class with Tatsuya and Hiroshi.

They started by bowing, then Tatsuya spoke to them at length about building character through persistent effort. Then they stretched and did pushups. Next, they practiced falling and rolling. Torr partnered with Blaire, and they did some simple take-downs, and then ran through a few leg locks they had learned previously, which were grappling techniques that involved wrapping their legs around each other in a proximity that made Torr blush. He survived that without totally embarrassing himself but stood apart from Blaire with relief. They finished with their arm lock flow. He and Blaire spent more time making their crazy faces at each other and laughing than doing the lock flows, until Tatsuya scolded them and made them each do fifty pushups.

At kickboxing class, they practiced footwork and some punching techniques, then they split into two groups. One group took turns at the punching bags with Elvis, while the other group went with Febo, who wrapped himself in a heavy canvas tarp and taunted them as they took turns punching him and kicking him with their shins. Then they assigned people to random partners, and they sparred. Torr was paired with Copper, who beat the crap out of him.

"Don't feel bad," Copper said, as Torr shuffled off the mat, nursing a bloody nose. "I did this for a living."

"I thought you were sworn to serve and protect," Torr said.

"I did. I served the law-abiding citizens and protected them from the drug-crazed psychos and feuding gangbangers. I had to get rough now and then."

Copper smiled smugly, and Febo handed Torr a square of gauze for his nose. "You were in Gaia United," Copper said. "I can tell you've had some training."

"A little," Torr said. "But we mostly relied on guns and artillery. Figured if it ever came down to hand-to-hand combat with the Tegs, we would've already lost."

"No doubt," Copper said dryly. "But you're getting faster. Don't be afraid to hit hard. It's the only way to learn. And stop pairing up with your girlfriend so much."

"She's not my girlfriend," Torr said.

"Not yet," Copper said with a teasing grin, and Torr felt himself blushing.

The last session of the day was Berkeley's meditation class. They lined up in neat rows and sat cross-legged, facing Berkeley, who sat comfortably in the front with his legs folded like a pretzel. Everyone set a small moon rock in front of them, and Berkeley told them they were to gaze at it until he rang the bell.

Berkeley's session was the most difficult. He told them to sit up straight, resting their weight on their butts and their knees. For most people, he rolled up pieces of canvas to make a little seat to perch on while they crossed their legs and tried to press their knees to the mat. Torr's seat was higher than most.

"You're too tight and rigid," Berkeley told him as he folded a third piece of canvas to raise his seat even higher.

"Thanks a lot," Torr drawled, dabbing the gauze at his nose, which had mostly stopped bleeding.

Berkeley chuckled. "Your muscles, I mean. Tendons and ligaments, too. But the body does reflect the mind, so you should try and be more flexible."

Torr scowled at him and sat on his cushion.

Berkeley told them to rest their hands comfortably on their thighs. "Make sure your legs are comfortable," he said. "Westerners aren't used to flexing their hips in this position, but you'll get used to it."

People fidgeted and shifted.

"Are your legs comfortable?" Berkeley asked. He looked everyone in the eye until each person grew still and nodded yes.

"Good. You will not move your legs or your hands for the rest of the session. Not one twitch. Your hands should rest heavy on your legs. Or they are light. It doesn't matter. Look at the rock."

Torr's legs grew numb and his back tired from trying to sit up straight over tight legs and hips. Berkeley was right. He needed to stretch more. But his aching body was not the biggest problem. He quickly grew bored of gazing at the rock, and his mind hopped around from thought to random thought.

"If you notice your mind wandering," Berkeley said, as though he were aware of Torr's thoughts, "return your attention to the rock. Or, if you prefer, you can focus on your breath."

Focusing on breathing was something Torr understood from sniper training, but here there was no gun and no target, and no purpose that he could determine. Simply pulling his mind back over and over to focus on his breath, or worse, the rock, made him feel like a horse with a bit shoved in its mouth and a bridle tightened around his jaw. It didn't help that one of his nostrils was clogged. He found himself fidgeting, wanting to blow his nose. He could use the excuse of his bloody nose, and no one would think the worse of him. He closed his eyes and inhaled through his clear nostril. He really needed to scratch the itch on his shoulder blade—badly. But he kept his hands still. The itch grew more intense, and Torr ground his teeth together. Why was Berkeley doing this to them?

"Focus on the rock." Berkeley's voice woke him out of his angry haze. Berkeley was speaking to the whole group. Torr was not the only uncomfortable one. Blaire was stretching her leg, and Roanoke furtively scratched his head.

Torr stared at the rock and sat up straight. But his back hurt. He had pulled it badly carrying concrete blocks when they were building bunkers at Scripps Ranch. He had let Mike stack too many in his arms and was too proud to put them down. His back had never been right since.

"Torr, I want you to focus on your breath," Berkeley said, his soft voice soothing.

Torr exhaled. Breathing he could do.

"Feel the breath exiting your nostrils," Berkeley instructed. "It tickles the hair above your lip. Focusing on the breath is better than focusing on a rock because your breath is always with you."

Torr felt the air brush his upper lip, exiting from his single nostril. That damned itch on his shoulder burned into him, down to the bone. He grew hot and sweaty, but he was not allowed to move his hands. *You will not move them for the rest of the session. Not one twitch.* Torr imagined himself at the shooting range with the 6 Creed in his hands.

"Relax your hands," his father said to him as he clutched the barrel of the gun, with his right index finger curled above the trigger like an eagle's talon. The shooting range spread out before him in a scruffy field of dried grass. His memory flowed to Gaia United training when he had surprised the Designated Marksman instructors. They were gathered in a group, watching him shoot. At each break they moved the target farther and farther away. He didn't miss until eighteen hundred yards, and the instructors huddled together, conversing in hushed tones.

It was all in the positioning. Like surfing. Finding the point of perfect balance. Elbows forming a solid base, holding his torso's weight. Rifle butt braced against his shoulder, with his face pressed against the cheek rest on the exact same spot every time. *Do not move your body. Do not move the gun one hair's breadth. Squeeze your finger. Absorb the kickback. Follow the bullet. Breathe. Light hands. Weightless against the trigger. Slow your heartbeat. Breathe. Feel your heartbeat in your chest. In your fingers. Beat. Squeeze.* Beat.

The bullet shot out of the muzzle, and Torr imagined its trajectory as it spun through the air, drifting one click with the easterly wind at six hundred yards out. Arcing downward at a thousand. It hit the hill with a puff of sand to the left of where he had aimed. He hadn't checked the wind. Reina would have told him right.

"Focus on the breath," Berkeley said, interrupting his thoughts.

He was talking to him, and Torr lifted his eyes. Berkeley gazed at him calmly, unmoving except for his sparkling eyes. "Do not lift your eyes when I speak to you. Look at the rock in front of you. Relax your gaze."

Torr dropped his eyes to the irregular moon rock he had chosen. It was a dark olivine green, riddled with tiny holes. He stared at it and wondered how it had gotten so many holes. Had it been hit by a solar storm? Pummeled by solar wind and dust over millions of years? Or had another element worn away over time leaving the little gaps? But there was no water or air on the moon. Nothing to erode it. Maybe the rock was from an asteroid and had once been inside a big ice ball and laced with dark ice that had burnt away on the harsh lunar surface, leaving the rock looking like Swiss cheese.

"Do not think about the rock," Berkeley said.

Torr met his eyes, and Berkeley glared at him.

"If you notice yourself inside a story in your head, shift your focus to the breath."

Torr dropped his eyes to the rock. It was a nice rock. Kind of shiny. Torr glanced around surreptitiously, his eyes darting from under lowered eyelids while he kept his head perfectly still. Raleigh was picking at a scab on his arm. Darla was crying silently, tears slowly trickling down her face.

"Do not let your eyes wander. Rest your gaze on the rock. But do not examine the rock. The rock is a resting place for the eyes. A place of nothing."

Torr dropped his eyes. *This is hard. Stupid rock.*

"Emotions are just thoughts. Let them go and focus on the rock."

Torr could hear Darla sniffing beside him.

Minutes dragged on and Berkeley remained silent. When Torr caught his mind wandering, he shifted his focus to the breath. Over and over.

After an eternity, Berkeley rang a little bell and released them.

When his numb legs had recovered feeling and the needles of pain subsided, Torr stretched his legs out, and then glanced at his watch.

It was noon. The other classes were wrapping up, and he gathered everyone around him.

"One lap around the perimeter road, then everyone can leave for the day," he said, to a chorus of groans.

"Jogging? With all this dust?" It was the little man named Gerbil, staring at him as if he were crazy.

"Wear a mask. Let's go."

"It's five miles," Sky whined.

"Yep," said Torr.

He led with whoops and hollers, then dropped back and ran circles around the laggards, encouraging them with kind words or curses, depending on the person and what Torr thought they would best respond to.

Most people had slowed to a walk by the time they got to the sundial. Some stayed with him as he set a slow but steady jogging pace back to the training camp.

Berkeley was waiting for them at the picnic tables with a stack of Light Fighters patches, needles, and thread. They each took a patch and sat at the tables or on tarps and sewed on their patches. Others straggled in from their jog and took a patch. Torr sewed his onto a front vest pocket, poking his finger with the needle more than once. Somehow, the patches made things feel more official. Torr could see that others were wearing their patches proudly.

When they were done, Torr and his friends headed towards the ration trailers. Blaire and Darla joined Cassidy and the other Smiths, who walked amongst the men. Jasper had disappeared for most of practice but had shown up for the meditation session and the run, and was walking with Berkeley, his new patch affixed to a vest pocket.

Raleigh nudged Torr with his elbow, and Torr followed his gaze. At the far corner of the training yard stood Jorimar and Helug. Torr lifted his hand in greeting, and the Scrids clapped fists to chests in their salute. Torr returned the salute and walked down the road, and the Scrids followed.

"I hope they don't want to join the Light Fighters," Torr said. Raleigh nodded in agreement as Jasper called to the Scrids in greeting. Torr rolled his eyes as the wild-haired men caught up to them, boot bells tinkling and stone clubs swinging at their sides.

"Mangarm," Jorimar called out to him with a toothy smile, then rattled on in his language.

Jasper walked up next to Torr and said, "He calls you *Moon Wolf.* He says your wolf is happy to see them and wants to go with you to their planet, Scridland."

Torr gave the Scrids a half-smile. "Yeah, yeah," he said dismissively, shivers running up his spine. He put his hand on the round pommel of his knife and hurried ahead of them, glancing around. He didn't see his wolf but was glad that he was there.

———————)———————

Torr and the Boyer brothers, Sky and Thunder, Fritz and Frank, and their neighbors Li-Jie and Zhang-Yong took an evening stroll. They stopped by the Smith camp to see if Blaire and Darla wanted to join them, seeing as how they were part of his squad and all. Blaire and Darla exchanged glances and joined them out on the ring road. They headed out Spoke Road Three to the no man's land of the western quadrant, when Torr stopped walking and motioned his friends to a halt. A gang of about a dozen men were walking towards them. Strutting, more like.

Torr regarded the cocky, aggressive postures of the young men. He did not recognize any of them. He considered running, but that would only invite further harassment later on. Torr placed one hand on his wolf knife and the other on his club.

"Yo," Torr called to the man he identified as the leader.

The dozen men spread across the road to block their passage. They were ten paces away. "You think you're hot shit?" the leader snarled at Torr.

"No."

"Well, you stink like you are." The man's shoulders were wide and thick with muscles.

"Let us pass," Torr said. Raleigh and Roanoke flanked him on one side, and Fritz and Frank on the other. Torr suddenly wished he had not invited the women along. He glanced quickly at the rest of his squad: Sky and Thunder, Li-Jie and Zhang-Yong, and Hawk. Not exactly a bunch of brawlers.

"We don't need no Pussy Fighters patrolling the roads," the leader said. "Or building a militia like you're the fucking king. You think you're the fucking king? President Metolius's goddamned fucking bastard son?"

Torr blinked. The man was ranting and barely making any sense.

"We have nothing against decent people," Torr said.

"We're decent, and we don't like your kind," the man said.

"Well, sorry to hear that. Come on," Torr said, motioning to his friends, and strode forward, intending to break through their line. The facing gang stepped forward a pace but stopped when their leader held up his hand.

"We ain't fighting no girls," the man said.

"They're in our gang," Torr said, and continued walking.

Torr hoped the men would back off, or simply let them pass, but when they were four paces apart, he could tell they intended to fight. Torr stopped. "No knives," he said, and tossed his knives to the side of the road. His friends hesitated, then followed suit.

The opposing gang members exchanged glances, then a couple of knives hit the dust by the side of the road.

"All of them," Torr said, and more knives followed.

"I'll fight you. One on one," Torr said. "Who's your strongest?" He looked to the leader who was flexing his shoulders. "You and me. What do you say?" Torr challenged.

"You got it," the man growled.

Torr lunged at him before the man had time to reach for the club at his side. It was a clean fight. Fists and holds. Torr avoided damaging the man's throat, and did his best not to break any bones, and took a few dizzying punches for his efforts. Finally, Torr got tired and took his opponent down with an Uchimata throw. The man landed in the dust and Torr stepped away, pressing a hand to his bloody lip.

The man got warily to his feet, and Torr's squad held their positions. The other gang was not so disciplined, and broke ranks to run at them. Torr fought off an attacker who came at him, and tossed the man to the ground. It was bedlam all around. Blaire and Darla were pounding a large man, two-on-two, while Raleigh was fighting off two men. Roanoke was throwing kidney punches at another who had Hawk in a headlock, and Roanoke took them both to the ground. Hawk broke free, and the brothers pounced on the man. Sky and Thunder were delivering punches and kicks to ward off two attackers while Li-Jie and Zhang-Yong and Fritz and Frank were working together, fending off four men. Torr turned to meet the leader, who was jumping at him from behind.

It could have been a minute or an hour that they fought. His squad instinctively formed a circle, facing out to protect each other's backs. Suddenly, it was over. Most of the attackers were on the ground, and his own squad was panting like they'd just finished a good sparring session.

Torr didn't notice any major injuries, and the opposing gang members slowly climbed to their feet, rubbing at jaws or dabbing at bloody noses. "You fight pretty good," Torr said, eyeing the leader, whose eye was swelling. "But a little sloppy. You want to train with us?"

The leader glared at Torr. "Fuck you."

"I'm not kidding," Torr said, chuckling. Torr met Blaire's eyes, and she gave a slight nod. He studied the man's perplexed face, and said, "I'm completely serious. Meet us at our training yard at 5L tomorrow morning at eight. We need more good men."

He and his squad retrieved their knives from the dust and continued their walk, leaving the battered men staring after them.

"Everyone okay?" Torr asked, glancing at each of them.

They all nodded, and Roanoke swaggered beside him. "That was fun," Roanoke said.

Torr smiled. He had to agree.

——————— ꒰ ———————

It was after night gong, and Torr sat across from Ming-Long, sharing a quart of beer Ming-Long had scored from Schlitzer.

"Nice shiner," Ming-Long said, gesturing at Torr's eye. "Blaire hit you back?" he asked.

"No," Torr said, returning Ming-Long's teasing smirk. "Just a little scuffle with some tough boys out on the perimeter."

"Oh, yeah. I heard about that. Sabo Vaclavich's gang. They're lightweights."

"I invited them to join the Light Fighters," Torr said, holding the cool glass bottle against his eye.

"Yeah? I'd be surprised if they joined. Sabo thinks he's an alpha wolf. But they could be worth something with a little training."

Torr nodded and took a mouthful of beer. "You fought the Tegs? Back on Earth?" Torr asked, lifting his gaze to meet Ming-Long's.

Ming-Long nodded. "Yeah. Bastards."

"Were you in an army?" Torr asked.

"Nah. Just street fighters. All the young guys got together, trying to keep the Tegs out of our neighborhood. Didn't work too well."

Ming-Long frowned, and Torr was afraid he had trodden on sensitive ground. "You were in Gaia United," Ming-Long said, gesturing to the Gaia United tattoo on Torr's forearm.

"Yeah. But we surrendered. I deserted."

Ming-Long nodded again. "Lucky."

Torr took a swig of beer and handed the bottle to Ming-Long. "Yeah, but not before I killed a couple of Tegs."

Ming-Long met his gaze. "Congrats. I killed a bunch, too," he said.

"Does it bother you?" Torr asked.

Ming-Long made a face. "I try not to think about it much."

"Yeah, me too. But I still feel kinda bad about it, sometimes," Torr said.

Ming-Long scoffed. "Bad about it? Why?"

Torr shrugged. "I don't know. Cause they're dead. And I killed them."

"Motherfuckers," Ming-Long said. "They deserved every bit of it. They murdered my family. I couldn't kill all the Tegs who came to our apartment building because I ran out of ammo. I wish I'd killed them all."

Ming-Long wiped his mouth and handed Torr the beer.

22

---)---

FOOL'S PASSION

A week had passed since Cassidy had made her arrowhead necklace. She stood on a ground tarp in the training yard, adjusting the three necklaces hanging around her sweaty neck. Ming-Long had warned her against wearing any jewelry, especially necklaces, and even had recommended that everyone cut their hair short or shave their heads, so that an attacker could not grab them so easily. No one had followed his advice.

Her squad had just finished their knife fighting class, and Ming-Long stood by the tables with his t-shirt hanging from his belt, his bare, broad chest glistening. He was in his customary cross-armed stance, his wide shoulders squared and relaxed, and his short spiky hair coated with dust. Cassidy liked looking at his body. She had become familiar with it over the past several days, watching him demonstrate knife forms and defensive poses. Her eyes wandered slowly over the rounded muscles under the silky skin of his arms. His large hands had their own character, graceful like a hawk's wings, yet deadly as talons.

He smiled and gestured at her, reminding her to drink. She smiled back at him, then took her canteen and gulped down most of it. Like usual, their knife fighting class had consisted of grueling strength and endurance exercises, as well as street fighting moves to disable and disarm the opponent. Not to mention repetitive drills of footwork and knife forms that left her muscles screaming.

She walked over to him. "Do you like torturing us?" she asked, teasing. Ming-Long continued to smile but did not answer. He did that often—ignoring her questions and grinning a wide, toothy grin.

She rolled her eyes and threw a knuckle jab at his chest, which he flicked away with the back of his hand as though it were a fly. He did not blink. "You are too predictable," he told her. "Your eyes betray your intentions. Distract me first, and then hit me."

She looked into his glittering black eyes and threw her knuckles at him again while at the same time turning in a half-circle and darting out with her foot to kick his knee. He held her eyes, caught her wrist, and lifted his knee away, all in one smooth motion.

"Better," he said. "But I taught you to kick from farther away, beyond easy reach of my arms. What good is it to kick me if I have your hand trapped?"

She scowled at him and tried to pull her wrist from his solid grip. He continued smiling as she wriggled her arm to try and slip it free while at the same time kicking at him. He lifted his leg, laughing harder when her boot connected with his shin.

"You notice how strong my hand is?" he asked. He was so close she could see the little black hairs in his nostrils. He twisted her arm another half turn.

"Yes, I noticed," she said, trying not to let on that it hurt or that she was becoming frustrated that she could not get free. He held the narrow part of her arm next to her wrist with a hand that engulfed half her forearm.

"When you're fighting a stronger opponent," Ming-Long said, "the best strategy is to keep your distance and use other tactics. Like running or throwing things. And don't trust anyone."

"How can I not trust anyone?" she asked, laughing with pain as he cocked her arm more.

"Stay aware at all times," he said. "Expect the unexpected."

She glared up at him and met his mocking gaze, shooting anger out through her eyes as he had taught her, her knees starting to fold from the pressure on her joints. She jerked her knee up with a feint between his legs as she wrenched her arm against his thumb. He crouched at the knee-jab and wrapped his other arm around her waist as she twisted into him in an effort to release her wrist. Her side was pressed against his hard chest, his body radiating heat.

"You missed," he said, with a warm chuckle as she pushed against him. His smell was strong and bitter, with a hint of honey. He released her the same moment she saw Jasper watching from his seat at the table.

Jasper's eyes were not laughing. "Don't play with her," he said, his voice cutting.

"I wasn't," Ming-Long said, wiping the back of his hand across his mouth.

Jasper gave Ming-Long a severe look. Ming-Long straightened and stepped aside. Jasper looked at Cassidy pointedly, then turned away to continue his conversation with Berkeley.

She glanced at Ming-Long and squinted apologetically. He smiled his usual smile, not annoyed in the least that she had started something that he took the blame for.

"Sorry," she said quietly.

"Don't worry," he said. "I've got your back. I've always got your back."

She nodded, glad he was there.

————————————) ————————————

Cassidy was at the Fen, inside the half-container, when she heard shuffling at the doorway. Ming-Long's silhouette was framed against the light.

"I thought I heard someone banging around in here," he said. "What're you doing?"

"Just looking for some crates. Berkeley said some are filled with junk that I can take to the Smiths for their craft business. But I can't get to the ones on the top—can you help me?"

He came over and with his long arms brought down two plastic crates from the top of the stacks. "Let me take them to the doorway for you, where there's more light," he said.

"Let me see if these are them, first," she said, prying off one of the lids. She looked up to see Ming-Long's eyes on her. "What?" she asked, tilting her head curiously.

"You just look kind of detached lately," he said. "Like you're not all the way here. Are you okay?"

She nodded and returned her attention to the crate. It appeared to be one that Berkeley had described, filled with nuts and bolts, nails and screws, scraps of wire and string, pieces of old bicycle tires and inner tubes, and other random items.

"Is the kidnapping thing still bothering you?" he asked gently, stepping closer and resting his hand against the stack of crates.

She stood upright and took a breath, meeting his eyes in the dim light. "No. Well, yes, and no. It's the war, really, that's on my mind a lot lately."

"Your parents?" he asked.

"Yeah. My parents. And everybody else. All the prisoners. The breeding centers. *Rape* centers."

"I'm sorry," he said, his eyes searching hers.

"Why is it all so ugly?" she asked. "Why is all this craziness and cruelty happening?"

Ming-Long shrugged. "I don't know, Cassidy. I don't understand any of it. But I know how much it hurts. I lost my family in the war, you know."

She shook her head. "No. I didn't know."

"The Tegs. They killed them all. My parents, my brother, my sisters. All of them." Ming-Long swallowed, his Adam's apple moving in his throat. "I was on the roofs, fighting. Sniping. I saw them drag each of their dead bodies from our apartment building. My family must have fought back. Most all my neighbors were taken out alive. But my family was dead. All of them. Covered in blood."

His face was like stone. Only the pulsing in his neck betrayed his feelings. "I'm proud of them," he said, his voice tight.

Cassidy went to him and wrapped her arms around him. They hugged, his heart beating against her chest.

"I ran out of ammo and couldn't even shoot the men who killed my family," he said, his voice breaking.

"Shhh," she said. "It's not your fault."

She lifted her head and found his dark brooding eyes, and suddenly he lowered his head and pressed his lips against hers.

"No," she said, pushing away, her heart hammering.

"Why not?" he asked huskily, pulling her tighter and seeking her lips again.

She held his kiss for a moment, then broke away and pulled out of his embrace. Her breaths came fast and shallow, and she felt flushed all over. "I'm sorry. I'm with Jasper," she said, backing towards the door.

"You don't act like you're with him," he said, following her and taking her hand.

"I know," she said, pulling her hand free. "But I am." She turned and staggered out of the container and into the front yard, her head reeling.

----------)----------

Cassidy invited Hawk into her tent and handed him the blue and gold book and the garnet.

His mouth dropped open. "Oh ... holy stars ...," he said, and stared down at the garnet. "This is a magic stone?"

"Yeah, I guess," Cassidy said, laughing.

"Look," he said, pointing to the introduction from Danute. "It's songs from all over the galaxy."

Cassidy nodded and held out her hand. "I need to copy them down," she said, "so we can read them even when we don't have the magic stone."

He passed her the book and garnet, then sharpened a pencil for her. Each page was printed on the right-hand side, leaving the left-hand pages blank. She copied the introduction as neatly as she could onto the blank facing page, and then turned to the next page.

They pressed the garnet between their palms and read the lyric together, then she carefully copied it down.

Arise

Arise, oh chastened ones,
For if the path were easy, the floodgates would open
And demons would charge across the heavens
Brandishing swords of flame
And chaining glowing angels with their curse

It is not for the faint of spirit
To be crushed under the stones of madness
Or hunted like stags in the forest
For the pleasure of the noblemen
Who would slay them for their crowns
And mount their heads in their halls

Arise, oh glorious ones
For your light is the only light
Your eyes the only eyes
Your hearts the only hearts
To raise us from the burning pyres
So that we can live again

"Geez, that's a depressing song," Cassidy murmured as she wrote. "I think it's cool," Hawk said. "Like a fairy tale."

"Yeah," Cassidy said. "But the princess always gets trapped in a tower in fairy tales."

Hawk peered at her. "You're right. That's not fair."

"Not fair at all," Cassidy said.

"But it's always the men who get killed. In fairy tales, that is," he said. "In real life, the women get killed a lot, too, and the men are sad."

She gazed into his big brown eyes. "I'm sorry about your mother," she said.

He shrugged and looked at his hands. She put his arm around him, and he leaned his head on her shoulder. "My dad says she would want us to be happy," he said. "And that we need to be strong and make her proud."

"That's what my dad would say, too," she said, patting his back.

"Where is your dad?" Hawk asked, lifting his head.

"In a Teg work camp, I think," she said, swallowing. "I think my mom is still free, hiding in the forest."

They held each other's gazes.

The canvas door parted, and Jasper peered inside. Cassidy and Hawk turned their heads.

"Hi. Sorry. Oh good," Jasper said. "There it is. I need that back."

"Need what back?" she asked, closing her fingers around the garnet.

"Come on, Cassidy," he said, cocking his head at her. He stepped into the tent and held out his hand. "Give it over. I need to see if the Murians know what my new crystal does. The one I got from Gabira."

"You're going to visit the Murians?" She squeezed Hawk's shoulder, then hopped to her feet. "And you weren't going to invite me?"

"Cassidy," he said, huffing out his breath. "I'm meeting my father there. They're teaching us how to play stones. We'll be there all night."

"So?" Cassidy said. "Maybe I want to learn how to play stones, too."

Jasper sighed. "Then we'll have to drag the Alphabet Boys all the way across camp and make them stay up all night. They're already getting comfy for the evening."

"They are not," she said, peeking out through the gap between the door flaps. Some of the Alphabet Boys were sitting at the picnic tables, and others were lounging on their bedrolls in the pavilion, reading. "They're getting bored. Copper told me," she said. "They'll be glad for a diversion."

"No, Cassidy. Not this time. We'll go another time."

She slipped the garnet into her pants pocket, crossed her arms across her chest, and glared at Jasper. She didn't know if it was frustration or exhaustion, but tears rose to her eyes, pooling at the edges of her eyelids.

"Oh, for star's sake," Jasper said. "Hawk, can you give a us a minute, please?"

Hawk put down the book and left the tent.

"Come here, Cassidy," Jasper said, sitting on her sleeping bag and patting the spot next to him. "Let's see if this garnet works between us."

"What are you talking about?" she asked, fighting back tears. She sat next to him. "We speak the same language."

Jasper chuckled. "I'm not so sure about that. Here, we'll hold it together, and then we'll talk."

"You're just trying to steal it from me," she said, wiping her eyes.

"It's already mine. How could I steal it?"

She fished the garnet from her pocket and held it out in her open palm. He placed his palm over hers, and they held hands with the garnet pressed between them.

Jasper looked into her eyes and said, "I love you, Cassandra Dagda. Do you understand me?" A grin turned up his lips, and despite herself, her mouth softened into a smile.

"I understand," she said, and her lips trembled.

"Your turn," he said, his voice low.

She took in a shuddering breath and dropped her gaze to their hands. "I am afraid I'm broken and no good to anyone anymore."

He gently lifted her chin, and she raised her gaze to meet his. His eyes glistened the moss-gold that she loved so much. "You are perfect to me," he said softly. "No matter what happens, you are the love of my life. I only wish I could protect you better. When you hurt, I hurt. And I blame myself."

All his cockiness was gone. He was suddenly the serious young man she had known on Earth, during the brief moments when his brashness and confidence fell away and his heart was stripped bare. She leaned in and touched her lips to his. They were soft and smooth and quivered under hers. They clung together and then parted, his breath warm on her skin. He kissed her again, and she wrapped her arms around his shoulders. He cradled her waist and pulled her close as their kiss deepened.

Their lips drew apart, and they tenderly kissed one another's cheeks as they spoke softly. "I want to come with you," she said. "I want to see if the Murians can help us."

He hugged her, rocking her gently. "Alright," he said. "But only for a little while. Then my dad and I are going to stay and play their stone game. Okay?"

She sighed. "Alright. If you insist. I'm tired, anyway."

"That's my girl," he said, kissing her forehead, and helped her to her feet.

She pulled on her Delosian boots and they left the tent together. They held hands, and she pushed away the memory of Ming-Long kissing her. She didn't need to tell Jasper about that. Suddenly, she realized she was not afraid of Jasper's touch or his kisses—Balthazar had never kissed her, so at least he had not ruined that for her. She stood tall and felt one layer of Balthazar's grime fall away. "Ha. Take that, you evil wretch," she said under her breath as Jasper gestured for Buck and Dang to come over.

"What's that?" Jasper asked, squeezing her hand.

"Nothing," she said. "I wasn't talking to you."

He studied her face for a moment, then turned to the men.

They invited Torr to come along, as well as the Boyer brothers and a few more Alphabet Boys to round out their security detail, and then headed across the dome.

———————)———————

Jasper led them to a forest-green container deep in the maze of shipping containers on the western outskirts of the dome and rapped on the metal door. They left their guards outside while Jasper, Cassidy, and Torr went inside. A bearded man named Jericho introduced himself and shook her hand, then guided them down a ladder and along a stone tunnel. The tunnel led to the underground spaceport, which was a stone cavern with two dusty speedsters parked along the back wall. Cassidy determined that the large metal wall on the far side of the hangar must be an airlock leading out to a landing tunnel.

Four other port guards stepped forward, greeted Torr by name, and smiled at Cassidy politely as they were introduced. Jasper's attention turned to a dark cleft in the back wall, where Cassidy detected movement.

"There they are," Jasper said, gesturing at the shadows. Cassidy squinted into the darkness, trying to make out details. Two forms strode forward into the light.

Cassidy took in a sharp breath.

The Murians wore long hooded cloaks, and their pale faces were obscured in the depths of the cowls. Hints of green light reflected off the inner edges of the cowls. She froze as clicking and hissing sounds came from one of the Murians. They were speaking with Jasper in their language, and Jasper made clicking sounds in response. Cassidy could see now that the Murians' cloaks were green—the color of shiny ferns. Jasper motioned for Cassidy and Torr to join them.

The cloaked men were as tall as Jasper and moved silently over the rock floor. They led the way through the gap in the rock wall into another long dim tunnel. The billowing robes made the Murians look as though they were floating. The shadows grew denser, and Cassidy's eyes adjusted to the deepening darkness. One of the Murians stretched out his arm, which was draped in a long, loose sleeve that hung almost to the floor. A waxy-white hand peeked out from the edge of the sleeve and was suddenly illuminated by a crystal shaft clutched in his fist, dispelling the darkness and exposing bare stone walls.

"Oooh," she said softly.

They entered a large cave, whose walls were studded with glowing purple crystal points. The room was spacious, with bedrolls of the same fern-green fabric arranged neatly against one wall. Baskets, bowls, and a cloth spread on the floor marked an eating area, where two other Murians set aside plates of food and rose to greet them. Jasper held the garnet and began clicking to the cloaked men.

Cassidy stepped back, startled by green eyes that glimmered at her from the depths of the cowls. Torr had described their eyes, but nothing could have prepared her for the huge neon-green eyes, wide-set and knowing, like cat's eyes, only with horizontal pupils, like goats. The skin on their broad faces was ghostly white. They spoke to Jasper, and he began to translate, but she snatched the garnet from his hand and stared at the Murians.

"Who are you?" she asked.

"Murugan, Guruhan," the first two said, the clicks and rasps of their voices morphing into words she could understand. They bowed with their left hands over their bellies, their heads bent low. She returned the bow. "We have felt you walk upon the surface," Murugan said. "Why has it taken you so long to visit us?"

She translated for Jasper, who shrugged guiltily. Cassidy swallowed, not knowing what to say.

Murugan continued. "The stars cast light of a thousand ages, crying for the coming of the Princess of Light. You must go to Muria. We must know if you are truly she who can awaken the Star Globe from its terrible, dreamless sleep. You must free it from the demon's curse. You must pull tears from stone and make the caverns weep with joy again."

She did not know what he was talking about. She pulled out her crystal shaft from a pouch on her belt. "Do you know what this does?" she asked, and Jasper translated her words into Murian for them. He reached for the garnet, but she held onto it and hid it behind her back.

The Murians' eyes burned brighter, and Guruhan took the shaft from her with long fingers tipped with luminescent green fingernails. The crystal glowed instantly—a cold white—and Cassidy shivered. Guruhan inspected the shaft carefully, pressing it to his cheek and closing his eyes. Glowing green eyelashes lowered like short fluorescent tendrils of a jellyfish.

"Teach me how to make it light up," Cassidy pleaded, reaching for the glowing crystal.

Jasper translated her request for them, then said, "Hold the garnet against his palm so he can understand you." She shook her head, frightened to touch the unearthly white hand.

"Does it not awaken for you?" Guruhan asked with concern, handing her the crystal. It dimmed as soon as it touched her skin. He clicked mournfully. "It cannot feel you. Your filaments are retracted. Open up," he urged her.

"Open up, how?" she asked.

Murugan and Guruhan peered at one another. "First let us introduce you to the others," Murugan said. "They are anxious to meet you. And the father of Jaz is already here, trying to learn our game." He let out a wheezing, coughing sound, which Cassidy guessed was a laugh. "He learns more slowly than a Murian sproutling." He laughed again.

"Come with us," Murugan said, motioning with his arm. The long draped sleeve drew back and revealed long fringes of glowing green filaments hanging from his forearm.

Cassidy looked at Jasper, who nodded reassuringly and placed his hand on her back. "It's okay," he said. "Their tendrils are weird, but they won't hurt you. Come on."

They turned and headed down another tunnel, deeper into the cave system. They passed by a tunnel branch, from which she smelled the distinct odor of a latrine. The Murians themselves gave off a pleasant scent like spicewood. Mounted on the ceiling snaked metal pipes with square air vents every several yards. They continued in the dark silence, broken only by Murugan's light crystal and the soft padding of feet on the stone floor. They emerged into another, smaller chamber lit by several white light crystals mounted on the gray rock walls. Kai was there with two more Murians. The men rose from the floor where they had been seated around several small polished black and white stones arranged in a pattern.

Murugan introduced Cassidy and Torr as the Princess of Light and the Prince of Dreams. Torr gave her a startled look as the two new Murians prostrated themselves on the floor before them, faces to the floor and arms outstretched. The Murians climbed nimbly to their feet and bowed with their left hands on their bellies. Cassidy and Torr awkwardly returned the standing bow, and Cassidy gripped Jasper's hand.

"How are you doing, Cassidy?" Kai asked, greeting her with a warm hug.

She shrugged. "Okay, I guess."

Kai gazed at her with concern.

"Biribar is our historian," Murugan said, introducing the shorter of the Murians. Cassidy interpreted for the others, still holding the garnet.

"What is that red stone you carry?" Biribar asked. "May I hold it?" She handed it to him. His hand was pale and unusually thin, with long fingers. "It's a translation stone," she said. "Can you understand me?" His waxen face lit up. He clicked rapidly, motioning for her to talk. "I can't understand you now," she said. "But I'm interested in learning your language."

He nodded and smiled, revealing greenish teeth, and handed the garnet back to her. "We have learned some of your language," he told her. "But with the stone, you make so much more sense." A hissing, wheezing laugh escaped his mouth, and a similar laugh came from Guruhan.

Jasper and Torr looked slightly disgruntled at her hogging the garnet, but she closed it in her hand.

Biribar said, "That is a legendary whisperer's stone. Cherished by priestesses and traders. They are very rare. It is said that the Blessed Guide of the last Princess of Light and Prince of Dreams carried one."

Cassidy's spine tingled, and she looked at Jasper. She told him what Biribar had said, and Jasper's face went pale. Kai regarded his son with a puzzled stare.

Torr gave a relieved chuckle. "See, Jaz? You were supposed to have it."

"Let me see that," Kai said, and she handed the garnet to him. He listened for a minute to the Murians and said, "They say the Blessed Guide travels across the galaxy to prepare the way for the Princess of Light and the Prince of Dreams." He looked confounded, his narrow face twisting into a frown. Cassidy squeezed Jasper's hand, which was cold and clammy. "Sounds like something Melanie would say," Kai said. He stared off into the distance for a long moment, and then his face brightened. "But this garnet is going to make it much easier to learn how to play stones."

They showed Biribar their other crystals, and Kai held Cassidy's light crystal, trying to make it glow.

"Do you know what this one does?" Jasper asked, taking back the garnet and handing Biribar the crystal he had bought from Gabira. It was not unlike Cassidy's light crystal—a simple shaft with six long facets ending in a point.

"Hmmm. No," Biribar said, with Jasper translating. "It's not a light crystal. If I were a priest, I could talk with the crystal and simply ask it its purpose." A wry grin twisted his wide mouth. "But the priesthood fell into disrepute, and my parents would not allow me to attempt the three trials. And so I settled for a life of analyzing the ancient texts." He pointed to a basket of rolled parchments. "I only brought a few of the key scrolls with me. Perhaps your whisperer's stone will help me better understand some of the ancient texts." He lifted his glowing eyebrows hopefully at Jasper.

"It works with written text," Cassidy confirmed.

"Yes, you can borrow it sometimes," Jasper said, handing the garnet back and forth to Biribar. "But everyone wants time with it these days," he said, casting a pointed glance at Cassidy. She smirked back at him.

"I'm interested in your scrolls," Cassidy said, taking the garnet from Jasper.

"Yes, Princess of Light, I would like to share them with you. Let me find the interesting passages and we can study them together."

She held out her hand to the Murian, and he pressed his palm against hers with the garnet between them. His hand was smooth and warm. "And magic," she said. "Can you teach us some magic? Something that can help rescue my friends, who are trapped?"

The Murian's brow furrowed, and glowing strands of hair that had escaped his hood floated in the air, reminding her of Brianna. "Trapped where? Underground?" he asked.

"Yes, underground in a bunker," she said. "How did you know?"

"That is where everyone holds captives," he said, matter-of-factly. "Except for the king, who has a stone fortress that withstands the Alts. Or unless one wants their captive to die, in which case they leave them exposed to the elements."

Cassidy nodded, understanding some of his meaning.

"There are ways to find captives in the rock," Biribar continued. "But I don't know this word, *magic.*"

"It's, uh ...," she said, searching for the right words. "It's something that is not ordinary. A power that cannot be explained."

"Ah," he said. "Crystals. Yes. They can guard a captive. Evil, tainted crystals. And other crystals can free captives. If you know them."

Cassidy tried to understand his meaning, turning down her mouth from the effort.

"Come on, Cassidy," Jasper said, interrupting. "We're going to play our game now. See you later?"

"Yeah, okay. Thank you, Biribar," she said, releasing the Murian's hand and giving Jasper his garnet. She pondered Biribar's cryptic words but could not make sense of them. Guard crystals? Evil crystals? She shook her head, not understanding how that information could help them rescue Balthazar's latest pair of sex slaves.

Four Murians and Kai returned to the stone game, and Jasper joined them.

Cassidy and Torr accompanied Guruhan and Murugan back into the main living chamber and accepted the Murians' offer of food. Without the garnet, they gestured to one another while eating strips of Murian gish and sipping from small cups filled with a fermented berry juice they called whafkan juice. The gish was salty and chewy, and the whafkan juice was sweet and tart.

Guruhan and Murugan drew a star map in the dust. Torr leaned over the drawing as the Murians pointed and named the stars and planets. Cassidy felt in her pockets. Her light crystal wasn't there. She searched her pack, but it wasn't there either.

"I must have left my light crystal in the other room," she said. "I'll be right back."

Torr waved distractedly as the Murians kept drawing.

She trotted down the passageway to the back chamber. The men were seated around the game pieces, but they were not playing. They were watching Jasper, who was holding her crystal up, and it was glowing brightly.

"Jasper, how did you do that?" she asked, walking over.

The men looked up at her, and the crystal faded.

"Cassidy, what are you doing back here?" Jasper asked.

"I came for my crystal."

Cassidy met his gaze and frowned. His eyes looked odd—glazed over. The corners of his mouth showed residues of green saliva. She glanced at Kai, and his lips also had the telltale green stains.

"Kai," she said, scolding. "You, too?"

"What?" Kai asked, putting his hands to his chest, feigning innocence.

"You took Greenwash," she said accusingly, then examined the Murians. She had attributed their green-stained teeth to their diet of gish but should have trusted her first thought upon seeing them. Her mouth watered at the thought of the drug, and the urge to take some fought with her internal warning to leave.

"Not Greenwash," Jasper said. "It's different."

"Don't lie to me," she said, and turned to Biribar, who was clicking and hissing at her in his language. She grabbed the garnet from Jasper's other hand, and the Murians' sounds morphed into a breathy version of Globalish.

"Jaz ran out of Greenwash," Biribar said. "This is something we call Fool's Passion. Greenwash is a narcotic. Fool's Passion is a hallucinogen. It shares the same fundamental ingredient as Greenwash, the Blessed Amrita, which is why everyone loves both drugs so much. Both are weak in the elixir, but even the smallest trace stirs the source of life. Hopefully you will extract pure Amrita when you go to Muria. The Princess of Light is the Blessed Water Carrier, and we need her help badly."

Cassidy nodded, not following his meaning. She turned back to Jasper and said, "You're stoned."

Jasper grimaced sheepishly.

Her gaze wandered across the blanket and alighted on a small leather flask lying next to a collection of polished game pieces. "Is that the stuff?" she asked, reaching for the flask.

"Yes, that's it," Biribar said. "Would you like some?"

"No, Cassidy," Jasper said, taking the flask and hiding it behind his back.

"You should stay away from that," Kai said.

Cassidy stood up straight. She *should* stay away from it, she agreed silently. Her mother always cautioned against becoming dependent on plant spirits. "The addictive ones are always evil tricksters," Brianna had said. "Disguising the journey towards death as a dance of joy."

"Let me smell it," she said, and darted behind Jasper and tore the flask from his grasp.

His reflexes were slow in his stoned state, and she hopped away easily, pulling off the cork and sniffing it. It smelled foul.

"It's mostly made from fermented mushrooms," Biribar said.

"She took a lot of Greenwash," Jasper said, getting to his feet and heading towards her as she backed away. "She shouldn't have any."

"Well," Biribar said. "If she's accustomed to Greenwash, then she will find Fool's Passion mild by comparison."

A small voice in her head told her to give the flask to Jasper and leave the chamber, but a mischievous imp possessed her body and raised the flask to her lips. She tasted the liquid, and her face pinched as she took in a small mouthful. It was bitter and numbed her tongue on contact. She swallowed it and closed the flask, giving it to Jasper as he reached for it.

"Cassidy," he scolded. "Torr is going to kill me."

She swallowed again and blinked. A familiar warmth permeated her body, and she smiled. "Ahhh," she sighed, and wrapped her arms around her ribcage, hugging herself.

Jasper rolled his eyes. "Oh, stars."

She rocked back and forth with the garnet clutched in her fist and gazed around the cavern for what felt like a single breath's time. Or was it many minutes? The light crystals in the wall sconces shone with multi-colored starbursts, and the whirr of the ventilation system grew louder. "Do you think I can make my crystal work now?" she asked.

"It takes a little while for the drug to take effect," Jasper said, handing over her crystal and glancing towards the entrance worriedly. "You'd better go before Torr comes back here. How much did you take?"

"Not much," she said, laughing. The sound of Biribar's voice brushed across her consciousness like feathers. He was saying something about the Blessed Water Carrier and Amrita. She turned to the Murian. "Can you help me make my crystal light up?" she asked. "Does the Fool's Passion help?"

Biribar understood her question and answered, "Yes. It will help your filaments unfurl. Your senses will be heightened. Perhaps you will connect with the light crystal, and it will glow for you." He smiled widely, reminding her of how her dog, Silver, used to bare his teeth in a toothy smile when she scratched his side.

"What did he say?" Jasper asked. "Let me have the garnet."

Cassidy translated and held up the light crystal with one hand while holding the garnet tightly in the other.

"Just wait for the Fool's Passion to soften your mind," said Biribar.

"Wait," repeated Cassidy, the word feeling round in her mouth.

Biribar pushed the hood off his head, revealing thick glowing green hair. She stared, mesmerized. It could have been bundles of solar filaments lit with the bright green of an aurora. Suddenly, an urge to empty her stomach took hold of her. She lurched to her feet, forcing back bile, and stumbled to a wall. Biribar caught her arm and shoved a bowl against her chest as she heaved a mouthful of yellow liquid into it. She knelt and threw up again, and then rolled back onto her heels, wiping her mouth. Her stomach felt better, although her head felt like she was being rocked upon ocean waves. The nausea passed, and she wiped sweat from her brow. She guiltily put down the bowl and returned to the blanket and sat next to Jasper.

Cassidy rinsed out her mouth with water from Jasper's canteen and gave him back his garnet. Blood buzzed through Cassidy's veins, making her skin hum. Her thoughts skipped and rushed in an endless current, as though pushed by a steady wind making its long journey across the sea. The colors of the cave wrapped around her in a sparkling shawl. Specks of jade green and cinnabar red glistened in the silvery rock. Had those colors always been in the moon rock? She had never noticed them before.

Guruhan appeared and then left with a rolled parchment and the garnet, and Cassidy wished they had never traded the garnet away. Her attention drifted back to the Murian sitting across from her. The tendrils on Biribar's head floated like her mother's hair, only more so. It was as though the glimmering strands were sniffing the air, which was redolent with the scent of Jasper, who sat next to her, staring at the wall above Biribar's head. Jasper smelled of cedar and bay leaf. She squeezed his hand and traced the veins on the back of his hand and forearm, and then ran her fingers through his hair. It was getting long, and the auburn locks were thick and tangled. She took his chin, turning his head to face her, and pushed her tongue into his mouth.

He returned the sloppy kiss but resisted as she tried to push him to the ground. "Not here. Not now," he said, his fingers gripping her hair at the scalp. His golden-green eyes met hers, and she giggled. Jasper disentangled himself from her, and Cassidy released him with a pout.

Kai was sitting with the four Murians, leaning over the stone game. His face was tense with concentration. He moved a white stone slowly across the blanket, and the Murians laughed at him, their clicks and hisses splashing across the cave like sprays of water.

Jasper had her light crystal in his hand, and it was glowing. He was completely absorbed by it. The crystal cast an orb of light, illuminating his face and making him look like an angel.

She wanted the crystal to glow for her and turn her into an angel. She sat next to him, feeling herself sink into the rock. It was cold, and she melted into it, the structure of the crystalline rock matrix teaching her cells how it was formed. Her cells mimicked the structure, turning her into a stone statue. She panicked as she tried to breathe, and then the molecules of her body spun into the ether, and suddenly she was floating, each cell separate from the other, tiny stars with eons of nothingness between them.

"Let me try," she said, reaching across the gaping chasm towards Jasper's hand, her voice drifting to her ears from far away.

He looked up, recognizing her, and handed her the crystal shaft.

"Oh," she said, wonder filling her heart. The crystal was not a rock, it was awareness. It observed her as she observed it, and it tremored with excitement—a strange creature vibrating with life. Her gaze melted into the bright orb of light, and she was surrounded by it. Strains of music filled her ears, unlike anything she had ever heard before. She tried to hum along, to memorize the melody. If she could paint the sound, it would be a sunrise after an eternity of darkness, vermilion and bronze, glowing like the inside of the sun itself.

When she finally parted from the light crystal, letting Jasper take it with his curious fingers, she met Biribar's approving gaze. Jasper stared at the glowing shaft, holding it aloft, while Kai sat quietly with the Murians, concentrating on the game of stones. Jasper moved over to watch, and Cassidy stood up. She suddenly felt hot, and turned in a circle, disoriented.

She was finding it hard to breathe, and she wanted fresh air. But she was surrounded by stone walls rearing up all around, closing her in. The men didn't seem to notice she was there, as though they were in a different world, in a different dimension. She tried to call out to Jasper, but her throat was swollen, and she could not utter a sound. She put her hand to her neck, trying to pull the rope away from her throat, but Balthazar was angry with her and was pulling tighter. He would not be satisfied until he rendered her unconscious. Maybe he would kill her this time, and she would never wake up. She ran for the door and suddenly was in a dark passageway. She turned around and around. Which way was out? She ran blindly and found three men crouched over a map, tracing shapes with their fingers. She recognized Torr's back, but he did not look up. He did not see her either. She wasn't really there. She was gazing into the bloody water of the bathroom sink, crying out to him, but her cry was a hoarse whisper. She ran into another passageway, searching for a way out. More men sat at a table, fiddling with knobs on a console. She was a wraith in a nightmare and ran down another passageway. It ended with a ladder. She scrambled up the rungs and found herself locked in a metal box. Men's voices laughed on the other side of the metal door, ignoring her. Guards who would not help her. Willfully blind to her captivity. Balthazar would come soon and drag her out of the box. Another ladder appeared in a dark corner. She scaled it and pushed open a hatch in the ceiling. The hinges rasped and squeaked, but still the guards laughed. She climbed up onto the metal roof, quietly lowered the hatch cover shut, and crawled to the center of the flat roof.

She lay down on her back and stared up. The stars stared back at her. They would help her if they could, she was sure of it. But she was trapped within a web of hexagons, a prison of metal and glass. Her muscles shook and her heart pounded. Sweat dripped down her neck.

She focused on a cluster of stars, and the pinpricks of light flared into balls of fire. White and gold flames. Cascading robes and gem-speckled crowns. Twelve goddesses in a circle, reaching out to her. Their hands outstretched, their eyes ablaze. Pleading for her to respond. Behind each woman sat a man robed in black, holding a chain attached to a metal collar fastened around the woman's neck. And behind the men stood another circle of men, robed in fiery red, with pulsating black ropes tied around the necks of the men in black. The ropes writhed like snakes, and Cassidy choked.

She turned onto her side, clutching at her neck, trying to breathe. She closed her eyes against the vision, but the three concentric circles of people stared at her, drilling her with their eyes. She spasmed and lurched on the metal roof, and all turned black.

————————————) ————————————

"Cassidy."

Torr's voice was urgent—but distant—as though in a dream.

"I found her. She's up here," Torr called.

"Cassidy," he said, shaking her shoulder. He rolled her onto her back and held her by the jaw, his big thumb and fingers squeezing her cheeks.

"What," she mumbled, pulling her face away.

"Cassidy, wake up."

"I'm awake," she said, cracking her eyelids open and squinting up at him.

"Stars, Cassidy," Torr said, hugging her head to his chest.

His heartbeat thudded in her ear. She was lying down on warm metal.

"Where am I?" she asked, propping herself up on one elbow and looking out over a sea of shipping containers.

"Outside the Murians' caves," Torr said.

"How'd I get up here?" She pulled away from him and rolled over onto her hands and knees and tried to stand up.

"A ladder," he said, helping her to her feet. "We couldn't find you."

"Oh. I don't remember," she said, wiping grit from the corners of her eyes.

"You took more drugs," he said, and guided her to a hatch in the roof. A ladder led down to the interior of the container.

She climbed down gingerly, and then hobbled outside. She leaned against the side of the container for support.

A bearded man she recognized was standing with the Alphabet Boys and the Boyer brothers. The men grew quiet and eyed her with concern. Footsteps clomped through the container behind her, and Jasper rushed out, taking her into his arms.

"Algol's hell, Cassidy, you scared the crap out of me." He squeezed her, lifting her off her feet. His sweat smelled sharp and acrid. He set her back on her feet, and Torr pushed Jasper's shoulder.

"You stay away from her," Torr said, backing Jasper across the dust. "You too, Kujo," Torr said bitterly. Kai emerged from the shadows of the container and stood next to Jasper.

"I'm sorry," Kai said.

"Get out of here," Torr said, his voice trembling, and pointed at the gap between containers.

Jasper and Kai turned and strode stiffly away.

Torr propped his arm around Cassidy's back, and together they walked slowly towards the road, their friends trailing behind them.

The ground felt mushy under her feet, and the air smelled flinty.
"Did I take more Greenwash?" she asked her brother.

"No. Something similar, I guess. They called it Fool's Passion.
A hallucinogen."

"Oh. How long was I passed out for?"

"A couple of hours. I just about died. You can't do this again,
Cassidy. No more drugs. Promise me."

"Okay," she said weakly, trying to recall what had happened. Vague
hints of sipping something from a flask and being lost in a cave and
a circle of chained women blurred together. She stopped trying to
remember and leaned against her brother as they walked.

"Hey, Raleigh," Torr said over his shoulder. "Radio Blaire and tell
her we found her."

"Yes, boss," Raleigh said, followed by the crackling of a radio.

"Blaire?" Cassidy asked weakly.

"Yeah. I thought maybe you ran to their camp. We went there
looking for you."

Raleigh handed Torr the radio, and Blaire's voice crackled through.
"Torr? Is she okay?"

"Yeah. Here," Torr said, and held the radio in front of Cassidy's
mouth. "Say something."

"Hi, Blaire," Cassidy said.

"Cassidy, oh my stars, we were so worried."

"I'm sorry," Cassidy said.

"What happened?" Blaire asked.

"I got lost. I'm sorry, I'm tired. We'll talk later." She pushed the
radio away, feeling dizzy. A fan pod whirred overhead, and the Milky
Way glowed red and gold.

She veered off to a porta-potty at the G-road intersection. When
she was done, she staggered out of the stinky hut and found Torr
waiting for her. She could walk by herself now and shuffled next to her
brother. She didn't know what spoke road they were on—all the tents
and people looked the same. A drum beat in the distance. The gravity
bar pulsed white in the center of the dome, and she headed towards it.

Next thing she knew, she was crawling into her sleeping bag,
her clothes still on. She pulled the covers up over her head and fell
fast asleep.

23

ATHENA

Ridge was in a bad mood. Hatred for Balty seethed in his blood, making his muscles twitch. Even selling his load of food and walking across the dome to Schlitzer's did not calm him down. He had overslept, and on his way out of the house he had heard Balty beating one of the girls in his room. The girl's yelps still echoed in his head and made him quiver with fury and guilt. Ridge was just as responsible, allowing that abuse to happen in his own household. And Jidna was his own sort of scumbag.

He couldn't bring himself to face Danny today. She saw right through him and knew him for what he was—a coward.

But he couldn't avoid the second brothel. At least Schlitzer did not pretend he was anything other than a gangster. Jidna walked with Schlitzer across the perimeter road towards the sundial, removing his sunglasses so that he could gaze upon the colors of Earth unfiltered. Today Eurasia was robed in green and gold, and the oceans shone a cobalt blue that made his heart hurt.

They reached the metal disk, and Jidna swept it off and checked his watch against it.

"Any progress?" Jidna asked.

"Yeah, kind of," Schlitzer replied. "I talked to Jaz."

"What did he say?" Jidna asked.

"Well, I didn't ask him directly, but he understood. I think he might want something big in exchange for the deeds."

"How big?"

Schlitzer fidgeted with his ponytail. "He mentioned a galaxy-class cruiser."

Jidna laughed, and then stopped laughing. He was talking a hundred Solidi or more. And then there was the contract for the Cephean or Delosian pilot that would need to be transferred with the ship. The Gandoops themselves only owned two interstellar cruisers, and they were always in use. He supposed he could give up one of them, but what if Schlitzer wanted one as well? He'd never be able to convince Ishmar and Ali to part with both of them, never mind Balty, who probably thought he owned them now. Jidna blew out his breath in annoyance. "That's a lot to ask."

"I know," Schlitzer said. "I laughed at him too, and then changed the subject. How much would you agree on for an outright purchase in gold?"

Jidna stiffened, feeling tendrils tickling his back. Schlitzer was trying to get a hold of him. Did Schlitzer think he wouldn't notice? Jidna knew Schlitzer used energy filaments to control people. When they'd first met years ago, when he was Ridge, Schlitzer had sent out tentative feelers into his abdomen, trying to understand his intentions. Ridge had sloughed them off like worms squiggling off a wet sheet of glass. Another time, Schlitzer had tried to get into his true eye. Ridge had grabbed it with his mind's hand and sent a jolt through it, sending the tendril curling back into Schlitzer's head. The pimp had recoiled with a shiver of pain. So, Schlitzer knew Jidna could sense the intrusions and had the power to repel them. The fact that Schlitzer was trying to get at him surreptitiously by going behind his back only irritated Jidna further and made him wonder what else the pimp was up to.

Jidna focused his attention on his back where the tendrils were crawling and envisioned an electromagnetic shield like the speedsters used. A small electrical current vibrated through his body for a brief moment as one of Schlitzer's tendrils tried to dig into the back of his heart area and encountered the shield. Schlitzer drew back, a flash of pain marring his normally placid countenance. The tendrils disappeared, and Jidna held the man's blue eyes until the pimp dropped his gaze uneasily.

"Trust, Schlitzer," Jidna said dryly. "What are you worried about? I'll cut you in. But I don't have that kind of gold lying around." Actually, he did, but he was investing it in Last Chance and socking some away in case things went completely to hell.

"I'm not worried," Schlitzer said, rubbing his solar plexus. "But times are getting tough around here. Might be time to pull up stakes and find another swamp to infest."

"Yeah," Jidna said, running his fingers idly through his beard. "I've been thinking the same thing. But there aren't any great options. I've invested too much of myself in my mining claim to abandon it now."

Schlitzer nodded. "We've gotten through tough times before. And you deserve to keep what you built. Maybe the kids will agree to sell the deeds, but they're not stupid. They know they're worth a lot. Gold might be the easiest way out of this. Think about it, you'd have clear title to the land. We could get them to sign them over to you and everything. Completely aboveboard. How about it?"

Jidna met Schlitzer's eyes. How much was he really prepared to part with for legal claim to Anaximenes? How much wealth would Balty let go of? What say did Balty have about any of this, anyway? Why was that fucker even in his life? Having that filth infiltrating his home and now his business felt like Balty's hands were down his pants, and it made him quiver with fury.

Schlitzer mistakenly thought the anger was directed at him and raised his hands defensively. "What happened to trust, Jidna?"

Schlitzer looked truly hurt, and it touched Jidna, drawing him out of his simmering rage. "No, no," he said. "I'm sorry, it's not you. It's my other ... partners. They're quite demanding."

Schlitzer lowered his hands. "Oh," he said, his expression shifting to concern. "I get it. I forgot about them for a second."

"Please," Jidna said. "Just try snagging the deeds instead. You must have guys who are good at that sort of thing. I'll pay you for your troubles—but not a star cruiser."

Schlitzer bobbed his head back and forth. "I do have talented men. But it could get tricky. The twins are in a well-guarded camp with the best security guards in the dome, aside from my own and Rodney's, of course. And the kids are guarded everywhere they go. But I'll see what I can come up with."

"I'd appreciate it," Jidna said, struggling to maintain a friendly aspect. Balty might not be so understanding, but it wouldn't help to antagonize Schlitzer.

———————)———————

"No, not yet," Ridge said.

"What's taking so long?" Balty demanded, turning away from the wet bar and glaring at him. His voice was like acid. "I thought you said it would be easy. If you were one of my men, you would learn that I do not take no for an answer."

It took all of Ridge's will to keep his eyes from registering terror. Instead, he concentrated on the tendril that was trying to wrap itself around his neck. It was fat and gray and pulsing. He finally got a hold of it with his mind's hand. Balty's attacks had gotten more aggressive lately, and Ridge had to take charge of this situation before he surrendered control completely to the powerful man. It was bad enough Balty was taking over the spaceport—Ridge would be damned if he was going to let him manipulate his energy body as well.

Ridge held onto the gray tendril and gave it a sharp yank, wanting to tear it from its root. Balty jerked forward, and his hand flew to his abdomen, his eyes bulging in pain.

"We suspect the kids carry the deeds around with them," Ridge said calmly as Balty gasped for air. "It's just a matter of securing them without creating any waves. I don't want to solve one problem only to create another. Surely, you would agree."

Garbled moans escaped Balty's mouth as the fat, gray tendril grew limp in Ridge's phantom hand and slowly disintegrated. Ridge held his ground as two of Balty's thugs rushed into the room.

"What's wrong, Balty?" one of them asked, hurrying to Balty's side and casting an accusing glare at Ridge.

The second thug grabbed Ridge by the arm. "What are you doing to him?" he demanded.

Ridge shook off the man's hand and replied stiffly, "People's own anger and aggression often turns back on themselves. You know, heart attacks and such," he said, making up the first thing that came to mind. Whatever he had done, it had worked.

Ridge held Balty's fuming eyes, and continued, "Often, what you wish upon others ends up happening to yourself instead. That's why I always carefully guard my thoughts. Particularly around certain people."

Balty's eyes narrowed. He knew Ridge had done something, but he didn't know what. And now Balty was probably wondering if somehow he had done it to himself. At the least, he would think twice before attacking Ridge again.

"Just be patient," Ridge said to Balty, and strode to the bar to fix himself a drink.

------------) ------------

As much as Ridge thought about abandoning his home to that scumbag, he couldn't get himself to actually leave. He stayed for the principle of it, despite the enslaved women, though that situation had taken an unexpected turn.

Balty appeared to actually like one of the girls. Her name was Athena. Ridge watched, fascinated, while Balty brought her out into the living room. He had never done that with any other girl.

Athena had long brown hair, unlike the blonds Balty usually preferred. He must have taken a liking to her immediately while perusing his options among the latest shipment of women.

Athena did not appear at all afraid of Balty. In fact, she seemed to genuinely enjoy him. She spent most of the time sitting on his lap with one arm around his thick neck and the other holding a glass. Balty was more relaxed than Ridge had ever seen him, and the two of them teased and giggled like teenagers.

Ridge examined the happy pair from the corner of his eye. He found it impossible to believe Athena honestly liked Balty. No doubt she was pretending for her own survival, but she definitely had Balty hooked. Maybe Balty had finally met his match, and Ridge wondered if she were part Cephean. Her eyes were a glittering green, and Ridge tried to see if her hairline came to a point, but her hair covered her forehead.

Ridge looked for energy tendrils and saw a mass of them bundled around the pair like ropes. He couldn't distinguish which were Balty's and which were Athena's. Some were pure and golden. Others were thick and dark. They attached in every chakra, front and back. Ridge did not know what to make of it. The whole mess reminded him of a writhing nest of snakes vying for dominance and survival. Balty and Athena were no doubt unaware of their entanglement, or rather, all too aware of it. They were under each other's spell, gazing dazedly into each other's eyes.

Balty's newfound connection with Athena didn't stop him from keeping a second woman in the back. Ridge had heard her crying. Since both girls shared Balty's suite, there was no way Athena could be unaware of his treatment of the other captive. Athena either was as sadistic as Balty or had enormous self-control and was doing whatever she had to do to save her own skin. Or maybe she was hoping her relationship with Balty would somehow save the other woman as well. Ridge wished her luck.

Athena was an interesting mix of gentleness, strength, and wit. Ridge watched as she pushed Balty's hand away when he tried to fondle her breast, taking his hand and sucking on one of his fingers instead, with her eyes locked onto his. This made Balty growl and tickle her, sending her into a fit of giggles. When she stopped squirming, she nestled her head in the crook of his neck, and Balty hugged and rocked her like a child, his eyes closed, singing some lullaby about the Soldiers of the Lone. Athena lifted her head and gazed into Balty's eyes, and then kissed him gently on the cheek, stroking his hair. Balty closed his eyes again and embraced her. It was the picture of perfect bliss.

Athena did not have any visible bruises. She only had a couple of dark love bites on her neck, but so did Balty. Ridge had never seen a hickey on Balty before—scratches, yes, but not a hickey. Probably, no one had dared suck and bite the cruel man's neck, or they had not been allowed to. Ridge retreated to his chambers to the sound of ice clinking in glasses and low warm laughter.

He sealed the door and entered the silent stillness of his bedroom, retreating into his own thoughts. He lay on the bed, staring up at the square of starry sky, and felt sorry for Giselle that she could never look at the stars. Or Earth. Or the sun, which would return to Gandoop in a matter of days. All because of her evil witch of a mother.

Or maybe Giselle stayed underground by choice. More likely, she was a victim of the madwoman, Gabira. Maybe she needed Ridge to save her. He closed his eyes and imagined her falling at his feet in gratitude after he rescued her from her mother's dungeon. He would pull her into his arms, and she would kiss him and let him lead her to his bed.

But how could he get at Giselle with Gabira spinning her dark web and ensnaring him? He would focus his efforts on outwitting Gabira, and then seducing Giselle. A smile slowly spread across his face. Yes, that would be best. Ridge would beat Gabira at her own tricks, lure Giselle to Last Chance, and settle her comfortably in his new den. Suddenly, the prospect of moving to Last Chance did not seem so bad.

———————————)—————————————

Ridge let Schlitzer work their plan, and left Gabira and Giselle to stew in their cave. He wasn't going to pressure any of them at the moment—sometimes things worked out if you just left them alone. In the meantime, he entertained himself as Jidna, enthusiastically pursuing his goal of clearing out the glut of food Balty had let accumulate in the warehouse.

It took him seven loads to get rid of all the perishables that hadn't made it into the cold storage rooms, which he discovered were filled to overflowing. Half of the produce on the warehouse floor was rotting, and he sent it reluctantly to the recyclers. The remainder of the fresh produce and other desirable items, such as hard cheeses and cured meats, made it onto his freighter and over to Peary. Every day, the Guild traders expected him, and gold flowed into his coffers.

After he'd cleared out most of the eggs and dairy products, he filled the entire hold with five-hundred-gallon tanks of spring water, and several kegs of beer and casks of wine for Schlitzer. And bottled beer, which weighed twice as much as canned beer, and cost twice as much. The water was at the request of several traders, but Jidna was still surprised at the price it brought. He'd assumed the dome was self-sufficient when it came to water. Water was recycled for the most part, and he knew Peary had several tankers that mined ice daily at Peary Lake and other deposits around the pole, but that was a slow process. Maybe Ramzy wasn't releasing any extra water for personal consumption. They had a strict rationing system, and each person was allotted only four liters of water per day. That would leave everyone thirsty in such a dry environment, although Jidna was sure Ramzy had calculated the required water for survival.

The following day, Jidna took wheat flour, whole grains, nuts, and dried legumes, plus some cases of hard alcohol for Schlitzer's bar, and cases of canned beer. The day after that, he took canned food and some medicines.

He had succeeded in clearing out several of the warehouse aisle floors and gotten rid of the most precariously towering stacks of pallets. And he had bitten into a small portion of the ten percent of goods owed to the Gandoops, a backlog that had grown beyond all reckoning.

An unexpected side effect of his food campaign was that Jidna was suddenly wildly popular at Peary Spaceport. Jidna wasn't sure it was such a smart thing for him to be attracting so much attention, but he reveled in it nonetheless.

One of the traders told him that a far side mining lord had said he'd gone to Gandoop to try to buy food but had been turned away.

"I guess it pays to do the Gandoops favors," Jidna drawled with a cocky grin, stroking his beard. "They take care of their friends."

The trader looked at him enviously, probably wondering how to get into the Gandoops' good graces himself.

24

HEARTSTRINGS

Torr found his father in a field. It was not the small sloping field of the coastal farm where he'd encountered him last. It was a vast flat field near the delta. Parallel lines of green and brown striped the land, converging in the distance in a haze of shimmering heat, with folded brown hills rising in the distance. Caden was bent over the black soil, planting green seedlings from a plastic tray. Dozens of men stooped under the hot sun, moving slowly along the endless rows. Here and there wagons dotted the land, stacked with racks of more seedlings waiting to be transplanted.

Several rows over, a Teg officer was mounted on a tall chestnut horse that stepped along the dry, cracked furrows between the rows. A bullwhip was coiled in the Teg's hand. Torr eyed him warily from where he stood near his father, shielding his eyes against the blazing sun with his hand. The officer's eyes scanned the field, passing over Torr. Or through him. Torr inhaled sharply, his heart hammering.

Without warning, the whip lashed out and struck a worker in the rear. The worker stumbled forward onto his knees while the officer yelled a rude curse. Struggling to his feet, the hunched man continued planting without looking at the mounted officer. A line of blood seeped through the fabric of his blue coveralls.

Torr sidled up to his father and took a seedling from the tray. He scooped a hole in the dirt with his hand and gently placed the plant into it, and then patted dirt around it. They looked like pepper plants.

Caden tilted his head towards him and jerked back with surprise. "Torr," he said, his voice barely audible. Caden's eyes filled with tears, and he grasped Torr's fingers. They held each other's hand in a small, silent embrace, their eyes locked in a gaze of joy and pain.

"Son," Caden said, dropping his hand and taking another seedling. "Are you dreaming?"

"Yes, but I am awake."

"Did you save your mother?" Caden's face was strained.

"Yes."

Caden's eyes closed, and his fingers sank into the dirt.

"She ran into the hills," Torr said in a hushed voice. "With a raven."

Caden smiled and nodded. He pressed dirt around a seedling and grabbed another from the tray. They moved a pace to the right and continued talking in undertones. "How is Cassidy?"

Torr hesitated, then said, "She was attacked. But she is okay. She is recovering."

Caden gave a little start and met his eyes again. "Attacked? How badly was she hurt?"

"Pretty badly. But she is safe now."

Caden drew in a deep breath and nodded. "Life is hard right now. We must all be strong."

Torr did not want to worry his father with the details of Cassidy's ordeal, and whispered, "We got to Peary Dome, and we saw our land. There's a large mining operation and a spaceport built on it. And there are Tegs there. I think they're using it as an outpost."

Caden's expression hardened. "I'm not surprised. The moon is strategic. The Tegs will want it—as soon as they're done here," he muttered, glancing around the field.

"Are you well?" Torr asked. It was a dumb question. His father was a prisoner. A slave. But he looked healthy enough. He had lost some weight and was burned by the sun, but his eyes had not lost their spark.

"As well as can be expected. They work us like dogs." Caden rose to standing, stretching his back and wiping sweat from his brow. Torr heard the whip before he saw it lash across his father's cheek, leaving a dark line. Its tip flailed past Torr as it recoiled. Caden stepped backwards, thrown off balance by the blow, but regained his footing and stooped over the dirt and grabbed a seedling with shaking hands.

"Work!" the officer barked, and pranced past on his horse. Torr's body went rigid. He was bent over the earth next to his father, whose skin oozed with bright red blood.

"Dad," Torr whispered in muffled anguish, his cheek twitching.

"I'm okay," Caden said, waving Torr's hand away as they both pawed at the dirt, pretending to plant. Caden pulled a scrap of fabric from his pocket and dabbed at the bloody gash. "At least he missed my eye."

Torr swallowed, fighting back rage. He withstood the urge to rush the officer and pull him from his saddle. "I should wrap that whip around his skinny neck," Torr growled.

"Don't do anything," Caden whispered sharply. "Leave it."

They moved slowly along the row, the sun beating down on Torr's neck. He didn't think anyone else could see him, but he didn't want to take a chance, and continued stooping like the others. The dirt was hot and crumbly, and the green leaves smelled pungent and alive. Torr scanned the field from the corners of his eyes. Guards with assault rifles loitered around the periphery. A group of them were sheltered under a tarp.

"I don't see how I can get you out of here," Torr whispered.

"I don't either. But just seeing you has brightened my day." Caden tilted his face towards Torr and gave him a warm smile. Torr's eyes teared up suddenly, and he wiped at them with the back of his grimy hand. His father dabbed at his cut again, but as soon as he took the kerchief away, the line oozed with blood. They both turned back to planting.

"Look," his father said, pushing a clump of dirt into the furrow on the other side of their raised planting row.

A long green garden snake with a gold stripe down its back was sunning itself on the baking earth. Caden poked at it with an empty tray, and it slithered a short distance, its little black tongue tasting the air.

"Ha!" Torr said, and leaned over, snatching up the snake with a darting motion. He stood up and held the writhing snake in the air, his fist clamped tightly behind the snake's yawning jaws. Torr strode across the furrows towards the horse, uncaring if the Teg guards saw him. He approached the horse from the front, waving the snake at the large animal. The horse's eyes rolled wildly, its ears flattened, and its big nostrils snorted out puffs of dust. It shied away sideways, trampling seedlings under its hooves.

The Teg jerked at the reins, trying to get his spooked mount under control. Torr didn't know if the horse could see him, but the officer clearly did not. Torr jumped forward and waved the snake at the horse's nose. The beast reared and lunged, throwing his rider off and kicking his hind legs in the air. The officer's leg twisted as he fell and his foot caught in the stirrup. Torr tossed the writhing snake at the horse's head. The horse screamed and lost its footing, rolling onto ground and over the officer's trapped leg before lurching to its feet and charging away, leaving the officer in a tangled heap.

The snake lay on the ground, stunned for a moment, and then skittered sideways and slowly disappeared into a crack in the dry earth. Torr stepped back as Teg guards yelled and ran to the officer's aid. The downed man was heaving and groaning with pain. Torr could see his twisted leg was badly broken.

Torr turned and caught his father's eye, which sparkled at him for a moment before he turned back to his work. Torr grinned and made his way towards Caden, weaving between the laborers.

A sun-darkened face peered up at him from beneath a sunhat. Torr recognized Felipe, who smiled at him slyly. "Brujo," Felipe said, and gave Torr a big wink.

They were back to full rations, and after lunch Torr stashed his whole loaf of bread in their tent for later. He had lost weight, and although he liked being lean and muscular, he knew he needed a fat reserve in case rations got cut again, or his body would start cannibalizing his own muscle tissue—the onset of starvation. The Fen's food supply had been recently restocked by Jasper, although he had warned everyone to make it last, since no one knew how long the latest food source would last. Jasper collected gold from everyone who had it, claiming that prices had skyrocketed. Torr had chipped in several Eagles, and he wondered if he shouldn't join the Traders Guild himself. But then he would need to hang out with Jasper all the time, and he grew angry every time he saw that smug, freckled face.

Jasper knew enough to stay away from Torr and Cassidy after the Fool's Passion incident, taking breakfast in his tent and leaving the camp before the rest of them departed for the training yard. He returned at dinnertime, and then disappeared again. The only problem was that Torr had been looking forward to a flying lesson.

"Hey, Cass," Torr said.

His sister was sitting on her sleeping bag, staring into that damnable crystal ball again. She had recovered from the Murians' drug, and although her face was drawn and her eyes hollow, she was nearly normal again—although still a sullen and brooding version of her former self.

"Hmm," she murmured, not taking her eyes off the small sphere.

"Do you think you could pilot the speedster yourself?"

She glanced up at him. "I flew it back here myself, didn't I?"

"Sorry. I know. I meant, could you teach me? Do you want to take it out for a spin?"

He gazed at her hopefully.

"I guess so. Why not," she said, a small smile turning up the thin hard line of her lips. "This dome is claustrophobic."

"Yeah, it is," Torr said. "I thought it was so huge when we first got here."

"Me too. When do you want to go?"

He shrugged his shoulders. "What are you doing now?"

"I was going to head over to the Smiths. I promised Bailey I would make her an arrowhead necklace today." Cassidy's hand went to the black arrowhead pendant at her throat. "It won't take very long. We can go after that."

"Perfect," Torr said. "I need to take care of something anyway. I'll walk you over there, and then pick you up after a bit."

"Okay," Cassidy said.

"I need to tell you something first," Torr said as he pulled a pair of stiff socks from a laundry line strung across the back corner of the tent. He sat down to pull them on and said, "I dreamt about Dad last night."

She listened intently as he related the dream of their father in the fields.

"I hate the Tegs," she said.

"Me too," Torr said.

"But at least it sounds like Dad is surviving," she said glumly. She squinted at him and asked, "You were able to hold the real snake? And the Teg saw it floating in the air?"

He thought back on the details of the dream. "The horse saw it," Torr said. "I don't know if the Teg did or not. But I was definitely able to grab it. It felt real. The Teg didn't see me, I'm sure of that. But Felipe did."

"Felipe? The strawberry farmer? That's very interesting," she said with a faraway look. "I wish Mom were here. She would know what it all meant."

Torr sighed. "I wish she were too."

"You are a dreamer, though, that is for sure," Cassidy said, meeting his gaze with a glimmer in her eyes.

"I suppose so," he said. "I just wish I could help Dad get out of that place. They're treating them like slaves."

Her expression reflected his helpless despair.

He stood up. "Are you ready to go?" he asked, frowning at the purple Delosian gown she was wearing.

"In a minute. I need to change," she said.

He left the tent to give her privacy. After several minutes she appeared in a new set of clothing she and Berkeley had made—a top made from a patchwork of shiny silver fabric and white neoprene, and a skirt made with long flaps of carbon fiber that fell below her knees and past the top of her dark-red Delosian boots.

"You're wearing that?" he asked.

She tilted her head at him. "Yeah. Why?"

"It's a skirt," he said.

"Yes, I know," she said.

"But you don't like skirts," he said with a puzzled frown.

"I like this one. It's like armor. It makes me feel good. And strong. I'm not ashamed of being a woman, you know. I'm tired of hiding who I am."

"Yeah, but ...," he said, struggling to find the right words. "It makes you ... vulnerable. And it's dusty out here. And we're about to go flying."

A half-smile quirked up her lips. "You sound like Mom. Don't worry, Berkeley made me leggings," she said, lifting the skirt panels to reveal her knees clad in the black stretchy denim. "And as for flying, you saw what I was wearing when I flew here. If you're worried about the length, this isn't long enough to get in the way of the foot pedals." She held out her foot and moved her toes in a circle. "Come on, let's go," she said.

He shrugged in surrender. His twin sister was changing in unexpected and confusing ways, morphing into a different person by the day. Although, who was he to judge? He supposed he must seem like a very different person to her than the high school graduate who had left home for the war just a few years ago.

"Alright, let's go," he agreed.

They left with a security detail of available Alphabet Boys, the Boyer brothers, Fritz and Frank, and Sky and Thunder, leaving Durham and Dang to guard the Fen. On the way through Center Ring, Torr made a stop at Montana's office. The administrator was at his radio table with earphones on. He pulled off the headset when he saw Torr and smoothed back his thinning hair, then stood to greet Torr.

"What can I do for you, young sir?" Montana asked.

"I was wondering if you have a map of the near side of the moon I can borrow."

Montana nodded. "Yes, I have several. Let's take a look."

Montana pulled a few rolled maps from a box and spread out three of them on the map table. "They're all similar. Depends if you're more interested in topographical detail, mineral makeup, ice deposits, underground lava tubes, or what."

"I'll take a topographical map."

"Sure," Montana said, handing him one. "You can keep it. I have a dozen of those."

"Really? Great, thank you," Torr said as he rolled up the large paper map.

"Want one of the far side, too?" Montana asked, digging through the box and pulling out another topographical map.

"Fantastic. Thank you," Torr said, rolling it together with the first map. "What do you do on your radio all day?" Torr asked. "Dome talk? Your ration guards?"

"No, I listen to Earth chatter on this. There's not much these days with all the Teg jamming. But I do get to talk with some folks on occasion. Most importantly, sometimes I can get through to Glamorgan. They're about the only free port anymore. I talked to them yesterday. I wanted to see if they could send us a shipment of rice, but they said all they can spare is potatoes."

"A whole shipload of potatoes?" Torr asked.

"Yep. Looks like we're going to be eating a lot of potatoes. But I won't complain. We need the food. I don't know how long it'll take us to consume a whole cargo load, though. Might need to store some down below in the women's cave, where it's cool. Then the trick will be to get them back out." Montana gave Torr a wry grin, and Torr nodded, trying to recall his visit to Gabira's. That entire afternoon was murky, ending with the attack, of which he remembered nothing but snarling faces and waking up in the infirmary.

They chatted for a few minutes, then Torr went back outside and he and his friends continued on to Spoke Road Three. He left Cassidy and the Alphabet Boys at the Smith camp, and then walked with the others into the maze of containers. He found the green container in the back and rapped on the door with the metal rod. A couple of minutes later, the door creaked open and Jericho peeked out.

"Torr," Jericho said in greeting, letting him in and locking the others out. "What's up?" Jericho asked, cuffing him on the shoulder. "How's your sister?"

"She's okay," Torr said, following him down the ladder. "I need to talk to the green men."

"Oh? Gonna give 'em shit for drugging her?" Jericho threw him a dour look as they strode side by side down the dim passageway.

"No. I don't know if they understand what's going on with Cassidy," Torr said. "Jaz and Kujo should have known better, though. At least they tried to stop her, or so she told me. That dude who held her captive really messed her up."

Jericho shook his head sympathetically. They stood together in the shadows at the back of the hangar, and Torr folded his arms across his chest.

"I'm sorry, man," Jericho said. "That's rough."

"Yeah," Torr said, glancing sideways at the stocky man. "But I guess I should be thankful she's alive and we got her back."

Jericho nodded grimly, and Torr knew Jericho was thinking of his own sister.

"It all sucks," Torr said, putting his arm around Jericho's shoulders and shaking him gently.

"Yeah, it does. Is it ever gonna end?" Jericho asked, meeting Torr's eyes.

"What, the war?" Torr asked, dropping his arm to his side.

"Yeah," Jericho said. "The cancer. The rot. Cephs invading Earth, and then the Tegs taking over. They're like a virus. We can't let them take over the moon, Torr."

Torr sighed. "You're right. They're strong, though."

"Strong don't matter out here," Jericho said, gesturing across the rugged hangar. "Smart matters. Wily matters. Magic matters. You got those three things, and you're gonna rule the moon." Jericho held Torr's gaze and raised an eyebrow. "You got those three things?"

Torr reflected and said, "I guess so. In small doses. But I need to get stronger in magic."

They exchanged wry grins, then Torr took his leave and headed down the dark corridor. When he arrived at the threshold of the Murians' living area, he stood for a moment until Guruhan noticed him. The Murian was hooded, but Torr recognized him by his tall, lean frame and slightly stooped shoulders.

Guruhan was alone, and the Murian jumped to his feet, pulling his long bell sleeves over his glowing arm tendrils and baring his many teeth in a welcoming grin.

The Murian rushed over, clicking and hissing and bowing obsequiously, and then ushered Torr over to the dining area and offered him a seat on a flat, square pillow. Murugan came out from the back, and they served Torr whafkan juice and a small selection of salty dried mushrooms.

Torr chewed the rubbery mushrooms and sipped on the sweet fermented juice. Without the garnet, they communicated with smiles and gestures, and conversed haltingly in the Murians' broken Globalish.

"Mapppph, yessssss," Guruhan said, finally understanding Torr's gestures. The Murian rose to his feet and disappeared into the back, then returned with a rolled scroll, nodding happily and waving the scroll at Torr. "Mappppph, yessssss."

Guruhan lowered himself onto his knees next to Torr and unrolled the scroll. It was the same one they had examined before—a thick, somewhat translucent parchment, made of real animal skin, and marked with dark indigo ink. Guruhan pressed his long fingers, with their glowing fingernails, down on the curled edges of the parchment to hold it flat on the blanket.

It was a detailed relief map of the near side of the moon, depicting elevation and contours with gradations of ink. Tiny, sparkling red jewels adorned the map in a random pattern.

The last time, Guruhan had explained that he had been given the map by a Murian priestess for his scouting mission on Earth's moon. The priestess had told him that when cosmic travelers journeyed between the planets on the paths of light, one of the most treacherous passages was between Muria or Delos and Earth when the planets were connected. The travelers had to make a hop off the moon to travel to and from Earth, and when they landed on the moon, void of oxygen or air pressure, they had only a number of seconds to make the next hop to the planet of their destination before their bodies swelled up and they lost consciousness and died. Some travelers didn't make it, and the Murians suspected that the face of the moon was littered with dead star travelers from the past many millennia.

Torr considered how long a corpse would last on the moon, given that there was no air or moisture for normal decomposition. But the heat and cold were extreme. Plus all the dust, and the endless barrage of solar wind and micrometeorites. He didn't know if there would still be any remains from the last alignment two thousand years ago, but he wanted to look.

Murugan pressed the rolled map to Torr's chest when he was ready to go.

"Find sssstar travelerssss, Sssstar Chhhild."

———————— ❭ ————————

Cassidy was sitting at a table with the four Smith sisters when Torr arrived at the women's camp. Darla was standing behind Cassidy, braiding her hair.

"Look," Bailey said to Torr, holding up an obsidian arrowhead hanging from a leather cord around her neck. "Cassidy made this for me."

"She's going to make one for each of us," Becka said, and Britta smiled. The two middle sisters could have been twins.

Torr met Blaire's eyes and returned her warm smile as he thought back on Judo class that morning when their limbs had been intertwined in every possible position.

"Obsidian has magical properties, you know," Bailey said.

"Oh, it does, does it?" Torr asked, returning his attention to the youngest of the sisters. "Cassidy has an obsidian knife," he said.

"I know," Bailey said, and Cassidy unsheathed her blade and held the snowflake obsidian hilt up to the sun. The white splotches glowed and glimmered while the black portion grew darker.

A shiver ran up Torr's spine. "You ready?" he asked as Darla tied a band around the end of Cassidy's braid.

Cassidy nodded and got to her feet, sheathing her knife. "Thanks, Darla," she said, inspecting the braid with her fingers.

"Anytime," Darla said with a little bow.

They left the camp with their security detail and headed towards the training yard.

The afternoon training sessions were in full swing, and Torr stood on the sidelines and noted a few new members whom he'd never met. There were two pairs facing off in Judo freestyle, and two sitting in meditation poses in the rows of students facing Berkeley. Torr had the distinct sense that Berkeley was watching him and Cassidy, even though Berkeley's eyes were cast downward in a glassy gaze, as if sleeping with his eyes open. Torr shivered again and rubbed his cheek, which had started twitching when they'd approached the training yard. It was a quality of twitching he had grown accustomed to since he'd joined the front lines at Miramar. It was not the sharp, insistent twitch of his childhood, nor the subtle throbbing that no one could see. It was an electrical current that branched across his face and skull and resulted in him squinting his eye—akin to the feeling of being watched or knowing danger was lurking around the next corner.

Berkeley was still observing them, and Torr gave him a small wave. Berkeley's motionless face registered no response. Torr gave him a bemused grin and shifted his attention back to the Judo class.

Two of the new men seemed to know what they were doing, although they seemed to be trying to look as though they did not, grappling together in a sloppy manner. They were too relaxed to be novices—too smooth in their holds and releases, as if anticipating their partner's moves. Torr peered at them and rested his hand on the pommel of the wolf knife. Lacy black trailers swam across his field of vision, and he squeezed his eyes shut to clear them. He opened his eyes, but the thin black lines were still there, waving back and forth as though in a gentle current. Torr frowned and tried to follow the lines. They seemed to terminate in the chests of the two new men. Torr tilted his head, then walked a few paces to the right. No matter what position he stood in, nor what angle the men faced him, the lines were attached to the fronts of their chests—in the center at the sternums. Torr lifted his hand from the pommel, and the lines disappeared. He held the pommel again, and the lines reappeared.

A soft jab in his ribs broke his attention, and he turned to his sister.

"What are you looking at?" she asked. "You ready to go?"

"Yeah, in a minute. But I was just noticing something weird. Lines or something in the air, coming off two of the new recruits," Torr said, motioning towards the Judo mat.

"Hmmm," she said, squinting. "I don't see anything. Where do the lines lead to?"

"Good question," he said, finding the lines again. They seemed to rise westward toward the dome's curved, glass roof. "Out to space, as far as I can tell," he said, rubbing his cheek.

"That's strange," she said.

"Yeah. I don't know what to make of it." He sighed and turned to Cassidy. "I want to show you something before we go," he said, and led her to the picnic tables.

He smoothed out the Murians' map and told her the story they had related to him about the lost star travelers.

"That would prove this whole thing isn't a myth," she said slowly.

"Exactly," Torr said, meeting her gaze.

"There sure are a lot of them," Cassidy said, inspecting the red gems. "To think that many people died trying to reach Earth. Or to leave Earth. But to find the bodies, don't you think we would need to get out and walk around?" she asked.

"Your speedster has spacesuits and oxygen tanks," he said, his eyebrows arching.

"Yeah," she agreed. "But I would be scared to open the doors and go outside. What if something went wrong? We'd be stranded. I would feel more comfortable if there were two ships, and if Kai were with us."

Torr nodded. "Me too. But I'm still sore at those guys. Let's do a scouting mission on our own first and see if we discover anything."

"It wasn't their fault that I took Fool's Passion," she said. "They told me not to."

"I know," Torr said. "But it's their fault they were doing drugs at all. Come on, let's get going."

The Judo students stopped grappling and stared at them as they climbed into the speedster. Cassidy lowered the doors and explained the instrument panel and basic displays and controls she said she had learned from observing her captor pilot his craft through her crystal ball. The hair on the nape of Torr's neck rose as she stated this matter-of-factly and pointed out the various switches, dials, and knobs as though it were not exceedingly odd and almost frightening that she knew all of this.

She showed him the hover controls and how to taxi as she swiveled out of their parking spot and glided onto the perimeter road. It was not very different from his mother's hovercraft in manual mode, and he took over the controls from the co-pilot's chair halfway around the ring road. When they arrived at the spaceport, he glided through an open loading bay. People turned to them with curious stares and friendly waves. A man operating a small crane angrily shook his fist at them as he swung a water tank out of their way.

One of Rodney's Rangers, Mazon, whom they knew from all the times they'd visited the spaceport searching for Jasper when they'd first arrived at Peary, waved with a bemused smile and guided them to a small-craft airlock. Soon they had passed through the dual decompression chambers. Cassidy piloted through the landing tunnel and out into the open.

A feeling of freedom lifted Torr's spirits. He sat back and gazed out across the lunar landscape as Cassidy flew above the gaping Peary Crater and then curved around and headed north towards the far side. Torr gazed out the windshield. He had never been to the far side before, but it was obvious when they crossed over. The nature of the landscape changed from smooth, dune-like ridges to clusters of small impact craters overlapping one another, marked by broken, jagged crater rims and fields of rubble. It was as though they had entered a war zone. He sat up straighter and searched for the radar screen controls.

"Here," Cassidy said, pressing a button. The green radar console lit up between them.

Torr could not detect any movement on the screen. The lunarscape was eerily desolate, from the endless fields of craters and scattered scree to the empty sky. Without Earth brightening the heavens, the stars were denser and brighter, and Torr was filled with a deep sense of loneliness.

"Let's go back to the near side," Torr said, shivering. "It's creepy out here."

Cassidy nodded and made a wide arc back towards the north pole.

Torr exhaled as they crossed over Peary Rim with the familiar dome glistening on the highest ridge.

"Let me take the controls," Torr said, nudging her hand away and grabbing the center stick. He placed his feet on the foot pedals and pushed on his side stick. "Let's check out the ice lakes," he said, descending into the cavernous pit of Peary Crater.

There were other craft down there, and Torr sat back in his seat, relaxed and confident. The speedster was a beauty, responding smoothly to his lightest touch. He pressed the foot pedals and moved the side stick gently from side to side, testing out the yaw and roll, and then banked into a sharp curve, pressing on the throttle.

"Don't get too fancy," Cassidy said, taking over the controls. She straightened out the craft and dropped into a gentle descent.

Torr pointed out three bright dots on the radar screen. "Those must be ice tankers," he said, pointing at a pair of stationary dots in the dark zone. "And this must be a patrol craft." He pointed to a dot moving slowly across the far end of the crater.

They headed for the dark patch where the two tankers were and crossed through a curtain of pitch black. The speedster's headlights illuminated the dark space in front of them in conical beams, which pierced the nothingness and revealed a profound void.

"Try going lower," Torr said.

"But I can't see the bottom," Cassidy said. "I don't want to crash."

"You've got a ways to go," Torr said, watching the radar console. "Turn the lights off," Torr said.

Cassidy switched off the exterior lamps and dimmed the console lights. Up ahead, two patches of light dotted the floor of the ice crater. Cassidy approached slowly, and Torr could make out the shapes of the tankers hovering over the ice, each with a large drill sunk into the ice bed. One of the tankers flashed their lights, and Cassidy returned the greeting signal, and then turned the speedster and headed up towards a brighter light, as though surfacing from the depths of the ocean.

They surfaced to find the dome glistening above them. Torr took over the controls and did a flyover, the dome's facets sparkling white and gold. As he passed above the apex, he detected movement outside the northern edge of the dome. "What's that?" he asked and navigated closer. Several men were outside the dome behind Air and Water control, garbed in grayish-white spacesuits and operating a collection of yellow earthmovers amidst a cloud of dust. Most of the heavy equipment was on a gradual grade that sloped down the back side of Peary Rim towards the far side. The men were busy pushing moon soil into mounds with bulldozers, scooping it into dump trucks with backhoes and shovel loaders, and unloading it into chutes connected to large metal contraptions inside the glass wall.

"I never noticed all that before," Torr said. "There must be a man-sized airlock back there, and those must be the oxygenators."

A few men glanced up and waved. Torr flew past the men, then curved around and skimmed along the plateau at the eastern side of the dome—the flat approach to the landing tunnel—and then headed back across Peary Crater. At its far edge, the mountainous rim descended in giant sloping steps to the broad expanse of the near side. Here, crater edges were smoother than those on the far side, and the crater floors flatter.

Torr passed the controls back to Cassidy and unrolled the Murians' map and the topographical map of the near side Montana had given him. He arranged them on his lap and compared them to the terrain stretched out below. Torr played with the buttons on the radar screen until he found the setting that displayed coordinates. He then tried to approximate the coordinates from the red gem markers on the Murians' map and tried to locate the spots on the more precise map from Montana.

"There should be one a little southwest of here, near 85-25," he said, pointing to a spot on the radar screen, and then to a red gem on the parchment. Cassidy adjusted course and slowed the craft. Torr kept an eye on the live coordinates readout on the console, and Cassidy descended slowly until they could make out details of boulders and the rims of small craters casting crescent shadows. The craft vibrated silently underneath him, and Cassidy brought them to an idling hover overlooking their destination.

They were inside another enormous crater, and Torr scanned the ground with his binoculars, looking for anything resembling a human body. Cassidy flew slowly back and forth in a search pattern, but nothing looked out of the ordinary. They finally gave up and went in search of the next closest red gem. It was the same fruitless search.

"We need to get out and walk around," he said.

"Yeah," she muttered. "Next time. With Kai."

He frowned but nodded.

They tried a third location, and then gave up.

Torr took a turn flying the craft. Cassidy said she wasn't sure about how to go into high gear—that it required setting multiple coordinates, trajectory, and other things she didn't understand. She found a thick flight manual and an operating handbook in a compartment, and they decided to take them back to their tent to study them.

After cruising around the cratered lunarscape for a while, they finally returned to Peary Rim. Cassidy took the controls and flew towards the landing tunnel. A tinny voice blared through the ship's radio, making them both jump.

"Peary Control. Identify yourself."

They scrambled to respond, finding the radio controls.

"Requesting permission to land," Torr said, guessing at what he was supposed to say. "But we don't know our call numbers. Sorry," he said, feeling stupid.

"Is this Torr?" the voice asked. "It's Mazon. You with your sister in the stolen craft?"

"Yeah," Torr said. "Hi, Mazon."

Cassidy entered the landing tunnel and hovered in front of the line of compression bay doors.

Mazon replied, his voice loud in the small cabin, "Ramzy already assigned your craft a call sign: *T-H-I-E-F.*"

"Ha ha," Torr said. "Very funny. Can you let us in? We're outside the landing bays."

"I know," Mazon said, and one of the doors began opening.

———————————) ————————————

Jasper showed up at the training yard the next morning and caught Torr by the water tank between sessions. "So, I heard you took the speedster out," Jasper said, crossing his arms over his chest.

"Nice of you to drop by," Torr drawled, glancing at Cassidy's speedster where it was parked nearby. Torr ignored Jasper's comment, preferring to needle his friend instead, and asked, "You here to train? I thought you were such an advanced wizard that you didn't need to learn hand-to-hand combat skills."

"I use wile and wit instead of muscle, if you must know," Jasper said. "How was the ride?"

"Sweet," Torr said, pulling on the tank tap and watching the stream of water fill his waterskin.

"So, I guess you don't need me anymore," Jasper said.

Torr flipped the tap closed and screwed on his waterskin cap. He looked at Jasper, whose chapped red lips were twisted into a smirk. "We need your water," Torr said. "And your food."

"But not my piloting skills."

"Jasper, grow up," Torr said, and walked away, joining his squad on the kickboxing mat.

He paired up with Blaire again. They warmed up and then went straight into sparring. Torr jabbed at Blaire's guarded face, trying to avoid hitting her eyes or nose or thinking about their kiss from the other day. Had it been a friendly gesture of compassion, or something more? She acted like it had never happened, and he tried to act the same. He dodged a hook aimed at his jaw, ducking and countering with a jab to her ribs, which landed with a soft thud. She grunted and responded with a flurry of jabs, which hit him harmlessly on his shoulder as he turned and danced away.

————————) ————————

Torr woke up from his afternoon nap, refreshed, and glanced at his wristwatch. It was twenty hundred hours. He frowned, having slept through dinner—and no one had woken him up. He hopped out of bed and went to the kitchen to scrounge for some food. There were a few hard-boiled eggs left from Jasper's latest haul, and he sprinkled one with salt and ate it in two bites.

The Alphabet Boys' pavilion was empty, and no one else was about. Berkeley came strolling in from the back, his cloak flapping and his beard points freshly oiled. He regarded Torr like a startled barn owl.

"Did I miss dinner?" Torr asked.

"Yes, oh Master, but we saved you some." Torr ignored the jest as Berkeley handed him a plate of rice and chickpeas mixed with chopped egg, onion, red pepper, and raw spinach. "Tatsuya insisted you needed your beauty rest, and no one can argue with Tatsuya."

Torr nodded and accepted the plate. "That's true. Thank you," he said. Berkeley tipped a large tin of olive oil, carefully drizzling some over the chickpeas. Torr added salt, and then devoured the plateful.

"Where is everybody?" he asked after he'd finished.

Berkeley was sitting at the table with him, busily braiding a bracelet from several strands of colorful embroidery thread that he was expertly intertwining in a complex pattern. "Girls are at the Smith camp with the Alphabet Boys. Most of the other guys crashed." Berkeley swept his hands towards the various tents.

Torr stood and cleaned his dish. "Well, I need to go on a little errand. Want to come?"

"Where?" Berkeley asked.

"Schlitzer's," Torr said. "Where's Jaz? Is he sleeping?"

Berkeley shook his head. "No. He took off a couple hours ago with Ming-Long and Khaled."

"Will you come with me?" Torr asked.

Berkeley agreed, and Torr woke Raleigh and his brothers, Fritz and Frank, and Sky and Thunder. They left the Fen, picked up Li-Jie and Zhang-Yong at their tent, and stopped off at Center Ring.

Outside the porta-potties, two Light Fighters walked over to them. "What're you guys up to?" the tall one asked, smiling and revealing perfect white teeth. Torr recognized them as the pair who had volunteered to join Cassidy's squad—Stanley and Gerbil—but she had chosen Sky and Thunder instead.

"Schlitzer's," Torr said. "Want to come?" More men were always better when wandering around Peary Dome, as far as Torr was concerned.

"Sure." The men's expressions brightened. "You buying?" Stanley asked, and Torr shrugged.

"Sure." He still had gold in his pocket, and then some. He was happy to buy his crew a drink.

They crossed the dome to 12L and ducked into Schlitzer's spacious pavilion tent. The place was busy, with standing room only at the bar. The floor pillows were crowded with Schlitzer's prostitutes and patrons. A loud comforting buzz of talking and laughter filled the air. The clink of bottles drew Torr and his friends to the bar.

"Beer?" Torr asked the guys, and they all nodded.

The woman behind the bar had long blond hair and bare breasts, drawing the eyes of the men sitting along the polished wood bar. A blue sarong was wrapped around her waist, covering her lower parts but revealing her shapely calves and red high-heeled sandals. Torr pulled his eyes away from her breasts, which were jiggling while she shook a drink she was making.

Schlitzer was sitting at the end of the bar, surrounded by a cluster of men and women. The pimp's eyes slid across the wood and rested on Torr. Torr gave a polite nod, and Schlitzer returned the gesture.

The bartender took her time getting to them, but after a few minutes she stood in front of Torr, well aware of how distracting her naked breasts were. Torr looked her in the eye, ordered the beers, and handed the cold, sweating cans to his men. He paid her, adding a generous tip. She winked at him, her thick mascaraed lashes dipping over large blue eyes. He let himself smile at her and received a grin in return. He took a breath and stepped away, chatting with his friends as they checked out the scene.

"Gonna get a girl?" Gerbil asked, his small eyes squinting up at Torr.

"No," Torr said flatly.

Gerbil stared lecherously after a hooker and her client as they left the tent. Stanley gave Torr a friendly smile, which could mean anything, or nothing. The guy was so suave, it was hard to tell if he was for real.

Torr's cheek had started pulsing again, and he pressed the cold can to his cheek to see if it would numb it and stop the nervous tic. It didn't. He gave up and took a swig of beer.

"Gerbil," Torr said, wiping his mouth. Gerbil jerked his head, apparently surprised at being addressed. "What's your real name?"

"Oh," Gerbil said nervously, clutching his fingers around his can. "Jervis."

Torr nodded. "Is that a family name?"

"No, it's where I'm from. Port Jervis." Gerbil smiled, showing crooked teeth.

"It's a good name," Torr said. He smiled at Gerbil and wondered why he put up with such a demeaning nickname. The buck-toothed man grinned back at him and lifted his beer to his mouth, slurping loudly.

Torr looked up as the crowd shifted to let Schlitzer pass. The pimp's head towered a few inches above most of the guests, his unruly curls free from the constraints of the ponytail tonight. His blue eyes met Torr's as he came to stand at his shoulder.

"Hey, Berkeley. Torr," Schlitzer said, greeting them. His tone was friendly, and he smelled like soap.

"Hey, Schlitzer," Torr replied, raising his beer can in a toast and taking a drink.

Berkeley nodded silently, and Schlitzer smiled his warm, welcoming smile.

"Is it true you have showers here?" Torr asked.

Schlitzer chuckled. "Yeah. Every camp should have 'em."

"Doesn't that take a lot of water?" Torr asked.

Schlitzer shrugged. "We've got a pristine carbon recycling system."

"Still, how many gallons does that take?" Torr asked.

"A lot. Gotta have showers for the girls, though. And the guys. Cost of doing business," he said with a crooked grin.

Torr grimaced. He supposed so. He tried to hide his disgust and took another swig of beer.

Schlitzer raised one bushy eyebrow. "Shasta?" he asked sardonically.

Torr looked down. He was still wearing his Shasta Mountaineering shirt. His vest had parted enough to reveal the insignia. "Yeah. What of it?" Torr asked.

"As in Shasta Shamans?" Schlitzer's tone was mocking.

Torr didn't feel like playing Schlitzer's juvenile game. The pimp and Jasper were friends. If Schlitzer were a spy worthy of the title, then he knew Jasper and Torr were both from Shasta. Torr leveled his gaze at him, unflinching except for his cheek, which was pulsating strongly. Schlitzer's eye slid to his tic, and the man stifled a snicker.

"What can I do for you?" Torr asked coldly.

Schlitzer chuckled. "You're in my camp. What can I do for *you?*"

Torr lifted his can. "Cold beer."

Schlitzer relaxed his face into a genuine smile. "Here," Schlitzer said, and flipped a gold coin Torr's way. Torr caught it as Schlitzer said, "I didn't realize Debbie had switched with another girl the other night. It was her night off. My bad." The man dipped his head apologetically.

"I'm keeping the tequila money, though. If you want that back, you'll have to talk to Debbie."

Torr nodded. "No worries. Thanks." He suddenly felt bright and warm inside. Maybe Schlitzer was not so bad, after all. But then he recalled that Jasper had said Debbie didn't even sell her services to patrons anymore and realized that Schlitzer was still spinning lies. Torr chose to ignore the man's bullshit and inspected the coin. "What's this?" he asked. The front had a head and nude torso of a woman, holding two spears crossed between her breasts. The reverse was of a strange bubble-looking thing on a narrow stem, like a wine glass.

"Let me see." Schlitzer peered at the coin. "Oh, that's a Spears, from Lingri-La. They're kind of rare." He smiled generously.

"Oh. Cool." Torr inspected the coin, his first off-world gold piece. "What's the deal with Lingri-La, anyway?"

Schlitzer lifted a glass of ice water to his lips and drank. "Ah, planet Lingri-La. A man's heaven, and a man's hell, right Berkeley?" Schlitzer smiled enigmatically.

"What do you mean?" Torr asked. Berkeley was listening with obvious discomfort. Torr looked between the two men.

"You don't know the story of Lingri-La?" Schlitzer asked with genuine surprise. "Jaz's mother is there."

Torr's froze for a moment. "Melanie?" He looked at Berkeley, who grimaced. "Does Jasper know?" Torr asked.

"Of course Jaz knows," Schlitzer said. "I'm surprised he hasn't talked to you about it. You being so close, and all."

Torr frowned. "Tell me."

"There's nothing to tell, really," Schlitzer said, sipping his water. "She's studying there. She's a priestess-in-training. I hear it takes a lifetime to be ordained a full priestess, if they even allow non-Lingris to be ordained, that is. Right, Berk?" The man's voice was rich and resonant—pleasant to listen to, as though vibrating from a fine instrument.

Berkeley shrugged, his expression pained. When had Jasper discovered the whereabouts of his mother, Torr wondered. And why hadn't he said anything about it? "Tell me more. What's the planet like?" Torr asked. He turned to Schlitzer, since Berkeley looked like he had just sucked on a lemon.

"Well, do you know who the Nommos are?" Schlitzer asked.

Torr nodded. "Yeah. I saw one of their ships at the spaceport. They're a tribe on Delos." *And they buy Earth women,* Torr thought to himself, not wanting to start a conversation that would inevitably lead to Cassidy.

Schlitzer bobbed his head from side to side. "Sort of. They came from a planet, Nommos, which they had to abandon several centuries ago when the polar ice caps melted and all the landmasses sank into the sea. They settled the ocean on Delos, through a treaty with the exiled Ilians, who had claimed all the land territory as their own, generations before. The Nommos built floating cities. Anyway, before that, the male Nommos population had become largely infertile. They rely on genetic engineering to keep their species alive. Because they don't need sex anymore to procreate, and the men apparently can be quite unpleasant towards women, the female Nommos told them to go to hell and took over Lingri-La, a small planet in the Taurus constellation. It's completely female, except for male consorts they allow in for their genetic material. Right, Berk?" Schlitzer asked, prodding. "Berkeley knows all about that." A sly grin spread across Schlitzer's face, and Berkeley's mouth twisted into a sneer. "He was a Lingri-La consort for a time, weren't you, Berk?" Schlitzer clapped Berkeley on the back, causing him to choke on his beer.

"You know I don't like to talk about that, Schlitzer," Berkeley growled, wiping beer from his beard. "So, lay off."

Schlitzer threw back his head and laughed a gay and pleasing laugh. "Anybody else would be proud," Schlitzer said. "That's what stories are made of. You're the only one I know with first-hand experience—you should be telling us stories all day long." He jabbed at Berkeley's shoulder. "I'll pay you." Berkeley's scowl deepened. "When are you going to loosen up, eh, wizard?"

"Lay off, I said." Berkeley swung his hand through the air, an arc of glittering gold sparks trailing his hand. Torr and Schlitzer backed away, and Schlitzer's laugh grew louder. Torr had never seen such a thing, nor had he ever heard such a threatening tone from Berkeley. Schlitzer must have really pushed Berkeley's buttons, and intentionally, it seemed. As much as Torr was itching with curiosity to find out what they were talking about, he kept his mouth shut. Berkeley tramped off towards the bar, where he pushed his way to a spot against the polished wood and stared sullenly into the mirror that glinted between shelves of bottles.

Torr turned to Schlitzer, resting his hand on the hilt of his wolf knife. He froze, trying not to betray his surprise at the slithering shadows that snaked from Schlitzer's abdomen and were attaching themselves to various parts of Torr's crew's bodies. They all seemed oblivious. Fritz, Frank, and the others were laughing and drinking in the noisy pavilion, eyeing the girls who lounged half-clothed on the colorful pillows. Most of the silvery threads attached into Torr's friends' backs up along their spines, and some delved into the back of their heads. A few writhed into bellies or chests, or into their foreheads. Torr noticed with horror that one had attached into his own heart area. Torr stood still, trying to calm his mind and understand what he was seeing. It was just like in his dream of Schlitzer and the snaking tendrils. He chugged his beer and set the empty can on the ground at his feet.

Torr slowly lifted his hand from his knife hilt, and the shadowy images disappeared. He replaced his hand, and the filaments were clearly visible. He took in a deep breath and closed his eyes for a moment, taking in the significance of it. When he opened his eyes again, Schlitzer was looking at him, his warm blue eyes dancing with mischief. Torr felt a tickling sensation on his back. He reached around, and his hand passed through what felt almost like strands of rubbery seaweed, slippery and writhing.

Filled with disgust, he instinctively slid the wolf knife from its sheath and whipped it behind himself, neatly slicing the slithering tendrils, and then cut through the one attached to his chest. Stepping forward, he carved the air around his mates, cutting the glinting threads, which jerked and recoiled as they were severed.

He danced around his friends, slicing front and back, their eyes following him with alarm as they stepped backwards or froze in place. In rapid succession, Torr severed a cord that was in Hawk's forehead, then one in Raleigh's abdomen. Sky and Thunder stared at him with horror as he sliced several that were digging into their backs. Fritz and Frank backed away and drew their own knives as Torr sliced the threads that had dug into their chests.

Stanley and Gerbil had gray ropes, thick and dark, firmly embedded in the fronts of their abdomens. Torr was taken aback at their solidity, surmising that they were old and had been there awhile, strengthening over time. He lifted the knife with a hammer grip and sliced down hard through them, and then slashed the knife in the form of the star as the severed ropes split into many and flailed about and then whipped out through the tent and into the dark sky.

Torr wheeled on Schlitzer, who was stepping towards him with a threatening sneer. Torr backed away and neatly sliced the tip off a tendril directed at his forehead, and then used a figure eight to sever one that was snaking through the air towards Berkeley. Torr crouched in his defensive stance. Schlitzer stopped, his eyes narrowing.

"These are my men," Torr snarled, twirling his knife to change his grip. "Keep your slimy tentacles off them. Though I see Stanley and Gerbil are yours already. I've relieved them of their obligation to you, for the moment." Torr's lips curled menacingly. "Don't try it," Torr warned as a mass of cords whipped from Schlitzer's belly towards him. He sliced through them all with one stroke of Lady's Fan. "Back off, or I'll sever them at their source," Torr growled.

Torr wondered if Schlitzer could see the silver cords as Torr could. Judging by the pimp's confounded expression, Torr did not think he could, though clearly Schlitzer felt something, as evidenced by the wrath rising in his eyes and directed at Torr.

"Put that knife away. No unsheathed weapons in the bar. Get out." Schlitzer's hand shook as he pointed towards the exit. Several men fell upon Torr and the others. Torr managed to sheathe his knife and let the thugs drag him by each arm and toss him onto the dust outside the half-lowered walls. He hit the ground hard and rolled, followed by thumps and grunts of his companions. Berkeley was last, though he held the bouncers at bay with a clawed hand pointed towards them, backing himself out of the tent.

"What in the hell was that?" Frank asked, beer foaming from the mouth of his overturned can, which he quickly righted. "What's with the knife, Torr, for Algol's bloody hell?"

"You're crazy," Sky cried, getting to his feet and backing away from Torr.

Torr stood and slapped the dust off his clothing, and then helped Hawk to his feet. "Sorry, buddy," he said, upset with himself for bringing the youngster along and exposing him to such a pernicious creature as Schlitzer.

Raleigh and Roanoke were examining him curiously, trying to figure out what he had done, and why.

"Did you see that, Berkeley?" Torr asked. "Did you see those snakes?"

"No," Berkeley said, shaking his head. At least he was not looking at Torr like he was insane.

"Let's go," Torr said. "Sorry about that." His friends limped after him as he sought to put distance between himself and Schlitzer. He was tempted for a moment to go back inside the tent and see what his Destroyer could really do, but he resisted. No sense stirring up trouble just for the fun of it.

When they'd gone a couple of blocks, he turned to Stanley and Gerbil. "You should go back to your master," Torr said. "I broke the leash, but now I can't trust you. I assume you'll go back sooner or later. Out of habit, or desire. Or obligation."

"What are you talking about, Torr?" Gerbil asked, whimpering at Torr's heels.

"You're a spy for Schlitzer. You think I'm stupid?" Torr's cheek twitched, and he let it, knowing it made him look like he could lose control at any moment.

"No, I'm not," Gerbil whined.

Torr wanted to punch the ugly little man right in his mouth and break those buck teeth. But Gerbil was too sad and stupid. He didn't have the wits to do anything other than what he was told, and probably had stumbled into Schlitzer's service the way water finds its way to the ocean. Stanley, on the other hand, was inspecting Torr with a measured regard. He knew exactly what Torr was talking about. Torr struck hard and fast, aiming for the man's jaw. Stanley was quick, however, and blocked the blow, and then whipped Torr to the ground, twisting Torr's wrist painfully. Torr winced as Stanley increased the pressure, and then inhaled as his wrist was released. Berkeley was standing over them with one palm extended, glaring down at Stanley, who sank to his knees. The man fell onto his side and scratched at his own throat, his face growing red as his legs kicked in the dust.

"Should I kill him?" Berkeley asked. Blood began trickling from Stanley's nose.

"No!" Torr said, pulling Berkeley's arm down. Stanley crab-crawled away, gasping for air, and then climbed to his feet and loped off with Gerbil scurrying after him. Torr let them go.

The rest of Torr's friends had backed away and were watching fearfully from across the road. A small group of passersby made a wide arc to avoid Torr and Berkeley. The two of them turned and continued walking towards the Fen, the others trailing behind.

When Torr had caught his breath and his pulse evened out, he asked, "What is that thing you do?" He inspected Berkeley's finely sculpted features, framed by the mass of dreadlocks and forked beard, which transformed a naturally beautiful man into a crazy shaman.

"Agh," Berkeley grunted, waving his hand dismissively. "Killing is so easy, it's scary."

Torr nodded in somber agreement.

"I've learned the hard way how powerful we are," Berkeley went on, "and spend most of my time trying to forget. You seem to bring it out in me, however." Berkeley glared sideways at Torr, looking gravely displeased. "You and Schlitzer, both. How about you tell me what you just did? You pissed Schlitzer off something awful. I've never seen him lose his shit like that before. And don't tell me it was just a crazy knife dance."

Torr wrinkled his brow and said, "He's got tentacles leashing everyone to him. Some sort of glamour spell or something. Some parasitic control thing, I don't know." Torr took a deep breath and peered at Berkeley. "You haven't noticed?"

"Oh, I've noticed. That's why I rarely go there, even though it is good practice." A humorless smile turned up Berkeley's mouth.

"You mean, you saw them, too?" Torr asked, relieved.

"No," Berkeley said. "You must be clairvoyant. You *see*. I'm clairsentient. I *feel*. I can feel him pricking me whenever I'm around him. I just brush him off like an annoying mosquito. But he's very persistent. It's good you can detect him. Most people can't." Berkeley eyed Torr with interest. "You saw tentacles, you say?"

"Yeah. Silver threads, more like. Except for Stanley's and Gerbil's. Theirs were dark, fat things. Like snakes."

"They're not really snakes," Berkeley said. "That's just the way your mind interprets it. They're energy filaments."

"Well, I severed them all," Torr said, unsheathing the wolf knife, half expecting the blade to be blood-stained. "Schlitzer didn't like it."

"No, he wouldn't," Berkeley agreed.

Torr laughed, and Berkeley joined him, their voices ringing through the dry, still air.

————————)————————

Torr sat on a table at the training yard with his feet on the bench and the wolf knife in his hand, watching the squads engaged in their practice sessions.

Berkeley dismissed his meditation class early and sat on the table next to Torr, crossing his legs in his meditation pose. "What's up?" Berkeley asked. "Sitting out Judo today? Are you feeling sick?"

"No," Torr murmured, his eyes half-closed, inspecting the Light Fighters one by one. "I'm trying to see something."

"See what?"

"I don't know," Torr said slowly, holding the hilt tighter. "Remember those snakes I saw coming out of Schlitzer? I'm trying to see if I can see any more. Find more spies among us." He frowned from the effort as he stared at a man who was jabbing at a punching bag. If Torr relaxed, he thought he could see shadows of lines around the man, like cobwebs that showed up for a moment and then disappeared again. "But I can't see anything solid."

"Well," Berkeley said. "Energy lines aren't solid. You probably saw Schlitzer's because he's so strong and was actively attacking us."

"But I should be able to see something," Torr insisted.

"Stop trying so hard," Berkeley suggested. "Try meditating with me. Come on."

Torr sighed, pulled his legs up onto the table, and folded them stiffly into a cross-legged position, sheathing his knife at his hip. He slowed his breathing and tried to calm his mind, but it was jumping all over the place.

"Focus on the breath," Berkeley said.

Torr turned his attention to his abdomen as it rose and fell. After a time, his mind quieted. His breathing was slow and easy. His hand rested lightly on the wolf knife's hilt at his belt, and he could feel the coarse texture of the sharkskin under his fingertips. The heavy stillness of the windless dome seeped into him. Sounds filtered through the air, striking his ear drums. He let them come and go. The slap of fists on skin. Grunts as a dozen bodies rolled to the ground in a new hip throw. He lifted his eyes and watched Tatsuya and Hiroshi walk slowly among the students. Tendrils of shadows crisscrossed the air in front of the two instructors, connecting bodies. Torr did not react but let the images float about. He steadied his gaze on Darla and Blaire, who were paired together. Thin lines connected them at various points on their bodies. The threads glinted gold, and then disappeared. Torr sucked in his breath and tightened his grip on the knife hilt.

He settled into his breathing rhythm again, relaxed his grip, and slowly moved his gaze to the next pair, Roanoke and Raleigh. Braided threads of gold connected the brothers in the forehead, throat, heart, and abdomen areas. Torr blinked, and the images disappeared. He relaxed again and detected faint flashes of gold as the brothers circled each other.

Sweat beaded on Torr's brow from the effort of concentrating. "The harder I try, the less I see," Torr muttered. He exhaled with frustration.

"Stop trying," Berkeley said. "Awareness just *is*. You can't force it. You must let your senses unfold like a flower. If you try to force it open, you'll tear the petals."

Torr tried to relax. As the minutes wore on, he saw glimpses of gold and silver threads connecting people, but as soon as they appeared, they disappeared again. He tried to imitate Berkeley's motionless pose. Torr settled into his body and let his heartbeat gently rock him. He patiently scanned the clusters of Light Fighters, glints of gold and silver appearing here and there.

A man in the kickboxing class drew his attention. A thick gray rope-like shadow extended from his belly and snaked into the distance where it disappeared. Torr stiffened and lost the image. He spent the next few minutes trying to get it back, but the sparring partners kept crossing in front of the tall brown-haired man.

Torr unfolded his numb legs and rubbed them until the painful tingling subsided, and then stood up. The classes were wrapping up. The Judo students knelt in lines and bowed, then began dispersing. Torr pulled his Gaia United whistle from his vest pocket and blew it sharply. The Light Fighters turned to the sound. He blew it again, the shrill sound reverberating off the glass dome.

"Line up!" he barked, striding forward. Torr pointed to the ground in front of him. "Line up for inspection. Squad leaders in front." He pointed out positions for the squad leaders, and the squads slowly formed lines behind them, regarding Torr with confused curiosity.

"Line up behind me," he told the instructors, who huddled behind him, looking more confused than anyone. "Ming in front," he said, and his friends slowly obeyed.

Torr had not asserted his authority since he'd led people on their first perimeter jog. He preferred to stay in the background, letting the instructors lead. But nobody questioned him. They looked at him expectantly, thinking something important was happening. Cassidy and Blaire peered at him, but he avoided their gazes.

"Line up straight," he said impatiently, and people shuffled from side to side, attempting to comply. Lieutenant James would be appalled at the lack of order of his troops. But Torr did not want to drill them on how to form ranks just now. He took a deep breath and tried to calm himself, not sure he could focus on his breath and reach a state of detached awareness with everyone staring at him. What was he doing? He suddenly felt self-conscious, but closed his eyes and tried to relax.

When he opened his eyes, everyone was still looking at him. He ignored them and walked slowly alongside the first line, which was a squad led by the loud-mouthed William, who stood silently for once. Torr softened his gaze and examined each person, looking for thick gray ropes of energy. "Stand straight with your hands down at your sides," he ordered. "Look straight ahead." People obeyed, and he continued his inspection, moving on to the squad led by Li-Jie and Zhang-Yong.

By the time he got to the fourth line, he was starting to see hints of shadows. Thin threads of silver or gold. He ignored these and made his way to the line where the tall brown-haired man stood. Torr stood in front of the man and ran his eyes slowly down the taut body. The man was fit and muscular and did not move a muscle, staring straight ahead. The man's hands were strong and well formed and stayed stiff at his sides. A trained soldier, from the looks of him. Torr's attention settled on the man's abdomen, where a thick shadow took shape.

It looked like a fat rubber rope extending as if it were an umbilical cord—similar to those Torr had seen attached to Stanley and Gerbil. Goosebumps prickled at the nape of Torr's neck, and he clutched the sharkskin handle of the wolf knife.

The snake-like shadow extended into the distance. Not towards Schlitzer's camp, but southwest towards the edge of the dome, where it disappeared. Torr furrowed his brow, thinking back on the encounter in Schlitzer's tent. He had assumed Stanley and Gerbil had been tethered to Schlitzer, but as he thought about it, he remembered the severed snakes had coiled away from Schlitzer rather than retracting into the pimp's body the way the severed tendrils from his campmates had. Torr took a deep breath. People shuffled and fidgeted around him, but the man under Torr's gaze did not move.

Torr could not figure it out, and he couldn't very well punish the man for having shadow snakes embedded in his belly. He wondered if he had unjustly accused Stanley and Gerbil. Torr released the man from his scrutiny and moved slowly down the line. People were nervous now, and Torr could sense their relief when he passed them by without lingering. He stopped next to the man who had been paired up with the first. He had similar gray cords slithering from his body and trailing off into the distance, in the same direction as the other man's. He studied him. Another fit man. Shorter. Compact, with hard muscles. A tense jaw. This man was as disciplined as the first one. Torr felt uncomfortable. There was something not right with these two men. Should he ask them to leave? There were plenty of former soldiers in the Light Fighters, but these two did not have the open confidence of the others. These men were hard and closed. He did not like them.

He clamped his teeth together and moved on, finishing his inspection by slowly examining the instructors—his trusted mates. To his relief, they all looked clean. Berkeley met his eyes and gave him a slow nod. Torr turned to the waiting ranks, cutting off whispers with a stern frown. He held them in position with his silence as he stood in front and observed the two men with snakes one last time. If he told them to leave without any explanation, it would be perceived as random harassment, and would erode the trust and confidence of everyone. People needed to understand the rules to feel secure. How could he tell them that no thick gray energy tentacles were allowed? He sighed and raised his hand.

"Dismissed," he said, suddenly exhausted. "Go back to your training."

He turned and sought out the water tank as people broke ranks, muttering amongst themselves.

———————)———————

Torr filled his waterskin at the Fen's water tank and followed Blaire with his eyes as she left the back and headed for the kitchen area. It was the quiet time of day when half the Fensters were still at the training yard teaching the afternoon sessions. Torr had gotten into the habit of stealing a nap during this time, as had the Boyer brothers and Sky and Thunder, who had already disappeared inside their tents.

Normally, Cassidy spent her afternoons at the Smith camp, but recently she had been inviting the Smith sisters and Darla over to the Fen. Berkeley was letting them use his sewing machine to make themselves new garments, and the five Alphabet Boys who guarded Cassidy during the afternoons were standing guard. Well, three of them were currently relaxing in their sleeping area in the shaded pavilion, while the other two were in the back standing guard.

Torr circled the wagon and sat at the picnic table across from Blaire. She was seated on the bench, and her head rested in her folded arms on the table.

"Tired?" Torr asked.

"Exhausted," she mumbled into her arms.

"Me, too," he said. "You wore me out at practice this morning."

"Ha ha," she said, lifting her head and smirking at him. "I'm going to find a new partner if you don't start being tougher on me," she said.

"I'm trying. I really am," he said, returning her silly smirk.

She grunted and lowered her head back into her arms.

"You really must be tired, if you're not going to come up with a smart comeback," Torr teased. "You don't want to sew?"

"I'm not much of a sewer," she said into her elbow. "Besides, there's only one machine, and Darla's hogging it." She breathed deeply and nestled her head into a more comfortable position.

"I'm about to take a nap in my tent. You can join me if you want," Torr said, the words escaping before he could stop them.

She lifted her head and raised one eyebrow. "Are you propositioning me?" she asked with a small grin.

He bobbed his head back and forth noncommittally, his face growing warm. "If you'd like," he said. "Or I'm sure Cassidy would let you borrow her sleeping bag. It's all the way on the other side of the tent." He smiled innocently. They had been wrapped in each other's arms all morning, although not in the way he was imagining.

She yawned and sat upright. "Okay," she said.

"Okay?" he asked, surprised.

"Yeah," she said, standing up. "Let me ask Cassidy if she minds if I sleep in her bed."

"Okay," he said, trying to mask his disappointment.

He stood up and waited for her to come out from the back, and they walked together to his tent. He held the door flap open for her and followed her inside.

They removed their boots at the doorway and went to opposite sides of the tent. She lay down on top of Cassidy's sleeping bag and curled up on her side facing him. She nestled her hands up under her chin and instantly closed her eyes.

Torr stretched out on his back and sighed silently, watching the dreamcatcher spin slowly one way and then the other. The sewing machine buzzed in the background, and Darla's laugh rang out, joined by Copper's.

The sound of Blaire's breathing was soft in the stillness of the muted tent, and her scent filled the air. He inhaled deeply, finding it impossible to relax with her not two yards from him. He turned his head and gazed at her sleeping form. The curve of her hips. Her peaceful face.

Her eyes opened and she met his gaze. Their eyes remained locked in a long silent exchange. He extended an arm in invitation, and she slowly rose up onto one elbow, and then crawled across the canvas floor and stretched out beside him. She settled into the curve of his arm, resting on her side with her head cradled in the hollow of his shoulder. Her body was firm and warm against his and set his skin on fire.

He stroked her hair and ran his fingers down her bare arm and shivered as she kissed his neck. She moved her leg over his, her thigh heavy and hot. He couldn't take it any longer and gently pulled her on top of him. She looked down into his eyes before lowering her lips to his. He closed his eyes, and the background noises of the dome hushed as they kissed. Any shyness he had harbored fell away, and he rolled on top and gazed down at her flushed face, their noses nearly touching.

"Hi, Blaire," he said softly.

"Hi, Torr," she replied. Her eyes were glossy, and her pupils were dark and deep.

"You're beautiful," he said.

"So are you," she said, and pulled his head down for another kiss.

───────────)───────────

They spent all afternoon in his tent. Blaire finally left the Fen with her sisters and Darla before dinnertime, and Torr sat at the table with his campmates, lost in a warm glow. His friends and sister didn't tease him or inquire about his personal business, but they exchanged knowing looks with one another. Torr was famished and focused on his food, and then retreated to his tent to be alone and bask in the memory of Blaire's skin against his.

He spent the evening in a blissful slumber. At night gong, Cassidy came in to go to bed, and he pretended he was asleep. When her breathing had settled into a steady rhythm, he drifted off again, and found himself on the hot rocky plains of Turya.

He strode through the abandoned city and into the great square. His friend Igotra and the others were singing the mournful strains of a song he did not recognize. Torr listened to the haunting melody until it began to repeat itself, and then headed across the square towards the red stone gate. He walked between the pillars of snakes and under the lintel of bat guardians, and they let him pass. After the long and tortuous climb up into the Ageless Mountains, he passed through the black stone gate and found himself at the peak with the gleaming black temple and crystal globe reflecting the red fireball of Uttapta.

Torr approached Father-Heart-of-Sky, passing between the flickering fire pits and up onto the gold dais. The massive sphere glinted with streaks of rainbows. Torr set his palms on the warm polished surface and gazed into it. He imagined the wonders this globe had seen—Star Children from ages past stepping into its glimmering depths, cosmic travelers riding across the galaxy on beams of light. He was surrounded by the glow of the crystal, and suddenly found himself squinting against a shimmering white light.

He lifted his head and looked around. He was high atop a mountain covered in white gritty snow, broken by jagged outcroppings of gray rock. No footsteps marred the textured summer snow. He gazed out over a panorama of forested valleys and misty hills. *Earth.*

He recognized the shape of this mountaintop and the contours of the land below. He had been here before. He was at the peak of Mount Shasta. To the north he could see clear into Oregon. To the southeast stood Mount Lassen, and beyond that a shimmering wall of clouds rose from the ground and formed a cloud cover overhead. The *Shaman's Shield.* It still held, and he was inside.

"Mom," he called out, cupping his hands around his mouth and shouting again. "Mom!" His voice rang through the crisp air. No voice called back to him. "Where are you?" Torr called again. "Mom?"

He closed his eyes and felt for her. It was dark and damp. The sharp smell of sweat, tangy with fear, alerted him to the presence of another person. He opened his eyes, and dim shapes slowly took form. A stack of cardboard storage boxes. An old washing machine and dryer. A faint light framing the outline of an air vent at eye level. He was in a cellar. Hard-packed dirt was underfoot, and floor beams loomed overhead, crisscrossed with pipes and wiring.

"Mom," he whispered into the dank space. "Mom, are you here?"

A fraught silence hung in the air, and then a tentative, "Torr?"

Rustling and footfalls tracked their voices as they found each other. They embraced, his mother's strong arms holding him tight.

"Oh, my stars. Torr," she said, loosening her grip and regarding him in the dim light. "Thank goodness you're here. I'm so scared." She grasped his shoulders. "Are you dreaming?"

"Yes, I must be," he said. "I was looking for you."

"Well, looks like you found me," she said with a soft chuckle. "You're getting quite good at this."

"I guess. Sometimes," he said.

"How's Cassidy?" she asked.

"Fine," he lied, giving her a strained smile. "It's tough up there, like you guys warned," Torr said, his smile faltering.

"I know, darling," Brianna said, grabbing his hand. "She went through something horrible, I sense."

Torr swallowed and nodded. "I wish you were there," he said.

"Why? What happened?" Brianna asked.

Torr took a breath. His mother's eyes bored into him. "She was kidnapped," he said. "And ... attacked. And drugged. But she escaped. She's safe now. She's recovering. Slowly."

Brianna nodded, her pained eyes searching his.

Torr squeezed her hand and said, "But I think she's addicted now. And I don't know what to do about it, other than to keep her away from the stuff."

"What kind of drug is it?" she asked.

"Some off-world drug from Muria. I think it's a narcotic. Or a sedative. Hallucinogen. I don't know. There are a couple different kinds."

"Murian, huh?" she muttered, releasing his hand and rubbing her chin. "I wouldn't know anything about that. Did you check the red notebook?"

"Yes, I did. Nothing presented itself. Cassidy had given Jasper a vial of one of your tinctures for addictions, but he sold it. The idiot. And that was the only one."

"Which herb was it?" Brianna asked.

"Douleia, I think," he said.

"Ah, yes," she said. "Douleia. I only had that one bottle. It's a difficult herb to get. It blooms for only two weeks, deep in the remote forests of the north. I had always prescribed it when people blamed themselves for harm inflicted upon them by another. I suppose that could be related to addiction." She shrugged her shoulders, a deep frown scoring her face. "Cassidy will have to work it out for herself, in the end. That's how it usually goes with addictions. It's helpful to support her as much as you can, but ultimately it's up to her to beat it." Brianna's eyes were dark and sad.

Torr sighed and said, "I visited Dad." Brianna's eyes shifted from one worry to another. Torr described the field workers and the Tegs, the whip and the snake, the horse and the fallen soldier.

"You were able to hold the snake," she said, inspecting him curiously. "Grandpa Leo used to tell tales of dreamwalkers who could do such things, how some shamans could shape the world around them in their dreams. You have proven your skill once again."

Torr shrugged. "I think I held the snake. Or maybe the horse saw me and got spooked. The snake felt real in my hands. But it could have been just a dream."

Brianna nodded thoughtfully. "Animals are very sensitive," she said. "And snakes are known to cross into other worlds."

The nape of Torr's neck tingled, and he asked, "But what about you? Why are you scared? I mean ... what happened?"

"I'm trapped," she said. "The Tegs have cordoned off the northern boundary, and to the south they are amassing people into camps. Patrols of Tegs and dogs are combing the hills south of here, searching for people hiding out, and slowly moving north."

"What kind of cordon?" Torr asked. "How many soldiers?"

"They've cut a firebreak through the forest and built lookout towers with floodlights. There's a Teg camp in a big field to the northeast. Hundreds of troops, I would guess. And beyond that is the river. They've blocked all the bridges."

"How far from here?" Torr asked.

"The firebreak is about five miles due north. The camp is perhaps ten miles northeast as the crow flies. I thought about trying to wade up the river, but the banks are too steep and rocky and the current is too strong."

"I'll go scout it out," Torr said, and suddenly he was outside a dilapidated house in a small homestead carved out from the forest. It was nighttime, and a half moon hung in the sky, bathing the land in a soft white glow. He stared up at it, looking for the north pole and Peary Dome where he slept. There was no glimmer of the dome—the moon looked as it always had.

A shadow stirred and Torr turned his head. A large raven peered down at him from a dead tree branch, its eyes glints of moonlight. Torr nodded to the raven and headed north.

His giant footsteps took him through the dense pine forest and to a firebreak of fresh stumps and dark upturned earth, which cut a wide straight path through the trees. A watchtower stood a hundred yards to his left, and another stood to his right. Floodlights lit the empty space, with the stumps casting short shadows in a haphazard grid from the lights on either side. Perhaps it would be possible to navigate the shadows, he considered.

He headed east and found the Teg camp. Tents, trailers, parked vehicles, cooking stations, and banks of porta-potties filled a large flat field. Small groups of soldiers sat around campfires. He skulked around the perimeter, where a border guard of lone men spaced a hundred yards apart stood watch or lounged in lawn chairs and idly scanned the camp's boundaries. Otherwise, it was quiet, save for a soft chorus of snores droning from the tents.

He regarded the thick forest beyond the camp, where the terrain grew rugged as the foothills steepened and civilization gave way to wilderness. Even if his mother could get past the Teg boundary, she still had a long journey ahead of her. First, she would need to contend with the Shaman's Shield. Even if she could get inside the magic barrier, Mount Lassen lay many miles to the northeast, and Mount Shasta was even farther away, due north. Winter would come at some point, bringing deep snows with it. Torr reasoned that the Tegs would move north to the Shaman's Shield once the populated areas were secured— if they weren't there already.

Torr sighed. One step at a time, he told himself. He skirted the camp and headed towards the river. Several long footsteps took him to a wide straight road lit with streetlamps and devoid of cars, except for soldiers sitting in parked vehicles every few hundred yards. He followed the road east to the river.

Parked jeeps blocked the bridge, and a few sleepy soldiers sat on rooftops and tailgates, with automatic rifles resting on their knees. The American River rushed below, tumbling over submerged boulders in a series of rapids that churned and frothed in the moonlight. Torr slinked away in the cover of shadows, and in a single breath was inside the cellar again.

He and his mother sat across from each other on dusty wooden chairs.

"You could crawl across the firebreak," Torr suggested. "They did not cut the stumps to the ground, and they cast lots of shadows." His mother nodded but did not look very confident. "Or the road is pretty exposed, but you might catch the guards sleeping," he said weakly, and she returned his glum look.

"You could swim across the river," he suggested, "and try to sneak past them on the mountain roads. It'll be harder for them to seal off those roads with all the twists and turns." Their family had taken road trips in those foothills when he was a child, exploring the small mountain towns and searching for wild herbs in the forest.

"Or, you could maybe cross through the camp," he said. "I didn't notice any dogs there."

Brianna's face pinched. "The dogs are with the patrols further south, as far as I could tell," she said. "But I'm too scared to cross the camp." Her eyes betrayed a helpless desperation that pulled at his heartstrings. "Crossing the river and using the cover of the forest might be the best bet," she said, her face creased with deep lines.

"Cassidy said you raised the wind when the Tegs came to our house," Torr said. "You could do that again."

She frowned and shook her head. "I can only do that in a deep meditative state. I can't call the wind and run at the same time. I suppose if I did raise it, that would create some chaos and an opportunity for me to run afterwards. But that was only the second time in my life I did that. I don't know if I can do it again."

"What about the plants?" Torr asked. "Can't they help you?"

Hope kindled in her eyes. "Yes, perhaps," she said slowly. "Can you bring me some samples from each area?"

"Okay," he said, and he was suddenly traversing the forest again in leaps and bounds.

From the firebreak he took a handful of wood chips and bark, stuffing them into his cargo pants pockets. He did not remember putting on his clothes in the tent, but in his dream he was fully clothed with boots and vest, and his three knives. He wondered if he closed his eyes and concentrated, could he change into his Miramar gear with his TAFT and Dashiel? But he was afraid that if he were successful, he would find himself in San Diego, far from his mother. He rested his hand on his wolf knife and peered into the shadows.

"Brother Wolf," he whispered. But he could not detect his spirit animal.

He took a breath and headed east. From the border of the Teg camp he took tufts of rye grass and a small stalk of prickly thistle. From the roadside he cut sprigs of fireweed, Scotch broom, and Queen Anne's lace. From the river's edge he took horsetail, live oak leaves, and rushes.

He returned to the cellar and held out his hands to show his mother what he had harvested, but the only plant that remained was the thistle. He set down the stalk of prickly leaves and purple flowers on an empty chair and dug into his pockets and pouches, but they were empty. He turned to his mother. "I had so many," he said, dumbfounded. He recited the plants he had collected, and she nodded.

"I'm impressed you were able to gather anything and bring it back at all." She picked up the thistle plant and ran her finger across a flower's fuzzy crown. "You got this from the camp, you say?"

Torr nodded, and her eyebrows knit together.

"Your instincts were correct," Brianna said. "I must cut through at their camp."

She sighed and stood, and then gathered her things and pulled on her backpack. His green Browning 6 Creed was strapped to the side of the pack.

"Ever use this?" he asked. "Still have any ammo?"

"I haven't shot it," she said. "It would make too much noise. Besides, I really don't want to kill anything. I'm surviving on plants and scavenged canned goods from abandoned homes."

He wondered if he would be able to shoot it in his dream state.

"Let's go," she said. "Dawn will come if we don't leave now."

Torr hiked with his mother through the forest. The raven hopped from branch to branch behind them, or flew ahead, leading the way. They came upon a hillside overlooking the camp when the sky was brightening to a pearly gray.

They got onto their bellies and crept up a small rise, which blocked their view of the camp. The hill was thick with grasses and tall thistles. They pulled up several of the prickly plants, and Torr laced them through the webbing on the back of his mother's pack. The long, spiny leaves poked up over her head and down over her legs in a sort of ghillie suit. She tucked some into the back of his belt and vest straps, the sharp prickles poking through to his skin.

They nodded to one another and crept forward over the rise. The camp spread out below them, murky in the encroaching dawn. Soldiers were stirring, and there were already short lines at the porta-potties.

They debated whether they should skirt the perimeter, weave their way between the tents, or cut straight through the center where a dirt road bordered by thistles bisected the camp.

His heart thudded in his chest when suddenly the raven took off, its wings whoosh-whooshing. It flew out over the camp and along the central dirt road and flapped slowly along its path, and then circled back towards them. Torr met his mother's eyes.

He took a deep breath and crawled on his elbows through the brush towards the camp entrance. His mother crept silently behind him. He reached the wood rail fence surrounding the camp. The entry gate stood open, and two soldiers in the front seats of a parked jeep were busily eating breakfast. A few dozen yards to their left, a guard's back was to them as he pissed into a clump of thistles.

Torr led the way under the rail fence, through the grass that bordered the camp, and into the overgrowth of grass and thistles that lined the dirt road. The sky brightened as the sun rose, and the camp stirred as soldiers slowly pulled themselves out of their slumber. The smell of coffee brewing wafted through the air, and a jeep rumbled by. A breeze rocked the grass and thistles back and forth.

Torr crept slowly, worming along on elbows and hips, and glanced over his shoulder. Brianna was a lump of thistles behind him, bobbing slightly as she moved forward. Torr took another breath and inched ahead.

They made their way painstakingly through the center of the camp, alongside the road that seemed much longer at ground level than it had from their vantage point up above. Occasionally a soldier crossed the road, or a vehicle drove by. But who would think that refugees would dare pass right under their noses?

They crossed the camp without incident and inched slowly across the outer boundary between two guard chairs, one of which was empty, and the other occupied by a Teg who was staring down at his handscreen.

They entered the undergrowth of the surrounding forest without any alarm being raised, and soon were beyond sight of the camp. They crawled for several more minutes, and finally rose to their feet. Birdsong surrounded them and pine boughs glowed gem-green in the morning light. Brianna removed the thistles from Torr's back and strung them through her front pack straps. He pushed aside a prickly leaf and kissed her cheek.

"I love you," he said.

"I love you, too," she said. "Tell Cassidy I love her and I'm sending her healing energy."

"I will," he said.

"If you see your father again, send him my love," she said, the corners of her eyes wrinkling with the effort to sound cheerful.

Torr nodded.

The raven descended with a smooth swoop and perched atop her backpack amidst a cluster of thistles. Brianna waved, stepped into a screen of oak branches, and was gone.

Torr opened his eyes. He was in his tent. Cassidy rolled over in her sleep, and the dreamcatcher hung motionless, staring down at him.

25

TENTMATES

"Jasper," Cassidy said across the dinner table.

He glanced up and met her eyes with the wounded expression he wore whenever he looked at her these days.

"May I please borrow the garnet?" she asked.

"Again?" he asked, his frown deepening.

"Yes. I need to translate the blue and gold book. There are a lot of pages."

He sighed and shoveled a forkful of rice into his mouth.

"You had it all day," she said.

"It's my crystal, Cassidy," he said with his mouth full.

She kept her eyes fastened on him until he relented and passed her the crystal. She took the garnet and stood up. "Come on, Hawk," she said.

"You're welcome," Jasper said.

"Thank you," she said, giving him a tight grin, and went to the wash basin to clean her plate.

Inside her tent, she and Hawk took turns holding the garnet and translating the passages from *Songs of Sirius*. She and Hawk came up with slightly different interpretations, and Cassidy attributed it to the different vocabularies they had adopted from living in different parts of the Free States and their different levels of education. They would both read a passage aloud, and then take the translation that was most easily understood, or in some cases, most elegant. It was poetry, after

all, she reasoned. Or, as the title of the book said, songs. She wondered
about the music that must have accompanied the lyrics.

The current lyric they were translating was called *The Ropes that
Bind Us,* and started like this:

> *Could be one rope or a thousand*
> *Silver and gold, silver and gold*
> *That bind us together*
> *Hearts and minds, hearts and minds*
> *Oh that it be love, oh that it be love*
>
> *Beware the dark bonds*
> *That enslave and kill us, enslave and kill us*
> *And suck the essence from our beings*
> *Body and soul, body and soul*
>
> *Around your neck*
> *On your knees*
> *Blade through the back*
> *Pierce the flesh, pierce the flesh*
>
> ...

Cassidy shivered as Hawk began translating the next passage, and
she glanced out through the thin gap between the door flaps.

"Someone's watching us," she said, and reached for her crystal ball.

"Who?" Hawk asked, setting aside the book.

"I don't know," she said, and gazed down into the rain-
bow-streaked sphere.

The vision of a man inside a tent came into focus. He was looking
through binoculars out a small side window. The vision zoomed out,
and Cassidy was able to see the location of the spy's tent in relation to
the Fen. It was in the second row of tents across the alley behind the
Fen's kitchen area, perfectly situated for an unobstructed view between
tents and through the back entrance of the Fen, straight at her tent.
The tarp she had hung back there had been pushed aside to allow easy
access to the alley. She shivered again and got to her feet.

"Get Torr," she said, not taking her eyes from the crystal ball.

Hawk hurried from the tent, and a minute later Torr pushed
through the door flaps with Hawk on his heels.

"What's up, Cassidy?" Torr asked.

She looked up. "The guy who's spying on us is in a tent behind the kitchen. Across the alleyway," she said.

Torr's mouth moved, but no words came out.

"What should we do?" Hawk piped up. "Should we go get him? Drag him out and beat him up?"

"No," Torr said. "I want to observe him and see if he's working alone."

"You mean, like, spy on the spy?" Hawk asked, his eyes bright.

"Something like that," Torr said.

"So do you believe me now?" Cassidy asked her brother.

Torr turned his gaze to her. "I never said I didn't believe you." She narrowed her eyes at him, and he continued, "Can you point out the exact tent?"

"Yes," she said. "But I don't want to tip him off. I can draw you a map."

"Or I can lend you some radios," Hawk said. "And Cassidy can direct you using her magic crystal ball from in here."

They both turned to Hawk, who was unclipping his radio from his belt. "Here," he said, handing his radio to Cassidy. "I'll get Raleigh to lend you his," he said to Torr, and ran from the tent.

Hawk returned with his two brothers. "We're good at sneaking around," Roanoke said. "We can be your scouts."

"Here, you can borrow mine," Raleigh said, handing his radio to Torr. "We have a private channel." He showed Torr and Cassidy how to tune to their band.

Cassidy set the radio aside, then pulled out her journal and began drawing a map. "Here's the tent," she said, drawing squares and an arrow pointing to the spy's tent. "I can alert you when he's about to leave," she said. "And you can follow him."

"I'll stay here and guard Cassidy," Hawk said, standing by the doorway and peeking outside.

Torr left with Raleigh and Roanoke, and Cassidy sat on her sleeping bag and stared into the glimmering sphere. The spy was still at his post, peering through binoculars in the direction of her tent. He would have seen Torr and the Boyer brothers coming and going, and she hoped they had sense enough to act casually and not walk directly up to the spy's tent. At that, the vision expanded, and she could see the

Fen's yard. Torr and the two brothers were leaving through the normal exit past the Boyers' tent, but instead of turning left towards Center Ring, they turned right onto Spoke Road 7.

Torr and the Boyers wandered the roadside, pretending to be interested in the assortment of wares displayed on ground tarps and checking in with Hawk and Cassidy periodically over the radios. Cassidy was able to maintain the vision in the crystal ball and reported that the spy had not moved.

After an hour had passed, the men came back to the Fen and sat with her in the tent while she kept her vigil. It was not until after night gong that the spy left his post and began snaking his way through the tent blocks towards the perimeter road. Torr and the two older Boyer brothers left to follow him, accompanied by Fritz and Frank. Cassidy directed them over the radio, and Torr's voice came through the speaker in a raspy whisper.

"I can see his energy trail," Torr said.

"What energy trail?" she asked.

"It's a line of energy coming from his belly, like a spider's web," he said. "Silvery, like a metallic thread, floating over the tents. I'm following it. I want to see what it connects to on the other end."

"He went into a tent near 10K," Cassidy said. "He's by himself. It looks like he lives there."

"Okay," Torr said. "Try to remember the exact location. I'm following the thread in the other direction."

Cassidy noted some landmarks around the spy's tent, then shifted her focus to her brother. He and his friends crept through empty alleyways and wove between clusters of tents, making their way towards the outermost blocks.

"I thought so," Torr said, standing in an alleyway and looking across Spoke Road 11 at a fenced-off camp. "Schlitzer."

The crystal ball widened its field of view, revealing an extensive fenced-in camp dominated by a large oval tent. The vision zoomed in through the tent's roof and took Cassidy inside a spacious pavilion. The floor was dotted with rugs and pillows occupied by small groups of men and women. A long wooden bar ran along one side of the tent, and two bare-breasted women were serving drinks. At the end of the bar sat a tall man with a mop of graying brown hair and a goatee, surrounded by a throng of people. She saw no threads attached to him, but the man glowed with a subtle silvery haze, and she surmised that he was the infamous Schlitzer. He flinched and looked around, as though he could sense her watching him. She shivered and covered the crystal ball with her hand, breaking the connection.

———————————)———————————

The next evening, Jasper and Berkeley drove into the Fen on a low-slung four-wheeler, the low whine of the electric engine quieting as the vehicle rolled to a stop.

Cassidy hopped up from the bench at the table. "Is that my moon rover?" she asked, walking over and fanning her hand through the cloud of dust.

"Well, technically it's Berkeley's. And mine for paying for the parts," Jasper said as he and Berkeley climbed out. It was a simple vehicle with a square frame, a roll bar, four large wheels, two lawn chairs serving as the seats, and a large engine mounted on the back with a metal bumper attached to the rear.

"It might be ugly," Berkeley said. "But it's a powerful little beast. Hank put in a jeep engine, so this thing really moves."

The Fensters gathered around to admire the makeshift rover.

"Can I take it for a ride?" Cassidy asked, brimming with excitement. With this thing, she could go where she wanted, when she wanted. "You say it's fast?" she asked Berkeley.

"Yep, and it'll climb over anything," he said. "Although it's flat as a pancake in the dome. You could crush some tents with it if you wanted," Berkeley said, running his hand over his forked beard.

"Could we take it outside?" Torr asked, walking over and sitting in the driver's seat.

"Sure, I suppose," Berkeley said. "If you have space suits."

"We have suits," Torr said.

"Get out. It's my buggy," Cassidy said, pushing on Torr's shoulder.

"Says who?" Torr asked. But he relinquished the driver's seat to Cassidy, and Jasper climbed into the passenger seat.

"You know how to drive a stick?" Jasper asked.

"Yeah. I drove my dad's truck. Remember?"

"Oh yeah. There's no key, just flip the start switch."

Cassidy pushed up the small metal switch, and the electric engine buzzed to life behind her and the vehicle vibrated underneath. She hiked up her long purple gown around her knees, and then pushed on the metal plate under her left foot, shifted into first gear, and pressed the accelerator. The buggy lurched forward, and then jerked to a stop. She tried again and drove slowly through the back exit and into the alleyway, heading south.

"Whoa," Jasper said, gripping the roll bar as she careened towards a tent and quickly steered back onto the path.

"The steering's too tight," she said, gritting her teeth.

"You'll get used to it."

She turned left onto a spoke road towards the spaceport and accelerated. The buggy lurched forward, and they zoomed along, pedestrians stepping out of the way. The breeze ruffled her hair, and she shifted into high gear.

"Whoa, slow down," Jasper said. "You'll tear up the road, and I'll hear it from Montana."

She down-shifted and turned onto the perimeter road in the direction of Earth, which floated above the horizon like a blue and gold lantern lighting the black sky.

At the sundial, she slowed to a stop, put it in park, and leaned back in her seat.

"Thanks," she said, meeting Jasper's gaze.

"You're welcome," he said, and frowned at her. "But don't get any harebrained ideas. It's still not safe to go out by yourself. We want to use it to haul the water trailer to the training yard and back."

"Okay," she said.

He opened his palm to her, and she put her hand in his. His skin was warm and sweaty, and his eyes glistened.

"Are you still mad at me?" he asked.

"No. I wasn't really mad at you." She held his eyes, and they glistened green like the ferns back home.

"Oh," he said, squeezing her hand. "I thought you were."

"No. I just don't feel good sometimes," she said, shifting her gaze towards Earth.

"I understand," he said.

They didn't say anything more as they held hands and gazed out at the heavens. Earth hung in the sky like a distant memory. The Seven

Sisters glimmered on the horizon, and the glowing bridge of the Milky Way spanned overhead, beckoning her to travel its starlit path.

————————) ————————

After night gong struck, she left Sky and Thunder's card game and walked the line of tents. Jasper was standing outside his tent, arms folded, watching her approach. She stood in front of hers and regarded him. She knew what he wanted, and she wanted it too, but her body seized up as though the reptilian brain sensed a predator—frozen like a lizard caught in the gaze of a hawk.

He unfolded his arms and removed his sunglasses, his eyes piercing hers.

She opened her clutched fists and poked her head through her tent doorway. "I'll be with Jasper," she said softly.

Torr was studying the speedster's flight manual and glanced up. "Okay," he said.

She let the canvas flap drop closed and met Jasper's gaze again. Without a word, she walked over to him and entered his tent. She removed her boots and placed them at the doorway.

He followed her and removed his own boots.

They didn't speak, but he watched as she pulled the Delosian gown up over her head, folded it, and placed it on a shelf. She stood there in bare feet, panties, and a white tank top. He stripped down to his shorts and got into bed, holding the sheet back for her to join him. She lay down next to him and settled into the warmth of his arms, and for a moment she was brought back to Earth with the familiarity of his scent and the beating of his heart.

He pulled her close, and she pressed her lips to the smooth, throbbing skin of his neck.

————————) ————————

They spent the night together. She didn't let it get sexual, aside from a few kisses, but she enjoyed the comfort of his body, and the next morning he was in a better mood than she had seen him in weeks.

As for herself, she felt conflicted. She liked being with him, but at random moments her body remembered Balthazar's and she was gripped with fear. Still, she was encouraged that she hadn't suffered a major panic attack and had been able to sleep in Jasper's arms the whole night through.

After breakfast, Jasper prepared to head off to his trading business. They slipped into his tent, where he hugged her and gazed down into her eyes. Their lips met in gentle kisses, and she pressed her cheek to his, breathing him in. It felt good, and normal, the way it was supposed to feel.

"See you later," he said, kissing her again.

"Okay," she murmured.

After he left, she stood in the center of his tent, feeling warm and glowing. But the pattering of her heart was laced with trepidation, and she cursed Balthazar for tearing her flesh and poisoning her spirit.

She sighed and stepped out into the light, then waited for the Boyers outside their tent to go to the training yard. Hawk came out with a grin on his face, followed by his brothers and father.

"We have a surprise for you," Hawk said, and held out two hand radios. "We made these for you and Torr."

"You did?" Cassidy asked. "I thought you guys had a backlog of orders." She glanced at Durham.

"We do," Durham said. "But they've waited months already, they can wait a little longer." He smiled, and Cassidy reached for a radio.

"I set you and Torr up with your own secure channel," Durham said, and showed her how to use the radio's controls. "Here's the Fen's channel," Durham said, tuning in to a different band. "And these are open Peary Dome channels." He cycled through several frequencies. "And there are some other channels I can show you later."

"This is great," Cassidy said. "Thank you so much. How much do we owe you?"

"Torr already paid us in advance," Durham said. "Let's go bring him his."

Torr was in the back with Berkeley, hooking up the training yard's water wagon to the moon buggy. Torr was thrilled with the radios, and he and Cassidy practiced communicating on their channel. When it was time to leave, Cassidy hopped into the buggy's passenger seat and rode with Torr as he navigated slowly over the roads to the training yard, with the Fensters trotting alongside.

Between training sessions, Raleigh showed her and Torr how to listen into the Guild's private channel, and the Rangers'.

"Can't hack into Schlitzer's, though," Raleigh said. "It's too secure. Don't know who set his up, but they know what they're doing."

"And don't let on that you have access to the traders' and Rangers' channels," Roanoke said, "or they'll change the encryption keys and we might not be able to get back in."

That afternoon, Cassidy left the Smith sisters at Berkeley's sewing machine, pulled the tarp curtain closed across the alleyway entrance, and retreated into Jasper's tent to be by herself. The woodsy scent of him lingered in the quiet space. She sat on the bed, gathering the panels of her carbon fiber skirt into her lap, and then pulled out her crystal ball and gazed into it.

The man was pacing outside his spy tent, probably frustrated that she had blocked his view. She wondered again why he was spying on them. Torr was sure the man was connected to Schlitzer. They had considered that maybe Schlitzer was keeping tabs on the Fen simply because they were one of the most powerful groups in the dome. In any case, they had decided the man did not pose an immediate threat, and it would be more valuable to keep surveilling him than to confront him or Schlitzer.

She shifted her attention, searching for Jasper. She found him inside the spaceport hangar with several other men, watching a compression chamber door slowly open. She unclipped the radio from her belt, tuned in to the Guild channel, and listened in. A dusty freighter exited the landing bay and floated slowly to a parking spot at the other end of the hangar. The scruffy pilot stepped down from the cockpit and was immediately surrounded by traders. The pilot led them to the back of the craft. Cassidy looked more closely. Something about the man struck her as odd. His stern bearing was incongruous with his unkempt clothing and overgrown hair and beard. There was something familiar about him, but she couldn't recall having ever encountered him before.

Cassidy spent the next hour watching in the crystal ball and listening on the radio as sacks of rice and crates of produce were unloaded from the freighter. There was constant chatter on the radio channel as traders verbally inventoried the contents for unseen listeners. She recognized Ramzy's voice among the mix, arguing with someone over how many sacks of rice he needed. Another voice popped in, asking if there was any booze.

Jasper appeared and disappeared from view, climbing in and out of the freighter as he helped unload and stack crates. The cargo hold was finally emptied and all the goods stacked to the side. Bidding ensued, and the closing bids were double the asking prices. The traders gathered around the cab of the craft, and the competition grew fierce as they bid on chewing tobacco, alcohol, chocolate, and coffee. She held her breath, then exhaled with disappointment as Jasper lost the chocolate to another man who kept doubling the bid. Jasper did manage to score two small bags of coffee beans, however, and her lingering resentment over his preoccupation with his trading business faded. After all, the Fen's supply tents were stocked with food again, and it was largely due to Jasper's efforts.

She held her breath again and shifted her focus. She landed inside the sadist Balthazar's rape room. The two current sex slaves were sleeping on the bed, huddled together. Cassidy's insides clenched. She closed her eyes, and two warm tears rolled down her cheeks.

————————) ————————

"Why don't you just move in with me, Cass?" Jasper asked that evening, holding her gaze across the Fen's table.

"Into your tent?" she asked, her insides fluttering.

"I would invite you to move into my mansion, but it's under renovation at the moment," he said with a half grin.

"Um ...," she said, twisting her fingers together.

"You don't have to," he said quickly. "It's just an idea."

She swallowed. "I'm afraid I'm not ready," she said, staring down at her hands.

"I know," he said gently. "But I miss you."

"That's because you work all the time," she mumbled.

"I know I do. But if we shared a tent, then we'd have more time together."

Deep in her belly, darkness oozed around a bright spark, clouding its brilliance. She curled her hands into fists and looked up at Jasper. His eyes were dark and brooding, as though she had already said no. "Okay," she blurted out.

His eyes widened. "Okay?" he asked.

"Yes," she said resolutely. "Yes. I will not let fear win." She raised her chin and held his gaze.

They smiled at one another, and her light grew a little brighter.

————————) ————————

After a few days of sharing Jasper's tent, it felt as though she had always lived there. She liked being part of his life in the little ways that living in the same space offered. She liked sleeping by his side and talking into the early hours of the morning. She knew he wanted to have sex, and she did too, but any time they began to get intimate she froze and had trouble breathing, bringing any advances to a halt. It didn't help that Torr and Blaire had taken advantage of her absence and spent their nights together in Torr's tent, the muffled sounds of their lovemaking audible through the canvas walls.

"I can't sleep," she said one night after Jasper had dozed off and Torr and Blaire were at it again.

"Huh?" Jasper mumbled as she pushed aside the blanket and got up.

"I'm getting some tea," she said.

"Okay, Cassafrass," he said, and turned over, wrapping the blanket around himself.

She put on clothing and went out into the yard. Ming-Long and Khaled were on guard duty and were sitting across from each other at the table, playing chess. She pulled the tarp curtain across the back exit to the alleyway. The spy had gone home for the night, but she felt better with the curtain closed anyway.

"You guys are keeping a close eye on things, I see," she said as she pulled a cup off the drying rack and turned on a burner to heat up some water.

"We rely on our ears," Khaled said. "You said you can't sleep and want some tea, and Torr and Blaire are in lust."

"You're so smart," Cassidy said, and sat next to Ming-Long while she waited for the water to boil.

Khaled continued talking while moving his rook up the board. "Buck snores like a chainsaw, Thunder is his very own farting orchestra, and some loser from across the alley dumped some garbage back there after night gong. We caught him and made him clean it up. Another exciting night at the Fen."

"You're an herbalist," Ming-Long said, glancing at Cassidy after capturing Khaled's bishop. "Can't you brew something to help you sleep?"

"I've tried different things," she said. "Nothing really helps."

What she needed was something to make her forget. She had looked through the red notebook more times than she could count, but it was always the same illegible scrawl. Just when she needed its help the most, the plant spirit medicine had abandoned her. But always lurking in the background was Greenwash. Several times she had been on the verge of begging Jasper to find more, but she was afraid he would actually get some and she would not be strong enough to resist. She knew the drug was bad for her, and she had promised Torr she wouldn't take any more. But it was always there in the recesses of her mind, reminding her of the rush of euphoria followed by a foggy slumber where time did not matter and memories were washed away. The other Murian drug, Fool's Passion, tasted foul and scared her a bit, so that was not so hard to avoid.

When the water was hot, she made tea for the three of them and sat down again to watch them play chess. If Ming-Long bore any hard feelings after she had rejected him for Jasper, he showed no signs of it. They had continued relating as normal in training class and as campmates, and he seemed to have forgotten all about it. He glanced at her, and she smiled.

"My grandfather was an herbalist," Ming-Long said, taking Khaled's knight.

"He was?" Cassidy said, perking up with interest.

"Yeah. I have his old book. Want to see it?"

"Sure," she said, sipping at her tea.

Khaled moved a pawn, and Ming-Long moved his queen diagonally across the board while he continued speaking. "He was an acupuncturist. Herbs are a big part of that practice. He used to take me with him to the mountains to collect plants. Those were the days." The skin around his eyes crinkled as he smiled nostalgically.

"What are the mountains like in China?" she asked.

Ming-Long described taking a train all day and night through the countryside to get to a chain of steep green mountains to collect leaves and roots and seeds. When they returned home, they dried them and ground them into powders.

Ming-Long beat Khaled at chess, then went into his tent and returned with a large book. "Here," he said, opening the leather-bound tome and setting it on the table in front of her.

She immediately became lost in its wonders, her senses absorbed by plant samples that had been pressed onto each page: leaves, flattened flowers, and thin cross sections of stems, roots, and seeds. The colors were faded, but she could still detect purples and yellows and reds lingering within dried petals. Tears came to her eyes, and she lowered her face to sniff at the pages, still pungent after so many years.

"They're so beautiful," she whispered. "Real plants. It's unbelievable." A wave of homesickness overwhelmed her. "I wish I had done this. All I have are drawings and a few pressed leaves and flowers, when I could have been collecting plant samples my whole life."

"You have bags of herbs," he reminded her.

"Yeah, but they'll be gone eventually, and these are ..." Her voice trailed off as she turned page after page to reveal leaves and flowers that were familiar, yet not. She recognized only a few, and the handwriting was in Chinese characters that she could not read. Earth was so vast that a country all the way on the other side of the globe had many varieties of plants she had never seen before. Her heart grew heavy. The other side of the globe, which now she would never visit. A world lost to her forever.

"Show me your drawings later," Ming-Long said.

"I will," she said, and turned the page to a collection of faded orange blossoms.

———————————— ❱ ————————————

Cassidy sat in Jasper's tent and opened the speedster's flight manual. She found the section on high-speed flight and skimmed the pages. It appeared that the safest way to navigate in high-speed mode was to use the auto-navigation feature. That required uploading precise topographic maps, setting target coordinates and altitude, and combining them with radar detection. Target coordinates could be saved and labeled. The good news was that there were no weather events on the moon to worry about, and the weak gravity and lack of atmosphere made the calculations simpler. She assumed Balthazar had uploaded moon maps, and he had hopefully saved the coordinates for the structure where she had been held, as well as Gandoop Spaceport. Probably Peary Dome was also stored in memory, and if she had known, she could have fled to Peary directly and arrived much faster, saving herself that long, agonizing escape flight. She went back to the beginning of the section and started reading in earnest. Some of the information was very technical, but she did her best to understand. It would be safest to try it the first time with Kai there. She would go to the speedster later and examine the controls, and see what maps and locations were already in the system.

She studied the manual until she couldn't absorb any more information—there were so many controls to learn. She yawned and hoped Kai would give her lessons. She left the tent and walked to the back area and found Berkeley in the workshop tent.

"Hey," he greeted her. "I was going to come find you. Look what I made for you," he said, handing her a bracelet.

"For me? Thanks, Berkeley," she said. It was one of the intricately braided bracelets he made from embroidery floss. This one was red and blue and green, with a pair of red coral beads hanging from the ends.

"Here, I'll tie it on for you," he said.

She held out her wrist. "What did I do to deserve such a gift?" she asked, smiling.

"Do you need to do something to deserve a gift?" he asked, fastening a knot at her wrist.

"Did you weave magic into it?" she joked, admiring the complicated pattern.

"Maybe a little," he said slyly.

She looked up at him, and he met her gaze with his big round owl-eyes. "What kind of magic?" she asked as the back of her neck tingled.

"Just a little protection spell. Nothing much. Just rub the beads when you remember to. The more you rub them, the stronger the spell becomes."

"Hmmm," she mused, rubbing the smooth round beads between her thumb and forefinger. "Did Eridanus teach you this one, too?" she asked.

"Yes, he did."

"Can you teach me?" she asked.

Berkeley shook his head. "No, I cannot. I would if I could, but I don't know how to teach you. It's an energy thing."

She tilted her head to the side. "Is he still alive?"

"I don't know. I think so. I hope so. I looked for him last time I was on Delos, but they said he had retreated into a cave to live in silence. Nobody would tell me where the cave was. I'm an outsider, after all."

"I want to meet him," she said, rubbing the beads.

———————————)———————————

The next evening, she spent some more time studying the flight manual, starting from the beginning of the thick book. When she'd tired of the dense material, she took out her green and yellow herb notebooks—the ones that contained her plant sketches and the few samples she had collected. She left the tent and went in search of Ming-Long to show him.

He and Khaled were in front of Ming-Long's tent, sitting on crates facing each other with another crate between them, playing chess.

Ming-Long looked up from the chessboard as she approached. "Shhh," he said, casting Khaled a furtive glance.

Cassidy pulled up a crate and sat down. "Shhh, what?" she asked. "What are you talking about?"

"Nothing," Khaled said, moving a pawn up the board.

Cassidy rolled her eyes. "Come on. What's the big secret? You talking about Becka again?"

Khaled blushed and shook his head.

"Nothing you'd be interested in," Ming-Long said, and took Khaled's pawn.

She kept her eyes trained on Ming-Long, and he lifted his gaze to meet hers. "If you really must know, we were talking about Schlitzer. And Gabira."

"What about them?" she asked.

Ming-Long sighed, and said under his breath, "They have the only stashes of Greenwash left in the dome, and they are charging crazy prices. That's all. But I shouldn't tell you that. Torr would be mad. So don't tell him I said anything, okay?"

"I don't care about Greenwash anymore," she said, lifting her chin defiantly. The mention of Greenwash made her skin tingle, and she tried to force the sensation down. But it was as though it were a living creature and the more she pushed it away the harder it pushed back. "Why are you talking about it?" she asked. "Do you take it?"

"No, I hate the stuff," Ming-Long said. "But other people are looking for it, so I thought it might be a good way to make some quick cash. But I don't have that kind of gold." He cocked one eyebrow at her.

"Well, don't look at me," she said. "I don't have any spare gold."

Ming-Long shrugged and returned his attention to the game. She wondered if rumors about her stash of gold had made their way around the Fen. If he was trying to hint that she could lend him some, she was not interested in helping anybody make a drug deal. She gritted her teeth and watched the men move their chess pieces, rolling her bracelet's red beads distractedly between her fingertips.

"Algol's hell," Ming-Long said as Khaled plucked a white bishop off the board and laughed gleefully.

"I'll show you my plant drawings later," she said, and stood up to leave.

"Oh. Okay. Sorry," Ming-Long said. "Don't forget."

"I won't," she said. She took her notebooks and headed for the back to find Tatsuya.

The elderly man was sitting at his tattooing bench, cleaning his needles.

"Can I visit your bonsai tree?" she asked.

"Yes, of course," Tatsuya said, and nodded towards his tent.

She removed her boots at his doorway, stepped into the quiet space, and sat on the meditation pillow. She set her notebooks on the floor, focused on the small fragrant tree, and tried to still her trembling limbs.

———————)———————

The next day, she crept out of bed at morning gong and sat inside the tent doorway facing the yard. The gonging faded and rustles of morning activity slowly broke the silence of curfew. Jasper stirred behind her.

A crescent Earth gazed down at her. Her mother and father were out there. Cassidy imagined them looking up at the moon, thinking of her and Torr and wondering if they were safe. Her mother would cling to the belief that Cassidy and Torr were on some sort of destined mission to find the Star People. That the lunar land had been passed down to them for a reason. That this was the moon of crystal sand.

She lowered her eyes to the crystal ball, which sat cool and smooth in her palm. Cassidy stiffened as the crystal shimmered with rainbows and resolved into an image of the dusky moonscape. The three massive Anaximenes craters loomed like vast pits. The image zoomed in on dark rolling dunes between the three craters and centered on a structure whose lines blended into the landscape, the surface of the building the same color as the surrounding dust. The view zoomed in and passed through the roof, and suddenly Cassidy was inside Balthazar's house, in the living room furnished with two large leather couches, an overstuffed chair, a wet bar, and a wall screen. The room was dimly lit, and empty.

She inhaled sharply as the vision shifted, expanding through closed doors and settling onto the bed where Balthazar had a girl pinned under him. They were both naked, and the girl looked to be about Cassidy's age. It took all of Cassidy's will not to close her eyes and lose the vision. The girl seemed to be begging Balthazar to stop as he wrapped a hand around her throat. In a panic, the girl clawed at his neck and face. A savage look gleamed from his eyes as Balthazar let go of her neck, captured both her wrists in one large hand, and with the other hand swung with an open palm, slapping her full across the face, and then grabbed her neck again.

The scene stabbed at Cassidy's core as though a sword cut up through her belly and into her heart. She couldn't breathe, and the view shifted from the bed and took her through the closet door to reveal a second girl huddled in the far corner of the dark bathroom, hiding in the shower stall, shaking. Cassidy tore her eyes away from the crystal ball and found herself back inside Jasper's tent. Her hands trembled, and the crystal ball rolled onto her lap. Her breaths came in painful spasms as she choked, gasping for air and straining to hold herself together. She wanted to run away from the vision. She wanted to run to save the women. She couldn't do either, and she couldn't pretend it was just her imagination.

"Jasper," she said, crawling onto the bed and shaking his shoulder.

"Mmm," he replied sleepily.

"We need to figure out how to get those girls out."

"What girls?" he mumbled.

"The new ones Balthazar is holding captive. Can you get some guns?" He cracked his eyelids open and looked up at her. "Those girls need help," she pleaded. "They'll never be able to get out on their own."

Jasper's lips tightened. "Cassidy," he said. "We can't control what goes on outside Peary Dome."

"That's our land," she said stubbornly.

"You own a piece of paper," Jasper said. "Powerful men occupy your land. We can't help everybody."

She rose to her feet, helpless anger boiling inside her. She pulled on her black pants and leather jerkin and stormed from the tent, looking for Torr. She heard him inside his tent with Blaire. It sounded like they were having sex. She turned, and Jasper was behind her.

"You don't have to run away from me, you know," he said. "We were having a conversation."

"You don't want to help."

"I do want to help," he said, his eyes flashing.

"You said we can't help everybody."

"That's right."

"It's like you don't even care."

"I do care."

"And who's everybody?" she asked. "If I were going to help everybody, I'd be calling the Star People down to Earth with golden armies." Sarcasm was acidic on her tongue. "I'm talking about the women on our land. There are two in there. They need our help."

"Cassidy," he said, taking her shoulders and holding her firmly as she tried to shake him off. "Listen to me." He caught her arm as she twisted away. "Knock it off. Listen." His hands were rough as they grabbed her upper arms. "Listen to me." He held her with steely eyes. "Cassidy. There's a regular black market trade in Earth women."

Cassidy's heart dropped. "Don't you think I know that?" she asked. "Where do you think Anna and Maria came from?"

He took a breath and loosened his grip.

"But tell me what you know," she said, her heart pounding.

He pulled her back inside their tent and spoke in a harsh whisper. "The Tegs and the Cephean Federation sell Earth females to other planets." She stopped breathing and slowly wrapped her fingers around his hands, squeezing them. His voice was hushed. "They bring them to the moon. By the ship full. They transfer them to interstellar freighters and send them off to slave traders on Delos, and other planets."

A flood of bile burned her stomach and rose to her mouth. She wanted him to stop, but he kept on, gripping her hands tightly. "They used to bring them through Peary Spaceport, before the Free Men won control. Now they take them through Gandoop." Jasper's large, warm hands held the two of hers that had somehow curled together into a single fist. "Why do you think I was so freaked out when you went missing?" Cassidy felt herself swallow. "Cassidy. If we rescue those two girls. Even if we kill that man, Balthazar. There will be more. More girls. More evil men. It will not stop."

Tears were running down her face, and she hadn't even noticed until one fell with a soft splat onto her jerkin. The tears had come of their own accord, springing from a depth that felt no anger, only sorrow. Jasper had stopped speaking, but she held his eyes, finding comfort in the knowledge that it pained him as much as it did her. She pulled one hand away and wiped her nose with the back of it. She found her voice, scratchy and hollow. "What do we do, then? Sit by and watch?" She sniffed loudly.

He shrugged helplessly, his face falling in surrender. His hands dropped to his sides.

"No," she said softly. "We take out the whole operation. We take over Gandoop Spaceport. Cut off the black market traffic completely."

"How?" he asked. "We can't attack the spaceport without destroying it."

She lifted an eyebrow meaningfully.

"No, Cassidy. We don't have the weapons to destroy a structure like that."

She held his gaze, and her jaw hardened. She would find a way. She had to.

26

NANA'S RING

R idge was holed up in the sitting room of his private chambers at the house, trying to relax on his couch. Balty's and Athena's drunken laughter filtered in from the living room. He couldn't tolerate their company any longer. Their relationship disgusted him. How could either of them pretend it was real? Did Balty think some virgin teenager he had raped truly had loving feelings for him? And was Athena stupid enough to fall for him?

Ridge inhaled the gray gloom of melancholy. And what kind of delusion was he weaving for himself regarding Giselle? He could tell she despised him. Did he think if he revealed his true identity—if he appeared as his clean-cut, filthy-rich self instead of a hairy, slobby outer rim mining lord—that she'd suddenly invite him to share her silken pillows? Not likely.

But he couldn't shake his obsession, as much as his rational mind told him he was being an idiot. Thoughts of Giselle tormented him day and night. And so he continued indulging his fantasies and plotting ways to fulfill them. Perhaps it was how their trap worked. Shove a thorn into his heart and leave him with no other option than to beg them to pull it out. But to do so he needed to figure out how to evade Gabira's trap. He didn't want to risk being stranded in her enchanted olive grove again.

His grandmother would have been able to outwit Gabira. He was her grandson, so he should be able to resist her magic as well. He got

440

to his feet and paced the floor. Unclipping the radio from his belt, he turned to his family's private frequency. "Papa," he said, sending the signal over his antenna towers and through the Gandoop facility's relays. "You out there?"

A few seconds later, Ishmar's gravelly voice came through. "Rjidna?"

"Yeah. Hi. Do you have any old stuff of Nana's? You know, trinkets, or jewelry?"

"I think so. A few things in a box somewhere. Come over and you can take a look."

Ridge stalked silently past the living room, hopped into his speedster, and flew over to Gandoop. He found his father in his underground chamber, sipping tea with pine nuts in it. Ridge accepted a cup, stirred in a couple of teaspoons of sugar, and waited while Ishmar finished his tea and told him about the latest drama of Ramzy calling and pleading with him to end the food embargo.

"I didn't know what to tell him," Ishmar said. "What am I going to say, some Teg general has us by the balls?" Ishmar shook his head, looking worn down. "He wants to know why we're letting some no-good outer rim mining lord make a killing off them, and why we won't open up normal trading channels." Ishmar arched his eyebrows at Ridge.

Ridge shrugged his shoulders. "I'm just having a little fun. I feel sorry for those poor bastards. What Balty is doing is not right."

"I know," Ishmar sighed. "But be careful. That man has a wicked temper."

Ridge nodded.

"Well," Ishmar said, sighing. "Hopefully Balty will tire of his dastardly little game and move on to something else, like setting his eyes on another planet or something. We can only hope." Ishmar smiled his kind smile, and Ridge smiled back, feeling like a liar giving his tacit encouragement of such a notion. Ishmar didn't know Balty like Ridge did. Balty was like a pit bull. He would never let go of the moon until he had conquered it.

"What do you want with Nana's things?" Ishmar asked.

They set down their tea cups, left the chamber, and entered a small storage room down the hall.

Ishmar pointed to a box on a bottom shelf. Ridge pulled it out, blew off a cloud of dust, and took it back to the chamber. He sat on Ali's cot to examine its contents, removing them one by one. The smell of the box reminded him of his grandmother, transporting him to her stuffy living room that smelled of wax candles and dried rose petals. He remembered sitting next to her on the hard couch and threading embroidery needles for her as she stitched a pillow cover with bright flowers.

Inside the dusty box were several small cardboard boxes filled with costume jewelry, a wooden box that used to hold letters and now was empty, and a brass letter opener with a hawk's head for a handle. A yellowed envelope held faded photos. He found photos of himself and Ali when they were young boys, so innocent and full of hope. A photo of Ishmar as a young man reminded him that his father used to be handsome. A wedding photo of his grandmother and grandfather looked to be from a different century. Ridge felt like he did not know them at all and didn't think he would want to. Most people smiled for their wedding pictures. This pair wore stern frowns. It made him shiver. His grandfather was a distant, flickering memory of a man who drove a taxi for a living, working two shifts every day, and on the rare days he was home only wanted to eat and sleep.

There were several photos of Ali's mother, including a wedding photo. She was an attractive woman, and Ali had her eyes. Ridge noted with a twinge of sadness that there were no photos of his mother among his grandmother's collection. Nana had never liked her second daughter-in-law. The photo of Ridge's mother that he kept stashed in his top drawer back at the house was of a beautiful, smiling young woman who always made him overwhelmingly happy and sad whenever he looked at her—so he kept her memory tucked safely away in its envelope, and only pulled it out when the sharp fangs of loneliness drove him to it.

He glanced up at Ishmar, who was seated on his cushion drinking more tea, and said, "I wanted something like that big black ring she wore. The one she was buried with."

Ishmar pursed his lips distastefully. "She wasn't buried with that."

"She wasn't?"

"No, I had them cut it off her. It was the ugliest thing. But she wanted you to have it."

Ridge sat up straight. "She did?"

"Yes." Ishmar rubbed his sagging eyes and pushed himself to his feet. "I forgot all about that. It's the ugliest damn ring. I always hated that thing."

Ridge hovered behind his father while Ishmar dug through a drawer filled with his own treasures: ancient Earth coins in little plastic bags, gold cufflinks and tie-clasps, key chains filled with old brass keys.

Ridge hadn't known his grandmother had left anything for him and felt a strange warmth bloom inside him. "I always thought she hated me."

Ishmar glanced over his shoulder at him. "Of course she didn't hate you. You were her favorite."

"I was? She yelled at me all the time."

"She yelled at everyone. She said you reminded her of Papa."

"Papa? Really?"

Ishmar's hand emerged with the black ring. "Here it is."

Ridge's blood surged. He took it and examined it in the light. It was heavy, featuring a large oval obsidian, pure black and shining like a glint of water at the bottom of a well. The stone was cut with one large central facet encircled by smaller facets and was bordered by several small fake black gems. It was truly hideous. Thankfully, it did not evoke the ghost of his grandmother but was simply a piece of volcanic glass. The copper band was cut, and the tarnished circle was slightly deformed where someone had cut it free from her finger and tried to bend it back into shape. He stashed the ring in his flight suit pocket and returned the dusty box to the shadows of the storeroom.

After sharing a simple meal of quinoa and chickpeas with Ishmar and Ali, Ridge left for his lab at Last Chance. Once there, he took the ring to his workbench. He carefully removed the stone from its cheap, corroded-green copper setting and removed the gaudy border of smaller glass gems. He polished the stone, and after drawing out its natural luster, found it to be intriguing. He fashioned a gold setting and band that fit his right ring finger. He fixed the large gemstone in its setting and put aside the small border gems. He gazed at the obsidian, trying to divine how his grandmother had used it. No secrets revealed themselves. The only way to discover its powers was to try it out on a witch.

———————— ☽ ————————

Ridge donned his Jidna disguise and headed for Peary before he lost his courage. He knew he would be harassed by the Guild traders for showing up without food, but he didn't have the patience to shuttle freight today. He climbed out of his battered Last Chance speedster in the Peary hangar, fending off the trader sharks who swarmed him. The only one who wasn't visibly upset at him for arriving empty-handed was the lone female trader, Phyllis. She walked with him to the front exit, and by the time they stepped out into the sunshine she had effectively placed an order for food she needed for her clientele. Jidna shook her hand, and she held it in her bony grip. Clasping his hand with both of hers, she turned it to inspect his ring.

"Expecting trouble?" she asked, squinting up at him with a friendly grin.

He examined her brown eyes and the crow's feet at their corners. Her gaze drilled right through him. He wouldn't be surprised if she knew he was wearing a disguise. He could practice using the ring with her. She didn't feel evil and conniving like Gabira.

"Care to help me figure out how it works?" he asked jokingly.

Her lips drew into a straight line. "Well, now," she said. "That kind of knowledge could cost you."

An answering smile spread across his face. "I have gold, if that's what you need."

Phyllis returned his grin and led him to her camp. She bustled him into a food storage tent, dragging in two lawn chairs with her and closing the door flaps. He could see why she wanted more food. Her storage shelves were almost empty. Maybe he would give her a price break on her food order, if she could actually help him.

He pulled out a handful of gold coins, found six Delosian Stags, and set them carefully on a plastic crate that served as a low table. She eyed the gold hungrily, then leaned over and took his hand, rubbing her thumb over the ring's black facets. "Let me see," she said, and closed her eyes.

After a minute of silence, she began speaking in a monotone. "I see you surrounded by dark gray storm clouds. Green leaves are snapping in the wind. Olives are falling from branches like rain, and crows are feasting on them. You are standing in the center of the storm, trying to recall who you are."

His spine shivered, and he pulled his hand out of her warm grasp.

She opened her eyes and spoke in a more normal tone. "It is important that you remember who you are, so the storm cannot harm you." She paused and frowned. "That's all I have for you, I'm sorry." She smiled hesitantly, afraid she had not given him enough to earn any gold.

He nodded slowly. He thought it was enough. He pushed the stack of coins towards her. "Thank you," he said, and took his leave.

————————————) ————————

The guards outside Gabira's cave recognized him by now and were learning to expect coffee beans and gold, and to not ask questions. He only had gold for them today, but they did not complain. Gabira was waiting for him out in the hallway, her hands on her ample hips.

"What do you want?" she snapped.

"I was in the neighborhood," he said brightly, acting as though she were glad to see him. "Thought I'd drop by and say hi. I know you must miss me." He flashed her a smug grin and let himself into the gilt-walled chamber. No doubt she expected him to demand his gold back. More important to him was getting at her daughter. The flamboyant peacock, not the frumpy pigeon. And avoiding her olive grove from hell.

He sat on a stack of rugs, noting their fine weaving. The top one had a tree of life on it, and he judged it to be of Pakistani origin. "Nice rug," he said. "My great-uncle used to deal in rugs." She frowned and pulled the cord behind her head and sat back with her arms folded.

"Why do you let me in here if you're so unhappy to see me?" he asked cordially.

She continued her silent treatment and picked at her fingernails. He regarded the mural of the olive grove painted over the backdrop of golden sunshine and wondered if the painting had anything to do with her magic. He thought not. After a few minutes of awkward silence, the door opened and two serving girls entered the room with tea and a small plate of candied almonds and dried brown apricots.

Gabira shot out her first exploratory tendril while he chewed on an apricot. He noted with delight how the dark tendril gravitated towards his ring but then bounced off one of the smaller facets to grope harmlessly in the air. He watched her eyes, and they met his, her displeasure palpable.

He kept his expression flat, wanting her to try again, and she did. The same thing happened, and he nearly let out a triumphant chuckle, but swallowed it back. He did, however, allow himself a small grin.

"Looking for something?" he asked.

She sneered, her raised lip revealing greenish teeth. So, she was still taking that foul drug, Greenwash. No wonder she was so grumpy. Addicts were always childishly selfish and unpleasant to be around.

"Where is your lovely daughter?" he asked.

"Daleelah?" she asked, lifting her eyebrows innocently.

"Yes," he said, playing her game.

She pulled on the cord again, and soon both Giselle and Daleelah appeared.

"What did you bring us this time?" Daleelah asked, her big brown eyes bright with anticipation.

"Just my charming company," he retorted. "What do you have for me?"

The question clearly flustered her. Her small hands flew together fretfully, and her eyes grew round with chagrin. Giselle and Gabira merely glared at him. Daleelah stood up, smoothing her teal-blue robe primly, and left the chamber.

Gabira's and Giselle's dark eyes trained on him as though he were a poisonous scorpion they were intent on crushing. Gabira's crystal pendant glinted at him. He took in a deep, silent breath. Now would be the true test of Nana's ring. He met their eyes bravely, his head swimming for a moment. He blinked, trying to steady his wavering vision, and realized he should not have come. Nausea welled up in his throat and sweat beaded on his brow. He dug his fingers into the rug, trying to maintain his balance and not fall over in a retching heap.

The gray-green olive leaves in the mural fluttered gently, a warm breeze bathing his face. Suddenly his stomach felt better, and he took in a great gulp of air through his mouth and exhaled slowly through his nose. Again he inhaled, and the scent of the olive grove calmed his nerves.

Gabira smiled sweetly at him. "More almonds?" she asked, passing him the plate. The gold brocade tent flapped joyfully in the dancing zephyr, and he returned her smile. "Wine?" she asked, tugging the cord behind her head.

The serving girls returned with golden goblets and a small jug of red wine that Giselle took from the girls. Her cleavage exposed itself nicely as she leaned over the table to serve him. A sloppy grin slackened his lips, and he took a sip. It was sweet.

Daleelah entered the tent as the serving girls left, and she came to sit shyly at his side.

"Here, I made this," she said. "You can have it. See? I painted it using the panther you gave me as a model."

He took a small lacquered box from her fingers. Painted on the top was a black panther crouched in a slinking prowl, its green eyes watching him guardedly.

"It's a very good likeness," he said appreciatively, "but I didn't give you a panther." He laughed softly, wondering if this dull-witted girl was mentally deficient.

She cocked her head at him as Gabira barked, "Daleelah, come here."

She ignored her mother, looking at him steadily. "You remember," she said, taking a small statuette of a panther from her pocket and balancing it on her palm. It was gold and covered with black diamonds that reminded him of the gems that had encircled his grandmother's ring. His mental clarity returned to him as though a loud bell had wrenched him from a deep sleep.

"Daleelah, you fool," Gabira snarled, and strode across the room, tugging at Daleelah's wrist. Daleelah's fingers curled around the statuette possessively as her mother dragged her around the table and sat her roughly next to Giselle.

He still had the little box in his palm and closed his hand around it, the large central facet of his obsidian ring catching his own reflection. Yes, he was Rjidna Gandoop, and this was a trap. He held his own eyes in the reflection, repeating his name to himself. He breathed evenly, counting his inhalations and exhalations, and blocked out the irate prattle of Gabira as she scolded Daleelah for being a brainless ninny. Ridge chastised himself for removing the fake gems from the border of the black ring. Maybe they had been obsidian after all, and a crucial component of the shield. He kept his eyes glued to his reflection, not daring to look up for fear of losing himself again. He realized Giselle was talking to him.

"Would you like some more wine?" she repeated, leaning over him so closely that he could smell her breath, which was sour with wine.

"No, thank you," he muttered, thinking he should leave while he still could. But the olive leaves were still fluttering in the wind, and the sound sickened him. The golden tent was gone, and clouds hung low in the sky, bearing down on him menacingly. His head pounded, and he could hear the blood rushing in his ears. "No," he said roughly, pulling his cup away as she tried to pour him more. He clumsily placed his half-filled goblet on the brass table, the clatter of metal-on-metal making his ears ring.

He breathed deliberately, fighting off motion sickness. These witches were strong, he acknowledged anxiously. He was outmatched. He thought of his grandmother. Her black eyes and sharp tongue. *Do not talk back to me, you little snot.* Her shrill voice echoed in his head, and he recalled the spoon shield for his true eye. He grasped for the golden goblet, pushing past Giselle's hip, and pressed the cool metal against his forehead, wine sloshing over his hand.

He shuddered in a breath. Ah, that was better. The coolness seeped into his skin, his eyes still concentrating on the obsidian ring. Giselle tugged at the goblet but he held on tight, wine spilling onto her dress.

"Damn it," she cried, dabbing frantically at her jewel-green robe, the ruby-red wine darkening the silk in an uneven splotch over her thigh.

His eyes slid to her bared ankle as she lifted her skirt to clean it, but he forced his gaze back to the ring. His hunted eyes stared back at him. He could hear Giselle retreat angrily to her seat. His hands were trembling, but he was safe.

He sat like that for what felt like hours. When he finally dared look up, Gabira and Giselle were gone. Daleelah was sitting on her stack of rugs across from him, the panther perched on a pillow beside her. The gray clouds were thick, but the branches were motionless.

"Where are we?" he asked weakly.

Daleelah's brown eyes were placid. "Oh, just in one of Ami's groves."

"But it's not real," he said.

Daleelah shrugged. "She thinks it is, therefore it is."

"You believe that?" he asked.

"She does. That's what's important."

"How does she make it? The olive grove?"

Daleelah met his eyes directly. They were free of their usual vacuousness and held an intensity greater than Giselle's. Ridge caught his breath. He did not recognize her. For a moment, she was a ravishing beauty; the next moment, she was a mourning dove, dull of feather with a brain the size of a pine nut. He shook his head, trying to clear it of a sudden fog and focusing on his obsidian reflection again. The eyes that looked back at him were frightened. He pressed the goblet to his forehead again. Maybe if he just stood up and started walking, he'd find the door. Or, more likely, he'd find himself deeper in this star-cursed illusion.

He sat back against the pillows, exhausted from staring at himself in the oval facet; but he kept his focus on the ring, as though clinging to a floating board after a shipwreck.

"She brought a piece of it with her," Daleelah said. "From Earth." Her voice was clear and round like musical notes. He wanted to look at her, but dared not.

"Really?" he asked. "You mean a piece of an orchard?"

"Exactly," she said, and stood up.

He heard the swishing of her robe and glimpsed her bare feet in his peripheral vision as she walked away, leaving him alone in the olive grove. The cushions and rugs were gone. The table was gone. He was sitting on dry crumbled soil, his arms clasped around his knees, holding a goblet in one hand and staring at a glinting ring on his other hand. He slowly opened his stiff fingers and inspected the lacquered box that had been clutched in his ringed fist. He opened the box with his thumb, and little brass hinges held the painted top open. Inside were a few small clumps of dirt, a single olive leaf, one desiccated brown olive, and a thin twig.

He looked up, and he was inside the cave room. The painted walls greeted him cheerfully. He sucked in his breath and stood on shaking legs. He set the goblet down on the brass table, snapped the lacquered box closed and shoved it in his pocket, then staggered to the door. He cracked it open and peeked up and down the empty hallway, and then ran like hell for the stairs.

27

BROTHER WOLF

After lunch, Torr went to Center Ring and stopped at the entrance of the PCA to chat with the guards, Bratislav and Sid. The Boyer brothers and Sky and Thunder stood to the side, waiting for him. Torr stopped talking as the Scrids approached them.

"Mangarm," Jorimar said, calling Torr by his name, Moon Wolf, and forwent the ritual chest-butt, to Torr's relief. The man spoke to Torr in his coarse language, with words Torr did not understand. Jorimar's amber eyes glowed, and Torr wished he had the garnet with him.

"Did your wizard arrive?" Torr asked.

"*Asbjorn Skr,*" Jorimar said.

"You want my crystal. I understand, Jorimar, I do," Torr said. "But the Bear crystal is mine, and you can't have it."

"Move along," Bratislav said, waving away the Scrids.

Jorimar growled something incomprehensible, and they stalked off, their boot bells jangling. Jorimar and Helug stopped a few paces away, talking quietly and eyeing Torr.

Torr ignored them and turned back to his conversation with Sid and Bratislav.

Sid's eyes were blue like Torr's father's and examined him with a calm intelligence that also reminded him of Caden. "I hear you and your sister are the Star Children," Sid said curiously.

"Who told you that?"

Sid shrugged. "Lots of people. Montana. Jaz. Berkeley. Ming-Long. Kujo. Everybody."

"So, you think the whole of Peary knows?" Torr asked, concerned.

"No." He shook his head. "Not everybody. Not yet."

Torr hesitated. "Do you think Schlitzer knows?"

"You can be sure of it," Sid said, casting a glance at Bratislav, who nodded in agreement.

"Do you think people really believe it?" Torr asked.

"Do you?" Sid asked, peering at Torr with a look of guarded hope that made Torr's skin prickle.

Torr turned up his hands. "Seems far-fetched, don't you think?"

Sid frowned. "Yeah, but we need something. Hell, if it's not you, then who? Then what? Are we just going to float out here in space and wait for the Tegs to take over the moon, too? That'll be the end of us all."

Silence hung heavily between them.

Fritz and Frank walked across the yard and joined them, freed from their morning guard shift at the Fen.

"What are you up to this afternoon?" Frank asked, crossing his arms. His skull tattoo stared at Torr from his upper arm.

"I don't know," Torr said. "Got any ideas?"

"Want to practice scouting?" Frank asked, his eyes flitting sideways without his head moving. Torr had told the twins how the reconnaissance portion of his sniper training had been cut short in the rush to man the front lines. Frank rested his eyes on Torr, then took sunglasses from his pocket and slipped them on.

Torr put on his own aviators and scanned the yard, which took on a warm glow through the amber glass.

They took a quick trip back to the Fen, where Torr found Blaire in the workshop tent with Cassidy, Blaire's sisters, and Darla. Five of the Alphabet Boys were in the small courtyard, lined up on Tatsuya's tattooing bench, knitting.

"Making me a scarf?" Torr asked Copper.

"I'm making Darla socks," Copper said proudly, holding up a half-finished purple sock.

"Impressive," Torr said with an amused grin.

Torr turned to the women inside the workshop tent. "Want to

hang out with us today?" Torr asked Blaire, sliding his hand around the curve of her waist and drawing her to him.

"Sure," she said, her eyes twinkling. He tried to kiss her, but she dodged him playfully until they both were laughing. She finally kissed him, then pulled away. "Let's go," she said, stepping out of his reach and placing her hands on her hips.

"I'm coming, too," Darla said, putting down a pair of scissors.

Cassidy and Blaire's sisters exchanged glances, and Cassidy nodded. "Good. Maybe someone else will get a turn at the sewing machine." She cast Darla a meaningful glare, and Darla smirked back at her.

"Fine. Don't break any more of Berkeley's needles," Darla said.

"Ready?" Torr asked.

They went out into the main courtyard and joined their friends.

"Keep an eye on things," Torr said to Durham.

Durham looked up from his repair bench and gave him a small salute. "I'm on it," he said.

Torr and the others followed Fritz and Frank back out to Center Ring.

"Watch without looking," Frank instructed as he led the crew across the yard to Spoke Road Twelve. "See without staring. Open your eyes to soak in the surroundings like it is bleeding into you."

"Relax," Fritz added. "Your peripheral vision is great at picking up movement. Use it."

"Like a hawk," Hawk said.

"Like a hawk," Fritz agreed.

"Hawks can see heat," Hawk said.

"Unfortunately, we cannot. Not without a thermal scope, at least," Frank said.

Torr suddenly missed his Dashiel and its scope. He had liked using the infrared setting to see all the critters that came out at night on the dry scrubland of Scripps Ranch. With thermal imaging, he could detect coyotes and rodents as they moved surreptitiously through the brush. A sense of longing and homesickness flooded through him, and he realized he missed the cadence of night and day. The soothing darkness of midnight, the freshness of dawn. The moon shining over Mount Shasta. The crickets chanting their lullaby, and owls hooting to one another.

Here it was constant daylight, and it made the days blur together like a never-ending dream. They trod quietly, Torr scanning the roadways without turning his head. His ears opened as well, and he heard tent flaps brushing aside. Footsteps as people passed on the road. The crunch and rumble of a transport as it rolled by.

Torr noticed how people observed others, watching from behind lowered eyelids. Sensing. Feeling. Giving each other a wide berth. People generally kept to themselves, walking in small groups. It was mostly males, and they checked out Blaire and Darla as their group walked down the center of the road. Two other young women were walking by themselves half a block ahead, looking over their shoulders to determine if Torr's group was a threat. Torr watched as a group of four men walking in the other direction towards the two women slowed and did not move aside, forcing the women to make a wide arc around them. Torr's jaws tightened as the men stepped sideways, blocking the women's paths and making lewd remarks.

Torr's squad exchanged glances. The four men were toying with the two women, probably not intending to do them harm, just having a little fun. The women were scared, though, and the men seemed to be having a little too much fun, enjoying the women's fear a little too much. One reached out and grabbed the breast of a woman, who backed away with alarm.

Torr and Blaire were in the lead, flanked by Raleigh and Hawk, Fritz and Frank. They moved forward in a flowing stride, like an ocean wave driven by the wind. They bowled over the four men in one slow rush, tackling them easily with takedowns that Tatsuya and Hiroshi had drilled into them.

Blaire and Darla each took a woman by the elbow, and Raleigh and Roanoke glowered at the four men while Sky and Thunder and the blond twins kept walking with the women. Torr and Hawk hung back with Raleigh and Roanoke as the men climbed warily to their feet, sizing up the four of them. The men's eyes fell on their Light Fighters patches and shifted nervously to their knives and clubs. They tried to explain themselves with feeble excuses and ended up apologizing.

"Don't apologize to us," Torr said, signaling to the retreating women. "Next time, be polite," he said sternly.

"What he means," Raleigh said, "is don't fuck with people." Raleigh put his hand to his club. "Got it?"

The men bristled and slunk away as the four Light Fighters followed them with a few threatening steps, and then slowed and watched the men hurry down the road. "I don't know which way is best," Torr said. "Being nice, or a hardass."

"Both," Raleigh said.

"Yeah, I guess," Torr said, scratching his chin.

They caught up with the others, who had been watching from the intersection. The two women lived around the corner on a ring road. The squad dropped them off, and then continued down Spoke Road Eleven.

"This place is a free-for-all," Torr mumbled, and Darla nodded.

"Pretty much every man for himself. Or woman," she said, frowning.

"Back to scouting," Fritz said. "Slow down and look around."

"See who's watching us," Frank said softly.

Torr checked. Half the people glanced up as they strode by. Others ignored them, lost in their own thoughts. They passed a ration trailer. The doors were open, and the ration guards sat on stools in the shade of the trailer and followed them with their eyes as they walked by. Torr tapped his forehead at them.

"That one," Roanoke said softly. "With the black shorts."

Torr peered from the corner of his eye at a man standing at the side of the road who was wearing sunglasses and looking towards Earth.

"What about him?" Torr asked quietly.

"He's watching us."

"He's looking at Earth," Darla said.

"No," Roanoke said. "He's watching us. He's only pretending to look at Earth."

"How can you tell?" Blaire whispered.

"See how he stands? His ears are focused on us. His body is tracking our movements. His eyes are anchored on Earth to fool us."

Torr could see that Roanoke was right. He never would have noticed, but suddenly it was so obvious.

"Probably one of Schlitzer's gang," Fritz said softly. "Their camp is down the road. He must be on border patrol."

"Let's spy on them, instead," Torr said. A bitter taste rose to his mouth at the thought of the worm-ridden pimp.

They continued on, striding easily down the long familiar road. When they reached the end of the spoke road, they crossed the perimeter road and the wide empty space to the sundial. Hawk and Fritz swept off the large disc, and they compared the mark of the shadow to the times on their watches. Taking his binoculars from his belt, Torr turned towards Schlitzer's compound, wondering if he could see any of the camp from there.

Fritz gently pushed down Torr's arm, shaking his head. "Don't," he said. "There's sure to be somebody watching. They'll see you." Torr scowled but put the binoculars away. Blaire nudged his shoulder, and Torr looked behind him. Across the road, close to Spoke Road One, stood Jorimar and Helug, watching them. Torr was slightly irritated that they kept following him, but he could detect no threat in their body language.

Jorimar caught his eye and thumped his fists to his chest. Torr returned the salute. He rested his hand on his wolf knife hilt and looked for energy filaments, but seeing nothing, he turned to Fritz. "How can we spy on Schlitzer's camp if we can't look?"

Fritz smiled. "Oh, we can look. We can just go there."

Torr frowned. "After getting thrown out the other night?"

"So?" Fritz gave him a crooked grin. "You think you're the first person to get thrown out of Schlitzer's bar? Jaz got thrown out a couple of times, but that doesn't stop him from going back."

Torr lifted his eyebrow curiously.

"It's a whorehouse," Sky said with pointed disapproval.

"It's a bar," Fritz said. "With women whose job it is to be nice to you. You don't have to fuck them if you don't want."

"Shush," Torr said. "There's a kid here."

"I know all about it," Hawk said.

"I bet you do," Fritz teased, laughing as Hawk blushed.

"I've been there already," Hawk said gruffly. "Ain't no big thing." His red face belied his words.

"We should take you back to the Fen first," Torr said, recalling Schlitzer's energy filament burrowing its way into Hawk's forehead.

"No," Hawk said, his voice pleading.

"He'll be okay," Raleigh said. "I'll take responsibility for him. Kids need to grow up fast out here."

Hawk puffed out his chest.

Torr put his hand to his wolf knife. He couldn't detect any tentacles slithering around Hawk now. Torr would want to come along too, if he were fourteen, and nodded his assent.

"It's not right for women to sell their bodies," Sky said.

Blaire and Darla were standing stone-faced at the edge of the circle.

"Knock it off," Torr snapped. The men fell silent, and Sky stood rigidly. "Let's go," Torr said.

"Where?" Fritz asked.

"To Schlitzer's," Torr said. Fritz was right. The best way to keep tabs on Schlitzer was to spend time at his camp. Besides, Torr wanted to let Schlitzer know he had not been scared off by the scene the other night. It remained to be seen if Schlitzer would allow them back in or not. Torr eyed Sky and Thunder. "You guys can go home if you don't want to come."

Sky and Thunder traded glances. "We'll go with you," Thunder said. "You have women along, you need a big squad."

"Tell Sky to pull the stick out of his ass," Fritz said, and stepped away from the sundial, leading the others towards Spoke Road Twelve.

Torr waited for Blaire and Darla, who were straggling behind. Blaire cocked her eyebrow at him.

"You okay with this?" Torr asked her. "We can take you home, if you want. Or we don't have to go at all."

"Should you really be hanging out there?" she asked. "Isn't Schlitzer dangerous?"

Torr blinked. She didn't know the half of it. "He is," Torr acknowledged. "Yet, he intrigues me."

"Hmm," Blaire said. "I think a fly is intrigued by a spider's web. No?"

He pressed his lips together. The analogy of a spider's web with its sticky filaments was more apt than she realized. "You're right," he acknowledged. "Better to know your enemy ...?" he ventured weakly.

She gave a half-chuckle, then bit her lip, thinking. Darla rolled her eyes behind Blaire's head, making a funny face.

Blaire glanced at Darla, and then said, "We'll go. I've been there before, you know." Torr raised his eyebrows at her. "For the bar," Blaire explained, giving him a tight grin. "But it's not a nice place," she said. "There's all sorts of stuff going on at that camp."

Torr nodded. "I know. That's why I want to go there. I want to understand what it's all about. We're just going to observe," he said. "Come on."

She gave a little shrug and walked alongside him, pushing her shoulder gently against his. He put his arm around her and stole a quick kiss as they walked.

They made their way down Ring Road L to the open gate of the block Schlitzer had fenced in. Two guards let them pass with a silent nod. Torr walked across the dust and ducked under the lowered tent sides, entering the large pavilion. The bar was busy and boisterous. All the stools were filled with men or women. More men stood behind the stools, drinks in hand, vying for a chance to converse with the pretty prostitutes. Another knot of men and women sat on the floor pillows. In the center of them sat Schlitzer, a young woman perched on his lap and Debbie sitting on a pillow at his side.

Schlitzer's laughter died, and Torr knew they shouldn't have come. Torr could think of nothing to do but smile. What the hell? What did he have to lose? He preferred not to ponder that question too closely and elbowed his way to the bar. He caught the barmaid's eye and set his hand on the bar.

The other barmaid approached him. She was nude from the waist up, large brown nipples covering nearly a third of her breasts. He lifted his gaze to her big brown eyes, thick with mascara and black eyeliner.

"Beers for all of us," he said, gesturing to his companions.

"Cans or tap?" she asked.

Torr saw an aluminum keg sitting behind the bar. "Tap." He laid a handful of assorted small coins on the polished wood.

She smiled and poured the beer into glass mugs, leaving a thick head of foam on each.

At least Schlitzer knew how to serve beer, Torr thought as the cold liquid made its way through the froth and down his parched throat.

Fritz shifted imperceptibly, alerting Torr that Schlitzer was approaching. Torr turned to face the tall man.

Schlitzer's sky-blue eyes were casually examining Torr's companions, his wild hair pulled back in a bushy ponytail, and his brown and gray goatee freshly trimmed.

Torr raised his mug as the man approached. "Good beer," Torr said. "How do you keep the head?"

Schlitzer threw back his head and laughed heartily, making Torr smile. He was a charming man, Torr reflected, as a warm sensation flowed through his body. *Best stay alert with such a one,* he reminded himself, and rested his hand on the wolf knife hilt. Torr could not detect anything amiss. Perhaps Schlitzer was keeping his tentacles to himself, or maybe Torr's mind was not calm enough to sense the energy filaments. Torr tried to focus on his breathing, but still he could see nothing. If Schlitzer had understood what had happened the other night, perhaps he wanted to avoid another confrontation.

"You have a way with words, Torr," Schlitzer said amicably, coming to Torr's side and putting his arm around his shoulders. Torr felt his friends relax under the man's jovial smile. "What brings you guys back to my humble establishment so soon after your last pleasant visit?"

Torr ignored the underhanded jab and took a mouthful of beer. The man smelled good, reminding him of the little shops in Shasta that sold candles and incense and essential oils.

"I see you've brought your own lovely ladies." Schlitzer approached Blaire and Darla and kissed each of their hands. "Blaire Smith, I do believe," he said, acknowledging her with a gracious smile. "I am honored. Welcome to my establishment. I have several fine studs who would love to let you ride them." He grinned suggestively and chuckled with delight as Blaire smothered a scowl. Darla's gaze moved to two bare-chested men lounging on the pillows who looked to be for sale. Torr stood by, trying to act cool.

"And who do we have here?" Schlitzer asked, shifting his attention to Hawk. "You ready to pop your first cherry?"

Hawk's complexion deepened to a dark crimson, and Schlitzer threw back his head and guffawed. He wiped at his moustaches and turned to Torr.

"How is that sweet sister of yours?" Schlitzer asked. "Has she recovered?" The man was suddenly serious and exuded genuine concern.

Torr lowered his beer mug and nodded. "She's doing as well as can be expected."

"I'm glad," Schlitzer said.

Torr held Schlitzer's steady gaze. He had met men like Schlitzer before. At Miramar—all buddy-buddy until you beat them at target practice and then they act personally insulted. On the ocean waiting on surfboards for the best waves—acting like they're your friends until they take a wave out from under you, leaving you to be pummeled by a ton of crushing water. Torr's strategy had normally been to stay away from such men, but here he was in Schlitzer's camp, drinking his beer and staring into his bloodshot eyes.

"Sit down, won't you?" Schlitzer asked. He motioned to a pile of unoccupied pillows.

Torr and his friends settled onto the cushions, and Torr watched from the corner of his eye as Schlitzer wandered off, mingling with his patrons. Schlitzer had subtly let him know this was his turf and he was letting Torr stay not because he had to, but because he chose to. Most likely, Schlitzer was as fascinated with Torr as Torr was with him. Particularly if the rumors of the Star Children had reached him. It wasn't like Schlitzer could just waltz into Torr's camp anytime he liked. Like Blaire had said, Schlitzer wove a sticky web, drawing his victims to him.

Torr settled back against a cushion. At this height, he could see beneath the half-lowered canvas walls. He surveyed the surrounding camp, which was a warren of courtyards, tents, and shipping containers. It was a busy little enclave, and from the feel of things had more going on than simply alcohol and sex. A small transport rolled by, sending up a cloud of dust. He could smell food cooking and his stomach growled petulantly. A partially clothed young woman and a dusty moon rat walked by, the teenaged prostitute disappearing inside a tent with her client. Torr swallowed with distaste. But who was he to judge? Maybe it was just what happened when there were so many more males than females in a population. He breathed evenly and sipped at his beer, enjoying the sharp tang of it. Torr found Blaire's hand and squeezed it gently.

Three men walked briskly into view and stood outside the pavilion, one of them lifting a canvas wall and peeking inside. Schlitzer broke away from the group he was entertaining and went outside. He sauntered off with the men and pushed aside a door flap, exposing the interior of a tent in which a picnic table took up most of the space. The flaps closed behind Schlitzer. No doubt the man had a thriving smuggling business. Plus a spy network. Torr wondered what kind of information passed through his camp, and what Schlitzer did with it.

After slowly drinking their beers, his crew rose and placed their mugs on the bar, and then made their way to a spoke road and headed across the tent city, not saying a word.

Torr thought the visit a complete failure. He didn't know what he had expected to learn. Maybe Schlitzer had a hook in him that Torr could not detect, and he was drawn back again and again, like a fish on a line.

"What did you notice?" Frank asked him as they walked.

"Not much," Torr said.

"How many people were in the tent with the picnic table in it?" Frank asked.

"Schlitzer and three guys," Torr said.

"No," Frank said patiently. "There were already two guys in there. In the back corner."

"Oh, I didn't see them," Torr said. "You must have had a better angle than I did."

"No, I was sitting next to you. If anything, my angle was worse."

"Well, I didn't see anybody."

"I saw their feet under the table," Frank said. "And there were two cans of beer on the table."

"Oh," Torr said, embarrassed.

"And what else was on the table?" Frank asked.

Torr shrugged. He hadn't seen anything else but was sure he must have missed something.

"A stack of gold coins," Frank said. "I think about ten Eagles. What does that tell you?"

"They were there to buy something?" Torr guessed.

"Right. Also, it must not be a sensitive trade, otherwise they never would have met in that tent, which is in plain sight. Schlitzer must have another place where he conducts his clandestine activities. So, how many people were in the pavilion tent?"

Torr tried to picture the scene in the tent and count in his head. He hadn't thought to count while he'd been there.

"Thirty-five when we first got there," Roanoke said, walking up next to them. "Two barmaids, seven female hookers, and the rest were males. One man left with a hooker, and then three men came by and Schlitzer left with them. Two more men left with a hooker each, then another hooker came into the tent. Of the remaining men, eight were there only for a drink, seven were trying to arrange for a prostitute, two were prostitutes themselves, and five were waiting to meet with Schlitzer privately."

Torr stared at his friend. How had Roanoke figured all that out?

"That's about what I thought, too," Fritz said. "Which ones were regular customers, and which were newcomers?" The two older Boyer brothers debated with Fritz and Frank over this until they arrived at a consensus. Torr felt like a complete fool.

"What else did you notice?" Frank asked, directing his question at the others.

"Schlitzer smelled like patchouli oil," Darla observed.

Now that she mentioned it, there had been a lingering scent of patchouli, which reminded Torr suddenly of Gabira. He wondered if that meant Schlitzer and Gabira had seen each other recently and embraced.

Others contributed details Torr had overlooked.

"And what did you notice about Debbie?" Fritz asked Torr of the prostitute they had taken to Schlitzer's the other night.

"She was at Schlitzer's side most of the time?" Torr ventured.

"Right. What do you make of that?"

"They're close?" Torr asked.

"And she was watching us," Frank said.

Torr tried to recall her observing them but hadn't paid much attention to her.

"I heard she hasn't taken a client in a year," Fritz said.

"Jaz told me she and Schlitzer are dating," Torr said, happy to be able to contribute something.

"Ah, that explains it," Fritz said, nodding.

"And what was Schlitzer talking about when he was sitting on the pillows?" Frank asked.

Torr hadn't heard anything, but the Boyers had caught bits and pieces of the conversation, and Fritz and Frank claimed they'd heard pretty much the whole thing. Torr was considering how they had accomplished that with all the noise at the bar.

Frank recounted the conversation. "The men asked about the food shortage. Schlitzer told them he had an inside deal with the best food source, and that he would sell them rice at the going rate, which fluctuated daily. When the men complained about the high price, Schlitzer explained it all depended on how many food shipments had come in that week, when he expected the next one, how much he'd paid for the rice, and how many bags he'd sold to Ramzy and at what price."

"Did you read his lips?" Hawk asked.

"Ah, smart boy," Fritz said, clapping Hawk on the shoulder.

They continued walking towards the Fen, and Torr pondered his pathetic observational skills. His sniper instructors would be ashamed of him. It was as though without the Dashiel in his hands, he'd forgotten how to take notice of his surroundings. He realized he was lost in his head at that very moment, oblivious to what was going on around him. He stopped thinking, opened his senses, and the dome suddenly came alive with sights and sounds and smells he hadn't noticed before.

Blaire told him she loved him between moans and quivers, which quickened Torr's blood and sent him flying through the stars. When they were spent and satiated, he spooned her, nuzzling her thick brown hair. He pulled her closer into the curve of his body. Their ribs rose and fell together as their breathing slowed. The hush of night curfew surrounded the tent, and he drifted off into a dreamless sleep.

He awoke to the sound of snuffling at his ear and warm breath bathing his face. Torr cracked open his eyelids. The large muzzle of his wolf was at his shoulder, its nose black and shiny and its golden eyes trained on his. Blaire was sleeping with her arm draped across his chest, and he was lying on his back with his hand resting on the wolf knife pommel on the canvas floor beside him. Torr did not move or breathe, or even blink. A part of his mind told him the wolf was not real, though he could smell its breath and see the individual hairs of its thick fur. He wondered for a moment if he were dreaming but abandoned his musings as the wolf stepped stiffly away and crossed the tent, nose down and ruff raised.

The hairs on Torr's skin stood on end. He moved his hand from the wolf knife and felt for his other knives on the canvas floor beside the bed. He lifted Blaire's fingers from where they were resting on his chest and transferred the combat knife's hilt to her hand. She stirred groggily, and he put his finger to her lips, gesturing for her to be quiet, and then pulled the sheath free for her. Her eyes popped open to full alertness and she hopped up in a silent crouch, naked, and tossed the blade to her right hand, her eyes scanning the dim interior of the tent. Torr stood up and unsheathed the wolf knife, holding it with a hammer grip, and took the antelope knife in his left hand.

The wolf stood at the rear of the tent, its ruff full and bristling as it sniffed at the back canvas wall. A deep growl came from the wolf's chest, and Torr froze. Torr could tell Blaire could not see or hear the wolf. A snake-like hiss pierced the back wall of the tent and a vertical line appeared in the canvas, slicing down like a laser cut, though there was no visible light beam. Torr raised his weapons as a man slipped noiselessly through the gap in the canvas. The man's face was concealed by a bandana and a brimmed hat. Torr could not determine any reason the man would enter their tent other than to cause harm.

The scene unfolded in slow motion. The man seemed startled to find them awake and armed—and naked. That momentary flicker of surprise allowed Torr to strike first, driving his left forearm against the man's arm that held a laser-knife and lunging at the man's neck with his blade. Torr was not fast enough, and the man caught his forearm, stepping aside and twisting Torr's arm away, sending the wolf knife tumbling to the floor. He gave Torr a sharp elbow to the side of the head, stunning him, and then kneed Torr in the groin and tackled him to the ground, his hands around Torr's throat. Blaire jumped onto the back of the man and sank her blade into the man's back with a sickening *thunk*.

The man's hold on Torr's neck loosened, and Torr pushed him off and staggered to his feet as three more men silently entered the back of the tent. Two men wrestled Blaire away, while the third clamped Torr in a chokehold and pressed a white kerchief to his face. Torr instinctively held his breath and fought against the man trying to suffocate him while kicking at the first man, who seemed merely angered by the knife in his back and was trying to get control of Torr's arms. Torr

swung and kicked and tried to sink his antelope knife into flesh, but
the blade swiped harmlessly through empty air.

Two men were on Blaire with a white kerchief over her mouth and
nose, her eyes wild and blazing. Torr started with surprise as he recognized the two men as the Light Fighters with the gray snakes coming
out of their bellies. He lurched with fury and twisted against the man
smothering him. They fell to the ground and rolled back and forth,
the man knocking the antelope knife from his hand, and the first man
throwing his weight onto Torr's legs. The pommel of the wolf knife
jabbed into Torr's hip. He grabbed the hilt and flailed at the men's
bodies wherever the blade could fall—on hips, thighs, abdomens, he
didn't know where. He struck again and again, driving the blade into
flesh and muscle. The shadow of the wolf leapt onto the man who was
choking Torr.

The man screamed and rolled away under the jaws of the wolf,
kicking and flailing. Torr spat as the kerchief fell away, then inhaled
a lungful of air. The first man waved the laser-knife at him, sending a
searing pain across Torr's bare chest. Torr grabbed the antelope knife
and struck the man's forearm with the blunt end of the haft, forcing
the laser-knife down, and drove the wolf blade into the man's neck.
The man grabbed Torr's wrist and struggled against him as warm blood
drenched Torr's hand. With his other hand, Torr stabbed the man in
the gut, pushing him backwards. The spirit wolf leapt onto the man,
driving him and Torr to the floor.

Torr pulled his blades free and rolled away as Faisal's head poked
through the front of the tent. Faisal stared in momentary shock, then
frantically cut through the canvas door ties.

Torr sprang to his feet and jumped onto Blaire's attackers, slicing
across the first man's back with Dead Man's X. Two dark gashes split
the attacker's shirt, and the man stumbled forward onto Blaire and the
other man. Torr dropped the antelope knife and with a two-handed grip
around the wolf knife's hilt, put all his weight behind it and plunged
the long blade into the man's back near his heart, and then yanked the
blade out, stepping on the man's back for leverage. Torr was shaking
as the wolf appeared at his side and leapt onto the man, growling and
gnashing at his neck. The man convulsed under Torr's foot. The other
man tried to squirm away, but Faisal leapt onto him and stabbed him

in the throat. The man clutched at his neck and blood spurted through his fingers, and the wolf leapt on him and tore at his face.

The tent filled with the sounds of gurgling moans, and then Jasper was there, pulling a man away from Blaire as Torr knelt next to her limp body and the wolf panted at his side. Suddenly, Cassidy was there, and Fritz and Frank, Ming-Long and Khaled, and more of their campmates were crowding into the tent and pinning down the attackers. Copper rushed in with Buck and Arden. Yells of confusion surrounded Torr as he held Blaire's head with his bloody hands, adrenaline pumping madly through him. Blaire's frozen eyes stared up at him. Helpless panic seized him, but he pushed it back. Tatsuya appeared and knelt across from Torr, feeling Blaire's neck for a pulse. Cassidy knelt at Torr's side.

"Herbs," Torr said, shooting a glance at the sodden kerchief that lay abandoned on the ground.

Cassidy fingered the white cloth, her face pinching with distaste, and cast it aside. "I don't know what it is. You're covered in blood," Cassidy told him, her face pale. Voices jabbered in the background.

Torr glanced down at his chest, splattered red with sticky blood. A horizontal welt striped his skin below his collarbone. He bent over Blaire and pressed his ear to her chest, listening for a breath or a heartbeat.

"Quiet!" he yelled, cutting through the yammering panic that had risen around him. He stilled his own breathing and quieted his mind, willing his thundering heart to hush. Yes, there was a faint thrumming of life in her chest. He brought his lips to her mouth and blew his breath into her lungs, then drew in fresh air and filled her lungs again. Over and over. Her breathing began on its own, in soft little puffs, as though she were sleeping. He continued helping her breathe until her chest rose and fell in a regular rhythm. Fear and relief pounded in Torr's chest, and he cradled her in his arms, rocking her and praying to the stars.

"We should take her to the infirmary," Tatsuya said as Cassidy wrapped a blanket around Blaire's nude body and their campmates swarmed the blood-soaked tent. Cassidy, Tatsuya, and Berkeley tended to Blaire while Torr quickly wiped the blood from his skin and weapons with a t-shirt and hurriedly got dressed. Torr gripped the wolf knife and glanced around the tent. The wolf was standing near Blaire, its golden eyes staring up at Torr. Its tongue was lolling out the side of its mouth, and its long fangs gleamed white.

"Thank you," Torr said. "We'll be okay now." The wolf blinked, then faded into the shadows.

Faisal handed Torr his combat knife, which he had last seen buried in the back of his enemy. It had been cleaned of blood, and Faisal held his eyes.

"Blaire did that," Torr said, a look of pride passing between the two men.

Torr secured his weapons and then scooped Blaire into his arms. He crossed the yard and strapped her into the passenger seat of the moon rover. Cassidy and Jasper perched on the back of the rover as Torr navigated out of the Fen, with Berkeley and the Alphabet Boys running behind.

28

AURAS

The two men shifted from foot to foot as they faced Balty in his office at Gandoop Spaceport. Ridge huddled by the door, wanting to slip away, but knew not to draw attention to himself during one of Balty's rages.

"All four of them are dead," Balty repeated ominously, his handsome face coloring to a deep crimson as he picked up a glass globe paperweight on the desk and set it down with a thud.

"It wasn't our fault," the smaller man whimpered, his wide scruffy jowls sliding to the side as he chewed at the inside of his cheek.

The tall one stood up straight, his arms at his sides. "It's my fault," he said solemnly. "I should have personally made sure they were asleep."

"Damn right you should have made sure they were asleep, you fucking maggots! What the hell did you think I wanted you to do? A night attack is supposed to be a *surprise attack,* you *mindless fucks!*" Balty got to his feet and glared at them, his eyes bulging. The tall man dropped his eyes with shame, and the small one peered out the corners of his eyes at the door.

"It doesn't get dark in Peary," the small one complained, his crooked front teeth overhanging his lower lip.

Balty turned to him with a scathing look that sent the man cowering back a step.

"Your only job was to give the signal when all was clear," Balty said

467

slowly and loudly as if the men were hard of hearing. "A simple task. Instead, you sent them into a tent facing two very awake people who were *ready and armed*. What the hell?! My *grandmother* could do a better job than you two incompetent cocksuckers!"

The small man shrugged defensively. Balty grabbed the glass paperweight and threw it across the room. It hit the wall behind the small man's head and fell to the concrete floor with a loud crack. "Don't you shrug at me, you steaming pile of *horseshit!*" Balty bellowed.

The man's lips tightened. "Our man told us they were asleep," he said defensively. "Yell at him."

Ridge cringed. No one in their right mind talked back to Balty.

"And you say it wasn't even the right girl?" Balty asked in a dangerously sweet tone, looking between the two men.

"It was his girlfriend, not his sister," the tall man said in a hushed tone. "We should have been more precise with our instructions. Now in retrospect it's clear that 'the fucker and that bitch' could be misinterpreted."

The small man shrugged again and said, "I watched her go into the tent with my own binoculars. It was a girl, anyway. But I couldn't get a good look at her. They shielded the best views of their camp with tarps." He stood defiantly, as though it were a forgivable mistake.

Ridge curled his hands into fists as Balty came around the desk and kicked over a guest chair. The two men dodged the chair, and Ridge pressed himself against the door, his hand on the doorknob. Balty clutched the small man by the neck with one massive hand and pinned him up against the wall. The man struggled, grasping Balty's bulging arm with both hands, squirming and kicking. Balty kneed him in the groin and pounded his midsection with his free fist, then battered his head, while the other hand squeezed mercilessly. The second hand joined the first, wedged up under the man's jaws.

Ridge held his breath as the small man's face finally went still, his legs twitching and his eyes glassy, gazing emptily at Balty's maniacal face. Ridge's heart pounded in his eyes and he wanted to sit down but leaned against the door instead, lightheadedness threatening to drop him to the floor. He watched with horror as Balty held onto the poor bastard's throat, squeezing. The small man's eyes bulged, and his tongue hung from his mouth. The smell of loosened bowels filled the room, and the stain of urine darkened the man's pant leg. Ridge's body shook uncontrollably.

When Balty was sure the man was dead, he released him, the body falling in a boneless heap to the floor. Balty whirled and faced the tall one. The man stood still, his face like marble. The two handsome men stared at each other as though they'd just entered a world they did not recognize.

Balty blinked. "Drink?" he asked cordially and walked to the liquor cabinet in the corner. "Scotch?" He took out two glasses and poured from a half-empty Scotch bottle without waiting for the man's response.

The tall man straightened his collar, taking the drink Balty handed him. The telltale widow's peak of the man's hairline was unmistakable as he pushed sweat-dampened hair back from his forehead. It was subtle enough to allow him to walk around unharassed in Peary Dome, but not enough to escape Ridge's detection as the man faced his half-breed boss, the similarity of their countenances pronounced enough to mark their shared heritage.

"Ridge, can you take care of that?" Balty asked, gesturing to the stinking corpse. "Then come right back."

Ridge cracked a smile and dragged the body to the door. He awkwardly propped the door open and dragged the dead man across the threshold, calling to two workers.

"Take him to the recycler," Ridge said.

The two men lifted the body by the shoulders and legs and headed towards the passageway to the cubes. Ridge trotted across the floor and got some cleaning rags and bleach, and returned to the office.

It appeared the other man was not to die at the moment. He was sitting in one of the guest chairs, sipping at his Scotch. "Fortunately for you," Balty said to the man in a friendly tone, "you have some talents worth keeping. Unlike that rat you kept as a friend. What, did he suck your cock? Is that why you kept him around?" Balty stared at the man as though he expected an answer.

The man took a sip of his drink before responding. "No," he said softly. "We grew up together. Jervis lived down the street from me. I felt sorry for him."

Balty's face fell in a sad frown. "Oh. I'm sorry." He looked genuinely contrite.

Ridge wiped up the urine on the floor and gathered the solid crystal globe, which was split perfectly down the middle. He left the office to dispose of the rags and glass. After washing his hands, he reluctantly returned to the office.

Balty didn't even glance at Ridge as he entered the room and closed the door behind him. Ridge righted the second guest chair and sat down.

"Stanley, I need you to take care of a minor business matter," Balty said to the man. "I need you to go to Delos and pay off some Nommos lords to get them off my back. Seems they're complaining some of the females they ordered are not virgins." Balty grinned wryly. "A couple have even been pregnant." He raised his eyebrows as though he could not fathom how such a scandal could have occurred. "Can't trust ship pilots these days. The guards are even worse. Tut, tut." He shook his head despondently.

Stanley nodded in agreement. "Can't get good help these days. It's a shame."

"You would think those fish-heads would be happy, seeing as how they can't father their own children. You'd think they'd be glad for some good strong genetic stock thrown into the shipment for free." Balty sneered a lecherous grin.

Ridge laced his fingers together, thinking he should escape to Delos himself.

Balty started laying out the plans for Delos with Stanley, and Ridge excused himself.

"Stop by later," Balty called after him. "I need you to track down those kids."

Ridge winced and fled to his speedster.

————————) ————————

"I wasn't planning on killing them," Ridge told Balty that evening. Had Balty forgotten he'd assigned the task to Ridge? They were standing in the kitchen at the house, where Balty was sipping on a tall glass of bourbon and coke.

Balty rolled his eyes. *"I wasn't planning on killing them,"* he mocked, imitating Ridge's accent. "You think getting hold of the deeds is enough?"

Ridge knew Balty wasn't really asking his opinion—he was telling Ridge it was not enough. "No," Ridge said, agreeing with Balty to pacify him. "I guess not."

"Damn right, it's not enough," Balty growled, heading back to the living room. Ridge followed on his heels and sat down across from him. "You don't want to kill them," Balty said. "Well, that's what I thought, too. Stupid me," he said in a rare moment of self-criticism. "Even though that bitch deserves the back of my hand. I thought just knocking them out and getting their fingerprints for the deed transfer would cause the least waves. You know, theft is one thing, murder is another."

Ridge tried not to stare at him—the psychopath had just killed a man with his bare hands.

Balty went on, "Didn't want to give that hound Ramzy reason to go sniffing about. Now I see that was a mistake. That boy fought off four men. What do you make of that?"

Ridge winced, afraid of saying the wrong thing. "He was a soldier?"

Balty huffed dismissively. "Rebels. What do they know?" Balty scowled darkly. "Apparently my guys were torn up like they had been attacked by dogs." Balty furrowed his brow, then went on. "I hear the kids are from Shasta." He peered over his glass at Ridge. "Maybe they used demonic magic."

"Maybe," Ridge said reluctantly.

Balty snorted loudly. "I've been thinking about it. The problem is, there's a record of the deeds in the system with their DNA data," Balty said. "The only way to be sure they can't claim the land is to kill them before they challenge us or transfer ownership to someone else."

"Unless they transfer ownership to us," Ridge said.

"My thoughts exactly. They transfer ownership to us, and then we kill them." Balty laughed roughly.

Us. Ridge's stomach turned. Just who did Balty think "us" was? Was Balty insinuating that he would claim title to Anaximenes, not the Gandoops? *Over my dead body.* Unfortunately, Ridge feared that was all too real a possibility. His eyes bored into Balty's hand, which was curled around the sweating glass.

"If they'd been killed," Ridge said, keeping his voice calm and reasonable, "we still might not have the deeds. Shouldn't we get a hold of the deeds first?" He knew he was treading on dangerous ground, questioning Balty's tactics. But what had possessed Balty to try and take the deeds from them in their own camp in the middle of a cluster of tents?

"If those dickheads had followed simple instructions, we would have the deeds already." Balty rose and poured himself another drink. "All they had to do was drug them quietly, with the most expensive drug in the galaxy, I might add, as if I have gold to waste. Get their fingerprints, take the deeds. In and out. Simple." Balty tipped the glass to his mouth, taking a long swig.

Ridge exhaled, relieved he hadn't triggered the man's temper. So, Balty had used the Hesychasm. It had been Ridge who'd gotten hold of the drug, not Balty, and he had given the bottle to Balty for free. Ridge was the one with all the trading connections and stacks of gold. If it weren't for the Gandoops, Balty would be piss-drunk in a far side mining hovel somewhere.

"We know they wear the deeds on their persons," Balty continued haughtily. "If they don't sleep with them on, the deeds would have been inside the tent somewhere." Balty chewed on a piece of ice. "No, fuck the transfer. Just get the deeds and kill them outright. I'm sick of pussyfooting around. We can get fingerprints off a corpse just as easily as a living body. That's the answer. This whole thing is taking much too long. I should just go in there and take care of it myself." Balty glared at Ridge and said, "I don't know why they had to have Metolius's seal on them, for fuck's sake."

Balty's expression soured again, somehow insinuating it was all Ridge's fault. It didn't help that he was drunk and rambling like a lunatic. He wasn't even making sense. Kill them. Don't kill them. Transfer the deeds. Don't transfer the deeds. It was unsettling that Balty did not know what to do.

The deeds bearing Metolius's seal must have put Balty in a difficult position, Ridge decided. He pondered what Metolius might do if he had intended for those kids to have the deeds, and then Ridge and Balty stole them. Ridge's insides turned over. Maybe Balty was working for Tegea, and the two leaders of the Global Alliance were feuding over the gateway to the galaxy—a territorial battle that Ridge had found himself in the middle of.

But if that were the case, why would Metolius send a couple of kids to claim the land? Unless the kids were powerful mages in disguise, doing Metolius's bidding. Or innocent pawns in a galactic power struggle.

This whole thing had gotten crazy. Ridge's head ached suddenly, and he leaned back in the leather couch. He and Schlitzer had had it all under control. Sure, their methods took time, but they might get only one shot and had to do it right the first time. But Balty had been running a parallel operation without telling him. Now the kids would be more on guard than ever. It was bad enough the abduction of the girl had made them paranoid in the first place, spurring them to hire the Alphabet Boys. Now the kids knew they were targets again. Ridge seethed to himself, careful to keep his face pleasantly neutral.

"So you used the Hesychasm," Ridge said casually. He had given Balty one of his three precious bottles after watching Balty brutally beat one of the new girls as he dragged her from the house's hangar to his bedroom. Ridge had figured it would be kinder to the girls if they were drugged and unconscious while Balty did his sordid business. Of course, Balty used Greenwash on them, but that was a mild narcotic compared to Hesychasm, which supposedly rendered one unconscious with a single breath. It hadn't occurred to Ridge that Balty would use it for the same purpose Ridge was planning. Now the twins would be on guard for that, as well. Balty was fucking everything up.

Balty smiled wryly. "Yeah. Lot of good the Hesychasm did, with those bumbling idiots. Now my four men are dead. At least now they won't talk," Balty said, slurring his words. "I don't think they would have anyway, but men will break sometimes under torture. Not Cephs, mind you, but Earthlanders will." Balty sipped at his drink and shrugged. "Not that Ramzy could do anything even if he did find out we had something to do with it."

Ridge cringed. *We.* He nibbled at some peanuts and waited for Balty to drink himself into a stupor so that he could slip away and find a few hours of peace.

———————)———————

It was early morning the following day, and Jidna sat at Schlitzer's bar. The shaded pavilion was quiet. Only a few young men sat at the bar with him, and two barmaids were working behind it, cleaning and stocking. They had shirts on. They didn't bare their breasts until it was busy and they got hot. The men liked when it got busy. Now the girls were down in the mouth, with dark circles under their eyes. Jidna gestured for the blonde named Bambi and ordered a ginger ale.

"Do I look like a flight hostess?" Bambi asked. "Who has ginger ale on the moon?"

Jidna dug into his bag and came out with a roll of damp paper. He laid it on the bar and opened it. It contained several gnarled brown roots. He held the cool roots to his nose and inhaled the scent of Earth. Bambi took one and pressed it to her nose, closing her eyes in bliss.

"Aaah," she breathed out. "Ginger."

"Mash it up, throw in some sugar, and let it sit for a few days," Jidna said, having watched his grandmother ferment ginger plenty of times.

"I know how to do it," Bambi said, and took the ginger roots and placed them on the lower counter. "Come back in a couple of weeks and I'll have some ginger ale for you." She smiled, showing straight teeth tinged with green. Jidna frowned. Schlitzer must be giving his girls Greenwash. Ridge had never tried it himself. That kind of stuff scared him.

"Where's Schlitzer?" he asked, eyeing the points of Bambi's nipples as they moved under her t-shirt while she worked.

"I'll get him," she said, and sauntered off, slapping a gray bar towel against her swaying hip as she left.

Giselle had ruined him. He'd never been particularly attracted to Bambi, but now he had no interest whatsoever. He hadn't even thought of stopping by to see Danny, he realized with a twinge of guilt. He sipped at a glass of ice water until Schlitzer entered the tent, grumbling and rubbing sleep from his eyes.

"Jid," Schlitzer drawled, pulling up a stool. Schlitzer waved his fingers, and the two barmaids and young men disappeared to leave them alone. Schlitzer turned his blue eyes to Jidna. "What the hell are you doing here so early? Did you hear about the raid?" Schlitzer asked.

"Yeah," Jidna said. "I heard."

"Was that your doing?" Schlitzer asked bluntly.

"No," Jidna said with disgust.

"Well, not to be crass," Schlitzer said. "But whoever fucked that up is making things harder for us."

"I know," Jidna said. "Believe me." He sighed and swirled the ice in his glass, reminding himself of Balty, which made him dump the ice from his glass with a jerk of his wrist. Schlitzer followed the ice with his eyes as the white chunks hit the dusty ground. No one threw away water on the moon, especially ice. Jidna raised his eyes and caught Schlitzer's gaze. Schlitzer had no idea how much worse things could get.

Jidna dug into his bag and retrieved a bottle of clear liquid. The bottle was disc-shaped—round and flat and the size of his palm. Molded into the clear glass was the symbol of a stag. Antler Kralj Pharmakon. He had paid dearly for that bottle. Well, paid lots of gold, that is. And he'd bought three. One had gone to Balty, one he'd kept for himself, and the third he handed to Schlitzer, who inspected it curiously.

"Hesychasm," Jidna told Schlitzer. "Very powerful sleep agent. Place a few drops on a cloth, cover the nose and mouth with it, and your victim will fall limp like a rag. It wears off after three to four hours, with no ill effects."

Schlitzer wrinkled his brow suspiciously and set it on the bar. "I heard they used this stuff in the raid." His eyes narrowed with renewed suspicion. "How'd you get a hold of it?"

"There was a shipment," Jidna said. "There are a few bottles floating around. I guess one ended up in the wrong hands." He stared down Schlitzer's accusing glare. "It wasn't my doing. I told you. I'm not as stupid as that. Just tell me what you know."

Schlitzer relaxed his scowl and related information Jidna had already learned, and then said, "Now they've erected fencing and guard towers around the twins' camp. And their Light Fighters gang has started sending out squads to patrol the roads. They seem to be intent on bringing law and order to Peary." Schlitzer chuckled cynically.

Jidna was not amused. He did not need the complication of a vigilante militia. This whole thing was promising to be much more expensive than he'd counted on. Oh, well. What did he care about gold? He had so much, he was unable to recall where he'd stashed it all. Which reminded him, he needed to take some more over to Last

Chance. Little by little. So Balty and his thugs wouldn't take notice. Not that it was any of their business. It was his gold.

Jidna turned to the bar and took out the Delosian coin with the castle on it and wondered if Gabira would like it. "You ever seen one of these?" he asked. Jidna handed over the coin, and Schlitzer examined it.

"No," Schlitzer said. His gray, cobwebby tendrils snaked through the air towards Jidna but seemed to lose their way when they got near Jidna's obsidian ring, wandering off towards the bar and then fading away harmlessly. Jidna contentedly polished his ring on his pant leg. It was a helpful little trinket.

"You keep it," Jidna told him. He had to get the rare gold coin out of his hands before he used it as an excuse to visit Gabira's cave. Thoughts of her daughters made him feel both aroused and afraid. He was completely confused about their true natures and how he felt about them now. He was still plagued with fantasies of seducing Giselle and had acquired a puzzled curiosity about Daleelah.

"We set up another stakeout, by the Light Fighters' training yard. Want to see?" Schlitzer asked.

"Sure," Jidna said.

"I'll hook you up. Wait here."

"Take it," Jidna said, pushing the bottle of Hesychasm towards Schlitzer.

Schlitzer huffed out a breath and stuffed the bottle into his pocket. He left the pavilion and returned a few minutes later with a man he introduced as Ankara.

"Take Jidna by 5L," Schlitzer said.

Jidna walked out of the camp with Ankara, and they made their way across the dome. Ankara led him to a tent in a sparsely populated block with a clear view of the training yard. Jidna sat shoulder-to-shoulder with Ankara and they took turns peering through binoculars out the small mesh window. Only a few men were there, sitting at a set of picnic tables or jabbing at punching bags. Jidna glanced at his watch. It was still early yet, only 7:45. He raised the binoculars and panned slowly across the yard, landing on Balty's speedster, which was parked on an abandoned patch of dust. A smile tugged at Jidna's lips. The girl had balls.

"They must be coming," Ankara said, elbowing him and pointing. Jidna shifted his binoculars and found two stocky Scrids standing at the intersection of Spoke Road Five. "The Scrids follow Torr around like dogs."

"Why?" Jidna asked.

Ankara said, "They think the kids are some sort of prophesied pair. Rumor has it they're the twin Star Children."

Jidna furrowed his brow. If the kids had a group of followers who believed they were the Star Children, some would be happy to die to protect them. Securing the deeds to Anaximenes was becoming harder and harder.

Jidna watched as several groups of people entered the yard and a four-wheeler pulled to a stop, towing a small wagon hauling a tank of water.

"That's their gang, the Light Fighters. There's the leader, Torr, climbing out of the driver's seat," Ankara said. A brown-skinned, long-legged woman climbed out of the passenger seat. "That's his girlfriend, Blaire, leader of the Smith gang. And his sister, Cassidy, is coming up in that big group behind them. She's the one wearing the red t-shirt and yellow vest."

Jidna examined Balty's former captive. She looked strong and confident—a completely different person from the skinny drug-addicted wraith he had seen slip into his home's hangar and steal Balty's speedster. He turned his attention to the couple Balty's men had attacked. Their expressions were grim, and they scanned the yard alertly as they talked. Torr was tall and broad-shouldered, with the solid muscles of someone who worked out, and held himself with the easy confidence of one who has confronted demons and slain them.

Jidna squinted. Something was odd about Torr. There was a flickering, purplish glow around his head. Jidna first thought it was an optical illusion, but it remained even as Torr crossed the yard and the angle of the light changed. Jidna could only see it if he relaxed his gaze, but it was definitely there, reminding him of flames. Jidna looked at others in the yard. Most people had a thin sheath of color around them, varying from muddy brown to bright blue or red, but Torr's was prominent and extended several inches around his frame, and was most pronounced around his head.

Jidna had seen auras before but never thought much about them, and normally suppressed his vision to avoid unnecessary distraction.

PALMER PICKERING

Auras were nothing more than the visible signature of the electromagnetic field that all matter radiated. But Torr's was particularly active. Jidna's gaze shifted to Cassidy. She had a large aura as well. He relaxed his focus, fascinated. She glowed a deep indigo blue, edged in a pulsating gold. The gold shimmered around her head in a subtle display of dancing light. He had never seen anything like it, and wondered if others could see it, too. It was almost angelic. A sudden, jabbing fear took hold of him. He could not let Balty get his hands on her again. She was like a rare flower—infinitely more precious than Balty could ever appreciate.

The only problem was, he did not know if Balty was continuing with his own plans to get possession of the deeds. He could only assume that he was. It was up to Jidna to get to her before Balty did. He was not so concerned about Torr, the young man could take care of himself. But he was determined to keep this beauty from Balty.

———————— ☽ ————————

Back at his lab, Ridge painstakingly reset the obsidian oval into its original copper setting and fastened all the little black gems into their mangled prongs. He wondered worriedly if some of the magic had been broken forever by his asinine mistake of disassembling it.

There was only one way to find out, and so Jidna returned to Peary Dome, making the effort this time to load the Korova with food. It had been days since he'd made a food run, and the traders were like starving dogs fighting over table scraps. Some were angry he'd made a deal in advance with Phyllis and demanded they all get a chance to place orders. Others demanded he split his load evenly among all of them. He brushed them off politely and let people bid on the unclaimed items.

After the ship was emptied, he helped Phyllis load her goods onto a transport.

"How much?" she asked.

"How about, let's see," he said, looking up at a skylight as if calculating. "Six Delosian Stags."

Her mouth softened into a smile, and she dug into her pocket, handing him the six coins he had given her the week before in exchange for her reading.

He climbed into the passenger seat of her transport, and she drove it slowly across the hangar, stopping at a lengthy security checkpoint. The spaceport guards were getting more aggressive of late, Jidna noted.

Finally, they rolled out into the sunshine.

"How did your ring work out?" she asked.

"Well, I'm still here," he said with a chuckle. "I added the original border back on." He took the gaudy ring from his pocket and slipped it onto his finger.

She glanced sideways at it and knit her brows together. "Oh," was all she said.

At her camp, he helped her unload, then they sat in the lawn chairs in the shade of the supply tent. She looked at his ring but would not touch it.

"I don't like those new gems," she said bluntly.

He frowned at his ring. "Me neither, frankly. But the other day while I was lost in the metaphorical olive grove," he said, not wanting to reveal the dead-on accuracy of her vision, "it occurred to me that perhaps I would have had an easier time of it had I not removed the stones from their original setting."

She was silent for a moment, then said, "I find it's always best to follow your gut instincts."

He puckered his mouth in agreement. "What do you think the small ones do?" he asked.

"I don't know, and I don't want to touch them to find out. That should tell you something."

It did. He removed the ring and hid it in his pocket again. He felt better with it out of his sight. She thanked him for the food and left to return the transport, and Jidna wandered over to Danny's. He stopped outside her pavilion, which was quiet for this time of day. He slipped on the obsidian ring and went to find her.

She was inside the pavilion, sitting on pillows with a couple of her girls, waving a fan to cool her face. She shooed the girls away, leaving her and Jidna by themselves. Her blue eyes wandered to his, still young despite her aging skin and drooping breasts.

"Are you here to fuck me and leave?" she asked.

He pulled back in surprise. She had never spoken to him like that before. He met her angry eyes with his startled ones. "Um, I hadn't decided yet," he said honestly.

"Oh, I see," she said tartly, turning her nose away and fluttering her fan.

"Danny. You know, I'm rich. I can give you money if you need it. Or food. It doesn't have to be like that. We don't have to have sex for me to take care of you."

She turned her head slowly and glared at him over her fan. It was decorated with the image of a bamboo forest and a panda bear. She lowered the fan. "Is that what you think I need? To be taken care of?"

He clamped his jaws shut. He thought he was being kind, but he had clearly said the wrong thing.

"Is that what you think I want?" she insisted. "A sugar daddy?"

"Well," he said, fumbling for words. "I don't know. What do you want?"

She rolled her eyes and gave him a dismissive snort. "If you don't know, there's no use in me telling you."

She stood up and straightened her gown around her hips, then walked haughtily from the tent. He stared after her, dumbfounded, and got up to follow her. He ducked into her tent behind her and gently grabbed her arm.

"What's the matter, Danny? What's bothering you?"

"I don't know," she said, turning around in the small space, which was taken up by a large bed with an actual wooden frame and headboard and voluminous pillows and bedding, and fell into his arms, sobbing.

He froze in confusion. This was completely uncharacteristic of the cool, loving Danielita he'd known for over ten years. He clumsily patted her back, not knowing what else to do. "Why don't you just tell me what you want?" he asked. "It'd be easier that way. I'm not a mind reader, you know. And I obviously don't understand women."

She lifted her head. Her eyes were red from crying. "I want a lover," she said bitterly. "What do you think I want?"

He stared at her. He was going to say that he would have sex with her, but he knew that's not what she meant. Jidna blinked, trying to find the right words, but he couldn't think of any. His eyes landed on his ring, where his hand was cradling her blond head. Fine golden energy tendrils were wrapped around the small black gems. He couldn't tell which were his and which were hers. Their energy threads seemed wrapped up in them, as though caught in a spider's web, and the ring was the spider, reeling in its catch.

She glared at him as he stood dumbly, his mouth moving but saying nothing. She pulled away from him and sat on the bed, kicking off her sandals and pulling her feet up onto the bed and staring glumly across the dim tent. He sat next to her and tried to pull off the ring without tearing at the delicate filaments. His heart hurt, and he could feel hers aching, too. This was not supposed to happen. They were not supposed to fall in love.

He yanked the ring off and shoved it into his pocket, his pulse racing. He took a deep breath, the surge of longing and guilt subsiding. She looked up at him, her eyes wide and confused.

"I care about you. You know I do," he said.

She sniffed and wiped at her eyes. "I know," she said, returning her gaze to the shadows.

He gently turned her chin and waited until she met his eyes. He kissed her tenderly on the lips and pulled her down next to him on the bed.

"Let's just hold each other," he said.

They lay together for a couple of hours. They didn't have sex, and he gave her no money. Nor did he offer her promises of love. In fact, they barely spoke at all. He finally kissed her forehead and said goodbye, and then left with a sad heart.

He didn't know what to think of the whole encounter, but he was sure the cursed ring had something to do with it. How very disturbing. And intriguing. He slipped the ring back on and found his way to Schlitzer's. Once inside the large tent, he settled onto a stool at the bar.

After two shots of Petron, Schlitzer appeared and motioned for him to follow. They ended up in his private consultation tent, which was hidden amongst a tight warren of tents and shacks, and sat in two lawn chairs, facing each other. Schlitzer opened a cold bottle of beer for each of them, and Jidna leaned back into his chair with a sigh.

"What do you do when a hooker falls in love with you?" Jidna asked.

Schlitzer laughed a deep, hearty laugh. "Happens all the time. Don't trouble yourself over it. Just tell them you love them, wipe away their tears, then kiss them, fuck them, and get on with your day."

Jidna stared at him with a sour grin, shaking his head. "You're heartless, man."

Schlitzer raised an eyebrow with a smug grin. "I'm telling you. It works."

Jidna sighed and stared at the ceiling. He didn't have it in him to be such a bastard.

Schlitzer suddenly switched topics, his voice unusually raw. "What the fuck is going on with the food situation, anyway?"

"Oh, it's bad," Jidna said, turning to him. "You're all fucked."

Schlitzer regarded him studiously. "Whatever you want me to do, I'll do it."

Jidna noticed Schlitzer's silver tendrils reaching hesitantly towards him, trying to make a connection—or to manipulate him. The pimp's conscious intention made the tendrils light up like solar filaments, unlike the muted threads of most people.

Jidna casually raised his ring finger and watched the obsidian catch a shaft of sunlight that streamed through the crack between the door flaps. The little gems scattered the light in all directions. Perhaps that was their function, to help diffuse attacks. He wished he'd had them in Gabira's chambers. Now he was too afraid to go back. If Daleelah hadn't sprung his trap, he'd still be down there now, he was sure of it.

"Hey Schlitz, what do you do when someone you thought was the sexiest wench on the moon turns into a total bitch from hell, and the frumpy thing turns into a goddess before your eyes?"

Schlitzer threw back his head and guffawed. "Jidna, my man," he said. "You must have had one hell of a week."

Jidna laughed with him. "I have had an interesting few days, that's for sure."

"You kiss the goddess's feet, that's what you do," Schlitzer said. "And ask for mercy."

"But what do you do when she keeps changing from a frump to a goddess and back again, in the wink of an eye?"

Schlitzer stopped laughing and examined him with an odd look. "That, I could not tell you."

Jidna noticed suddenly that Schlitzer's tendrils had all converged on the ring and looked to be tangled there, the snarls getting worse as Jidna moved his hand to scratch at his beard. Jidna unobtrusively swirled his hand in a little circle, and the tendrils wrapped more tightly around the ring. Schlitzer's eyes popped a bit, as though he were a fish hooked in the mouth. Ridge looked more closely. The threads were snagged in the little black gems and their copper settings, like hair caught in barbed wire.

"But seriously, Jidna, for Algol's hell," Schlitzer cursed. "The stress is getting to me. Why can't you equalize the food situation? Why are you guys doing this to us?"

"There's some shit going on at Gandoop," Jidna muttered, distracted by the behavior of Schlitzer's snagged tendrils as he moved his ring hand back and forth. It was as though Jidna had grabbed hold of Schlitzer's heartstrings, or the pimp was a marionette that Jidna could pull this way and that.

"What kind of shit?" Schlitzer pressed. "I can help."

Jidna met his eyes. "It's bigger than both of us, my friend," he said, feeling the surrender seep into his bones. "I fear we're both pawns in a cosmic game."

Schlitzer wore a pained look, and Jidna suspected it was not just from the shortage of food. Jidna did not know how to free the tendrils from the ring, so he slid the ring off his finger and slipped it into his pocket. Schlitzer's face twitched with a spasm of relief, and he visibly relaxed, exhaling with a loud breath.

"But I am asking for your help," Jidna continued. "You know—the problem you're helping me solve? How is our little plan going?"

"I've got some solid leads," Schlitzer assured him. "But what about food? Does our project have anything to do with food?"

"I'm afraid not," Jidna said, too ashamed to tell him it would probably make things worse.

———————————)———————————

Ridge stood next to the pool table, chalking his cue. Balty lined up his shot and sank two balls on the break.

"Lucky," Ridge said flatly, and watched as Balty sank three more balls in rapid succession and smiled smartly at Ridge. But there was no way Balty was going to make this next shot.

He didn't, and scratched, cursing foully.

Ridge sank his first four balls easily, then had a complex shot to set up. He sank two balls on that shot, which left only one more on the table for him and two for Balty. He could hear Balty fuming, pacing back and forth behind Ridge and rubbing chalk agitatedly onto the tip of his cue. Ridge considered letting the bastard win, but then thought better of it. Balty liked to get all riled up, then beat him at the end. That's what made Balty happiest—losing and then winning. It really got his blood boiling. Their typical pattern was Ridge would win a game or two, then Balty would get all fired up and win a game or two. Balty always had to win the last game, or Ridge could not escape the game room.

Ridge sank his last ball, finishing the game. Balty glowered at him, his face red.

"What?" Ridge demanded. "You left the table wide open."

Balty scowled. "What's going on with your assignment? Why the fuck is it taking you so long?"

"Assignment?" Ridge asked, not knowing what he was talking about. "Oh. You mean the deeds?"

"What the fuck do you think I mean?" The whites of Balty's eyes showed above his lower lids. Never a good sign.

Ridge tightened his shoulders, then twirled the obsidian ring surreptitiously on his finger, curious to see how Nana's little helper would work on this maniac.

Ridge casually rested the butt of his pool cue on the ground and folded his two hands over the long, slender shaft, the ring facing Balty.

Balty didn't notice the atrocious thing, but Ridge saw Balty's fat, gray tendrils creeping towards him, hoping to catch him unawares. Balty's tendrils were different from other people's. They genuinely looked like octopus tentacles, sticky and grasping, unlike the simple threads he saw on most people. Ridge watched, fascinated, as the tentacles crept towards the ring, as though sniffing it. Suddenly, they were caught in the barbs of the little gems, and started writhing and thrashing, trying to get free.

But unlike Schlitzer, Balty was truly a big fish. A whale, or a shark—a predator in his own right—and the big man followed the tension of the snagged tendrils and lunged at Ridge with his pool cue raised, striking Ridge in the ribs with the butt end of the stick.

Ridge collapsed onto his knees, his breath driven from him with a bolt of pain. Balty's cue swung through the air and caught him upside the head, cracking loudly, the thin tip breaking off and spinning across the room as Ridge fell onto his side, clutching his head. He gasped and scrabbled to yank off the ring. He closed it in his grip and squeezed his eyes shut against the next blow, which did not come.

He opened his eyes and saw Balty glaring down at him, the broken cue still raised in his hand. Balty slowly lowered the cue, his eyes darting around as though wondering where the onslaught had come from.

Ridge took the hand Balty offered and let the big Teg pull him painfully to his feet.

"Sorry about that," Balty said nonchalantly, walking across the room to trade out his broken stick for a new one. "Lost my cool for a second. This deed business is an untimely annoyance. We'll have to expedite things. I'll see what I can figure out on my end." Balty spoke with the calm efficiency of an administrator.

It was the first time Balty had ever struck him, but the man seemed totally unfazed by it. Ridge stuffed the ring into a pocket and staggered to a chair, his ribs screaming and his head throbbing. Athena poked her head inside the doorway.

"Everything okay in here?" she asked brightly.

The girl had balls to come into the room at the sound of a fight, Ridge reflected with respect. Either that or she was a fool, and Ridge would be burying her soon out in the regolith.

"Yeah, yeah," Balty said. "Just a little friendly competition. Be a babe and get me another drink, won't you? And get a towel and some ice for Ridge, here."

"Sure, Balty," she said, and disappeared.

"I've got everything under control," Ridge said, rising gingerly out of the chair. His ribs felt like a spear was lodged in them, and it hurt to breathe. "It's just taking a little time to set everything up. I think you broke my rib," he huffed.

Balty turned and raised an eyebrow. "Really? Hopefully I didn't break your skull, too. As long as there's a lump, you'll be fine." Balty racked up the balls, then went to the end of the table and lined up his shot.

Ridge bowed out of the game and took his speedster straight to the main facility and found Yen. The doctor told him it was only a cracked rib, and the knob on his skull was nothing to be concerned about. They would both heal on their own. Ridge flew himself over to his Last Chance lab, wincing against the jabbing pain in his chest as he worked the controls.

The whole day had been a series of minor fiascos, and he blamed the little black gems. Clearly, their power broke down people's inhibitions and unleashed suppressed emotions—and not in a good way. He wondered if the ring was why his grandmother had always drawn people into conflict. Or perhaps her combative character had imprinted itself onto the black gems. Or, maybe Ridge had just set them the wrong way in his clumsy ignorance of magic.

At the lab, he hobbled over to his workbench, took a pair of pliers, and pulled every evil little black gem from its copper teeth, collecting them in a glass dish. He painstakingly reset the large obsidian oval into the plain gold setting he had fashioned and slid on the elegantly simple ring. His ribs and head complained the whole time, but this could not wait. He unceremoniously dumped the glinting gems into the refuse recycler and pushed the button. The recycler buzzed with a sharp grinding sound, and Ridge watched a cloud of glittering black dust pass through the transparent outflow duct and land in the glass receptacle. He waited for the dust to settle, black flecks flashing at him like glimpses of his grandmother's eyes. He pressed a button, and the dust shot out through the refuse airlock and disappeared from view.

———————————)———————————

The next day, Ridge looked through binoculars from the lab's port-hole window out over the Black Mare as the Silox detonated. His little side project—a porous silicon and liquid oxygen explosive device. It caused a satisfying burst of light, illuminating the black basalt for a brief, brilliant moment. He checked his stopwatch. Twenty minutes exactly. His timed fuse mechanism was working beautifully. Rock debris formed a small cloud of projectiles hurtling through the void, with a few pebbles hitting the lab dome like hail. He needed to move his test site farther from his buildings, and drill deeper holes. Most mines only blasted inside craters to avoid such fallout. Even so, blast particles came back to the moon eventually, occasionally hitting structures and causing friction between the mining lords. Maybe if he covered the target area with carbon fiber cloth first it would contain the debris. Either that or spew carbon fiber everywhere. He missed Earth's gravity and atmosphere.

He hadn't bothered taking off the spacesuit after dropping the small canister into the bore hole and retreating to the lab, so he immediately left again through the airlock, drove his four-wheeler to the blast area, and surveyed the damage. It had created a nice mound of rubble, easy for his earth movers to haul to the rock crusher, one of which he'd transferred from Gandoop to Last Chance. After a couple dozen more consistent blasts, he would feel comfortable letting his men use the Silox to break up the basalt and start mining the mare in earnest.

Then, once he was confident his Silox design was working perfectly, he would experiment with a shorter fuse time for hand-thrown grenades. For grenades, he'd have to make sure the timing was precise, and would need to measure the blast radius to make sure it was shorter than the throwing distance. With gravity. He admitted that grenades were not very practical on the lunar surface, where gravity was one-sixth that of Earth. They could work indoors, he mused, but then they could damage a structure's integrity. Maybe he should design a launcher. He sighed. He didn't know what he'd actually do with grenades, but it gave him a sort of dastardly delight just to design them and imagine tossing one into Balty's big mouth.

At the same time, he was designing a new remote-controlled detonation device using radio signals instead of a wire. That design was more practical on the moon, if not slightly more complicated, and had a different set of challenges and risks. He retreated to the lab and removed his spacesuit.

He radioed Murphy to get some men to gather up the rubble, crush it, and run it over to Gandoop to be processed into titanium, magnesium, oxygen, and iron. He wasn't planning on installing the equipment at Last Chance that he'd need for a fully independent production facility. Rock crushers were one thing. Furnaces, reactors, condensers, and gas compressors were quite another.

Eventually, he'd train his men on how to make the Silox, and then work on an automated fabricator for mass production, which he would house at Last Chance as their first manufactured product. The Silox had already proven to be much better at breaking up the hard moon rock than the explosives the moon mines were currently using. Ridge would soon have a new stream of revenue from his Silox, in addition to a steady output of titanium and other minerals and gases. Now if he could somehow keep knowledge of the Silox from Balty and keep all the profits for himself.

He took off for Gandoop, and once there went in search of his brother and father down in their little hideaway in the bowels of Cube Two, which was in the tunnels underneath the smelter and other processing equipment. The heat and noise of the main level receded to echoing silence as he climbed down the stairs to the lower chambers. One side of the underground facility housed the mine workers, whose domain consisted of four dormitory rooms, six private chambers for senior employees, a common area with kitchen and tables that doubled as a recreation room, and bathroom facilities. The other end held the Gandoops' personal storage rooms and various offices, one of which had been converted into a living space that Ishmar and Ali shared.

Ridge knocked on the metal door and pushed it open. Ali looked up from his cot where he was sitting and holding a small screen displaying the workers' schedules. Ishmar was sitting on a thick pile of rugs at the low brass table and stirring sugar into a pot of tea. He motioned for Ridge to join him. Ridge leaned over and kissed his father on both cheeks, nodded to Ali, and sat down as Ishmar poured him a glass of steaming tea.

"Where've you been?" Ali asked, setting the screen aside.

"Busy." Ridge blew on the hot tea and took a small sip. It was sweet and smelled of cardamom.

"Why do you keep shaving your head?" Ali asked with a disapproving frown.

Ridge brushed at the new fuzz on top of his head. "Keeps the dust off."

"You look like a skeleton."

Ridge shot his brother a sharp glance. "Kind of you to say so."

Ali managed a sardonic smile, then came over to sit on the rugs and poured himself a glass of tea.

Ishmar inspected Ridge with tired eyes. His father had aged, his skin hanging in dry folds from his cheeks and jowls. Ishmar had been handsome at one time. Strong and robust. Ridge smiled gently and asked, "How've you been?"

Ishmar bobbed his head ambiguously. "How do you think? There are a hundred of them here now. That man is like a crowbar, and we're the crack in the door."

Ridge nodded and sipped at his tea. "What should we do?"

Ishmar looked vacantly at the wall behind Ridge's head and finally said, "What can we do? Leave? Start over?"

The room was silent, and steam from the teapot rose in feathery wisps.

Ali broke the silence. "He'll never want to run the mine."

Ishmar snorted. "No, he'll just take all the product."

"Ten percent," Ali said, persisting in his optimism.

"Ten percent?" Ridge snapped. "Balty is not the Cephean Federation. Why should he get ten percent?"

Ali shrugged and said, "I'm just saying. Ten percent would be fair."

"How is that fair?" Ridge asked. "What has he done for us?"

"He makes deals," Ali said.

Ridge rolled his eyes but did not bother arguing any further.

Ali opened a tin of candied almonds and crunched on one absently. The pink sugar-coated almonds reminded Ridge of weddings he'd attended as a boy.

"Should we find women?" Ridge asked abruptly, taking an almond.

Ali stopped chewing and stared at him, and then started laughing.

"What's so funny?" Ridge snapped.

"Like Balty?" Ali's mouth turned down in disgust.

"No," Ridge said with irritation. "Wives."

Ali sat back, laughing at the ceiling. "What have you been smoking? What woman in her right mind would want to live here?" Ali shook his head, still laughing.

"It's better than going to a breeding center on Earth," Ridge muttered.

Ali shrugged. "Maybe. If she never wants to breathe real air again."

"We've got real air."

"You know what I mean." Ali popped another almond into his mouth, crunching on it and looking at Ridge as if he were still his stupid little brother.

"I saw Gabira and her daughters the other day," Ridge said, turning to meet Ishmar's eyes.

His father's face lit up. "Really?"

Ridge smiled. His father was still enamored, even after all these years and Gabira's flat refusal.

"I get Giselle," Ali said.

"No, I get Giselle," Ridge said, his temper flaring.

"Ha!" Ali laughed. "Fat chance of that. You can have her sister."

Ridge was suddenly angry, sick of Ali and his presumptuous ways just because he was born first. Ridge wanted to slam the glass down but held his temper and merely glowered at him. Ali raised his eyebrows at Ridge, challenging him to dispute his right as the eldest. Ridge wasn't going to get sucked into this argument again and was sorry he'd even mentioned the women. "You can have her," Ridge scoffed. "She's a bitch."

"A sexy bitch," Ali said, a crooked leer spreading across his face.

Ridge chose to change the subject, not wanting to think about her. "I got some furniture for Last Chance. A couple of freighters came in from LAX the other day. They're stripping the hotels. Got some nice stuff."

His brother and father stared at him blankly.

"It should be ready to move into in another couple of weeks. We can move there together."

"I'm not leaving," Ali said stubbornly.

"Have it your way," Ridge said and poured himself more tea.

Ishmar watched his two sons and said nothing.

———————⟩———————

Ridge stood next to Ali while they watched a Cephei-bound freighter being loaded up at the far side of the hangar. Ali stood with his arms crossed, observing casks of wine as they were carted up the cargo ramp. Ridge loved his brother. Ali was a rational, warm-hearted man, who was unfailingly courteous and respectful to everyone; he was only an arrogant, obnoxious prick to Ridge, and only in the privacy of their quarters. Ali had a thing about being the eldest. He always had. Ridge half-suspected it was because Ridge excelled at everything, and Ali was merely competent. Being the firstborn was the only thing Ali had over him. Or maybe Ridge was the only person Ali felt comfortable enough with to be human. Ridge took the abuse and returned it in kind. But when it got right down to it, they were all they had. Ishmar would not live forever—then it would be just the two of them. Ridge laid his hand on Ali's shoulder. Ali's head turned sharply at the unfamiliar display of affection.

"What?" Ali asked, thinking Ridge must want something. Ridge suddenly couldn't speak, and he was afraid the moistness in his eyes might be tears. Ali stared at his face. "What's wrong?"

Ridge swallowed and uttered anxiously under his breath, "I think Balty might kill me. Us."

"No," Ali said, brushing off his comment as ridiculous.

Ridge tightened his grip, and Ali glanced down at his hand like it belonged to some wild creature. "I just want you to know you've been a good brother," Ridge said.

Ali made a disgusted noise and shrugged his hand off. "Stop that. Stop talking nonsense."

"Okay," Ridge said, regaining his composure. "It's just that if something happens to me, I wanted you to know."

Ali wore a pained expression and met Ridge's gaze. "Cut it out," Ali said. "Nothing's going to happen to you."

Ridge nodded and took a breath. "I want you to move to Last Chance with me and Ishmar. It will be safer for you there."

Ali took in a quick, annoyed breath. "Rjidna Jibrail, stop now." Ali's voice had grown a touch more gentle. Ridge had nearly forgotten his full name, it had been so long since anyone had spoken it. The unexpected tenderness of it made tears spring to his eyes again, and he stiffened his face to hold them back.

Ali gave him a truly stricken look, the pooling tears no doubt frightening him more than the ominous words. "Come with me," Ali said brusquely, and Ridge followed him into the empty corridor that connected the spaceport to the cubes.

Ali turned to him and grasped him by both shoulders, holding his eyes with a stern, level gaze. "What happened? Tell me."

Suddenly, Ridge was eight and Ali was his big brother, and a sob shook Ridge's chest like some wave that came out of nowhere, and he was in Ali's arms. Ridge moaned from the jab of pain from his cracked rib, and Ali patted his back awkwardly. Ridge wished he could sink into the floor and disappear. "Balty's going to take everything," Ridge said, choking out the words.

"No, he's not," Ali said.

"Yes," Ridge said fiercely, and pulled back from the embrace, gripping Ali's shoulders in return, forcing him to meet his eyes. "He is."

Ali clung to his denial, and Ridge suddenly realized that if anyone was going to stop Balty, it had to be Ridge. If anyone was going to save their family fortune—save their lives—he would have to do it himself. He straightened and patted Ali's shoulders, his normal, stern countenance returning as quickly as it had left.

"Don't worry," Ridge told him. "You're right. We'll be fine. Just keep doing what you've been doing—being a good man." He gave Ali a stiff smile.

Ali looked at him oddly, one side of his lip curling up in confusion. "I think you must be getting ill or something," Ali said. "Maybe you should get some rest."

"You're right. I'm feeling a bit under the weather. I'll go back to the house after I take care of a few things."

Ali nodded, his brow furrowing from the strangeness of having glimpsed Ridge's soul.

Ridge and Ali walked back into the hangar together. Ridge gathered his energy to make another food run to Peary.

"Where you going?" Ali asked, as if he almost appreciated Ridge's company.

"Taking food to Peary."

"Again?"

Ridge nodded.

"Why?"

"Because they're hungry," Ridge said.

"What do you mean?" Ali asked.

Ridge glared at his brother. Was he blind, or stupid? Or dulled by Balty's tentacles? "Don't you see all the food rotting in the warehouse?" Ridge asked.

Ali shrugged. "Yeah. I guess."

"Well? It's intended for Peary," Ridge said. "But Balty has placed a food embargo on Peary. Haven't you noticed?"

Ali's face grew pale. "What do you mean?"

"What do you think I mean?" Ridge asked. "What do you think Ishmar and I have been talking about for the past few months?"

"Oh." Ali's face grew grave. "I didn't realize."

Ridge turned and started towards the warehouse to take stock of the latest food shipments from Earth. Ali caught up with him and walked by his side. "Can I come with you?"

"No."

"Why not?"

"Because I go over there disguised as that scummy outer rim mining lord, remember? If you come with me, you'll blow my cover."

"Oh."

Ali stopped walking, and Ridge left him behind, hoping he had enough sense not to tattle to Balty.

———————)———————

Jidna sat with Schlitzer in the pimp's private consultation tent.

"I have a plan for the girl," Schlitzer said, sipping a glass of ice water. "But the boy is proving more difficult. I know you said you didn't want to kill them, but it could turn out that way if he doesn't lower his guard. If you really want his deed, it may come down to us or them. And I don't want it to be us."

Jidna nodded silently and sucked on a piece of ice, considering his options. Did he really need the second deed? The main facility was on the girl's parcel. Wasn't that enough for him? He thought of his beloved home on the nexus of the three craters, and the rare-earths mine in Anaximenes H. He could survive without them, he supposed. But was it reasonable to expect that he could steal the girl's deed, and then the twins would take over the neighboring parcel peacefully? It would be the start of a long-standing feud. Best to end it now, he determined, sinking his head into his hands.

"What's wrong?" Schlitzer asked.

Jidna lifted his head wearily. "I'm not very good at all this intrigue and plotting. I'm an inventor. An engineer. I just want to live my life in peace."

"I know," Schlitzer said kindly. "That's why you hired me. Right?"

Jidna nodded, a weight lifting from his shoulders. "That's right," he agreed. "This is your area of expertise. Just tell me what you need."

"Well," Schlitzer said, setting down his glass. "I could use some weapons."

Jidna's back stiffened. "What kind of weapons? Can't you get whatever you need yourself?"

Schlitzer's eyes narrowed, and his lips turned up in an expression of scheming delight.

"I was thinking," Schlitzer said, "that we could use a few of those Teg weapons. You know, the black ones. The ones that make no sound, cause no bleeding, and kill on contact. You think you can get us some of those? I hear they're not even made of metal, so they can get past the metal detectors if Rodney's Rangers should decide to do their jobs all of a sudden and inspect your goods."

"Lectros," Jidna said. They were elegant weapons, he had to admit, and were made of some sort of Cephean fiber that could probably make it through Peary security. Rodney's guards routinely inspected his food shipments, but Jidna barely noticed. He hadn't been smuggling anything, and everyone was always so focused on the food that the guards did a cursory inspection and quickly moved out of the way to let trading begin.

He nodded slowly. Shipments of Teg weapons regularly passed through Gandoop Spaceport. "I'll have to see," Jidna said, and took a sip of water.

29

THE JAİL

Blaire lay sleeping in his arms as Torr gazed up at the dream-catcher dangling from the peak of their new tent. The past few days had sped by in a chaotic blur. Blaire had recovered from the attack with no ill effects other than some bruises and abrasions. Torr had also suffered some scrapes and bruises, but nothing serious. The burn across his chest was the only thing that still hurt.

The medics had determined that the substance on the white ker-chiefs was a strong sleep agent from Delos called Hesychasm, which was used for anesthesia on that planet, and was astronomically expensive. They had found a bottle of it on one of the men and were thrilled to add it to their surgical supplies.

Two of the attackers had died in the tent, and the other two died a few hours later in the infirmary. The one whose face had been torn up was conscious long enough to tell the medic a wolf had attacked him. The medic attributed it to delirium but was confounded by the nature of many of the wounds, which did look exactly like dog bites.

Torr had caught his campmates and fellow Light Fighters regarding him warily, and rumors circulated that Torr was a shaman shapeshifter and could take the form of a wolf, despite Faisal confirming that Torr was in his human form during the attack. Faisal could offer no expla-nation for the strange wounds, however, other than postulating that

Torr's wolf knife was magic and inflicted wounds as though it were the fangs of a beast.

Torr reflected with morbid curiosity that he felt no remorse for killing the men. He had been caught up in the heat of defending himself and Blaire and had reacted by reflex, as his training had taught him. He supposed shooting the men at Miramar had been no different, only he had been conscious at the time that Matthew was running away, and still he had decided to pull the trigger. He only hoped these four men would not visit him in his dreams.

The most disturbing thing was that the second man, before he died, had confessed to the medics that they had been hired by a very wealthy far side mining lord to subdue them with the Hesychasm in order to steal two lunar deeds, and that they were supposed to transfer the fingerprints of Torr and Blaire onto the deeds. Ink pads were found in the pockets of each of the men. Torr could only surmise that the attackers had confused Blaire with Cassidy. The man had said that they had been told not to kill them, and that they were to sneak in undetected and leave no trace behind. They were only to take the deeds.

In the days immediately following the attack, the Fensters had installed tarp fencing around the perimeter of the Fen and constructed a watchtower at each corner. Six men were assigned night watch. Still, Torr couldn't sleep.

He gently disentangled himself from Blaire and stepped out into the quiet of night curfew. Torr glanced over his shoulder at the tower behind Jasper's tent, and Raleigh tapped his fingers to his forehead in a salute. Torr returned the salute and made the rounds with Fritz, checking the perimeter and nodding silently to each of the guards. He joined Frank, who was sitting on the table, looking half-asleep. Durham appeared and crossed the courtyard on his crutches.

"Can't sleep?" Durham asked Torr.

"No. You either?"

Durham shook his head and leveraged himself up onto the table.

"Me and Durham will take the rest of the shift," Torr said to Fritz and Frank. "This is the second night in a row for you guys."

The blond twins didn't argue and retreated to their tent, leaving Torr and Durham to watch and listen.

————————)————————

Torr and his friends wandered the dome in the afternoon, searching for some sort of clues about those who had attacked them. Torr didn't think they would discover anything, but it was better than sitting around and worrying. No one in the Light Fighters had befriended the two attackers Torr had spotted with gray snakes coming out of their bellies. The PCA administrators and the guys who distributed tents hadn't been able to place the men, saying people came and went all the time, and everyone looked pretty much the same. It was the same story at the spaceport, with Rodney's Rangers and the customs guards shrugging and apologizing.

They stopped at each ration station, asking the guards if they had seen anything strange or noticed anyone new. Had any of their regular patrons suddenly stopped showing up? They got the same response everywhere—polite and friendly, but with blank expressions. No one had noticed anything unusual.

They walked the perimeter of Schlitzer's fenced block. Torr suspected the pimp but didn't want to enter his turf and suffer Schlitzer's snide remarks. Not far from Schlitzer's, the shoemakers' shop opened up to the roadway, and Torr slowed his pace.

The shopkeepers behind the table nodded with nervous recognition. Torr nodded in return, and one of the shoemakers waved him over. Torr frowned and approached the table.

"Sorry to bother you, Mister Torr," one of them said. "I heard you were attacked. Are you okay?"

"Yes," Torr said, examining the man's face. "I'm sure you didn't have anything to do with it," Torr drawled.

"No, no," the man said quickly, his eyes widening. "No. It wasn't us. I swear."

Torr furrowed his brow. "Well, did you notice anything strange? Any unusual activity from Schlitzer's camp?"

"No, no," the man said, shaking his head vehemently. "We don't never see nothing from over there." The shoemaker raised his hands defensively. "We just sell shoes."

"No new deals with slimy characters?" Torr asked.

"No. I swear. We don't talk to nobody. We just sell shoes and mind our own business." The other shoemaker nodded, and the three heavy-set guards shifted on their feet nearby.

Torr sighed and nodded to his friends. "Let's go."

"It's just," the shoemaker said hesitantly. Torr turned back to the man. "We were wondering if you've had a chance to talk to anyone about letting us visit our cousin Shiraz. Do you know when he will be released?"

"Oh," Torr said, exhaling. "Sorry. I completely forgot about that. No, I haven't had a chance. I'll check right now."

"Thank you. Sorry for the trouble," the man said obsequiously, and bowed his head.

Torr led his friends away from the shoemakers and headed towards the spaceport.

"Why do you want to help those guys?" Raleigh grumbled, but Torr did not answer.

Inside the spaceport, Torr found Rodney and asked him about the prisoner.

"You're concerned about your attacker?" Rodney asked wryly. "Why?"

"I don't know," Torr said. "The guy has a family."

"You're a good man," Rodney said, patting him on the shoulder.

Torr was surprised at the man's gesture and held his eyes.

"I was in prison, you know," Rodney said. "Life is complicated."

"It is," Torr agreed. "How long are you going to keep him in there?"

Rodney shrugged. "It's up to Ramzy. If we were on Earth, he'd probably get five years for aggravated assault and conspiring to kidnap. But seeing as it's the moon, Ramzy will let him out eventually. My guys are already complaining about guarding him and cleaning up his slops."

"Can his wife and kid visit him, at least?" Torr asked.

Rodney rubbed his chin. "Yeah, that should be okay. I'll check with Ramzy. I'll be right back."

"Thanks," Torr said.

"No, thank *you.* "

Rodney left and returned a few minutes later with Mazon.

"Hey, Torr," Mazon greeted him.

"Hey, Mazon," Torr said as the two grasped forearms. Mazon was short and compact, with a mass of braided hair and a big smile.

"Mazon will take a transport to their shoe shop and take the wife and kid to see him. Want to go with him?" Rodney asked.

Torr shrugged. "Okay. Never seen the jail."

He and Mazon left the shadowed hangar in an open-roofed jeep. Outside, Torr's friends scowled and trotted after them.

They parked in front of the shoemakers' camp and spoke with a brother of Shiraz. Half the camp wanted to accompany the wife and child, so Torr and Mazon drove to the jail by themselves and waited for the shoemakers and Torr's friends to hike across the dome.

Two more jeeps pulled up, and several Rangers climbed out and greeted them. Torr walked with Mazon into the area behind the infirmary. Mazon rapped on the door of a shipping container. He introduced Torr to the guard, Dunning, and then led Torr through the guard shack and into a small yard of bare, packed dust. The yard was enclosed by a rectangle of shipping containers topped with barbed wire and stinking of human waste.

Torr held his breath and followed Mazon to one of the containers. He took a turn peeking through a small viewing slit in the door. It took a moment for his eyes to adjust to the dim space, which was lit by several small air vents, but eventually he made out a figure sitting on the edge of a cot and eyeing the door. It was Shiraz. His beard had grown longer, and his clothes were ragged. And it stank.

"Don't you guys ever clean the cells?" Torr asked, backing away from the door.

"We do, but sometimes the prisoners get pissed and kick over their slop bucket." Mazon shrugged. "We don't make much effort to clean up after they do that. They just do it to get the guards to let them out into the yard while they clean the inside. If we let them out like that every time, they'll just pull that shit every day."

"They don't get to go outside?" Torr asked, following Mazon to a slit in another container's door.

"Once a day, for an hour. Or less, if they give us trouble." Mazon peered into the slit. "Yo, Jefferson," the Ranger said.

"Mazon?" A voice came from inside the container. Shuffling footsteps crossed the inside of the container.

"Why don't you make the prisoners clean up their own messes?" Torr asked.

"We just throw moon dirt on it and scoop it up with a shovel," Mazon said. "Can't give a shovel to a prisoner, they could beat you over the head with it. Right, Jefferson?"

A chuckle came through the slit in the door.

Mazon reached into his pocket and passed a tin of chewing tobacco through the slit.

"Thanks, man," the gruff voice said. "I owe you one. When are they letting me outta here?"

"Don't know," Mazon said and threw Torr an apologetic look.

Torr got a sick feeling in his stomach as he realized Jefferson must be the Ranger who had taken the bribe to allow the crate carrying Cassidy to pass through without inspection.

The Rangers continued chatting, and Torr wandered back to the guard shack. Dunning was out front, talking with the other Rangers who were waiting for Shiraz's family to arrive. Torr's friends were already there, gathered in a group next to the infirmary. Raleigh gestured at Torr to leave.

"I'm taking off. Thanks," Torr said.

"You don't want to see the family reunion?" Dunning joked.

"Nah," Torr said.

He nodded at the Rangers, and then walked over to his friends, kicking at the dust and reflecting on the effect of a person's actions. If it weren't for the two prisoners—if one of them had done the right thing—then Cassidy would never have been abducted and abused, and he would still have his joyful sister at his side.

———————)———————

After night gong, they knocked down the spy's lookout tent and pinned a note to it: *We are watching you.* There wasn't much to see since they had erected tarp fencing around the entire Fen, but still the spy arrived at his post every day and watched the back alleyway entrance to their camp.

At morning gong, Torr waited while Cassidy gazed into her crystal ball. As soon as she saw the spy leave his home tent to walk over to the lookout tent for his daily shift, Torr and Raleigh hopped into the buggy and sped to his tent near 10K, with Cassidy guiding them over the radio.

They found it and pinned another note to the tent door: *Tell Schlitzer to watch his step.*

30

THE OFFER

She felt like a crazy person. Some days she was fine, and other days she could not leave her tent and Blaire had to come get her. Today was such a day, and Cassidy stood trembling inside the threshold of Jasper's tent, waiting for Blaire to realize she wasn't coming out on her own. It didn't take long.

Footsteps fell outside the tent.

"Cassidy?"

"Yeah."

"Are you coming to training?"

"I can't."

"Can I come in?"

"Yeah."

Blaire poked her head inside and entered the tent. Blaire gently guided her outside and to the spoke road.

Men followed Cassidy with their eyes as she shuffled by. They were all waiting for an opportunity to grab her and steal her away. To sell her back to Balthazar. Tents rose and fell like drowning waves as she placed one foot in front of the other. Gray walls all around, closing in on her. Suffocating her. A rope around her neck. He was going to kill her this time.

"Ahhh!" she yelled, jerking away from the hand grasping at her arm.

She stumbled backwards into a soft bosom.

"Sorry," Darla said, standing across from her.

The tent city resolved into the clarity of the present moment, the tent lines stark and geometrical. Sounds were suddenly sharp, and the gunmetal smell of moon dust was acrid in her nose. Blaire had her arms around her.

Cassidy didn't remember Darla joining them. They sometimes met up with Blaire's sisters and Darla and the other Smith squad members in Center Ring and walked to the training yard together. But she didn't remember walking through Center Ring. She glanced up at a road post. 4F. She had no recollection of anything since leaving the Fen.

"Are you okay?" Blaire asked, helping Cassidy regain her balance.

"Sorry," Darla repeated. "I didn't mean to startle you. I was just saying how the fabric is getting grimy, and I wonder if a little water would make it worse, or maybe we should try brushing it clean."

Cassidy glanced down at her sleeve of white neoprene—the dust was attacking it like it did everything else.

"Oh. Yeah. I'll try brushing it," Cassidy said vacantly as she wondered why she was even wearing this shirt to training. She didn't remember dressing that morning. She looked down at herself. At least she'd had the sense to put on her black pants instead of the paneled skirt.

Everyone was staring at her. Wondering if she had lost her mind again. The Alphabet Boys hovered on the periphery, waiting for her.

"I'm fine," Cassidy said, shaking her arms and taking a deep breath. "Let's go. We'll be late."

Later that afternoon, the Smith sisters and Darla were at the Fen with her, listening to Fritz and Frank play music. The women sat at the picnic tables while the identical twins strummed their guitars and launched into a familiar tune.

Earth was visible in the gap between the dining area's shade tarp and the horizon of tents, and Cassidy choked up as she thought of her parents. Her father was in a work camp, but maybe her mother had made it to the Shaman's Shield by now. Cassidy glanced at Blaire's smiling face, which glowed with infatuation as she watched Torr talk and joke with the Alphabet Boys.

Blaire and her sisters had never spoken of their parents to Cassidy, but Torr had told her that they'd most likely died in Denver. Darla had confided in Cassidy about how she had left Earth—her father had been killed when Tegs came to their house in New Orleans. She had escaped through the neighborhood and made it all the way to Houston, hitch-hiking. There she had traded sex with a ship's captain for passage to the moon. Cassidy examined the woman sitting next to her. Her head was freshly shaved, showing off her shiny dark-brown head. Leather bands with bright beads decorated her wrists, and her usual silver hoops lined her ears and nose. Darla turned and met Cassidy's gaze.

"Whatcha thinking about, Miss Cassafrass?" Darla grinned, her dimples showing.

"You."

"Me? What about me?" Darla moved over to sit closer and looped her arm through Cassidy's, leaning against her.

"That you're a survivor."

"Shit, Miss Cassidy. We're all survivors here. You, me, and every other soul in this godforsaken place." She waved her delicate hand across the dome. "Last survivors of a doomed civilization. Stuck on a desert island, waiting to die." She giggled as though she'd said something funny.

Cassidy gazed out at the stars beyond Earth, wondering if their salvation really existed out there somewhere, or if Darla were right. Or maybe it was up to each one of them to do something—anything—to fight back against the encroaching darkness.

———————)———————

Cassidy cornered Torr in the kitchen supply tent while they were helping prepare dinner, blocking the exit.

"What?" he asked, holding a large can of stewed tomatoes.

"I was just thinking," she said. "Maybe you can use your Destroyer crystal as a weapon, and we can go rescue those women now."

He frowned and shook his head. "Good idea, but I'm not good enough at it yet. I need to spend more time practicing."

"Why?" she asked. "You were hitting the rocks Roanoke shot from his slingshot the other day."

"Yeah, but I can't control the thing very well. It takes too much concentration. Half the time I can't get it to work at all, and when I do, I often have to try several times. And even when it works there's usually a long lag time."

She folded her arms and glared at him. "You should practice more, then," she said. "That thing is magic."

He shrugged. "Yeah, clearly. Okay, I'll work on it." He stepped forward. "May I pass, now, Your Royal Golden Cloud?"

She made a face at him and stepped aside.

———————)———————

"You should sell the deeds," Jasper said, the next morning. They sat with Torr and Blaire at the Fen's tables, finishing up their breakfast. The other campmates had already eaten and gone off for a few minutes of private time before leaving for the training yard.

Cassidy pursed her lips at him. He insisted on bringing up the same topic over and over again.

"We already talked about this," Torr said. "We're not selling them."

Cassidy's gaze ranged between the two men, who were sizing each other up. Torr was no longer the meek adolescent Jasper had left on Earth, and Cassidy thought Jasper didn't quite know what to make of him. Cassidy didn't quite know, herself. Torr had fought off four men, killing them all—well, with the help of Blaire and Faisal, and his spirit wolf, supposedly. Still, he had proven himself a formidable warrior. His arms were corded with thick muscles, and though he looked relaxed with his forearms resting on the table, his fingers were alert and slightly bent, as if ready to reach for his weapons.

"Why not?" Jasper insisted, tearing at a hunk of bread with his teeth.

Cassidy glanced at Blaire, who was inspecting Torr with a calculated look. Blaire had been surprised when Cassidy and Torr had first told her about their lunar deeds, but now she seemed to be considering the possibilities. "What are you going to do with them?" Blaire asked, her eyes darting between Cassidy and Torr.

"I don't know," Torr said.

"Why?" Cassidy asked Jasper. "Do you have a buyer?"

Jasper gave a little shrug, and his eyes shifted.

"Aha! See?" Torr said. "I thought so. Don't tell me it's Schlitzer." Jasper's eyes widened innocently. "Did you tell him about them?" Torr demanded, his forearms tightening as his hands curled into fists. Cassidy felt her fists doing the same. Jasper was infuriating.

"No," Jasper said, holding his hands up defensively as Torr pressed his palms onto the table. "I didn't need to. He knew already," Jasper said quickly.

"He what?" Torr demanded. "How do you know? You discussed them with him?" Torr's face was red.

Cassidy's heart pounded, and she wanted to shake the scheming red-haired shyster.

"No, no. Well, yes. Will you calm down?" Jasper asked. The men glowered at each other.

"Tell me exactly what was said," Torr said. The wolf knife was in his hand.

"Put that thing away," Jasper said, looking nervously at the shining blade. Torr slipped it into its sheath, and Jasper continued, glancing guiltily at Cassidy. She stared at him coldly.

"I ran into Schlitzer at the traders pen. It was a while ago. I didn't tell you because I didn't want to make you nervous," he said hastily as Torr and Cassidy glared at him. "He hung around my container while I was portioning out a shipment of nuts and raisins I scored. Schlitzer never hangs around unless he wants something. In fact, he rarely leaves his camp. He must have been looking for me. Or one of his spies was watching me and let him know where I was."

Torr growled, "You should have told us right away. Why didn't you?"

Cassidy tensed at Torr's enraged expression, and Jasper rubbed nervously at his beard.

"Because you already said you didn't want to sell them. And because you hate Schlitzer. And because I was distracted by your sister." His gaze shifted to Cassidy, and her eyes hardened.

"Don't try putting this one on me," she snapped.

Torr's hands relaxed.

"Anyhow," Jasper said, lifting his chin and sliding into his storyteller's voice. "I said, 'Schlitz, what do you want? Wanna buy some nuts and raisins?' Schlitzer takes out a few coins and we make the trade, and then he just stands there, watching me. I think he was waiting for the other traders to leave, which they finally did. Then he says, 'Do you happen to know of any land for sale?'"

"'Land for sale?' I say. 'No.' Then I thought, what a crazy question, out of the blue like that. Well, it would be crazy, if I hadn't known exactly what he was talking about. So I look surprised. He just looks at me, and says, 'Well, if you did know of any, what price do you think it would bring?'" Jasper had made his voice low and sultry as if imitating Schlitzer's. Cassidy's lips turned up with amusement despite the fact that her pulse was thumping in her veins. She had never met the pimp and spymaster, but his reputation was of a conniving and dangerous man.

"At this point, I'm intrigued," Jasper went on. He laced his fingers together, enjoying having a captive audience. Cassidy's stomach felt hollow. Schlitzer knew about the deeds. How did he know? Who had told him? Whom had he told?

"'Well,' I say, acting like I don't know what he's talking about, 'A small outer rim parcel might bring, oh, I don't know, a couple million global credits.' I was just guessing, of course. I don't think gold really changes hands for moon land anymore. I think it's all traded on the black market for debts or favors."

"What did he say?" Cassidy prompted, kicking his foot under the table.

Jasper grinned at her, clearly enjoying dragging out the suspense. He continued, "So Schlitzer stood there eating raisins, as if it were a random question that he didn't really care about. Except, he's still standing there, which he never does. So I lock up my container, and he walks out of the cage with me. Then when we get out to the M ring he says, 'What if it were a prime piece of regolith land? Say, a major crater?'

"I turn to him, tired of his little game, and say, 'I don't know, Schlitz. What're you asking me for? You in the market for some land? Getting claustrophobic in here? It's worse out there,' I say." Jasper gestured to the glass hexagons looming overhead. Cassidy's mind was spinning.

"'I was just thinking,' Schlitzer says, real casual-like, 'that a major crater would bring a real good sum. Especially if there's a mine already on it. You know what I mean?' Then he looks at me with those baby-blue eyes like he wants to take me for one of his bitches. Anyway, I told him, 'Good luck with that,' and turned to leave. And he fucking follows me. I mean, this guy is desperate. He never follows me. He says, 'I think a crater like that would bring more gold than you could ever imagine. Think about that,' he says, and then shrugs and makes like he's going to leave.

"Then I say, 'What about a speedster? You hardly use yours.' Schlitzer loves that thing, but he nods like it's a good idea, and looks at me kind of funny. Because of course since I said that, he knows that I know that he knows that I know. He knew it all along anyway, so no reason to hide it," he said defensively at Cassidy's and Torr's angry scowls. "Then I say, 'For that matter, a crater with a big producing mine would be worth a galaxy-class cruiser.' And he nods at that! Like it's reasonable!"

Cassidy latched onto the idea of selling the deeds for a galaxy-class cruiser, excitement lifting the dread that was sinking into her bones at the confirmation that Schlitzer was after the deeds. With a star cruiser, they could go anywhere they liked, whenever they liked. The new ones had limitless power sources. All they'd need to do was restock air, food, and water. They could take on passengers in exchange for gold. They could travel the galaxy for the rest of their lives. Find Ramesh on Muria. Explore Delos. Sneak back to Earth under the guise of Delosian traders and rescue their parents. But, she considered, if they could get their craters back, they'd own an entire strategic spaceport. They could collect fees and buy a whole fleet of cruisers. Why sell the barn for one horse?

"For sure Schlitzer was talking about Gandoop," Jasper said. "And he's willing to pay anything. Can you believe it?"

"Yeah, I can believe it," Torr snarled. "That no-good scumbag. I bet it was his guys who attacked me and Blaire. He's gonna pay."

Jasper shook his head. "I don't think it was him."

"Why not?" Torr demanded.

"He never would have said all that to me if he was going to turn around and try to steal them. He's not that stupid. No, it was somebody else who attacked you."

Cassidy's blood went cold, and silence echoed as they gaped at Jasper. Thinking they knew the enemy was vastly more comforting than not knowing.

"Those men who attacked you were soldiers, Torr," Jasper said.

Cassidy and Blaire exchanged glances. Cassidy had thought they'd looked like soldiers, but hearing Jasper say it out loud made her want to crawl into a hole and disappear. If they were Tegs, how had Torr beaten them? Well, that was obvious. That wolf knife was something abnormal. There was magic in it for sure—and had the wolf taken solid form, with real fangs? Who could defend against something like that? But why had the men tried to drug Torr and Blaire instead of simply killing them?

"Maybe we *should* sell them, Torr," Cassidy said.

"No," Torr said with conviction. "Don't you see? If they want them so badly, they must really be worth something."

"True," Cassidy admitted, keeping her voice low as their campmates started gathering to walk to the training yard. "It's the second-largest spaceport on the moon, and the largest mine. Of course they're worth something."

"No, I mean something more. Something invaluable. We can't sell them." Torr's voice was shaking.

Cassidy wondered if he was getting a little cracked in the head from all the stress. Maybe he'd suffered another concussion. His eyes were bulging, and the wolf knife was in his hand again, and his other hand held the fluorite crystal. Cassidy exchanged worried glances with Blaire.

"Something to do with who we are," Torr said in a hoarse whisper.

Cassidy thought about the blue and gold book, and Avala, and the moon of crystal sand.

The four of them stood up wordlessly, then gathered their things and left for the training yard.

———————)———————

"Want to get some fresh, ice-cold water?" Jasper asked. They were sitting at the Fen's picnic tables with their friends, finishing up a dinner of rice and hummus.

Cassidy cocked her eyebrow at him. "There is no way in Algol's hell I am going back down into that witches' den."

"Not from Gabira," he said. "From Peary Lake. Our water tank is getting low."

Cassidy's attention turned to the large tank sitting on the wagon under the shade of the tarp. The water was almost gone. "You get your own water?" Cassidy asked.

"Yeah. It's free that way. Tanks of water are too expensive nowadays. Even for me. I don't know how your brother keeps shelling out gold for the Light Fighters' water," he said, throwing a glance at Torr.

"Anyway, if I work a few shifts for the guys, I get a tank as payment. Come on." Jasper stood up and stepped away from the picnic tables.

"You are very enterprising," Torr said, joining him.

"Gotta survive in this place any way I can," Jasper said. "It's all about relationships. You guys coming?" he asked, turning his gaze onto the Boyer brothers.

"Us?" Roanoke asked, and Jasper nodded.

The Boyers' expressions lifted, and they stood up to join them.

"You, too," Jasper said to Durham. "If you want."

"Sure," Durham said with a surprised grin. He swiveled around on the bench and grabbed his crutches. "I've always wanted to see the ice lake."

Jasper got Berkeley from the back, and Ming-Long and Khaled joined them. Jasper headed for the spaceport in the buggy with Durham in the passenger seat and his three sons hanging off the back. The rest walked and met them at the spaceport.

The two customs guards were playing cards at the inspection table and waved them through. At the far end of the enormous building, several craft stood in a line. One was a tanker, and two men were coiling a large hose and stowing it in the cockpit as a tanker truck rolled away.

"Hey, Jaz," they greeted him, eyeing Cassidy.

"It's all ready for you," one of them said.

"I'm due for a tank after this run," Jasper said.

"Yeah, yeah," the man drawled. "Sure you are."

"I am," Jasper insisted.

"I know. I'm just messing with you," the man said, grinning.

They exchanged a few more words, then Jasper motioned for Cassidy and the others to climb on board.

The cockpit had an open area behind the two pilot seats. A thick pole in the center of the floor was connected to the tank wall by a series of pipes and gears and had a large red lever at its base. Jasper sat in the pilot's chair, Ming-Long took the co-pilot's chair, and the rest of them squeezed into the open area and sat on the hard metal floor with their backs against the walls.

"You guys do this often?" Torr asked. "Is it easy to fly?"

"Yeah, much easier than a speedster," Jasper said. "Me and Ming-Long usually take turns getting water for the camp. Ming-Long had a regular ice run for a while, didn't you, Ming?"

Ming-Long nodded. "Yeah, that was the first job I ever had here. They made me do all the grunt work at first, but finally they taught me how to fly these hunks of junk."

The ship lumbered through the decompression chambers and shook as the large tanker quaked and lurched down the landing tunnel and lifted off, finally steadying as it flew over the gray expanse of Peary Crater.

"I thought you could make water from the elements in moon soil," Torr said to no one in particular.

Berkeley answered, "You can. Oxygen and hydrogen are produced from decomposing the moon's soil. But, generally, the big moon mines sell oxygen and hydrogen separately. Water can be made from combining them, but we mostly save the elements for breathing and for fuel. For drinking water, there's ice in the dark zones of craters. Or we import water from Earth. And recycle it, of course."

"Peary Crater has a bunch of smaller craters filled with ice," Ming-Long said. "Peary Lake, we call it. The ice never melted because it's so deep and dark. It never sees the sun. There are lots of pockets of ice at both poles, actually. We have rights to everything immediately around the north pole."

"We're here," Jasper said. Just then a curtain of black cloaked the craft.

Cassidy's stomach lifted as the tanker plunged downward into the sunless depths of the crater. Her eyes adjusted until she could make out the faces of her travel companions in the light cast by the multi-colored controls of the tanker's instrument panel.

Jasper navigated using a radar display, and the craft drew to a halt, hovering just above the floor of the crater.

Berkeley hopped to his feet and pushed down the large red lever. The gears started turning, and the pipe made loud crunching noises and then settled into a steady vibration. When the vibration stopped, a loud screech brought Cassidy's hands to her ears. The screech was followed by a loud thud, and then the sound changed to a low whir.

Cassidy went to the front of the cockpit to look out. An opaque white expanse gleamed eerily up at them from below, lit by spotlights shining down from the underbelly of the vehicle.

"It's kind of creepy out here," she said.

"Look," Torr said, and pointed out a speck of light off to their right. "Must be another tanker."

Jasper flickered his lights in greeting. The other ship did not signal back.

"What ship is that?" Jasper asked Ming-Long.

Ming-Long was peering through binoculars. "I don't know. Don't recognize it."

"The radar doesn't tell us anything," Torr commented, pointing out the blob on the radar screen.

"We'll go check it out when we're done here," Jasper said, taking out his binoculars and raising them to his eyes.

Cassidy took a turn with Jasper's binoculars and focused on the speck of light in the distance. The ship was quite a ways away, but a light shone down from the bottom of it, illuminating the lake below in a pool of milky white. The ship itself was lit with small lights that glinted at them like so many eyes. She could just make out the pipe protruding from its belly and buried in the ice bed.

"How does it get the ice out?" Cassidy asked, handing the binoculars back to Jasper.

Berkeley answered, "The pipe takes a core sample of ice, melts it, and pumps it into the tank. Then does it again until the tank is full."

As if on cue, more noises came from the pipe, and Berkeley pulled up the red lever. The pipe retracted, Jasper inched the tanker forward, Berkeley pushed the lever down, and the cycle repeated itself.

It seemed to take forever to fill the tank. Jasper illuminated the cabin, and they sat in a circle on the floor and played cards while they waited.

When the tank was full, Khaled raised the pipe, and Ming-Long took over the flight controls and glided slowly towards the other tanker.

"Which ship is it?" Berkeley asked.

"Too far away to tell," Jasper said.

"I'll get closer," Ming-Long said. "It's not a Peary Dome tanker, I can tell you that," he said, raising his binoculars and squinting at the ship.

"More trespassers?" Berkeley asked. "Jaz, call your dad."

"His shift's over," Jasper said.

"They're not allowed here?" Hawk asked.

"No," Berkeley said. "When the Free Men won control of Peary, we made a treaty with the mines for water rights. Peary Lake belongs to the Peary Dome camp. There are other pockets of ice that the mines claimed. So they're trespassing right now."

"Wait a second … Check this out," Jasper said. "What does that say on the side?"

Cassidy watched Torr as his hands gripped his binoculars. "Gandoop," Torr said ominously.

"Gandoop?" Berkeley and Cassidy echoed.

Ming-Long let out a low whistle. "That's not good."

"No, not good at all," Jasper said, anxiety straining his voice. "Why would Gandoop be out here?"

"I told you, Tegs are at Gandoop," Cassidy said, her throat tight. "They must be asserting themselves. It's like a message to us, saying, 'We're claiming our power here, and don't try to stop us.'"

"They must be looking for a fight," Berkeley said. "They have ice rights on the western rim of Hermite and don't need to come over here." He paced back and forth in the small compartment.

"Look, there's a second one," Torr said, lifting his binoculars to his eyes and peering over Ming-Long's shoulder.

Ming-Long decelerated as they drew closer to the Gandoop tanker, which was still hovering over the lake, its pipe implanted in the ice. The second craft was approaching from the far right.

Cassidy watched it on the radar screen, then took Jasper's binoculars again and focused on the approaching craft.

"That's no tanker," Cassidy said. "That's a speedster."

"Yep," Berkeley said, zooming the radar screen in on the smaller craft as the Boyers and Khaled huddled around the screen. "It's a speedster, alright."

"That's a Gandoop craft, too," Torr said. "It says 'Gandoop Patrol' right on the fuselage."

"Let's go," Ming-Long said and accelerated the tanker, turning in a wide arc and pulling up in a slow ascent.

Cassidy handed Berkeley the binoculars and watched the ships fall behind on the radar screen. "They're not chasing us," Cassidy said. "The speedster is next to the tanker now. They're just sitting there."

"Dad," Jasper said into his radio. "You home?"

A long moment passed, then the crackling voice of Kai came through. "Jaz? Yeah, what's up?"

"We're on an ice run, and there's a Gandoop tanker out here."

"Again?" Kai asked.

"What do you mean, again?" Jasper asked.

"We caught one heading out over the northern rim last week."

"They have a speedster with them," Jasper said.

"Where are they?" Kai asked. Jasper told him the coordinates. "I'll send someone to escort them out," Kai said. "Don't confront them."

"We didn't. We're leaving. I'll come by later," Jasper said, and signed off.

They reached the rim and headed into the sun towards Peary Dome, leaving the dark depths behind.

31

GRAY SNAKE TRAIL

Torr realized he was dreaming when he found himself walking up Spoke Road Eight, alone and unconcerned for his safety. He arrived at the stacks of staff trailers and climbed the ladder to a container on the third level, where Kai lived, and rapped on the metal door.

The door cracked open, and Edgemont peeked out, squinting against the light.

"What are you doing here?" Torr asked. "For star's sake, can't you leave me alone?" Edgemont smirked and backed away as Torr stepped inside. "Is Kai here?"

Kai appeared out of the shadows, wiping sleep from his eyes. "Hey, Torr," Kai said, and drew him into an embrace. "This is a surprise. Is something wrong?"

"No, no," Torr said, sitting on the edge of a cot. Edgemont sat on a cot against the opposite wall, and Kai stood in the center, looking between the two of them as though he knew the Teg. "I just need to figure something out," Torr said. "Those men who attacked us in my tent. The two who had been Light Fighters. They had strange energy snake things that extended from their stomachs and out into space. I want to know who they attached to on the other end."

Kai lifted a perplexed eyebrow, and Torr turned to Edgemont. "Where are those guys now?" Torr asked. "I mean," he said, waving his hand through the air. "They're dead. Are they here? Wherever *here* is."

Edgemont leaned back against the wall and folded his hands over his flat belly. "Not that I know of." Both of Edgemont's eyes were intact, and his forehead was unbroken skin. He regarded Torr curiously. "But maybe I can help."

"How?"

"I don't know. Come on, let's find their bodies."

Torr, Edgemont, and Kai ended up at a long Quonset hut tucked behind Air and Water Control. A transport was backing through a large open garage doorway at one end, and they followed it inside. They were inside Waste Control. Torr covered his nose and mouth against the rank odor. Mounds of trash took up one end of the building. A long fat drainage hose was being inserted into the back of the transport, and the stink confirmed that the composting toilets' waste was processed there. Torr followed Edgemont to a set of long racks against a side wall. Four body bags were laid out end to end on one of the shelves. A worker was shoveling garbage into a large maw of a machine that made a loud ripping noise as the garbage passed through the industrial shredder. Torr didn't want to be around when the bodies were fed through its metal teeth.

"Is this what you're looking for?" Edgemont asked, lifting what looked like a long gray shriveled worm that hung from one of the body bags like an umbilical cord. Torr gagged as Edgemont ripped the desiccated tendril from the zipper of the body bag, coiled it around his hand and elbow, and followed it along the dusty floor of the Quonset hut and out into the sunshine. Edgemont, Torr, and Kai followed the tendril westward across the perimeter road where it lay half-buried in the dust. Edgemont continued to gather it from the ground as they walked, adding its length to the fat coil that now hung from his shoulder. They reached the western outskirts where banks of shipping containers sat locked and abandoned. The tendril led to one.

Edgemont tugged at the thick padlock. "You have a key?" he asked Kai, who shook his head. "Try using that thing," Edgemont said, nodding at the Destroyer that had somehow made its way into Torr's hand.

Torr sent a purple stream of light slicing through the lock, and the heavy padlock fell to the ground. Kai stared at the crystal shaft with trepidation, while Edgemont laughed with delight. They stepped into the dim container, and Kai closed the door behind them.

It looked like an office on Earth but smelled like the moon. Gerbil was pressed up against the wall with a large black-haired man bearing down on him. A gray snake lashed from the tall man's chest and wrapped around Gerbil's neck. Torr stepped backwards and grabbed Kai's arm. Torr jerked, startled, as the man whose arm he was holding was not Kai, but another tall, lean man with olive skin, a shaved head, and wearing a black flight suit. Torr dropped the man's arm and leaned back dizzily against a metal door and gaped with horror at the scene unfolding before them. Edgemont sat on the edge of a desk and watched with fascination as Gerbil slowly choked to death from the gray garrote and finally crumpled to the floor.

The large man turned away from the corpse and faced Stanley, who stepped out from the shadows. Torr froze with recognition. The murderer and Stanley bore a striking resemblance—both of them tall and muscular, with bright green eyes and a widow's peak at their dark hairline. The large man wore a gray military field jacket with the Teg emblem sewn onto a chest pocket. The blood-red shield was emblazoned with two gold stars. The name tape over the right pocket read, *Balthazar*. The Teg wiped his hands together, his face sweaty from the effort of strangling Gerbil. His emerald eyes looked startled as he locked gazes with Stanley.

A gray rope of energy extended from each of the two tall men's bellies and met in a tangle, struggling for dominance. After a long moment, like an evenly matched arm wrestle, the cords trembled, and the men reached a draw. The cords merged together, and the two men were connected. Their stiff countenances broke, and their faces relaxed.

"Drink?" Balthazar asked and turned to a small liquor cabinet. Torr pressed himself against the door, but the two dark-haired men did not appear to see him.

Gerbil, on the other hand, screamed at Torr from the floor where he was being dragged away by the lean man. "I didn't do nothin', Torr. I didn't have nothin' to do with them attacking you. I swear. They just wanted us to keep a lookout. I didn't know."

Torr glared after Gerbil as he was dragged out the door. Slowly Torr made the connection and walked over to Balthazar. The man was oblivious to him. Torr lifted the Destroyer and shot a stream of purple fire to sever the fat cord connecting Balthazar and Stanley. The two men flinched slightly as the cord melted and fell away but registered no further reaction. They lifted their drinks in a silent toast and tipped back their glasses.

Torr left the room and followed after Gerbil. Two men carrying the corpse disappeared through a doorway at the far end of the large Gandoop hangar. Torr ran to catch up and slipped through the doorway after them. He pressed his back against the metal wall and looked around, disoriented. He was in the smaller hangar in Gandoop Spaceport. The metal room was empty except for seven small craft. There was no sign of Gerbil and the men carrying him.

The room was square but for the ceiling that curved overhead. His breathing echoed across the room, bouncing off two lines of speedsters closely parked wing to wing. Two red beauties and one that appeared to have been freshly painted battleship gray lined the back wall. Torr walked slowly past, inspecting them. The red ones appeared untouched, with dust coating the paint in a faint sheen. They were identical to the two at Peary.

In the front line closest to the compression bays were two older gray speedsters. But what really interested Torr were the two craft parked at the far end. Mantas.

Torr approached the first Manta and examined its wings. They were wide and curved and pointed at the ends. The exterior of the craft was coated with a dull gray pebbled material. He ran his hands over the hull. It felt like rough sandpaper, reminding him of the sharkskin hilt of his wolf knife. He skimmed his hand along the Manta's wing and stepped in front of its wide hollow nose, which was more like a mouth—dark and bottomless as a well—framed by two smaller wings that curved downwards. Above the mouth was a wide front windshield of dark tinted glass. Torr strained to see through it.

The Manta reared up at him, its wings arching overhead, its mouth stretching open, spewing green fire. Torr fell back, throwing his arm over his eyes.

"*Torr!*"

His eyes jerked open. He was scrabbling back over pillows and blankets, his arm shielding his head. He backed against the canvas tent wall as Blaire hovered over him.

He sputtered for breath and sat upright. "Oh," he gasped. "I was

dreaming." His breath came fast and heavy, and his heart pounded in
his ears. "A Manta. I saw a Manta. It was attacking me."

Blaire knelt in front of him and laid her hand on his shoulder,
peering anxiously into his eyes. "Are you okay?"

He nodded, wiping sweat from his brow. "Yeah. It felt real." He
took in a deep breath and held her hand. "I think it's alive," he said.

———————)———————

Torr ordered another inspection at training. The Light Fighters lined
up by squad and shifted nervously as he walked slowly up and down
the ranks. He didn't detect any shadowy gray snakes, so he returned to
the front and announced that any new recruits had to be approved by
him first. People peered at him with timid curiosity. They didn't know
what the inspections were for but did not question him.

Ever since the tent attack, people kept a wide berth around him,
and only those he knew dared talk with him. The distance made him
uncomfortable, but Torr didn't blame them. He was afraid of himself
and what he'd done in that tent. What the wolf knife had done. He felt
for the cold, round pommel at his hip.

"Good wolf," he said under his breath.

———————)———————

Early that evening, he recalled his dream and went into the back courtyard and found Hiroshi.

"What'd you do with the rest of that sharkskin bag?" he asked the
small man, who was polishing the blade of a hunting knife.

Hiroshi put aside the blade and polishing cloth and dug into a
small crate, emerging with scraps of sharkskin.

"This should do," Torr said, pressing the Destroyer against the
strips. They were longer than the crystal shaft, and a bit wider.

"Making a sheath?" Hiroshi asked.

Torr nodded. "Berk," he called. The whirr of the sewing machine
stopped. "Can I use your sewing machine?"

"No," Berkeley called back.

Torr ignored him and borrowed a cutting tool from Hiroshi. He
went into the craft tent, cleared the table of lengths of bright blue

fabric, and cut two strips of sharkskin to size. He salvaged a third piece and cut two slashes so it could slide onto a belt.

He took the sharkskin to Berkeley and showed him what he wanted. Berkeley changed sewing needles and in a matter of minutes assembled the three pieces into a sheath. The long six-sided shaft of the Destroyer fit snugly into it, with the butt end of the crystal sticking out far enough that Torr could grab hold of it.

He thanked his friends, stacked a pyramid of moon rocks on the Antler Kralj crate, and proceeded to unsheathe the crystal and practice wielding its power.

————————) ————————

A few days later, two new recruits were sent over to him. Thick gray tendrils trailed unmistakably from their abdomens and floated through the air past the southwestern edge of the dome, where they disappeared into space.

"Welcome," Torr said cordially, trying to give them a relaxed smile even though his cheek was twitching. "You want to join the Light Fighters?"

"Sure do," one said, and the other nodded. They were about thirty, with short hair and new growth on their faces. They looked fit and healthy, like they'd been eating well and working out. They were clearly not long-time moon rats, and since all the accessible spaceports on Earth were closed to free citizens except Glamorgan, Torr instantly deduced they were spies even without the gray cords. "You from the Great Isles?" Torr asked, testing them.

"No," one said. "LA. Got out just in time."

"Oh," Torr said, acting like he believed him. "You flew out of LAX?"

"Sure did."

"Lucky," Torr said. Both men nodded with confident smiles. Lying bastards. "You know how to fight?"

The men shrugged. "A little," said the man who was speaking for both of them.

"What kind of fighting? We need experienced fighters. You know any martial arts? Or boxing?"

"Some."

"We're pretty good," the quiet man said.

"Great," Torr said with a broad grin. "Because we're only taking new recruits who know how to engage in hand-to-hand combat. We'll have to test you, though, hope you don't mind."

The men exchanged glances. "Okay."

"Good. We'll make it a bit of a competition. In fact, we're looking for more instructors, so if you're really good, you can run a class. Would you be up for that?"

"Sure," the first man said, his face brightening.

"Cool," Torr said. He called over his squad and all the instructors. "Tatty, Hiro," he said. "We're going to test these guys. I want you two to grapple with this new recruit. See how long he can fight you off before you pin him to the mat, okay?" The two small Japanese men nodded and stood by the first recruit, who eyed Tatsuya and Hiroshi with a confident grin. "Febo, Elvis, you take the other guy. Drop him and pin him, but don't knock him out." Torr gave the quiet man a gracious smile as Febo and Elvis stood opposite the man. He did not look nearly as confident as his companion.

"Okay. Go," Torr said.

The men all slowly circled one another until a quick jab from Elvis started things off.

It was a true fight. The new men were skilled. Torr was afraid for a few moments that he had overestimated the abilities of his friends. But in the end, both men were pinned firmly on the ground.

"Don't let them up," Torr commanded, and strode briskly to the tarp overshadowing the tables and cut it down, clipping off two of the securing ropes. He cut each rope in half and tossed a length to Ming-Long, nodding towards the recruits. "Tie their wrists securely behind them."

"What? Why?" the men asked, fidgeting against the men holding them down.

Ming-Long's smile widened. "Sure thing, boss," he said.

Torr distributed two other ropes to his companions. "Tie their ankles," he said, and tied the second man's wrists himself.

"What is this?" the man first complained loudly as he struggled futilely against the many hands and knees that held him down.

When the two men had been bound and hauled to their feet, Torr faced them. "I'm sending you back to your master," he snarled. He rested his hand on his wolf knife pommel, and the gray snakes undulated as they stretched from the men's bellies and trailed off into the sky.

"What master?" Berkeley asked. "Schlitzer?"

"No," Torr said, shaking his head. "Worse." He took in a deep breath. "Give me a minute."

He walked by himself off to the side of the yard, ignoring the Scrids who were holding their constant vigil at the far corner of the large block. He hadn't considered how he would get these spies to Gandoop. He paced back and forth with his hands clasped behind his back, considering his options. He didn't think Peary Spaceport security would let him drag in two bound men and throw them onto a freighter. The men hadn't done anything wrong.

Maybe Jericho would let him take them out from ASB. But he'd need a pilot and a craft. There had been two old speedsters at ASB, maybe he could use one of those, and get Jasper to pilot it. But then Jasper would have to fly into Gandoop with the captives and get trapped in there with a bunch of Tegs. No, that was a dumb idea. And Cassidy's speedster was out of the question, for the same reason and more.

He went back to Berkeley. "Call Jaz on the Guild channel and tell him to get on the Fen's channel."

Berkeley got on his radio, and soon Jasper came through on the Fen's band.

"Torr. What's up?" Jasper asked.

Torr unclipped the radio from his belt and spoke into it. "I need a transport."

The radio was silent and Torr could almost hear Jasper grumbling on the other end. His tinny voice finally came through. "For what? Use the four-wheeler."

"I need a bigger one. Hurry."

"What do you think I am, Torr?"

"Just get it. Bring it to the training yard." Torr released the talk button and clipped the radio onto his belt. Jasper was still objecting when Torr turned down the volume and headed for Center Ring. He entered the PCA administration tent and waited in line, jittery with impatience. The lines were long, with several moon rats waiting their turn. Finally, he approached an administrator. The man behind the table looked up at him.

"Do you have any work permits for Ridge Gandoop?" Torr asked.

"Just got twenty, twelve are gone already."

"I need two," Torr said.

The man peered at him over his glasses. "Only one per person. Are you on the waiting list? What's your name?" The man tapped his fingers on a pad of paper with several names scratched in pencil.

"No, I'm not on the waiting list," Torr said, clenching his jaw. "I need two." He dug into his pocket and slapped two gold Eagles on the table.

The man's eyebrows knit together. "We don't take bribes," he said, his mouth turning down with disapproval.

Torr exhaled loudly. He took his Eagles and left the tent. He circled around to the front of the rec tent, where Bratislav let him through. Torr went to the back office and found Montana at his ham radio. Torr poked his shoulder, and Montana flinched and pulled his headphones off.

"I need two work permits for Ridge Gandoop," Torr said. "And I'm not on the waiting list."

Montana climbed wearily to his feet. "Sorry, you need to be on the list. You don't want to go there, anyway. It's a work camp."

"I know. The permits aren't for me."

Montana shook his head. "Sorry. No can do."

Torr ground his teeth together. He turned his back and retrieved his deed and map from his waist belt, then handed them to Montana.

Montana frowned and spread the parchments out on the table. Torr watched his face as Montana read the deed and mapped the coordinates.

"Cassidy has the parcel with the main crater," Torr said somberly.

"Damn," Montana said softly. "I didn't believe it."

"Well, they're real," Torr said. "I found a couple of Gandoop's spies trying to join the Light Fighters. You're aware that two of the men who attacked me and Blaire were Light Fighters, right? These guys have the same vibe. I want to send them back to Gandoop. I figured if the men had work permits, Rodney's men would let me send them out on a freighter, even if they are tied up." Torr gave Montana a half-smile, not sure his plan would work.

Montana scratched at his scruffy gray beard. "How do you know they're spies? How do you know they're from Gandoop?"

"I happen to know they're friends with the guys who attacked me and Blaire," he said. It wasn't much of a lie. "They had old Gandoop work permits on them," he lied again.

Montana let out a sigh. "I don't know about all that. Doesn't seem like proof to me."

Torr frowned. "Do you believe Cassidy and I are the Star Children?" he asked.

Montana inspected him for a long silent moment, his expression unreadable.

Torr drilled Montana with his eyes until the man's shoulders slumped in surrender.

"Wait here," Montana said. He returned a few minutes later with two squares of paper titled, *Work Permit, Gandoop Mine, 3-Year Contract.* The name fields had been left blank, but each permit had a round red-ink stamp, still wet and glistening, with an illustration of the geodesic dome and the words, "PCA Official Transfer."

Torr accepted them with a deep nod of thanks, folded the papers and stashed them in his leg pocket, and then left the PCA.

Jasper showed up at the training yard with a box truck, annoyance plain on his face. His scowl deepened as he observed the two men lying on the ground. They had been gagged and blindfolded and lay quietly. The rest of the Light Fighters had resumed training and stole glances at the truck and the bound men.

Torr and his squad loaded the men into the back of the transport, and then climbed in and sat on the floor along the walls of the cargo area, with the two men face down on the floor between their feet. Blaire sat next to Torr, and he rested his hand on her knee. Jasper drove them over the bumpy roads. When they arrived at the spaceport, Torr climbed out. They were parked at a closed garage door at the front of the building. Jasper unlocked it and rolled up the tall metal door, and then drove the vehicle through the loading bay and through another garage doorway into the main hangar. They were met by two of Rodney's guards.

"Is Rodney here?" Torr asked.

The men hailed Rodney on the radio, and after a short time the big man strode across the hangar floor.

Torr led him to the back of the transport. Torr's squad looked out at them, and the two prisoners lay motionless on the floor.

Rodney threw Torr a stern glare. "What's this?"

"They're not dead," Torr said, slapping one of the men's boots. The man's leg twitched. "They're just pouting."

"What are you doing?" Rodney asked, placing his hands on his hips. "You hankerin' for a spell inside a jail container?"

"Caught them spying on the Light Fighters. They're friends with the guys who attacked me and Blaire." Torr produced the two work permits. "I'm just getting them a ride to their new job." Torr smiled.

Rodney pursed his lips and inspected the permits.

Torr leaned against the corner of the transport, folding his arms across his chest. "What do you say?" Torr asked.

Rodney sighed with disapproval and pushed back a handful of braids. His brown eyes met Torr's, and Torr could see the moment when he relented.

"Trouble seems to follow you," Rodney muttered, and then nodded at his two Rangers. "These guys are going to Gandoop," he said, gesturing at the men lying in the back of the truck. The Rangers peered curiously at Rodney and Torr but didn't say anything as they proceeded to frisk everyone for weapons, including the bound men.

Jasper walked up from where he'd been scouting out the line of freighters. "*Starflower's* going to Gandoop," he said, pointing at a dusty Earth freighter.

"Alrighty, then," Torr said, rubbing his hands together. "Let's send these two guys on their way, shall we?"

Jasper backed the transport up to the loading ramp of *Starflower*.

Torr and Raleigh dragged one man out by the feet, and Roanoke was kind enough to catch the man's shoulders before his face hit the concrete floor. Others in the squad carried the second man and stood him next to his partner.

Torr negotiated their passage for three Eagles apiece. The Earth pilot eyed the men warily.

"Don't worry, they won't get free. Besides, you're doing them a favor, taking them home. Take off their blindfolds," he told Raleigh and Roanoke, who cut the canvas strips and let the blindfolds fall away.

The men shook their heads and glared at Torr.

"Tell your boss—what's his name? *Balthazar.* He's a two-star general, isn't he? Tell General Balthazar I'll send the next ones back in body bags." He approached the quiet one and held the tip of the wolf knife at his throat. "Understand? *Tell him.*"

Torr pressed the tip of the blade harder, and the man tightened his lips, his eyes staring forward. "Okay," Torr said. "I get that you can't acknowledge the bastard. Tell him anyway." He drew the blade across the man's skin until a thin line of blood appeared. "I'm sure you'll remember." The man swallowed, but otherwise did not move. Satisfied, Torr cleaned and sheathed his blade.

He folded and tucked a work permit into each of their chest pockets, buttoning them closed, and then he and his squad herded the men into the hold and lashed them to the side of a container. Torr watched as the pilot raised the ramp and sealed the cargo hold with a hiss.

Jasper cast Torr a parting glare, then left to return the transport and get back to his trading business. Torr waited until *Starflower* glided into a decompression chamber, then led his squadmates outdoors and headed back to the training yard.

———————————)———————————

That afternoon at the Fen, Torr stared at Cassidy where she was sitting at a table talking with Blaire, her sisters, and Darla. A thick, charcoal-gray energy filament was anchored in his sister's back.

"Hey, Cassidy," he said, his hand on the wolf pommel.

The women looked up, then Darla returned her attention to Cassidy, continuing the conversation he had interrupted.

"The barmaid had green teeth," Darla said. "I know for a fact Schlitzer gives his girls Greenwash as a reward for 'good behavior.'"

Torr clenched his jaw as he watched a storm of emotions play across his sister's face.

"Cassidy," he repeated. "Please come here. I need to check something."

She glanced up at the sharpness in his voice. She stood up, climbed over the bench, and followed him to his tent. Inside the dim space, he gently turned her shoulder so that he could examine her back. He took off his sunglasses and peered at the ghostly filament, which was buried in her lower spine, squirming like a parasite. He swallowed and shivered, gripping her shoulder tighter.

"What are you looking at?" she asked. "What's the matter?"

"Hold still," he said. "I need to do something." He unsheathed the wolf knife.

"Get that thing away from me." She shrugged off his hand and stepped back a pace. "You're acting crazy. Knock it off."

"No, I'm not. Come here. He's connected to you."

She lowered her brow and examined his eyes. "Who? What are you talking about? What do you see?"

"Energy filaments. Like cords, or snakes. Do you still feel connected to your captor?"

"No," she said angrily, her hands on her hips as she glared at him.

"Well ... I want to check something out. Did you say his name was Balthazar? He's a very bad dude."

"No shit," she said, her eyes narrowing. "What's going on?"

Why was her captor after their deeds, he wondered to himself. *And why was Balthazar connected to everyone with gray energy snakes? Who was he, and why was he messing with their lives?*

Torr squinted and looked more closely at the energy cord writhing from Cassidy's back. He could study this strange phenomenon with his sister. Try to understand how these things attached themselves. Maybe figure out what they were made of. *Were they light? Matter? Electricity?* Torr gripped the knife hilt in his hand and noticed fat bundles of gold connecting him to his sister at several points on both of their bodies.

"Come on, Cass. You complain I don't believe in magic. Well, I can see things that I don't understand. Something is digging into your back. A line of energy connected to you. It seems to be coming from beyond the glass dome in the southwest." She stared at him, the blood draining from her face. "Lie down," Torr said.

She examined his face for a moment and then lay face down on his blankets.

"After all that herbal therapy you torment me with," he teased, kneeling next to her, "it's my turn." He chuckled, but she was not laughing.

"Is he really connected to me? Get him off," she said, her voice trembling with panic and disgust. "Hurry up."

He gripped the knife pommel and softened his gaze, and the cord became visible again. It was like a pulsing vein, a living thing that Torr was afraid to touch, but he reached out hesitantly, groping through the air with his fingers. As he tried to grab it, the cord faded into an insubstantial shadow, still visible to the eye but not present on the material plane.

He changed tactics and located the spot where it had buried itself into Cassidy's lower back. He approached her carefully with the tip of the wolf blade and pressed it gently against her shirt. The fabric parted like water. He held his breath and went deeper, keeping the blade close to the throbbing cord, her flesh parting in layers under the blade. There was no blood, and Cassidy did not so much as flinch. The blade sank in without resistance until it met something that made the knife tremble and buzz, sending shivers through Torr's hand. He quickly pulled the blade out. Impaled on its tip was the snakelike head of the cord, a mouthlike orifice opening and closing in front of where the blade had it skewered. The long tail thrashed about, and a jolt shot up Torr's arm to his head, making him nearly drop the blade as a blinding pain sliced through his skull. He hung onto the knife hilt with both hands and staggered backwards as the creature's head struggled to free itself with such force that Torr was dragged from side to side. Cassidy jumped to her feet and gaped at him as he stumbled around the tent.

"Get out!" he yelled at her.

She scrambled from the tent, and he faced off with the creature, the part of Balthazar that was not ready to let go. The head flung itself off the knife and, finding itself free, hovered in the air for a moment before darting at Torr's neck. In its instant of hesitation, Torr grabbed for the Destroyer, pulling it free from its sharkskin sheath, and shot a purple flame at the snake as the head bit into Torr's throat, a sharp pain dropping Torr to his knees.

He froze in the clutches of the energy line's current, then collapsed onto his blankets and spasmed uncontrollably. The snakelike cord sizzled with purple flames from the Destroyer and melted before his eyes. Suddenly, the cord was gone, and his throat opened, air rushing in with a loud gasp. He rolled onto his side, sucking in mouthfuls of air, his heart pounding. He ran his fingers frantically over his throat and grabbed Grandma Leann's mirror. His skin was warm and sweaty, but unblemished, with no evidence of having been attacked. With the Destroyer still pulsating in his hand, he rolled onto his back and stared up at the tent ceiling, panting, and wondered what Balthazar had felt on the other end.

32

SMUGGLERS

Ridge was crossing Gandoop's hangar when Balty threw open the office door and made a beeline for an Earth freighter. Ridge followed, curious to see what had the man so agitated.

Two men were standing next to the freighter, rubbing their wrists. When they saw Balty, they stood at attention and stared straight ahead. "Come with me," Balty barked, and turned on his heel. "You, too," he said to Ridge.

Ridge suddenly wanted to disappear but followed them to Balty's glassed-in office, where they were joined by one of Balty's Teg officers, Harbin. Balty sat behind his desk, and the others stood in front of it.

"What are you doing back here?" Balty demanded of the two men.

"The boy, Torr, tied us up and shipped us back here, sir," one said sheepishly. "He knew who we were."

"What do you mean, he knew who you were?"

"He knew your name, sir."

"What do you mean, he knew my name?"

Balty's complexion darkened, and his fists tightened on the desk. Ridge tried to shrink into the corner.

"What do you mean, he knew my name?"

"He knew your name, and that you are a two-star general, sir. He said, 'Tell General Balthazar that I'll send the next ones back in body bags.'" The man swallowed and met Balty's protruding eyes.

"How did he know that?" Balty's voice was low, and the men squirmed under his glare.

"I don't know, sir," the man said quietly, his hands stiff at his sides.

"Well, how do you think he knew?" Balty insisted with a syrupy voice that made Ridge cringe.

The second man hesitated, then said, "They say he has magical powers."

Balty threw back his head with a loud guffaw, then stood and rested his palms on his desk, leaning over and glowering at the two men. "Do you believe that?"

"No, sir," the soldier said apologetically. "I don't know, sir."

Balty lifted his lip in a menacing sneer and turned to Harbin. "Get them out of my sight. Put them on the tunneling crew. I don't want to see their faces up here again."

"Yes, sir." Harbin saluted, then ushered the men out the door.

Ridge let out his breath and turned to leave, but Balty called him back. Ridge drew in his breath and closed the door. He stood in front of the desk as Balty sat heavily. The room was quiet with just the two of them, and Ridge watched the two men and Harbin through the one-way glass as they hurried across the hangar floor and disappeared from view. The men were lucky to have escaped Balty's wrath, and Ridge hoped he wouldn't suffer any residual effects of their failure.

"Sit down," Balty said, heaving a great sigh. The large man leaned back in his chair.

Ridge sat in a guest chair and returned Balty's gaze.

"We've got a spy," Balty said.

"Yes. It appears so," Ridge said, anxious to appease him and get out of there.

"When I find him, I'll kill him," Balty said.

Ridge gave a small nod. "Yes. I believe you will."

"The kid must have his own spies. He may be more of a challenge than I'd first thought. Your operation may have to take over," Balty said, drumming his fingers on the desk.

Ridge masked his relief, though he didn't trust Balty to tell him what he was really up to. "Sure thing. I'm on it. Things are progressing well," he assured Balty.

"Progressing at a snail's pace," Balty said grumpily.

Ridge rose from his chair. "Slow and steady wins the race." He smiled, but Balty did not smile back. "See you back at the house," Ridge said.

Balty grunted in response, and turned to his desk screen, giving Ridge silent permission to leave.

———————————)———————————

Ridge reflected morosely on the past as he watched Balty's crew work the shipping floor. It had seemed like providence shining down upon the Gandoops when Global Alliance business had arrived at their new spaceport. When the spaceport had first been completed, traffic had been slow. The Gandoops had ceased trading at Peary, forcing traders who wanted to buy their minerals and elements to come to them. But the ships always arrived empty, having traded away their loads at Peary first. The Gandoops weren't making any more money than they had before, and the thriving spaceport Ridge had envisioned was no more than a fancy oversized loading dock for their mining business.

Just at the point when Ridge had begun to regret their huge investment, the Gandoops had been approached by the Global Alliance for a contract to discreetly host Cephean and Earthlander dignitaries as they transferred between Earth-Lunar shuttles and Cephean interstellar ships. After all, Gandoop Spaceport was new and clean, and elegantly quiet, with a firmly disciplined staff and no questions asked—the opposite of Peary's dirty, noisy hangar filled with spitting, cussing mining lords, smelly off-world traders, and the Peary staff who rudely inspected every load to decide what they would allow through. The Global Alliance contract had been worth a goodly amount of gold.

Balty had arrived a couple of months into that arrangement. He had been introduced to Ishmar as a retired half-breed Teg general who spoke Cephean and would serve as a liaison for the Cephean pilots and dignitaries, who spoke little Globalish and needed a proper host of suitable rank for their brief stopovers on the moon.

Later, Ridge learned that Balty had been pulled out of the chain of command and sent to the moon for bad behavior at a politically sensitive time. Balty had ranted to Ridge one drunken evening about how he'd made Teg general at the age of forty and was in line for a Global Alliance post, when he'd gone to Delos on holiday and gotten into a drunken brawl, breaking the jaw of some "snotty arrogant bastard twenty-year-old" who happened to be the nephew of King Pelagon of Delos, of the Antler Kralj.

"Ilian pure-blood highbrow cuntlicker. *Royalty.* Didn't that go out with the last millennium?" Balty had stormed.

Apparently not on Delos. Balty had been sent to the moon to get him out of the way. Put on "special assignment." Balty had confided in Ridge that it had been either the moon or he'd have been exiled to Tree Nut. Ridge didn't want to point out that the moon felt like exile to him.

Balty had ended up at Gandoop, by far the best accommodations on the moon. Far enough away from Peary Dome, but not too far. It was an ideal location for the Tegs to keep an eye on things. Of course it would not do for a Teg general, no matter his status, to sleep in the tunnels of the mining facility, so the Gandoops graciously welcomed Balty into their lavish home. Balty and his bodyguards had moved into the two guest suites, and they never left.

It had been Balty who had arranged the next deal. Ancient and historical artifacts were being stripped from Earth as Tegea's forces swept across the planet. The remaining free nations were giving Ramzy grief about allowing Earth's cultural treasures to pass through Peary, so when Ramzy started turning away those cargoes, they ended up at Gandoop. The pilot of the first such load was short on gold, and Balty took advantage of the pilot's desperation and negotiated a ten-percent cut for the Gandoops. Ishmar followed his lead and imposed the same tariff on other shipments.

The first big haul that came through was from Alexandria. They had allowed the ship to sit at Gandoop for two years, in exchange for the outer rim parcel—Last Chance—and ten percent of the cargo. The captain had adamantly refused to let anyone inside his cargo hold for inspection. Rather than turning him away, Balty had suggested they simply take ten percent of the square footage of the cargo hold, which was documented in the ship's specs, in the equivalent volume of gold bars. The cargo must have been worth a fortune, because the captain had agreed to the terms and sent the gold in a separate shipment. After that lucrative deal, other artifact shipments were paid for with gold, or with ten percent of the goods, which they found was generally worth more than straight gold but required patience to convert to currency. Slowly, their storage areas had filled up with priceless treasures.

That had given Ishmar the idea of purchasing and storing other kinds of hard goods, to wait for the right buyer at the right price. They converted what was going to be a spacecraft repair shop into a warehouse—to store their goods until they could sell them for a hefty profit—and made do with a corner of the hangar for spacecraft maintenance.

Balty went on and negotiated for the Gandoops a ten-percent cut on all Cephean Federation black market goods—the kind that were outlawed at Peary—in exchange for a ten-percent cut of Gandoop mine's output for the Cephean Federation. Ridge didn't see how that was fair, but Ishmar had agreed to the deal, and Ridge kept his mouth shut. It had turned out to work in their favor. The black market traffic attracted other ships and opened up trade at Gandoop, resulting in the busy port they enjoyed today. Not to mention, it gave Ridge access to all sorts of interesting things from across the galaxy and introduced him to many important trading contacts. The Gandoops had even bought two of their own interstellar cruisers to hand-carry certain high-value items to anxious buyers, for ridiculous fees.

Balty had arranged another ten-percent deal with the Global Alliance to allow Cephean military supply ships to pass through Gandoop. Soon, the Gandoops were raking in gold hand over fist.

When female slaves started coming through Gandoop, Ridge had tried to put a stop to it, but they were in too deep at that point to stop the deluge of illicit traffic. It was then that the Gandoops realized Balty had gained control of key aspects of their spaceport operations. The Gandoops couldn't figure out how to get rid of him without ruining their burgeoning business and admitted to themselves that Balty had become a permanent fixture.

It took a few days of Ridge monitoring the Gandoop Spaceport radio chatter until word of a weapons shipment from Tree Nut caught his attention. He left the smelter and crossed the passageway into the spaceport. The bright white airiness of the spaceport lifted his spirits.

He inhaled deeply and brushed a few specks of ash from his otherwise spotless flight suit.

Ali was there, and together they stood with another one of Balty's Teg officers, Flanders. The Teg wore the standard disguise of mismatched Earth military surplus gear, like all Balty's men did. Flanders wore faded green cargo pants and a desert camo field jacket over a black t-shirt. Moon rat clothing could not disguise the humorless and disciplined demeanor of the Teg officer, but the fact that Balty was trying to disguise his men worried Ridge more than if he were open about the Teg presence. Ridge shrugged off his concerns and turned his attention to the Cephean trading vessel that had just arrived.

Flanders walked up onto the loading ramp and began taking inventory. Ridge squinted, trying to discern what he was looking at in the dim shadows of the hold. Two large cube-shaped things filled most of the space. An enormous silver dish was folded down on top of each, and massive treads snaked around the edges of the cubes. Ridge wondered aloud to Ali, "Are those Cyclops?"

Ali followed his gaze. Ridge had seen Cyclops before on the inventory logs but had never thought too much about them. None of the Cephean weapons ended up in Gandoop's warehouse; they all went directly from interstellar vessels to Earth freighters, and the Gandoops collected their ten percent in gold.

Ridge stepped forward and peered inside the ship.

"Are those Cyclops?" Ridge asked.

Flanders nodded, and Ridge regarded the big square machines. A thrill ran over him. They were monstrous, gorgeous hulks of machinery, created to produce blasts of such power as to destroy whatever stood in their paths. Suddenly, the Silox were but children's toys. With a Cyclops at Last Chance, he could churn up titanium-heavy rubble like a tiller plowing through a field.

Ridge looked over his shoulder and gestured excitedly for Ali to join him. Ali strode reluctantly across the floor. Ridge plucked the small screen from his brother's hand and flipped through the day's inventory. He saw that the two beasts had already been entered into the system. They were listed as "Flying Excavation Devices," or "FEDs." Ridge searched the inventory records for more FEDs and found that over a dozen had passed through Gandoop in the past two months.

"I'll take one of them," Ridge announced.

Flanders blinked at him, his face unmoving.

"We get ten percent of everything," Ridge said matter-of-factly, waving his hand between himself and Ali.

Ali backed away a step, pressing his palms forward. "We don't need one of those."

"Of course we do," Ridge said. "Have the men put one in a corner of the hangar until I figure out how to get it outside to test it."

"Uh ...," Flanders said, clearing his throat. "Excuse me for a moment." Flanders stepped away, and Ridge eavesdropped as the Teg spoke in a hushed tone into his radio. "Sorry to disturb you, Balty, sir, but, uh ... Ridge ... um, wants one of the Cyclops, sir."

There was a moment of silence, then a faint hiss over the radio. "What?"

Ridge glanced across the floor to the mirrored glass of his old office. The door swung open and Balty's broad frame lurched out, reminding Ridge for a moment of an angry orangutan he had seen at the zoo as a child, bursting from its pen into the outdoor enclosure. Ridge instinctively retreated a pace, then caught himself and stood up straight, preparing to confront the man.

"What's this?" Balty blustered, waving his arm impatiently at Ridge. "What's all this about?"

Ridge assumed a relaxed stance, forcing a half-smile to remain on his face. "Just taking our ten percent."

"You can't have a Cyclops, you nutcase." Balty sneered at him, and with a quick flick of his hand sent Flanders scurrying out of earshot. Balty turned on Ridge and glared at him. "Did my pool cue knock a few screws loose in that bald head of yours, Ridge?"

Ridge kept his lips turned up, as though this were a friendly conversation. "I don't understand the issue, Balty," Ridge said patiently. "We get ten percent. More than a dozen have come through just in the last few weeks. I want one for the mine."

Balty lifted his hands jovially, his face transforming into his friendly, negotiating façade. The suddenness of the transition almost made Ridge lose his casual smile. Familiar icy prickles on his back made his spine stiffen despite himself. Balty was trying to attack him with his energy tentacles in order to control him, and it made Ridge cringe inside from the cold invasiveness of it. As usual, Ridge sloughed them off, making Balty's smile harden with thinly veiled rage.

Ridge thought Balty would be accustomed to this dance by now, but he seemed oblivious to anything except that his power was being denied. Ridge was almost sure it was this mysterious response that made the man tolerate him—Ridge was to him both infuriating and intriguing, a skilled adversary of sorts, one whom Balty respected and wanted to conquer before killing.

Balty's sugary voice broke through Ridge's thoughts. "You can't have one of the Cyclops, my dear friend, because they are expected at Moffett Field day after tomorrow." Balty smiled apologetically and motioned for Flanders to proceed with organizing the transfer of the hulking beasts to the waiting Earth freighter.

"Just like the Nommos lords expect their shipments of females," Ridge drawled.

Balty turned his emerald eyes fully on Ridge, but Ridge did not flinch. Balty's mouth fell open, and Ridge felt a shiver of distress from his brother. Ridge had forgotten for a moment that Ali was standing there. He wasn't shielded against the bastard's tentacles, and Balty liked to take out his anger on Ali when he couldn't get at Ridge.

"Ali," Ridge snapped. "Go get Ishmar." Balty's tendrils didn't stick as well when the victim was not in Balty's direct line of sight, Ridge had observed, although some sort of connection seemed to persist across distances. At least he could send Ali out of Balty's view, down into the shelter of the shielding rock of the tunnels.

Ali threw him a sour look and took the radio from his belt and spoke into it. "Ishmar, please come up to the hangar."

Ishmar's clipped voice came through. He was on his way.

Ali knew Ridge had meant for him to leave the hangar. Ridge had his own radio and could have reached Ishmar himself. Ali was either being stupid or stubborn, or Balty's hooks were so firmly lodged in him that he would take Balty's side over his own brother's.

Balty had turned away and was regarding the Earth freighter as it maneuvered into position to load the Cyclops. Ridge stepped up next to him, finding himself in a reckless, intrepid mood.

"You just drive them off the freighter, right?" Ridge asked cheerily. "How do they work?" Ridge ignored Balty's sneer and sauntered up into the hold, shouldering past Flanders. Harbin appeared at Balty's side, and Ridge heard them conferring in gruff tones.

Ridge inspected the Cyclops, trying to get a look at the sides and back, which were hemmed in tightly, not allowing him the space to walk around either of the contraptions. He could not detect any controls. He scanned the rest of the shadowed hold, most of which was stacked floor to ceiling with black boxes that Ridge recognized as cases of Lectros. He recalled his original purpose for approaching the vessel, mentally checked off his accomplished aim, and then returned to his newest fascination.

At the back corner of the hold, Ridge spotted what looked to be two control pods: standalone man-sized cabs with a seat surrounded on three sides by control boards, levers, and black screens. Ridge quickly understood that the Cyclops were controlled remotely by the pods and grew even more pleased. He could run the thing from the comfort of the hangar at Last Chance, with massive blasting power under his fingertips.

He climbed up onto a Cyclops tread, grabbed hold of the edge of the laser dish, and pulled himself up onto the roof.

"Ridge, what are you doing?" Ali called up to him from the hangar floor.

Ridge pretended he didn't hear him and inched his way around the dish while admiring the technological beauty, then swung down into one of the pods.

He lowered himself into the seat, studying the controls. They were all marked in Cephean, a language he had only a rudimentary understanding of. But controls were controls. All modern Earth spacecraft designs had borrowed heavily from Cephean technology, and the layout seemed to follow a pattern not completely unlike that of his speedster's cockpit. Still, it would probably be best to test the thing outdoors, with the blasting dish facing away from any structures.

A Teg entered the bay, climbed over a Cyclops, and hopped into the second pod.

"You driving one out?" Ridge asked, unreasonably excited.

The Teg smiled at his enthusiasm, and Ridge leaned over as the Teg showed him the controls for land navigation. Ridge watched the man start up the first Cyclops and direct it slowly down the cargo ramp.

Ridge convinced the soldier to allow him to remotely drive the second one out, and the man instructed him as he did so. Ridge managed it smoothly.

"How do you get it to fly, and how does the blaster work?" Ridge asked.

The Teg started to explain the controls when they were interrupted by Balty's heavy footsteps clomping up the ramp. The Teg avoided Balty's glare while Ridge looked up with an innocent grin of delight.

"This is going to be great, Balty. Think of how easy it'll be to break up the sub-layer with one of these babies!" He would not tell Balty he planned to take it to Last Chance and put his little Siloxes to shame. First he needed to get a Cyclops into his possession, then after Balty forgot about it Ridge would quietly transfer it to Last Chance; the man paid little attention to the mining operations other than how much gold the products sold for.

Balty folded his arms and scowled at Ridge. Ishmar's voice reached his ears, and Ridge climbed out of the cab and squeezed past Balty, who stood rudely in his path. Ridge ignored him and listened as angry footsteps followed him down the ramp. Perhaps he should back off a bit. Best not to send the man into a total rage. Perhaps Balty was truly obligated to deliver the shipment of Cyclops on time—maybe his ass was on the line with Teg command. Ridge decided to change his tactic.

He turned to Ishmar. "Let me see our contract with the Global Alliance," he said to his father.

Ishmar lowered one gray eyebrow and reluctantly pulled his screen from his pocket. Ridge took it and searched the records. He could have easily found it on his own screen, but he wanted Ishmar as a witness. Ishmar was the one who had signed the agreement, but Balty had not signed for the Global Alliance. It had been a week-long negotiation, with a representative from Tegea's own staff sent to finalize the agreement—a stuffy administrator type who had kept to himself, spending most of his time in Ishmar's suite where they had put him up.

"Let's see," Ridge said. "It says here, 'All goods passing through Ridge Gandoop Spaceport subject to retention by Gandoop family of ten percent of goods, or ten percent of transaction, with choice of payment in goods or currency determined solely by Gandoop family.'" Ridge kept his eyes on the screen as he jumped to the end of the multi-screen contract, and his heart leapt. He'd remembered correctly. The gentleman had been a Teg general. "Signed by, 'General Peter H. Pachinaw.'"

Ridge raised his head and met Balty's boiling eyes, and told him reassuringly, "You're only doing your job—seeing to it that the terms of the contract are strictly adhered to. We all know that Cephs and Global Alliance officials are sticklers for administrative details. Right, Balty?" Ridge smiled, then dug in his last barb. "And we'll take ten percent of those Lectros while we're at it. Can't be too careful with mining security these days."

Balty's hands curled into fists at his sides, and Ridge had the urge to duck, fearing he'd pushed the man too far. Instead, Ridge leaned towards Balty and in a conspiratorial whisper said, "Might need the Lectros for our little mission at Peary." Balty stared at him for a moment and then slowly uncurled his fists.

"Give Pachinaw a heads up, and let him deal with the shipment shortage," Ridge suggested. Balty's eyes bulged, but he expelled cheekfuls of air in angry surrender, and Ridge flashed him his most charming smile.

————————) ————————

Jidna stood on the Peary hangar floor as the Guild traders unloaded his latest shipment of food. He had learned what was in shortest supply and highest demand but favored the staple foods Ramzy needed over the delicacies that brought the highest prices. He saved those goodies for the cockpit, and the small quantities demanded outrageous sums.

He stood by nervously and watched crates of eggs, lettuce, spinach, tomatoes, red peppers, string beans, and cucumbers make their way off the Korova and onto the floor next to sacks of potatoes and onions. He kept a cocky smile on his face and snatched a can of beer from a case he'd just sold to Schlitzer's men. He bent the tab back with his utility knife and chugged it down in two long draughts, letting some dribble down his chin and into his beard, as the other traders watched thirstily.

He crushed the empty can, stashed it in his leg cargo pocket, and belched loudly. He had brought several dozen sacks of rice and beans and made sure that Schlitzer's men got them all. He directed a cargo loader to a pallet of rice and guided it down the ramp. With the pallets of fifty-pound sacks lined up on the hangar floor, Jidna told the other traders to divvy up the produce evenly among them. This led to fierce arguments, and the traders quickly turned to him and started a bidding war. He didn't care who got what—it would all make its way into Peary's food supply. Right now, his only concern was the sacks of rice and beans, and it was all he could do to look unconcerned. He cut off the bidding before it got too high, and randomly allocated the goods among the traders, charging the same fixed price for everything. The traders accepted his deal, each one happy to have gotten something.

The security guards approached, shouldered their way past Schlitzer's men, and ran their metal-sensing rods along the edges of the stacked burlap sacks. Jidna maintained his casual demeanor, turning away to collect his gold. He watched from the corner of his eye as the security guards finished with the rice and beans and started tearing open a crate of fresh produce. He exhaled silently and went to chat with Schlitzer's men. They had already been ordered to take the food directly to Schlitzer and were too well disciplined to steal any for themselves.

The traders were all waiting for Jidna, and he finally went into the back of the cargo hold, where he quickly sold the remaining goods: vacuum-sealed bags of dried meat and fish, ten-pound sacks of sugar and wheat flour, and a few cases of butter that nearly led to blows.

He then led the gaggle of traders to the cockpit, where he quickly dispatched the chewing tobacco, chocolate, coffee, and bottles of booze he'd grabbed randomly from the warehouse shelves. He'd thrown in a few toiletries and cosmetics: biodegradable soap, toothpaste and toothbrushes, dental floss, tooth picks, shaving gel, razors, skin cream, lip balm, hair pomade, deodorant, cologne, and perfume. These were wildly popular, especially the dental products and lip balm. Jidna was partial to the hair pomade, which he'd discovered during his search for something to replace the stuff Janjabar had given him, which was almost gone. He held back two small tubs of the stuff, and after the traders had all wandered off tossed them to two of Rodney's Rangers who were hovering nearby. The men caught them and looked at him, surprised.

"Looks like your hair's getting kind of dry," he told them. They nodded, both of them feeling their frizzy cornrows.

"How much?" one of them asked dubiously.

"Oh, hell, you can have them. I made a killing today." Jidna flashed them a toothy grin and sauntered to the main exit, submitted to a pat down, and left the spaceport.

———————)———————

"Did you bring my special delivery?" Schlitzer asked, gesturing for Jidna to join him inside the container where the traders had unloaded the sacks of rice and beans. Schlitzer closed the door behind them.

Jidna had only been in there a couple of times—a container at the back edge of Schlitzer's camp, which the pimp used to conduct his most illicit business. Schlitzer managed to keep the container both discreet and heavily guarded—not an easy feat. The sacks of rice and beans shared the space with stacks of empty beer kegs and cases of empty liquor bottles at one end of the large container. At the other end were two ratty couches facing one another, with a coffee table between them. The place smelled of sour beer, and a bare electric light bulb lit Schlitzer's face.

All the traders smuggled things into the Peary camp hidden in sacks of rice. It was the oldest trick in the book. The only contraband Peary security was really concerned about were firearms, and their metal detectors picked those up easily. Everyone was willing to risk the guards finding a stash of drugs, as long as the price it would bring on the black market balanced out the occasional confiscation. Most things made it through security. When contraband was found, some guards took a cut and turned their backs. Others turned the traders in. The busted trader would be roughed up a bit and his Guild license suspended for a few months. It happened only rarely. Peary was a trading port, after all, and Ramzy relied on its gold.

Jidna went to the pallets, loosened the binding straps, and lifted sacks off the top until he found one sealed with orange thread. He grabbed an empty bucket and neatly sliced open the sack in the center of its fat belly. The bucket at his feet caught the spillage as he deftly pushed his hand through the grain until he felt the textured surface of a Lectro case.

He pulled it free, brushed rice dust off, and opened the case. Schlitzer lifted the Lectro from its foam bed and turned it over in his hand.

"Wow, this is a lot lighter than I'd expected," Schlitzer said. "How many did you bring?"

"Three dozen."

"Three dozen?!" Schlitzer exclaimed. "What am I supposed to do with so many?"

Jidna shrugged. "I'm sure you'll think of something."

"You don't want me to pay you for these, do you?" Schlitzer asked.

"No," Jidna said. "They're for our project."

"Well, I don't need all of these. I suppose we could sell them," Schlitzer said thoughtfully, inspecting the Lectro's trigger mechanism. "How much do they go for on the black market? Never seen any for sale."

"You can't buy these on the black market," Jidna said.

"Well, how much did you pay for them?" Schlitzer asked.

"I don't know," Jidna said. "I didn't check."

Schlitzer gave him a puzzled look and said, "Well, I'm sure I can find some buyers. I'll split the profits with you fifty-fifty, seeing as how they're so hard to get."

Jidna shook his head. "I'd hang onto them, if I were you. Things are going to get ugly around here. Sooner rather than later."

"What do you mean?" Schlitzer asked, concern wrinkling the corners of his eyes.

"Well," Jidna said carefully. "First, everyone is going to get very, very hungry. There will probably be riots. You'll need to protect your camp."

Schlitzer nodded, eyeing Jidna attentively.

"After that, I'm not sure what will happen. Nothing good, I can assure you of that."

Schlitzer continued nodding, his fingers feeling the gun as though trying to memorize its shape. "Did you bring extra ammo?" Schlitzer lifted the single clip of snake jaws from a slot in the case. "There's only six of those doo-hickeys in the clip," Schlitzer said, snapping the clip into the gun's empty magazine.

"Don't wave around that loaded thing near me," Jidna said, and Schlitzer removed the clip and returned it to the case.

Jidna dug his hand into the rice again and felt around until he found a box of snake jaws. The box held ten six-round clips. He had brought two ammo boxes per Lectro. He fished the second box from

the sack, sealed the burlap sack with duct tape, and started searching for the other cases. Some Lectros he had hidden in rice, some in
beans. He had stitched the burlap sacks closed on the industrial sewing
machine himself, using an orange thread. Together, Jidna and Schlitzer
found the remaining thirty-five sacks and set them aside.

Jidna removed another Lectro from a case, and he and Schlitzer
inspected it together. Harbin had shown him how they worked, and
he showed Schlitzer. How to engage the safety. How to aim and fire.

"They discharge on contact," Jidna said. "So after they hit anything,
they're done. They only discharge if they're released from the gun, so
you can throw the snake jaws around as much as you want, and they
won't activate. The beauty of this weapon is it's precise at long range,
it makes no sound, there is no explosion, no heat, and no blood. And
supposedly, it causes a painless death. If the projectile strikes anywhere
on the body, or even most clothing, it will instantly kill the target
and any other person who is touching the target. So be careful not
to shoot at someone your buddy is holding." Jidna repeated Harbin's
instructions robotically, trying not to think of the true purpose of their
transaction and what it could mean for the male twin.

Schlitzer nodded as he inserted and removed a clip. "Are there extra
snake jaws to reload the clips?"

"No," Jidna said. "I didn't find any. But you should have more
than enough with what I brought." Jidna calculated how many Tegs
Schlitzer's men could kill if Tegea's army invaded the dome. Maybe he
should have brought more. "For our immediate purposes, you have
more than enough," Jidna said meaningfully. "Hopefully you won't
need to use them. But if things drag on much longer, you may not
have a choice."

Schlitzer looked up at him. "We'll have to handle them carefully
and retrieve the spent cartridges. Once Ramzy figures out what's going
on, he'll tear the camp apart to find them."

"I'm sure you can figure out how to hide them," Jidna said
with confidence.

Schlitzer sighed and nodded. "I guess so."

"You look worried," Jidna said.

"I am worried," Schlitzer said. "About a lot of things. But first and
foremost, I'm worried about my men. Let's set some terms," Schlitzer said.

"What kind of terms?" Jidna asked.

"The price for the job. It's getting way more complicated than a simple theft."

Jidna nodded, and they began to negotiate. They came to an agreement after three beers.

Simple procurement of the deeds would earn Schlitzer five Solidi apiece. If assault on the twins was required, the cost would jump to ten each. In addition, anything that involved fighting would cost ten Eagles for each of Schlitzer's men, whether or not they recovered the deeds. Serious injury to any of Schlitzer's men would add an additional ten Eagles per person, assuming the man would recover from his injuries. Any permanently disabling injury, of which they discussed a dozen, added an appropriate cost that they attached to each injury, from dismemberment to loss of an eye to paralysis. Any death on either side, whether murder by, or death of, one of Schlitzer's men, would add one Solidi per death. Any jail time would cost an Eagle per day per man. Unless it was Schlitzer who was jailed, in which case, it would cost Jidna one Solidi up front, plus five Tetras per week of jail time. Any action that required any of his men to flee Peary Dome would cost two Solidi per person—unless Schlitzer had to flee, in which case that would cost Jidna twenty Solidi, plus passage for him and two other people to anywhere in the galaxy.

"Give me two weeks," Schlitzer said.

Jidna agreed. He hoped he could keep Balty placated for that long. Jidna took a tattered journal from an inside pocket and jotted down a cryptic reference to the terms along with the list of cost per injury, making a copy for each of them.

"When I've got the goods, I'll radio to confirm your order of raisins," Schlitzer said.

They discussed other details of Schlitzer's plan, and Jidna gave Schlitzer a prepayment of two Solidi. When they were both satisfied with the agreement, they sealed it with a handshake.

33

RED HALO·

Torr sorted through the loot he had plundered from the family who had bought *Moon Star*. He considered the diamond rings for a moment, but decided it was too soon for that. He settled on a necklace with a simple pendant of gold petals with a small center diamond, in the shape of a plumeria flower.

He presented it to Blaire before they went to bed that night.

"Ooooh, a plumeria," she said. "What's this for? Where did you get it?" Blaire asked, her eyes sparkling.

"Just a little trinket I picked up along the way," he said, reaching over and kissing her lightly on the lips. "I thought it would remind you of Earth."

"It does," she said, her expression growing somber.

"What's the matter?" he asked.

"Nothing," she said, rubbing the diamond under her thumb. "It just reminds me of my mother, that's all. She had a necklace like this, only hers was pink and white instead of gold."

"I can give you something else," he said quickly. "I didn't mean to make you sad."

"No, it's okay," she said, lifting her gaze to meet his. "Maybe it's a sign. Maybe she's watching over me from up in heaven."

The import of her words—the assumption that her mother was dead—made his heart hurt. He drew her into his arms. "I'm sorry," he said.

She sniffled, and he squeezed her tighter. "She got it in Hawaii," she said. "We went there once when I was little. But we never got to go back, because of the war."

Her tears were hot on his shoulder, and he rocked her back and forth.

———————————)———————————

Aside from their afternoon naps, he and Blaire were unable to sleep soundly ever since the attack, especially during night curfew. And so they took turns staying awake and keeping watch. That night, Torr had volunteered to take the midnight shift. As was their habit, they made love before settling in. Even during their lovemaking he was unable to completely let down his guard. He was on top, and when she closed her eyes and started moaning with pleasure, he reached for his wolf knife and held onto the shagreen handle as he moved, surreptitiously peering around the tent for his spirit wolf.

Torr found the spirit wolf sniffing around the front door, and he peered over his shoulder at the insubstantial wraith.

"Don't stop," Blaire murmured, wrapping her legs around him.

The wolf settled down onto all fours with its muzzle resting on out-stretched paws and its nose tucked under the door flap, unconcerned.

Torr released the knife and returned his attention to his lover.

Afterwards, Torr sat next to Blaire as she slept, afraid that if he lay down he would fall asleep and awaken to an intruder trying to kill them. He knew in his rational mind that a second attack was unlikely, with guards posted at the watchtowers, but he had jerked awake in a panic too many times to think tonight would be any different.

He gazed down at the woman at his side, her hands curled under her chin in an idyllic slumber. He reflected that he might be genuinely falling in love with her. At first it had been lustful infatuation, although he had been sure at the time that it was love. But as time went by, he became more concerned with her feelings than his, and found himself being patient in ways he had never been before.

He only had his high school sweetheart, Emily, and Reina to compare his feelings to. He had been sure he and Emily would get married, but then she went off to college up north and he went south to the border. They talked every night at first, but then during basic training Torr was sent off into the hills without any devices. And then later at Miramar he had been sent out to help construct bunkers and build roads, living in tents far from the base, with no network available to reach her. By the time he had been assigned squad leader in one of the new bunkers, Emily had found a new boyfriend, and Torr had not even been that upset.

Then there had been the slowly deepening friendship with Reina, which had turned into love, although he had never expressed his romantic feelings for her prior to their escape. By then it had been too late. The thought of her still pained his gut—a sharp hot knife in his side as he admitted she was probably still alive and suffering in a work camp.

He took a deep breath and examined Blaire's long dark eyelashes fanned across her smooth skin. She was unlike either of the other women, each of whom had been young and hesitant with him. Blaire was strong and forthright, and not shy about her physical desires. And she challenged him intellectually, questioning his assumptions and forcing him to think things through before arriving at conclusions.

But he had not resolved his biggest dilemma. His quest as a Star Child demanded that he leave the moon and discover the pathway to the stars. He would like to have Blaire at his side, but she had told him firmly that she would not leave her sisters behind. Or Darla. Or many others in her gang whom she felt responsible for. It had been their only argument and had left him with a deep sadness.

Now he wondered if his quest to find the Star People was a crazy, desperate attempt to prove something to himself. To prove that there was still hope, even though by all measures the Tegs had already won. The Cephean infestation had taken over Earth, and their Teg agents were now on the moon. It should be enough if Torr could somehow help keep Peary Dome free and well fed, as the specter of a Teg invasion of the dome grew more and more likely. Even the mission of saving Peary Dome felt overwhelming. The idea of traveling the galaxy and rescuing Earth with the help of some mythical saviors felt, well ... nuts.

But Igotra. He was real, wasn't he? Turya really existed, didn't it? How could his dreams fabricate such a place? He shook his head, picked up his wolf knife, and looked for Brother Wolf. The shadow spirit was still dozing by the doorway, a faithful friend who had stayed by his side every night since the attack, disappearing during the day to do whatever spirit wolves did.

Torr glanced at his watch. Four o'clock. He gently shook Blaire's shoulder. After a few more gentle shakes, she groggily sat up for her guard shift, and he laid his head in her lap and instantly fell asleep.

————————)————————

"I don't think we can do it," Torr said to his sister as they sat alone at the table after breakfast.

"Do what?" Cassidy asked, stirring honey into a second cup of tea.

"Find Turya. Save the world. You know, be legendary heroes. I think it's a bunch of bunk."

She shrugged her shoulders and kept stirring. "I just want to save the women from that creep," she said, and lifted pained eyes to meet his.

"I know, Cassidy," he said. "But I don't even know how we can do that."

Her wounded expression made him sorry he had voiced the truth. The image of the monstrous Teg general strangling Gerbil with his energy tentacle reared in front of Torr's eyes, and the thought of his sister having been enslaved to that man brought on a surge of horror and despair.

She pursed her lips and tears pooled in her eyes. "I know," she said weakly. "I feel so powerless. I hate it."

"It's not our fault. The Tegs are too strong," Torr said. "I think if we can somehow fortify our defenses in Peary Dome and keep it free, that will be the best we can hope for."

Cassidy stared into her tea and nodded.

————————)————————

"Ready to go?" Torr asked Blaire. He reached out and touched the gold plumeria necklace where it hung glistening against her smooth dark skin. From the center of the sculpted petals the small diamond glittered at him. He and Blaire kissed, then left the tent.

A tremor of excitement hummed throughout the dome. They waved to the campmates who had pulled guard duty and were stationed at the Fen lookout towers. Everyone else left the camp and joined the flow of people streaming up Spoke Road Seven and filling

Center Ring. They found the rest of the Smith gang on the opposite side of the vast yard.

Torr and Blaire held hands and gazed towards Earth as the sun approached the planet on its path towards a total eclipse.

The crowd grew thicker. They stood elbow to elbow, waiting in anticipation. Torr spotted Montana standing on top of the red container at the edge of the PCA compound.

"Come on," Torr said to Blaire and Cassidy. "Let's go up there."

They took Blaire's sisters, Darla, and the Alphabet Boys, and left the rest of the Fensters and Smiths, and threaded their way through the crowd.

Bratislav let them into the PCA tent. The Alphabet Boys stood outside with Bratislav, and the rest of them made their way to the interior courtyard and climbed the ladder of the red container, where they found Montana and Sid gazing out over the crowd.

Montana touched his forefingers to his hat brim in a salute and returned his attention to the sky.

"Hello, Smiths. Hey, Star Children," Sid said. "The stars are aligning. Isn't it about time you left the moon to go find the Star People?"

"Ha ha. Everybody's a comedian today," Torr said, shielding his eyes with his hand to block the sun as he looked at Earth. Torr had seen eclipses of the moon from Earth but had never considered the reverse point of view.

The ladder rattled. Torr turned as Jasper climbed onto the roof, followed by Berkeley.

"Hi, beautiful," Jasper said, tugging on Cassidy's ponytail and kissing her forehead. "And you four moon goddesses," he said, giving a courtly bow to Blaire and her sisters.

"What about me?" Darla asked, cocking her shaved head at Jasper. Sunlight caught the row of small silver hoops lining her ear.

"Miss Darla, the supreme empress of charm and sarcasm," Jasper said with a deep bow.

Darla punched his arm, and they all turned to face Earth. Berkeley began explaining how Earth would obscure the entire sun in a red flash, casting a red glow on the Moon. "But don't look directly at it until the drumming starts, or you'll burn your eyes out. Then stop looking at it when the drumming stops."

Down below, the crowd was growing raucous, blowing whistles and hooting and hollering. A few stray drums thumped in half-hearted rhythms.

"Not those drums," Berkeley said.

Someone else climbed the ladder, shaking the container. Torr was surprised to see Rodney lugging a tall wooden drum up onto the roof. Rodney nodded to Torr and surveyed the crowd down below, his muscled shoulders sloping under his black t-shirt. His beard and precisely sectioned cornrows were meticulously groomed, as usual. They were soon joined by Ramzy, who also carried a tall standing drum. He was wearing his customary desert camouflage pants and long white tunic. He ignored everyone and set his standing drum next to Rodney's, resting his hands on the drumhead. Torr had never seen Ramzy out amongst the people before, and several in the crowd below stared up at him.

The throng in Center Ring was overflowing onto the spoke roads. Torr took out his binoculars and detected another crowd gathered at the foot of Spoke Road Twelve at the sundial. He lowered his binoculars. Earth was impossible to look at as the sun inched closer.

Torr lowered his gaze as the dome slowly darkened into gray twilight. An excited hush fell over the tent city. Noise resumed as people talked among themselves and milled about, waiting. Yells and whistles pierced the air. The minutes stretched on. The sun slid behind Earth, and a howl went up as a thin sliver of gold gleamed on one edge of the dark disc.

Torr forced himself to avert his eyes until the disc flashed in a bright flare. The crowd exploded in an uproar, screaming and yelling and howling like wolves.

A-woooo ... A-woooo.

Torr and Blaire joined in with the howling, and the sun's corona danced in a fiery red ring around Earth. The flare-up quieted to a thick halo, and suddenly the bleak moon was bathed in apocalyptic crimson.

Torr raised his arms and hollered in the red-tinged darkness, then put his fingers to his teeth and whistled shrilly. Cassidy's whistle answered his. His blood was filled with fire, and he yelled at the top of his lungs, his voice lost in the uproar. A loud thump stopped the roar as Ramzy and Rodney hit their drumheads in unison and gazed out over the crowd. Another deep thump echoed off the dome, giving Torr goosebumps. Other drums joined in from below, and then a thunder of drums rumbled from the direction of the Scrid camp, bouncing off the facets of glass overhead and filling the vaulted space.

Blaire tugged on his sleeve, and he turned to look behind him. The normally white gravity bar was a vibrant red, the monolith glowing like a steel rod pulled from a forge.

The crowd roared again and broke into a primal, chaotic dance. Torr and Blaire, Cassidy and Jasper, Berkeley, Darla, and Blaire's sisters, and even Sid and Montana jumped exultantly on top of the metal container, pounding out the rhythm with their feet. Rodney and Ramzy struck their drums in unison, rocking back and forth.

An ember-like glow permeated everything, as though they were in a giant fire pit. Above, the sky was a field of black studded with stars, and the Milky Way was a dark river cutting through it, with riverbanks of luminous clouds.

Torr pulled out the Destroyer and Bear crystals and lifted them over his head, the red ambient light catching the crystals and making them glow like the gravity bar. Cassidy pulled out her crystal ball and shaft, and Jasper held up his new crystal shaft. Blaire and Torr danced together, then apart. Torr spun in place and lost himself in the throbbing pulse.

Drumbeats of a higher pitch reverberated off the dome in a harmonic chorus. Torr tried to determine the source of the high-pitched drums, but he could not. It sounded as though they came from the top of the dome—a distinct rhythm in a different voice, as though they were talking with the drums on the ground.

Torr danced to the phantom drums, stomping his feet and staring out at the red, coppery sky. The smell of sulfur flooded his nose and mouth. He held his breath against the rotten-egg stench, breaking the foot pattern of his dance. He stumbled to a stop and stared around him.

He was encircled by concentric rings of half-clothed drummers. They were all men, on their knees with drums tucked between bare legs, hitting the drumheads in a frenetic rhythm. Torr and the hundred drummers were inside a red stone pit with tall walls and a stairway carved into the curved rock wall. From the rust-colored sky above, the massive Uttapta beat down on Torr.

He stood in the center of the circle of Turyan drummers, and next to him in the open space danced a brown-skinned man with gold luminescent hair that hung past his waist. A large drum hung from the Turyan's shoulder harness. He was oblivious to Torr's presence, as were the other drummers, who rocked back and forth in a trance-like state.

Torr found himself hopping up and down to the drumbeat. His crystals were still in his hands, glowing with the smoldering red light of Uttapta, but he slipped them into his pockets so that he could tap on his abdomen along with the Turyan drummers. The rhythm was too complicated for him to follow, so he tapped out a simpler beat as he jumped and turned in a slow circle, imitating the movements of the lead drummer.

Torr raised his eyes and met the gaze of a kneeling drummer who had stopped beating his drum and was staring at Torr, mouth agape. The elderly man rose to his feet, and with his drum tucked under his arm hobbled in between the rows of drummers to the center and squinted, looking Torr up and down.

Torr stood still and stared back at the man. "You can see me?" Torr asked.

The man could not hear him over the booming of the drums, but he broke into a wide smile, revealing toothless gums. The man's skin was wrinkled and sagging, but his hair and beard were a shimmering reddish-gold, as were his eyes.

Everyone else ignored the old man as he knelt at the edge of the open central circle and motioned for Torr to join him. Torr knelt, and the man set the drum on the ground between them and beat out a short pattern, and then gestured for Torr to hit the drum. Torr repeated the pattern, and the man laughed gleefully, the sound of his laughter lost in the noise, and pounded out the same pattern again. Torr repeated it. Then they both hit the drum together, in time with the others, and Torr realized they were playing one part of the complex cadence. The rhythm pulsed through Torr's body, and he became one with the flow.

Torr's elderly partner stopped drumming, and Torr stopped with him. The man smiled encouragingly, then pounded out a different pattern. It was a second part of the cadence. As Torr learned one part after another, his ear began to sort out the multi-layered rhythm into its individual components. There were a dozen parts, and just when Torr had learned the twelfth, the drumming ended with a unison of three thunderous beats. The drummers stood and stretched and milled about, sipping from metal flasks or climbing the stairway to exit the pit.

The lead drummer turned to Torr's teacher, and the two men talked excitedly. Torr's teacher gestured at Torr, and the lead drummer looked blankly in Torr's direction, tilting his head left and right, trying to see him. Torr examined the leader, who was nude except for a loincloth and the large drum hanging from its harness. He wore a large flat gold crescent strung on a leather thong around his neck. The gold had been hammered, and its dimpled surface reminded Torr of craters on the moon. The man turned his shoulder and the light of Uttapta caught the crescent, flashing a blinding shaft of light into Torr's eyes. He raised his hand to shield them.

"Don't look at it," Blaire said, her tone scolding.

The gunpowdery smell of lunar dust filled Torr's head. He lowered his hand and peered at Blaire, then glanced out through the dome's hexagonal grid at the sky. It was black and starlit. The sun was peeking out from behind Earth, framing one side of the planet in a brilliant crescent of golden-red light.

"Don't look!" Blaire said and turned his chin to face her. She looked at him oddly. "Are you okay?"

He was standing on top of the red container, feeling dizzy. He held Blaire's shoulders to steady himself and nodded. "Yes, I'm okay."

The drumming in the dome had subsided. Ramzy and Rodney were trundling towards the container's ladder with their big drums, and the Scrid camp was quiet. Only the chaotic percussion from a drum circle down below still echoed off the glass dome, making Torr cringe from the amateurs' attempts at keeping a rhythm. The crowd was starting to disperse as the red tinge of the blood moon transitioned to a pale silver. Night gong must have struck sometime during the eclipse, but no one seemed to care.

Torr and his friends sat on the edge of the container with their feet dangling over the side, enjoying the dusky penumbra of the partial eclipse. They waited for the full light of the blazing sun to stream into the dome before finally wandering home to the Fen.

Blaire fell asleep as soon as she hit the bed, her breathing slow and regular. Torr lay on his back, wide awake, and stared up at the dream-catcher as it spun slowly away from him. He closed his eyes and tapped his fingers quietly on his abdomen, practicing the parts of the Turyans' drum cadence.

34

TRADER

Cassidy lay in bed, happy for the chance to sleep in. Torr had declared a day off from training, and Jasper had left immediately after morning gong for the spaceport, saying he had a ship to meet. She drifted in and out of sleep as the sounds of the dome inhabitants slowly stirring filtered in through the canvas walls. Blaire's and Torr's voices came from the neighboring tent, and the Alphabet Boys joked and laughed from the direction of the pavilion. Cassidy rose and pulled on her purple Delosian gown. She sat cross-legged on the bed, gazed into the crystal ball, and searched for the fear and despair that rippled across her consciousness. She found its source and watched the two captives in Balthazar's rape room sitting on the bed, holding each other and rocking back and forth. One of the captives was thin, and her bare skin was covered with bruises of various colors. The other woman was shapely, with long dark hair. Her skin was unblemished, but she was crying harder than the battered woman.

Cassidy's chest was tight, and she struggled to draw air. She guiltily pulled her attention away and shifted focus to the adjacent room. The leaden weight on her chest grew heavier as she watched Balthazar rise from his bed. She knew what would come next and closed her eyes against the sadistic monster. She drew in a breath and opened her eyes, finding Balthazar's housemate, Ridge Gandoop, climbing into his speedster in the house's hangar. He passed through the decompression chambers and flew out over the lunar terrain. He was running late today.

She exhaled and breathed in again, calming herself in order to maintain her focus.

The loner wore his black flight suit, as usual, and his scalp was freshly shaved. He headed towards the white spaceport and black cubes that sat on her land and parked in the small hangar where she and Torr had fled Gandoop. He strode across the main hangar floor, and Cassidy watched him direct a crew loading food onto a freighter. Small cargo loaders ferried pallets of food from the warehouse and into the cargo bay, and Ridge Gandoop stashed various items into the cockpit. When the ship was full, he climbed into the pilot's seat and passed through the airlocks. He piloted the craft southeast. Earth floated above the horizon, a sparkling aquamarine gem against a stark black sky.

The tent door rustled. Cassidy could see in her peripheral vision that it was Blaire but did not break away from her crystal ball.

"Are you coming to breakfast?" Blaire asked.

"Later," Cassidy mumbled.

"What do you see?" Blaire asked hesitantly through the parted door flaps.

"I'll tell you later," Cassidy said.

Cassidy felt her friend inspecting her with a mixture of curiosity and apprehension.

"I'll bring you some tea," Blaire finally said.

"Okay," Cassidy said, and focused in as a compound came into view and the loner pulled back on the throttle.

Two large connected rectangular buildings and a small white dome a short distance away stood upon the shores of a vast sea of black basalt. The loner banked the craft in a slow tight curve and parked the freighter inside one of the rectangular buildings.

She barely noticed Blaire setting a mug of tea on the canvas floor next to her as the man with the metal hand and four other workers transferred the cargo from one freighter to another. She followed the loner as he climbed into the freshly loaded cargo ship and flew from the rectangular building to the white dome, parking in a small hangar that doubled as a single airlock. She watched as he went into a small living area, peeled off his black flight suit, and donned a disguise of a tangled wig and beard and shabby clothing. In minutes, he transformed from a severe rigid man into a portly slob.

Her tea sat untouched as she watched Ridge Gandoop pilot the freighter across the barren moonscape to Peary Dome and park inside the spacious hangar. Jasper was one of the traders who flocked to the craft as the imposter climbed down from the cockpit and opened the cargo bay door.

She reached with one hand to locate her radio on the floor nearby and fumbled with the controls while keeping her eye on the crystal ball.

"Jasper," she spoke into it, watching as he carried a crate of eggs and placed it on a stack.

"Algol's hell," she cursed under her breath. He would be tuned into the Guild channel, not the Fen's. She could not contact him to tell him the trader's true identity without revealing that the Boyers had hacked into the private Guild channel, which she and Torr had sworn not to tell even Jasper.

She broke away from her vision and quickly changed into her silver skirt and white top, zipping the shirt up over her rune belt, and then clasped on her utility belt, heavy with her weapons, radio, and two black pouches. She slipped the crystal ball and light crystal into one pouch, and a few coins and other odds and ends into the other. Finally, she pulled on her velvet boots, grabbed her daypack, and left the tent. Blaire and Torr were sitting with Berkeley and the Boyer brothers in the pavilion with the Alphabet Boys, listening to Fritz and Frank play their guitars.

"I need to go to the spaceport," she said. "Who wants to come?"

They all did.

"Let's take the buggy," Torr said. He and Berkeley unhooked it from the wagon. Torr hopped into the driver's seat, and Blaire took the passenger seat. Cassidy and Berkeley hopped onto the back bumper and held onto the roll bar as Torr left the Fen through the alleyway, with the others trotting at their flanks.

At the end of Spoke Road Nine, Torr parked the buggy along the front wall of the spaceport. Torr and Berkeley went inside with Cassidy, leaving the others outside to wait for them.

The cool building felt good after the heat of the dome. The last of the traders were carting away goods from the freighter, which was already locked up. Jasper was not among them, and the bearded imposter was nowhere to be seen. Berkeley spoke with one of the men, who motioned across the floor.

Cassidy spotted Jasper standing alone at the far end of the hangar, where the large interstellar spacecraft parked. A loud creaking turned her head. The largest of the compression chambers was opening. Its wall-sized doors parted slowly, and a Nommos ship floated silently into the cavernous hangar. The oblong craft shone bluish-silver and was covered with long spikes. Her abdomen clenched at the sight and sweat broke out on her upper lip.

"A blowfish for the fish people," Berkeley said. "I didn't know they were arriving today."

"What are they doing here?" she asked. "Are they here to traffic women?" A sudden wave of lightheadedness overcame her, and she took Torr's arm.

He put his arm around her shoulder. "You okay?" he asked.

"No," she said. "They're here to transport Earth women to Delos. I know it. We have to stop them." Her legs were trembling, and a clammy sweat was sticky on her skin. She stepped forward as the ship obscured her view of Jasper.

One of Rodney's Rangers appeared and stood in her path, an assault rifle slung across his chest.

"Only Guild traders allowed," he said. He motioned to the main exit. "Please wait outside."

Berkeley stepped forward. "Hey, Garfield," he said. "I think she wants to talk to Jaz."

"Hi, Berk," Garfield said. He glanced at Cassidy, then turned back to Berkeley. "You can wait inside the traders pen, if you want, but they can't pass. Nommos trading is by appointment only. Jaz got the first slot. He won't want to talk to her now, I can assure you. Catch him later." Garfield waved them away with a shooing motion, then turned to help guide the dirigible-shaped craft down the cargo lane.

Cassidy gritted her teeth, and Berkeley took out his radio. "Jaz," he said.

A crackling noise came from the tinny speaker, and then Jaz's voice. "What. I'm busy."

"Cassidy wants to talk to you."

"I'll talk to her later."

"We're at the port," Berkeley said. "You got a Nommos trade lined up?"

"Yeah. Gotta go."

The radio went silent, and Berkeley shrugged his shoulders at Cassidy. "It's okay, Cassidy," he said. "Nommos can't do any human trafficking out of Peary. But they have a lot of gold and always stop here to trade. Let Jaz make his deal."

"So, what, then? They go to Gandoop after this and pick up women there?" she asked, panic gripping her throat. "I want to see these evil fish creatures." She stepped forward, but Garfield glanced over his shoulder with a stern frown. Another Ranger had joined him, blocking the way to the rows of parked craft.

"Come on, Cassidy," Torr said gently, turning her towards the exit. "There's nothing we can do. We'll meet Jaz back at the Fen."

She walked woodenly across the floor and outside, and then climbed onto the back while Torr drove back to the Fen.

Cassidy watched Jasper conduct his trade through the crystal ball from the still silence of her and Jasper's tent.

She had expected the Nommos to look like fish in some manner, with slimy, scaly skin, or spiky spines along their backs. But they looked like Earthlanders. Tall with white skin, pronounced noses, overhanging brows, and wearing long flowing robes. There were two of them standing with Jasper. One had long silky white hair hanging loose and wore an ivory-colored brocade robe over ivory pants and polished black boots. The other's head was wrapped in a dark amber scarf to match his russet robe.

Cassidy hunched over and peered into the crystal ball in her lap, causing the image to zoom in. The russet-robed Nommos was exchanging cases with Jasper. The cases were the size of small suitcases, or more resembling ice coolers. The one Jasper handed the Nommos was white and lit with several small blue lights. The case Jasper received in return was identical, but the lights were dark.

Cassidy's heart thudded in her throat. Jasper had sworn to her that he would stop dealing drugs, and yet there he was, making a drug trade while lying to her about it. She wondered why the Greenwash required such a high-tech container. Maybe the space journey required it. Temperature control, or pressure, or something. Or maybe it was another substance he was hiding from her. Indignation replaced curiosity as she continued to spy on him. She had thought she and Jasper had agreed to be honest with one another and not hide anything. She had tried to share her feelings with him honestly, and every night she related what she had done that day. He only ever gave her a brief summary of his day, explaining that the details of a Guild trader's day would bore her. He said it required a lot of waiting around, broken up by brief periods of haggling with unsavory characters.

Gold exchanged hands, and Jasper counted the coins twice. Finally, the men bowed to one another and parted.

Jasper crossed the hangar to the traders pen, carrying his white case, and then disappeared into his storage container. She set down the crystal ball, rose to her feet, and paced back and forth, considering how to confront him.

———————————)———————————

All of Cassidy's carefully planned words devolved into a screaming fit when Jasper finally returned to the Fen and found her in their tent.

"You swore you would stop dealing drugs," she yelled, not caring who heard. Her blood seethed, and she pinned Jasper with an unbending glare.

They stood across from one another, eyes locked.

"Cassidy," Jasper said. "Shhhh ... Calm down. I'm not dealing drugs. I told you."

"Liar! I saw you," she said, incensed that he would keep up his pretense and lie to her face.

He looked taken aback. "You spied on me?" His eyes flared. "What kind of trust is that, spying on me?" he asked.

She set her hands on her hips. "Oh. So. When you get caught, you try to turn it into I'm bad because I'm spying on you—when it's you who are lying through your teeth. You dirty drug dealer. You know, Schlitzer uses that shit to control his hookers. Still. To this day. Did you know that?"

Jasper's eyes grew wide again.

"Of course you did," she said, contempt thick in her voice.

"It wasn't drugs. And I gave Torr all the Greenwash I had. Schlitzer was one of my customers. He bought several vials from me, a while ago. I'm not surprised he still has a stash. But that's not my fault."

"Not your fault," she drawled sarcastically. Her eyes narrowed. "But what do you mean it wasn't drugs? What was in that white case if not drugs?"

Jasper dropped his gaze to the floor.

"What?" she insisted. "What's in that case?"

"The case is empty," Jasper said, avoiding her eyes.

"Well," she said, glaring at him. "What was in the case you handed the Nommos? The one with the blue lights. I'm sure they would not give you piles of gold for an empty case."

"I can't believe you were spying on me," Jasper said, meeting her eyes defiantly.

"Stop avoiding the question and answer me." She folded her arms across her chest and tilted her head. "I'm waiting."

He pursed his lips, and finally said in a small voice, "Eggs."

She wrinkled her brow, confused. "Eggs?" Her pulse grew weak. "What kind of eggs?"

Jasper's eyes shifted away again. "Human eggs."

His words hung in the air, and for a long moment she could not process them.

"Human eggs," she repeated as the meaning slowly sank in.

"Yes," he said, and took a heavy breath. "The Nommos males are infertile, and they're desperate to keep their race going. They buy eggs, still thinking that if they could get the right egg, their sperm will work." He shook his head. "They refuse to admit their sperm is bad. They're insane that way. And they pay crazy amounts of gold for eggs. They buy sperm too but won't pay a premium for that. I guess it's easier to get. And they have huge egos, despite everything, and want their own DNA passed on, not someone else's."

Cassidy felt a sneer turn up her lips. "That's sick."

Jasper nodded. "It is," he said. "In the meantime, they have become master geneticists, and cultivate embryos in jars with eggs and sperm from other races. They inject their own genetic material into the mix to keep their bloodlines alive. Or so they tell themselves."

Cassidy fell to her knees, and Jasper knelt next to her.

"Where do you get the eggs?" she asked in a trembling voice, afraid of the answer.

He hesitated, then answered reluctantly, "From Earth."

"From the Tegs," she said slowly, heat rising to her face.

He did not answer.

"From enslaved Earth women." She met his guilty eyes. Her shocked horror retreated and a flood of rage rushed to her head, turning her vision red. Her ears rang from the blood screaming in her veins. "From the work camps," she said. "Jasper, that could have been me in one of those camps."

"From clinics," he said defensively. "Fertility clinics. The women give the eggs freely."

"You mean *for free,* because they have *no choice.* And they're not fertility clinics, they're breeding centers. *Rape camps.*"

His eyes were wide, evasive. "At least I don't sell women. The Nommos prefer live women. And they pay a fortune."

Cassidy slapped his face, hard. His head turned to the side, and he kept it there for a long surprised moment. Her palm stung, and she struggled to her feet, but he grabbed her hand and pulled her back down to her knees.

She wrenched her hand free and stood up. "Don't you try to make excuses, Jasper Manann. You are shameless. Despicable." She scowled down at him, then stormed out of the tent onto the dusty ground.

A smoldering rage rose in her belly and up through her lungs like flames catching tinder. What right did men have to do this, and why did other men let them? Why did women let them? Why did *she* let them? Anger tore from her throat and burst from her body like shards of lightning. Her fingertips burned and her hair crackled, and light blazed from her eyes. Raking her fingers through the air, she clawed for something solid, grasping for air molecules to hurl through the heavens, to pull the air from the lungs of Balthazar and the Nommos, to suffocate every person who preyed on others.

Cassidy spun in the middle of the Fen's courtyard, spinning faster and pulling the air along with her in a whirlwind, wanting to roll the horror and sadness into a ball that she could cast into the flames of hell to burn for eternity. Tents rocked on their poles and shouts of alarm sounded from the camp. The creaking of tent supports and the ripping of canvas tore through the air around her, but Cassidy did not stop. She raised her eyes and her hands, commanding the cruel madness to end, or she would halt everyone in their tracks, let them draw no more breaths, let them say no more words, let them think no more thoughts. Dust columns swirled around her, gaining speed and whipping her hair across her face.

Torr burst across the yard and caught her wrists. They stood together in a frozen dance, arms raised over their heads, their eyes searing into one another's.

"Stop it, Cassandra!" Torr yelled. "Stop it, right now!"

She glanced at him dizzily, his gray eyes flinty and sparking.

Torr released her wrists and grabbed her chin. "Cassidy!" he yelled. "Look at me!"

She stared. It was Torr. She was on the moon. She gasped for breath. The whirlwind subsided, dust hanging in the air. Her hands and legs shook violently. Torr's eyes flitted to her hair, which was loose and wild and dancing with static electricity.

"Cassidy, what the hell?" Jasper asked, appearing at her side and tugging at her shoulder.

Breaking free of Torr's grip, she pushed Jasper aside and ran into their tent, which was collapsed on one side and its shade cover torn away. She ducked under the sagging ceiling, grabbed her daypack and utility belt, and then ran across the yard to the moon rover. She revved its silent engine and tore across the Fen, careening around the kitchen tents and out into the alleyway.

Voices called after her as she drove down the alley through hazy dust clouds and turned left down a spoke road. Tents lay collapsed or in tatters all around, and cyclones of dust floated along the road like ghosts traveling the night. People milled around in confusion, gaping at the remnants of the wind storm in a dome where there was not supposed to be any wind. She stepped on the accelerator and raced past them.

At the perimeter road, Cassidy turned right and drove towards Earth floating above the horizon. Dust was slowly settling to the ground, hovering in a pale cloud layer. Her inner core of strength that had expanded and harnessed the air to her will slowly contracted and folded in on itself. She was inside her body but at the same time outside of it, looking down at herself. It was as though she could see the fragile shield she had constructed around herself slowly crumbling. She was powerless to stop it and watched the fault lines deepen. Jasper. Her love. Her best friend. His betrayal sank into her heart like a cold sharp blade. He was part of the whole sick trafficking operation, exploiting women and selling them for parts.

She swallowed back dry tears. She was numb, but not numb enough. Pain and anguish throbbed in her heart. When would this nightmare ever end? *Greenwash.* Its pungent smell and bitter taste invaded her senses. It would wash away all the hurt. Stop her from caring. She could shatter into a million pieces and it would not matter. Voices jabbered in her head, pleading with her to be reasonable. Telling her that the pain would pass on its own. Echoes of her mother's voice explaining the mechanics of addiction. She ignored them.

35

SEARCH PARTY

"Cassidy," Torr said into the radio.

Silence greeted him.

He blew out his breath and turned to Blaire. "She's gonna be the death of me," Torr said.

"She'll be fine," Blaire said, laying her hand on his shoulder. "You'll be fine, too."

Blaire unclipped her radio from her belt. "Becka."

A moment later Becka replied, "Hey, Blaire."

"Cassidy ran off," Blaire said. "Has she shown up there?"

"No. When? Did you guys have a wind storm over there?"

"Yeah. It was Cassidy's doing. Then she hopped in the moon buggy and took off. She was upset about something."

"Whoa, really? Okay. We'll send out a search party," Becka said.

"Okay, thanks. We're sending out patrols, too," Blaire said. "Can you guys check the training yard?"

"Sure," Becka said. "We're on it."

Torr turned to the Fensters gathered around.

"You guys check the spaceport," he said to the Alphabet Boys. "Blaire and I, and you guys," Torr said, motioning to the Boyer brothers and Sky and Thunder, "we'll go to the Scrid camp. We'll check Center Ring on our way over there. Jasper, you go secure ASB."

"Okay," Jasper said.

Torr searched Jasper's eyes. They were shifting with guilt, and his lips drew into a hard, thin line. "We will talk later," Torr said acidly. Jasper averted his gaze and fiddled with his radio.

"I'll go with you," Berkeley said to Jasper.

"Khaled and I can check the sundial and Schlitzer's," Ming-Long volunteered.

"Okay, thanks," Torr said. "Fritz, Frank, Faisal. You guys patrol the perimeter road. Start at the greenhouses."

"I'll guard the Fen with Tatsuya and Hiroshi," Durham said. "We'll radio you if she comes back here."

"Okay," Torr said, sighing and rubbing dust from his eyes.

Torr strapped his belt around his waist, then he and Blaire strode towards Center Ring, with their friends trailing close behind.

36

⸺ ☽ ⸺

THE EXCHANGE

C assidy reached the sundial and took a hard right onto Spoke Road Twelve, then turned right onto Ring Road L. She abandoned the moon rover at the entrance to Schlitzer's camp, a fenced-in block she had passed many times in her aimless wanderings and visited briefly in her remote viewing sessions.

A distant voice in her head told her to stop. It sounded like her mother's voice. Or a younger, wiser version of herself. But her legs moved on their own. The guards at the open gate glanced at the buggy but ignored her as she entered the camp. A few tarps and some litter had been scattered by the wind, but the compound showed less wind damage than the rest of the camps she had passed.

She followed the sounds of voices and laughter to the large pavilion-style tent and ducked under a canvas wall that was rolled up halfway from the ground. She glanced around. A polished wooden bar backed by a mirror and shelves of liquor bottles stood along one side. A barmaid walked over as Cassidy approached the bar. Her blood was racing and she felt a bit off balance, but she set her jaw and perched on a stool.

"Hi. Can I help you?" the barmaid asked, flashing her a friendly smile.

Cassidy noted the greenish tinge to the barmaid's teeth and could almost taste the Greenwash. "Is Schlitzer here?" Cassidy asked. She held the barmaid's eyes.

The barmaid raised one manicured eyebrow and said, "Yes. I'll get him." She gave Cassidy a glass of cold water and left the tent.

Cassidy sipped the water, savoring the coolness, and drummed her fingers on the solid wood bar. She identified Schlitzer from across the tent as he entered with the barmaid and scanned the space, his eyes landing on her. He strode over with an air of easy confidence—a man accustomed to getting his way. Cassidy gripped her glass.

"Well, well," Schlitzer said, and sat next to her. "I believe I am blessed by the presence of the Star Child. Am I not? Cassidy, is it?" He bowed his head deferentially. "To what do I owe this honor?"

She felt herself relaxing. "Well," she said quietly. "I hear you may have some ... Greenwash?"

Schlitzer raised both eyebrows, and then threw back his head and laughed. His laughter trailed off into a soft chuckle, and he ran his fingers over his graying moustaches as he examined her. "Aren't you dating Jaz?" His smile deepened. "Oh, that's right. He got rid of his stash. Pity."

He held her gaze. His eyes were a piercing blue. "I may have a spare vial," he said.

Her pulse throbbed insistently. "I'd like to buy it. I have gold."

"Really ...," he drawled, settling back on his stool. "Greenwash is worth much more than gold right now. I have the last stash in Peary, and more gold than I can spend."

She swallowed. "What, then?" she asked. "What do you want for it?"

"Hmmm," he said, pulling his mouth to the side in thought. "I may be able to part with a little. Come with me. I'm sure we can think of something."

Schlitzer led her to a tent furnished with a large mattress and two pillows covered with purple sheets and pillowcases, a real wooden coffee table, a real wooden chair, and a dark-red throw rug. She turned around in a circle, then faced Schlitzer with a hand on her hip and met his smug look.

"What's this?" she asked, disdain heavy on her tongue. "You want sex? Don't you get enough of that? I mean, you're a pimp. Right?"

He laughed again. "I like your directness," he said, sitting on the mattress on the floor. He patted the bed next to him. "I happen to love my job," he said, his smile widening. "Do you want some Greenwash or not?"

She scowled at him, but her feet were planted solidly on the dusty red rug, and the euphoria of the drug hovered just beyond her reach.

Her spirit twisted painfully, and then gasped and departed from her body. It floated above her and watched with detached pity as she shrugged the daypack off her shoulders, removed her utility belt, and lowered herself onto the bed. She lay down on her side, and Schlitzer stretched out next to her and ran his hand over the curve of her hip. Her body shivered as he moved his hand up underneath her top and brushed his fingers across her bare skin.

"What's this?" he asked, stopping at her waist. He lifted her white armored shirt and felt around her waist belt. "I've heard about these," he said with a hint of awe as he snapped open the clasp and stared at the belt. "Berkeley made this, right?" He glanced up to meet her eyes, as though theirs were a casual conversation between friends.

"Yes," she said as he tossed the rune belt gently aside.

He ran his fingertips along her jawline and trailed them lightly down her neck. Her body suddenly seized up. She was unable to take a breath, and he pulled his hand away as her heart thundered in her chest.

"I'm not going to hurt you," he said softly, and tried again, brushing his fingers across her cheekbone and moving a stray strand of hair away from her eyes. "You can breathe now," he said.

She sucked in a mouthful of air and held her breath again.

He sighed and sat up, then peeled off his shirt and pants and turned to her. "It would help if you removed your clothing," he said with a half-grin. She stared past him and did not respond.

"I'm not going to force you," he said, lying on his side several inches from her. "Take your time."

Her limbs were leaden. She knew she should leave the tent but was anchored in place by a force greater than her will. What did it matter, anyway? Her body was already worthless. Balthazar had made sure of that. She pushed herself up and robotically removed her clothes, then wadded them up, placed the bundle next to the mattress, and lay back down. The warm air of the dome brushed against her bare skin, and she wanted to pull the sheet up over herself, but she and Schlitzer were lying on top of it.

He propped himself up on one elbow and regarded her. "You are not the first woman who has come to me after being brutally raped, you know," he said.

She met his eyes. They gleamed sky blue, speckled with gray.

"It gets better," he said, stroking her hair. She flinched under his touch but did not resist. "You'll see," he said.

His words were hollow, echoing in a dark cave. He leaned in to kiss her, but she turned her mouth away. He kissed her cheek, then her neck.

She squeezed her eyes shut and inhaled. He smelled of sandalwood soap. She could stand it for just a little bit longer, she told herself. Greenwash would make it all go away.

She gritted her teeth as his fingertips ran lightly over her skin. He tried stimulating her in various ways, but when she did not respond he finally sighed, grabbed a bottle of lubricant, and then lowered himself over her, spread her legs with his knees, and penetrated her. She winced and stared at the ceiling, while at the same time staring down from above at herself and the back of the man on top of her. He was much gentler than Balthazar, she reflected numbly, from a cold analytical part of herself that registered distant sensations, while at the same time feeling nothing at all. She exhaled and turned her mind to memories of swimming in the ocean, the waves rising and falling, buoying her up under a vast cobalt sky.

Before too long, it was over. Schlitzer handed her a towel and stood up to get dressed. She turned away from him, prickles of self-loathing stinging as she reluctantly returned to her body. She put on her clothing and snapped the rune belt around her waist.

Schlitzer was waiting for her. She turned to him, avoiding his eyes. He pulled a silver vial from his pants pocket and held out the dropper.

"I don't get the whole vial?" she asked, her eyes fastened on the green liquid.

Schlitzer laughed. "No. Sorry. Two drops."

"I said I wanted a vial," she said, anger displacing her shame.

"I don't believe I agreed to that," he said calmly. "I'm sorry if you assumed so. But I cannot spare that much."

"Well," she said, trying to recall their conversation at the bar. "But ... I normally take the whole dropper-full," she said, meeting his gaze.

He raised one eyebrow. "Normally?" he asked, one side of his mouth quirking up. "I define normal around here. Do you want it, or not?" He squeezed all but a small portion into the vial and held the dropper out to her.

She frowned but tilted her chin back and opened her mouth.

He chuckled and handed her the dropper. "You can do it yourself," he said. "You're not a baby."

She took the rubber dropper with trembling fingers.

"I might get sick and pass out," she said.

"That's okay," he said. "I'll bring in a bucket. You can stay here as long as you want. And we have our own porta-potties." He motioned over his shoulder. "Just follow the smell."

She inhaled and squeezed two drops onto her tongue.

─────) ─────

Cassidy threw up violently into the bucket, but it didn't matter. The familiar feeling of well-being permeated every cell of her body, and she floated back to the bed and sprawled across it, enjoying the soft mattress and pillows. The smell of Schlitzer was still on her, but she didn't mind. The sheets were purple, and her memories were like gossamer cobwebs, everything swirling together into one pleasant blur. Life was beautiful, after all. Was it not? Butterflies, the sharp thorns of a rose bush, the sticky mud of a bog. She loved everything. Even herself. That was the best thing about Greenwash, she reflected. That she loved herself, no matter what. Even though Balthazar had stripped her of her dignity. Even though she loved Jasper, who was trading in human eggs. Even though she had slept with Schlitzer. Life was a colorful kaleidoscope, ever shifting into new configurations, each better than the last, and none lasting for long.

The weave of the canvas ceiling was fascinating. How the threads crisscrossed in perfect precision, making something sturdy out of thousands of thin strands. The tent door rustled and footsteps approached. Two men knelt down next to her, and she looked up at them.

"Ming-Long," she said. "Khaled. What are you doing here?"

"Here you are," Ming-Long said, leaning over her. "Everyone's out looking for you. What are you doing here? Are you okay?" he asked, concern etched in his brow.

"I'm great," she said, smiling up at him. "How are you?"

"Oh, Cassidy," he said, and glanced up at Khaled. "She's stoned."

Khaled moved around to her other side and took her hand. His skin was calloused and cool under hers.

"Here, Cassidy," Ming-Long said. "Let me wipe your mouth. Looks like you got sick."

He pulled a white kerchief from his pocket and dabbed at the corner of her mouth. Khaled took her other wrist and his grip tightened as Ming-Long pressed the cloth over her nose and mouth.

"Uhhh," she moaned. The cloth restricted her airflow, and he pressed down harder. "Stop that," she mumbled, trying to turn her head. "I can't breathe." The pressure lessened, and she inhaled.

37

---)---

LAST CHANCE

Schlitzer had notified Jidna that the raisin order should be coming in any day now, and that he would need to be ready at a moment's notice to receive his goods. So Jidna had spent the past three days at Danny's, telling her he was in a bit of a jam back at the mine and asking if she would mind putting him up until the tension passed. She was more than happy to accommodate and had set him up in a private tent.

The call came not too long after an odd wind storm had swept the dome, leaving everyone in a state of confusion.

"The first batch of raisins has arrived. The sweet raisins." It was Schlitzer's voice. "Meet at the arranged location."

"10-4," Jidna said.

The radio went silent and Jidna clipped the radio to his belt. He brushed at his beard with his fingers and pulled his shoulders back. Jidna rejoined Danny where he had been helping her and her girls set up tents that had blown over.

"I must be going," he told her, kissing her hand.

"Now?" she asked. Surprise and disappointment flashed across her face, but she quickly put on her practiced expression of friendly neutrality.

"Yes. I'm sorry," Jidna said. "Things have calmed down back at the mine, and a piece of machinery has broken. I must take care of it right away." He bowed graciously. "Thank you for your generous hospitality." He kissed her hand again, but it lay limp in his hand. Her eyes were suddenly hard, and he wondered what she had expected. He deposited a Tetra into her cold palm, and her fingers closed around it.

He bowed again and stepped away, then quickly gathered his things and left out the back alleyway. He exhaled with relief when he turned onto a spoke road. With that delicate exit accomplished, the prospect of his next task tightened his shoulders as he strode quickly over the hazy roads.

He waited at the north wall of Peary Spaceport, fidgeting in the narrow lane next to the solar inverters. This area was a vacant no-man's land, with the stink from the moats the most prominent presence. Jidna tugged nervously at his rat's nest of a beard and gazed out through the glass panels of the dome at the line of solar dishes, which were perched on the ridge like huge sunflowers that turned slowly to always face the sun.

It was not long before a small box truck drove down the narrow lane and pulled in between two inverter shacks, parking out of view of the main road. Schlitzer's two men hopped out from the front seats. They exchanged code words with Jidna and introduced themselves quickly, and then the one named Khaled opened the back of the truck. Jidna peered inside.

The young brown-haired beauty was curled on her side, with wrists tied behind her back, ankles bound, and a white kerchief soaked with Hesychasm tied over her nose and mouth. Her eyes were closed, and she looked to be in a peaceful slumber. He reached out and shook her shoulder gently. She was breathing in a slow steady rhythm—passed out cold.

"I'll take it from here," Jidna said, and nodded at the two men. He gave them each two Solidi, as per the agreement with Schlitzer. They quickly pocketed the gold, and the one named Ming-Long handed him the truck key. The two men grabbed backpacks from the cargo area and left in a hurry towards the front of the spaceport and disappeared around the corner.

Jidna climbed into the back of the truck and lowered the metal door. The cargo area was lit by a small skylight. Jidna knelt next to the unconscious woman and cut her bonds. He did not want to be found with a bound woman in Peary. Human trafficking was not tolerated here. That was one thing Ramzy had gotten right, which was more than Jidna could say for Gandoop Spaceport, or himself, now.

Schlitzer had told him that the young woman carried a small crystal ball that Gabira was desperate to get a hold of, and it would serve as his bribe to get into the cave. Jidna quickly found the crystal ball and another crystal shaft in a utility pouch on her belt. He slipped the crystals into his pants pocket and rummaged through her other belt pouch. His fingers closed around a familiar object. He withdrew his hand and opened his fist. The key fob to Balty's speedster sat in his palm. He smiled and returned the key fob to the pouch and continued sorting through its contents. He found a few copper and silver coins, some tenth-gold bits, a stale hunk of bread, and a small photo strip that showed two snapshots, which Jidna realized were of Cassidy and Jaz when they were teenagers. He gazed at their silly, happy faces, and a stab of guilt cut through him. He was taking Jaz's girlfriend away from him. His heart tightened with shame, but there was nothing to be done. Jaz would thank him if he understood the alternatives. Unfortunately, Jidna couldn't tell Jaz about it, so the man would undoubtedly go insane with worry. Jidna returned the coins and other items to the pouch.

A small green daypack sat on the metal floor next to her. A metal flower pinned to an outside pocket and a Light Fighters patch marked it as hers. Jidna inspected its contents—bags and bottles of herbs, notebooks with sketches of plants and herbal prescriptions, a smaller canvas bag with a fountain pen and a jar of ink labeled *Black Guya*, and a folder with scraps of old writings in what looked to be ancient Delosian. Jidna replaced everything. He did not want to steal from the girl. It was bad enough he was giving her to that witch. Let Gabira figure out what to do with her belongings. If Gabira were pleasant, Jidna would even let the greedy woman have the crystal shaft.

He held his breath and tentatively lifted the bottom of her shirt but found only bare skin. He furrowed his brow. Schlitzer had confirmed that she wore a waist belt hidden under her shirt. His jaws tightened. Could the two men have stolen the deed right out from under him? His pulse quickened as he assessed the situation, torn between saving the girl and chasing after the moon deed. He couldn't very well leave her here. But wait. Schlitzer had said the belt had a concealing glamour on it.

Jidna ran his fingers along the silky skin of her waist until it met stiff resistance. Jidna grasped the invisible fabric. It felt like a canvas waist belt. His skin prickled as it did whenever he discovered something unexpected that opened his mind to new possibilities. What kind of technology had made such a thing? He found the clasp and unclipped the belt, and it suddenly appeared. He pulled it from around her waist and inspected it curiously, then finally opened the pouch.

Inside, he found several papers. His hands trembled as he pulled out a square of parchment and unfolded it. *Lunar Deed* stared up at him in elaborate script. A small tremor of excitement shook him. A second parchment contained a map. Jidna plotted the coordinates and noted with a pang of relief that the entire main Anaximenes crater, which held Gandoop Spaceport and the black cubes, was contained within her parcel.

He perused the deed and noted the Salmon Seal of Metolius alongside the signature and fingerprints of the President of the Global Alliance. Jidna shook his head in wonder. He was holding genuine, valid deeds to his land. He gripped the parchment with elation.

But suddenly, Balty's face appeared in his mind's eye, glaring at him accusingly. What would that bastard do if he found out that Jidna—Ridge—had the deeds and didn't tell him? He would probably kill him. The memory of the rat-faced man twitching against the office wall brought bile to his mouth.

He pursed his lips. The land was his, and his brother's and father's. They had slaved for two decades to make it what it was today. Then, when all the hard work was done and they were ready to reap the rewards, Balty comes swooping in like a crow raiding a nest. Well, not this time. Fortune had smiled down upon him. With this invisibility belt, he'd unexpectedly stumbled upon a way to keep the deeds from Balty forever. He would tell Balty the girl had disappeared, and that would be that. There would be nothing in Algol's hell Balty could do about it. Triumph filled him to bursting.

He reined in his exuberance and returned to the task at hand. He wasn't out of the woods yet. Jidna scanned the deed again, uncertainty creeping back in. He examined the signature and fingerprints of Metolius more closely. What if these kids were actually sent by the President for some secret mission, and he was about to defy one of the two most powerful men on Earth?

Jidna held the moon deed flat on the metal floor under his knees, then fumbled with the ink pad in his pocket and awkwardly took the girl's right hand. He wiped her index and middle fingers clean with a damp cloth, which he'd brought just for that purpose. He dried them with a corner of the cloth, then carefully rolled each fingertip across the ink pad and pressed them to the parchment below her child-sized prints, next to the spot where he would forge her signature. Jidna blew on the ink and admired her perfect fingerprints, marveling at how they were exactly the same patterns as the smaller versions above it.

Jidna attempted to wipe the ink from the girl's fingers, then gently placed her fine-boned hand at her side. He took a deep breath and rifled through the other papers in the pouch and found her passport. He flipped to the identification page. Her signature was there, in a more adult script than the careful child's signature on the deed. He'd forge this one onto the deed later.

He quickly examined the other papers, which were the girl's DNA birth certificate. Jidna folded them up with the deeds and slid all the documents back into the pouch. The belt pouch was oddly heavy. Feeling inside, he found two Solidi and six Tetras. That was a surprise. How did she get that much gold? Nervousness crept back in as he considered the unsettling connection between her and Metolius.

He slipped the solid gold pyramids into his pocket, his mood lifting a tiny bit. He could always use more gold.

He closed up the waist belt pouch and inspected the odd rune embroidered into the fabric, then clasped the belt around his own waist below his pillow stuffing. The pouch disappeared behind the thick padding. Jidna reached up under his fake, fat belly, and could feel the pouch, but it was not until he unclasped it that it became visible again. He clicked it closed again, lowered his padding, and then reached around his waist and could not feel anything, even through his thin undershirt. This was truly intriguing, but further inspection would have to wait until later.

Jidna unclipped her outer belt that held her pouches, a radio, a short wooden club, a slingshot, and two knives. The radio was turned

off. He popped open the back of the small hand radio and removed
the battery, then closed up the back again and stuffed everything into
her pack. He guiltily unzipped her silver and white top and peeled it
off, then removed her silver paneled skirt, revealing long shapely limbs.
His gaze traveled over the curves of her body, now covered only by
black leggings, a tight pink t-shirt embellished with a jeweled butterfly
that glimmered over round breasts, and knee-high velvet boots that
reminded him of Delos.

Jidna grabbed his sack and pulled out a traditional long silk robe
from his part of the world, which he had found in the warehouse,
and slipped it over her head and arms. He awkwardly tugged it down
until it covered her body. It was a small effort to disguise her and make
Gabira's guards believe she was actually his niece. At least they'd have a
truthful story to tell if they were questioned. The robe was a rich indigo
blue and embroidered with intricate scroll patterns of gold thread at
the neckline, cuffs, and hem. He rolled up her dusty clothes along with
the utility belt and stuffed them into his sack.

He adjusted Cassidy's face cloth, checking to make sure she was
still unconscious. She was sleeping like a baby. He smoothed down
her hair, which was loose and tangled. He clumsily tucked wayward
strands behind her delicate ears. If she were his wife, she would be
wearing gold earrings, but her earlobes were bare of any ornamenta-
tion, though she was wearing gold necklaces. He gently lifted a coin
pendant that had slipped down the gold chain into the soft hair at the
nape of her neck. It looked to be pure gold and bore the image of a
nude woman pouring water from an urn. On the reverse side was a
Delosian Heaven's Window symbol, with its three eyes staring out at
him. It made him shiver, and he dropped the pendant.

Another pendant was hidden in her thick brown hair. He gently
pulled it free. It was another Heaven's Window triangle, but with blue
gems for eyes. It reminded him of one of his grandmother's amulets
that warded off the evil eye, and it, too, was staring at him. Also around
her neck was a thin black cord that held an arrowhead of black obsidian. All three pendants made him feel exposed and ashamed, as though
someone were watching him. He shrugged off the feeling and carefully
placed the pendants in the little hollow at the base of her throat. She

was a pretty thing. At her wrist she wore a watch and a woven bracelet of many colors tied with red-beaded strings. He left them on her wrist.

Jidna slung her small backpack along with his own sack over his shoulders, pulled the white rag down around the girl's neck, and then hoisted her in his arms and carried his prize to the doorway leading to Gabira's cave. He had paid off the two guards in advance, and they opened the door for him, one of them crossing the alleyway to close the back of the truck.

"My niece finally made it," Jidna told the third guard manning the inside of the airlock. "What a relief," Jidna said, smiling.

The man raised an eyebrow and let him pass.

Cassidy was not light, despite her feminine build. Jidna was huffing by the time he made it to Gabira's olivewood door. He kicked at it loudly with the steel toe of his boot.

The door swung open, and Gabira's large almond-shaped eyes rimmed with thick black eyeliner peered out.

"I've brought my niece," he announced. "And your crystal ball."

Gabira looked startled, then her brown lips formed an "O." She swung the door into the room and closed it behind him as he lowered his heavy burden onto a pile of rugs. He tried to catch his breath and placed his hands on his hips, proud of himself. *He had done it.* He let himself wallow in self-congratulations for a moment, and then turned and smiled at a curious Gabira, who studied him with slitted eyes.

"That is not your niece," she said.

"She is if I say she is," Jidna retorted. He brought out the crystal ball and held it up to the light cast by the solar filaments. Gabira reached for the crystal, but he pulled it away and hid it in his pocket. "Not so fast." He snickered at Gabira's peevish expression. "Is she my niece?"

"Yes, Jidna, she's your niece. Let me see that crystal. Did Schlitzer send you?"

"No. Schlitzer is working for me. And if I don't stop by his camp in an hour, he and his girlfriend will come down here looking for me and haul you to the surface, so don't think you're going to trap me again, my little sorceress."

She threw him a sharp glance, her mouth working like a cow chewing her cud. He avoided making eye contact with her and fingered his obsidian ring. All he had to do was radio Schlitzer when he got home, but she didn't need to know that. And he really didn't know if Schlitzer and his supposedly gifted girlfriend, Debbie, could withstand her witchcraft any more than he could, but he had determined the mission was worth the risk—he just needed to get out of there fast.

"You're not leaving her here," Gabira said gruffly.

"Oh, yes I am. And you're going to take good care of her. And not let her out." He cast a meaningful look at the matronly woman whose plump face scrunched up with displeasure. "That is, if you want the crystal." Gabira eyed the crystal ball as Jidna produced it from his pocket again and rolled it around on his palm, watching as the light glinted through the cloudy crystal. He wondered why the witch wanted it so much.

"It will cost me more to feed her than that crystal is worth," Gabira complained.

She was lying, of course, but then again, food had recently become very expensive. He reached into his pocket and produced the crystal shaft. He was not about to give her the Solidi. "What do you think this is worth?" he asked innocently. Her expression grew ravenous, and he knew he had her.

"Let me say hello to your daughters," he said, making sure to keep his voice even, though he was obviously begging. He pocketed the crystal shaft.

Gabira turned down one corner of her mouth but took a deep breath and shuffled to the wall and yanked the gold rope. *"Giselle! Daleelah!"*

Jidna cringed at her loud voice and looked down to make sure it hadn't awoken Cassidy. He bent down and cut away the white cloth from her neck and shoved it into his pocket. He was not about to leave Hesychasm within reach of the wicked women. In fact, he shouldn't stay there much longer. He was beginning to feel giddy. Soon he would be caught in her trap, if he were not careful. Just a few more minutes. Long enough to get an eyeful of Giselle, and maybe touch the silk of her robe and get a good whiff of her. He rolled his eyes at himself. He was pathetic. He gave Gabira a lopsided grin and sat down on a stack of rugs, and then realized with a spike of fear that he had left the little panther box Daleelah had given him back at the house on his bedside table. The little box of dirt and the dried olive could have protected him from getting lost in her olive grove again, and he attributed his oversight to Gabira's lingering, pernicious powers. *He should leave—now.*

The scowling woman peered down at him angrily, still standing. "Did you bring any food?"

Jidna frowned. It must have taken a lot for her to ask that of him. Her supplies must be dwindling. "I'll have some delivered to you, via Schlitzer," he promised. He stood up and reached into his sack and held up a large bar of Swiss chocolate. "I brought this for Giselle." He could delay just a little bit longer and give the chocolate to Giselle himself. He smiled at Gabira, and she held her tongue.

A small snort startled him. Cassidy's head lolled to one side, but she was still fast asleep. Jidna looked at Gabira impatiently. "She won't sleep forever," he said, but Gabira merely glared at him.

A few moments later, the door opened and Giselle swept into the room, followed by Daleelah. He searched Daleelah's face for a hint of the intelligent, mysterious woman he knew was hiding in there somewhere, but he only saw the mousy version of herself. Perhaps her other self had been the illusion, and this timid thing was all there was to her.

The sisters instantly spotted Cassidy and huddled around her.

"What a pretty dress," Daleelah said breathlessly, fingering the fine embroidery.

"What's she doing here?" Giselle asked. Her voice was gravelly— not the dreamy, melodic voice he remembered.

The sisters did not seem at all concerned that Cassidy was passed out.

"She's going to stay with us," Gabira said sourly, sitting heavily on her stack of rugs.

Giselle stood upright and stared at her mother, who nodded at Jidna. He held up the crystal ball, and Giselle relaxed, a wide smile revealing her pretty white teeth. She held out her long fingers, and Jidna handed her the chocolate instead, earning a frown in return. He stepped across the room and handed the crystal ball to Gabira, who snatched it away from him and held it to her large breasts.

"What's in here? Is it hers?" Giselle asked, nudging Cassidy's pack with her toe. Jidna nodded. Giselle opened it and pulled the contents out, laying them on the brass table.

"A bunch of teas and herbs and papers," Giselle told her mother. She opened a red notebook and flipped through it. "Spearmint tea," she read, "relieves nausea." She flipped through a few more pages. "Chamomile tea, soothes the nerves. White willow bark, treats pain and fever." Giselle closed the book.

Gabira replied idly, distracted by the crystal ball, "Let her keep them. She can be the nursemaid down there. Maybe she can keep those whiny women from crying to me all the time."

Giselle stuffed the herbs and notebooks back into the pack. Jidna handed her Cassidy's bundle of clothing, and Giselle unrolled them and held them up against herself.

"Those are too small for you," her mother snapped.

Giselle frowned at her mother and tossed the clothing onto the brass table. Next, she examined the utility belt with the weapons and radio, turning the dead radio on and off. Jidna noted a radio repeater mounted on the stone ceiling in the corner and wondered how he could get into Gabira's good graces enough to access her private channel.

"Give me that," Gabira said, holding out her upturned palm.

Giselle dropped the radio into her mother's hand, then dug into the pouches. She pocketed Cassidy's few coins while her mother was fiddling with the radio, sniffed the heel of stale bread, and then put it back in the pouch and snapped it closed. She showed no interest in the knives or other implements and set the belt aside.

Daleelah was perched on the stack of rugs, stroking Cassidy's hair. "She's stirring," Daleelah said softly.

Giselle leaned over Cassidy and held the two gold pendants in her fingers, and then pulled them and the obsidian arrowhead up over Cassidy's head, tearing the necklaces free from strands of hair. The necklaces went into Giselle's pocket just as Gabira rose from her seat.

"Give me those," Gabira demanded, and Giselle's face fell in an angry pout.

Jidna's gaze wandered over Giselle's wide hips as she turned to her mother and handed her the necklaces. The young woman spun around, feeling Jidna's eyes on her backside. Her expression was scornful, but it made him want to kiss her lips even more.

"Thank you, Jidna," Gabira said sharply, dismissing him, and rose to her feet. "What about that other crystal?" she asked haughtily.

He took out the crystal shaft and turned it until it caught the light. "I was thinking that perhaps ...," he said, suddenly losing his confidence, "... Giselle would like to live up on the surface." He rushed on, feeling his face flush. "I built a new residence. It has a window, and a skylight. I was thinking of building a small greenhouse."

Gabira scowled darkly at him. Jidna stole a glance at Giselle. She was pointedly ignoring him. Daleelah looked up at him shyly, then dropped her gaze.

Gabira stashed the crystal ball in a pocket and placed her hands on her hips. "Don't you think that leaving me with this vagrant girl is enough? Now you want to lure away my daughters? How am I supposed to take care of all the women by myself? If you wanted a wife, you should have kept your ... niece," she said, and then laughed snidely. "I suppose you don't want me to speak of her to anyone?" She arched her eyebrows menacingly.

"That's right," he said, shifting on his feet, and slowly passed her the crystal shaft. She grabbed it and shoved it into her robe's side pocket.

"You may go now. Do you remember the way out?" Gabira smirked at him. "Don't get lost."

He hesitated for an awkward moment, and then nodded goodbye to the two sisters. They ignored him. Giselle was kneeling on the floor, removing the watch from Cassidy's wrist. Daleelah was gently patting Cassidy's cheek. "Wake up, little bird," she said in a sweet voice.

"Think about my offer," he said to Giselle, whose eyes flashed to him.

Gabira stepped between them and pushed his shoulder towards the door. Jidna stopped outside the open doorway and gave Gabira a polite bow, and then stole a last look at Cassidy.

"You will send food," Gabira reminded him.

"I will," he assured her.

She stepped out into the hallway with him.

"You'll take good care of her, right?" he asked.

"What do you care?" she asked roughly, pulling the door closed behind her, leaving the two of them alone in the silence of the rock tunnel.

"I feel horrible," Jidna admitted.

Gabira knit her drawn-on black eyebrows together. "Why?"

Jidna shrugged. "I've taken away her freedom."

Gabira let out a harsh laugh. "Oh, don't be silly. We all lost our freedom when General Tegea chased us off Earth." She leaned her face close to his with a twisted smile, and growled in a low voice, "We're all trapped on this star-forsaken rock, *Mister Ridge Gandoop.*"

Jidna stepped back with surprise. He glanced nervously down the long hallway in the direction of the stairway, which disappeared up into the shadows to the guard room. At least she'd had the sense to keep her voice down. He turned to glare at her.

She stood back on her heels and folded her arms across her chest, her gold bracelets clinking together. She wore a smug grin. "You think I don't know who you are? How many outer rim mining lords do you know with the kind of gold you have? Huh?" She raised her lip in a sneer. "Everyone's struggling to survive out here. Except you. I hear you're hoarding all the food. And now you're selling it at five times the normal price. Do you feel horrible about that, too?"

She tried to catch his eyes, which he deftly shifted away. What could he say? That he was the puppet of a sadistic Teg general? How long would that information stay in this cave?

She watched him, enjoying his discomfort. How had she discovered his true identity? She must be in Schlitzer's confidence. Schlitzer's betrayal bothered him more than Gabira knowing his secret. Or maybe she remembered Ishmar after all and had put two and two together. He avoided her mocking stare.

"We do what we must to survive," he said.

Gabira nodded. "That's right. We do. And I can only imagine that giving me that girl has something to do with your survival."

"Or my death," he said. He met her curious gaze, then without another word turned and stalked down the hallway and up the long set of stairs.

The guard politely released the airlock, looking too bored to have heard any of their conversation. Jidna took in a deep breath, brushed past the two other guards, and stepped out into the light.

38

CONTAINER YARDS

"Torr."

Ming-Long's voice scratched over the radio. Torr grabbed the radio off his belt as Ming-Long continued speaking rapidly. "One of Schlitzer's scouts found the four-wheeler. It's out past the container yards in the western quadrant. Between Spoke Roads Two and Three, out by the moats. Cassidy probably climbed up onto one of the container roofs again."

A surge of relief unwound the tension in Torr's shoulders. "Okay, great. Thanks, Ming. Where are you?"

"I'm at the spaceport. The Alphabet Boys just left."

"Okay, cool," Torr said. "We're headed out now. See you there."

"Do you think you need me?" Ming-Long asked. "There's an ice tanker here. The guys said Khaled and I could take their shift and they'd give me a tank of water for the training yard. What do you think?"

"Sure," Torr said. "That'd be great, thanks. Our tank is almost empty."

"Sounds good," Ming-Long said. "Hope you find her soon."

"I'm sure we will," Torr said. "See you later."

"Out," Ming-Long said.

"Jasper," Torr said into the radio. "Did you hear that? You said she's not in ASB or with the Murians, right?"

"Right," Jasper said in a tinny voice. "Jericho is keeping an eye out for her. We should have looked out by the moats. But we went to check the maintenance buildings, and now we're at the infirmary. Where are you guys, are you close to the container yards?"

"Yeah, we're at the Smiths," Torr said. "We're on our way over there now. I'll let you know when we find her."

"Okay," Jasper said, and the radio went silent.

39

———)———

PEAKS ⊙F
ETERNAL LİGHT

Schlitzer had assured Jidna he could distract Jaz and Torr long enough for Jidna to deposit Cassidy in Gabira's cave and leave before anyone determined Cassidy had gone missing again and locked down the spaceport.

Jidna walked around the massive spaceport building to the front door and entered the dim hangar. Things felt relatively normal, although Rodney's Rangers were out in force. He still had time.

He nodded to the guards as he crossed the floor to his cargo ship.

"When are you bringing another load of food?" Rodney called up to him as he climbed into the cockpit.

He smiled down at the tall stern man. "Soon," Jidna promised.

"Bring some apples," Rodney said.

"I'll try," Jidna said and turned away, guilt searing through him.

Jidna piloted the ship through the decompression chambers, drumming his fingers on the throttle while the chambers took their sweet time lowering the air pressure and releasing him. He finally made it through the second chamber and glided through the landing tunnel and out into the bright light of Peary Rim. No one followed him, and he relaxed back into the pilot's chair and marveled at how the sun always shone up here on the Peaks of Eternal Light.

He set the coordinates and launched into high gear, leaving Peary Dome behind.

40

THE MAZE

Torr and the others left the Smith camp and headed west. He followed Raleigh's gaze and glanced over his shoulder. Jorimar and Helug were trailing them at a distance—his constant companions. The Scrids' obsession with him had not waned after all this time, and Torr wondered what they expected from him. He acknowledged them with fists to his chest, and they returned the salute.

Torr reached the collection of shipping containers sprawled haphazardly across the western outskirts of the dome. His cheek began twitching, and he swatted away the annoying sensation. The Boyer brothers strode beside him as they entered the warren of metal boxes. Darla had joined them, and walked with Blaire, Sky, and Thunder.

Torr found a container with an exterior ladder and scaled it to the roof. He stood on top and took out his binoculars and scanned the sea of dusty shipping containers. Green, blue, red, orange, turquoise, dingy-white. There was no sign of Cassidy on the patchwork of rooftops, but the container yard extended for several hundred yards in either direction. She could easily be lying on a container farther away and he would not see her. He climbed back down to his waiting companions.

"Let's find the four-wheeler first, then we can organize a methodical search," Torr said. The others nodded, and they navigated their way through the maze towards the edge of the dome.

41

PASSAGE

At the lab at Last Chance, Jidna went inside to shower and change into Ridge. He peeled off his wig and beard, threw his dusty, stinky clothes into the laundrobot, and then unclipped the mysterious waist belt and inspected it, considering its secrets. There was nothing odd about it on its face, aside from a neatly embroidered rune of a language he did not recognize.

Ridge removed its contents. His hands shook as he examined the deed more closely. It really was it. Legal title to Anaximenes. All he needed to do was forge her signature, which would be easy to do when he had the time. He left the papers on the little table in his private living quarters and showered.

As the hot water ran over his bare scalp, he considered his next move. He could hide the deed here. Or bury it outside somewhere. Or, with the invisibility belt, he could carry it safely with him, hidden under his one-piece flight suit. No one would ever find it, unless he were dead.

After toweling himself dry, he sorted through the girl's papers. He would keep the deeds and passport with him until he transferred the signature, then he could get rid of the passport. He did not think he needed her DNA birth certificate and stashed it on a shelf in his workshop to recycle later. He placed the folded deed and passport inside the belt pouch, buttoned it closed, and clipped it around his waist, watching with delight as it disappeared from view. After he pulled on his flight suit, he examined himself in the mirror and patted his belly and back. There was no evidence of the belt whatsoever. No bulge around his waist. No feel of it under his fingers. It was truly amazing. He smiled, went out to the lab's hangar, and climbed into the freighter to head over to Gandoop Spaceport.

————————) ————————

At Gandoop Spaceport, Ridge found Ming-Long and Khaled lurking in the shadow of a Peary ice tanker, waiting for him, with Harbin hovering nearby.

"Ridge, sir," Harbin said, striding briskly over to him. "These gentlemen say you have arranged passage for them to Delos."

"Yes, yes," Ridge said. "I'll take care of it."

"Very good," Harbin said. "What should we do with this tanker?"

Ridge frowned at the craft with the name *Ice Princess* painted on the side. "Have some of your men abandon it in a crater on the far side."

"Yes, sir," Harbin said. The Teg bowed curtly and walked away.

Ming-Long and Khaled fidgeted nervously as Ridge approached. He introduced himself as Ridge Gandoop and shook their hands. No recognition registered on their faces that he was the same man as the slovenly Jidna Gandi, outer rim mining lord.

He let them use the toilet while one of the forklift operators went to fetch sleeping bags, a crate of food, and a drum of water Ridge had set aside for their journey.

Ming-Long and Khaled returned, and Ridge led them to the interstellar ship and introduced them to the pilots. Ridge watched as the two men handed over two Solidi each to the captain, who pocketed the gold and nodded to Ridge. The pilots spoke little Globalish and stepped aside to inspect the last of the freight as it was brought out from the warehouse.

Ming-Long and Khaled talked excitedly as they walked with Ridge to the cargo bay.

"Have you ever been to Delos?" Ming-Long asked Ridge.

"I have," Ridge said.

"What's it like?"

"Oh, it's pretty," Ridge said. "Lots of forests. A single, huge ocean.

Castles and villages. Like Earth used to be." Ali had come to stand at
Ridge's side and listened curiously.

The men grinned and nodded. "What kind of women are there?"
Khaled asked.

Ridge shrugged. "Delosians look pretty much like Earthlanders.
The natives are dark-skinned and normally live in the mountain forests
and remote villages. They usually only come down into the valleys to
trade. Those descended from the Ilians are the dominant race now and
are of different lineages. The ruling class is usually blond. The merchants, priests, and such are darker. You've seen plenty of the Monger
House traders at Peary, I'm sure."

"Antler Kralj are the royalty," Ming-Long recited, counting off on
his fingers. "Monger House are the merchants. Teller House are the
religious advisors. Handler House are the craftsmen."

"That's right," Ridge said, and watched the workman load the
freighter with the trip supplies, depositing them into a half-container
at the front of the hold, which Ridge had arranged for the men to
camp out in during their trip. The container had a ventilation fan,
and the cargo hold had environmental controls suitable for passengers.
A cargo loader buzzed by with a portable composting toilet outfitted
with a space-friendly waste-trapping system that he unloaded into the
back corner of the container.

"There's no military on Delos?" Khaled asked.

Ridge shook his head. "No. Only the nobility. Knights and such.
But they don't fight. Not since they fled the war on Iliad. They
only hunt."

"Then there are the Nommos, and the Scrids," Ming-Long said.
"They live there, too."

"The Nommos live on floating islands on the ocean," Ridge said.
"There are a few small colonies of Scrids on Delos. Craftsmen, mostly.
And black market traders. And outcasts. The planet Scridland is still
wild and free. Most of them still live there."

"I've met some Scrids," Ming-Long said, chattering on about how
the Scrids thought Cassidy and her brother were the Star Children and
how their wizard wanted to steal them away.

Flanders was inspecting the freight with the captain as the last of
the ship's cargo was being stowed, but Ali checked his screen out of

habit, comparing the freight inventory against the bill of lading. He looked up at Ridge with concern. "This ship's not ...," Ali said, but Ridge cut him off with a stern glare. Ali clamped his lips shut.

Ming-Long stopped talking and looked at Ridge.

"This ship's not supposed to leave until tomorrow," Ridge explained. "But we're moving up the schedule for your convenience." Ridge put on a gracious smile, and Ming-Long's grin returned, a small scar next to his mouth pulling at the side of his lip. Ridge took a breath and watched the loading crew double-check that everything was strapped down securely as Ming-Long burbled on in the background.

Finally, the ship's captain motioned for Ming-Long and Khaled to board. They hoisted on their backpacks and shook Ridge's hand enthusiastically.

"Have a good trip," Ridge said kindly. "Thank you, and best of luck to you."

The two men bowed their heads and thanked him. They climbed up the ramp and stepped into the container. The captain bolted shut the metal box, raised the ramp to close the cargo hold, and then climbed into the crew's cabin with his shipmates and sealed the ship's airlocks.

The freighter moved slowly across the floor and disappeared into a large decompression chamber. Flanders walked off to inspect an inbound freighter.

Ridge let out a pent-up breath and turned to Ali. "Those guys did some work for me that I'd rather not become common knowledge."

Ali's nostrils flared, but he said nothing. They both knew somebody in the family had to do the dirty work, and that usually meant Ridge. Ali was glad to let him deal with such things—it allowed Ali to keep his pristine self-image intact. In exchange, Ali afforded him the benefit of the doubt, tacitly accepting that Ridge did what needed to be done.

Ridge went on, more to justify it to himself than defend his actions to Ali. "If I sent them to Delos, they could turn around in a year and find their way back here. If I sent them to Earth, they could join the Tegs and show up here as well. Sending them to the Cephean planets, I know they'll never come back. Slaves on Tree Nut never escape." Ridge smiled sadly, then left to check on the smelter.

42

SOLDIERS OF THE LONE

Torr found the four-wheeler abandoned at the edge of the dome. The glass triangles loomed overhead, and the moat stank of pond scum. Peary Rim dropped off sharply at the western edge of the dome and the panorama of the lunarscape spread out down below, vast and glorious. A sharp line divided dark from light, and Torr imagined the waning moon that must be visible from Earth. His parents would be looking up, wondering if he and Cassidy were safe.

Torr circled the moon rover, searching for footprints with the Boyer brothers. There were many, from years of foot traffic, but none marred the fresh buggy tracks, and none that they could find resembled Cassidy's small Delosian boot soles. Torr went around again to the driver's side to look once more but found only large male footprints. He turned to his friends and rested his hand on the vehicle's roll bar, tightening his cheek muscles against the insistent twitching.

"Her boot soles were made of tire treads," Torr said. "So her footprints could be mixed in with all these tire tracks. Let's just start here and move south." Torr gestured to the collection of containers. "We need to find one with a ladder. Cassidy's got to be on a roof nearby."

"Cassidy!" Hawk called out. "Where are you?"

"Cassidy!" Blaire echoed.

"Cassidy!" called Darla.

A sharp buzzing was followed by a gasp of air escaping Hawk's lungs as he slumped and fell to the ground.

"Hawk," Roanoke exclaimed and ran to his brother's side. Another buzz struck Roanoke, and he tumbled over and collapsed onto the dust.

"Everyone get down!" Torr yelled. "Get behind the buggy! *Lectros!*"

The scene unfolded in slow motion as Torr scanned the container rooftops for the sniper while leaping over the buggy towards Blaire.

Another buzz, and Sky grunted and fell, tumbling over and landing limply in the dust.

Buzz.

Thunder grunted and fell.

"Get down," Torr yelled, tugging at Blaire's arm.

"Get down," Blaire echoed. She pulled away and jumped in front of Darla, shielding the smaller woman's body with her own as another buzz split the air. Blaire fell on top of Darla as a snake jaw glinted in the sunlight, attached to Blaire's back. Torr froze, horrified, as a gray sheath of energy flashed across Blaire's and Darla's bodies as they clung together on the ground. Both women twitched and then went still, and Raleigh fell down beside them, his face frozen in a warrior grimace, a throwing knife dropping from his hand.

Torr dove underneath the buggy and crawled to the other side, crouching behind the metal frame as he listened to two people drop from containers and hit the ground, footsteps crunching towards him. Torr peeked over the rover. Two men dressed in dusty moon rat camo were striding towards him, black Lectros in hand.

"We don't want to hurt you," one called to Torr. "We just want your moon deed."

"My deed?!" Torr cried. "You killed my friends for the *deed?*" Disbelief and fury rose in his throat and turned his vision red. He wanted to rip the deed from its hiding place around his waist and fling it at the men, yelling at them to take it. But it was too late. Blaire was dead. All his friends were dead.

"Just hand it over and we can work something out," the other man said.

"Like hell we can," Torr said, rage and grief seething in his blood. "Where's my sister?!" He crept around the wheel, but the men split up and came towards him from either side.

Pounding footsteps drew the men to a sudden halt. Torr peered around the buggy.

Jorimar and Helug were running towards them.

"No!" Torr yelled. "Get back. They have Lectros."

The two attackers backed away, Lectros raised.

The Scrids stormed closer, red hair flying and boot bells jangling.

The attackers fired their weapons. Snake jaws glinted in the air but clattered against crystal shafts raised in the Scrids' clenched fists and fell harmlessly to the ground. More snake jaws were parried by the Scrids with their crystal shafts and lightning-fast reflexes.

The attackers cowered as the Scrids thundered forward and fell on them with knives and clubs. The attackers fell under the blows, and Torr ran around the buggy.

"Blaire," he said. His body trembled violently and his legs threatened to give way under him as he stumbled towards Blaire's motionless body.

She was face down in the dust. Darla's dark eyes peeked out from beneath Blaire's shoulder, staring up at the sky. Raleigh was sprawled next to them. A single choking sob escaped from Torr's throat, but he bit back the next one, chomping down on the inside of his cheek, mindless of the taste of blood seeping between his teeth.

The fight died down in the background, and Torr vaguely noticed Helug pounding out a rhythm on the side of a metal shipping container with a wooden club and knife.

Tat-a-tat, ta-rat-at-tat.

Sounds grew muffled and time distorted as Torr knelt by Blaire and plucked the snake jaw from her shirt, tossing it aside like a venomous insect. He gently moved Darla's arm aside and pulled Blaire by the shoulder, rolling her onto her back and cradling her dusty head in one hand. She looked up at him with unseeing eyes.

Pressing his fingers to her neck, Torr felt for a pulse and put his ear to her mouth, listening. There was nothing. He sealed his lips to her mouth and exhaled heavily into hers, filling her lungs. He pushed several breaths into her, but it was not like when she'd been put under by the Hesychasm. That had been a living body absorbing the life-giving oxygen. This body was a lifeless shell. Blaire was dead.

A wave of anguish flooded through him. He looked into her black dilated pupils. Even though her body had died, maybe her soul was still inside, looking out at him. Lowering his cheek against hers, he pulled her into his arms and steeled himself against the rush of panic and grief. His voice quavered as he spoke in her ear. "I love you, my sweet, sweet Blaire. I'll find the Star People and defeat the Tegs for you." He clutched her thick hair as sobs shook his chest. The lullaby Grandma Leann used to sing to him came to his lips, and he sang it through his tortured throat, rocking her back and forth.

> *The moon is bright on the willows*
> *We can't be far from home*
> *The gods they watch us from the stars*
> *Their shields protect and hide us*
> *From the Soldiers of the Lone*

Torr laid Blaire's limp body tenderly on the ground, turning her face so that she could look up through the dome to her resting place in the heavens. He let Jorimar help him to his feet. With tears streaming down his face, Torr pulled away and knelt next to each of his fallen friends—straightening their limbs, folding their hands across their chests, and saying a short prayer. Darla. Raleigh. Roanoke. Hawk. Sky. Thunder.

Torr looked up in annoyance as Jorimar took him by one arm and Helug grabbed the other.

"Leave me alone," Torr said, trying to pull his arm from Helug's iron grip, but the two men firmly led him away from the dead bodies.

"There may be more men," Jorimar said haltingly. "Come. Come."

"We need to find Cassidy," Torr said, trying to wipe tears from his face with his shoulder.

"She is not here," Jorimar said.

"Where is she?" Torr asked.

"I don't know. She is not here," Jorimar repeated.

Three more Scrids appeared up ahead, running towards them along the line of moat tanks.

"Let go," Torr said crossly, trying to free himself from their grip.

Stump and two others stopped in front of them, and the five Scrids pulled and pushed Torr away from the corpses and headed south. Torr struggled, but the burly men dragged him off his feet and lifted him to horizontal, wrapping their arms around him as though he were a tree trunk.

"What are you doing?" Torr yelled as they carried him off. "I can walk by myself. Let me go!" They ignored his pleas and hurried him across the vacant strip of land.

Torr tried to twist and kick his way free, but his muscles felt like jelly and the Scrids had him securely pinned. They carried him swiftly across the dust, their pounding steps jarring Torr's bones. Blaire's lifeless face filled Torr's vision. Then Hawk stared up at him. Then Raleigh, and Roanoke. Sky, and Thunder. Darla.

Pain and guilt crushed Torr's chest, making it hard to breathe. He should have known crystals could stop the snake jaws. Edgemont had told him as much in his dream. His Destroyer hung in its sheath on his belt, a powerful weapon left unused. He could have saved Blaire. He could have saved them all.

Then his thoughts turned to his sister. What if the men with the Lectros had found Cassidy first?

"Let me go!" he demanded, but the Scrids ignored him.

They carried him through the maze of containers and across the perimeter road into the blocks of tents, and finally arrived at the Scrid compound. Torr found himself inside the Scrids' circular tent, surrounded by a dozen more Scrids who were gabbling furiously in their language.

Torr was too dazed and distraught to struggle much as several rough hands held him down and removed his vest and weapon belt. They set everything on the large cylindrical slab made from a cross section of a gravity bar. In the center of the slab a crystal stood on its end and pointed straight up towards the top of the dome. It was similar in size and shape to Torr's Bear crystal. Stuck upright into the ground in a circle around the slab glowed several light crystals.

An elderly Scrid pushed through the men to stand over Torr. He had the heavy-boned frame of the younger Scrids but lacked the solid mass of muscles. His head of hair was thinning and gray, as was his long trailing beard. Torr met the man's amber eyes, and his heart lurched in his chest. The man's gaze felt like a knife slicing through his awareness. Torr tried to scramble away from the man but was held firmly by several hands.

Torr didn't even bother struggling as Helug and Stump bound his arms against his sides with coils of thick rope and tied his legs together in a similar fashion. They laid him on the stone slab on his back, and he watched with numb shock as the old man stood next to him and began swaying back and forth, chanting in a deep voice and shaking a rattle.

Jorimar hopped up onto the platform with them. The others stood in a circle around the slab outside the barrier of light crystals and joined in with rhythmic chanting, stomping their belled boots in time with the rattle.

The chant beat against Torr's ears like a drum.

Andi stiga
Fara lopt
Heimili heita
Gaumr far

Andi stiga
Fara lopt
Heimili heita
Gaumr far

They repeated the same phrases over and over. Torr felt the sound vibrate through the white stone, sending ripples through his body as though he were made of water and the sound waves were swirling him in a circle. His lips mouthed the words of the chant, his hoarse whispers drowned out by the deep sonorous voices of the Scrids. He closed his eyes as the effects of whatever they were chanting pulled him into a groggy haze and the gentle vortex swallowed him in its soothing darkness.

Torr was pulled into the whirlpool of a dream. The four men he'd killed in the tent swirled above him, caught in a funnel of cold black water. They flailed their arms and legs, frantically trying to swim to the surface, but were pulled relentlessly downwards into the darkness with Torr. The gashes the men wore from the blade of the wolf knife seeped a dark purple blood, almost black, which flowed out of their bodies and streamed into Torr's eyes, clouding his vision. He swiped the blood away, peering upwards and searching for a hint of light that would show him the way out. A speck of light glimmered in the distance. Holding his breath, Torr scrambled against the swirling current and grabbed at the foot of the nearest man, then climbed hand over hand up the struggling man's leg. The body sheared off at its center, the gash across the back of the man's ribcage yawning open like the mouth of an angry beast, and the body tore in two, plunging Torr further down into the maelstrom. Torr swam against the current again, climbing upward, clawing at the bodies that spun in his path. Their skin tore off in ribbons under his claws, shredding into long strands of purple blood that coursed around him like ink from a giant octopus. He was pummeled by waves of blood that beat him down into the waiting abyss.

43

FRIENDS OF A SORT

Ridge stood under the rainbow skylight in his living room, watching Balty pour drinks for the two of them. Panic was rising in Ridge's throat, but he swallowed it down, afraid Balty would sense it. What madness had compelled him to hide the deed from Balty and carry it around with him, strapped to his waist? What if Balty's creeping tendrils could detect it? He should run to his chambers and remove it. He should burn it. He should get his gun and fill Balty with bullets. He had a Lectro now—he could shoot one of those snake jaws at Balty's broad back, and the scumbag would drop dead. Ridge could blame it on a heart attack or something. He hovered between confessing to Balty and fleeing.

But the deed was safe in the invisibility belt. Balty would never know. If the Teg could sense it, Ridge would have known by now. Ridge tried to gather the courage to tell him the girl had disappeared, but then what? Balty would hunt her down and torture her to find the deed. She wouldn't have it, of course, and then the bastard would kill her. Balty would get desperate and angry, and he'd find out about Ridge's alter ego. He would beat up Ridge and find the belt strapped to his waist, then strangle him to death. Ridge should bury the deed in a crater somewhere, before it was too late. But Balty would still beat the crap out of him, probably killing him in a crazed rage.

Ridge dismissed his paranoid fantasies. He would have to lie to the man, but he didn't have to do it this second. Let Balty search Peary Dome for the girl himself. He'd never get past Gabira's defenses. Maybe she would trap the bastard in her olive grove from hell, and Ridge would be rid of him forever.

Ridge smiled as Balty turned from the bar and handed him a drink. Ridge would get hold of the boy's deed tomorrow and give that one to Balty. The maniac could have the house, but Balty would have to kill Ridge for the spaceport and mine.

The Teg's peaked eyebrows rose. "What's the status of the deeds?"

"My men will get them both tonight," he told Balty calmly. "We'll have possession of them tomorrow."

Balty smiled. "Great news." He clapped Ridge on the shoulder.

Ridge followed him into the game room and stood beside the pool table as Balty took a few practice shots. Ridge's hands had stopped sweating by the time Balty racked up the balls for their first game. Balty gestured for him to break. Ridge bowed his head courteously, determined to win the first game.

"What is this I hear about you running a black market with our food?" Balty asked as Ridge lined up his break shot.

Ridge froze, keeping his eyes fixed on the balls while his pulse pounded in his ears. He took his shot, sinking two balls. He put away two more balls, then turned to Balty.

"I meant to thank you for that," Ridge said smoothly. "You've succeeded in driving up the price five-fold."

"Put a stop to it," Balty said, holding his gaze. His emerald eyes were unyielding. "Those outer-far-side-rim whatever-the-fucks who've been sniffing around the spaceport have been told to piss off. There's to be no trading with moon rats except for minerals and elements. You got that?"

Ridge swallowed. He had one more trip to make to Peary. After that, he wasn't planning on going back to Peary for a long time to come. Regardless, he wanted to let Balty know there was one person in this establishment who would not jump at his every word. And that person was Rjidna Jibrail Gandoop, founder of Ridge Gandoop Mine and Spaceport. He deserved some respect.

Ridge peered at Balty, who was holding his pool cue casually. Ridge's rib still bothered him a bit, and he had no desire to feel Balty's wrath again. He took a breath and replied, "Do you intend for ten thousand people to starve? For what? Your entertainment?" Ridge was surprised to hear his own voice talk back to Balty, and Balty looked just as startled. "I don't see why we can't make this work to everyone's advantage," Ridge said stubbornly. "Sell the food at an inflated price. Cause Peary some pain but keep the food flowing."

Balty strode around the table and took the collar of Ridge's flight suit in his fist, the sleek fabric stretching across Ridge's shoulders. Balty's iron grip lifted Ridge onto his toes. Ridge sucked in his breath in an unwilling reflex but managed to keep his eyes on Balty, whose furious face now loomed close enough for Ridge to smell his stinking alcohol breath.

"I would prefer to keep your blood from flowing," Balty said tightly, his teeth bared. "But if you keep pushing me, I will have no choice. Do I make myself clear?" Balty twisted his fist, tightening the fabric painfully across Ridge's throat.

Ridge struggled to breathe and played his trump card. He had been hoping to win this argument outright and somehow keep food shipments flowing to Peary, but no sense in him dying along with everyone else. He croaked through his throttled throat, "I had to smuggle the Lectros in somehow, Balty, now let go."

Balty's eyes drilled into his a moment longer, then he slowly loosened his grip. Ridge breathed in, rubbing at his neck, and pushed Balty's arm away. "Algol's hell, Balty. Can't you give me a little credit, after all this time?" Ridge straightened his flight suit and cast Balty an admonishing glare.

Balty exhaled loudly through his nose and stepped back onto his heels.

"Why do you want to starve them out, anyway?" Ridge asked.

Balty leaned on his pool cue, his eyebrow cocked with something close to amusement. "You really are something, Ridge," Balty said with a chuckle.

Ridge shook his head, smiling with one corner of his mouth. He wondered if he and Balty were friends of a sort, after years of sharing the same roof amidst the bleak isolation of the moon. But the collegial thought was quickly replaced by the image of fighting dogs circling for the opportunity to rip each other's throats out.

"There's one more food shipment I need to make, to complete our business deal for the deeds." He held Balty's gaze, daring him to object.

Balty flared his nostrils and said stiffly, "Make sure it's the last."

Ridge wasn't going to argue. He wouldn't be going back to Peary anyway. The whole thing made him sad. The Guild traders would become desperate after Jidna failed to show up. Probably they would come to Gandoop themselves, only to be turned away. The inhabitants of the dome would fight over scraps for a few weeks. Next, they would strip the greenhouses and storage trailers of every last morsel of food, and then start killing each other.

Ridge took a deep breath and nodded.

44

PINE FOREST

When he awoke, Torr was surrounded by dozens of Scrids, their bulky chests lit by a blazing bonfire, and their backs darkened by the blackness of night. Torr lay on the dirt, bound in ropes and flat on his back beyond the heat of the fire but inside a circle of chanting, dancing Scrids. Boot fringes waved and chimed as they stomped by. A circle of many drummers surrounded the dancers, and a familiar cadence entrained Torr's heartbeat. Torr stared up at a dark sky glittering with white ribbons of starlight. The air was cool and fresh, and smoke from the fire mingled with the scent of the thick conifer forest surrounding them.

Torr tilted his head to the side and regarded a jagged tree line that drew a black silhouette against the starry sky. Flickering orange flames cast a glow upon the nearest trees towering overhead. He guessed that he was on the planet Scridland. He closed his eyes and let the repetitive beating of the drums lull him back to sleep.

45

❧

RAISINS

Ridge lay in his king-sized bed, staring up at the skylight. He was not enthusiastic about leaving this luxurious home. He'd been intending to move out for months but had never gotten around to it. He supposed he was purposefully procrastinating. He didn't want to leave—not really. He'd always hoped in the back of his mind that he would find a way to get rid of Balty. Or that the scumbag would announce one day that he was going back to Earth—that his parole had ended and he had been given a job on Tegea's staff. But no such luck.

Ridge reached over and felt for the Truthsayer. He let it dangle from his fingers, the small blue crystal emitting a soft glow above his solar plexus. "Should I leave this house?" he asked.

The Truthsayer slowly circled counterclockwise. "Yes," he said into the silent room. A snort of laughter escaped his nose. The crystal stilled.

"Was it necessary to kill the boy?" He sincerely regretted the decision, but it had been the right thing to do. It wasn't fair to risk the lives of Schlitzer's men with another attempt to restrain him and steal the deed, when one death would solve the problem.

The pendulum hung motionless and glowed brighter.

Ridge sucked at his teeth in disgust. "There's no magic in you. You're not a Truthsayer."

He tossed the pendulum into the little box on his bedside table, where it made a soft thunk as it landed on the velvet and slowly dimmed.

The radio chirped at Ridge's hip. He carefully finished sealing the chamber that held the silicon of his latest Silox, wiped his hands, and took the radio from his belt.

"Yeah," he said.

"Hey, can you talk?" It was Schlitzer.

"Yeah. What's up?" Ridge asked, standing and pacing around his small lab. He'd been waiting to hear from Schlitzer for twenty-four hours now, and the anxiety had twisted him into a knot.

"Couldn't get a hold of that other raisin shipment," Schlitzer said.

Ridge's blood chilled. "What? Why not?"

"The Scrids stole the shipment out from under us."

"The Scrids?" Ridge fumbled for words. "What do they want with raisins?"

"They think raisins are something special. That they hold some magical properties or some bullshit like that. I don't know. But they got them."

"Can't you get them back?" Ridge asked, his throat tight.

"No. Don't think so. Seems the Scrids, uh, ate them all already."

Ridge frowned, trying to decipher Schlitzer's meaning. Had they killed the boy? What about the deed? "What about the, uh, written contract ... uh ... parchment?" Ridge asked.

"They got that too, I guess. We can't retrieve anything. We raided the Scrid camp, but it all seems to have ... disappeared. Taken through their portal, or something."

"Disappeared," Ridge said slowly. "Portal. That's not good."

"No. And besides that, we lost nine Solidi in the negotiation."

Ridge paused. "Nine?" *Nine people dead? Whose men?* "From which side of the negotiation?" Ridge asked.

"Both."

Ridge was silent. "Shit."

"I know," Schlitzer said, and Ridge heard him sigh. Schlitzer continued, "At least the other part of the deal came through. Right?"

"Yep. Pretty clean, in comparison. I put the, uh, shipment in storage. And sent the other traders happily on their way."

"Good."

The radio was silent.

"What now?" Ridge asked emptily.

"Sit and wait, I guess," Schlitzer said. "See if we can learn anything else. See if we can track down the missing raisin shipment."

"Right," Ridge agreed. "Hey. Thanks a lot. And sorry."

"I'm sorry too. Let me know if you need anything else," Schlitzer said.

"Right. I'll stop by tomorrow," Ridge said.

"Okay. Ciao," Schlitzer said.

"Ciao," Ridge replied.

The radio went silent. Ridge stared at his half-finished Silox. How could he tell Balty he had nothing? He had been depending on the boy's deed to appease him. The Teg would suspect he had been betrayed and would confront Ridge. Well, at least the bastard would never find the girl's deed. No way in Algol's hell was that bastard going to take their land out from under them.

Ridge set aside the Silox and cleared a spot on his workbench. He spent the rest of the day finishing the forging tool he'd been working on. It was a two-pronged device. One prong traced the signature on the passport, and the other prong held a fountain pen, which laid down ink in a perfect copy. He'd even built in a sensor that measured the thickness of the stroke and converted it to pressure on the pen side. It was pretty sweet. He drew several practice signatures on thick paper and tweaked the device until it was perfect. The only thing was, he had no vellum to test on and he was concerned the ink would set differently on the parchment's animal skin than on wood pulp paper. He would have to risk it.

He removed the deed from the waist belt, clamped it onto the bench, and held his breath as he watched the ink flow smoothly onto the vellum next to the girl's petite fingerprints. He smiled with relief. It was flawless. He congratulated himself and waited patiently for the ink to dry. He carefully signed his own name on the document and added his fingerprints, as the new official owner. A warm glow of pride filled him. It didn't have an official seal of transfer, but it was good enough. He set aside the invisibility belt, rolled up the deed, and stuffed it and the girl's passport into a metal tube and sealed it. Donning his spacesuit, he drove his four-wheeler out to fetch the drill borer. He drove the drilling rig to the front side of the lab, where the regolith was already disturbed from driving heavy equipment in and out of the landing bay over the years, and drilled a shallow hole. He took the exact coordinates of the spot and committed them to memory. Then he dropped the metal tube into the hole, pushed rubble and soil into it, and drove the rig's wide metal treads over it several times to wipe away any trace.

———————————)———————————

The next day, Jidna gathered his nerve and left Last Chance's lab hangar with his Korova packed full of food, bound for Peary Dome. He knew there would be a lockdown there. He also knew he had to pay Schlitzer and get food to Gabira. Why prolong the inevitable? He had reasoned it through every which way, and this was the only logical course of action. He might be a scumbag, but he wasn't going to let Gabira's women starve. One load of food would last them several months. By then, the crisis should be over, one way or another.

His instincts told him he should probably stay away. But if he were Jidna, and if he were innocent, he would show up at Peary with a load of food like normal. Jidna wouldn't know anything about a kidnapped girl, nor the strange disappearance of the leader of the Light Fighters after a massacre. Only if Jidna stayed away would it signal his complicity in the recent events. No. Jidna was innocent. He was cheerful and brave. Sly and cunning. Good-natured and greedy. He was the happiest outer rim mining lord on the moon, with an exclusive contract with Gandoop to sell food to Peary. Why should he suddenly avoid the gold bleeding out of Peary Dome?

He rode silently, going in and out of high gear with barely a gasp. He circled slowly, lined up his approach to the landing tunnel, and announced himself to Peary Control like he had done so many times in the past few weeks.

"Last Chance 2224, requesting entry for Guild business."

The radio was silent, forcing Jidna to bypass the tunnel and circle around again. Two security speedsters raced up from behind and flanked him. The radio blared suddenly. *"We're on lockdown."*

"Again?" Jidna asked.

"Yes. You got food?"

"Yes," Jidna said, gripping the throttle.

"Hang on."

Jidna cruised slowly along the crest of the crater, gazing down into the gaping pit where the ice-filled craters of Peary Lake lay hidden beneath a shroud of darkness.

"Bay two, Last Chance."

"Got it," Jidna said. His heart was hammering in his chest, but he forced himself to execute his plan. He banked his craft and headed into the tunnel. He made his way through the compression chambers, taxied to a parking spot, and climbed out of the cockpit.

Ramzy loomed in front of him and shoved an envelope into his hand.

"Give this to Ishmar Gandoop," he told Jidna. "We're confiscating your cargo. We'll pay you the old rate once I hear back from Ishmar. You won't be allowed back until then, so get your fat ass to Gandoop and tell those selfish, greedy bastards we've had enough of their games."

Jidna swallowed but met Ramzy's bulging eyes with an even glare. "That's less than what I paid for it," Jidna said.

"Tough luck. You've been running a racket for too long now," Ramzy said. "It's over."

Jidna considered putting up more of a fuss but didn't want to push things too far. This was Ramzy's territory, after all.

"This was a special order for Gabira," Jidna said, afraid of giving away the location of the girl, but more afraid the women would starve. "She said they're running low on food, and I promised I'd take care of her."

Ramzy blinked, and then exhaled loudly. "I'll see to it she gets what she needs," Ramzy said curtly.

Jidna nodded. "Good enough," he said. He tucked the letter into his breast pocket and watched Rodney's men unload the cargo from the hold and cockpit, while more Rangers held back the complaining traders. When all the cargo was unloaded, Jidna climbed back into the cockpit. He considered entrusting Schlitzer's payment to one of his men, but it was an awful lot of gold. Who could trust anyone with so many Solidi? The pimp would have to wait for his gold until ... whenever. Or, he could come to Last Chance and get it himself. Jidna backed the Korova out of its parking spot and headed for the decompression chambers.

Ridge stood in the Last Chance lab and tore open the envelope of Ramzy's letter. He unfolded the crisp paper.

Dear Ishmar,

I had thought we were friends, but it seems I was mistaken. It saddens me to wonder what has become of you that you should intentionally threaten ten thousand souls with starvation. Or is it your intention to send us all into the arms of the Global Alliance? Or perhaps you expect us to flee back to our beloved Earth, where many of us shall need to surrender ourselves if you do not stop your crazy game.

Please, I beg you. Whatever has brought about this time of madness, let us work together to resolve it. I have tried contacting you every day, with no response. None of our normal radio frequencies are active. Or perhaps they are jammed? Why?

I have tried coming there directly, but your Space Control will not even speak with me, other than to tell me that all local lunar traffic is prohibited at Gandoop except by prior appointment, and that all appointments are by invitation only. I feel like a new recruit being hazed by an elite force who wants to break me. But I fear this is no hazing, and that I am on the wrong side of the battle.

Please contact me at your earliest convenience.

Urgent regards,

Ramzy

Ridge crumpled the note in his fist and let it fall to the floor.

———————)———————

"Ridge!"

The faint voice pulled Ridge out of a hazy dream. The radio hissed at him again. "Ridge, pick up the damn radio." It was Balty.

Ridge pulled himself to a seated position on the hard narrow lab bed and turned up the radio's volume. He couldn't avoid this forever.

"Hey, Balty," Ridge said into his radio.

"Where have you been?" Balty demanded. "I've been calling you for hours."

"Sorry," Ridge said.

"Well. Get your ass over to the house. I need to talk to you."

Ridge got dressed and flew his speedster over the deathly still moonscape, steeling himself for the inevitable confrontation. He had nothing for the Teg, and Balty wouldn't like it.

Balty gruffly greeted him in the living room and turned to the wet bar.

Ridge flopped onto a couch. "I need a drink."

The Teg threw him a curious look, then disappeared into the kitchen and returned with a bucket of ice.

"Thanks," Ridge mumbled as Balty handed him a drink.

"When are you going to install that ice-maker in here?" Balty asked, delaying his urgent need with dangerously idle conversation.

"Oh, yeah. I'll get to it," Ridge said.

"And what about the motion sensor?" Balty asked as he sat down in Ishmar's chair, glancing with annoyance at the upper corner of the room where the tiny gadget had been broken for weeks, forcing Balty to turn the lights on and off with a wall switch.

"Right. I'll take care of them both at the same time," Ridge said.

Balty narrowed his eyes and inspected Ridge. "Are you done with your food smuggling?" he asked.

"Yeah," Ridge said. *If he could call selling his own damned food smuggling.*

"So," Balty said casually. "Do you have the deeds?"

Ridge tried not to grimace. "Well," he hesitated, and met the steady, humorless gaze of the Teg. "It's like this. We killed the boy's guards, but the Scrids rescued him. He's disappeared. People tell me the Scrids have some sort of portal to their planet that only they can navigate."

Balty lowered his brow, his handsome lips pursing skeptically. "Oh?"

"Yeah," Ridge said, waving his hand. "I know it sounds ridiculous."

"It does," Balty said grimly. "What about the girl?"

"Well. She got kidnapped again and has gone missing. Hopefully she and her brother will show up at some point, and then we can get the deeds." Ridge shrugged apologetically and took a sip of his drink.

A malicious smile curled Balty's lips. "And you don't suspect foul play?"

"Oh, I do," Ridge said. "I just can't do anything about it. Not right now."

Balty nodded slowly and swirled the drink in his glass. "So. That's it? That's everything?" Balty's eyes examined his, and Ridge felt Balty's energy tendrils groping around his body.

Ridge relaxed his gaze in order to see the filaments. There were several of them. Thick and gray, and insistent. Ridge raised the glass with his right hand, directing the obsidian ring towards Balty. The tendrils veered off, but as soon as Ridge lowered his hand, they came back again. One tried to insert itself into Ridge's throat, and he nearly choked as he mentally yanked it free. Ridge could see Balty was not going to back off this time. The tall man rose to his feet and towered over Ridge, the tendrils converging on Ridge, some slipping past the ring and wrapping themselves around Ridge's neck and limbs.

Ridge staggered to his feet. "What are you doing, Balty?"

"What am *I* doing?" Balty asked coldly and grabbed Ridge by the neck. Ridge's glass fell to the rug, and he pulled at Balty's thick forearms, trying to break free from his tightening grip. "Why are you lying to me?" Balty demanded and threw Ridge onto the couch. Ridge cowered as Balty loomed over him, his face and neck red with anger. "I know you got the girl's deed, and I know you sent her down to the women's caves. So, where is it?"

Ridge stared up at him. Who had told him? It could only have been Schlitzer, and the betrayal stabbed at Ridge's heart. He had been a fool to trust him. Ridge should have known Balty would get to Schlitzer, and the pimp would have no choice but to work with him. He sat upright and rubbed at his throat as Balty's tendrils retracted.

The Teg turned his back to Ridge and poured himself another drink, then sat back in the easy chair, regarding Ridge with calculated intensity.

Ridge stalled for time, frantically trying to figure out how to get out of this mess. It was too late the get the Lectro from his bedroom and kill the man. Balty would be ready for that, and carried his own Lectro under his jacket, as usual. Plus, his thugs were lurking in the corridor. Ridge's pulse throbbed. He had employed the wrong tactic all these years—investing in a work force for the mine, all the while subjugating the workers and brewing resentment, when he should have been building up an army and cultivating loyalty.

"Look, Balty," he said, trying to decide if he should continue lying. He finally sighed, resigned to his fate. "I have the deed. It's mine, you know. The land. The spaceport. The mining operation." He raised his eyebrows at Balty, daring him to disagree.

"Of course it is," Balty said, waving his hand with irritation.

"So, what's the problem, then?" Ridge asked.

"The problem is," Balty said, "I need to take possession of it."

"Of what?" Ridge asked, his ire rising.

"The deed," Balty said.

Ridge scowled at him. "I already signed it over to myself."

"Well, hand it over, and you can sign it over when the time comes."

"When the time comes for what?" Ridge asked.

Balty cocked his head and let out a sardonic laugh. "What, did you think I wanted it for myself? You think I'm going to claim the land? Sign it over to myself?"

Ridge stared at him mutely.

Balty broke into a true laugh. "I'm flattered that you think I'm so powerful. No, idiot. I'm a soldier. I follow orders." His smile faded, and the two men locked gazes. "Get the damned deed."

Ridge glared at Balty stubbornly. "I won't."

Balty held his gaze, his emerald-green eyes hard and glistening. "Let me tell you something, Ridge. You bring a lot of value to this place. Plus, I even kind of like you. And I can't say that about many people. And your brother, Ali. He's a skilled administrator. Excellent with people. And a hell of a nice guy. Keeps the mining operation running like clockwork." Balty took a sip of his drink and chomped on an ice cube. "But Ishmar. Now, he's a good man. But he's getting old. Doesn't contribute much anymore. My men have got the business side of things handled. The diplomatic tasks have fallen to me." Balty shrugged and looked innocently into Ridge's horrified eyes. "I've got guards down in the lower level of Cube Two right now. Making sure he doesn't leave his chamber. Making sure he's comfortable. Well fed. With a steady flow of oxygen."

Ridge's heart fell, and Balty smiled.

Ridge dug up the metal tube and took it into the lab. He removed the moon deed and read it slowly. The document he'd coveted for so long, finally in his hands. Why should someone else get legal title to the land Ridge had slaved to develop for more than half his life? But the reality was that Balty had already taken control of the spaceport—what did it matter who held the piece of paper? He exhaled in painful surrender, tossed the girl's passport onto the workbench, and headed back to the house with the deed.

He was flying slowly over the spaceport and mining facility when his thoughts were interrupted by Gandoop Control, asking him to identify himself.

"Don't you recognize my speedster by now, you fucking morons?"

"Sorry, Ridge, sir. Just following protocol."

Ridge huffed loudly and returned his attention to the facility spread out below. It was a thing of beauty. A work of art. His soul manifested in the form of elegant structures and complex machinery. He'd figured out how to sustain life on the inhospitable moon. He should be rewarded, not robbed. Tears welled up in his eyes.

At the house, he met Balty in the living room. They stood facing each other. A feeling of numb detachment fell upon Ridge as he held the deed out to Balty. He reluctantly released his grip as the Teg took it from his hand. A look of satisfaction spread over Balty's face as he inspected the document and plotted the coordinates on the map.

"Excellent," Balty said. "Nice work." It was as though Ridge had never lied to him. Maybe Balty had expected it. "Here," Balty said, reaching into his pocket and handing Ridge an ink pad and a fountain pen. "Might as well sign it over now. In case you should ... disappear."

Ridge swallowed uncomfortably, but he placed the document on the coffee table and sat heavily on the couch, with the Teg looming over him. It felt like he was draining his blood onto the parchment as he carefully signed his full name. He laid down his fingerprints, blew on them, and handed the deed back to Balty. The Teg folded it and slipped it into an inside pocket of his jacket. Ridge watched gloomily as the deed disappeared from view.

"Who did I just sign it over to?" Ridge asked.

Balty looked down at him. "I don't know. Not me." His voice held none of its usual sarcasm, and Ridge was reminded that Balty was under the thumb of his own master.

Balty went to the wet bar, returned with two glasses of whiskey, and lifted his glass in a toast.

Ridge returned the gesture and downed his whiskey, bitter despair burning into him with the alcohol.

"Why didn't you just kill the girl?" Balty asked. "Or bring her to me, like I'd asked you to?"

Ridge set the glass down on the coffee table. It always astounded Ridge how Balty could sound so relaxed when he spoke of killing people or raping his girls. "I couldn't," Ridge said.

Balty snorted and gave him a disappointed frown. "And I had such high hopes for you."

Ridge waved away the intended insult. He thought of the beautiful girl whose life he had stolen away, sending her into a life of captivity. He was a horrible, spineless, no good, stinking scumbag, just like Balty. He liked to tell himself he was superior, but he was no better than the corrupt, arrogant man facing him.

"Don't worry," Ridge said. "I'm as bad as you'd hoped. You're in good company."

Balty's scowl broke, and he let out a roaring laugh. "I like you, Ridge. You're not afraid of me. It's refreshing."

"Yeah, well, the girl's a prisoner," Ridge said glumly.

At least Ridge had kept her out of this madman's hands. At least she wouldn't get beaten and raped, though now that Balty was in love with Athena, Cassidy might have gone directly to a slaver's ship bound for Nommos. Ridge took a deep breath, feeling a bit better about having given her to Gabira.

"I'll get her out," Balty said, a leer spreading across his handsome face.

Ridge swallowed and met Balty's gaze. "I hope you like olive groves," Ridge said, raising an eyebrow in a challenge.

Balty's arrogant countenance faltered for an instant, and then hardened again. "What's that supposed to mean?" Balty asked with a derisive chuckle.

"Oh, nothing," Ridge said. "She has a mural of an olive grove in her chamber, that's all." Ridge smirked at Balty. It was unlikely Balty would try and retrieve the girl himself, and Ridge was confident none of Balty's lackeys had any magical powers to speak of—surely none strong enough to evade Gabira's first line of defense in her audience chamber. If they did resist the befuddlement, they would not make it out of the phantom olive grove, he was sure of that. The magic that had frustrated Ridge so badly was now a comfort to him, and he admitted a grudging respect for the sorceress.

Balty refilled their glasses and lifted his to Ridge in another toast. "To General Tegea," Balty said happily, tapping his chest where the moon deed was safely stashed.

Ridge silently downed his whiskey. He stood up and turned his back on Balty, strode directly to the hangar, climbed into his speedster, and flew out over the barren moonscape.

PART THREE

SHAMANS

46

————) ————

GRAY FEATHER

Torr climbed the mountain path, the fire of Uttapta blazing down on him and burning his exposed skin. He covered the back of his neck with his bandana, wishing he had a baseball cap with a brim. He adjusted his sunglasses on his sweaty nose, the amber aviators turning the smooth cliffs of the Ageless Mountains into polished copper.

At the top, he strode beneath the black stone gate, passed the winged lion statues, and paused. Last time he had been there, the lions had been sitting with their wings folded. Now, the solid gold creatures were standing on all fours, their wings partially outstretched. They were staring at Torr, their yellow eyes piercing.

Torr tilted his head at them quizzically. The two statues were similar, but not identical. One blinked, and its metal skin was suddenly a tawny fur rippling over smooth muscles as the creature ruffled its wings and twisted its maned neck back to rake its fangs through golden wing feathers.

"So, you're spirits, then," Torr said.

The second lion also became flesh and blood, and the pair followed Torr, padding on silent paws as he approached the stone circle where the giant Star Globe shone majestically from atop its gold dais, surrounded by flickering fire pits.

An old man was standing in front of the crystal globe, staring into its glassy depths. He wore a plain white robe whose hem brushed against the ground. His white hair and beard were long and stringy, emitting a shimmering, golden luminescence. The man's bony hand was pressed against the globe's surface, and Torr examined the lined face that reflected back at him.

The old man turned as though he saw him, but his gaze passed right through Torr and the lions, who faded with a ripple in the air and returned to their seated, golden forms overlooking the hazy vista.

"Can you see me?" Torr asked, waving his fingers in front of the man's glinting red eyes.

The man cocked his head, his eyes searching the air, and then returned to gazing into Father-Heart-of-Sky.

Torr stood at his side, placed his palms against the glassy surface, and gazed at their reflections in the solid sphere. The man's eyes widened and his jaws flapped noiselessly, as though searching for words. The man stood there, stunned, staring at Torr in the reflection.

"Hi," Torr said.

The man jerked backwards, breaking his palms away. He looked frightened and gathered his long robes in his hands, then ran across the rocks towards the black and gold temple that dominated the high plateau.

Torr ran after him, towards faint strains of a female chorus, mournful as the wind that whistled across the mountaintops.

"Ribhana," the old man called out, scuttling up the broad steps and through a wide, open doorway into the shadows of the temple. "Ribhana, come quickly. Father-Heart-of-Sky. I saw something. A young man. *Flying Star!* He's here—inside the globe."

Torr thought the poor man was going to pass out as he panted and leaned against a gold pillar to hold himself up.

Seated on red pillows in a circle on the polished black marble floor, a dozen white-robed women sat together, gazing at a knee-high crystal ball that sat in the center on a short gold pedestal.

They were singing in such close harmony that Torr could not distinguish one voice from the next. It was an eerie tune that made Torr picture himself hurtling through the cosmos without a ship or a spacesuit, unable to breathe and fearing for his life.

A woman wearing a long red sash draped down over her chest broke her gaze from the crystal sphere and turned her eyes to the old man. He was catching his breath and wiping his brow while her eyes sidled slowly across the dim space and rested on Torr.

Ribhana stopped singing abruptly, and the other voices faltered and trailed off. The women all turned their heads, following her gaze. Some lit upon Torr with wide-mouthed shock. Others searched the shadows vacantly, squinting, and asking, "Where? I don't see anything. What are you staring at?"

From the glistening crystal ball, an ethereal figure emerged, paused for a moment, and then rushed across the floor towards Torr, her hair lifting in a glowing mane of light-snakes, gold and red, like the rays of Uttapta.

Torr staggered backwards, then turned and ran, leaping down the steps three at a time, and found himself running headlong through a forest of tall gray pines. The straight, stately trees stood quietly, one looking like the next as he dashed between the trunks. The land gently sloped up a hillside, the ground carpeted with brown pine needles that softened his frantic footfalls. He drew to a stop and turned in a circle.

The monster woman had not followed him into the forest. He had the sense he was dreaming and tried to wake himself up. He pinched his cheek, hard. The trees stood like pillars, their branches spreading overhead, enclosing him in a dense, dark canopy. He smelled the faintest whiff of a campfire and followed it. The air was still, and soon he saw wisps of blue smoke rising above the next fold of land.

He climbed over the rise. His mother was bent over the small fire, stoking it with a long stick. He ran down the hillside.

"Mom? Mom!" he called.

His mother looked up, sniffing the air.

"Over here," he said, running to her.

Her eyes focused on him, and a broad smile spread across her face. She took him in her arms, and suddenly he was crying on her shoulder.

"Torr, honey, what's wrong?"

"I'm lost. In a dream. I can't get out."

"Shhh, shhh," she said. "Where are you? Are you still on the moon?"

"I don't know," he said, pulling himself together and looking into her eyes. "I don't know where I am."

Torr's eyes popped open. He was bathed in sweat and his heart pounded. Sunshine filtered through green branches overhead, and yellow gems of dew glittered on pine needles like so many stars. The air was cool and moist, and Torr breathed deeply, filling his lungs. He jerked himself up to sitting, remembering where he was.

The trees in the Scridland forest were older, and the trunks more massive, than those in the dream he had just left. He was camped out in the open air next to the trunk of a towering tree, in a bed of animal hides on a mound of pine needles set between thick exposed roots. At least his bonds were gone—as was his belt. The Scrids must have determined there was nowhere for him to go, and without weapons he was no threat. They were probably right. Scrids were too strong for him to fight bare-handed, and he wasn't about to go wandering off into a thick forest on an unknown planet.

The fight in Peary Dome rushed back to him—Blaire's dead face stared up at him. He buried his face in his hands, unable to comprehend all that had happened. Why had those men killed Blaire, and Raleigh and Roanoke and Hawk, and Sky and Thunder, and Darla? For him? For the deeds? None of it made sense. He was suddenly racked with shaking sobs.

Worry for his sister pushed the blade of grief deeper. What if she had been felled by snake jaws as well? The agony was too great. *No*, he told himself. *She had survived. She had found more drugs and passed out on a container roof, oblivious to the carnage below.*

When he had cried himself out, he wiped his cheeks and looked around. He'd been curious about the planet Scridland, but now that he was here, all he wanted was to get back to the moon, find his sister, and lay Blaire's body to rest. He would carry Blaire's and Darla's bodies to the Smith camp and kneel before Blaire's sisters, begging them for forgiveness. Then he would take the bodies of Raleigh, Roanoke, and Hawk to Durham, look their father in the eye, and say that their death was his fault. He would say a prayer over Sky's and Thunder's bodies himself, along with Cassidy, because no one else besides his sister and Durham would mourn their passing. But instead, he had disappeared, leaving the senseless slaughter for Jasper and Cassidy to find. Cassidy would blame herself.

Torr rubbed his eyes. What did the Scrids want with him, anyway? Jorimar was standing across the clearing on the other side of the glowing embers of the previous night's bonfire, talking with a gray-haired man—the wizard, Torr supposed—the one who had brought him here. Torr recognized no one else. Some of the men from the feverish dance the night before were stirring in their bedding. Some got up and walked out into the woods, while others emerged from huts and poked at the embers and tossed on logs, sending up fountains of sparks.

Jorimar and the wizard glanced at Torr and returned to their animated conversation, the wizard gesturing at the sky. Torr realized Jorimar was holding Torr's triptych, the small three-paneled painting of Jesus and the angels descending on shafts of light, which he had nabbed from *Moon Star*. He rolled his eyes. More proof for the superstitious Scrids that he was a Star Child. Now they would never let him go.

A round white cross section of a gravity bar stood beyond the fire near Jorimar and the wizard, the companion to the slab at the Scrids' Peary camp. At the center of the stone slab stood a large crystal. It looked like the one in the Scrid camp—perhaps it was one and the same, though he didn't recall the wizard holding it. Torr would need to get on top of the slab, chant like a madman, and send himself back to Peary. He wondered grimly if he would need the wizard's help to do so. Trying to remember the words of the chant, he closed his eyes and brought his mind back to the day before.

Andi stiga
Fara lopt
Heimili heita
Gaumr far

He smiled with satisfaction. He was not completely brain-dead, despite his stiff and aching body. He needed to return to the moon right away. Cassidy and Jasper would be crazed with worry. He rubbed his whiskered chin.

Jasper and Berkeley, Kai and Montana, Ming-Long and all the others would be tearing apart Peary Dome, looking for him. Cassidy must have been discovered by now, hiding out on top of a shipping container. A niggling fear stirred in the corner of Torr's mind as he recalled the men's footprints around the moon buggy. What if she had been abducted again? The possibility was too disturbing to imagine, so he pushed it out of his mind. No, her footprints had simply blended in with the tire tracks. She had been found and would be sick with guilt and grief over the death of her friends. And now Torr had gone missing. Maybe the Scrids who'd stayed behind had told them where Torr was, or someone had seen him dragged off to their camp. They would figure out he had been taken through the portal. That would be better than not knowing. They wouldn't be able to get through the portal to rescue him, he was fairly certain, though Jasper and Berkeley would no doubt attempt it.

He reached out with his senses to try and connect with Cassidy, but all he got was a vague, foggy feeling, confirming his suspicions that she had found more of the Murian drugs, and now she was sleeping it off. He shook his head, wishing his mother were there to help Cassidy shake the addiction.

He returned his attention to the Scrid camp and examined the white slab from his vantage point of many yards away. His back grew rigid as he saw that there was a neighboring slab—a smaller version of the large white portal slab. On top of the small round slab, glinting in the sun, sat his knives and crystals. Forming a circle around his things were six light crystals, standing on their ends on the slab and glowing as though they were sentries. His vest and belt were sitting on the ground nearby. The belt was empty save for his short wooden club and his waterskin clipped to it. How dare they take his personal things. The knives he could understand, but the crystals were no threat to them.

He frantically reached up under his shirt, and his fingers met the stiff canvas of the rune belt. He exhaled with relief and silently thanked Berkeley for his magic—although what good would moon deeds and Solidi do out here in the middle of nowhere?

He stood up on wobbly legs. Jorimar saw him standing, and carefully propped Torr's open triptych on the small stone slab outside the circle of light crystals and gave him the two-fisted salute. Torr thumped his fists against his chest in return. The wizard gave Torr a little bow, and Torr lowered his head briefly. He did not want to alienate the two people who could help him get back to Peary. Jorimar motioned to a couple of Scrids, who disappeared into a long lean-to roofed with rushes. They reappeared carrying bowls and a waterskin and headed his way. As they approached, Torr realized they were women.

He had always wondered what female Scrids looked like and was pleasantly surprised. They were thick-boned, like the males, but their waists narrowed below plump breasts, and rosy dimpled faces smiled happily, framed by masses of red curls that bounced as they walked. They handed him a small slab of wood piled high with slices of roasted red meat and greens from the forest, a small wooden bowl full of yellow berries, a bowl filled with white mush, and a leather waterskin. He accepted the food gratefully and sat and ate it all, relishing the gamey meat, pungent greens, and tart berries. The skin was filled with some sort of sour wine. Even the mush had a savory flavor. The two young Scrid women squatted nearby and watched him eat. They wore leather pants and fringed boots like the men, but instead of bear hide vests, they wore loose, tan suede tunics decorated with colorful seeds and small stone beads and cinched at the waist by braided leather belts.

It was surreal being here, and his mind bounced between vivid images of Blaire's dead eyes and his other fallen friends, and the view of the dense green forest, which sang to him as a light wind played through the branches far overhead and sent an occasional smattering of water droplets to the ground. His campmates would have found his friends' bodies and taken them to the Smith camp and the Fen by now, where their families and friends would mourn them.

He needed to return to Peary before the bodies were taken away to the recycler. Torr wanted to see Blaire one last time before she was shredded and reduced to water and elements, never to exist again. Tears rose to his eyes, and he choked on his wine. The Scrid women stared at him curiously. They appeared to be his age or younger. He drank half the wine and left the empty tray and bowls for the women to clear.

Torr stood up and took the half-filled wineskin with him and strode across the yard to stand with Jorimar, the wizard, and an old woman who had joined them. The white-haired woman leaned on a cane, and her skin was drooping and wrinkled, but she looked up at him with keen, fire-yellow eyes.

"Vaka," Jorimar said, telling Torr the wizard's name.

Torr bowed his head to the gray-bearded man. "Vaka," he repeated.

"Salima," the woman said with a scratchy voice, introducing herself. Torr nodded a silent greeting.

The wizard's rheumy amber eyes seared into him as they had when they'd first met, making Torr dizzy. He lowered his gaze, not liking the feeling. Salima stood beside him and poked at Torr's upper arm and said something to Jorimar.

"Strong," Jorimar translated, smiling widely. Torr memorized the Scridnu word. *Terkr*. He wished he had the garnet.

"Thank you," Torr said, and Jorimar translated. *Kappo*.

Torr stalked past them and reached across the small slab for his knives and crystals.

"Jeng," Jorimar called out with alarm. He grabbed Torr's shoulder and pulled him back. Jorimar frowned sternly at him, then gestured for Torr to watch. Jorimar slowly moved one finger between two of the light crystals, and a line of white light shot out between them, catching Jorimar's finger. Jorimar jerked back his hand with a high-pitched squeal, which made Vaka and Salima cackle with delight. Jorimar blushed and showed his finger to Torr. A dark red welt encircled it. Salima fished a leaf from inside her gum and handed it to Jorimar, who wrapped it around his finger. He grinned at Torr.

Torr rubbed his chin, wondering if Cassidy's light crystal could also work as a shield when combined with other light crystals. Undaunted by Jorimar's burned finger, Torr leaned forward and slowly moved his left hand towards the invisible barrier while the Scrids watched with amused smirks. He frowned, intent on defying the crystals, and thrust his fingers towards the wolf knife. He yelped as a flash of light cut across his fingers, and quickly pulled his hand back, clasping it with the other.

Vaka and Salima laughed with hoarse, coughing laughs, and Jorimar suppressed a smile. A dark red line scored Torr's knuckles on both sides. He shook his hand and hopped around in a circle, the pain traveling up his arm. He poured wine over his hand from the wineskin while Salima clucked and hurried off, returning a minute later with a cheekful of herbs, which she handed to him in a green wad. It was slimy from her spit, but he pressed it to his skin, and the herbs instantly cooled the burn. She wrapped his hand with a length of soft chamois leather to hold the herb compress in place and tied it with a simple knot.

"*Kappo,*" he said, bending and unbending his knuckles. She chortled happily and patted his arm.

Defeated, Torr snatched the triptych from the slab, folded it, and tucked it into his cargo pants leg pocket, then picked up his belt and vest, glaring at them to try and take them from him. Jorimar did not object but pulled Torr's amber aviators from inside his bear hide vest and perched them on his fat nose, grinning with childish delight. Torr rolled his eyes and held out his hand for the sunglasses, but Jorimar pursed his lips in a pout.

Torr put on the vest and clipped on his belt, realizing his binoculars were also missing. "Where are my binoculars?" he asked, putting hollow fists to his eyes. "And my radio?" He moved his hand to his ear.

Jorimar motioned over his shoulder. Sitting inside a lean-to, one of the young women was looking at him through the binoculars.

Torr made a face at her, and she broke out in a fit of giggles.

A teenaged boy, who was sitting on a log nearby, had removed the battery from Torr's radio and was turning the knobs and pressing the radio to his ear. Torr shook his head and glanced over to the far edge of the clearing, where a group of young boys huddled together. One cocked back Torr's slingshot and launched a pine cone into the woods. The other boys stared into the woods, then hopped up and down and grabbed at the slingshot for a turn.

"Fine," Torr muttered. "Give them back to me later."

Jorimar ignored him and gazed around, mesmerized by the tinted glasses.

Torr checked his vest pouches and found his collection of miscellaneous items was still there: a few coins, a carabiner, a small spool of hemp cord, lip balm, a stale heel of bread, a seashell Blaire had given him. His heart thudded heavily as a wave of grief crashed over him. He closed his eyes and let the feelings swell and subside, letting his thoughts come and go as Berkeley had taught him. After a few steadying breaths, he opened his eyes.

The wizard was regarding him head to toe and scanning the air around his body. Torr wondered if the purple flames were still there.

He asked Jorimar, "What are you going to do with me?"

The man smiled. "Wait," he said.

"Wait," Torr repeated. "That's what you're doing with me? I thought Vaka wanted to train me?" He looked towards the stooped man, who had turned and was walking away with Salima.

"Wait," Jorimar said, nodding.

Wait was what he did for the next few days, spending most of his time lying in his pine needle nest and bear hide bedding and staring morosely up at the tree branches, interrupted by bouts of choking sobs that snuck up on him in random surprise attacks. He tried to distract himself by repeating the Scrid words he was learning and plotting his escape, but soon his mind would wander back to the massacre of his friends and send him into a weeping fit again. He was sure by now he had missed their funerals, and the bodies had no doubt been recycled.

Frustration was a constant companion, as it became clear that he was trapped here and there was nothing he could do about it. Other young men slept under neighboring trees, and a few had made attempts to interact with him—but he was often angry and distraught, and so they left him alone.

Torr was thankful for the cloaking privacy of nighttime, something he'd missed at Peary Dome. The air was pristine, and with no ambient light other than firelight the dark forest felt alive, creeping up to the edges of the hamlet and surrounding it. When the fire turned to coals, legions of stars pressed down from above and cast a ghostlike glow over everything. There was no moon.

His watch had stopped. He assumed the journey through the portal had been too much for it. Torr marked the passage of daytime by the journey of the small white sun across the sky, however long that took, and the nights were broken up by the hunters leaving and returning.

The only times he left the base of his tree were for meals or to trek to the latrine, which was a long hand-hewn board with holes in it, situated over a rock crevasse with the sound of a stream flowing far below.

After his first meal, he either had to join the Scrids around the fire, or he would not eat. The choice was easy—he was starving, and the food was delicious. The typical meal consisted of roasted meat or fish, forest roots and greens, and the boiled mashed grain cooked with animal fat, and a spicy orange root that added flavor.

Vaka liked to stare at him. Torr felt hot and prickly whenever the old man did that, as though he were feverish and afflicted with a sudden rash. It was an unsettling feeling, and Torr avoided the wizard's eyes as much as he could. Vaka didn't force him to meet his gaze but made a habit of sitting next to Torr when they ate meals around the fire. No matter where Torr sat, Vaka ended up sitting next to him, often without Torr realizing the wizard was there until he felt the tingling presence of the man. Vaka made Torr nervous, but if he got up and moved, the wizard appeared next to him a few minutes later. He tried to steel himself against the strange reaction he had to the man, but it was no use. Finally, Torr gave up trying and attempted to study the phenomenon instead.

At first he'd thought the effect was magnetic, because he felt a strong physical pull towards Vaka, but if he got too close to him, he felt repelled, as though some sort of barrier surrounded the wizard. Lately, he'd noticed that when Vaka sat next to him for a time, Torr felt like a pot of water sitting on a fire, his energy churning and rising to the brink of boiling. He wondered if this were some sort of preparation for training—a kind of energy transfer. His mother and grandmother had spoken of such things—a technique the shamans used to prepare apprentices. Or perhaps the Scrid wizard was simply overflowing with power.

Torr sat on his bedding, his back against the rough bark of the giant pine tree, and studied the small village, which consisted of a few huts and lean-tos arranged around the central clearing and massive campfire, whose embers were kept alive day and night and served as cookfire, heat, and light. A small river flowed nearby and provided a constant shushing sound in the background.

Vaka was at the white gravity bar slab with his back to him, talking to Jorimar and two other men. Vaka didn't look at him, but Torr could feel the man's presence as a force of attraction, even at this distance, like a light that continually drew the eye. It was late-afternoon, and women, children, and elderly people were busy doing chores. Most of the young and middle-aged men were napping, in preparation for the nightly hunt.

The village was home to about a hundred people, made up of several families, including a half-dozen round, red-haired toddlers. It was impossible to tell the little boys from the girls, except for the really small ones who sometimes scampered around naked. Scrids were built just like Earthlanders. The older children ran around in packs, sneaking into the woods, climbing trees, and dropping pine cones onto their elders' heads or throwing them from the surrounding forest. The adults thought this a game and caught the pine cones, trying to tag the child back with it before the attacker disappeared behind a tree. Several of the boys had made slingshots copied from Torr's design and using a stretchy animal sinew. Torr recalled Jorimar catching the rock Roanoke had shot from his sling and understood now why Jorimar had not been upset. In fact, it was a sign of affection when a child targeted an adult for their game. Torr saw only one child disciplined, with a sharp cuff to the backside after a badly aimed pine cone hit a baby's head.

Jorimar seemed to be the leader of the tribe. They called their tribe and village *Gray Feather.* One of the curly-haired young women was Jorimar's daughter. Her name was Frija. She appeared to be in her late teens, and was good-looking, as Scrid females went. Jorimar, Frija, and Jorimar's mate, Osma, had sort of adopted Torr, making sure he got his share of food and tending to his needs. Though, what he really needed was to go back to Peary Dome. Jorimar smiled and ignored him every time Torr mentioned it.

More days passed. Torr had forgotten how alive a forest was. It wasn't just the plants and the creatures that croaked from the shadows. The wind was alive. It whispered through the treetops, telling a tale that Torr was sure he would understand if he listened long enough. He'd never realized how much he loved the wind.

Torr took to wandering in the woods, venturing ever farther from Gray Feather village as he became familiar with the terrain. He was usually shadowed by two or three stocky men. They had no intention of letting him escape but seemed to respect his curiosity. Perhaps they were more concerned that he might get lost. Torr discovered other Scrid settlements up and down the river. They were all about the same size as Gray Feather. Torr's guards—or guides—knew everyone and showed off Torr as though he were an exotic animal. Torr understood by their body language and his limited Scridnu vocabulary that the tribes were all related. Though they all appeared warlike, Torr felt no hostility between the tribes. Perhaps they were just hunters, with no need to kill each other as long as there was enough game to go around.

Torr ventured away from the river on either side, crossing gravel fords where the river widened and grew shallow, and exploring the wooded hills. The farther he went from the river and villages, the more the woods were wild. Huge downed trees were stacked and tangled together, blocking his progress and forming treacherous thickets where he could easily break a leg. Deep ravines cut through the rocky land, filled with clear rushing streams. Torr found himself waiting for his companions and letting them lead the way. They seemed to enjoy showing him their home. Game trails snaked through the woods, invisible to Torr until the Scrids pointed them out.

Hunters went out at dusk and returned in the middle of the night with prey hanging from their shoulders or from saplings propped between them. Torr asked to go along, but they said no. When Torr asked why, Jorimar told him it was because the villagers "had to eat." Torr supposed that meant if Torr went along, he would ruin the hunting. Probably it was true. Not having grown up in these forests, nor having learned to tread silently the way the Scrids did, he would alert the prey. The Scrids also had phenomenal vision and hearing, perhaps because they were still hunters, whereas few Earthlanders hunted for their survival anymore.

The hunters caught large wild fowl with flat heads and spiky beaks, furry animals similar to raccoons, and another animal that was sort of like a rabbit. Occasionally they came back with small goat-like creatures, or large blue fish with webbed feet. Torr tried to stay awake, waiting for the hunters to return, curious about this strange land and what the forest held. Then he would sleep late into the morning along with the other men and rise to a large meal of meat and wine.

He often had vivid dreams, which wrenched him from his slumber, leaving him drenched in sweat. The dreams with Blaire were the most disturbing, if only because he was happy in his dreams and miserable when he awoke. One morning he'd awoken and sat up, crying like a baby. Frija and her friend were watching him, giggling. Frija ran off and returned with a small leather skin that Torr had seen parents use to feed their babies. He got the joke and wasn't amused, but grabbed the skin from her hand, curious about what was in it. He sucked on the skin, much to the delight of the women. It tasted like fermented goat's milk. He drank it all and burped, then handed Frija the skin. She was laughing so hard, her face was a deep crimson. He curled up on his side and went back to sleep. When he awoke again, he felt a warm body snuggled against his back. He started and found it was Frija. She looked at him with big amber eyes.

"No sad," she said in hesitant Globalish.

His eyes filled with tears, and her face fell. She had obviously taken the effort to learn the phrase from her father in an effort to make him feel better. The kindness made him cry harder, and he climbed to his feet and hurried into the forest to be alone. That night she came to his bed again, but he sent her away. He did not want anyone but Blaire, and she was gone forever. He curled into a ball and fell into a haunted slumber.

He dreamt he was at Miramar, lying on the shooting platform and peering through the scope of his Dashiel at the thinning Shaman's Shield. Next to him lay Blaire, propped on her elbows and looking through binoculars. "That guy has a Lectro," she said.

"I know," Torr said, training his sights on two Teg soldiers leaning against the vehicle and looking their way. "That's Edgemont. He's always watching me."

"Did you know that if two people are touching, the Lectro will kill them both?" she asked, glancing at him with her golden-blossom eyes.

"Yes, I know," he said, pain jabbing at his heart. "Edgemont told me. How do you know that?"

"From when I was holding Darla. The snake jaw bit me, but it killed Darla also."

Torr swallowed, holding her calm, happy gaze. She did not seem at all disturbed that she was dead. "Are you okay?" he asked, his voice breaking.

"Of course," she said. "Everything is fine here. Are you okay?"

"No," he said. "I'm miserable without you."

"Oh," she said, crestfallen. "Don't be sad. You must go on without me. I'll be looking over your shoulder, though, don't you worry." She smiled again, her eyes sparkling.

"Why does it hurt so much?" he asked, putting aside his gun and pulling her into a hug. He ran his fingers over the fabric of her shirt, feeling the firmness of her back muscles, the warmth of her body. "It's like my heart is actually broken. It's physically painful."

"Oh, Torr," she said gently. "It's just because our heartstrings were severed. It hurts."

"It feels like a dagger is embedded in my heart," he said.

"Yes, it does feel a bit like that, doesn't it?" she agreed.

"I'm going to let the dagger stay stuck in there," he said. "The pain will always remind me of you."

"I'm not sure that's such a good idea," she murmured in his ear.

"It's a great idea," he said, hugging her with all his strength.

Next he knew, they were walking together on the brown hills of Scripps Ranch behind the bunkers, where sandbags were piled up for target practice. Blaire held his hand tightly, dragging him with her as she bent to pick tiny purple flowers that poked through dry golden grasses. She handed them to him, adding to the growing bouquet.

"Is that guy Edgemont one of the men you killed?" she asked as she handed him a fuzzy yellow bloom.

"Yeah, one of them," Torr said. "The other one was Matthew."

"Oh," she said, and pointed out an alligator lizard that stood in a frozen pose, hoping they wouldn't see him.

Torr poked gently at the small lizard with a stick and watched it scurry into the underbrush. Suddenly he was in the bunker again, deafening rounds of gunfire echoing off the cinderblock walls. Torr clutched his Dashiel and fired, the stock kicking back against his shoulder. He reloaded and peered through the gunsight, looking for Teg soldiers, his pulse throbbing frantically in his fingers. Fires blazed in the distance as Teg vehicles burned, and the pops of artillery guns on the next hill were answered by booming explosions that sent flaming streamers into the ash-filled air.

Torr rolled over and stared up at a screen of tree branches, slowly remembering where he was. The campfire crackled and popped, orange flames licking up into the air. He sat up and waited for the dream to fade and his heartbeat to normalize. He rubbed his eyes, missing Blaire.

It was dark out, and the Gray Feather hunters had returned. Some were stoking the fire while others strung up two small boar-looking animals from a thick bough to hang until morning, when the women would skin the animals and prepare the meat for cooking. Torr climbed out of bed to join the men for their nightly ritual of drinking wine around the fire.

They welcomed him, handing him a skin fat with wine, and told him the story of the hunt as though he could understand. Torr watched their gestures and recognized some of the words, but mostly just enjoyed their company. One man was busy carving a design into a stone club, which was for his son who was soon to reach manhood. The son was one of the boys who slept under a tree that neighbored Torr's. The boy was about fourteen and was not allowed to set eyes on his battle club until he was taken out on his first hunt, so his father only worked on it at night or from the shelter of a lean-to behind a curtain of animal hide. Torr asked with grunts and gestures why Helug's club was smooth and polished, with no carvings whatsoever.

This question brought forth chortles of glee at the mention of Helug, who Torr learned was the son of one of the men sitting around the fire. The aging man sprang to his feet and proudly displayed his own club, which was smooth as well, but of a dark gray stone, not the red of Helug's. The polished club was apparently a family tradition. He told Torr through pantomime that crafting a perfectly smooth and symmetrical club took more skill than the rough designs his tribesmen carved. A friendly debate ensued, but the old man smiled smugly as if to humor the others and sat back down at the fire.

Torr glanced over his shoulder, trying to sense Blaire watching over him, but all he saw was the dark, looming forest.

———————————)———————————

The wind howled in the cold night, and the tall bonfire roared and set everything aglow. Torr stood with the women behind the drumming, dancing, chanting warriors as Vaka stood on the slab and frantically shook his rattle.

Andi stiga
Fara lopt
Heimili heita
Gaumr far

"Is he going to Peary?" Torr asked, grabbing Frija by the arm.

She smiled, and repeated, "Peary."

Torr's heart jumped, and he added his voice to the chant, letting himself be swept up in the momentum of the rolling rhythm. He pushed through the women and drummers and dancing men, and jumped up onto the platform with Vaka, stomping to the beat, unable to resist the pull of the chant.

The drummers did not break their rhythm, but the circle of dancing warriors fell apart into a jumble of confusion, as though Torr had violated a sacred rule. The men knocked against one another as they stumbled to a halt, their eyes darting between Torr and Jorimar while the sonorous voice of the wizard droned on.

Torr felt the tug of Vaka's chant pulling him into a churning vortex. The old man and the drummers were caught in the inexorable pulse and could not stop. Torr attuned his voice to Vaka's, his throat hoarse. A large hand clamped around Torr's elbow, and the ground pitched beneath him as he tumbled off the pedestal head first, his face meeting the furry vest of a stunned dancer, a copper medallion cutting into Torr's cheek.

Vaka's voice did not break, but reached a fevered pitch, and then was drowned out by the thundering drums and ululations of the women. Torr twisted around, and the white stone slab glimmered. Vaka was gone.

Jorimar and three others dragged Torr to the edge of the clearing and sat him roughly on his bedding, beyond the glow of the fire. Blood dripped down his face. They bound his torso tightly against the base of the tree and left him there, immune to his threats and curses as they returned to the circle and resumed their dancing and chanting. It was a new chant Torr did not understand, nor did he care to understand. All he wanted was to get on the slab and go back home to Peary. His cheek was twitching suddenly. He exhaled in angry frustration. Everything was out of his control. He was a prisoner on another planet, bound to a fucking tree. He was bleeding, and he couldn't even still his own damned cheek.

He closed his eyes and recalled Berkeley sitting in front of the rows of meditating Light Fighters. "Follow your breath," Berkeley said for the thousandth time, with the patience of a father speaking to a beloved child.

Torr sat under the tree and did as he had been taught, letting all thoughts float away when they arose and focusing on his breath. His belly rose and fell. There was a space between breaths and a gap between thoughts. The space and the gaps became longer, until he became aware of himself as a universe of cells holding themselves together with some mysterious force. His nerves were highways running through his body, following the channels of the blood vessels and branching out to feel everything. The nerve in his cheek was a jagged offshoot, shaped like a bolt of lightning, which surged and then fizzled over and over as it kept firing, making his cheek react with a painful twinge each time. He became fascinated with the nerve. Something was wrong with it to keep firing like that. He followed the branching nerve up its trunk and into the brain, where it ended in a tangle of nerves, which had curled in on itself like a ball.

He was in a dark cell. The stone walls dripped with water, and a thin sliver of light filtered in from high on the dungeon wall through a chink in the stones. He was lying naked on his side on a damp dirt floor, curled in a tight fetal position, with his knees pulled up to his chest and his arms wrapped tightly around his shins to try and conserve body heat against the biting cold. The rattle of the jailer's keys startled him, making him lurch to his feet and cower in a corner. *Not again.*

The jailer opened the door and two guards came in, kicking him in the head and back and hauling him out by the arms, as if he had any strength left in him to resist. Darius had concluded that the men enjoyed inflicting pain just because they could—the only power they had in the world.

Darius was forced roughly into a stone chair and bound by thick ropes around his torso, pinning his arms at his sides. Again, needless effort for a man who was staring at death.

The Delosian priest came into the room with a rustle of velvet and silk brocade, the aroma of wood sap drifting in with him. Darius closed his eyes and let the scent fill him. White pitch from the skeleton trees of the northern Delosian mountains, where Darius had been born. Pitch supported more than one family Darius had grown up with.

Darius was pulled from his pleasant reverie by firm hands clamped painfully on his jaw. The priest stared him in the eye as Darius flinched from the shooting pain, which branched from his jaw up to his eye.

The abscess from the last tooth they had extracted to torture him throbbed madly under the priest's thumb.

"Are you ready to tell us where your sister is?" the man asked pleasantly in Darius's native tongue.

"I'm sorry, I don't know," Darius lied.

The priest backhanded him, the gem on his ring catching Darius under the eye. Warm blood oozed down his cheek. Darius swallowed and met the man's presumptuous gaze. Darius held his breath as the acolyte handed the priest the extraction tongs.

"Pssst."

A pine cone landed in Torr's lap. He jerked his head up, sweat running down his forehead and stinging his eyes. He was still bound by the ropes, unable to move his arms. A young boy was crouched in front of him, peering at him worriedly, and then ran off. Remnants of Torr's dream haunted him, but the twitching of his cheek had stopped. He explored the inside of his mouth with his tongue. All his teeth were accounted for. He leaned his head back against the tree trunk with a sigh, the scent of pine gentle on the air. "Darius," Torr mumbled sadly.

It occurred to him that he had dreamt of Darius while in a waking, meditative state, like his Grandpa Leo used to do. The Memory Keeper was fifty paces away on the slab. Maybe the crystal had awoken his memories like a box long sealed with a rusty lock, which once opened would never close again. Did his twitching cheek come from Darius? Was it a stored memory that triggered a physical response, or had he actually been Darius, and some remnant of muscle memory still remained? He tried to recall if his cheek had twitched before he'd received the fluorite crystal from Great-Aunt Sophie. He'd been about seven at the time. He couldn't remember his cheek twitching before that. Surely he would have been taunted by the other children in Shasta if he'd had that nervous tic back then. He clearly recalled being bullied over it at his new school in San Jose, until he had punched the biggest bully in the mouth, busting his lip and making him cry. They hadn't taunted him after that.

His musings were interrupted by Frija and her mother returning with the boy. Frija came over to him, frowning with concern. She leaned down and covered Torr with his bear hide, then gave him a drink from his waterskin. Osma nudged her aside to examine his face and began cleaning his wound. The copper disc had cut him under the cheekbone next to his nose, and she gestured that he was fortunate it had missed his eye. She clucked and left, while Frija squatted and smiled at him. Osma returned with a torch and her cheek stuffed with herbs. In her other hand she carried a shallow bowl filled with a red liquid. She handed the torch to Frija, numbed his cheek with the wad of herbs from her mouth, cleaned the wound with the red liquid, and then proceeded to give him several stitches using a bone needle and sinew.

After they left, he was alone in the dark and watched as the villagers settled down for the night. He evidently was not going to be freed to visit the woods to relieve himself and wondered with distress how long they intended to keep him tied up. A slow fire of rage smoldered deep within his belly. He became agitated, squirming against the tight ropes. Vaka had left without him.

The bonfire slowly burned down to a bed of glowing coals. Torr resisted dozing off, afraid of rejoining Darius in the torture chamber. The hunters left and returned a few hours later with three large hares. One by one, the men wandered off to bed. Torr fought against sleep, his head nodding down to his chest then jerking up again. He pretended he had pulled the night shift at Miramar and was on the platform with his Dashiel, scanning the darkness with his night scope.

At first light Jorimar appeared to untie his bonds.

"Free," the husky man said with a smile, his hair tangled from sleep.

Torr scowled and rose stiffly to his feet. After shaking out his tingling limbs, he went immediately to the latrine to empty his bladder and bowels. Jorimar did not follow, and Torr took his time. He scanned the forest, wondering if he dared strike out on his own. He decided against it. The white stone slab was his only way out.

Back at the campfire, he strode over to the large white slab. He stood outside the circle of light crystals that stuck up from the dirt, not understanding their purpose, since he could pass between them unharmed. He swung his foot between two of them, but nothing happened. He glared at his crystals and knives where they sat on the other slab, still under the protection of the six guard crystals. Vaka must have put some sort of spell on those to keep his crystals and knives from him.

Anger reared its head again. They were keeping him here against his will. Just like Zinz had kept Darius. Torr had previously entertained the idea of coming to Scridland to learn from the wizard. But now that they had brought him here by force, he wanted nothing to do with Vaka.

Jorimar came to stand by his side and folded his arms across his broad chest. Jorimar gazed at the portal slab and the large crystal at its center, then beamed at Torr, as though sharing admiration of the power of it all.

"When is Vaka coming back?" Torr asked. "Where did he go?"

Jorimar's forehead wrinkled like it always did when he tried to understand Globalish. Torr repeated his questions more slowly. Jorimar's face lit up with comprehension.

"Sister," Jorimar said.

"Sister," Torr echoed, his jaw tightening.

Jorimar nodded, his smile broadening. "Cassit. *Marglod Sky,*" he said. "*Golden Cloud.*"

Torr's blood boiled. "No!" Torr said, pushing at Jorimar's beefy chest. "You're not kidnapping her, too. You leave her alone!"

Jorimar's eyes widened with surprise as he took a heavy step backward. *"Marglod Sky,"* Jorimar repeated, as if that made their actions okay. He appeared genuinely puzzled that Torr was upset, apparently thinking this whole thing was an honor.

Torr had to return to Peary. He had to get to Cassidy before Vaka did. The hot blood of fury rose to his face, and he hopped on top of the slab and stood at its center by the large crystal. Jorimar stayed on the ground and watched Torr with narrowed eyes. Torr started stomping in a circle like he'd seen the Scrid warriors do. He wished he had Scrid boots with fringes and bells and Vaka's rattle. He started chanting loudly, unconcerned that most of Gray Feather was still in bed. He recited the familiar chant:

> *Andi stiga*
> *Fara lopt*
> *Heimili heita*
> *Gaumr far*

He nurtured the hope that the warriors would take pity on him and join in the chant, circling the slab and lending their voices to help

speed him on his way. But they did not. They did stumble from their
sleeping huts, however, and watched with stern frowns. They glanced
nervously at Jorimar, but the leader did not move. He seemed confident that Torr would be unable to harness the energy required to open
the portal and transport himself to Peary. After a few minutes, the
curious crowd grew bored and went back to bed. Only Jorimar, Osma,
and Frija stayed to watch. Torr felt small stirrings of energy enter his
feet and travel up his legs, but they always died before reaching his
abdomen. The warm, swirling energy seemed to get stuck in his groin
area, and fell back to his ankles like a fountain fed by a weak pump.

His voice grew hoarse. At long length, he gave up and sat discon-
solately on the slab and glared sullenly at Jorimar, who grunted and
walked away. Osma and Frija had already left.

Torr sat wearily on the slab, liking its warmth despite his impotency
in making the portal work. He muttered aloud to Blaire, as though she
were there with him. "Stuck on the planet Scridland. A forest prison
no better than a stone dungeon. Well, a bit better. Quite a bit better,
in fact. But a prison nonetheless."

He frowned. Blaire was dead. She could not hear him. What would
she do if she were here, he wondered. What would Cassidy do? What
would Jasper do? What would Darius do?

Torr gazed at the smaller slab and rested his eyes on the fluorite
crystal. "Darius," he said aloud. "If you can help me, I need you now,
buddy. I need to get the fuck out of here."

The Memory Keeper sat inertly on the slab. After staring at it for
some time, silently begging the crystal to help him, he shifted his
gaze to the wolf knife and entreated Brother Wolf for his help. Torr
inspected the shadows, but there was no wolf.

Discouraged by his failures, Torr slid off the slab and stood by
the fire. *Fire.* A thing of power and beauty. He tossed a log onto the
smoldering coals and watched as is slowly ignited, the blaze growing
and creeping across the dry fuel, transforming wood into ephemeral
flames. He had not seen fire since the battle at Miramar. Fire had been
strictly outlawed on the moon. Kai had told him it was the thing the
Peary leadership feared the most. A fire in the tent city could rage
through the dry canvas structures and consume all the oxygen. *Fire.*
The ultimate force of destruction.

Orange and yellow flames danced across the log. Torr clamped his jaws together and ripped the rune belt from his waist and dangled the canvas pouch over the bed of glimmering embers. *His damnable moon deed.* The cause of death of Blaire and his other dear friends. Tears of pain and frustration pooled in his eyes as he held the pouch over the coals, tempted to hurl it into the center of the fire where the flames grew ever higher. The deed ... his Solidi. Why did he need any of it? If it hadn't been for the deed, Blaire and his friends would still be alive today.

But ... he considered, clutching the rune belt in both hands. If it weren't for the moon deeds, he and Cassidy would never have escaped Earth. He and his family might have gone to José and Felipe's farm together, and without Torr's dream body they would have all ended up in Teg camps. Cassidy's fate in particular could have been even worse than what she experienced with General Balthazar.

If it weren't for the deeds he would have never met Blaire. If she had never met him, she wouldn't have been murdered. The bitter irony forced him to his knees, where he crushed the belt in his hands and his tears dripped onto the dirt at the edge of the fire. He cursed his fate. *A Star Child.* A supposed savior? His was a path of death and destruction. And for what? He hated his life. He hated himself. He should throw himself onto the flames and be done with it.

He sat back on his heels and wiped away his tears, then slowly clipped the belt around his waist and stared glumly into the fire.

———————— ⟩ ————————

Bright sunshine and the smell of roasting meat woke him up. He climbed out of his pine needle nest and shared in the midday meal around the fire, and then left the village and strode into the woods, wandering aimlessly. He was angry and didn't want to stay at Gray Feather any longer. But neither did he want to get lost in the endless forest. He caught glimpses of his guards from time to time as they followed him silently through the trees, but they let him be. He spent all afternoon wandering and contemplating his predicament. The Scrids wanted to bring Cassidy here, too. To do what? Torr guessed that maybe the Scrids thought their planet was the key to the new configuration of the pathways of light, and that the presence of the Star Children would make it so—or attract the Star People—or something.

Torr tried to recall the various Star Seeker legends for some sort of clue. He should have read the blue and gold book. *Songs of Sirius.* Cassidy and Hawk had translated a lot of it with the help of the garnet, but Torr hadn't taken the time to look at it. He scolded himself for neglecting the book, and his eyes teared up at the thought of Hawk. He wiped at his cheeks. The book was supposedly the journal of Danute. *The* Danute. She would have known some things. Or rather, she had transcribed lyrics. In those days, Torr figured, there would have been bards who passed along history and wisdom through song.

Whatever the reason the Scrids held him, he was a prisoner, and the Scrids wanted to imprison Cassidy, too, just like the priests on Iliad.

When he'd tired himself out and returned to the camp, dinner was being served. He went to join Frija, and they ate in silence. When night fell and the hunters left camp, Torr retreated to his bed under cover of the pine trees and burrowed into the warmth of his bear hides. The darkness of the thick forest pressed in around him, and Torr slowly sank into the arms of sleep.

Darius and Danute sat at the feet of Rigel on the dirt floor of the forest priest's simple hut. They were ten years old, and the priest was holding a small crystal shaft in his slender fingers.

"This crystal," Rigel said in his low, warm voice, "is not a rock," he said, correcting Darius. "It is an ancient species with intelligence beyond our comprehension."

Darius exchanged skeptical glances with Danute. She put on a funny face that made him laugh, and Rigel's serious face softened into a gentle smile.

"Don't try to understand with your mind," Rigel told them. "Just remember to respect the crystals. Feel them with your senses, and you will have some understanding of the depths of their beings. They communicate with one another," he said, and waggled his bushy brown eyebrows at them meaningfully. "So don't try any sneaky stuff on them. They will tell each other." He gave them a menacing look, and Danute broke out in giggles.

"They do not talk," she said to Rigel.

"They do. They talk to each other," Rigel said. "In their own language that we cannot understand. At least I cannot understand them."

His voice lowered to a whisper. "But if you try hard enough, one day you may understand them."

Danute's eyes grew large, and she took the crystal that Rigel handed her. She brought it to her lips, covering it slyly with her hand and whispering to it, her eyes glinting, and then lowered her hand and said more loudly, "Now don't tell Darius." Dimples marked her cheeks as she laughed and handed the crystal to Darius.

Darius held it to his ear but heard nothing. He let it rest on his open palm and waited to see what he could feel. He thought he felt the gaiety of Danute radiating off it, as though it were laughing with her.

A night bird woke up Torr, its eerie call thrusting him from his dream into the cold Scrid night. The camp was quiet. The hunters had not yet returned. Torr rose from his bear hides and approached the slab. Most people slept in the shelter of the lean-tos, except for the single young men who slept under the trees as he did, and most of them were out hunting. No one stirred. Two guards toured the perimeter of the camp, but they ignored him. They were used to him staying up at night, waiting for the hunters to return. The bright starry sky met the line of jagged treetops that surrounded the hamlet.

Torr climbed onto the large slab and gazed up at the sky. The guards did not bother him—he had rested there that morning and Jorimar had not objected. The wolf knife glinted at him from the small slab nearby, catching the low flames of the dying fire on the metal pommel. Torr felt a longing for the wolf, as though it were a close friend he was prevented from being with. The Memory Keeper shone a cloudy green, and the Destroyer and the Bear crystal looked at home among the light crystals.

Danute had spoken to a crystal in jest, but it gave Torr an idea. He slid to the ground and crept over to the smaller slab. The wolf stared up at him from the metal pommel, seated in his front-facing pose, his ears alert. Torr whispered softly to the crystals, feeling silly and a bit crazy.

"Memory Keeper, can you please tell the light crystals that you belong to me, and it's okay if I take you back?" The green double-pyramid sat on the slab, inert. Torr didn't know what he'd expected, but he had expected something. "Destroyer, Bear crystal, I want to take you back. Please tell the light crystals they can let my hand through."

He steeled his nerves, warily moved his hand between two guard crystals, and was struck with a flash of light that caused him to jerk his hand back. A red welt appeared on his fingers. He cursed under his breath and went in search of cold water.

———————)————————

The next day, the chanting began again, led by Salima. Two dozen swaying, stomping Scrid warriors encircled the slab and danced and drummed as though in a trance. After a long while, in a flash of blinding light, Vaka appeared on the slab and fell to his knees.

Salima and Jorimar helped the wizard down off the slab as the drumming came to a thunderous halt.

The three elders conferred, then Jorimar turned to Torr.

"*Marglod Sky,*" Jorimar said, making a hand gesture through the air. "No find."

"No find?" Torr asked, part relieved and part scared.

"Hide," Jorimar said, covering his head with his hands in pantomime.

"Ah," Torr said. "Hiding from Vaka, no doubt. Smart girl." Torr grinned smugly at Jorimar. She was not stupid. After Torr had gone missing and their friends killed, the Fen would be locked down like a fortress. Cassidy had probably retreated to her tent again, using her crystal ball to surveille the surroundings, and perhaps search for him.

Jorimar returned a confused frown.

"She doesn't want to be a prisoner, Jorimar," Torr explained, but the Scrid's face scrunched up with the effort to understand his words. Torr chided himself once again for trading away the garnet. Torr shrugged and lifted his palms at the Scrid in a gesture of helplessness. "Sorry, Jorimar. But I can't help you from here. Send me back to Peary, and maybe we can work something out."

Jorimar shook his head and turned back to Vaka and Salima.

47

THE JADENS

Cassidy raised herself onto her hands and knees and vomited into a bucket. When there was nothing left to throw up, a woman with long dark hair dabbed at Cassidy's mouth with a towel and offered her a cup of water. Cassidy gratefully drank a few mouthfuls, then curled up on the floor and sank into a dreamless slumber.

Cassidy awoke to the sound of a bell. She was lying on a hard stone floor, her head throbbing. She propped herself up on one elbow and peered around in the murky darkness. The large stone chamber was lit only by a square of red glowing coils and a single flickering candle that moved slowly through the blackness. Rustles and soft complaints murmured around her. Cassidy tried to remember where she was. It felt like a dream, but the stone beneath her was real, covered by a thin rug of roughly woven wool. She was covered in the same scratchy wool as the floor rug, which hung heavily from her shoulders in a long poncho-like cloak that was stitched up the sides and had deep side pockets. Underneath the woolen cloak, she was clothed in a silk robe over thin woolen undergarments. On her head was a scratchy woolen hat, and she wore thick woolen booties with flat leather soles. She sat upright as more candles sputtered to life. Soon, Cassidy could make out rows of women on sleeping rugs, sitting up and rubbing their eyes blearily or rolling away from the light to steal a few more winks of sleep.

Knowledge of her surroundings came back to Cassidy bit by bit. The roving candle was held by Agapantha, a large rotund woman with graying blond hair that hung in curls below a funny pointed hat of the same rough-spun wool as her multi-colored cloak. In her other hand, Agapantha swung a large brass bell, which sent sharp tones reverberating throughout the cave. Agapantha lumbered heavily along the rows and nudged slumbering women with her toe.

Their group of women was housed in the jade cave, named for the cave's low hanging rock ceiling, which was streaked with mineral veins of a lustrous green. They called themselves the Jadens, and there were twenty of them. Twenty-one, now. Several other groups of women lived in similar caves that branched off a main tunnel.

Cassidy's sleeping rug was in the center of the rows of women. To one side of her was Carmen, and to the other side was Prissa. Yesterday, they had mined ice. Cassidy opened her hands, revealing calloused palms from swinging a pickaxe and wielding a chisel and hammer. It was slow, hard work. Today, they would be chipping away at a stone tunnel Mother Gabira wanted widened.

"I don't want to work today," Cassidy muttered. Her back and legs were sore, and she was always cold down in the tunnels.

"Stop complaining," Prissa said crossly, sitting up. The sixteen-year-old's short blond hair was mussed, but her hard gray eyes were wide awake. "Ice duty provides us water. You should be thankful Mother Gabira shelters us."

Cassidy turned and met Carmen's dark brown eyes. Carmen's full mouth turned up in an exasperated grin, sharing Cassidy's sentiment. "Don't pay any attention to Prissa," Carmen told Cassidy. "She's just sore you were put between us so she can't elbow me in the night any longer."

Prissa's pinched face tightened further with annoyance. Cassidy stood up and walked to the sitting area at the side of the cave where the electric space heater cast waves of heat from its red coils. The sitting area was marked by several small rugs scattered across the stone floor and a half-dozen large kilim-covered cushions woven in patterns of blue dancing stags. An electric teakettle sat atop a square chunk of rock, which was table height and served as a counter. Beside the rock slab stood a large wooden water barrel. A metal box hanging from the wall powered the electric devices, which were snaked together by black and red cords. Cassidy sat on a pillow, waiting for the water to heat up for tea.

Agapantha shuffled over to the rock slab, set the candle in its holder, and slumped heavily into her stone chair. "Wake up, my Jadens," she called out, ringing her bell again.

Cassidy covered her ears, her head pounding.

Prissa paced the rows, giving laggards a sharp kick in the legs to rouse them. No one seemed anxious to start another day of chiseling rock.

Cassidy wondered how long she'd been a Jaden. It could have been days, or weeks, or even months. She had no wristwatch, and the hours blended together in an endless cycle of working and sleeping in the perpetual darkness of the caves. She drew her knees up to her chest inside the warm cloak and wrapped her arms around them. Carmen came over and sat next to her, and Cassidy whispered, "I can't remember anything." They had the same conversation every morning. Neither of them could remember how they had gotten into Mother Gabira's cave. They had vowed to try to remember in their dreams. "I still don't know where I came from," Cassidy said under her breath.

Carmen leaned in close to her. "Me neither. Every time I almost remember, I get the worst headache."

"Me too!" whispered Cassidy, raising her hand to her throbbing head. "Is that what is causing my headaches? Trying to remember?"

Carmen nodded. "I think so. Whenever I forget about it, the headaches go away."

Cassidy frowned and vowed not to forget. She had come from somewhere. There had to be something before her first day at Mother Gabira's, and she had to remember what it was. She was almost certain Mother Gabira was not her true mother, but she could not remember who her real mother was. A stab of pain lanced through her temple, and she winced, pressing her hand to her head.

The water finally boiled, and Cassidy and Carmen prepared tea, and then served themselves a small portion of cold rice left over from the night before. After eating the meager breakfast, they went to the latrine, which was a large cave with a long pit in the floor and several mounds of decomposing refuse piled in the back, covered with a thin layer of lye to try and mask the smell. Another group of women was leaving when they arrived.

"Agate Sisters," Carmen whispered to her. "Their cave is dark and cold." Cassidy waved at a couple of them, glad she had been placed with the Jadens.

Back in the jade cave, Cassidy left with Carmen, Prissa, and the others for the caverns. Cassidy rubbed at the calluses on her palms as she walked. Stone was actually easier to chisel than ice. Once she understood the matrix of the stone, she could work with it to knock sections loose, whereas the ice seemed to be one solid mass that required brute force to break.

It took a long time to make their way down the steep, winding tunnels. Stairs were carved into some of the steeper sections, and other passageways were strewn with piles of rubble that Cassidy carefully climbed over. On their backs they each carried a large basket fitted with wide leather straps that hung from their foreheads and across their shoulders. The air grew colder, and Cassidy pulled down her hat's ear flaps and tied the red braided yarn under her chin.

They finally arrived at their assigned spot. They were making a tunnel that followed a wide vein of dark yellow rock. The vein angled down, making the tunnel gradually descend, but that's what Mother Gabira wanted. It didn't make any sense to Cassidy, but she did as she was told. Another thing that didn't make sense was why the gray rock surrounding the vein could be left in a pile, while the chunks of yellow rock needed to go into the baskets and carried all the way back up top.

Cassidy shuffled to the pile of stiff leather gloves and slipped on a pair. Next she donned a pair of scuffed goggles, chose a medium-sized hammer and chisel set, and then set to work next to Carmen, removing chunks of gray rock from the wall to expose more of the yellow rock. Prissa was nearby, swinging at a section of the yellow wall with a heavy pickaxe, while another Jaden broke the yellow rock into smaller pieces once it was on the ground. More of their group worked farther down the passageway where another vein of the ochre-colored rock had been found.

Cassidy straightened and stretched her sore back and shoulders. She caught Prissa's stern glare and went back to work. When they had a good-sized mound of yellow rock, Cassidy filled her basket and followed the others up the long winding passageway to a large cave where another group of women was working.

Cassidy deposited her load onto a pile. She then placed some of the rocks into one of the short wide metal pipes that stood upright in a row. Cassidy stood on the base plate of the pipe, holding it steady with her feet, and grabbed the handle of the crushing rod and pounded at the rocks. When the pieces were small enough, she dumped them in front of one of the women sitting on the ground around bowl-like depressions in the stone floor, where the women ground the small chunks with metal rods until they were reduced to a yellow powder.

Along the wall stood buckets of powder, waiting for Giselle and Daleelah to come with their wagon to cart them away.

Cassidy and her fellow Jadens crushed rocks until their backs and shoulders were burning, and then descended to the yellow vein and repeated the process.

"Why are we mining the yellow rock?" she asked as she filled her basket. "What's in it?"

"It's none of our business," Prissa retorted. "It's Mother Gabira's business."

Carmen shrugged. "Iron? Copper? Gold?"

"It's not very shiny," Cassidy said, turning a chunk of the reddish-gold rock in her hand and bringing a candle closer to get a better look.

"Whatever it is," Prissa said haughtily, "it helps Mother Gabira feed us."

Cassidy tossed the rock into her basket and bent down for more.

After working all day, they finally returned to the jade cave. Cassidy's headache had subsided, reminding her that she hadn't spent any time trying to unearth memories of who she was.

She took a candle and went to her bed, where she sat cross-legged and flipped through the red notebook in her lap. A purple satin sack filled with herbs sat by her side. Mother Gabira and Sisters Giselle and Daleelah had given her these books and herbs so that she could help take care of the Jadens. She paged slowly through the notebook. It felt so familiar. A pounding ache racked her skull. She ignored it and turned to a random page and read.

Peppermint – Steep a large pinch of mashed leaves for ten minutes in a cup of hot water. Relieves cramping, coughing, and muscle pain.

Cassidy searched in the purple bag and found a paper bag labeled "Peppermint." She opened the bag and breathed in the intoxicating fragrance, took a pinch of the crushed green leaves and placed them on her tongue, and then resealed the bag. The leaves were sharp and pungent on her tongue and reminded her of ... something. Turning the pages of the book, she came upon more entries.

Valerian – Place one teaspoon of dried root in a cup of hot water. Cover and let sit for one hour. Relieves stress, migraines, stomach cramps, and insomnia.

Yarrow – Place two pinches of flowers in hot water for fifteen minutes. Relieves colds, headaches, and cramps.

Chamomile – Pour boiling water over the flowers and steep for five minutes. Reduces anxiety, pain, inflammation, and insomnia.

Cassidy climbed to her feet and took two paper bags of herbs to the counter: peppermint and chamomile. She reached down into the open wooden barrel, dipping the ladle into the few inches of water remaining at the bottom, and filled the kettle. The barrel was replaced each day and was to sustain the twenty-one Jadens. Each person was allotted twelve ladlefuls a day, which they carried in waterskins, and it was closely monitored by everyone. If anyone was caught sneaking more than their share, their hands were tied behind their backs for a week, except when they were working in the mine. Or so Prissa had told her. Every night, a bit extra remained in the bottom of the barrel, which they split, or was given to anyone who was sick or had their period. Ever since Cassidy had arrived with the herbs, they had all agreed that letting Cassidy make tea for them to share was the best use of the extra water.

Cassidy turned the teakettle on and waited for the water to boil, turning it off as soon as the loud roiling noise quieted to boiling and steam issued from the mouth. She poured the water into a bowl where she had placed a large pinch each of the peppermint leaves and chamomile flowers. There was not an endless supply of herbs and she wanted to make them last, while at the same time making sure the tea had flavor. She leaned her head over the bowl and breathed in the fragrant steam as the herbs steeped. Carmen leaned in next to her, enjoying the aroma.

Carmen pulled back her long black hair and the red braids of her hat before they fell into the steaming water. "Peppermint today?" Carmen asked. Cassidy nodded. "And what else? What are those little white flowers? They're so beautiful."

"Chamomile," Cassidy said, tugging playfully on the red braid of Carmen's hat. "It's soothing, so you won't cry in your sleep tonight."

Carmen gave Cassidy a crooked smile. "I can't help it if I have nightmares," Carmen said.

Cassidy had been having nightmares too. Usually, she was lost in crystal caves and endless tunnels. Last night she had dreamed of the flowing script in the red herb notebook. The careful, cursive writing had come alive and followed her off the page and chased her as she ran, frightened, down dark winding tunnels. The writing had wrapped around her forehead and turned her to look into the eyes of a beautiful woman with almond-shaped green eyes and billowing black hair. She looked so familiar, yet Cassidy couldn't place the face. Staring into the woman's eyes, she got the same kind of deep ache in her heart that she got whenever she read the herb descriptions written in the flowing handwriting. The ache felt like homesickness, but she didn't know what for.

Cassidy shook off the memory of the dream and tried to stave off a pounding headache, turning her bracelet distractedly around her wrist as she waited for the tea to steep. The bracelet was made of braided red, blue, and green embroidery threads, and hanging off the knot were two red beads that she liked to rub.

"Where did you get that?" Carmen asked, as she did every day.

Cassidy shrugged. "I still don't remember." The bracelet made her sad, but she didn't know why. Carmen wore a necklace made from multi-colored thread in an intricate weave, with glass beads of various colors woven into it. It was a short necklace tied tight against her throat like a choker, and hanging in the little hollow at her throat where her collarbones met was a small silver pendant in the shape of an upside-down hand with an eye etched into its palm. Carmen didn't know where she'd gotten the necklace either, but it made her heartsick as well. Carmen said she hoped that if Cassidy could remember where she'd gotten the bracelet then it would help Carmen remember where she'd gotten the necklace.

Cassidy ladled a small portion of tea into each of the Jadens' personal ceramic drinking mugs, each mug glazed with a unique pattern. Everyone came to fetch theirs and returned to their sleeping rugs to nurse the few tablespoons of tea. Afterwards, everyone lay down on their rugs, wrapped in their cloaks. The last candle was extinguished and the room plunged into darkness, except for the faint red glow cast by the heater, which reflected a dull orange off the prone bodies lined up in neat rows across the cave floor. Cassidy fell asleep rubbing the two red beads between her fingertips.

48

───────── ☽ ─────────

MEMORY KEEPER

That night, the stars were bright. Jorimar pointed out a constellation that had risen above the horizon. The stars formed a V, as though they were a skein of migrating geese.

"Orr," Jorimar said, tracing a V in the air, and Torr committed the word to memory.

The drummers gathered in a large circle around the fire. Jorimar pointed at the stars again, and Torr surmised it was some sort of ritual or prayer to the stars, reminding him of the Star Seekers in Shasta who gathered in drum circles in an attempt to communicate with the Star People.

Torr sat in the outer ring of young teenagers, each of the youngsters grabbing a pair of sticks to strike a steady background beat. Torr was older than the young men and women he sat with but was relegated to the back row, as though sent to the kid's table at Thanksgiving dinner. He didn't mind. The teenagers were good-spirited—always pulling pranks on the adults, and, along with Frija, watched over Torr with concerned regard.

Vaka launched the drum cadence, and shivers ran up Torr's arms. The rhythm was familiar. An old song speaking to him. More shivers lifted the hairs on the nape of his neck.

It was the cadence from Torr's dream of the drum circle on Turya. The same pattern but stripped down. Torr listened carefully and discerned six of the twelve parts. Two of the rhythms were not quite right, interrupting the enchanting flow he had felt in the stone pit on Turya. When the song ended, Torr hopped to his feet and walked over to the pair of Scrids who had beat out one of the wrong cadences.

Everyone frowned at him, but he ignored their glares and knelt down on the dirt.

"It goes like this," Torr said. He put down his sticks and tapped out the rhythm that the old Turyan drummer had taught him, striking the drumhead with his hands.

The two Scrids stared at him, and then followed his pattern, practicing Torr's variation.

"And you," Torr said, moving over to the pair with the other incorrect cadence. "Like this."

He tapped out the slightly different pattern, and the pair took it up. The others joined in, and the larger cadence flowed in an uninterrupted current. The drummers swayed back and forth, their faces lifting to the stars in ecstasy.

When the song concluded, Vaka and Salima walked over to him, looking him up and down. They spoke in their own language, and the circle of Scrids murmured in agreement.

"Mangarm," Jorimar said, his eyes aglow.

"Yes, I am Moon Wolf," Torr said. "I thought you knew that."

If any of the Scrids had harbored doubts about who he was, those reservations were gone now. The entire village gazed upon him, their amber eyes glowing.

"There are more parts," Torr said, waving his hands to the drummers. "But I can't remember them."

Jorimar squinted, trying to understand.

"Maybe," Torr said, pondering, "if you let me get my Memory Keeper, perhaps it will help me recall."

Jorimar did not understand his words but followed him to the slab. Torr pointed at the fluorite octahedron. "I need that," Torr said, lifting his eyebrows at Jorimar.

Jorimar frowned and consulted with Vaka and Salima. After a heated discussion, Salima closed her eyes and spoke softly, waving her hands through the air. The guard crystals grew dimmer, and Salima reached inside the circle of sentinels without a problem, retrieved the green crystal, and handed it to Torr.

Torr grinned and gave her a small bow.

"Thank you," Torr said, closing his fingers around the warm crystal.

"Tanka oo," Salima repeated, grinning back at him. She closed her eyes and waved her hands again, and after a few moments the guard crystals glowed brightly, sealing the protective circle around his belongings.

Torr frowned at her. Those were his things.

She met his eyes. "Mangarm," she said, as though that explained everything.

"Yeah, yeah," he muttered, and walked over to the ring of drummers.

"Now," Torr said, dropping to his knees and sitting back on his heels, as the Turyan drummers had. "Let me borrow your drum," Torr said to one of the men in the drum circle. He gestured at the Scrid until he understood.

The man exchanged glances with Vaka, then passed the drum to Torr.

Torr slid the fluorite crystal into his inside vest pocket, then closed his eyes. He didn't know if this would work, but if Darius could store his memories in the crystal, then Torr should be able to store his own memories, too. Right? But could he retrieve them? He calmed his mind, breathing evenly until empty spaces opened up between his thoughts.

The drum circle on Turya filled his vision. The elderly Turyan knelt across from him, his skin wrinkling in a wide toothless smile, nodding with encouragement as Torr imitated the newest rhythm.

Torr tapped it out on the drum, and he vaguely heard the Scrids tapping along with him. He opened his eyes, and the Scrids continued the beat. Torr nodded. They practiced it, adding in the original six cadences. After a time, Torr held up his hand for them to stop. He calmed his mind again until he returned to the Turyan drum pit, and then sought out the next rhythm. The Scrids tapped along with him.

They did this a total of six times, until Torr had transferred the knowledge of all the remaining drum cadences. Then he sat back and listened as the Scrids slowly added one rhythm to the next, old and new, until all twelve cadences were interwoven into one celestial symphony.

————————)————————

Darius lay on the ground in the cold dark cell, wondering at the irony of the Star Child dying in a dungeon. Such a glorious ending to a blessed life, he thought dourly. It was the warring Ilian and Cephean priests who had destroyed the Star Globe, but they blamed the Star Children to save their own purulent hides. Darius and Danute were no use to them after the destruction of the portal to Turya, so who better to blame than the twins?

Darius rolled onto his scabbed back, which was healing slowly from the last flaying they had inflicted on him, though a fever still raged in his starving body. The lock rattled at the door, but Darius did not bother to respond. Nothing they could do to him would make him reveal Danute's escape route. He would die with the knowledge. But it was only the guard leaving a small cup of water for him. The lock clicked shut again, and Darius crawled to the sound and carefully felt the hard ground for the cup, grateful at least that they had stopped shackling him a few weeks ago, after he could barely stand from a particularly brutal beating. He drank the tepid water in one long draught. It was never enough. He crawled to a wall and licked at the water that dripped down in some places. He sat back on his heels and considered something that had been percolating in his mind for days.

His spirit wolf appeared every dawn when a faint light filtered in through the chink high in the stone wall. The wolf would emerge from a dark corner and dig at the ground in front of the cell door, and then whimper and claw at the door itself. Darius had tried digging alongside him, scraping his fingernails into the hard dirt, only to expose a subfloor of solid rock. He had been beaten severely for trying to dig his way out.

But the door—it was metal. The lock was metal. Danute had told him of her priestess's training where she had learned to melt through metal with her mind. He had never learned the technique himself, but if it were possible ...

Metal was nothing more than melted ore, which had a crystalline structure, if he understood correctly from the swordsmith. Darius knew how to deal with crystals. When he had one, that was. Of course his Destroyer had been confiscated, along with all his other possessions. He thought back on how he had exploded the diamond, which had led to Zinz's death. He winced again at the recollection, still feeling a twinge of guilt at the satisfaction the memory brought him. He had used the Destroyer to target the diamond, but as he had learned from Rigel, crystals were merely a focusing tool to amplify his intention.

He still had his intention. That was one thing the priests could not steal from him.

Darius stood on weak legs, wavering until he maintained his balance. He faced the door in the darkness, knowing from memory the location of the lock on the exterior of the door, having seen it many times while being dragged back to the cell after a torture session. It was a simple padlock that hooked over flat metal hasps. The hasps were not as thick as the padlock itself. Darius gazed towards the spot on the other side of the closed door, envisioning the metal, imagining he was directing the Destroyer at it. He pointed his hand at his target and breathed deeply. He focused his thoughts, pulling in the grounding energy from the rock floor and the enlivening energy from the air—two sources of power the priests could not block. Red light and white light mixed together in his heart, and when it was full, he shot out a stream of purple light from his fingertips. He heard a thin creaking, but nothing more. He inhaled and relaxed, gathering the energy again. He wondered if the guard could see the purple light, but whenever he had listened, the guard's footsteps had always faded away. Why guard the door in a dank pit when he could sit at the top of the stairs in the corridor by the window?

Darius breathed in and tried again, shooting another stream of light. Nothing. He was proud of himself, at least, for harnessing any energy at all in his weakened state.

"The first stage in learning to melt or cut through metal," Danute had said, the conversation echoing in his head, "is to ask permission of the crystal essences."

Darius had laughed. "Yeah, right. Oh Crystal Being, please allow me to strike you asunder," Darius said.

"Smart-ass," she said. "It's a thing of respect. Crystals are sentient beings."

"If you say so," Darius said, though Rigel had said the same thing, so he did not argue.

Darius came back to himself, trapped in his tomb, and tried again. "Oh crystal metal being," he said aloud, not caring if he sounded crazy.

"Let me free you from the bonds of the stupid metal shape the black-smith hammered you into, so that you can commune with the ground again, from whence you came."

Danute would have chided him for being sarcastic, if she were here. But he was serious. Why would a crystal being want to be stuck attached to a door, holding a lock? What a miserable existence.

Darius reached out with his senses and felt himself merge with the metal clasps, and then pointed his fingers and shot purple light through them.

A loud thunk came from the other side of the door—the heavy padlock landing on the ground. Darius opened his eyes and staggered to the door. He pressed his ear to the cold metal. Could it be? No sounds of the guard reached his ears. He hesitantly pulled at the door handle, and slowly the door creaked open. A tickle on his bare legs drew his hand downward, and he felt the bristly ruff of his wolf.

"Coming with me?" Darius asked softly. "This could be the final moments of my life. Thank you for being my faithful companion all this time."

Darius was filled with a strange calm. It felt infinitely better to walk into the jaws of death than to die from torture and starvation. They would have to kill him this time, before he would let them drag him back into this cell. He would fight and force the guard to strike him down with his axe.

Darius crept through the doorway into the dimly lit corridor, leaning against the stone wall for support. He slowly made his way up the stone steps and peeked out the open doorway at the top, squinting against the light.

The corridor was empty. A waterskin and book sat on the guard's stool under the window. Upon the stone window ledge sat his Memory Keeper, the green octahedron catching the light and glowing from within. Darius grabbed it and clutched it to his chest. "Ah, my beauty," he said.

Next, Darius grabbed the waterskin and drained it until his belly was taut, then considered his next move. He had always been dragged down the corridor to the left, where light shone from a series of windows. The wolf's shadow ranged down the corridor to the right. And so Darius went right, into the darker corridor towards he knew not where. He snuck along the vacant hallway with his wolf in the lead, and then down a narrow staircase and along a servant's corridor. This part of the castle complex was removed from everything else. No one wanted to publicize that the Star Child was being held prisoner by the Star Priests, even if they had painted him as a traitor—he knew for a fact that some of the common people hated the priests as much as he did.

A door stood ajar. Darius pushed it open and peeked inside. It was a storage room. He slipped inside to take a breath and calm his pounding heart. He sat on a bench and sucked in lungfuls of fresh air. Servants' clothing hung from hooks overhead. He looked down at his naked body, his ribs prominent underneath his emaciated flesh, and puckered scars crisscrossing his thighs and torso. He found a uniform that fit him: dark-blue trousers and a matching jacket. He slipped the Memory Keeper into a pocket, and then fumbled with the buttons, his fingers twisted from where they had been broken. He pulled on a pair of worn leather boots, and then found a servant's cap, pulling it down over his forehead. There were several dark-skinned Delosian mountain slaves among the servants, and Darius hoped no one would give him a second look. He glanced at the wolf, who was staring up at him with yellow eyes.

"What do you think, wolf? Ready to go?"

The wolf blinked at him.

"I agree. Let's be off," Darius said.

He grabbed a broom and left the storage room, using the broom as a walking stick and straightening his posture as best he could, and shuffled down the hallway as though he belonged there.

———————————)———————————

Torr awoke from his dream. He was Darius. Darius was him. He sighed and clutched the Memory Keeper. "I guess the story had a happy ending, of sorts," he said to the crystal. "At least I hope it did. At least now I know he didn't die in the explosion of the Star Globe."

First light brightened the sky with a pale glow. A group of women and children with baskets on their heads filed off silently towards the river. The Gray Feather men were sleeping soundly, along with the pair of guards whose routine was to stand watch while the rest of the men were out hunting and then creep into their huts to sleep at dawn when the women and children rose.

Torr took advantage of the quiet early hours and climbed out of bed, grabbed a bundle of clean clothes, and headed to the latrine. He then took a quick dip in the men's frigid swimming hole, submerging his head, and then treading water for a few seconds until the icy cold drove him shivering to the shore. Sounds of the women and children splashing and laughing upriver drifted through the trees. He toweled himself dry with a square of chamois cloth, then clipped on his rune belt and put on the new set of clothing Osma and Frija had made for him: animal skin pants and tunic, his very own bear skin vest, and hunter's boots lined with fur but without fringes or bells. The clothing was soft and comfortable. He gathered his dirty clothes and made his way back to the village.

Torr ate a quick breakfast by himself, then wandered over to the small stone slab. The wolf knife and Bear crystal, along with his other two knives and the Destroyer, sat inside the circle of glowing guard crystals.

The wolf pommel was face up, and the metal image of the wolf sat upright and stared at him with glowing gold eyes.

"Hello, Brother Wolf," Torr said. "I would like to free you from your trap. Would you like that?"

The wolf continued staring at him.

"I thought so," Torr said, and regarded the guard crystals, which glowed and pulsated, as though listening to the conversation.

Torr considered that the metal in the blade and pommel were of crystalline steel. Perhaps the wolf in its metal form could talk with the guard crystals.

"Brother Wolf," he said. "Talk to the light crystals. Convince them to let me retrieve you and the other knives and crystals, so they won't burn me, okay?"

The wolf stared at him, ears alert.

Torr furrowed his brow and examined the six glowing crystals. "Hey," he said quietly to them, feeling silly. "Please let my hand through without burning me."

The crystals pulsated back at him.

He closed his eyes, as Salima had done, and waved his hands through the air, repeating his plea. He opened his eyes, and the crystals were still pulsating.

Torr readied himself, thinking how stupid he was to subject his hand to crystal fire again. He inhaled and mustered the courage Darius had displayed. He concentrated and relaxed at the same time, drawing in grounding energy through his feet and quickening energy through the top of his head, combining them in his heart and letting the energy flow down his arm and into his hand. He peered through slitted eyes at his hand until he detected the faintest flicker of purple.

He extended his hand slowly, watching the light crystals warily as his fingers approached the space between them. His arm clenched as a glimmer of light appeared between the six crystals in a faint, glowing haze. He resisted the reflex to withdraw his hand and inched his fingers forward until they entered the light, which brightened and danced around his hand. He forced himself to hold still. The light was cool this time, not burning. His fingers darted into the circle and grabbed the hilt of the wolf knife and withdrew it. He grinned at the wolf in the pommel, who was howling at the moon. One by one he went in to retrieve the other knives and crystals.

He stashed them away with a feeling of triumph and wished he could show Salima what he had achieved. An idea occurred to him, and he reached for one of the guard crystals, wondering if he could take the six of them as well. He closed his fingers slowly around one of them, but before his grip could tighten, a jolt of pain shot up his arm. He let out a surprised gasp and drew back his hand. Apparently, the crystal did not want to go with him. He felt sheepish. It would have been stealing. He bowed his head to the six light crystals. "I'm sorry. Thank you," he said softly. He thought the crystals glowed a bit brighter in response, and a smile played across his lips.

Torr walked nonchalantly back to his bedroll. He was breathing quickly and concentrated on calming himself. He had not expected to succeed, but now that he had he didn't know what to do next. Jorimar would surely confiscate the knives and crystals as soon as he discovered them missing.

Torr's buoyant mood deflated, and he sat on his bedding, trying to devise a plan. He could force Vaka at knife-point to take him back to Peary. He shook his head, his mouth pulling down. No. The Scrid warriors would overpower him, and Vaka was too strong in magic to be forced to do anything. He wrapped his arms around his knees and gazed up at the pale sky through the tree branches.

Despite the wild beauty of Scridland, he missed Peary Dome. He didn't know when he'd started thinking of Peary as home. Except now it would be empty without Blaire. His mournful thoughts wandered to Raleigh, Roanoke, Hawk, Darla, Sky, and Thunder. A deeper, gnawing ache reminded him of Reina and Bobby and their Miramar squad-mates, and their unknown fates. And then there were his parents. Caden was a prisoner at a work camp, and probably would be for the rest of his life. But his mother, she was still free—he hoped. She should have reached the Shaman's Shield by now and would have either gotten through somehow or was still hiding out in the forest south of the barrier and living off the land.

He scanned the forest surrounding Gray Feather and imagined Blaire lurking in the morning dusk, watching over him. Two glinting spots, like eyes, caught his attention. He held still and stared but saw only trees. Surely his mind was playing tricks on him, or one of the Scrid men had gone into the woods to relieve himself. The other men were still asleep, snoring from their beds under the trees or inside their huts. Distant laughter drifted up from the river.

Torr stood and rested his hand on the pommel of the wolf knife. Two chips of reflected light appeared in the same spot as before, staring at him. They were definitely eyes, standing lower than a Scrid's. The hair rose on the back of his neck. What creature was watching him? Could it be a deer? Wild boar? A bear? Everyone used bear hides, but the hunters had never brought back one of the large beasts, nor had he encountered one in his wanderings. Torr's heart hammered in his chest as the eyes bored into him. He crouched low and tiptoed forward, curiosity driving him to see what was staring at him.

The form of a wolf took shape in the shadows. Torr stopped, crouching in silence. It was a large creature, the ruff of its neck full and magnificent, framing calm, golden eyes. Shivers ran up his arms. It was his wolf. *Brother Wolf.* His hand tightened around the hilt of his knife, which grew warm in his hand. He drew the blade from its sheath and glanced down at the pommel. The vortex side stared up at him, swirling slowly. Torr turned the pommel over, and the wolf was staring at him from the metal, standing as it was in real life. He looked up, and the wolf was still there in the shadows. It turned and trotted a few paces into the forest, and then stopped and turned to stare at Torr again.

Torr broke out in a sweat. He slid the blade back into its sheath and removed his hand slowly from the hilt. The wolf remained visible in the shadows, only dimmer than before, like a dark cloud with a head, four legs, and two glinting eyes. Torr gripped the knife again, and the form solidified. The wolf went another few paces and turned again, waiting for him.

Torr looked around the quiet camp. He'd adjusted to the rhythm of life here. In time, he would learn their ways and be accepted as one of them. He'd be allowed to go out on the hunts, and one day he would get over Blaire and marry, and breed a few fat, red-haired, laughing Scrid babies. His anger would fade into the past, and he would train with Vaka and become a powerful wizard and learn to travel the galaxy.

He returned his gaze to the wolf, who was waiting patiently. The thought of following the wolf filled him with fear. It was crazy to head away from the safety of Gray Feather and into the black forest, following an apparition. The scar under his cheekbone pulled tightly as he grimaced, trying to decide what to do. A few minutes ago, he had been afraid of being trapped here. Now, he was afraid to leave. He shook his head. He was a coward. But what if he left, and then Cassidy appeared with Vaka? Torr would be lost in the woods, and Cassidy would be trapped at Gray Feather by herself. But if he stayed, then they would both be prisoners.

He frowned at himself. Excuses. What kind of shaman's son was he? His mother had run to the hills by herself, with only a raven at her back, leaving Caden in the hands of the Tegs. What were the crystals and wolf knife good for if he was too scared to work with them—too afraid to explore the magic of the unknown? He gritted his teeth and returned to his bedding. He stood for a moment, considering what he was about to do. He took a breath and walked casually over to the lean-to that held the food supplies. Torr filled his waterskin from the stone cistern, then took handfuls of dried meat, fresh greens, and berries, and wrapped them in a large chamois cloth. He looked around and grabbed a coil of hand-braided rope and a small chunk of grayish-green flint, then left the storeroom. He returned to his bedding

under the tree, rolled the bundle of food and his Peary clothes in one
of the heavy bear hides, made a sling and shoulder straps with the rope,
and hung the whole thing across his back. He stepped behind the large
tree trunk and surveyed the forest.

Torr took a deep breath and skulked silently into the woods where
he had last seen Brother Wolf. He gripped the knife hilt anxiously,
searching for the glinting eyes and furry shape. Disappointment and
doubt crept in as his eyes cast desperately from empty shadow to empty
shadow. A brushing against his leg made him jump. Brother Wolf was
at his side and looked up at him with wide knowing eyes. Torr exhaled
with silent relief.

At its shoulders, the animal reached the height of Torr's hip. Torr
went to sink his fingers into the thick fur of the wolf's back, but in
so doing let go of the hilt. The form became a shadow that loped
out ahead of him. Torr followed, taking care to observe the ground
in front of him before stepping, so as not to snap a twig or crunch a
pine cone. He stole a glance over his shoulder. Gray Feather village was
already hidden by the dense forest, and no one was following him—he
normally slept late like the other men and went on his hikes after the
midday meal. No one would expect him to wander farther than the
latrine or swimming hole this early in the day.

He moved furtively through the shadows, unsheathing the knife
and carrying it in his hand so he could clearly see the ghost-like wolf
as it ranged in front of him. Soon, Torr found himself on one of the
Scrids' wide walking trails that connected Gray Feather to the settlement several miles downriver. Torr followed the shadowy figure, which
trotted several lengths in front of him. He picked up his pace, jogging
and feeling the weight of the bear hide bundle on his back. They crested
a low rise and descended down the other side. Torr relaxed, confident
he had passed beyond hearing range of the Scrids at Gray Feather.

The wolf kept up a steady pace, and soon turned off the main path
onto a narrower hunting trail that led into the hills. As the minutes
stretched on and Torr heard no shouts of alarm from Gray Feather, he
let himself think about what lay ahead. He had no idea what he was
doing or where the wolf was leading him. He stopped wondering and
focused instead on his breathing and the rhythm of his feet hitting the
ground. A shiver of excitement passed through him as he became more

confident that he'd escaped and was embarking on a new adventure guided by his spirit wolf.

This was how it should always be, he decided. He and his spirit guides would lead the way, not wizards or priests, or anyone else who wanted to steal his power. *I am Mangarm,* he told himself, *Moon Wolf of the Star Children, and the fate of the galaxy rests in my hands. Mine and Cassidy's, and no other.* Well, maybe Jasper had something to do with it, he acknowledged. Regardless, he would be a slave to no one. If he were to be trained, it would be on *his* terms. Otherwise, he'd figure it out on his own.

The sun rose above the hilltops and oblique rays filtered through tree limbs, casting shafts of golden light onto the trail in front of him. Torr lifted his face to a gentle breeze. The air was cool and crisp and smelled of pine. He smiled, and with the wolf knife in his hand, ran towards his fate.

49

RİDDY NİDRAZAM

Lines of script floated off the page and chased Cassidy down the dark passageways. She panted loudly, tripping on the uneven ground and crashing into the rough stone walls with her palms and elbows. The snaking cursive text caught up with her and wrapped around her wrist, twisting her around to face the flashing pen of a woman sitting at a kitchen table and bathed in sunshine streaming through a window with bright yellow curtains. The pen had a golden nib and black ink flowed through it. The ink itself flowed from a tree far away, across the ocean and beyond fields and mountains. The great gray tree bled black sap from a gash in its bark through a metal peg pounded into its trunk that made the ink *drip drip drip* into a bucket. *Sleep sleep sleep* said the drip drip drip.

"*Sleep to awaken,*" wrote the raven-haired woman with green eyes the color of the lichen growing on the gray bark as the ink flowed from the tree through the woman to the pen and onto the paper.

Gong gong gong rang the morning gong to wake Peary Dome from its nighttime curfew. Cassidy propped herself up on an elbow. "Torr!" she called out, gripped by a sudden panic, her clenched muscles jerking her violently awake. Shifting shapes and sounds of women awakening pulled Cassidy out of her slumber, and she remembered where she was and recited to herself, "*I am in the blessed shelter of Mother Gabira. I belong in the jade cave. I am a Jaden.*"

A match flamed from across the room as Agapantha lit a candle and set it on the stone counter. The Jaden's cave mother continued ringing her brass bell. The sharp sound filled the air as Agapantha hauled her obese self across the room, one heavy step at a time.

Carmen was lying on the rug next to Cassidy and looked up at her with bleary eyes. "Who's Torr?"

Cassidy blinked. "Torr?"

"Yeah, you yelled it out in your sleep."

Cassidy sat up and rubbed her eyes. She couldn't remember. She could remember something about a strange green-eyed woman who wrote in script that flowed with ink from a big tree. Script like the handwriting in the red herb notebook. She shook her head. It was so strange.

"Think! Who is Torr?" Carmen insisted, sitting up and grabbing Cassidy by the shoulder.

"I don't know," Cassidy said, shaking off Carmen's hand and dropping her forehead into her hands as a splitting headache sliced through her skull. "Ow," she moaned, rocking back and forth with her head in her hands.

The headache had still not subsided when it was time for the women to descend into the tunnels to work. She had not been able to hold down her morning's rice and tea, but spit it right back up, making a mess that Carmen and Prissa cleaned up. Agapantha clucked over her and told her she would have to stay behind today.

Cassidy curled into a ball on her rug after the women left, thankful for the silence. She begged Agapantha to extinguish the candles, which she did except for one. Agapantha, as the Jaden's cave mother, stayed in the room all day and took care of things. Cassidy pulled her hat down over her ears as Agapantha shuffled around the room, straightening the sleeping rugs with her foot. The large woman finally completed her circuit, then collapsed heavily into the great stone chair that looked as though it had been carved just for her. Cassidy rolled restlessly onto her other side.

"Can't sleep?" Agapantha called gently across the room.

"No," Cassidy moaned, sitting up and resting her head on her knees, searching for a position where her head did not feel like it was going to crack open.

"Shall I make you some tea?" Agapantha offered. "Maybe one of your herbs cures headaches. Look in your book."

"Okay," Cassidy mumbled. She took the red notebook from the satin bag but could not read a thing. The script was wavy and illegible in the faint, flickering candlelight. "I can't see with my headache. Everything is blurry," she whined to Agapantha. The woman waddled across the floor, took the book from Cassidy, and made her way back to her chair and candle to read.

Agapantha sang out in a cheerful voice, *"Riddy Nidrazam – The beautiful thing about this flower is the effect it has on sleep. Sleep becomes a tender place to rest your aching head and feet. The head nestles upon a soft pillow of dreams, and the feet float gently in the heavens, where all burdens will be brushed away by angels' feathers. Life sparkles fresh as when a cool rain washes dust from leaves beside a heavily traveled path, leaving green gems that glisten with morning's glory.* Ahh, that sounds divine," Agapantha said, sighing. She continued reading, *"One drop for calm. Two drops for repose. Three drops to cat nap. Four drops to sleep like a babe."*

Cassidy grimaced from the pain of her headache but took the purple sack and staggered over to Agapantha. She took a dancing stag pillow and sat at Agapantha's feet, then searched inside her sack and found a small brown bottle with a white label that read in flowing script, *"Rddhi Nidram Azam – Sleep to Awaken."* Cassidy's heart froze as the memory of the wild-haired woman in her dream came flooding back. *Sleep to Awaken.* Her head pounded.

Agapantha and Cassidy got their cups and split a ladle of water between them. Cassidy unscrewed the herb bottle's dropper and squeezed four drops into her own cup and four into Agapantha's. The woman's pudgy face screwed up into a pout. "Only four?" she complained.

Cassidy looked into Agapantha's blue eyes, which drooped downward at the outer corners. "Four drops to sleep like a babe," Cassidy reminded her.

"I am bigger than a babe," Agapantha complained, popping two hard candies into her mouth from the stash she kept in her pocket, not offering Cassidy any. "I always get double everything." The candies made a small mound on the side of her cheek.

Cassidy eyed the woman's bulging belly and stout legs, then added four more drops into Agapantha's cup. After helping Agapantha lift her trunk-like legs onto a stack of pillows and propping a pillow behind the woman's head, Cassidy returned to her sleeping rug and curled up to keep warm. She hoped the Riddy Nidrazam would work fast, before her head split in two.

———————————)———————————

Cassidy floated through a dark olive grove, flying through the air with the full moon shining brightly off gray leaves. She floated over a hill of scrub brush and to the valley beyond. Spread out before her was a silvery field of misshapen shadows. It took several moments for her to discern what she was looking at. It was a graveyard of felled tree limbs and trunks, reminding her of bleached bones, and stacks of branches with wilted leaves clumped like matted hair. The horror of it made her gasp. At the head of the moonlit field crouched three figures. Cassidy moved to them and hovered silently, unseen. One form was a weeping woman on her knees, her arms and forehead pressed against the ground.

"My trees," the woman sobbed, "My beloved trees." Two young teenaged girls huddled nervously at their mother's side as she wailed loudly. "Who would do this?"

"Shhh, Ami," the younger girl said anxiously, patting her back. "Hush, Ami, we must go back to the caves. The soldiers will hear you and come back. There's nothing we can do for the trees now. Come. Hurry!"

The woman labored to her feet. She was large, with round, bulging breasts that swung under her loose robe. The older girl sniffled with her mother and took her arm while the younger daughter led the way, stepping over the severed limbs. They disappeared into the shadows of a cave, and Cassidy flew behind them into the still blackness. The younger daughter lit a candle, sheltered the flame with her hand, and led her sister and mother down the sloping tunnel and through a series of small chambers. Families of crystals grew in clusters from fissures in the wall. Some crystals were clear, and others were a smoky quartz with veins of gray webs inside them. Orange specks glimmered within others, as though tiny ancient creatures had become trapped and were suspended in the matrix of the quartz.

Rustling noises were followed by tramping footsteps, and an acrid smell entered the chamber. The women froze. The girl blew out the candle, but orange light and black shadows played across uneven rock walls, and two men entered the far end of the chamber, each bearing flaming torches.

"Aha! I told you!" the man cried, his words slurred with drunkenness. "Women!"

The two men wore dark gray uniforms with blood-red emblems on their chests, high black shiny boots, and weapons hanging from their belts. They raised their torches and staggered drunkenly towards the women, who backed away and pressed against the cave wall while Cassidy hid up in the shadows.

A blood-curdling snarl ripped through the chamber as the mother grasped a crystal shaft and broke it from the wall with a deafening crack. The men hesitated and stepped backwards as the crazed woman leapt at them, yelling in her native tongue and flailing the crystal about the men's heads. Their hands went to their weapons too late as the woman crunched the crystal into the temple of one man and stabbed the other through the eye. The woman yanked the crystal from the oozing eye socket and sank it into the man's neck, blood spurting forth. Both men fell twitching to the ground, and the woman watched, glassy-eyed and shaking, as they bled out. When the men became still and pale, she gathered her daughters in her arms, and shadows danced from the torches where they sputtered on the ground.

—————————————)—————————————

Cassidy was a small child and stood on the hillside next to the slender woman with the raven hair and fiery green eyes.

"What do you do?" the woman asked the small scraggly bush that grew from the chalky ground. A single five-petaled white flower bobbed in the hot wind alongside round green seed pods that made the delicate stalks bend under their weight.

Ripples of heat rose from the dry dust, and a fine sheen clung to the flower. White fuzzy stamens waved and bowed over the shiny green pistil, from which a light green mist floated up, intoxicating the dancing pollen heads. The five white petals rose to surround the mating dance, like white taffeta skirts of a graceful ballerina. The ballerina flower spoke in the thin voice of the singing wind.

The black seeds of my soul are my gifts to you
Inebriated with alcohol, we bleed red blood that stays with you forever
Swimming in water, we leach yellow blood that disappears until fire
brings it forth
My blood of any color soothes pain of the body and spirit

"What are you called?" asked the slender woman who was swaying with the stalks, her hand clasping little Cassidy's, who swayed with her, mesmerized by the graceful ballerina.

That which I lift and send to freedom from the depths of your despair. I am called Black Sorrow.

"*Cassidy! Cassidy!*" The raspy whisper roused Cassidy from a sweet slumber. She opened her eyes to find Carmen shaking her by the shoulder.

Carmen's wide brown eyes stared down at her. "Oh, thank the stars," Carmen sighed as though a great burden had been lifted. She sat on the ground with a grunt, and Cassidy raised herself on one elbow. The jade cave was empty except for Agapantha, who sat snoring in her chair, her feet resting on a pile of pillows. The rugs of the other Jadens lay empty in tidy rows. Cassidy sat up and picked crusty sand from the corners of her eyes.

"Where is everyone?" she asked Carmen. Her tongue was pasty, and her mouth tasted sour.

"Working."

"Why didn't you wake me?" Cassidy asked. "Why is Agapantha sleeping?"

"I came back to get my hat, and you guys were out cold. You looked so strange, and Aggie was talking in her sleep. I've been here all day trying to wake you up." Carmen spoke in a hiss, as though afraid someone would hear her in the empty cave.

Cassidy stared at her, not understanding. "What do you mean? Aggie and I just took a nap. I had a headache." At least her head did not hurt anymore. She crawled stiffly to her feet and drank deeply from her water mug, and then joined Carmen, who was shaking Agapantha's shoulder and hissing in her ear, "*Agapantha!*"

Worry creased Carmen's brow as Cassidy lifted one of Agapantha's fleshy eyelids. The large woman's blue eye stared, unseeing. Cassidy placed her ear against the woman's nose and felt air tickle her cheek as Agapantha breathed in and out. She patted her cheek but got no response. Cassidy knelt next to the stone chair and clutched Agapantha's pudgy hand, praying she would wake up.

Their sister Jadens eventually filed wearily into the chamber. They each came to check on Agapantha and asked Cassidy and Carmen what had happened. Cassidy repeated her story of the sleeping herb as each woman frowned with concern. The Jadens gathered in small groups, glancing nervously at Agapantha.

"We just wanted to sleep," Cassidy explained to Prissa, who stood with her hands on her narrow hips. "I had a splitting headache," Cassidy said. "And you know how Agapantha has trouble sleeping."

Agapantha had a ritual. At night before bedtime, the Jadens took turns helping her with her pillows. Twice a night, her foot pillows fell over. Her surprised gasp would wake all the Jadens, and whoever's turn it was scrambled to gather the pillows and lift her heavy legs back onto them. But now her small round feet sat perched neatly on the pillows just as Cassidy had placed them hours ago. The woman had not moved. Cassidy scratched her head and met Prissa's gray eyes, which squinted meanly at her.

"It's you and your herbs," Prissa said, her voice thick with accusation. "If she doesn't wake up, it's your fault."

Cassidy's shoulders rose in a shrug, and she met Prissa's scathing glare. "Mother Gabira gave them to me, to be the Jadens' nurse," Cassidy said, and raised her nose in a challenge, daring Prissa to say anything against Mother Gabira.

Prissa crossed her arms over her flat chest. "Nurses *help*. Putting Agapantha to sleep forever is *not helpful.*"

"How do you know?" Cassidy demanded. "It was Aggie's idea—she wanted to take the herbs. She told me to give her double, like she always gets. Maybe she was exhausted."

The tall skinny teenager pursed her lips and snorted before turning on her heels and stalking off.

Cassidy rested her fingertips against Agapantha's wrist. She thought she felt a feathery pulse, but she couldn't be sure it wasn't her own. The confidence she'd displayed to Prissa faltered as she knelt next to the sleeping woman. *"Aggie!"* she whispered loudly, hoping to wake her before the sisters came with their dinner. *"Aggie!"*

Agapantha smiled but did not awaken. Cassidy sat back on her heels, relieved at least that Agapantha's face had moved and she didn't appear to be having nightmares.

Vague recollections of her own dreams nudged at her consciousness. Dreams that had felt real, as sometimes her dreams did. In one dream she had been flying through caves. She loved when she flew in dreams and wished she could fly in real life. But in this dream she had seen a shrieking woman who reminded her of a young Mother Gabira. She shuddered at the memory of the eerie and violent dream.

In another dream, which seemed bizarre now, but had seemed perfectly normal at the time, she had learned the name of a plant from its singing flower. What was it called? Ah, yes, *Black Sorrow.*

She went to her bedding where she'd left the purple sack and looked through the bags and bottles. She froze when she found a paper sack whose label read, *"Black Sorrow. For pain."* Tingles ran up and down her spine. With trembling fingers she took the red notebook and flipped through the pages, and found *Black Sorrow* written on a page in clear flowing script.

Black Sorrow – Soak seeds, leaves, and roots in water for two days. Drink the resulting juice to relieve pain, inflammation, and depression.

Her eyebrows knit together as she considered the obvious fact—her dream had revealed something real. Had that little girl been herself as a youngster? Had the dream been a memory retrieved by the strong sleeping herb? If so, who was the dark-haired woman with green eyes? Was it her mother? Pain seared through her temples, and she squeezed her eyes shut. *No, not another headache.* She breathed deeply and went to the sitting area, rummaged through the crates of supplies that sat against the wall, and found a spare cup. She took a pinch of dried Black Sorrow and placed it in the bottom of the cup, poured half a ladle of water into it, and set the mixture aside to soak.

Cassidy saw Prissa watching her.

"What?" Cassidy demanded.

"Is that the sleeping herb?" Prissa asked suspiciously.

"No. It's for pain. I still have a headache."

Prissa's mouth tightened, and she continued glaring suspiciously.

Cassidy sighed with irritation at nosy Prissa and the piercing pain in her temples. She returned to Agapantha, knelt by her side, and held the sleeping woman's hand. Carmen came to join her. They looked at each other and then at the sleeping mound of a woman, wondering wordlessly when she would wake up.

Giselle and Daleelah came with their food and glanced at Agapantha, who usually helped them unload the food. Carmen told them Agapantha was not feeling well and had just dozed off. Cassidy rushed to help with the bowls of rice and beans, then helped roll the full water barrel down the wagon ramp and load the empty one. She let her breath out with relief when the two sisters left without raising an alarm and without Prissa ratting on them.

Carmen and Cassidy shook Agapantha anxiously. There were bad smells coming from her. The woman's eyes suddenly popped open. She gave a great yawn and stretched like a contented cat. "Oh, my, what a lovely sleep I had," she purred. "And the dreams! I dreamt I was back home, walking through fields of flowers. And then I was eating lemon cake with pink icing and fresh raspberries, and chocolate rum ice cream drenched with hot caramel sauce. Yum!"

"Well, I'm glad you're finally awake," Cassidy said. "You slept all day."

"All day!" Agapantha exclaimed. "Oh, my, no wonder I feel so fabulous. Is dinner ready?" She stretched again with a loud fart, then dug into her pocket for two pieces of candy that disappeared into her mouth. She rose gingerly to her feet and shuffled towards the latrine.

Lemon cake with pink icing and fresh raspberries. Those things sounded so familiar, yet so foreign. Familiarity tugged at Cassidy's mind, but her head rebelled with a sharp pain. There must be another world out there. A world Mother Gabira was keeping from them. Embers of anger flared inside her. This must be some sort of prison. A dark dungeon that she must find her way out of. Her skull felt as though she'd been struck with a chisel and hammer. The sharp pain drove her to her knees.

"Cassidy," Carmen cried out with concern, kneeling at her side. "What's wrong?"

"We have to get out of here," she said hoarsely, and clutched at her pounding head.

50

RITE OF PASSAGE

Torr's elation at being free waned as the days passed one after another. Brother Wolf was always at the edge of his vision, urging him forward. When the wolf blended too much into the shadows, Torr held the hilt of the knife and the wolf solidified as it leapt through the forest, leading Torr ever deeper into the wilderness.

Torr was far beyond the land he had come to know while at Gray Feather and had not encountered any other Scrid settlements. From what Torr could tell, the Scrids only settled in the river valley. This land was high forest.

He was utterly and truly lost, and he fluctuated between hysterical panic and a morose desire to bury himself in a bed of pine needles and sleep forever. Exhausted by his emotions, he trotted behind the wolf, his leg muscles numb and his feet aching. Hunger was more urgent. He'd finished the last of the food from Gray Feather two days before. The wolf disappeared at night—Torr assumed to hunt—but never brought back anything to share. He wished he'd paid more attention to his mother when she'd tried to teach him about plants.

Torr scanned the forest as he followed the wolf, giving most of his attention to the rough path before him, which was strewn with rocks and branches. Most of what grew here were pine trees—monstrous giants twice the girth of the redwoods back home, and just as tall. He could carve out a hole in one of them and live comfortably. Some trees formed natural gaps between their roots where he sometimes huddled at night. There was very little undergrowth with the trees forming a solid canopy that trapped the sunlight. Torr knew that the tender new shoots at the tips of pine branches back home were edible, and he'd taken to eating them here, suffering no ill effects. Still, his gnawing hunger was never satiated.

Torr was not a trained hunter, and without a gun he was useless. He longed for his bow and arrows, or even his slingshot, and tried throwing rocks at birds and the furry creatures that lived in the trees, but they were sharp-eyed and flew or scurried off when he came near. Probably they could smell him—he stank. When it became dark and he stopped his trek for fear he would turn an ankle or break a leg, he would crouch for hours with a knife in hand, waiting for a hapless prey to wander across his path. None ever did.

During the day, he stopped and knelt by streams, looking for fish, but they darted beyond his reach. That morning he had found two small crustaceans under rocks in a little spring and had eaten them whole, shell and all, after snapping off their little heads and claws. He hadn't even waited for their legs to stop flailing before crunching them between his teeth. They were delicious, and he dreamed of catching more, but he could hear no trickling water nor see any of the telltale green growth that hugged the mountain brooks.

As he walked, he thought about a design for a trap. He could scrape out a pit and cover it with branches and pine boughs. He could make a spear. Yes, that was it. He would carve a wooden point or look for more flint and knap a spearhead. He should have taken more than the small chunk of flint he'd stolen for starting his fires at night, which he lit to stay warm and feel safe in the limitless wilderness. He should have asked Cassidy to make him an arrowhead. He should have insisted Jorimar teach him to hunt. He should have taken more seriously the Boy Scouts wilderness survival training and gone out on a week-long survival expedition. They should have given them survival training at Miramar instead of making them build roads and pour concrete for bunkers.

He sent a prayer up to the stars. *Golden stars, guide me in your shining light. Open the pathways to eternity. Golden stars, shine down upon me. Let your golden light wash over me. Lift me into your arms. Guide me to the heavens.*

He did not know how many more days of this he could tolerate. Hunger and exhaustion weighed upon his every step. He considered admitting defeat and begging the wolf to lead him back to Gray Feather, but sternly dismissed his thoughts and forced himself forward.

Sunlight filtered through the trees up ahead. That meant a clearing. Perhaps there would be a stream. He stopped to listen but did not hear the flowing of water. One thing he could be thankful for was that fresh water was abundant in these hills. He proceeded forward and entered the clearing, which was bathed in warm dappled sunlight. He stopped to catch his breath. He enjoyed hiking, but not from sunrise to sunset. His legs ached, and his feet were sore and blistered. He gazed around at the grass and shrubs, which competed for light. The wolf lay down at the edge of the clearing, seemingly glad for a rest. He knew the wolf would prefer to sleep during the day and travel at night, but Torr was no wolf.

It was an idyllic forest meadow, and Torr stretched out on the grass and gazed up at the cloudless sky. The sky was pale blue, and the sun was a small, white disc, which was too bright to look at. It had only rained a few times since he'd been on Scridland—thrashing downpours, which if they went on long enough penetrated the forest canopy and sent him and the rest of the young men of the tribe scurrying under the lean-tos, where they would sit together as the rain pelted the roofs and dripped through the bundled rushes. The sun was directly overhead now, and he closed his eyes.

He dozed off, enjoying the warmth of the sun. When he awoke, he saw that the wolf was sitting on its haunches, peering alertly into the forest. Torr rose silently to his knees, wondering if the wolf had found prey and if Torr would be able to share in its kill. His stomach growled loudly. He tried to see what Brother Wolf was looking at. The animal seemed to be staring at a brown tree trunk mottled with shadows and partially screened by a low-hanging bough. As Torr stared, a form began to take shape. It appeared to be a Scrid, and Torr held his breath, his heart pounding in his ears. The perfectly still, camouflaged figure stared back at him with wide amber eyes.

It was a female, and Torr let out his breath. He was confident he was days away from the river settlements, and that this female was not

part of any tribe that would hunt him down and return him to Gray
Feather. Caution quickly turned to relief. He would not die out here.

Vor varmr dagr, he called to her: the formal greeting to a woman,
which he understood to mean, *May the glorious sun warm your days.*

She peered at him curiously, no doubt wondering at his strange
accent, and replied with the greeting for a man, *Vedr visa veidr,*
meaning *May the wind guide your hunt.*

The young woman raised her eyebrows at him, the corners of her
mouth turning up. He realized he was grinning at her. She reminded
him a bit of Frija, with full breasts, a round face, thick tumbles of dark
red curls, and burnished-gold eyes. This woman seemed a bit older
than Frija, closer to Torr's age. She wore the usual animal skin pants
and tunic, and a bear hide vest. The beige and brown tones blended
perfectly with the tree trunk and shadows. He sat back on his heels,
not wanting to scare her off.

He was in the middle of the small clearing, and it occurred to him
that perhaps she had come here to enjoy the sunshine as he had. He
slowly rose and backed away, taking his bundle of belongings with him
and leaving the grassy knoll. He squatted down at the forest's edge to
see what she would do, without taking his eyes off her. She was his
lifeline; he could not let her disappear back into the forest. Perhaps she
had been trailing him and had let herself be seen, and if so, he hoped
that meant she would help him. Hunger and desperation roiled in his
belly. He forced himself to hold still and be patient.

She peered warily at the wolf, and Torr realized with surprise that
she could see it. The wolf turned away and circled through the trees,
coming to rest a few paces behind Torr, where it settled down onto all
fours, its pink tongue lolling out the side of its toothy mouth.

Torr and Brother Wolf watched as the Scrid woman padded silently
into the clearing. She kept one eye on them while she methodically
dug up the roots of a wide-leafed plant and plucked new shoots from
another, putting them into a leather sack. Torr salivated as he saw two
of the rabbit-like creatures tied to her sack, hanging by their hind legs
and still pliant. They had died recently, and he wondered if she had
trapped them. He watched as she pulled up pine seedlings by the roots
and tossed them aside. It occurred to Torr that she was keeping the
glade from becoming forested. Perhaps she was even cultivating the

plants for food, or at least protecting their delicate ecosystem. She then went to the edge of the clearing and pushed aside a screen of leaves to expose a small trap made of sticks that formed a cage. It was empty.

She let the leafy plants fall back over the trap, then slung her sack and rabbits over her shoulder. She lifted her eyes and met his gaze for a long moment, then stepped into the forest. Torr rose, with the wolf at his side, and quickly crossed the clearing to examine the trap and its trigger mechanism, which was a simple stick weighted with a small rock. Torr hurried after the Scrid as she strode silently through the woods. He and Brother Wolf trailed her by several paces—not so close as to alarm her, but not so far as to lose sight of her. He could tell by her posture that she was tracking him by the noises he made as he clumsily tramped through the forest after her. She was letting him follow.

After several minutes they came upon another clearing. Torr and the wolf watched from the shadows as she went through the same routine of harvesting roots and shoots, checking traps, and pulling up pine seedlings. This clearing had a white flowering plant, and she collected the blooms and added them to her sack.

She apparently had a network of glades, and Torr shadowed her as she stopped at a half-dozen. Torr watched as she slowly opened a sprung trap, grabbed the animal by the scruff of the neck, and with a deft twist, snapped its neck. She lashed it with the others and slung them over her shoulder. He wanted to start a fire and cook the rabbits right there but dared not approach her. His stomach ached, and he felt lightheaded with hunger. He hoped that she would eventually guide him to her home and feed him. Otherwise, now that he knew about the clearings and the traps, he could check the traps himself, though that would be stealing. No matter—he could inspect their construction more closely and make his own.

Her next stop was a small stream. She took off her boots and waded into a knee-high pool and stood still, crouching over the water and gazing into it. In one hand she held a long thin spear with a glinting stone fastened to its tip. Torr watched from the bank at a safe distance as she stood still for several minutes. She reminded him of a heron, graceful and poised to strike. Her spear darted out, and she jammed it into the streambed. The water churned, and she reached into it, pulling out a thrashing fish. It was the length of her forearm, blue with little feet that waved in the air as its whiskered mouth opened and closed. She glanced at Torr, and he gave her the Scrid hand signal that meant *good*—a wave of the pinky and thumb. She flashed him a smile and climbed to the bank several yards upstream from him and severed the fish's head in one sharp stroke of her knife. She cut off the little legs, then tied it by its tail with the rabbits.

Torr took the opportunity to kneel at the edge of the stream and search the submerged rocks for the little crustaceans and found one. He thought of giving it to her but was too hungry to be polite. He snapped off the head and claws and popped it into his mouth, chewing noisily. He found another and ate it as she eyed him curiously.

She forded the stream barefooted, then stopped on the far bank to put on her boots. Torr was afraid she would leave without him and hurried to remove his boots and roll up his pant legs, then splashed gracelessly through the water and quickly pulled on his boots on the other side. He thought he saw her laughing, but she turned her head and headed into the forest. The wolf was pacing back and forth on the opposite side of the stream, and Torr whistled softly for him. He stopped at the whistle and his ears pricked up. Torr hurried after the Scrid woman and heard the wolf splashing across the stream after him.

Not long after, Torr followed the woman into a large clearing. She glanced over her shoulder at him, then trotted over a path that cut through a field of scrubby green bushes and wild flowers. At the end of the clearing stood a collection of lean-tos. A knot of tension unwound inside Torr as he rested his hands on his knees and took in a great, shuddering breath. He said a quick prayer of thanks to the stars, then stood up to inspect the small settlement.

A middle-aged man stood at the border of light and shadow and watched Torr approach. The young woman ran up to him and spoke softly, looking back at Torr and the wolf. Torr could see that the man was able to see the wolf as well, and curiosity instead of fear lit the man's face. He had the typical thick, squat Scrid frame, and his long curly hair and beard were a mixture of auburn and white. Torr wondered if he was the girl's father.

Torr stopped in the middle of the clearing and called out the greeting, *Vedr visa veidr.*

The man returned the greeting and strode out to meet Torr. Torr stood his ground, wondering if the man would chest-butt him. Torr gave him the two-fisted salute to the chest, and the man returned the salute, but did not lunge to strike his chest against Torr's. Torr felt an instant sense of comfort with the man.

The Scrid regarded him with interest. Though Torr's beard had grown out during the time he had been on Scridland, he was too tall, lean, and fair to be mistaken for a Scrid.

The man spoke to Torr, and Torr struggled to decipher his speech, understanding a word here and there. Forest. Village. River.

Torr nodded and pointed east from where he had come. "Gray Feather," he said in Scridnu, *Sot Vaengr*. "Jorimar," he said, but the man only tilted his head. "Vaka," Torr said, and the man's eyes blazed with recognition.

"Vaka," the man repeated, his eyes flitting to the wolf.

Torr nodded and pulled the wolf knife slowly from his sheath, offering it to the man. The wolf on the pommel was sitting and looking straight ahead. There was no moon. The vortex spun slowly.

The man reached out and took the knife, looking from the pommel to the wolf, whose shadow stood among the field of flowers, and his cheeks grew red. He handed the knife back to Torr and struck his fists to his chest again. Torr knew that such a salute after an initial greeting was a sign of respect and recognition, and Torr returned the salute. Either this man was a wizard, or Torr had learned nothing of Scrids. The man motioned for him to follow, and Torr strode towards the lean-tos after him, while Brother Wolf faded into the forest.

───────── ⟩ ─────────

They fed him a stew of fish, root vegetables, and greens, and prepared him a bed in the shelter of a lean-to that blocked the wind. He slept the night through, got up to eat a meal of rabbit and wine, and then went back to bed until nightfall. He rose to eat again, relaxed by the fire until he found himself dozing off, and then went to his lean-to to sleep some more. By the following day, he felt revived in both body and soul. The calming presence of the two Scrids was like a salve, and their generous kindness made him feel welcome and safe.

He knew enough of the language to learn they were father and daughter and lived out here by themselves. The man was named Bjarg, and the young woman was Velspara. They were self-sufficient and lived well in the forest.

They conversed with a combination of words, gestures, and objects. Bjarg asked him where he was from, and Torr pointed to the sky, and when night fell, he searched the stars for Earth's sun. He had no idea where it would lie in the sky in relation to Scridland, which he knew was located somewhere near the Orion constellation, but Bjarg understood that Torr had come from another planet. Scridland did not have a moon, so Torr did not try to explain his exact origin. Coming from another star system across the galaxy was good enough.

Bjarg showed Torr a squarish crystal that looked similar to Torr's Bear crystal, but smaller. Bjarg motioned questioningly to the sky, then swirled his arm over his head in a circle. Torr understood the question and recited the chant that had brought him here.

Andi stiga
Fara lopt
Heimili heita
Gaumr far

Bjarg jumped up and down around the fire with excitement, his eyes gleaming as he gestured and spoke rapidly to Velspara, who nodded and listened intently, glancing at Torr as her father spoke. Bjarg's gestures told the story of a slab of cylindrical stone, and Torr nodded. *Grundhalda,* the gravity bars were called. Bjarg chanted like Vaka had and mimed a swirling whirlpool and flying through the sky.

Bjarg stopped and looked at Torr for confirmation. Torr nodded. That was what had happened. The father and daughter kept talking, and Torr gathered that she was asking how it worked. Bjarg told her to watch, then gathered a pile of pine needles, which he climbed onto. He began the chant again, urging them to join in. The three of them stomped and chanted, and at one point, Bjarg ran off to a lean-to and returned with a rattle that looked like a large seed pod on a stick and resumed chanting. Torr and Velspara danced around Bjarg, who wore boots that were fringed and belled, and slowly the pine needles lifted from the ground and swirled around Bjarg, rising to his shoulders and then above his head. The rattle stopped, and Bjarg was silent. Torr and Velspara stopped chanting and looked anxiously at the swirling cloud of pine needles, which stopped in midair and then fell to the ground with a dusty whoosh.

Bjarg stood in the center, his arms raised, smiling proudly. Velspara stomped her feet with approval, and Torr added his praises, wishing he had bells on his boots. Bjarg came to Torr and grabbed him by the shoulders, pressing his forehead to Torr's in the Scrid gesture of affection, which Torr had seen fathers do to sons. Torr was touched—and impressed. Bjarg was surely a wizard.

After several attempts, Torr was able to convey that he had been brought here against his will, and that he wanted to go home. Furrows of concern etched Bjarg's brow as he appeared to ponder this problem. Torr gestured that maybe he should go back to Gray Feather and use Vaka's grundhalda and try to invoke traveling again. He didn't dare ask Bjarg to come with him. He didn't imagine Vaka would much like another wizard coming into his village to help Torr escape Scridland.

Velspara asked Torr something that he did not understand. Bjarg tried to say it in a different way, and finally Torr realized they were asking him why Vaka had brought him here.

Torr could feel himself blushing. Finally, he tapped himself on the chest and spoke the name Jorimar had given him, "Mangarm."

Bjarg's and Velspara's mouths dropped open, and their faces grew pale. They looked at one another, and then at Torr. "My sister, Marglod Sky," he told them in broken Scridnu, aided by gestures, "is still at my home, and I must get to her before they bring her here."

The father and daughter stared at Torr, seeming to understand enough. Torr went to the lean-to for his belongings and returned to the fire, where Bjarg and Velspara were conferring in low voices. They looked up as he stood before them. He reached into his bundle and brought out the Bear crystal. "Asbjorn Skr," he said.

Torr thought the wizard was going to faint, but slowly color returned to the Scrid's face. After several combinations of words and gestures, Torr understood what Bjarg was saying. He would teach Torr how to use the Bear crystal, and how to get home.

Torr learned that he could use his Bear crystal and a slab of the white stone, grundhalda, to travel. Bjarg knew of another grundhalda somewhere in the vast forest west of their camp. Torr also learned that the crystals Vaka had used to bring him to Scridland worked in pairs and resonated at the same vibration, allowing for passage between two locations without the need to carry a crystal. With only a single crystal, such as the Bear crystal, it had to be carried; that meant only one person could travel at a time, and the person traveling needed to be a wizard. Torr understood that he would need to become a wizard himself in order to get back to the moon using his Bear crystal, and the idea both excited and terrified him.

Torr set his mind to the task and worked to memorize a new chant Bjarg was teaching him. It was a grounding chant, and Torr did not know why he needed to waste time learning how to stick more firmly to the ground when what he needed to do was release from it. But he did not argue and chanted the new words with Bjarg.

> *Jar fjall veurr honla hlif*
> *Bergrisi festa hjarta*
> *Bjoda fang hoettr seidr*
> *Varda vandr taufr vegr megin*
> *Holdr Bergrisi halda festa*
> *Glegpa sol festa jord*

After he'd memorized the chant, Bjarg made him practice. While Bjarg chanted the traveling chant, working himself into the frenzy that lifted the bed of pine needles to swirl around him, Torr chanted the grounding chant. As Torr sank into its sonorous rhythm, feeling it in his bones while he stomped against the hard ground, he realized that he was providing an opposing force to Bjarg. As Torr intensified his chanting, feeling it resonate in his belly as though he were a drum, the swirling tornado of pine needles slowed and began turning in the opposite direction, slowly churning downward. They practiced like that, Bjarg churning the pine needles upward, and Torr pulling them back down, like a swirling tug of war.

In the evening around the fire, Bjarg and Velspara acted out the words of the grounding chant, until Torr puzzled together an interpretation he could understand.

Iron mountain protector, seize the shield
Hill-giant, strengthen the heart
Challenge and wrestle the dangerous enchantment
Guard against the wicked talisman, diminish its power
Hero hill-giant, hold fast
Swallow the sun, strengthen the ground

At last, he understood why Bjarg had taught him this first. What good would it do for Torr to learn to travel to Peary, only to have Vaka capture Torr in his enchantment again and whisk him right back to Scridland? This chant was the counterspell to the traveling spell. Torr thumped his fists against his chest to Bjarg, and the wizard came and pressed his forehead to Torr's.

Torr asked them to explain the meaning of the traveling chant, and from their exuberant pantomimes, he understood its meaning, and now was able to feel the power in his mind as well as his body:

Spirit walker
Travel the skies
Home calls
Heed the cry

Andi stiga
Fara lopt
Heimili heita
Gaumr far

The words to this chant were simpler, but invoking the spell was harder. He knew he could do it; he had felt the swirling movement under his feet on the grundhalda at Gray Feather when he'd tried to escape, but there he'd had the help of the white slab. Bjarg communicated to him that if he could rally his strength here, without a traveling stone, then when he did stand on the grundhalda he would be filled with the power to travel the skies.

Torr practiced the traveling chant for several days, with only the faintest rustling of pine needles at his feet to reward his efforts. One evening around the campfire, Velspara presented him with a new pair of boots she had made for him. They were of sturdy bear hide: smooth suede on the outside and luxurious brown fur on the inside. The boots were strung with fringes, and Bjarg presented him with a carved wooden bowl filled with little copper bells and discs. They were the symbols of the warrior, he told him. Scrids earned an ornament for each of their kills. Torr would be a warrior wizard, an *Odinn,* Bjarg explained through their now common language of gestures and words. If he successfully traveled using the Bear crystal and a grundhalda, he would have earned the title and the boot ornaments.

Torr sewed the bells and discs onto the fringes himself, with a bone needle and sinew Velspara provided. He learned a chant to sing as he sewed, to imbue the boots with power.

> *Speed of the wind*
> *Bind to my soul*
> *Strength of the rock*
> *Harden my bones*
> *Song of the rain*
> *Ease my journey*

> *Vindr skunda*
> *Binda hug*
> *Styrkr bjarg*
> *Festa bein*
> *Songr regn*
> *Audr for*

Every day, he practiced stomping and chanting. And each day, the pine needles swirled a little higher, until he could raise them in a spinning sheath that extended above his head and hold them there for several minutes. The feeling was exhilarating, as though every molecule in his body spun and flew and sang. Afterwards, he felt energized, a buzz lingering in his body for hours.

But niggling in the back of his mind was Cassidy. Anxiety brought him to Bjarg once a day, asking if he was ready. Every day, Bjarg told him not yet, and then Torr would ask Bjarg to lead him back to Gray Feather. Bjarg told him to be patient, that he was making great progress.

The day finally came when Bjarg told him he was almost ready. Only one thing was left for him to do. He must die.

Torr stood staring at Bjarg. Bjarg described what he meant in various ways: he lay down on the ground with his eyes closed; he showed him the carcass of a rabbit; he showed him a rotted bird with maggots crawling out of its eye sockets.

"I don't want to die," he told Bjarg in Globalish. Bjarg understood his facial expressions and tone well enough.

"You have to," Bjarg told him. "Or you won't be an *Odinn.*"

Torr considered this for several minutes. He was desperate, but he wasn't crazy. He had stumbled into a world he did not understand, governed by rules he did not know. But he knew what death was, and he could not risk everything to gain everything. Could he? Risk his life? That was insanity. How could he help anyone if he were dead? There was too much left for him to do. He was the Star Child. He needed to complete his quest, which he had barely begun.

He lay awake all night, laboring over the problem. By morning, he'd concluded the only reasonable path left to him was to return to Gray Feather. Filled with sadness, Torr pulled on his new boots and rolled his belongings in his bear hide. He thanked Bjarg and Velspara, who pressed their foreheads to his. Torr headed out of the clearing with his hand on his knife hilt, whistling for the wolf. Emptiness filled Torr's entire being, as though he were abandoning his life, instead of the other way around.

The wolf did not appear, and after several miles of following a game trail that headed roughly east, Torr began to worry. He'd followed the wolf the whole way here, and it had taken several days. The likelihood of him finding his way back to Gray Feather on his own was next to nil. When the sun reached its zenith, the wolf still had not appeared to guide him through the dense forest. Torr stopped and glared at the wolf on the pommel.

"Are you going to help me, or what?" Torr demanded. The wolf sat upright with ears alert. "You're not, are you?" he admitted reluctantly. "Stubborn bastard," he grumbled, wondering if he was speaking to the wolf or to himself. He found a stream and drank deeply, and then with a sinking despair, turned around and headed back to Bjarg's.

Bjarg made Torr dig his own grave in the forest a few hills beyond their homestead. It took all day with the rudimentary stone pick and ironwood shovel. He was drenched in sweat, and his muscles burned and shook from fatigue. He kept his frantic thoughts at bay by focusing on one shovelful of dirt at a time. Dig. Lift. Toss. Finally, the tall, circular hole was deep enough for Torr to stand in. Torr stripped out of his clothing, and Bjarg eyed the rune belt curiously as it winked into view when Torr unstrapped it. The Scrid asked if he could hold it. Bjarg studied the rune carefully, and then set it on Torr's pile of clothing.

Bjarg instructed him to slather himself with bear grease, and helped Torr cover his back with the gooey gunk. Velspara eyed his naked body with interest from a few paces away. He felt neither embarrassed nor excited at her curious gaze; he was too consumed by nervousness.

Torr did not believe Bjarg intended for him to truly die. He had realized on his hike the previous day that it must be some sort of sha-man's ritual—an initiation rite. Still, initiation rites were known to be difficult and dangerous, otherwise they wouldn't be powerful.

Bjarg had encouraged him to eat and drink water all day as he dug, and now he handed Torr a full waterskin and watched him drain it. Bjarg made him finish a second skin as well, which left his stomach uncomfortably full. Torr lowered himself into the hole and stood stoi-cally while Bjarg filled the hole with dirt, burying him up to his neck. The wizard stomped the earth around him, packing it firmly. Bjarg placed a pointed bear hide cap on Torr's head and tied it securely under his chin, and then left the glade with Velspara. Torr watched them go with a dull terror. Brother Wolf had not reappeared; he had abandoned him when he'd needed him most.

Torr had thought he'd be able to dig himself out if he wanted, but when he tried to move his limbs in the embrace of the dirt, it was heavy all around him. He pressed at the air pockets, which simply filled with more dirt. Soon he could only move his fingers and toes and started to panic. He tried to calm his heartbeat and his breathing, and eventually they quieted on their own. His body was helpless, and it quickly surrendered to that fact. His mind, however, became more and more agitated as the sun sank towards the horizon.

How long was Bjarg going to leave him there? Torr had asked the Scrid that question several times, but the man had simply smiled. What if Bjarg were an evil wizard posing as a good one, and was part of some secret plot to get rid of the Star Children to serve his dark master? Or it could be an elaborate ruse to steal Torr's moon deed. Or maybe it was true that Torr had to die to become a warrior wizard, only Bjarg hadn't told him warrior wizards were actually only spirits and that his body would no longer be needed.

But Torr didn't want to die. He loved his body. He loved his life, even if his heart hurt like hell half the time. He couldn't abandon Cassidy, or Jasper, or his parents.

Thoughts of Blaire crept in even as he tried to shut them out. Would he find her in the afterlife? Was she watching him now? Waiting for him? He wished she had never died and he had never left the moon. He wished they'd gotten married and raised kids and found a way to free Earth and live a normal life. He wished he could stop crying, because his nose was stuffing up and he couldn't wipe it. He forced himself back to his senses and cleared his nose by blowing a stream of snot onto the dirt, then stared into the deepening dusk.

He hadn't considered the creatures of the forest, but they came out as the last vestiges of sunlight faded from the sky. Bright masses of stars shed an eerie glow across the little clearing, creating enough light for Torr to detect movement of gray against gray. Little blobs moved slowly around the perimeter of the grassy glade. Then there was rustling. Then more rustling. Torr breathed silently, hoping they wouldn't see him, though of course they would smell him. Whatever they were. Soon he saw that they were the rabbit-like creatures Velspara trapped. Their long hind legs were what reminded Torr of Earth rabbits or hares, but they had long bushy tails and small pointy ears. They scratched through dead leaves, looking for insects. Torr counted almost a dozen of them. They made their way further onto the grass and began digging with short front legs, burying their noses under the turf. When one found something, others would come running, and then snarl and hiss and try to push each other out of the way, until one finally ran off into the woods with the prize. The animals peered at him cautiously and maintained a distance of several yards around him.

Torr overcame his fear and watched the creatures until they left and the clearing was still again. The night dragged on, with night birds and insects clacking and buzzing from the trees, and more rustlings off in the forest. The air grew cold. Eventually he stopped trying to hold his water, and let himself piss, feeling the warmth run down his leg before it soaked into the dirt.

A pack of wild boars entered the clearing. Torr stiffened, hoping they wouldn't notice him. Boars were not so gentle as those other little creatures, and Torr clamped his teeth together, nervous sweat beading on his brow. The boars were not shy, and the adults were as big as medium-sized dogs. Several juveniles trailed behind the adults, running under their parents' legs and nipping at one another. The creatures with their long snouts snuffled loudly along the ground. One headed slowly towards Torr, white tusks curling out of snorting nostrils. When it wandered close enough for Torr to see its beady black eyes, he yelled sharply. The boar hopped backwards, startled, and then approached again. Torr held it off with sharp yells, until it realized Torr was not a threat, and then ventured closer. Torr sang loudly, a raucous space chanty Fritz and Frank liked to sing. The boar appeared undaunted, but it made Torr feel better to sing.

The snuffling boars hunted for whatever bugs or plants they were looking for, coming within inches of Torr's face, but did not touch him. Their foul breath didn't stop him from singing, and soon they wandered off, leaving him with a sore throat and his nerves tied in knots. He cursed Bjarg out loud, screaming hoarsely. *"May you die in Algol's stinking hell, with lice crawling up your dick and shit stuffed up your nose!"*

The rabbits woke Torr as dawn crept across the sky with fingers of gold. The little animals scratched and dug, and then slipped away as the sun peeked through the trees and sent shafts of light into the clearing.

Torr had survived the night and waited expectantly for Bjarg to free him. It hadn't been so bad. A little claustrophobia. A little fright. Nothing too serious. He was proud of himself.

The day passed slowly. Bjarg did not come. Torr was hot and thirsty, and his head ached. Birds and insects fluttered and fed in the clearing. He soiled himself, gazing sullenly at the trees. He hated himself. He hated Bjarg. He hated Jorimar, and Vaka, Salima, Helug, Stump, Frija, and Velspara. He hated everyone. He screamed at the birds pecking for worms in the grassy glade, delighted when he scared them away, and angry when they returned and ignored him.

"Blaire!" he called out. *"Blaire!"* he called louder, his voice fading into the forest. *"Why'd you fucking have to go and die?! Why didn't you come to me instead of trying to save Darla, you stupid, selfless ..."* He choked, and his nose filled up, tears stinging his eyes. He held himself quiet, staring at nothing until his mind went numb.

His stomach cramped with hunger and his mouth was pasty. His muscles ached, and his bones were cold. His head felt like an axe had split it. His cheek was twitching every few seconds. He closed his eyes and followed the firing branch of the nerve and found the agony of Darius huddled in his dungeon cell. Torr forced his eyes open again, feeling the nerve of his cheek relax. He was not Darius. Darius and Danute were dead. He was Torr, and his sister was Cassidy, and they had to survive.

Night came again, and he looked into the shadows for Brother Wolf. He called for him. He howled. Begged. Cried and yelled. The wolf did not come. Bjarg had kept the wolf knife at their hut, a mile away. The wolf had only ever appeared to Torr when the knife was near at hand. Darius seemed to summon his wolf at will, but Torr was not Darius.

The boars came again and ignored him as they had the night before. He spat at one, missing its eye and hitting the tusked snout instead. The boar jumped back a pace, eyed Torr warily, and then continued foraging. Torr mused numbly about what it would feel like if the boar jabbed its tusk into his eye. The boars wandered off, and insects chanted from the trees. The stars glistened in the sky, unconcerned with his fate.

"You know," he said to the glittering sky, "if you're out there, Star People, and I die, you're fucked." The stars winked at him, and he spat again, watching his spittle fly several paces and land on the dark grass.

Everyone had abandoned him. Even Edgemont had not appeared in his dreams. "Oh, I get it," Torr said into the night. "You torment me for your amusement, but then when I really need help, you're nowhere to be found. Selfish motherfucker."

The only one who had been able to reliably touch him at a distance was his sister.

"Cassidy!" he called, beckoning his sister from across the heavens.

"Cassidy!!" He called her name until his throat hurt. He waited expectantly for the familiar tug of her, a nudge, a sense of her. Anything. Nothing came. She was too far away. "Dad!" he called. "Mom!" Hunger was making him weak, and he closed his eyes, wanting to cry for his mother like a child, but lacked the energy.

He was awoken in the night by a cold rain slapping against his pointed cap and stinging his cheeks. The rain grew heavier. He tilted his head back and caught raindrops in his mouth. The water was cold and fresh. He let it bathe his lips and tongue and collected small mouthfuls in the back of his throat before swallowing gratefully. When the worst of his thirst was quenched and he tired of craning his neck and collecting rainwater, he let the icy water trickle off the hat and down into his beard. He intermittently dozed, then drank, and then dozed again. The rain kept up all night, petering out as dawn approached.

Morning came, and Bjarg did not. Torr followed the progress of the small sun as it slowly traversed the sky. Night fell. By midday the following day, he cursed himself for not drinking more rainwater as thirst and hunger battled for his attention. His tongue was sore and swollen, and all he could think about was cold stream water and the little crustaceans. He felt alternately dizzy and sleepy, but forced himself to stay awake, afraid he might never wake up.

That night, he felt the grubs. First, they were between his legs, tickling his balls, and then tried to climb up his ass. He squirmed and wriggled, trying to get them off, but they kept coming. He felt them crawl down his legs and up his chest. Torr lifted his head and stared at the heavens and said the prayer Grandma Leann used to say at bedtime when he was a child.

Shine down upon us, oh golden stars, source of life. Visit us on rays of light. Descend to Earth and fill us with your fire. Make us whole again. Unite mother and father, parent and child, brother and sister, enemy and friend, strong and weak, rich and poor, joyous and sorrowful, the dead and the living. Make us one. Bring us peace.

He said it over and over, until his eyes closed and he fell into darkness.

————————) ————————

Torr was floating in the black expanse. Stars beckoned from all directions. "Me, me," they called to him. "Come to me, to me." Torr swam towards them in the black waters of the heavens and dove into one, burning into a million embers, which formed more stars that called to him. The more stars he dove into, the more stars there were. He incinerated himself again and again, his cells breaking apart into small universes that were born and loved and died.

He was floating on his back, staring up at the moon. He found Anaximenes crater and saw that it crawled with black ants scurrying into and out of a deep hole. A torrent of water cascaded down the sides of the massive crater and filled the ant hole. The ants swam to the surface, flailing their little legs frantically before growing still and floating away. A great black queen ant floated up near Torr. It perched on six legs and skirted over the surface like a water bug. The creature came to Torr and climbed up onto his floating chest. Torr lifted it between his thumb and forefinger and stared into its black eyes, the long antennae swaying back and forth. He squished the ant in his fingers. It made a loud popping sound and white goo spurted out, covering Torr's fingers. He flung the ant away with disgust, but the goo stuck to his skin.

Torr looked up, and he was in the woods. It was a mixed forest of deciduous trees and conifers. The air was warm and fragrant. It was midday. His mother was kneeling on the ground, digging up plants by the roots and laying them on a pile next to her.

"Mom," he called.

Brianna flinched and turned, finding his eyes. She climbed to her feet, peering at him, and then rushed into his arms. He hugged her tightly, smelling the herbs and sweat in her hair. "Mom," he repeated, anxious and relieved, scared and elated—emotions tumbling forth in a confused rush. "Where are you? Where is this?"

She looked at him, stroking his head. "Your hair has grown," she said, smiling lovingly and examining his face. "And you have a beard." Her brow furrowed. "What's wrong? Where are you?" she asked.

He swallowed. "It's bad, Mom," he said, wanting to cry. "I was on the moon, and my girlfriend got killed because of me and my moon deed." He buried his face in Brianna's hair and let the tears flow. She hugged him, rocking him back and forth, and let him cry. He told her about Blaire until his throat constricted and he couldn't talk anymore.

"How's Cassidy?" she asked gently.

He took a deep breath, drew himself up, and cleared his throat. He met her dark green eyes. "Cassidy's fine," he said, wiping at his cheek. "She and Jasper are going out. But she's still addicted to that drug."

"I wish I were there to help," she said.

"Me too," Torr said. "But I'm not there anymore." Torr told her how he'd been taken to the planet Scridland by a wizard and a pair of twin crystals, and how he was there now, buried in a hole and suffering through an initiation rite. "Do you think I'll die?" he asked.

"I hope not," she said somberly. "I don't think so. But I think you need to learn something before you will get free."

"What do I need to learn?"

She frowned and shrugged. "I don't know."

"But how will I get out if Bjarg doesn't free me? My arms and legs are immobilized. He didn't give me any tools. He took everything away."

"He didn't give you *anything?*" she asked, searching his eyes. "Are you sure?"

"Nothing," Torr insisted. He took a deep breath. "But what about you? Where are we?" he asked, looking around. They were clearly in the mountains.

"The foothills. The Shaman's Shield is a couple of miles that way." She gestured north. He could just make out a wall of white clouds looming in the distance. "It still holds," she said. "But I can't get through. I try every day, but I can't crack the code. Whatever Remo and the other shamans have done, it's effective." She looked impressed. She also looked thin, and lines of worry formed a permanent crease between her eyebrows. All the same, her skin and eyes shone with a vibrant energy.

"It suits you out here," he said.

She smiled. "I like nature. But I really need to get inside the Shaman's Shield. The Teg troops seem to be leaving the deepest forest alone, for now. But the altitude is too high here. I need to move on before the snows come."

He could see the strain in her body and wished he could help. He was clothed in his cargo pants and t-shirt, but also his bear hide vest and fringed boots, and his knives hung at his side. He pulled the wolf knife from its sheath. The wolf showed his profile and howled at the moon. The vortex was not spinning. He resheathed it, and a loud clicking sound made him look up into the branches of a scrubby oak.

A large black raven was tossing acorns to the ground and clucking proudly. Torr clicked back, and the raven looked at him sideways.

"I see your friend has followed you," Torr said.

"Yes. He followed me this whole way," Brianna said, grinning. "He's helping me gather acorns." The raven squawked loudly and hopped to another branch, sending a shower of acorns to the ground.

"He can't help you cross the Shaman's Shield?" Torr asked.

"The raven can get through, actually," she said slowly. "I thought at first he would get Balor to come for me, but the silly bird just comes back after a couple of minutes as though he's waiting for me and can't figure out why I don't follow him."

Torr helped Brianna gather acorns and went with her to a shelter she had built in a little hollow under a large pine tree, with a roof of cut saplings and pine boughs. She had gathered roots, plants, and nuts, which she was storing in hand-woven baskets. It looked as though she'd been here for a while. His bow and quiver of arrows were hanging from the low ceiling. He picked up his 6 Creed, which was leaning against a bough. It was loaded, and the safety was on. He peered through the scope out into the woods. It felt good to hold it again.

"You been using this?" he asked, putting it down.

She smiled proudly and nodded. "I got a deer," she said, her face falling. "I didn't want to kill it, but ..." Her voice trailed off, and she led him through the woods to a tree where strips of dried venison hung several yards up in the air from a rope that was strung over a high branch and anchored to a boulder nearby. "I don't want the bears coming to my camp. They're attracted by the meat," she explained. "Rodents still get up there, but there's not much I can do about that." She showed him the deer's hide, which was stretched across two saplings, with two large holes where bullets had pierced it.

Brianna led the way across the forest floor until they found a game path heading north and followed it, with the raven flying from tree to tree. Torr tucked the belled fringes into the tops of his boots to quiet them. The wall of clouds appeared before them as they crested a rise. A while later, they were standing at its base. The Shaman's Shield was sheer and white, like a cliff of ice that extended far overhead.

Torr threw a stone at it, and it bounced along the cloud wall like a stone skipping over water, and then fell to the ground with a soft thud. Trees grew half in and half out of the Shaman's Shield. The raven landed on one such tree—an enormous old oak—and hopped from branch to branch until it disappeared inside the white mass of the Shaman's Shield. A minute later the raven hopped back out, squawking loudly, its black wings fluffing as it screeched.

"He likes that tree," Brianna said. It was large and sprawling, with some of its great, thick branches growing along the ground like tired arms.

"Have you tried climbing the tree to cross over?" Torr asked, shivers running up his spine.

His mother cast him a sharp glance. "No. I should have thought of that. I did get a spirit reading from that tree, though. Here," she said, digging into her pack and pulling out a green notebook. She read aloud:

"Grandmother Oak–Eat two fruits to follow the whispering wisdom lost to your kind."

Torr held his mother's eyes. They were green and shiny like the oak leaves, and as ancient as the tree. "Here," she said, passing the book to him. "What does it tell you?"

He looked down at the page of wavering scrawl. Like a nest of writhing snakes, the lines squiggled until they finally separated out into a legible phrase. *"Grandmother Oak,"* he read aloud. *"Eat two fruits to die unto yourself and become another."* Torr shuddered.

The raven cawed from the great oak, and Torr and Brianna knew what they had to do. They hiked back to her little den and packed up as many things as she could carry. They left the shelter intact and walked out of the clearing. Torr carried bundles of food and flasks of water strapped across his back. Brianna carried her heavy pack and wore the 6 Creed across her chest. They stopped to take as much venison as they could carry, leaving the rest on the ground for the bears, and rolled the deer hide and strapped it awkwardly on top of Brianna's already bulging pack. It was heavy, but his mother insisted on taking it.

When they reached the grandmother oak, the sun was low in the western sky and sent shafts of light slanting through the forest. The light rays that hit the Shaman's Shield disappeared into it like water soaking into cotton. Torr stood nervously at its edge and craned his neck to look up. The cloud cliff seemed to rise forever. He had never stood so close to the magical barrier, not even at Miramar, where they had been prohibited from walking right up to it. A vibration emanated from it and ran through him in a noiseless buzz.

Torr followed Brianna, who approached the grandmother oak and laid her hand on its massive trunk. Even the raven stayed quiet, waddling silently across a broad branch while Torr held his breath and tried to listen for the whispering wisdom of the tree. He heard nothing but the shiver of wind passing through the leaves.

Torr scanned the ground, which was littered with golden-brown acorns, and collected several to fill one of his vest pockets. He held two in his hand and joined his mother who had two in her palm. They twisted off the caps, placed the acorns on a stone, and rapped them sharply with the butt of his antelope knife. The thin shells split easily, and Torr popped a smooth nut into his mouth. His face puckered as he bit into it. It was sharply bitter, but he chewed and swallowed it, and then ate a second one. His mother did the same. They washed them down with water, and then examined the tree and the Shaman's Shield.

Brianna pressed her hand to the tree trunk and closed her eyes. Torr stepped over roots and felt the gray, wrinkled bark. The trunk was wider than Torr was tall and stood completely outside the Shaman's Shield. Only its sprawling branches on the far side crept into the shimmering white barrier and disappeared. Several fat branches snaked across the ground. They were wide enough to walk on, and Torr hopped onto one and gave his mother a hand up. She insisted on leading, and he did not object. She held her hand out behind her and he took it, feeling like a little boy again. He wasn't ashamed to admit he was scared. The half of him that didn't believe any of this was real was what kept him from jumping down to solid ground and folding his arms in stubborn refusal.

The raven hopped along on a branch above them, and Torr felt the rough bark of the branch under his feet as he walked forward, holding his mother's delicate hand. He had never noticed how small her hands were before, but now he felt he could crush her bones with one good squeeze.

The Shaman's Shield shimmered as they got closer. Torr knew that since a stone, and even a bullet, bounced off the thing, only magic would allow them through. He looked at his mother, her hair floating around her face and her eyes bright like stars. On the branch above their heads, the raven kept up its waddling march and stepped right into the solid wall as though it were a normal cloud of water vapor. Torr exchanged glances with his mother, and she stepped forward. The cloud buzzed as her foot hit the barrier. Her whole body vibrated for a moment. The shock jumped from her hand to his and shivered up his arm. She lurched forward and was gone.

Torr felt himself being pulled forward by her hand and placed his foot in front of him to break his fall. His hand went numb, and then his foot, as each entered the Shaman's Shield. He felt suspended in time, his limbs heavy and unfeeling, reminding him of those strange dreaming-awake nights when his arms and legs would not move on the bed, no matter how hard he tried.

Brianna's hand pulled him forward with a hard jerk, and an icy pain rippled over his face. Suddenly, there was no sound. He was in a dense grayish-white cloud. It was not cold, and it was not hot. Torr vaguely felt the branch under his feet and the pressure of his mother's fingers. He called to her, hearing his voice for an instant before it faded and died. He called out again. As though in a muffled snowstorm, the sound traveled a few inches from his mouth before being absorbed. He could see the ghostly shape of his mother creeping through the gray mist in front of him. Overhead, the small dark blob of the raven bobbed side to side as its short legs carried it forward.

Torr could see only a short distance in the dense fog and had no sense of direction. When he'd watched the Shaman's Shield dissipate at Miramar, it had shed particles of ash that fell like snow. He waved his hand through the whitish-gray blur, trying to determine its true composition, but it parted without giving him a clue. They crept forward. Torr expected the branch to end, but it did not. As long as the branch kept stretching out in front of them, they would be alright, Torr told himself. It would take them through the magic and drop them out on the other side. Only, the branch did not really end, it met and merged into another branch, which veered off in a different direction. They stepped onto it, and soon that branch met three others, which diverged three different ways. Brianna and Torr followed the raven, who chose the center branch and kept waddling forward.

Soon, the raven was trailing behind instead of leading, and with a flap that nearly made Torr lose his balance and teeter off the branch, the large bird hopped over Torr's head and landed on Brianna's shoulder. Torr and his mother steadied each other as she jerked and swayed. The raven settled its feathers, Brianna and Torr regained their balance, and they crept forward once again.

The raven rode happily on Brianna's shoulder but offered no assistance when they met the next jumble of branches. Brianna turned and looked through fingers of mist into Torr's eyes, worry creasing her brow.

The raven cocked its head and gave a muted squawk.

"Some help you are. Let's just keep going, Mom," he said, leaning forward so she could hear. "It's got to end somewhere." His legs ached with every step, growing heavier as the surreal day wore on. His eyes stung, and his throat and nose felt irritated. Weakness and lightheadedness took hold of him, causing him to lose his step more than once. His mother's firm grip was all that allowed him to keep his footing. He dared not let go of her hand, as afraid of becoming lost forever in the mist as he was of falling.

The branches led them this way and that through the otherworldly fog. Some branches they had to climb up to reach, others they had to climb down. They found themselves in a three-dimensional maze of interlocking trunks and branches with no ground and no treetops, no beginning and no end.

After what felt like hours of creeping through the twisting labyrinth, the dispersed light faded into murky darkness. Torr and Brianna sat on a branch wide as a terrace and leaned their backs against a wider trunk, where they shared dried venison and water, the raven begging for bits of meat. As much as Torr ate, he still felt thirsty and empty inside. They each ate two bitter acorns, afraid of losing the magic of the trees and becoming lost in the Shaman's Shield forever. Torr's mother leaned against him, and soon her head was resting on his shoulder and she was asleep. Torr let his eyes close and drifted off.

When they awoke, the muffled silence was heavy all around them. The raven stretched its wings, and Torr yawned. They hadn't spoken but a few words since they'd entered the Shaman's Shield and didn't speak now. There was nothing words could do to bring them back to reality. Torr was in a dream inside a dream and feared he would never get out. At least he was with his mother.

A fatigue heavy as stones weighed on him. He could not rise and tried to relax his quivering muscles. His body was buried on Scridland, dying of thirst. Brianna knelt at his side and peered with concern into his eyes.

"My body is dying, Mom," he said faintly. "I don't think I can go on."

"You must," she said urgently, clasping his hands. She held her waterskin to his lips, but even as he drank, he knew it would do no good. He pulled his mouth away. "No, you drink it. It won't help me," he said. "I'm not really here."

"You are," she insisted, and dug frantically into her bag. She searched through her various herb notebooks, then made him eat two more acorns and drink bitter drops from several vials.

"There," she said with a loud exhalation. "That should do it."

He raised one eyebrow skeptically but was able to get to his feet and maintain his balance under his awkward load of supplies. He held her hand as they headed into the shrouded lacework of bridge-like branches that stretched into nowhere and walked across whatever branch appeared in front of them. They walked for what felt like hours, one branch looking like the next, and thick fog pressing in on them from all sides.

"Mom, I think we're lost," he said as they trod across yet another branch. His pulse pounded in his temples.

She squeezed his hand but did not reply. Torr recalled all her warnings about getting lost in magic. So this is what she meant, he reflected anxiously. His mother stepped onto another branch that appeared out of the ashen fog. He tried to quell his rising panic and followed her. The raven turned its head from its perch on Brianna's shoulder and held Torr's eyes. The raven did not seem concerned, and Torr focused on his breath until his heartbeat normalized.

A gentle wind picked up, and they stopped.

Brianna tilted her head to listen. "There shouldn't be wind in here," she said.

"Maybe we're close to the border," he said hopefully, not really caring if it was the interior border of the Shaman's Shield or the exterior. He just wanted to get out of there and stand on solid ground.

"No," she said, shaking her frizzy mane of black curls. "Shhh."

Torr listened more closely. He could hear it too. The wind was coming from only one direction and didn't seem to actually reach them; he could not feel movement on his face, and the surrounding leaves were still. The sound was like the susurrus of a field of ripe wheat as it swayed and rattled. Torr hung onto Brianna's hand as she crept towards the sound, choosing the right hand fork of a great branch.

The wind grew louder as they headed towards it, though the air still did not move. Torr thought perhaps his mother was right. It was not wind at all. It sounded like leaves brushing softly together, but the air was not moving them. His spine tingled, and goosebumps rose on his arms. If it wasn't wind, what was it?

Shivers rose up his spine as he realized what the sound reminded him of. The old women of Gray Feather liked to sit in groups grinding seeds, making rope, or working hides. When Torr walked by them, their voices always lowered to a whisper, their bright amber eyes following him like hunters following a buck. It always unnerved him a bit—a half-dozen grandmothers talking about him. He did not know what they said, but in his imagination they were either making fun of his skinny hairless body, or they were admiring him and arranging his marriage. That's what the trees sounded like: whispering grandmothers. Dozens of them. Hundreds. Watching. Mocking. Discussing his fate.

The rustling murmurs stayed a few branches ahead of them. Torr's legs quivered with fatigue, but he kept on as they followed the whispers. The raven became excited, bobbing its tail up and down and curling its talons into Brianna's shoulder. The light grew brighter up ahead, and the mist began to glow a pearly white. Hope drove Torr forward, and they quickened their pace. The whispers and the light converged into a sparkling dance before them, as though sprites spun and swirled in the air, flitting through the web of thinning branches. The fat branch they were on sloped downward and buried itself in leaf-covered dirt. Torr's boots struck solid ground, and he said a silent prayer as the eerie whispers faded away. He stepped through the edge of the mist with an icy cold shiver, and emerged into the warm autumn air, white light filtering through the canopy of clouds far overhead.

"We're inside the Shaman's Shield," Brianna said, joy lighting her face. The raven launched from her shoulder and flapped overhead.

Relief surged through Torr's blood, and he hugged his mother.

They parted and gazed around at the familiar landscape. Two snow-capped peaks looked down on them like grinning gods. Lassen was large and close, and Shasta loomed in the distance. Pine-covered hills rose in folds between them and the towering peaks. Torr knew it was less than a hundred miles to reach the little city of Mt. Shasta that sat at the great mountain's base. His mother could make that journey in a few days. He turned to her and kissed her cheek.

"I need to go back to Scridland," he said, "and rejoin my body before it's too late."

His mother held his cheeks in both hands and looked deep into his eyes. "It's not too late," she said. "You saved me. Go back and find the Star People. I love you. And tell Cassidy I love her. And Jasper. And Kai."

"I will. I love you, too," Torr said, choking on his words. He strapped the food and water he had been carrying to the back of her pack and adjusted the 6 Creed's strap across her chest.

Tears glistened in her eyes as she kissed his cheeks, then she turned and followed the raven into the forest.

———————❖———————

It had been a long season of hibernation, and the bear shifted in his earthen den. The fragrant dirt was packed warmly around him, protecting him from the elements. Only his head was free. He began to nose the dirt aside, taking great mouthfuls with his strong jaws and flinging it away in clumps. He could smell grubs below the surface, and a ravaging hunger rose in his belly. He used his long claws to dig at the encasing dirt. Before long, he freed his forelegs and scooped masses of squirming grubs onto his tongue. Swallowing the delicious crunchy creatures, dirt and all, he dug for more, working his hind legs to free himself. The bear hauled his great bulk out of the pit, his hind legs scrambling for a hold, stiff and numb as they were. He was weak, and he nearly fell over as he shook the dirt from his matted hide.

Ahhh. The air was clean and fresh, and the wind sang in the trees. He detected the scent of a stream across the rolling hills and headed in its direction. On the far side of a hill, he came upon a settlement of two-leggeds who foraged and stored their food in wooden dens. The bear lumbered over to one of the dens, pushed his way through a hide that hung down on one side of the raised structure, and climbed up inside. He found a hollowed-out stone filled with water and sank his muzzle into it and drank. When he'd had his fill, he nosed around inside little nests of wood and reeds. One held seeds. Another held roots. Yet another held dried flesh of the tusked horn-foots. He ate from each, ravenous, and scooped up seeds with his tongue from where he'd spilled them onto the wooden ground.

He froze. The rank scent of a wolf hit his nostrils as the air shifted. The furry, staring creature was at the hide entrance. The bear turned and rose on his haunches, claws bared, a deep growl ripping from his throat and his head butting up against the flimsy covering of boughs and bundled grasses.

A male two-legged appeared next to the wolf, brandishing a stick. The bear was cornered and backed against the den's wall, pushing against the saplings that swayed but did not give way. The two-legged screamed in a high-pitched wail and shook a seed pod at him, making a horrible rattling sound, like when the winter winds tore branches from the trees. The wind whipped at him, and a branch struck him on the head. Dizziness overtook him, and he stumbled onto his side, vertigo and darkness pulling him into a swirling river current, drowning, drowning.

51

BLACK SORROW

assidy brewed another batch of Black Sorrow. She shared some
with Carmen and strained the rest into a small empty bottle she
found in her pack. She found a black ink well and fountain pen in
the purple sack, and carefully wrote on the glass's faded label, *Black Sorrow.*

She and Carmen were free of headaches all that day, and the next.
Cassidy gave Agapantha four drops for her aching legs and feet, and the
woman begged for some the following day. The other Jadens began coming
to Cassidy for various ailments, and she looked through her red and black
notebooks until she found the appropriate herb. Even Prissa came to her
to relieve cramps. Cassidy made her a tea of Cramp Bark, reading in the
book that the herb would also help with irritability. Prissa was noticeably
more congenial the following day, and Cassidy smiled smugly to herself.

The next night, Cassidy was kept awake by several women who had
caught cold down in the ice caves. Hacking coughs woke her every
time she was about to drift off. When she finally fell asleep, she dreamt
of the green-eyed woman again. Cassidy was four years old and sat
up in bed, unable to stop coughing. The beautiful young woman was
sitting on the side of the bed and gave Cassidy a spoonful of something
that made her mouth pucker.

A small boy was coughing in the bed across from her. He had short
blond hair and big gray eyes. The woman was Cassidy's mother, and
the boy was her brother.

"Here, Torr, honey," her mother said, going to him and giving him a spoonful of the same medicine in between bouts of coughing.

"Yuck," Torr said, making a sour face that made Cassidy laugh and cough. "What is it?" he asked.

"It's called Maiden's Wand," their mother said, patting his back.

"What's Maiden's Wand?" he asked.

"A maiden is a young woman, and a wand is a magic stick."

"Oh," Torr said. "I want a magic stick."

Their mother laughed and hugged him. "I'm sure you do," she said, rocking him happily.

Cassidy woke up in the jade cave to more coughing. When Agapantha lit the morning candles, Cassidy took a taper and paged through the red notebook by its flickering light. The book was strange. Most pages were filled with writing that was wavy and illegible. The pages whose writing she could read seemed to always give her the answer she was looking for. This time was no different. *"Maiden's Wand"* was clearly written in neat, flowing handwriting. *"Take one spoonful of strong tea every four hours to relieve cough, bronchitis, toothache, and skin ulcers."* This time, she was not surprised that her dream had led her to the medicine. Still, shivers ran across her skin, making the little hairs stand on end.

Carmen sat up sleepily, and Cassidy leaned in close to her ear. "Torr is my brother," she whispered, a dagger of pain lancing through her head.

Carmen's eyes grew big. "How do you know?"

Cassidy took the bottle of Black Sorrow from her bag and let two drops fall onto her tongue before answering. "I know from my dream. And I've seen my mother. She's beautiful, with long black hair and emerald-green eyes."

"Oh," Carmen said. "You're so lucky. I can almost remember something, but not quite." She lowered her head to her hand, and Cassidy gave her two drops of Black Sorrow.

"What is that?" Prissa's voice cut through the air.

"For headaches," Cassidy answered, turning to meet the sour woman's eyes. "You want more Cramp Bark?"

Prissa scowled at her, and then nodded. Cassidy gladly gave her some.

Cassidy found a small sack of the Maiden's Wand herb, boiled two pinchfuls in a few inches of water, and then gave a spoonful of the strong tea to everyone who was coughing. She set another batch of Black Sorrow to soaking.

"Here," Carmen said, "I want you to have this." Carmen held out a flat round flask of green-glazed ceramic that was no bigger than her palm. The ceramic flask had a prowling tiger molded onto each side and was sealed with a little cork stopper and had two notches near the mouth for a cord. "You can use it for your herbal remedies," Carmen said.

"Oh, I couldn't," Cassidy said.

Carmen insisted. "Yes, you need it. I can't remember where I got it, anyway."

Cassidy bowed her head and accepted the flask. "Thank you," she said.

Those with the worst coughs stayed behind that morning, and Cassidy told them to take Maiden's Wand every four hours.

Two mornings later, the sick women felt better, but Cassidy, Carmen, and Agapantha had all come down with the hacking cough. Cassidy's throat was sore and swollen, and her head throbbed. Giselle and Daleelah stopped by and chose three women to serve them that day. It was supposedly a great honor.

The two dark-haired sisters backed away from Cassidy and Carmen, who were coughing badly, and covered their mouths and noses with their sleeves. They hurried away with the three women in tow. The rest of the Jadens went down into the tunnels to work, but Cassidy and Carmen stayed behind with Agapantha to nurse their coughs.

Cassidy boiled another batch of Maiden's Wand and decided to throw the soaking Black Sorrow into the kettle with the bubbling Maiden's Wand, then watched as the herbs simmered together in a dark red brew. When the tea was ready, she poured a small amount into her cup, as well as Carmen's and Agapantha's, and then filled the tiger flask with it and poured the remainder into the spare cup she'd used to soak the Black Sorrow.

They all drank the bitter liquid, and Cassidy sat on her rug, coughing. She pulled a length of blue yarn from the edge of the rug and used it to tie the tiger flask around her neck, and then tucked the flask under her gown.

Carmen was the first to run to the latrine. Cassidy and Agapantha soon followed. They knelt or squatted next to each other over the pit, alternating between violent vomiting and diarrhea.

"Sorry," Cassidy gasped. "I guess I shouldn't have mixed the two herbs together." The other women were too busy heaving to answer.

The nausea finally subsided, and they hobbled back to the jade cave. Cassidy arranged the pile of pillows under Agapantha's feet, and then joined Carmen on their sleeping rugs. Cassidy took the red notebook and a candle, curious about what had caused such a violent reaction to the mixture of herbs. She found the page with Black Sorrow, struggling to read it in the dim light. She drew the candle flame closer to the paper. Flowing script slowly appeared on the blank white page below the main entry, the invisible ink turning first yellow, and then red. *Boil with Maiden's Wand to heighten senses, enter the spirit realm, and ward off magic. Intense vomiting is followed by six hours of illumination.*

Cassidy looked up at Carmen with alarm. Carmen gave her a puzzled frown. Cassidy clamped her lips shut, and then chose her words carefully. "I believe I just made a hallucinogen. Don't be afraid. It will wear off before the other Jadens return."

Carmen's eyes widened in mild fright. Cassidy told Agapantha, and the two young women grabbed pillows and sat at Agapantha's feet. The three of them sat huddled together, glancing at each other nervously, and waited.

"Do you see anything?" Cassidy asked.

"Colors are bright," Carmen said, staring at a blue stag pillow.

They were. Vivid and dancing. Cassidy could hear the distant pinging of chisels on stone. She could not normally hear at such a great distance, but the sound was clear and distinctive. The shadows in the corners seemed alive, and Cassidy clutched her arms around herself, fingers of fear creeping up her back. Agapantha stared off into nothingness, a thoughtful expression on her face. They each drifted off into their private worlds.

Cassidy jerked back, startled, as she suddenly noticed an old man leaning against the stone wall, watching her. He was a slight man with cinnamon-colored skin, which was heavily wrinkled and sagged from his bare arms and chest. He wore a wispy gray goatee and moustaches, and his fingers traced the whorls of a conch shell that hung from a brown fiber cord around his neck. The white and brown shell was big as a fist.

The man looked real, but she could tell that he was a plant spirit. She could not determine if he was from the Black Sorrow or the Maiden's Wand, or perhaps he was formed from the combination of the two—a new concept to her. Her mother had not talked of any such spirit. The old man looked at her knowingly, reminding her of Tatsuya.

Her mother. Tatsuya. It all came rushing back to her. Who she was. Earth. The moon. Peary Dome. The Fen. *Ming-Long and Khaled.* They had betrayed her. *Schlitzer.* She inhaled with a small gasp. The betrayal by her friends hurt almost more than the self-betrayal and shame of trading her body to the pimp for two drops of Greenwash. Why had Ming-Long and Khaled turned on her? How had they known she was in Schlitzer's tent? What had ever possessed her to have sex with Schlitzer? Her breathing was shallow and shaky.

Jasper and Torr. They would be sick with worry. They would tear the camp apart as they had before. Move every tent to look for holes underneath. Only they wouldn't find her. Surely they would come to search Gabira's cave. *And get drunk on her enchantment.* She gritted her teeth. *Gabira.* Her jaw clenched with hatred. What had that witch done, now? How had Cassidy gotten here? Had Ming-Long and Khaled brought her here at Gabira's command? She could remember nothing after the drug-dazed moments in the tent when Ming-Long and Khaled had suffocated her. Her next memory had been of Gabira's tent in the gentle breeze of the olive grove. She shook her head. That olive grove was not real.

She patted at her belly and reached up inside her robe. *Her rune belt and deed were gone. And all her gold.* She felt the pockets of her robe. Her crystal ball was not there, nor was the light crystal. Her neck was bare, all her pendants gone. Her heart raced. *Gabira, that wicked thief.*

She thought of Torr again, and a strange sensation came over her. A faint scent of forest brought on the image of a stand of towering pines. Shaking her head against the incongruous thought, she caught the eyes of the plant spirit man who was still looking at her while calmly tracing the spiral conch shell. Cassidy climbed to her feet and marched over to him.

"Who are you, and how do I get out of here?" she demanded.

The man laughed and gazed at her kindly. "Ah, very good. You can speak with me. I thought for a moment you assumed I was not real." His voice was soothing, but scratchy, like two branches rubbing lightly together.

"I know what you are," she said, her anger at Gabira tart on her tongue. "You're a plant spirit. You've come to help me."

The man laughed again—a rustling, whispering laugh. "Have I, now?"

"Yes. You've come to get me out of here. Me, and Aggie, and Carmen. *Carmen,*" she repeated, and whirled around to look at her friend. "Carmen," she called across the room. Cassidy ran to her and grabbed her hands. "Are you Berkeley's Carmen? Ramzy's daughter?"

Carmen stared, her eyes and mouth round. "Cassidy? Where are we?"

Cassidy hugged her. "Don't be afraid, Carmen. It's okay. The spell is broken. Do you remember who you are?"

Carmen pulled away and looked at her, tears streaming down her face. Carmen nodded, sniffing loudly. "My father sent me down here. To keep me away from Berkeley." She erupted into sobs. "How long have I been here? How do you know my father and Berkeley?"

Cassidy held Carmen's hands as the distraught woman got a hold of herself. Cassidy answered, "I know them through my friend, Jasper. Jaz."

"Jaz," Carmen said, recognition in her voice.

"I think you've been down here for two years," Cassidy said.

Carmen burst into sobs again. "Two years!" she moaned. "Oh." She rocked from side to side, and Cassidy hugged her again, patting her back.

"It's okay. It's okay," Cassidy said.

"Berkeley. He must have forgotten about me by now." Carmen's voice was thin and plaintive.

"No," Cassidy said firmly. "He has not. He misses you terribly. He tries to come visit you, but Gabira always bewitches him, and he forgets until he leaves the cave. It's always the same."

"That witch! Bloody Algol's severed head," Carmen cursed through her tears.

Agapantha's twittering laughter turned both their heads. "That Gabira," Agapantha chortled, "she's had us tricked this whole time. Wow, she's good."

Cassidy met Agapantha's bright blue eyes. "You think that's funny?"

"I think it's amazing," Agapantha said, her eyes glinting. "She's much more powerful than I ever thought." She clutched her hands together with excitement, and then her round face turned down in a frown. "She promised she'd teach me magic. But she hasn't taught me a thing. What a no-good liar. She took my gold and then trapped me down here in her enchanted web." Agapantha's eyes narrowed to thin slits. "She's a treacherous thief."

Cassidy nodded in agreement. "We have to get out of here," Cassidy whispered, suddenly afraid their voices would carry and Gabira and her daughters would hear them. "We have to leave before the herbs wear off."

"How?" Carmen asked.

Cassidy shrugged. "Walk. It can't be that far if Giselle and Daleelah come here every day."

"Yes," Carmen said. "And the serving room is not too far either, I believe." She looked like she was trying to remember a dream. "It's all foggy. They only called me to serve them a couple of times. Probably they were afraid someone would recognize me." Her face hardened, her weeping replaced by a stony scowl.

"Do you see that man?" Cassidy asked Carmen and Agapantha, nodding towards the conch shell man who was leaning against the stone wall, watching them calmly.

"No. See who?" Carmen asked.

"Nobody. Never mind. A vision," Cassidy said.

Agapantha peered around the cave and shook her head. "I don't see anyone. Just lizards climbing the walls."

Cassidy shivered and stared at the walls, not seeing any lizards. Her gaze fell on the man again. He smiled at her and nodded with encouragement. She turned back to her friends and said, "We can just walk out. Let's get our things."

"What if they catch us?" Carmen asked.

"I can't walk that far," Agapantha said anxiously.

"Yes you can. You have to. And I need to find my crystals," Cassidy said, panicking. *And the rune belt.* If Gabira had put it on her own body, Cassidy wouldn't be able to find it unless she could feel it against Gabira's skin. Her mood darkened. She would have to leave without her possessions. She could make more Black Sorrow and Maiden's Wand brew and confront the witch later. She stood up. "Come on. Hurry."

"What about the others?" Carmen asked, her eyes red from crying. She stood with Cassidy, brushing off her cloak.

"We'll have to come back for them later," Cassidy said.

Agapantha struggled to her feet with the help of Cassidy and Carmen.

Cassidy glanced over at the old man. He pointed towards the wall. "She's coming."

"Who?" Cassidy's heart jumped into her throat as heavy footsteps approached behind her. Cassidy turned to see Gabira's broad form blocking the back entrance to the cave. The proud woman strode towards them, purple sleeves fluttering against thick forearms that clinked with gold bangles.

"Mother Gabira," Agapantha and Carmen said fearfully. Carmen dropped to her knees and touched her forehead to the ground in a subservient bow. Cassidy quickly imitated her. She heard Agapantha fall heavily back into her chair and break into a coughing fit.

"Rise, Carmen and Cassidy," Gabira said in an almost kindly voice. "My daughters told me that a bad cough had broken out down here." Agapantha stopped coughing, her hand clapped over her mouth. Gabira peered at them. "I hope it is not the Peary Flu. Have you been throwing up as well?"

The three of them nodded silently. Cassidy glanced furtively at Gabira through lowered lashes, not wanting her to discover that the spell had been broken. She cast a darting glance over her shoulder. The old man was still there, looking on with interest. Gabira did not appear to see him.

"Don't you have herbs for this?" Gabira asked Cassidy.

Cassidy was shaking with nervousness. "Yes. I made some tea, and we all drank it. We're feeling better now," she said, trying to sound confident, but started coughing instead.

When the coughing spasm subsided, Gabira caught her eyes and held them. Cassidy tried to break the gaze but could not. Gabira's concerned expression hardened, her eyes turning cold with suspicion.

"What is your name?" Gabira demanded of Cassidy.

Cassidy swallowed. "Cassidy."

"What is your last name?"

Cassidy hesitated. "I don't know," she lied. What would she have said an hour ago? If she pushed past the glaring woman right now, she could escape. She could grab Carmen and they could escape together. But her herbs were scattered on her bedding. She'd need to leave them there, and Gabira had her crystal ball. That meant once the herbal brew wore off, she'd be unable to break Gabira's spell and free the others. And if she got caught again, she would have no way of escaping. She could feel the warm ceramic of the tiger flask against her breastbone. She still had that, which would be enough for one more dose. She eyed the distance to the dark tunnel from which Gabira had emerged.

Gabira gave her a hard look but spoke in a friendly, conversational tone. "Well, you certainly do look awake."

"Yes, ma'am," Cassidy said, her voice wavering. "I mean, I'm tired from being sick."

"But you see clearly." The woman's eyes were stony behind her smile.

Cassidy swallowed. "Yes, Mother Gabira. My vision is fine."

"Your vision is fine," Gabira repeated, her voice overly sweet. Cassidy was afraid she'd said the wrong thing. Did Gabira know she was no longer entranced? A nervous sweat broke out across Cassidy's brow. Gabira had her trapped in her gaze. A crystal shaft glinted ominously from Gabira's ample cleavage.

Cassidy felt a moment of lightheadedness, but quickly recovered. She could run past Gabira and find her way through the dark tunnels, but Gabira would follow. Gabira knew the way, and Cassidy did not. Surely the woman would catch her. Cassidy could tackle her right now with a simple swipe of the legs—knock the woman unconscious if she had to. Then she could take a candle and lead Carmen and Agapantha out. "I'm leaving," Cassidy announced, edging towards her bedding. She'd get her herbs, and then leave.

"You want to go back up top?" Gabira asked, as though it were a simple thing. "Why didn't you just say so?" The crystal shaft at Gabira's bosom glinted in the dim candlelight.

Cassidy's breath caught in her throat, and she fought back a cough. "You mean, I can leave?"

Gabira threw back her head and laughed. "Of course you can, sweetheart. Did you think you were a prisoner?"

Cassidy's face was hot, but she did not answer.

Gabira gestured towards Cassidy's purple sack and herbs where they lay in plain sight. "Gather your things. I'll take you now."

A breath of relief escaped Cassidy's lungs. "Oh. Really?" Could she trust the woman? It was clear the spell was broken; what power could the witch have over her now? If it came down to it, Cassidy could strike her on the back of the head and flee.

Gabira did not smile but nodded curtly. "Yes. Hurry up. It's cold down here." Gabira had dropped all pretenses, and Cassidy found Gabira's gruff manner oddly comforting.

"Carmen and Agapantha, too," Cassidy said. The two women glared at her, looking terrified.

Agapantha said quickly, "No, no. I'll stay here."

Gabira looked coldly at the two women, and then back at Cassidy. Cassidy's chest tightened. She had just revealed that her two friends were also free of Gabira's enchantment and was instantly sorry she had spoken.

Carmen pressed her lips together, her face growing pale.

Gabira sighed. "I'll get your father to fetch you," Gabira said to Carmen. "Ramzy will want to escort you. You stay here until I see Cassidy safely to the surface and send word to your father. Cassidy, get your things," she ordered.

Cassidy scurried to her bedding and stuffed the herbs and note-books into the purple sack and slung it over her shoulder. She ran to Carmen and hugged her. "I'll wait for you," she whispered in her ear. "I'll get Berkeley, and we'll wait outside the exit for you."

Carmen nodded and squeezed her in a tight hug. Cassidy went to Agapantha next and gave her a quick hug. "Tell the others I said goodbye." She met Agapantha's eyes, trying to tell her with a look that she would come back for her. Agapantha squeezed Cassidy's hand and wished her well.

Cassidy took a deep breath, turned away from her friends, and followed Gabira. They stepped into a stone tunnel and left the jade cave behind.

52

WARRIOR WIZARD

Torr woke up to cold water splashing on his face. He sputtered and opened his eyes, gasping for breath. The silhouette of a man stooped over him. A waterskin was shoved into his mouth, and Torr closed his eyes and sucked on the nozzle, gulping down the cold water until the skin was empty.

Bjarg stood over him, muttering in Scridnu. Torr was on the floor of the supply lean-to, and Velspara stood by, holding a torch and looking down at him worriedly. Torr opened his mouth as Bjarg cradled his head and placed another waterskin spout in his mouth. This time it was a salty, sour drink. Torr drank it all, and then Bjarg laid his head gently on the hard floor. The side of his head hurt, and he felt for a lump, slipping his fingers under the pointed bear hide cap.

Velspara and Bjarg knelt to either side of him and scraped dirt-caked grease off his bare skin with a stone tool they used for scraping hides, and then washed his naked body with warm water scented with fragrant oil. Torr lay limp as they washed him a second time, turning him over to get every inch of his body, and then smeared him with a pungent salve. He closed his eyes as four hands kneaded his muscles.

When they were done, they rolled him in a clean hide and propped him up to a sitting position against the back of the lean-to. Velspara left, and Bjarg held Torr's face, looking into one eye, then the other, and talked to him in the guttural Scridnu language. Torr stared dumbly at him. Velspara returned with a bowl of gruel and fed him with a flat wooden spoon. After Torr finished the gruel, Bjarg made him drink a bitter brew. Then they laid Torr down, and he slept.

They woke him up several times that night and throughout the next day for food and drink. Bjarg and Velspara knelt by him anxiously as they fed him gruel and water. In the afternoon, they stripped him and massaged him again with the herbal salve, and then helped him hobble to the trees where he pissed in a dribble onto the leaves. He slept again. He awoke later to find Velspara kneeling next to him with a steaming bowl of meat and root stew, and a brew of bitter herbs.

By the next day, he could feed himself, and by the following day he was walking normally.

That night around the campfire, Bjarg acted out the story of how he'd found Torr. The Scrid had awoken to a thunderous roar and found a huge bear in the supply hut, penned inside by Torr's wolf. Bjarg knew the majestic ursine creature was Torr—shapeshifted into a bear—by the pointed cap that was perched on the bear's head. Bjarg had summoned Torr's spirit from the bear, and Torr had transformed back into himself, covered with dirt from head to toe.

Torr grunted in response. What a bunch of bullshit. Bjarg had probably dragged him from the jaws of death at the very last instant and was weaving this tale to make it seem like some mystical, magical event. The man had nearly killed him with his crazy ritual. Bjarg saw his silent scowl and insisted Torr had passed the initiation rite and had proven himself a most powerful *Odinn*. Torr glared sullenly into the man's fervent, golden eyes. The Scrid wizard truly believed his own story, or at least wanted Torr to believe it.

Torr vividly recalled a dream he'd had of his mother, lost in the Shaman's Shield in a tortured maze of massive oak branches, with a raven riding her shoulder. They had followed the whisperings of the grandmother oak trees through the endless fog to the other side. The memory almost made him smile. He only vaguely recalled a bizarre dream of being a bear and clawing himself out of an earthen pit. He admitted to himself that there could possibly be some truth to what Bjarg was saying, but Torr was not about to approve of the man's methods. There were other ways to induce delirious dreaming besides half-killing someone. The wizard took a step back as Torr rose to his feet and glowered at the man.

"Mangarm," Bjarg said, reaching out to take his arm.

"Go to hell," Torr said, shoving the man so hard that he fell to the ground. Torr turned on his heel and retreated to the lean-to, where he rolled himself up in his bear hide bedding and fell into a fitful sleep.

At dawn, Torr left the camp by himself. He followed the trail over the hills and found the clearing where he'd been buried. The pit was still there, partially filled with dirt, with mounds of freshly turned soil surrounding the hole. Torr knelt down and examined the marks in the dirt. It had clearly been disturbed by creatures over the past few days during his recovery. He could see cloven hoof marks from the boars, and little claw marks from the rabbit creatures. He froze as he found what he had been afraid of finding. Large five-toed clawed prints marked the dirt in several places. The foot pads were massive, the paw prints bigger than his own hand. Deep furrows that could only have been made by long claws scored the sides of the pit. Torr sat heavily on the ground and his heart beat wildly in his chest. The possibility was too strange to accept.

Finally he got to his knees and pushed the dirt into the hole, filling it as best he could. When he was done, it formed a small mound that looked like a fresh grave. He scoured the edges of the clearing and found a knee-high rock. He levered it loose with a sturdy stick and scraped off dirt and leaves to reveal the softly shining white mineral that had been hiding underneath the grime. He examined it and concluded it was the same stone as a grundhalda. Torr rolled the small boulder across the clearing and up onto the dirt mound. He surveyed his work. Satisfied, he left the clearing to go apologize to Bjarg.

———————————⟩—————————

Torr had regained his strength and felt like himself again. Over the next several days, Bjarg made him practice the chants over and over, and Torr was pleased that raising the whirlwind of pine needles had become much easier since his bear-death.

After one such successful practice session, Bjarg clapped his fists to his chest, saluting Torr respectfully, and told him that he was truly a Warrior Wizard and was ready to travel the stars.

The next morning, Bjarg and Velspara presented him with two parting gifts. One was a rattle made of a large, round, shiny black seedpod attached to the end of a short black stick. It made a sharp shushing sound when Torr shook it. It was the pod of a black dream flower, Bjarg communicated to him, which Velspara had harvested and dried for Torr before she'd ever found him. Torr raised an eyebrow, unsure if he'd understood correctly.

They insisted, explaining with pantomime and guttural Scridnu that Velspara had dreamed of him since the great bird star in the sky reached the zenith of the heavens, the season when the river runs high and the sun shines the warmest. She had thought the dream was of a Scrid adolescent boy because of his skinniness and lack of thick Scrid man-hair. She had dreamt of him walking the forest with a wolf flanking him on one side and a bear on the other. Torr got goosebumps and met Velspara's eyes as she smiled proudly. Torr thanked her and shook the rattle, returning her grin, then tucked the black stick through his belt. He felt a respectful fondness for his spirit animals, resting one hand on the pommel of the wolf knife at his hip and the other on the Bear crystal that hung from his neck in a bear-suede sling Velspara had made for it.

The second gift was a long hooded cloak of soft suede. Torr rubbed the suede under his palm. It had a short velvety nap of a dusky charcoal-gray color that when he rubbed his hand against the nap turned a deep slate blue. The cloak was smooth under his fingertips and was feather-light. He swirled it around his shoulders, and it flowed like silk, draping down with its hem skimming the ground in a silent swish. He pulled up the hood, and his head disappeared inside, sheltering his eyes in what felt like a secret cave.

Torr threw back the hood and smiled with delight. "Wow," he said. "Fit for a king."

Bjarg and Velspara tilted their heads at him, not understanding. He searched his limited Scridnu vocabulary, settling on words that meant, "Glorious stars, a hide for a tribal chief." It was an awkward phrase, but they understood his sentiment, and their faces lit up with delight.

"Mangarm," Bjarg said, pressing his forehead to Torr's.

Velspara in turn pressed her forehead to his, then carefully took the cloak from his shoulders. Her amber eyes met his. *"Varda,"* she said, *Watch,* and drew the cloak over her own shoulders. She pulled the large hood over her head, tucked her hands inside the sealed cloak, and disappeared.

Torr stared at the empty air, astonished. He turned to Bjarg, whose eyes met his, gleaming mischievously. Bjarg laughed, and Velspara reappeared, throwing the hood off her head and joining in with her father's laughter. Torr swallowed, unable to speak. She cloaked herself again, and he reached out and pawed the air where she had been standing. He felt nothing. She reappeared suddenly, and he found his hand pressed against her chest.

He drew his hand back apologetically, then took the cloak from her and tried it himself. He pulled on the hood, lowering it so that the large cowl completely enshrouded his head, leaving only a small gap to see out of. He pulled the front closed across his chest and could tell by their expressions the moment he disappeared. He drew in a deep breath, overcome with bemused elation.

"Hey, can you hear me?" he asked. They registered no response. He stepped next to Velspara and touched her shoulder with his hand sealed inside the cape. He could feel her shoulder through the soft suede, but she did not react. He pressed against her shoulder but could not move her. She held her ground as though he were not exerting any pressure at all. He walked around Velspara and her father, whistling loudly. No response.

Drawing back the hood, he regarded them with open-mouthed wonder. "What in Algol's hell is this?" They smiled widely. He repeated his question in Scridnu, using one of their expletives, which translated to, "What in the fire of dawn is this?"

"*Grimkott,*" Velspara said, and lowered her hands to the ground where she prowled on all fours like a feline.

"Ah, a cat," he said, and then switched to Scridnu. "How big?" he asked.

Bjarg told him it was large, holding his hand at the height of Torr's hip.

"Ah, a big cat." Still, it must have taken several of the beasts to make such a cloak.

"Big cat," Velspara repeated in Globalish.

"*Grim,*" Bjarg said, pointing to his shadow.

"Oh, a shadow. Shadow cat," Torr said.

"Shadow cat," Velspara parroted, smiling proudly.

Torr wouldn't have minded staying there and teaching her Globalish and improving his Scridnu, which he was just beginning to grasp. But he was growing anxious from letting so many weeks slip by. Cassidy had surely found more trouble by now, or at the very least was wondering hopelessly where he was, while here he was laughing and playing with an invisibility cape.

Not that such an incredible tool would not come in handy. It was truly a precious, invaluable gift. He couldn't wait to show Cassidy, and Jasper, and Berkeley. Jasper would try to trade something inconsequential for it, downplaying its worth. Torr had learned his lesson with the garnet. How much easier would his time on Scridland have been if he'd had the translation crystal? His hand went to the hilt of the wolf knife. It had been a fair trade, he reluctantly admitted. He looked down at the pommel, and the metal wolf stared out at him expectantly. Yes, he agreed, it was time to go.

He bowed his thanks to Velspara and Bjarg, and they pressed foreheads again. Torr was suddenly filled with sadness. And fear.

"Will the shadow cat cloak help me travel?" he asked in Scridnu.

"No, Mangarm," Bjarg answered. "It will help you afterwards. Find the light of the stars and bring the golden trail to Scridland."

Torr did not know what the light of the stars was, or how he would bring a golden trail to Scridland, but he nodded solemnly.

After a hearty meal, Torr gathered his things. He rolled his few belongings in his bear hide and strapped it across his back, then draped his new cloak over the whole bulky thing. The cloak still fell perfectly to the ground, brushing the grass silently as he walked.

They left the hamlet together as the sun rose higher in the sky, then hiked westward all day until the sun fell below the horizon, turning the sky a pale purple. Velspara led them to a small clearing, where she freed a rabbit from a trap. Bjarg would not allow them to make a cookfire, saying it would drive the bear spirits away. Torr knew better than to shrug off Bjarg's comment, and the nervousness that had been following him all day took hold of him and dug into his belly.

Torr tried not to think about what he was about to attempt. If he thought about it, his rational mind told him it was impossible to traverse the heavens to the grundhalda at the Scrid camp in Peary Dome.

No chants, rattles, drums, bells, or crystals could possibly help him accomplish such a feat. Then he recalled the whispering grandmother oaks—and shapeshifting into a bear. Plus, he reminded himself, he had made it here with Vaka. He took a deep breath. It was better if he didn't think about it.

They spent the next day tramping across rolling hills covered with tall pines that grew so closely together no sun shone through. They crossed a wide rushing stream, hopping over a series of jutting white rocks, then climbed the hill beyond. The ground here was rocky, and soon there were no trees, only fields of yellow lichen and clumps of small scraggly bushes that managed to find a hold on thin patches of dirt.

They had gained elevation, and Torr looked back from where they'd come, taking in the broad vista of green forested ridges that turned blue, then misty gray as they receded into the distance. He breathed deeply. This planet was sparsely inhabited. A primal, untamed land. There were no spaceports, Jorimar had told him, and therefore no threat of Tegs or the Cephean Federation snooping about. It was a wild, free place, and Torr felt the urge to stay. He inhaled the pristine air and turned his eyes upward. Earth was out there somewhere. The moon. His sister. He sighed and hurried to catch up with Bjarg and Velspara.

After cresting the next ridge, another hill rose gently before them and glowed white in the sunlight. Torr stood and gazed upon it, squinting against the bright reflection from the smooth, sloping white rock that spanned the whole of the hillside. The hill was formed entirely of grundhalda, Torr realized with a shiver of excitement.

They trod across the broad flat rock, hopping over little crevasses to a large expanse of unbroken stone. Torr felt the familiar comfort of the white gravity bar mineral. He shrugged off his cloak and bundle and lay down on the ground, gazing up at the pale blue sky and letting the heat of the sun-soaked stone warm his back. There was so much of the grundhalda in one place, its pervasive calm seeped into Torr's blood, relaxing every cell in his body. He rested his palms against the rock, and his heartbeat expanded in his chest until his whole body pulsed with the heartbeat of the ground, matching rhythms in a deep throbbing cadence.

Bjarg called to him, and Torr reluctantly climbed to his feet, gathered his things, and followed the wizard up the gently sloping hillside until they came to its peak. Green hills unfurled below them in all directions. They stopped where the stone ridge widened onto a small plateau in the shape of a rough circle. In the middle of the circle stood a large white boulder, twice Torr's height and as wide as it was tall.

"Up there," Bjarg said, pointing to the grundhalda boulder.

Torr and Velspara circled around it. The back face of the rock was jagged, and Torr was able to find finger and toe holds to pull himself to the top. Velspara stayed down below with Bjarg, and they gazed up at him with poignant expressions.

"You will travel from the grundhalda," Bjarg said to him in Scridnu. "You will wait for the bears. They will send you flying through the stars."

With that, Bjarg and Velspara pressed their fingers to their foreheads in the Scrid equivalent of throwing a kiss, then turned and strode away.

"Wait!" Torr called, his heart jumping in his chest. "Are you leaving?" He lowered himself down from the rock and jogged after them, but they did not turn around. Their backs were stiff, and Torr could read from their body language that they did not intend to look back, and that Torr was not to follow. He stopped and stared after them, tears coming to his eyes. He wasn't ready for them to leave. He had thought they would help him. Lend him their power. Dance and stomp around the boulder to speed him in his way. Say a proper goodbye, at least.

He breathed heavily and tried to slow his heart as the two Scrids headed down the slope. *"Kappo,"* he called, sending his thanks to them, though no words could express his true gratitude. "May the stars shine upon you," he called in Globalish, and then tried to cobble together the blessing in his rough Scridnu, *"Foera stjarna skina ayo!"*

He thought he saw their steps falter for an instant, but with heads held high, they continued towards the forest.

53

THE ICE-MAKER

Ridge turned around in the small living space of the Last Chance lab. He really should move into the permanent quarters next door. He had all but moved out of his house, and the Last Chance residential quarters were more or less complete. It was just so big and empty over there. Ishmar kept putting off joining him, and Ali refused to discuss it. Murphy and the workers lived in their little bunkroom in the back of the hangar and were too scared of him to offer any sort of real companionship. Ridge sighed and gathered his things for his latest project. It was time to install Balty's new ice-maker.

Balty had been bugging him about it for weeks, but Ridge had needed to fashion a new cherrywood cabinet and a smaller set of shelves to replace the existing shelving where the ice-maker was to go under the wet bar. He loaded the carefully constructed cabinet into a Korova, along with a bag of tools and the other equipment, and climbed into the cockpit. His palms were moist with nervous sweat, and he wiped them on the legs of his flight suit. Before he could get through the lab's decompression chamber, they were moist again. He tried to calm his pulse as he flew over the bleak moonscape.

Balty was in the living room, on his way to becoming drunk, with Athena staggering around with him. Three of Balty's bodyguards sat at the kitchen table, playing cards and looking bored. Balty half-heartedly offered the services of one of his men to help Ridge, but last time one of them had helped him build a cabinet in the game room, the idiot had cut all the shelves an inch too short. Ridge declined the offer, and the guards looked relieved.

"This place is going to be a work zone for a few hours," Ridge warned Balty and Athena, "so take whatever you want into the kitchen for now."

They lugged liquor bottles and glasses into the kitchen and then retreated to the game room with their drinks, leaving Ridge by himself.

He had installed the plumbing the week before for the water intake and drainage. All he had to do was wire the electrical, install the cabinetry and the ice-maker, and rig the motion sensor.

The ice-maker sat in front of the wet bar on the floor. Ridge had removed the old shelves when he'd done the plumbing, and a gaping hole awaited the new cabinetry and appliance. Ridge tested the fit of the new cherrywood cabinet. He slid it into the gap. It fit perfectly. He slid it out again and rested it on the floor. Now was the tricky part. Cables hung off the top back of the cabinet and had to be handled carefully.

Balty walked through the end of the room on his way to the kitchen. "How's it going?" he asked.

Ridge stood with his hands on his hips. "Good, good. The cabinet fits perfectly. I built some lights into it that I'll wire into the new motion sensor, along with the lights that frame the liquor shelves over the bar."

"Excellent plan," Balty said, and disappeared into the kitchen.

Ridge got a ladder from the hangar and set about replacing the motion sensor, which was mounted onto a corner of the ceiling over the wet bar. There was actually nothing wrong with it. Ridge had loosened the connections intentionally months ago when he'd first hatched his plan. He needed to replace it with the one he'd brought with the tiny video camera embedded in it, which would feed a signal up to the antenna where he had installed a new transmitter. No one would detect the video signal the way he was encrypting it and interlacing it with the radar deforming signals he broadcast from his antenna arrays. As long as Ridge was within range of one of his antenna towers, he'd be able to pick it up, decrypt it, and watch and listen to whatever was going on in this room. That meant he could watch from the comfort of his Last Chance lab. He suppressed a devilish smirk as Balty staggered through the room again, two glasses clutched in his hands.

Ridge fished the antenna cables from inside the wall behind the motion sensor fixture, hooked the video camera into the antenna and the electrical, and mounted the new motion sensor device onto the ceiling. That done, he removed the molding that ran along the top of the wall over the wet bar, ran new cables from the motion sensor and antenna, and mounted them across the top of the wall. Then he drilled a hole above the wet bar, dropped the cables behind the wall, and heard them snake down and land on the floor. He replaced the molding and fished the cables out from under the wet bar's sink.

So far, so good. It had all been accomplished with minimal mess, and with no questions from Balty. The next part was the tricky part. Connecting the motion sensor to the lights was no big deal—it was the other set of cables he was nervous about.

He had tested his Silox with the remote-controlled detonation mechanism and antenna extension dozens of times out on the mare, so there was no reason to doubt his design. Still, sweat beaded on his brow, and his fingers trembled as he gently slid forward the cabinet with the false top that hid two Silox devices. He only really needed one Silox to do the job. He had put enough explosives in each of the metal canisters to blow the entire compound to Algol's hell. But in case one failed, he wanted a backup.

If there was a flaw in his design, he would discover it when he messed with the cables now, although he'd have no chance to realize it while being blown into star dust. Or he'd discover it when he triggered it remotely and nothing happened. He'd get to watch the event in any case, or at least right before. A sick grimace tugged at his mouth. He took a deep breath and wired the wet bar lights into the motion sensor. Then he held his breath as he spliced the Silox trigger cables into the roof's antenna cable. Sweat soaked into his flight suit and dripped down his clean-shaven scalp as he sat back on his heels and regarded his work. He was still here. A smile crept across his face.

He carefully arranged the Silox cables, then gently slid the open-backed cabinet into place without incident. Next he maneuvered the ice-maker into position, then lay on the floor while he connected the plumbing and electrical. When he was done, he pushed the ice-maker all the way into the cabinet, opened and closed the finely crafted cher-rywood door, and then turned on the ice-maker and listened as water rushed through the narrow pipe. He stepped into the kitchen to wait for the lights to go out, and then went back into the living room. The lights went on. Nothing exploded.

He slid in the set of shelving he'd fashioned for the remaining space, and then admired his handiwork. It was beautiful. He put away the ladder, cleaned up the mess of dust and cable fragments, and then neatly lined up liquor bottles on the new shelves. The various colors of glass bottles and liquor glowed in the lighting, creating a pleasing display.

Ridge poured himself a glass of tequila, then sat on the couch and waited for there to be ice.

———————)———————

Ridge sat in his Last Chance lab and watched on his handscreen as Balty stood at the wet bar in the living room. Ridge laughed out loud. It was ridiculously perfect.

His handcrafted Silox remote control activator sat on the work-bench within easy reach. He picked it up, licking his lips as he smugly watched Balty bend to fill a glass from the new ice-maker and then pour golden whiskey over the ice. Ridge could hear the crackling of the ice as the liquor hit it, and Ridge nodded with satisfaction—the video camera's far field microphone was sensitive enough that he would be able to hear conversations in the living room if he wanted to.

Ridge rested his finger on the Silox's remote control trigger mecha-nism and took a deep breath. If he were lucky, the deed to Anaximenes was either on Balty's person or stashed in his private quarters and would disintegrate with everything else, bringing that unfortunate chapter to a close.

Athena appeared on the screen and walked up behind Balty to accept a drink. Ah, now there was the rub. Ridge would have to blow up that beauty when he took out the slimeball and his thugs, plus the second girl who was locked up in the back. That was unfair. But neither was it fair that Ridge would end up destroying the love of his own life: his house. His masterpiece. He had put his heart and soul into that building, and Balty had come in and stolen it out from under him.

Ridge imagined the handsome general blown to bits in front of his eyes. To get the full effect, Ridge would need to take the remote control out in his speedster within view of the house—but not too close. It would be like the Silox explosions out on the basalt mare—a flash of light followed by an expanding cloud of debris and dust. Anything within range would be hit with hunks of hurling metal.

Ridge pondered the aftermath as he watched Balty and Athena lounge on Ridge's couch as if they owned the place. If Harbin were smart, he would suspect Ridge. Who else could engineer such a spectacular explosion? What if word of his Siloxes made its way back to Gandoop? He hadn't trained his men at Last Chance on using the devices for mining yet, but they might talk of Ridge's repeated blasts during their infrequent trips to Gandoop. He couldn't keep his workers totally isolated, unless he wanted to do all the supply runs himself. And eventually he wanted to manufacture the devices and sell them to lunar mines for a hefty profit. He chewed at the inside of his cheek.

Maybe no one would suspect anything. Maybe they'd figure the house blew up from some random malfunction. He wrinkled his brow. Like what? They didn't have anything there that was massively explosive. The nuclear generators were incredibly stable. Oxygen tanks would cause only minor damage. Maybe he had over-engineered his solution.

Maybe Harbin would be glad to be rid of Balty and would quash any investigations. Maybe Ridge should bribe him. No, that was a stupid idea.

Maybe Harbin would suspect Peary Dome of staging an attack. Harbin would call in more Teg troops and they would attack Peary. Ramzy would resist, and General Tegea would order Harbin to destroy the dome. Ridge exhaled as Balty and Athena happily sipped their drinks.

Ridge relaxed and withdrew his finger from the trigger. He could still blow up the motherfucker right now, but he preferred to watch Balty's face. The man was so smug. So arrogant. So completely oblivious to the fact that Ridge held Balty's life and death at his fingertips. Ridge smiled to himself. Maybe tomorrow.

54

SHARDS

Cassidy followed Gabira down a long winding tunnel. Gabira held a candle that sputtered every now and then, forcing them to stop until the flame steadied and carved a little dome of light out of the darkness. They did not speak. A gust of warm air blew the flame out. Gabira cursed into the black air and fumbled with matches. Cassidy held the candle while Gabira lit it again, then handed it back to the grumpy woman, the smell of sulfur lingering in the air. Gabira seemed to be sore that someone could break her spell. Cassidy wanted to gloat but was distracted by a growing sense of unease.

They turned a sharp corner and headed down a long incline. "Where are we going?" Cassidy asked.

"Outside," Gabira said simply, and did not break her stride.

Cassidy held back a rush of panic. She should turn and run the other way, but what if she got lost? She remembered the first time she'd found herself in these caves and escaped. She had crept up a winding passageway from one of the rooms Gabira was excavating. That time, she had been given a glimpse of the path by her crystal ball. Now, she did not know where the jade cave lay within the maze of tunnels. She glanced behind her and saw the old plant spirit man trailing at a distance, just within the soft halo of light cast by the candle. The conch shell hanging from his neck glowed in a softly gleaming spiral. His presence gave her small comfort. He had not revealed his purpose, and maybe he had none. She set her jaw and decided she would follow Gabira just a little bit further. If they did not come to the way out soon, she would turn around and brave the darkness.

The tunnel seemed to go on forever. She tried to memorize every turn. Just as she was gathering her courage to flee, the air brightened and a musky fragrance reached her nose. She inhaled deeply. It reminded her of Earth, and her anxiety slipped away. Everything was going to be okay.

The tunnel widened to a round grotto with a sandy floor. Filtered light shone through the far passageway. Cassidy felt a surge of longing and ran towards the light. She emerged from the cave and found herself on the side of a hill. The sky was hazy, and clouds obscured the sun. Below her stretched an orchard of greenish-gray olive trees. The ground was hard and dry, with tufts of straw-colored grass poking up here and there. Homesickness for Earth welled up in her chest, and she looked to the gray sky, confused. Was Earth up there, or was she on Earth now?

Cassidy climbed down a series of terraces to a small valley and walked between rows of trees, running her fingers over smooth leaves. There were no olives. Last time, Daleelah had been harvesting ripe fruit, and the leaves had fluttered in a warm breeze. Now, everything was still. There had been a golden tent pavilion before, grand and majestic. Now, there were only rows of gnarled trees that ran the length of the small valley and lined the hills on either side. If she went over the hill, would she find the golden pavilion and discover the way out? Would the pavilion then turn into the room with the olive mural that would lead out to the corridor and up the stairs to freedom?

Cassidy stepped gingerly over the dry earth, and Gabira followed a few paces behind. The conch shell man picked his way slowly through the orchard, stooping to examine fallen branches.

Cassidy had the vague sense that she should not stray so far into this strange land, but fascination kept her moving forward. What was this place? She made her way to the facing hill and mounted the terraces towards the top, wanting to know what lay beyond. When she reached the crest, she saw a hazy panorama of distant hills, blue and gray in the distance. Below her lay a field of butchered trees and branches. There was no pavilion. There were only gray limbs stacked in rough piles or strewn indiscriminately. Cassidy's breath caught in her throat. These were the trees from her dream. The trees young Gabira had been crying over. The trees that had made the woman go mad with grief.

Cassidy glanced over her shoulder at the older woman, who was huffing from the effort of climbing up the terraced orchard behind her. Gabira's snarling, triumphant smile greeted her as the heavy woman swung a thick piece of wood at Cassidy's head. Cassidy was caught by surprise, and before she could twist around to block the blow or duck out of its way, the club met the side of her skull, and all went black.

———————)———————

Cassidy rose onto her elbow, awakened by her own coughing. Her head pounded painfully. She gingerly felt the side of her head and found that her hair was sticky with blood and a big lump had formed. She rolled onto her back and stared up at the gray sky. The air was hot and dry. A wrinkled brown face peered down at her. She sat up with alarm, then recognized the conch shell hanging from the old man's neck. Slowly, as if piecing together fragments of a dream, she recalled what had happened and where she was—on a ridge in Gabira's enchanted olive grove.

"That bitch," Cassidy mumbled as she fingered her blood-matted hair and the tender lump on the side of her head. She rose unsteadily to her feet, suppressed another cough, and searched the ground. All she found was her discarded wool hat. Her purple sack of herbs was gone. "That bitch," she repeated, and gazed despairingly at her surroundings. To one side of the ridge stretched the desolate field of felled trees. To the other side was the small green valley and hill where they had come out of the cave. Cassidy spotted the purple of Gabira's robe through the trees as the woman climbed the terraces to the yellow chalky outcropping where the entrance to the cave stood. Cassidy wanted to run after her, but a wave of dizziness forced her to sit back down and hold her head in her hands. By the time the dizziness passed and she got to her feet again, Gabira was gone. Cassidy peered at the hillside but could not locate the entrance to the tunnels.

The conch shell man stood calmly by her side and smiled at her dumbly.

"Can you help me?" she asked. He just smiled. "Please, can you help me?" she repeated.

He tilted his head at her and continued smiling as though it were all very entertaining. He was no help. She would have to get out of this trap on her own. She made her way down the terraced hillside, heading back the way she had come.

Her head throbbed. She stuffed the hat into her pocket and walked across the small green valley, stumbling over the rough ground in her long woolen cloak and ducking under olive branches that snagged her hair. She stopped and rested her hands on her knees, waiting for a wave of nausea to pass. After several deep breaths, she kept walking. The man walked beside her as she crossed the orchard. What if she could not find her way out? She'd be stuck in this eerie likeness of Earth, which was much too still and silent to be real. Cold tendrils of panic wrapped around her throat, but she forced them away. She had to think clearly.

She tripped over a rut in the ground and fell against the old man. He caught her with strong hands. Up to this moment, she had thought him to be an incorporeal being, not flesh and bones.

"Whoa, there," he said, grabbing her arm to steady her. "Easy, now."

Cassidy stared at him. "You're real," she said breathlessly.

He shrugged with an amused smile. "I'm as real as this place, I suppose." He laughed a dry laugh. "As real as you are—here." He held her arm with a firm grip as she stood on unsteady legs.

"Where is *here*, exactly?" she asked, studying his wizened face.

"This," he said, gesturing to the trees and hills, "is a fragment of another reality. Brought into existence by that powerful shaman you call Gabira." He shook his head in wonder. "She is something, isn't she? I've only seen the likes of her a few times." He grinned broadly.

"Another reality?" she asked. "A fragment?"

"Yes. A fragment is a sort of parallel reality. A piece from another place and time brought into being by the power of a shaman's will. This one is quite something." He drew in a deep breath through his nose, smelling the air, and waved his hand across the small green valley filled with olive trees.

"Can we get to Earth from here? Are we on Earth?" Cassidy asked, and then coughed, sending a stabbing pain through her head.

His eyes widened. "Earth? No. We are nowhere. We are here, but not here." He cackled.

"How come the herbs didn't break this magic spell?" she asked.

"Because this is not a spell. It's a fragment, as I told you. The herbs broke the spell of forgetfulness and confusion Gabira had placed on you, that's all. That was a powerful spell, I must say. She threw in a good dose of murky muddlement as well, with the help of that sparkly crystal shaft she wears around her neck. Even your herbs couldn't completely ward off the power of that crystal. Gabira is very powerful to keep so many people entranced for so long. But a fragment is something completely different."

Cassidy let out a short breath. "How will we get out of here?" Panic clutched at her again and she stepped away, wanting to run for the chalky hill, but his bony fingers wrapped around her wrist.

"Chasing her won't help," he said. "She has gone to the other side."

"You mean we're trapped here," Cassidy said, with a deepening despair.

The man shrugged casually, as though it were no big thing to be lost in another reality.

Cold fear washed over her, making Cassidy's skin prickle. She turned to face him. "I need to get out. How can I get out?" Her pulse hammered painfully in her head, and she suddenly found it hard to breathe.

He held up one finger. "You need a shard."

"A shard," she repeated, not understanding. She counted her breaths to calm herself, recalling sitting in the meditation class with Berkeley and staring at a rock. If she lost her head now, she could be stuck here—nowhere—forever. She turned her eyes to meet the old man's. They were small and black and glittered. He knew how to get out.

She grabbed his wrist, fear seizing her again as another thought rushed in. "When the herbs wear off, will you disappear?"

"Yes. I am Yachak. When the influence of the Natema wears off, I will return to my realm." His face was grim.

"Natema?" she asked. "The red brew?"

He nodded. "You are a plant spirit medicine woman, are you not? Only shamans know how to combine the plants to make Natema."

Cassidy tried to piece together recent events. Had it been six hours since she'd drunk the combined potion of Black Sorrow and Maiden's

Wand? She tried to calculate how long she'd sat with Carmen and Agapantha, and then the journey through the tunnels with Gabira, and now the minutes—or hours—spent in the olive orchard. There was a strange timelessness in the caves, and out here it was even worse. Cassidy lifted the ceramic tiger flask from inside her woolen cloak and uncorked it, bringing it to her lips with trembling fingers. She tilted it and drank all of the bitter liquid. She squatted and waited for the vomiting to come. It rose quickly, and she emptied her stomach onto the dry ground, and then hid behind a tree to release her churning bowels. Natema was a wretchedly inconvenient concoction, she thought, as she cleaned herself with handfuls of dry grass. She sat under another tree and waited for the sickness to pass.

She found Yachak nearby, rummaging through fallen branches.

"What are you doing?" she asked.

"Collecting shards," he said. "You should as well."

"What is a shard?" she asked.

The conch shell man stood and regarded her. "A shard is a piece of the fragment that you carry back with you. If you can bring a shard back to your base reality, then you can use it to cross into and out of fragments."

"Any fragment, or just the fragment you got the shard from?" she asked.

He pursed his brown lips. "For a shaman, a shard from any fragment will work. For normal people, it must be a shard from that same fragment." He saw her worried look and assured her, "You are a shaman, don't worry about that, otherwise we would not be talking right now."

She felt a spark of pride at the confirmation, but her delight was quickly smothered by anxiety. "If I have to bring the shard out before I can use it, how can I get out in the first place?" she asked. Shamanism did not make sense. The rules were all backwards.

"I will lend you one," he said, his eyes glinting. "I have two."

Relief swelled inside her, and she found herself able to breathe again. She squeezed his wiry arm, not wanting to let go. His hand went to the large conch shell hanging from his neck. He lifted it to show her. "This is the first shard I ever got out myself. I almost didn't make it. That shaman was cunning, that one. He'd made a fragment of an underwater cave. I had to hold my breath until I almost burst, swimming out." He cackled again. "That shaman was treacherous."

"But how were you able to carry the shell between the worlds?" Cassidy asked.

"A friend had given me a shard." Yachak showed her a green-rimmed copper coin that had been pierced with a hole and was strung onto the cord that held the shell. "I carry it still. My friend got it from his teacher. I don't know how his teacher got it. Here." Yachak untied the knot of the cord, pulled off the copper piece, and handed it to Cassidy. She clutched the tarnished coin tightly in her fist.

Yachak tied on his conch shell necklace, then kicked at the sticks at his feet. "Gather some bits of wood. Those from the oldest trees are best. I saw a good one across the way. Come on."

She held onto his thin bare arm as he led her through the trees. An ancient tree stood in the center of younger ones. Its trunk was wide and knotted. A section of the trunk had died and had fallen into a jumbled heap. She and Yachak pulled at the dried wood, looking for loose pieces. Cassidy pulled a section off that came apart in several pieces the size of small daggers. She found one she particularly liked. It was smooth and had a notch for her grip. She stuffed several other wood shards into the deep side pockets of her cloak and clutched her favorite shard in her hand with the coin.

"Is this good?" she asked Yachak, showing it to him. He smiled and nodded. "And these?" She showed him the contents of her pockets. "I'll be able to give these to my friends?"

"Yes," he said. "If you can get the shards through to the other side. Come on. Let's go." He had gathered a few shards of wood for himself and stuffed them under his belt. Cassidy took his arm, and they headed for the hill.

Yachak led Cassidy to the shadowed cleft in the hillside, where they entered the sandy mouth of the cave system and ventured into the deep blackness.

———————)———————

"Yachak?" Cassidy called, feeling around in the pitch-dark cave. "Yachak!"

Echoing silence answered her. The air was thick and cold as she reached through the nothingness until she bumped against a rock wall, hard and rough against her calloused palm. The stale air caught in her throat. She called out again for the skinny little man. His arm had been strong and wiry in her grip, and then it was gone. She leaned back against the wall, calling for him. Panic rose in her throat. His copper coin was gone, and she clutched the shard of wood to her chest, happy for a moment that she had carried a shard between the worlds. She reached into her pockets, and her fingers met several other smooth pieces of olivewood.

Her satisfaction was quickly overtaken by nervousness. She was deep in the caves and could not possibly retrace her steps. She rallied her courage and crept forward, keeping one hand against the wall and the other hand wrapped around the olivewood shard. The tunnel descended slowly, taking her deeper into the rock. Maybe Yachak had left her on the correct trail, and all she had to do was follow it.

Then she came to a fork. She held her breath and headed left. After more intersections, she admitted to herself that she was hopelessly lost. Fear surrounded her, pressing in from all sides. There was nothing to do other than stagger forward. Perhaps she would die in here. Perhaps that's what Gabira had wanted all along.

It could have been minutes or hours that she stumbled through the endless tunnels, forcing herself to take another step, to take another breath. A distant *tap tap tap* brought her to a standstill. Was it her pulse pounding? No. She dropped to her knees and pressed her ear to the ground. *Tap tap tap.*

She rushed forward, and then paused again to listen for the faint sound. She followed it through the winding darkness, finally detecting light ahead. Her blood rushed and she emerged into a long low room lit by flickering candles set on the floor. Relief flooded through her, and her legs grew weak and trembly. Her toe hit a chisel, making a clanging sound as it hit the metal hammer next to it. A dozen women looked up from their work chipping stone and stared at her, their faces transformed into dancing shadows by the flames. Cassidy recognized the women. They were the Jaden's neighbors from the agate cave. She stepped forward gratefully.

"Jaden?" one of them asked. "What are you doing here?" The women looked dazed; they were under Gabira's spell.

"I got lost," Cassidy said, trying to steady her shaking voice. "I was, uh, taking ice up to the cistern and I must have taken a wrong turn. Stupid me. Glad I found you." She tried to look innocent and hoped no one would notice that she was not carrying an ice basket. The Agate sisters nodded and smiled, and then returned to the wall where they were laboriously widening it one chip at a time.

Cassidy bent down and quietly took the small chisel and hammer at her feet, and slipped one into each pocket, thinking they would give Gabira a good lump on the head to match her own. Or cut the bitch's throat. She felt a gloating, wicked guilt at the thought, and wondered if she would really do such a thing.

She straightened and took a breath, her head throbbing. She noted idly that her coughing had stopped. Perhaps the Natema was a cure for coughs, after all.

"Can someone show me the way to our chambers?" she asked, taking a candle from its holder. "I've never been to this room before."

One of the women took another candle and led Cassidy through the tunnels. After a few minutes, Cassidy recognized where they were, and the woman left her to return to work.

A flicker of light played along the rock walls, and faint voices drifted through the tunnels. Cassidy trotted forward and the passageway opened up. Cassidy passed the other women's chambers and came upon the jade cave, and a sigh of relief escaped her lips. Agapantha was in her chair, and Carmen sat on a pillow at Agapantha's feet. Cassidy rushed to them, and they looked up at her with surprise.

"What are you doing back from the ice cave so soon?" Agapantha asked. "Are you still sick?"

Disappointment sank into her as she looked from Agapantha to Carmen in the flickering candlelight. "Don't you remember?" Cassidy asked plaintively. "Gabira took me away. To leave the caves. But she tricked me."

Cassidy could tell from their blank expressions that their Natema had worn off and they were under Gabira's forgetfulness spell again.

Carmen stood up and peered at her with a furrowed brow. "The side of your head is covered with blood." Carmen hurried to the water barrel and spooned a bit of water onto a square of fabric and dabbed at her head.

"I fell. Ouch," Cassidy said, letting Carmen examine her head and pick away the dried blood.

Carmen tutted and wiped at her scalp and hair until she was satisfied. "You have a nice lump there, but at least it's stopped bleeding."

Cassidy thanked her but was filled with loneliness, realizing she'd have to escape by herself. But if she did not act fast, her last dose of Natema would wear off as well, and she'd become as dull-witted as her two friends—and Gabira would have won.

"Wait," Cassidy said, joyous hope springing forth. "The cup!" She had drained the remainder of the Natema into a cup for later. She ran to the stone counter. There would be enough for Carmen and Agapantha, and they could all three escape up to Peary Dome. She grabbed the cup and froze. It was empty. "How?" she demanded, shaking the cup at her friends. "Did Gabira come back and empty this?" Clearly her friends had not drunk it.

They shook their heads, frowns of confusion on their faces.

"I did." A thin voice wavered from the rows of sleeping rugs.

Cassidy spun on her heels. A figure rose from the floor rugs, having been camouflaged by the woolen cloak she wore. "Prissa," Cassidy cried. She had wasted the precious Natema.

Prissa shuffled unsteadily across the floor. Her face was streaked with tears. She looked nothing like the rigid, bossy teenager from this morning—she seemed fragile and scared. "I started coughing," Prissa said, whimpering. "So I came back. They told me the cup of herb tea would cure the cough, so I drank it all." She sniffled and wiped at her nose. "But then I got sick to my stomach. I'm scared I have the flu."

Cassidy wrapped her arms around Prissa's thin shoulders to comfort her. The trembling teenager kept talking. "And I don't know what I'm doing here or why it's so dark and cold. My brother brought me here to be safe, and I thought it was nice and pretty down here. But it's an ugly cave. I don't understand."

Prissa started sobbing on Cassidy's shoulder, and Cassidy patted the poor girl's back. "Shhh. It's okay," Cassidy said. "Gabira had us all under her spell. The herbs broke the enchantment. Quiet, now." She did not want Prissa's sobbing to alert Gabira. She realized she and Prissa could escape together. Cassidy glanced sadly at Carmen and Agapantha, wishing they had drunk the remaining Natema instead of Prissa, but it was too late. Happily, Prissa did not seem nearly as annoying as when she was under Gabira's spell.

"Listen," Cassidy said, taking Prissa by the shoulders and looking into her bloodshot eyes. Cassidy shook her gently. "We can get out of here. Now. Will you help me?"

Prissa sniffed and nodded, a brave look hardening her eyes. That was more the Prissa she knew, but in a good way. Cassidy smiled. "Good. Now stop crying. Maybe we can take Carmen with us," she whispered, "but not Agapantha. She'll slow us down." She felt guilty saying that, but Prissa nodded in agreement and wiped the tears from her cheeks.

"How will we get out?" Prissa asked. "Mother Gabira's chambers line the tunnel that leads to the outside."

Cassidy squeezed Prissa's bony shoulders with excitement. "You know the way out?"

Prissa shrugged. "Sure. I've served there lots of times. I've seen which way the visitors come and go. There's a long staircase that leads outside."

Cassidy felt warmth and gratitude towards Prissa and hugged her tightly. "Okay. Hurry. Get your stuff."

Cassidy had no belongings to bring other than what she was wearing. Gabira had taken her bag of herbs and notebooks. "I wish I could get my herbs back," Cassidy said as Prissa rolled up her sleeping rug. "Why are you taking that?" Cassidy asked.

Prissa shrugged. "I like it." She secured it with a long scarf, which she made into a sling, and hung it across her back.

Cassidy did not want to take her own rug. She didn't even want the heavy cloak, but it was warm and held her wooden shards, and the chisel and hammer.

"Can you lead us directly to the way out?" Cassidy asked.

Prissa nodded. "But I thought you wanted your herbs?"

"Gabira stole them," Cassidy growled.

"We can try to get them back," Prissa said. "Maybe she put them in the kitchen. That door is always unlocked."

"Really?" Cassidy hesitated. "That will delay us. I don't want them to discover us." She thought for a moment. "Gabira has my crystals, too." *And her moon deed.*

"Crystals? Are they magic?" Prissa asked, her gray eyes growing big.

Cassidy nodded. "Yes. One is for sure. And the other one glows."

Prissa's expression was shrewd. "Then you have to get them back. It's not right to let Gabira steal things, especially things that make her more powerful."

"But how?" Cassidy asked. "Do you think they're in the kitchen, too?"

Prissa frowned. "I doubt it. She probably has those locked in her bedchamber. She keeps the keys in her pocket." Prissa's eyes narrowed and regarded Cassidy. "If we can find your herbs ...," she said slowly. "What is that herb that made you and Agapantha sleep all day?"

Cassidy hugged Prissa in a burst of affection. "You are brilliant! If we can feed some Riddy Nidrazam to Gabira, then she'll be knocked out cold, and we can find my crystals."

Prissa grinned mischievously. "Exactly."

"But how will we get her to drink any?"

"Leave that to me," Prissa said confidently, and pulled Cassidy towards the sitting room area. She lit two candles and handed one to Cassidy.

"Carmen," Cassidy said, approaching her friend who was standing nearby, watching with a concerned look.

"Where are you guys going?" Carmen asked.

"Home," Cassidy said. "We're taking you with us." Cassidy took Carmen by the hand, but Carmen pulled away fearfully.

"But I am home," Carmen said. "The jade cave is my home."

"It is not your home," Cassidy hissed, bringing her face close to Carmen's. "It's a prison, and Gabira is the jailer."

Carmen's eyes grew large with indignation. "She is not."

Cassidy sighed heavily. Perhaps it was not a good idea to bring an enchanted person along, even if she was Cassidy's best friend. Agapantha was watching them, a dark scowl on her round face.

"What kind of no good are you girls up to?" the cave mother asked suspiciously.

"Nothing, Aggie," Prissa said pertly. "We are going to help Mother Gabira. She asked me to come help her." Agapantha and Carmen peered skeptically at Prissa but did not question her. "She needs three of us," Prissa continued in her old bossy tone. "There is a big party of men coming, and she needs more servers." Prissa grabbed Carmen's hand. "That means me, Cassidy, and you." She glared at Carmen.

"Okay, I'm coming. You don't have to squeeze so hard," Carmen complained, pulling her hand from Prissa's.

55

NİGHT AT BEAR ROCK

Torr turned desolately away from the retreating backs of Bjarg and Velspara and climbed to the top of the grundhalda boulder. The wind picked up, whistling as it careened across the rock face of the hillside and coursed through the narrow crevasses. He turned and gazed at the three-hundred-sixty-degree view, settling on the two dots of his friends as they made their way to the lichen-covered hill, and then disappeared over its ridge. He felt more alone than he ever had. More alone than when he'd been buried in the ground, where at least the creatures of the forest had visited him each night. More alone than running from Gray Feather when he'd had the company of Brother Wolf. He pulled out his knife and gazed at the pommel. The wolf was lying down with his muzzle resting between his front paws and his eyes peering up at Torr, the way he did when he wanted to stay in the confines of the Ilian steel.

"Fine," Torr said to the wolf, and sheathed the blade. "Leave me alone to the wailing wind and the spirit bears." He tried to sound brave, but he was afraid of night falling and that Bjarg was not kidding about the bears. Bears wouldn't be able to climb the boulder, Torr hoped. But could they really help him travel? He sat on the flat top of the grundhalda and drew his knees to his chest, wrapping his arms around them. He didn't know if he was more afraid of the bears actually coming to help him, or not coming at all. He reviewed details of the odd dream of his bear spirit while he'd been buried. Anything to avoid thinking about what the real terror was: traveling through the vast reaches of space by himself. How would he ever find Earth's moon in that infinite abyss?

He couldn't even really believe it was possible, though he'd traveled to Scridland that way. He couldn't remember any of that journey. One moment he'd been caught in the whirlwind of Vaka's chant, and the next moment he'd awoken on the grundhalda at Gray Feather.

Torr watched Scridland's small sun as it fell to the horizon and slipped behind it, leaving a wash of cobalt sky edged with purple mountain ridges. Cobalt turned to orange, then red, then gray, and finally black. Stars popped into view like a million fireflies. Cold fell quickly, and the white rock hilltop glimmered as though it were a sheet of ice. Frost had visited them the night before as they'd climbed elevation. Tonight would be no different. Torr pulled his shadow cat cloak around himself and wore the silly pointed bear hide cap he'd worn during his initiation. It was comfortable and warm. From his belt hung his knives and the Destroyer. In his vest pocket he felt for the fluorite crystal, making him wonder if Darius had ever encountered such a lonesome, impossible challenge—and then he remembered the dungeon, and felt like a coward. He sat up straighter and left the hood of the shadow cat cloak hanging down his back, the grayish-blue hide covering the bulge of his bedroll that was strapped to his back. No sense making himself invisible to the bears if they were supposed to help him, though the knowledge that he could hide himself made him feel a bit safer.

Bjarg had told him to wait until the Three Spears were directly overhead. Torr identified the constellation on the eastern horizon. He had some time.

Torr forced himself to stay awake, standing and jumping up and down on the boulder to keep warm. The forest was too far from the white stone hill for him to gather wood and make a fire. Besides, he did not want to encounter any lurking bears. His breath formed clouds when he exhaled, and he blew streams of mist up to the stars with his prayers. He did not want to admit that he could die trying this crazy feat, but he knew it was true. What was to stop him from getting lost during the transition and disappearing forever? He had no idea how traveling worked. If he got lost in between, no one would ever know. A cold panic gripped him. His existence would blink out as though he'd never been. The idea of dying alone in some invisible dimension filled him with dread. At least Blaire had died with Darla in her arms and Torr whispering vows of love and singing lullabies in her ear. Somehow this comforted him as he realized she had not died such a bad death after all.

56

SLEEP, MY PRETTIES

Prissa led Cassidy and Carmen to the spot where Giselle and Daleelah always entered the back of their chamber, and they left through the dark gap in the wall. They hurried through the passageways, Prissa cupping the flickering flame with her hand. Cassidy's candle guttered out, and she relit it from Prissa's and handed it to Carmen. They pressed forward again.

The tunnel wound around and continued for far longer than Prissa thought it should have. It wasn't long before Cassidy realized they would soon be lost again. Prissa had thought she knew the way, but clearly she did not. Cassidy led them back to the jade cave, jittery with frustration and urgency. She should know how to get out of there. If she had the crystal ball, she would be able to see the paths. If she had the skill of clairvoyance of her childhood, she wouldn't need the crystal but would be able to sense everything around her and spy on Gabira and her wretched daughters whenever she wanted to.

Cassidy went to the water barrel and stared down into it, clutching the sides. The barrel was half full. Her own reflection looked back at her, orange and shadowed from the candlelight.

"Come on, water," she growled. "Show me how the hell to get out of here." Her twisted face glared up at her. She jiggled the barrel and ripples marred the glassy surface, but nothing else appeared. *"Aargh,"* she growled.

"Aggie, let me borrow your goblet for a minute," Cassidy said, taking the golden goblet Agapantha had borrowed from Gabira's serving chamber. Mother Gabira agreed that she needed a big drinking goblet, Agapantha had explained to Cassidy.

Cassidy plunged the ladle into the barrel and filled the goblet half full, then bit into the tender flesh inside her cheek and spat a mouthful of bloody saliva into the water. "Wait," she said breathlessly, and looked into the gold shimmer of the metal reflecting through the water.

Her faint reflection glimmered up at her, then faded into dark ripples that converged and swirled and resolved into a reflection of the cave. She stared into it, and slowly she was pulled into a view of the tunnels as if she were flying through them. She held her breath, not wanting to lose the vision. The path from the jade cave forked a couple of times, led to a chamber with a ceiling of sticks, and then to a short curving tunnel. The tunnel ended at a door that led to a long straight hallway lined with several doors and ending at a stairway.

Cassidy pulled away and hurried her friends to the back of the cave, carrying the goblet of water and a candle and ignoring Agapantha's indignant questions. They entered into the silence of the passageway, and Cassidy led them along the path she'd seen in the water, and then stopped in confusion. Where were the forks? The path only curved around to the right, deeper into the endless warren of tunnels that led down to the ice. She turned in a circle, flustered and distraught. Prissa looked at her expectantly, and Carmen's eyes were foggy.

She gazed into the goblet again, seeking that place of surrender where her own concerns dropped away. The water glimmered and showed her the caves. The path forked not far from the entrance to the jade cave. Then it split again. She had seen no forks in the passage-way. Her pulse pounded insistently. She didn't have time for this. They retraced their steps, and staring down into the goblet's golden water, Cassidy saw the first fork. She looked up at the wall. There was no fork there. She felt with her hand until she came upon a gap in the solid rock, cloaked in the shadows of the wall.

"This way," Cassidy said, and took the dark passageway, which she suspected was hidden by more than mere shadows. Prissa held her candle up and followed, pulling Carmen behind her. They discovered the second fork the same way, and then passed through a chamber

hung with a low lattice ceiling of dead tree branches and solar filaments. They hurried through the cave and into another tunnel, and
soon came upon a door. The door was unlocked, and Prissa led them
into a long straight stone hallway lit by a cluster of solar filaments
suspended from the ceiling.

Cassidy held her breath and gazed into the gleaming goblet. The
water unveiled a series of dark chambers behind the wooden doors.
Two chambers at the far end were bright with light. The first chamber
revealed three serving women sitting on a stone bench. Across the hall
from the servers' room, the second chamber showed Gabira, Giselle,
and Daleelah lounging on stacks of rugs and leaning against colorful
pillows, sipping at goblets of their own.

Rage roiled inside Cassidy at the women who were enslaving them.

"The kitchen," Prissa whispered, tugging urgently at Cassidy's sleeve.

Cassidy tiptoed towards a door on their right. Her hand shook as
she opened the door and peeked inside. She motioned to her friends,
and they slipped inside and closed the door behind them. It was dark
except for the candle flames. Cassidy's heart was pounding in her chest,
and she set the goblet on a wooden chest and gently touched the lump
on her skull.

They explored the room. On a long counter made from several
wooden crates were four large rice cookers and four hotplates holding
pots with fragrant steam escaping the edges of the covers. Several more
cooking pots hung from the wall, and a dozen wooden barrels were
lined up near the door. Stores of dried goods were stacked against the
walls: sacks of rice and dried beans, bags of wheat flour and sugar,
tins of oil, bags of fresh onions and potatoes, large cans of vegetables
and fruits, cans of peanut butter, cans of tuna fish and salmon, crates
of eggs, and large rounds of cheese. On metal shelving were bags of
nuts, dried fruit, a case of fresh apples, a case of oranges, and a tin of
almond candy. Aside from rice and beans, none of the food had ever
made its way down to the jade cave. Next to tins of tea and a jar of
coffee beans lay Cassidy's purple sack. She hurried to the shelf and
rummaged inside her sack. It was filled with her bags and bottles of
herbs, and the four notebooks. Relief steadied her staggering pulse.
She found a bottle of the sleeping herb, Riddy Nidrazam, and held it
aloft for Prissa to see.

Prissa grinned, and Cassidy slung the herb bag over her shoulder, ignoring Carmen, who stood nervously in a corner gazing wide-eyed around the room.

"Now," Prissa said. "To the servers' room. Hush, now," she warned Carmen, who had started asking a question in a normal tone of voice. "Mother Gabira does not like her serving girls to speak, nor to look anyone in the eye. Remember that," Prissa said firmly to Carmen, who nodded mutely.

Cassidy took Agapantha's goblet, and they crept back out into the empty hallway. She led them past two more doors on the right and stopped in front of a third, which stood across the hall from the large wooden door with the brass dog knocker and matching door handle. Cassidy's heart raced as she led Prissa and Carmen into the serving chamber.

Three young women stood up with surprise from a stone bench carved into the wall. They wore the brightly colored silk robes that everyone wore under their cloaks, and their woolen undergarments had been removed, baring the skin at their throats and wrists. The forms of their naked breasts pressed clearly against the thin silk. Disgust filled Cassidy—Gabira was parading the nubile women in front of enchanted men for their pleasure. She wanted to shake the women and ask if they knew what Gabira was doing. But she clamped her lips shut and watched Prissa as she masterfully handled the confused serving girls.

"Now," Prissa said tartly. "Are Mother Gabira and Sisters Giselle and Daleelah inside their painted cave?" The servers nodded. "Are there any visitors?" The women shook their heads no. "Good. Are they ready for refills? What are they drinking today?"

One of the young women answered, "Yes, they should be almost ready. We're waiting for the bell. They're drinking wine."

Prissa smiled. "Perfect." She grabbed a jug of red wine from the counter and turned her back to the women. Cassidy bent over the jug and unscrewed the bottle of Riddy Nidrazam. She stood next to Prissa, and they pressed their shoulders together so that the women could not see as Cassidy added enough of the sleeping herb to put Gabira and her daughters out for the entire day.

"Excellent. Mother Gabira should be happy," Prissa said. The women looked at her dazedly. One of them started to say something, but they all jumped as a loud clanging interrupted her. The brass bell hanging from the ceiling jerked loudly back and forth on its cable, then quieted.

The serving women nervously rushed to place dishes of nuts and dried fruit on trays, then left with the jug of wine. Cassidy waited anxiously with Prissa. They sat on the cold bench and pulled Carmen down beside them. "It'll be our turn to serve next," Prissa whispered to Carmen, to stop her questions.

Carmen pressed her lips together unhappily. Cassidy stared down into her goblet, calming herself to summon her vision, when suddenly Prissa jumped to her feet. "Give me the herb bottle," Prissa hissed. Cassidy handed her the Riddy Nidrazam, and Prissa leaned over the cups of water the serving girls had been drinking from. "How many drops for them?" Prissa asked. Cassidy smiled, seeing Prissa's wisdom.

"Four each," Cassidy said.

Prissa let four drops fall into each cup. Cassidy stashed away the remaining Riddy Nidrazam, and then gazed down into Agapantha's goblet. She found the gilded room in the bloody water and watched as a serving girl filled Gabira's and her daughters' goblets with wine. Cassidy held her breath as the three witches raised the goblets to their mouths and sipped. She exhaled when no look of alarm disturbed Gabira's plump face. Cassidy clutched the stem of her goblet and watched Gabira and her daughters continue to sip at their wine.

"How did it go?" Prissa asked the serving girls when they returned, checking the wine jug and handing it to Cassidy. It was empty. They smiled at each other, and Cassidy returned her gaze to the scrying goblet, where Gabira, Giselle, and Daleelah were lounging comfortably against their pillows and yawning.

"Fine," one of the serving women said, seeming to gather a shred of her frayed wits. "What are you guys doing here?"

"It's our shift next," Prissa said, standing up with Cassidy to let the serving women sit on the bench. "We got here early so I could show the new girls what to do," Prissa said. She glanced at Cassidy and Carmen.

"Oh," the woman said, accepting the explanation. Cassidy watched as the three serving women drank their water. She tried not to stare but could not help it. They looked at her oddly, but soon they each had drained their cups and were leaning lazily against the back wall. Within minutes, their heads lolled back, and they were sound asleep. Cassidy and Prissa carried them to the floor and stretched them out, squeezing them one next to the other in the open space, while Carmen moved her feet out of the way and watched, her mouth round and confused.

Cassidy sat down on the stone bench and consulted her goblet. Gabira's head was leaning back against the gilded wall. Her eyes were closed, and her mouth hung open. Giselle and Daleelah were leaning against each other, with Daleelah's head on Giselle's shoulder. Cassidy waited a few more minutes, and then whispered, "Okay. They're asleep," and gestured towards the door.

They left Carmen with the serving girls, and Cassidy set the golden goblet on the countertop and crept across the hallway with her herb sack over her shoulder. Cassidy silently cracked open the wooden door, and the scent of patchouli hit Cassidy's nostrils. She pressed her ear to the narrow gap. "Snoring like pigs," she whispered. She gathered her courage, and they slipped into the room.

Gabira, Giselle, and Daleelah were sprawled across the stacks of rugs in a heavy slumber. Gabira's head was tilted to one side against a cushion, and her mouth hung open as she snored. Daleelah's head was in Giselle's lap.

"Sleep, my pretties," Prissa muttered, and flashed Cassidy a wicked grin.

Cassidy was too nervous to share in Prissa's levity. Her pulse fluttered as she warily approached Gabira. The crystal at Gabira's bosom glinted sharply, and Cassidy shielded her eyes against it.

"You," Cassidy hissed at the crystal. "Are you helping that witch? You're coming with me." Cassidy reached towards the glinting shaft but felt a burning sting before she could get close. It reminded her of a poisonous plant, and she hesitated. She did not want to touch it. She felt up around Gabira's corpulent neck and found the gold chain that held it, holding her breath so she wouldn't smell Gabira's sour wine breath. The chain was hot, but not burning. There was no clasp, so Cassidy pulled it awkwardly over Gabira's head, catching a strand of hair. The woman snorted loudly, and Cassidy jumped. Gabira's breathing settled back into a rhythmic buzz, and Cassidy gently pulled the chain loose from Gabira's gathered hair and let the crystal swing back and forth, not daring to look directly at it. It seemed to flash with rage. She dangled the crystal over Gabira's empty gold goblet and let it clink into the metal cup, followed by the gold chain that slithered into the chalice, and then Cassidy slid the whole thing into the purple sack.

Next, she reached around Gabira's neck again and unclasped the chain holding the large bejeweled pendant Jasper had traded to Gabira. "You don't deserve this either," Cassidy muttered quietly. She pulled it loose and held the Pleiades pendant in her palm. She fastened the necklace around her own neck, and her eye fell on a ring that encircled Gabira's fat forefinger. It was a man's ring, gold and round and set with similar gems as the pendant. She tugged at the ring, but it would not budge.

"Stop pillaging," Prissa scolded in a harsh whisper, elbowing her aside. "Did you find the keys?" Prissa reached into a side pocket of Gabira's robe and pulled out a ring of big brass keys. Her eyes glinted proudly. She dug into Gabira's other pocket and produced Cassidy's crystal ball.

Cassidy gasped and took the crystal sphere, cupping it in her hands. "Oh, thank you," she said, and slipped the crystal ball into her pocket.

Prissa continued delving into Gabira's pocket, and her hand emerged with a small silver vial.

"Let me have that," Cassidy said, and snatched the vial from Prissa's hand.

"What is it?" Prissa asked.

"Nothing," Cassidy murmured as she unscrewed the cap and filled the dropper with Greenwash. She gazed at the green liquid glimmering in the translucent dropper.

Terror and euphoria coursed through her veins, battling for dominance. The lure of unsurpassed joy welled up to drown out the memories of pain and humiliation, fear and shame. She held her breath, tuning out Prissa's insistent questions and regarding the vial of heavenly bliss—and the hellish horrors that were mixed up in it.

The vial shook in her trembling fingers. The pinnacle of ecstasy was two drops away. In Greenwash's comforting arms, fear would not torment her as it had in Balty's closet. Shame would not bury her as it had in Schlitzer's tent. She gritted her teeth. It was as though the

Greenwash were reaching out with its fingers and wrapping them around her throat. Panic choked her. *No,* a voice in her head commanded. *You are the Star Child. The fate of the universe rests in your hands. Pain and suffering are a part of life. And live you must. Clear-eyed through it all.*

Cassidy exhaled and squeezed the dropper. The green liquid fell onto the carpet at her feet, staining the red carpet a deeper shade of crimson. She tilted the vial, and its contents drained onto the wool fibers and soaked into them. Cassidy shook the vial and dropper until they were empty, and then rinsed them out in Daleelah's water goblet and dumped the water onto the carpet. She screwed on the cap and slid the empty vial into Gabira's pocket.

She lifted her chin, and then ground her heel into the dark stain and left the chamber.

————————————) ————————————

"How many crystals did she steal?" Prissa asked.

"Just one more. And some jewelry, plus a document I need badly. Come on," Cassidy said, grabbing Prissa's arm.

Prissa tried the keys on the first door down the line. She found one that fit and pushed the door open. "This is Gabira's chamber," Prissa whispered. "Come on." They slipped inside. Prissa found a wall switch, and an electric crystal chandelier lit up the room.

The chamber was cluttered. The walls were stacked with crates and bolts of fabric, and piles of jewelry sat on three wooden dressers. An armoire was bursting with silk robes, and sandals tumbled out onto the floor. Wall shelves held bottles of perfume, carved wooden statues, bronze sculptures, and tiny glass figurines of animals and birds. A tall basket held long sticks of polished olivewood.

They began searching for Cassidy's other belongings. "Look for a crystal shaft," Cassidy said, indicating the length with her hands. "And necklaces with a triangular pendant, a gold coin, and a black arrowhead. And a belt wallet of tent canvas with a red rune embroidered on it."

Prissa nodded and began looking through the piles of jewelry while Cassidy searched through dresser drawers, pulling out silk scarves and chemises, wrinkled robes, and stacks of satin sheets and pillowcases.

Cassidy found a large wooden chest at the foot of the bed, which doubled as a bench. It was locked with a small brass padlock. Cassidy tried all the keys, but they were too large. She took the hammer and chisel from her cloak and struck at the lock. The metal clanged loudly, but Cassidy kept at it until the lock broke. Inside the box, glimmering up at her, sat her light crystal on a green velvet tray. It responded to her touch by glowing brightly. "Look," she said to Prissa. She held up the glowing shaft, and Prissa gazed at her with wonder.

"Wow. Good," Prissa said. "What about the other things?"

Cassidy looked through the chest's contents, lifting out layers of velvet-lined trays overflowing with crystals and jewels of every kind. In the last tray on the bottom, she found her Golden Falcon and Heaven's Window pendants, and the obsidian arrowhead. "Found them," she said happily, holding the necklaces up for Prissa to see, and then pulling them over her head to hang from her neck with the Pleiades pendant. "Now we just need to find a canvas waist belt with a document in it," she said anxiously.

"Is it valuable?" Prissa asked, looking nervously over her shoulder at the door.

"It's the most valuable," Cassidy said reluctantly. She wanted to leave Gabira's chamber as much as Prissa did. Just being in the woman's bedchamber made her skin crawl. She didn't know how long the Riddy Nidrazam would last on a powerful shaman like Gabira. But she needed the deed, and the Solidi and Tetras. "Let's look a just little bit longer."

After frantically tearing apart Gabira's room and not finding the belt, they went into the next chamber down the hall, which appeared to be shared by Giselle and Daleelah. This room was much more orderly. To Cassidy's delight, stuffed in the back of a cabinet she found her green daypack with the clothing she had been wearing when she was captured. She put the extra wood shards into the pack along with the chisel, hammer, and light crystal. She then quickly changed into her pink butterfly t-shirt and black leggings, her white and silver top and carbon fiber skirt, pulled on the velvet Delosian boots, and clipped on her utility belt. Her combat and snowflake obsidian knives were still on the belt, and she seated them firmly in their sheaths next to the wooden club and slingshot. The radio was in two pieces, but she stuffed it into the daypack. Lastly, she rolled the sapphire blue silk robe and tucked it into the pack along with her purple herb sack, then put the crystal ball and her favorite wood shard into a belt pouch at her hip. The key fob to her speedster was sitting in the bottom of the pouch, and memories came flooding back. She frowned and determined that Gabira must not have known what the key fob was for, otherwise she would have sold it. She stood up, feeling much better in her own clothing. The woolen undergarments and heavy woolen cloak, hat, and booties she left in the cabinet.

But they did not find the rune belt. Torn between determination and fear of being caught, Cassidy realized with horror that the rune belt could be on Gabira's person. Cassidy found Gabira in her crystal ball. The witch and her daughters still appeared to be out cold. Cassidy steeled her nerves, and they slunk back into the gilded room. Gabira was snoring, and the two sisters were curled into balls on the thick stacks of rugs, sleeping peacefully.

Cassidy cringed and leaned over Gabira. The proximity of Gabira's face made her nervous, but she slid her hand down the woman's front between bulging breasts and felt around cool rolls of belly fat. The belt was not there, but something else was.

A cord encircled Gabira's waist, and Cassidy could feel three soft leather bags hanging from it. Cassidy's heart was hammering, but she tried to stay calm as she carefully slid her obsidian knife down Gabira's dress, sawed through the cord, and then dragged the bags out. Each bag was no larger than Cassidy's palm, and they were decorated with various symbols, reminding her of medicine bags. She untied the knots that held each one closed and peeked inside. One held clumps of dirt. One held shriveled black olives and olive pits. And the other held small olivewood sticks and desiccated leaves. Cassidy suspected they had something to do with Gabira's olive grove magic and tucked them into her daypack.

Cassidy turned back to the sleeping matriarch, drawn to the woman's hand. The small version of the Pleiades pendant glinted up at Cassidy from the ring on the woman's index finger. Cassidy furrowed her brow.

"I need that," she said aloud, and stood over Gabira. Cassidy found another water goblet and dunked Gabira's hand into it.

"What are you doing?" Prissa hissed. "Don't wake her up! We have to go!"

"I know. Hang on," Cassidy said, trying to twist the ring off Gabira's fat, wet finger. Cassidy spit on it, and finally the ring loosened and slid off. Cassidy rinsed it off and put it onto her own thumb, and then returned Gabira's hand to her lap.

She glanced around the room. Where could Gabira have hidden her rune belt? Cassidy frantically searched behind pillows and lifted the multiple layers of rugs of the makeshift divans. Prissa joined in her search and helped her roll Gabira aside to check under the layers of rugs she had sat upon. Next, they moved the sleeping sisters and checked their stacks of rugs. Cassidy snaked her hands slowly down the backs of the dresses of the two young women and felt around their waists, finding nothing but bare skin. The sisters did not so much as twitch in their sleep despite being groped and shifted this way and that. Cassidy finally expelled her breath in defeat.

"My waist belt is not here," Cassidy said to Prissa. "One last search of Gabira's chamber."

Prissa nodded reluctantly. They left the sleeping women behind and returned to Gabira's bedroom. Cassidy knelt by the large wooden chest again, feeling a tug of curiosity. She removed the velvet trays and felt along the bottom of the box, and then slid the tip of her obsidian knife blade along the bottom edge. A hidden panel lifted, and Cassidy carefully removed it. Her eyes widened as the sheen of gold glinted up at her. The bottom of the box was fist-deep with gold coins. She dug her hands into the hoard and let the coins slip through her fingers with a soft jingle. Prissa knelt by her side and stared. There were Tetras, Eagles, and gold coins of all different designs. But no Solidi. And the rune belt was not there.

"Should we take some?" Prissa asked guardedly. Cassidy frowned at her. "She stole from us," Prissa said. "My brother gave her gold to give me a good life, but instead she cast a spell over me and used me for slave labor. And all the other women, too."

Cassidy nodded—Gabira had stolen her Solidi and Tetras, after all. Their eyes locked, and they smiled. They scooped up the gold, and Cassidy filled the pockets of her pack and her belt pouches with the loot. Half-buried in the coins was a small blue velvet bag filled with more gold coins. Cassidy stuffed it in her pack. Prissa made a carrying sack from a large green silk scarf and filled it with the remainder of the coins, then knotted it closed.

"Should we keep looking for your waist belt?" Prissa asked, her face glistening with nervous sweat.

Cassidy bit her lip. "No. We should leave." She could not risk her freedom, and that of Prissa and Carmen. Not even for her deed. She took a deep breath, and they left the room.

In the serving room, Carmen stood up anxiously from the bench. "Where have you been?"

Cassidy stepped over the sleeping serving girls and took Carmen's hand.

"Come on," Cassidy said. "Mother Gabira wants us to run an errand up top. She said you should come."

Carmen looked at her, not understanding. "Up top?"

Cassidy tried to be patient. "You'll see. Here, take this off."

She pulled the heavy woolen cloak up over Carmen's head, and Prissa removed hers as well. "I don't want this anymore," Prissa said, kicking her rolled rug aside.

Prissa's canary-yellow robe and Carmen's vibrant fuchsia robe would make the women stick out in Peary Dome like peacocks amongst a flock of pigeons, but it couldn't be helped. They left the keys on the counter, and Cassidy took Agapantha's golden goblet, the blood-tainted water reflecting her face back at her. She drank the blood-tinted water, stuffed the goblet into her pack with the other one, and then led Prissa and Carmen down the long hallway.

At the top of the stairs, a guard stood up from his stool.

"Gabira's business," Cassidy told the man, and gave him a gold Eagle. He stared at the coin, and then at the other women.

"I can't let you leave," he said, stepping forward.

Cassidy smiled up at him, and the next moment her hands were around his throat, pressing on the arteries as Tatsuya had taught her. She kneed the guard in the groin and swiped his feet out from under him, falling with him to the ground, her hands still fastened tightly around his throat. She had caught him by surprise, and although he tried to fight her off, she was ready for his tricks. She just needed to hang on for a few more seconds, she told herself as she tucked her chin tightly and closed her eyes against his grasping fingers as she wrapped her legs around him and the two of them rolled back and forth on the landing. He suddenly went limp beneath her hands. She held his throat for another few moments, then released him.

"Hurry," she said to her gaping girlfriends as she bounded to her feet. "He won't stay passed out for long."

She opened the airlock and stepped into the antechamber, meeting the startled gazes of the two outer guards.

"Gabira's cage is open, and the birds are flying free," Cassidy told them. They looked dumbfounded, and one reached out to stop her.

"Run," she yelled to her friends as she deflected the man's hand and punched him in the windpipe, then landed a flying kick on the side of the other man's kneecap. The men stumbled away from her, and she lunged for the open doorway.

Warm air hit her in the face as she followed Prissa and Carmen out onto the dusty ground and slammed the door shut behind her. She was nearly blinded by the sunlight but grabbed their hands and ran.

57

DANCE OF THE BEARS

When the Three Spears constellation was directly overhead, Torr got to his feet and withstood the urge to jump from the boulder and find his way back to Bjarg's. He exhaled and closed his eyes, feeling the rock beneath his feet and breathing in the cold air, loving this galaxy and this life, and those still living. He thought of his mother and father. He thought of Cassidy and Jasper. He thought of Reina, Bobby, and Mike. He prayed to the stars like he had never prayed before, pressing the Bear crystal against his chest where it hung from his neck in its sling.

Bjarg had said it was best to keep it strapped close to his heart, so that he would not drop it at a critical moment, or all would be lost. With his other hand, Torr took the black dream flower rattle from his belt and shook it to the frantic beat of his heart.

Torr's boot bells jangled as he stomped his feet and danced in a tight circle, pushing all doubts aside. Once he committed to this, he could not turn back. He had to surrender to the unknown. When the hillside and boulder made of grundhalda stone lent him the energy he needed, then he would be pulled into the swirling clutches of magic. Bjarg warned him that if he let fear ride with him during the transition, he would surely die. He must believe wholeheartedly, or he must not try at all.

The chant rolled from his lips. It felt like a part of him and sang in his blood.

Andi stiga
Fara lopt
Heimili heita
Gaumr far

Spirit walker
Travel the skies
Home calls
Heed the cry

He was going home. Home to Peary Dome. A familiar euphoria lifted his spirits the way it always did when the energy of the chant and the dancing took hold of him. The rattle resonated with the bells on his boots, and the air around him shivered. His eyes were open, and he gazed at the dark forest and the blazing panoply of stars as he circled round and round.

He could not see Earth's sun from here, nor the moon, but he could feel them. He shied away from the burning fire of the sun and leaned into the cool stillness of the moon, where he felt the magnetic pull of Peary Dome's gravity bar and the lesser pull of the grundhalda in Jorimar's camp. That was his destination. He felt it the way a compass points north, pulling at him unerringly once he locked onto it.

Now all he needed was the energy spike to cast him forth. The resonance of the grundhalda hummed at his feet, adding its strength the way the relentless surge of the ocean pushes a wave to shore. The wave built and built but was not strong enough. He needed a tsunami. He needed a circle of warriors dancing around him, adding their swirling energy to his. He needed drummers lending their beat, feeding his, raising him the way a spinning top bounces and flies off the table, the way a slingshot lets loose a rock to hit its mark. But he had no warriors. He had no drummers. Why had Bjarg and Velspara abandoned him? Why was Brother Wolf hiding in his knife? Why were the stars mocking him?

He stomped harder and chanted louder. He shook the rattle and squeezed the crystal. His eyes pleaded with the glowing white rock below him to lend him more strength. Dark shadows dappled the white hillside. They were moving. He could not break his rhythm—the momentum was too strong. But the frenzied dance sharpened his senses, and he could see that the moving shadows had legs and heads, round ears and glowing eyes.

Bears.

A dozen of the great black beasts loped towards him and encircled the boulder. The chant rang from Torr's throat, and he called to the heavens. The bears rose on hind legs and rocked back and forth, noses sniffing the air. Torr stomped in a circle on the grundhalda boulder, and the bears danced on the ground in a swaying trance. A slowly spinning cyclone of energy surrounded Torr, and he lost all sense of space and time.

A low growl came from one bear, and then the others. A loud roar shook the air as the dozen bears bellowed together. The ferocious sound vibrated through Torr, followed by a wave of ecstasy, and then a great wind lifted him in a flash of white light.

He was falling into a black abyss. There was no sound, no light, no smell. There was only softness all around, and he was falling, falling, blindly, down a well that spiraled into infinity. He could not breathe, and his blood did not flow. He was dead, yet he was aware. Waiting. Sensing the grundhalda slab at Peary, feeling its heartbeat. It beat in his ears and all around him, yet it was not his heart. It was the heart of the mother, and he was the babe in the womb. He was being squeezed. Pushed out. He was being born.

58

FREEDOM

Cassidy stopped running when they passed the intersection of 9H. Gabira's guards were nowhere to be seen. She stood panting with Prissa and Carmen. This block of the spoke road was relatively empty, except for a couple of men loitering outside their tents and a transport that rumbled slowly by. Cassidy looked up through the triangular glass panels and found Earth. It was nearly full. Tears came to her eyes, and she saw that Prissa and Carmen were also staring at the glistening blue planet, their mouths hanging open.

"Do you know who you are now?" she asked Carmen.

Carmen nodded, tears trickling down her cheeks.

Prissa said with a taut voice, "I hope my brother hasn't left the moon."

"Who's your brother?" Cassidy asked.

"His name's Slav."

"Bratislav?" Cassidy asked. "Big guy? Blond hair? Doesn't smile much?"

Prissa looked at Cassidy, her eyes brightening. "Yes, you know him?"

"Yes. He guards the PCA tent at Center Ring." She pointed towards the center of the camp where the gravity bar shone as a beacon of glimmering white.

Prissa grabbed Cassidy's arm. "He does? Do you think it's really him?"

Cassidy described him further and could see the resemblance to Prissa. "It must be him," Cassidy said.

Cassidy's thoughts flitted from the Fen to Center Ring, trying to

decide where to go first. She did not know what time of day it was and
found her watch inside her pack. It was fourteen hundred hours. Jasper
would probably be at the spaceport, trading, and Torr would most
likely be at the Fen with Blaire.

"Carmen," Cassidy said. "Do you want to find your father first,
or Berkeley? It's probably safer to find Berkeley first. Gabira's cave is
directly below your father's office."

Carmen did not hesitate. "Berkeley," she said. "My father will just
send me back down to Gabira's. I never want to speak with him again."
Carmen's eyes flashed with the same stubborn glare as Ramzy's.

"Okay," Cassidy said, grinning at the family resemblance. "Berkeley
lives with us at the Fen. But he's probably teaching right now...," she said,
faltering. She did not want to run into Ming-Long and Khaled at the training yard. She needed to find Torr first and tell him what they had done to
her. "We'll find Bratislav first, and then we'll go to the Fen," she said.

They took off at a trot. Near the 9G ration trailer stood a lookout
tower, manned by two men she did not recognize. The guards wore
bright blue headbands and followed the three women curiously with
their eyes as they ran past. There had been a guard tower at the perimeter road intersection as well, which Cassidy had raced by. People leaving
the ration trailer carried only a half-loaf of bread and a water jug. No
one carried metal camp plates, and no aromas of hot food came from
the trailer. Cassidy's stomach growled with hunger, but she kept jogging.

Cassidy felt as though reality had shifted while she'd been gone, and
the Peary Dome camp was not the same one she had left. She suddenly
realized she had no idea how long she had been down in Gabira's cave.
It could have been days, or weeks, or even months, for all she knew.
Could it have been a year?

They found Bratislav on guard at the corner of the PCA tent, with his
bare arms crossed over his chest as usual, and a stern expression on his face.
He wore a bright blue headband that bore the Light Fighters symbol at the
center of his forehead. Prissa took off at a run and jumped into his arms.
Cassidy laughed with delight at his shock as he hugged his sister.

"Prissa!" he said. "What are you doing here?"

"Aren't you glad to see me?" Prissa asked, backing away from his
embrace. "Gabira had me trapped down there. Why didn't you come
get me?" She planted her fists on her hips and glowered at her brother.

"I ... I thought ...," Bratislav said. "I thought you were safe. I tried to visit you so many times, but somehow I could never get Gabira to bring you up to see me." He shook his head, his mouth turning down in confusion.

"She's a witch, that's why," Prissa said. "She's evil, and horrible."

"Oh ...," Bratislav said, furrowing his brow. "I ... I didn't know. I'm sorry."

"Never mind," Prissa said, waving her hand through the air. "Cassidy said I could live with the women at the Smith camp. So you don't need to worry about me."

Bratislav's gaze shifted to Cassidy. "Were you down in the caves, too?" he asked.

"Yes," Cassidy said. "Torr must be so worried. I'm afraid to go to the Fen, though, because ..."

"Cassidy," Bratislav interrupted. His voice was grave.

"What," Cassidy said, ominous prickles rising on the nape of her neck.

Bratislav took a deep breath and said, "Torr is gone, and Blaire is dead."

"What?" Cassidy asked, her mouth falling open. "What do you mean? Wait, what?" She must have misheard. "Blaire's what? Where's Torr?" she asked, shaking her head to clear her muddled brain.

"Torr and his squad had gone out looking for you," Bratislav said. "After you took off in the four-wheeler. No one knew where you went. They were attacked back in the container yards. Blaire was killed, and Darla, and those three brothers, and the other two."

"Darla, too? What brothers? What other two?" Her heart was pounding, drowning out her thoughts. She held onto Carmen's arm for support.

"The southern boys," Bratislav said. "And the tall Black guy, and the snotty one with the spiky blond hair."

A void descended upon her, numbness freezing her thoughts into single images. Blaire. Darla. Hawk. Roanoke. Raleigh. Sky ...

"Berkeley?" she asked as she clutched Carmen's arm.

"No," Bratislav said. "The other one."

"Thunder," she said, exhaling and feeling guilty that she was relieved it was Thunder and not Berkeley. "But no," she said. "It can't be. Why would anyone kill them? And where's Torr?" She released

Carmen and stepped forward, grabbing Bratislav's arm with both hands, her thoughts suddenly racing. "Where's Torr?" She realized she was yelling. Her hands shook, and Bratislav took them in his large, warm hands.

"The Scrids said they saved Torr from the attack," Bratislav said. "They said they took him to their planet to protect him. They were looking for you, too, to take you there."

Nothing made sense. She gazed into Bratislav's blue eyes, wondering if she were still caught in Gabira's illusion and this was all a nightmare.

"Two guys no one knew killed them, with Cephean weapons," Bratislav continued. "They died, too. The Scrids killed them before anyone could question them."

Cassidy's hands were clutching his, not wanting to let go. "Where are Blaire's sisters? Are they alright?" she asked.

"Yes. They're running the Smith camp. They're probably at the Light Fighters training yard right now, though."

"Let's go," Cassidy said, releasing Bratislav and turning to Carmen. "Berkeley's probably there, too. You coming with us?" Cassidy asked, turning to Prissa.

"Yes," Prissa said, holding her brother's shoulders and kissing him on the cheek. "Come find me at the Smith camp later," she told him.

"But ...," he said, "I just ... You just ..."

But the women had already turned away and were trotting across Center Ring, his voice fading into the background as they headed towards Spoke Road Four.

———————⟩———————

As they approached the training yard, Bailey saw her first and broke away from the Judo class. She ran towards Cassidy, followed by her two sisters. The three Smith sisters converged on Cassidy and they hugged in a group embrace, and suddenly Cassidy was crying.

"Blaire, and Darla," Cassidy said through her tears.

They all cried, and the sisters asked where she had been. "We were so worried about you," Britta said. "We thought you got taken back to that man."

"No," Cassidy said. "I was down in the caves below the spaceport. How long have I been gone?"

The sisters looked at each other. "Three months?" Becka ventured.

"Three months?" Cassidy repeated. The memories of her days underground were a faint blur.

She glanced towards the training mats. The Alphabet Boys were hurrying towards her, and Hiroshi and Tatsuya had stopped their Judo class and were coming over as well. Berkeley stood up from his meditation pose, and his round eyes grew rounder.

He and Carmen stepped hesitantly towards one another, and then rushed into each other's arms. Berkeley lifted Carmen off her feet in a bear hug, and they cried and laughed.

Cassidy turned to the Alphabet Boys and Hiroshi and Tatsuya, who had surrounded her and were asking where she had been. "I was down in the women's caves, with Carmen and Prissa," she said. "Prissa is Bratislav's sister. She was stuck down there, too. Where are Ming-Long and Khaled?" She searched the mats for the knife-fighting class, but Faisal stood with the Alphabet Boys at her shoulder, and Khaled and Ming-Long were nowhere to be seen.

"They disappeared the same day you and Torr did," Hiroshi said, bowing to her in formal little bows. Tatsuya was peering at her curiously and nodding at her with a reassuring grin.

"They took an ice tanker out," Buck said. "And they never came back."

"Well, they kidnapped me, that's why, and sold me to Gabira," Cassidy said, anger flushing her cheeks. "They got away with it and escaped."

Everyone gaped at her silently.

"We suspected something," Copper finally said, shaking his head. "I never trusted that guy, Khaled. But Ming-Long?" He shook his head again.

Relief washed over her, replacing her indignation, as she realized she wouldn't need to worry about them anymore.

Faisal stepped forward and took her shoulders. "Are you okay?" he asked, pushing up his sunglasses to perch on top of his head. His large black eyes gazed into hers with concern.

"Yes," she said. "But I need to find Torr. I heard the Scrids took him. Where's Jasper?" From behind Faisal's shoulder, Montana was looking on. "What are you doing here, Montana?" she asked.

"He's running the Light Fighters," Arden explained. "Ever since Torr disappeared. We're the dome's security force now."

She gazed around. The Light Fighters forces had grown, and everyone was wearing the blue headbands. Most people she did not recognize. A watchtower stood at the spoke road's intersection at the perimeter road, and her speedster sat on the vacant stretch of land where she had left it, coated in dust.

"We haven't seen Jaz for a few days," Faisal said. "But last time I saw him, his teeth were green."

Cassidy scowled at him.

"Yeah, I know," Faisal said. "He found a stash somewhere. We checked Schlitzer's, but Jaz wasn't there."

Cassidy's skin bristled at the mention of Schlitzer, but she held her emotions in check and said, "I bet I know where Jasper is. Can you guys come with me?" She turned to the Alphabet Boys.

"Of course," the men said, nodding. Arden, Buck, Copper, Dang, and Guy gathered around her. Elvis's and Febo's hands were wrapped in their boxing wraps. "Except you two," Cassidy said, nodding towards the kickboxing mat.

"We'll come, too," Becka said, frowning. "You're not disappearing on us again."

"Don't worry," Cassidy said. "I don't want those drugs anymore."

Becka's frown deepened.

Cassidy sighed. "I'm sorry I'm such a fuck-up," she said. "It's all my fault."

"It's *not* your fault," Berkeley said, approaching with Carmen. "We'll come with you," he said.

"Meditation class is canceled," Berkeley called over his shoulder at the rows of students still seated on the meditation tarp. They slowly unfolded their legs from the cross-legged position and stretched, glancing curiously at the strangers who had caused Berkeley to break his disciplined practice. "I'm glad you're safe," Berkeley said, pulling Cassidy into a hug.

"I can't believe the Boyer brothers and Sky and Thunder are dead," she said into his shoulder, tears welling up again. "Durham must be a wreck," she said.

"He is," Berkeley said, squeezing her tight. "The whole Fen has been turned upside down. But you and Carmen are back, so things can only get better. Let's go find Jaz," he said. "He's been in a deep funk this whole time."

"Do you think he's in the Murians' cave?" Cassidy asked.

"That's my bet," Berkeley said. "Let's go see."

"Let me check, first," she said, and pulled out her crystal ball. She calmed her mind and gazed into the small sphere until it filled with rainbows and resolved into a murky image of purple-speckled shadows. Slowly, the inside of the Murians' cave came into focus, its gray walls lit with points of purple crystals embedded in the cave walls. A sleeping body was curled up in a green blanket in a corner, and a shock of auburn hair poked out from one end.

"He's there," she said, and closed her eyes. "Let me see if I can find Torr."

Her friends were hushed around her. She opened her eyes and gazed into the crystal ball again, searching for Torr. A dark swirling sensation overtook her, as though she were being sucked into a spinning vortex. It made her dizzy and nauseous, and she broke her gaze away. "I can't look," she said, meeting Berkeley's eyes. "I don't know," she said, shaking her head. "Let's go get Jasper."

————————) ————————

Cassidy found Jasper in the Murians' caves behind Auxiliary Spaceport B, just as she'd seen in her crystal ball. He was curled in a ball in a tangle of green blankets, his eyes rolled to the back of his head, and a string of drool connecting his mouth to the ground.

"Jasper." She shook his shoulder. *"Jasper!"*

He responded with a groan. She shook him, but his body was limp under her hands, and he smelled of urine.

The Murians glanced over from where they were conferring with Berkeley, their eyes glowing green like cats' eyes at night.

"How could you let him get like this?" she asked, standing up and glaring at the hooded men.

The one named Guruhan pushed back his hood to reveal his glowing green hair. "He's free," the Murian told her in Globalish, his accent strange and breathy. "He knows Fool's Passion. He likes to drink it." The man made a gesture with his fingers to his lips, then pulled his hood over his head and returned to his conversation.

She turned back to Jasper and shook his shoulder but got no response. A mound of green blankets lay in a clump nearby. She found one that was not too nasty and rolled it into a pillow. She pulled Jasper over onto his back and attempted to straighten his limbs that wanted to curl back up, then propped the pillow under his head. His muscles twitched, and the whites of his eyes showed between slitted eyelids.

"Algol's hell, Jaz." She untangled his blanket and spread it over his shivering body, tucking it in around him. She borrowed Berkeley's waterskin and tried to get some water into Jasper's mouth, half of it dribbling down into his scruffy beard. After drinking some herself, she wet a corner of the blanket and wiped his face clean.

She dug into her daypack and pulled out the red herb notebook, but the writing was indecipherable. She looked around for something that could help him. The flask of Fool's Passion sat on the Murians' dining blanket, and the sight of it made her feel slightly ill.

Cassidy sighed and sat on the floor next to Jasper. She lifted his shoulders into her arms and pressed her cheek to the top of his head.

A faint rasp came from his lungs. "Cassie?"

"Yes, Jasper," she said, squeezing him and kissing his head. "I'm here."

He trembled in her arms. "Where?" he asked.

"We're in the Murians' cave," she said. "We're safe."

"No, where were you?" he asked.

"Gabira's," she said, holding him tightly.

"Aaah," he said. "That bitch."

She held him, and his head nestled against her breasts. His shoulders shook, and she realized he was crying. She kissed the top of his head and stroked his unruly hair.

"I can't live without you," he said into her bosom. "I wanted to die."

"Don't say that," she said. "Don't ever say that."

"I couldn't take it, Cassidy."

"I know, Jasper. I know." She kissed his forehead and his eyes. "But it's okay now."

He tilted his chin up, and she kissed his lips. They were dry, and his breath was sour. She kissed him again, and then hugged his head to her chest and continued rocking him.

"Is Torr here yet?" he asked.

"No," she said.

"He's on his way back," Jasper mumbled.

Cassidy gave up trying to run her fingers through his matted hair and said, "They think the Scrids took him to their planet."

"He's flying," Jasper said. "I hope he is not lost."

"I hope not," she said, reminded that Fool's Passion was a hallucinogen.

"I have a wicked headache," Jasper muttered. He reached out and scrabbled around on the stone floor in the shadows by the wall, finding his waterskin. He unscrewed the cap, and she helped bring the nozzle to his lips, and then recoiled in horror as a green liquid filled his mouth and seeped from the corners of his lips.

She yanked the flask away. "What are you doing?!"

He swallowed with a sick smile, meeting her eyes with his dilated pupils. "Just a little, Cassie, honey, to make the headache go away."

"No more!" she said, screwing the cap closed angrily.

"I'm sorry," he said. "I'm a horrible person."

"No you're not," she said, and tossed the waterskin aside, ignoring the niggling little voice that told her to take a sip. *Just a tiny little sip.* "It's the drug that's horrible," she said. "And people who use drugs to control other people. They're horrible, not you."

"You're not still mad at me?" he asked, settling his head onto the pillow.

"Mad at you?" she asked, taking his cold, clammy hand.

"For ... you know. Dealing in eggs. You raised the wind and took off, and I never saw you again. I thought it was because you were mad at me."

The pain in his eyes pulled at her heart. "Well," she said. "I was angry at the time, but it seems so long ago now. The reason I didn't come back was because I was kidnapped, by Ming-Long and Khaled. They must have sold me to Gabira."

"Ming-Long? Khaled?" he asked. His pupils nearly filled his entire irises, and he spoke slowly, as though he were drunk. "Those bastards. I suspected something when they disappeared the same time you did. I thought maybe they had sold you to the Nommos. They always talked about striking it rich and moving to Delos." She leaned closer to catch all his words as his scratchy voice grew quieter. "My dad thought their tanker was hijacked, but I always thought they used it as their getaway vehicle. Ugh," he said, and crawled over to a metal pot and started throwing up.

She scowled as she watched him, remembering all the times when it had been her puking her guts out before being pulled under by Greenwash. The flask of Fool's Passion sat in the shadows, taunting her. She closed her eyes and remembered sitting in on one of her mother's consulting sessions, recalling the words Brianna had spoken to the man who was struggling with addiction.

It's not always possible to conquer an addiction with brute force. Sometimes the best we can do is keep it at bay. Tell yourself you can have some, only not right this instant. Later. Always a little bit later.

"Maybe later," Cassidy whispered, opening her eyes and staring at the stone wall of the Murians' cave, and then turning her attention to her breath as Berkeley had taught her. *The breath brushes your upper lip as it leaves your nostrils. Focus on that. When you catch your mind wandering again, return to the breath.*

Cassidy attempted to focus on her breath until Jasper returned to the bedding and crawled under the blanket.

"So you don't hate me?" he asked, wiping at his mouth. "Can you ever forgive me? I thought about it a lot while you were gone. I realized I shouldn't have hidden things from you. It's almost the same thing as lying."

"No. I get it," she said slowly. "I'm not mad anymore. I just feel a sense of ... I don't know ... loss. I used to believe certain people were good and other people were bad. Now I realize everyone has the potential to be bad under certain circumstances, and it makes me sad."

"Oh," he murmured. "I'm sorry I made you sad."

"It's not just you," she said. "It's everybody. It's how life goes, I guess."

"But not you, you're good," Jasper said.

"Even me," she said, holding his hand.

"You couldn't help that you were kidnapped," he said.

"Not just that," she said. "I've made other ... bad decisions. Things I'm ashamed of."

"Really? Like what?" he asked. His eyes were nearly crossed.

Fear and self-loathing rose in Cassidy's chest—then a suffocating shame. Jasper would hate her if he learned she had willingly slept with Schlitzer. She pushed the memories back down into their dark hole. With her free hand, she dabbed at the sweat on Jasper's brow with the blanket, stalling. If she waited long enough, he would fall into a stupor and she could avoid the question. But he kept staring at her and squeezing her hand.

"Things I don't want to talk about," she said, squeezing his hand in return. "Not right now, anyway."

He drew his mouth to one side. "I suppose that's fair," he said. "Tell me later. But ... do you love me?" His glazed eyes held hers. "You never said you did. So maybe you don't. Especially now."

She sighed. "I love you, Jasper. I have always loved you."

Their fingers intertwined, and his gaze softened. "But do you *love* me?" he asked.

She wanted to say, *Of course I do,* but she could not force the words out. Finally, she said, "You are my friend, Jasper. I love you, and I forgive you. But I don't know what I want right now. I don't even honestly know who I am anymore." The look of pain on his face broke her heart. "We'll work it out," she said, leaning down and lightly touching her lips to his.

Before he had a chance to return the kiss, she drew away and clasped his hand in both of hers and held his wounded eyes. "I just need some time," she said.

He swallowed. "Okay. I have all the time in the world. As long as you're here and you're safe, I am a patient man." He flashed his cocky grin for a moment, but his lips quickly turned down again, and he said, "At the moment, I'm worried about Torr. He must be very careful to not let his thoughts stray, or he could get lost between the stars."

"What are you talking about?" she asked.

"I don't know, exactly. All I know is that he's flying, and that it's very dangerous. A few days ago, I was sure he was dead. Now I'm sure he's flying."

She frowned at him, and he turned his eyes to the ceiling, staring vacantly. His muscles were limp, and his hand grew flaccid in hers as the drug took over. She lay down next to him on the cold stone floor, suddenly exhausted.

"Berkeley," she said, propping herself up on an elbow. "I'm going to stay here with Jasper while he sleeps off this dose," she said.

Berkeley nodded, then consulted with the Murians and brought her two blankets. "I'll wait for you here," he said, eyeing Jasper's flask suspiciously.

"Thanks," she said, rolling up one blanket for a pillow and wrapping herself in the other. "Don't worry, I don't want any of that," she said, glancing at the flask.

He didn't look convinced but went to join the Murians. She stared up at the rock ceiling, trying to sense her brother, but all she felt was complete abandonment and an overwhelming dizziness, as though she were caught in a whirlpool and was being pulled into its drowning depths.

<hr />

A tingling wave pulsed through Cassidy's body. It felt as though a spacecraft had launched from Moffett Field, and her eyes popped open. The walls of her bedroom morphed into gray stone walls studded with purple crystal points, and she remembered where she was.

Jasper stirred at her side and gazed at her sleepily. The drugged glaze of his eyes had cleared. Cassidy sat up on the hard floor, wondering how long they had slept. She took out her crystal ball and peered into it. The walls of the Murians' underground dwelling reflected back at her.

"Where's Torr?" she asked the crystal. "Show me."

Rainbows glistened, and she saw the circular tent structure of the Scrid camp. Shivers prickled up the back of her neck. "Come on," she said, tugging at Jasper's blanket. "Let's go to the Scrid camp. I think Torr is there."

"No, he's not there," Jasper said. His voice was clear and rational. "We checked a bunch of times. Besides, it's too dangerous. They'll take you to their planet."

"We have to try to find him," she said. "Come on," she insisted, pulling Jasper to his feet.

He looked like hell. His clothes were stained and smelly, and his hair and beard were tangled.

"Do you have any clean clothes Jasper can borrow?" she called over to Murugan and Guruhan, who were sitting in the dining area with Berkeley.

"Clean clothes," Berkeley repeated, followed by a clicking, hissing series of sounds.

Murugan nodded with understanding and rose from the blanket. He rummaged in a basket, then brought her a bundle of green cloth. She thanked him and shook out the fabric. It was a pair of loose green pants and a wraparound tunic like the Judo gi Tatsuya wore.

Jasper changed into them and raked his fingers through his hair. She put her foot on his waterskin as he bent to retrieve it.

"You're not taking that," she said.

"But," he said, tugging at it. "It's only Fool's Passion. I paid a fortune for this. The Murians never sell the stuff, but I convinced them."

She grabbed his ear and twisted.

"Ouch!" he said.

"Leave it," she said.

He scowled but let go of the waterskin and grudgingly followed her and Berkeley from the cave. Jericho shook his head at Jasper with a disapproving frown but said nothing as he led them up the ladder.

They emerged from the container, and the sound of rhythmic drumming came from the direction of the Scrid camp, bouncing off the glass triangles of the dome in an amplified chorus.

The five Alphabet Boys and the five women were waiting for them outside the container, sitting in two circles. They stood up, yawning and stretching. Cassidy went to embrace the Smith sisters and Prissa while Carmen went to Berkeley's side.

"You look like something the dog spit up," Copper said to Jasper.

"Thanks a lot," Jasper said.

"And smell like it, too," Arden added.

Cassidy smiled sweetly at Jasper and shrugged a shoulder at him. His lip curled down, and she held back a chuckle.

The drumming grew more intense.

"To the Scrid camp. Hurry," she said, and took off at a loping run. She heard Dang calling Montana for backup on his radio as her friends fell into step behind her.

59

HOME

A violent wind assaulted Torr, pummeling him and whipping him from side to side. His lungs were compressed and burned from wanting to breathe. He arched his back in agony as he was thrown down, his shoulder and hip landing hard on unforgiving stone. He gasped and took a breath. The air seared his lungs. He coughed and curled up on his side, trying to stave off a swirling dizziness.

When he regained his equilibrium, he opened his eyes. His bundle was still on his back, and the shadow cat cloak was twisted around him. He was clutching the Bear crystal in one hand and the rattle in the other, and his pointed cap had stayed snugly on his head. Around him danced chanting Scrids, their red hair and beards flying as the dance reached its climax. Torr jerked up to a sitting position.

He understood now why it had felt like he'd hit a tornado as he landed. He was on the grundhalda in Peary, and Vaka was on the rock with him, spinning in a frenzy. The wizard was about to travel in the opposite direction, and the energy was rising to carry him to Scridland. Torr had hit the disturbance and been tossed about like a rag doll. He quickly realized that he would be sucked back to Scridland in the wizard's vortex if he did not get off the grundhalda.

Torr hopped to his feet and lunged off the grundhalda. His

trajectory was broken by the thick arms of a Scrid, flipping him through the air. He landed on the ground at the feet of another dancing Scrid, the breath knocked out of him. Strong hands lifted him and threw him back onto the grundhalda. It had taken but a moment for the warrior dancers to see what was happening and to react. The wizard and drummers had not missed a beat, and Torr could feel the vortex spinning around Vaka, pulling Torr into its center.

He recovered his breath, and by instinct started chanting, as though his body knew the words better than his mind did.

> *Jar fjall veurr honla hlif*
> *Bergrisi festa hjarta*
> *Bjoda fang hoettr seidr*
> *Varda vandr taufr vegr megin*
> *Holdr Bergrisi halda festa*
> *Glegpa sol festa jord*

> *Iron mountain protector, seize the shield*
> *Hill-giant, strengthen the heart*
> *Challenge and wrestle the dangerous enchantment*
> *Guard against the wicked talisman, diminish its power*
> *Hero hill-giant, hold fast*
> *Swallow the sun, strengthen the ground*

Torr clutched the Bear crystal and shook the rattle while he chanted furiously, kicking the warriors back as they reached out to push him towards Vaka. He chanted louder, feeling the pull of Vaka surging against his own warring current.

Torr turned and met the wizard's eyes. Vaka stared at him with bleak horror as the traveling chant continued to roll off the old man's tongue. Torr chanted faster, and Vaka lifted his voice ever higher. Torr drew slowly away from the pulsating vortex of the wizard, clinging to his grounding chant as though it were a life-line keeping him from being carried over a plunging waterfall. His throat was sore from yelling, but he raised his voice even louder and drilled the words into Vaka's face, which grimaced with the effort to pull Torr with him.

Vaka glared at him, surprise mixing with anger and determination. How had Torr learned the counterspell, Vaka's eyes asked. And where had he gotten boots with bells, a black dream flower rattle, and a shadow cat cloak? Torr pulled against the relentless current, and inch by inch reached the edge of the grundhalda. He hopped backwards off the platform and turned away from the screeching wizard, whose chant had fallen apart and was replaced with a stream of threats and curses. Torr circled menacingly, keeping Vaka and the warriors at bay with the rattle and his chant.

Torr let the Bear crystal fall to his chest in its sling, unsheathed the wolf knife, and brandished it at the Scrids. He felt the wolf brush against his leg as he slowly wove between the bewildered dancers and drummers. The men parted as Torr and his spirit wolf made their way towards the exit tent.

A shriek and a moan erupted from behind them as Vaka took up a new wailing chant that Torr did not recognize. A mound of rock creaked and groaned like a dragon rising from the ground and reared up before him. Torr froze, his neck craning as a stone cliff grew before his eyes until it reached halfway to the ceiling of the dome. Torr circled, dumbstruck. All around them, enclosing the small inner courtyard of the Scrid camp, was a ring of glistening white rock, sealing Torr inside with the warriors and Vaka.

The wizard's voice silenced, and Torr stared at him. Vaka's arms were raised high, with a small chunk of white rock clutched in one fist and a crystal in the other. He wore a triumphant grin and met Torr's eyes as if to say, *Try getting out of this one.*

Torr was stunned. Bjarg had not anticipated this and had not taught Torr a counterspell for a cliff that rose up out of nowhere. Torr laid his hand upon the jagged wall of stone. The white rock was warm and solid. He shoved his shoulder against it. It did not budge. A clatter filled the air as the Scrids beat their stone clubs and knives together as they did when celebrating a particularly successful hunt.

Torr backed up against the wall and glowered at the gloating men, daring them to defy him and his wolf. They did not try to attack, knowing they had him penned like one of Velspara's hapless rabbits.

Torr was trapped. Again. He wanted to explode with rage. Kill all the Scrids. But what good would that do? He would still be stuck in here with a bunch of corpses that he would end up mourning later. He knew some of these men. Helug. Stump. Others who'd saved him from the Lectros. The same men who had kidnapped him and sent him off to Scridland. Anger burned in his belly. If he killed Vaka, would the wall remain and doom them all to starve inside? Could they scale it and get out? Was it visible from the outside, and would others hear their cries for help?

Torr huddled against the wall as Vaka eyed Torr's black dream flower rattle and glared at him suspiciously. Torr glared back, lifting his chin, and said in Scridnu, "You are not the only wizard in the wild woods, my friend."

Torr smirked as Vaka's face turned purple.

After a time, the Scrids gathered in a circle to eat bread and drink water. Torr was hungry; all his food was gone, but it appeared the Scrids were going to make him watch them eat. He had a bit of water left and drained his waterskin, then sat on the ground, leaned his head back against the hard stone, and tried to think of a way out. All they would need to do was wait for him to fall asleep, then tie him up and send him back to Gray Feather.

He sank into dark despondency. All his efforts to escape Scridland. His long trek through the woods. His training in harnessing the power of the chants. Almost dying in a standing grave. All for nothing. Well, not all for nothing. He had helped his mother cross the Shaman's Shield. That was something. Now if he died, he could rest in peace. Sort of. There were still Cassidy and his father to consider.

He sighed and stared up at the geometric pattern of the glass dome. If only he could climb out of this stone cage. He laughed bitterly. He'd need to fly to do that, and he didn't have wings, last time he'd checked. He could disappear in his shadow cat cloak and steal bread. Yes, that was a good idea, except he could not very well hide in the cloak forever. Even letting his hand leave the shelter of the cloak to grab the bread would reveal himself. Eventually, the Scrids would grab him, and Vaka would steal his magic cloak. No, there was no way out of this. The Scrids had all the time in the world, and eventually time would defeat Torr.

Helug glanced over at him and beat his fists to his chest happily. Torr gave him a stony glare and looked away. Vaka was ignoring Torr, or so it appeared, although Torr could feel the strange quickening in his blood that he felt whenever the wizard was nearby. Vaka was trying to exert his influence on Torr. Trying to hook his energy somehow. Torr did not like it. He pushed back, and the wizard scowled and stuffed a piece of bread into his mouth. Torr licked his lips and lowered his gaze.

A tremor in the rock made him sit up straight. The stone at Torr's side rippled, and suddenly Cassidy stepped through as though the rock were nothing but a silken curtain to be pushed aside. His breath caught in his throat and he hopped to his feet. She was crouching and alert, like a hunter, her crystal ball in one hand and a short wooden stick in the other. The Scrids stared at her, and Vaka climbed slowly to his feet.

"Oh, good, you *are* here, Sundance," she said to Torr cheerfully, as the stone solidified behind her.

"Get back!" Torr cried, pushing her behind him as the Scrid warriors hopped to their feet and crept forward curiously. "How did you get in here? Can you get back out?" he asked as he brandished the wolf knife and searched for Brother Wolf in the shadows, hoping the warriors would see his spirit animal and back off.

A sharp clinking sound made him turn to his sister. She was crouched by the wall with a chisel in one hand and a small metal hammer in the other. She tapped gently, and a palm-sized sliver of stone came off in a neat chunk. She tucked it into a pouch and went for another. Since when did she have a chisel and a hammer? And how did she know how to work stone so skillfully? He stared at her for a moment as she chipped off the second piece and started on a third.

A shriek erupted from Vaka. He babbled something in Scridnu about Cassidy being a medicine woman and exhorting the men to stop her.

"Keep them away," Cassidy told Torr as she quickly chipped off a fourth chunk. "I'm almost done."

"What in Perseus's name are you doing, Cassidy?" he asked as he waved the wolf knife threateningly at the hovering men, who looked as perplexed as he was.

"I'm getting some shards," Cassidy said breathlessly as she chiseled off another piece. "I think he created a fragment."

"A *what?*" Torr asked, spittle flying from his mouth as he stood between her and the burly men who looked to be gathering their courage to obey the screaming wizard.

Vaka sputtered something incomprehensible, raised his rattle, and lurched towards them.

"Come on," Cassidy said. She shoved a stick into his hand and grabbed him by the wrist. She tugged at him and walked into the wall, her body disappearing the way Brianna's had when she'd entered the Shaman's Shield. Torr held his breath and followed, shutting his eyes against a stinging blast of dry gritty air. After a moment of rushing silence, he emerged on the other side of the rock wall outside of the Scrids' circular tent structure.

"Oh, good. You made it," Cassidy said, dropping his wrist. "You *are* a shaman."

"What did you ... how did you ...?" he stammered.

"I'll tell you later," she promised, and he followed her gaze.

Waiting for them was a crowd of Light Fighters, all wearing bright blue headbands and all staring up at the white stone wall. Their eyes fell on Torr and Cassidy, surprise and joy lighting their faces. Right hands rose to foreheads in a salute. Torr returned the salute and searched the crowd for familiar faces. Berkeley had his arm around a tall woman wearing a bright pink robe and raised his hand to Torr with a wide grin. Jasper came running up, wearing loose green clothing. His face was gaunt and his eyes were haunted. He shared one brief look of anguished relief with Torr, then turned to Cassidy and wrapped her in his arms, hugging her tightly and lifting her off her feet.

"That was too dangerous," Jasper said as she laughed in his arms.

Jasper put her down and turned to Torr, grabbing him in a big hug. "Glad you made it, man," Jasper said. "Seemed like that was a rough journey. You're gonna have to teach me how to do that someday."

Torr looked at Jasper oddly. "How do you know ...," Torr started to ask, but Jasper turned back to Cassidy, hugging her again. Out of habit, Torr looked for Blaire, and then with a jab of pain settled on the faces of Becka, Britta, and Bailey, who stood in a group and looked at him with a mixture of joy and sorrow. They came forward, and he met them in a huddle of heads and arms. He pressed his cheek to each of theirs. They were so like Blaire, yet they were each their own person, alive and strong. A strangled sob escaped Torr's throat as he lifted his face to gaze upon each of theirs.

"I'm sorry," he said, choking on his words. "I couldn't save her."

"We know," Becka said, pulling his head down to meet her forehead, reminding Torr of the Scrids' gesture of affection. "It's not your fault," she said.

He swallowed back his tears, forcing himself to be strong. He took a deep breath and looked around. Beyond the sisters, leaning on his crutches, stood Durham. Torr left the arms of Blaire's sisters and walked to meet him.

They clasped each other in an embrace. "I'm sorry about your boys," Torr said.

"I am too," Durham said, meeting his eyes. "But I'm so glad you've returned. I was afraid I had lost a fourth son."

Tears ran down Torr's face. "How long has it been?" he asked, not sure at all that time on Scridland matched time here.

"Three months," Durham said, resting a hand on Torr's shoulder.

"Three months? Is that all?" Torr wiped away his tears and looked around him. Everyone's blue headbands had his Light Fighters emblem embroidered or painted on the front, and there were many people he did not recognize. Those he knew smiled at him with glowing affection. Everyone looked skinnier than he remembered, bones prominent on faces, wrists, and elbows.

Two Scrid guards were bound and lying face down on the ground, guarded by Montana and several Light Fighters. Montana tipped his hat at Torr with a grin, and Torr returned the smile. A pulsating ripple broke the still air, and a loud scraping made Torr cover his ears. He looked behind him to see the white stone edifice shimmering and shifting.

"Come on," he called out to the Light Fighters. "The wall is coming down. To Center Ring!" he commanded. He gestured to Durham, and then turned to the Smith sisters.

"Go," Torr urged them. "Hurry. Get everyone out of here. Berkeley, you, too. Go!"

Becka and Berkeley led the charge of Light Fighters down the spoke road. Cassidy and Jasper left with them, running hand in hand. Torr, Durham, and Montana hustled the crowd away from the Scrid compound while Faisal and a few of the Alphabet Boys appeared at Torr's side, clapping his shoulders in quick, heartfelt greetings, before helping Durham and Montana move everyone along.

Torr unsheathed his wolf knife and shook his rattle at the disintegrating barrier, trying to ward off Vaka, whom he expected to emerge at any moment.

They left the two bound Scrids on the ground, and Torr took a parting look at the white wall, which was fading to a transparent glimmer. Torr turned and fled with his friends at his side. The Ilian steel of the wolf blade caught the sun in a bright flash, and the specter of Brother Wolf flitted in and out of view at his heels.

They headed towards Center Ring. Behind Torr the road was empty, but a blue and white Earth shone in the sky, urging him on. Before him, the white gravity bar soared high into the air, glimmering with a subtle glow. Torr grinned as he ran, mindless of the strange looks he attracted in his billowing shadow cat cloak and pointed bear hide cap, with his black dream flower rattle and crystalline blade, and the shadow of a wolf running at his side.

He was home.

Book Three of MOON DEEDS Trilogy –

ANAXİMENES

The explosive conclusion of the Moon Deeds Trilogy brings us the final battle for the moon.

The forces behind the Tegs' lunar invasion are even darker and more sinister than anyone knew. Only magic and bravery can hope to save the moon—and the galaxy—from the hands of those who want to control it all.

Also from Palmer Pickering –

Heliotrope

GENRE: HEROIC FANTASY - SWORD AND SORCERY

Teleo is a retired soldier descended from Mages, who were cast out of power generations ago. After years of war and sorrow, he wants nothing more than to live a quiet life on his farm and work his stonemason's craft.

His wife and daughter had been murdered during a war raid several years earlier, and his young son stolen by the enemy side. He spent years unsuccessfully searching for his son and returned home broken-hearted. At the local castle, he comes upon a war orphan stolen by his side from the enemy and rescues him from abuse, adopting him as his foster son.

Teleo is working on a stone mosaic for the Queen at the castle, when he finds himself in the middle of a coup. This launches a journey to protect his new family, uncover the secrets of the ancient ways, and reclaim the magic of the Mages.

Made in the USA
Monee, IL
04 March 2022